LAURELL K. HAMILTON

SUCKER PUNCH

An Anita Blake, Vampire Hunter, Novel

HEADLINE

First published in the USA in 2020 by
BERKLEY
An imprint of Penguin Random House LLC

First published in Great Britain in 2020 by
HEADLINE PUBLISHING GROUP

1

Cataloguing in Publication Data is available from the British Library

Hardback ISBN 978 1 4722 4182 5
Trade paperback ISBN 978 1 4722 4183 2

Offset in 11.70/16.15 pt Janson Text LT Std by Jouve (UK), Milton Keynes

Printed and bound in Great Britain by Clays Ltd, Elcograf S.p.A.

Headline's policy is to use papers that are natural, renewable and recyclable
products and made from wood grown in well-managed forests and other
controlled sources. The logging and manufacturing processes are expected
to conform to the environmental regulations of the country of origin.

HEADLINE PUBLISHING GROUP
An Hachette UK Company
Carmelite House
50 Victoria Embankment
London EC4Y 0DZ

www.headline.co.uk
www.hachette.co.uk

This one is for all of you, because you let me know that my imaginary friends are your friends, too, and that like all good friends they help you get through the tough times. I am so happy to be able to share the next adventure with you. I hope it finds us all safe and sound and out in the world again seeing each other in person, but no matter how far apart we are, you know that other people are picking up this book and reading the same words right along with you. Readers are never truly alone, because we are united in the stories we share and enjoy together.

SUCKER PUNCH

1

THE TINY PLANE landed in the dark on a runway that felt way too short. When the plane finally skidded to a stop, I couldn't make my right hand let go of the armrest. Literally I'd held on so tight that my hand had locked up, as if holding on tight would have done a damn bit of good if the plane had wrecked. The pilot turned his head to look at me and give me a thumbs-up. I just stared at him, my heart in my throat. I was phobic of flying, and this bumpy trip in a four-seater Cessna hadn't done a damn thing to quiet my fears.

He took off his headset and said, "Oh, come on, it wasn't that bad, was it?" He smiled when he said it. I glared at him until his smile faltered. I was projecting badass while the only mantra in my head was *I will not throw up. I will not throw up.* Only knowing that a man's life hung in the balance had gotten me to climb into the progressively smaller planes until this final one.

"Well, welcome to Hanuman, Michigan, Marshal Blake," the pilot said at last, and opened the door.

As I pried my hand free of its death grip, I wondered again why I was doing this. Because it's your job, I thought. I kept telling myself that as I gathered my bags and fitted the big one through the door ahead of me.

The pilot said, "That bag's big enough to hold a body."

"Only if it was my size or smaller, though I guess I could cut it up and make almost anyone fit," I said as I got the rest of me and the smaller bag through the door and down onto the tarmac.

"Very funny," the pilot said.

I gave him the flat look until he said, "What's really in the bag?"

"Weapons," a man said as he walked toward us in the last light of the setting sun.

I'd had just a moment to see the forest, and then it was dark as if someone had turned the lights off. You know you're in the boon-docks when it's that dark even before you step into the trees; in their shade, it would be cave dark.

I smiled at Marshal Winston Newman. He was as tall as the first time I'd met him, as in over six feet, but had more meat on his bones as if he was either gaining weight or gaining muscle. I'd have to see him in better light to be sure whether he was hitting the gym or hit-ting the donuts. His hair was still short underneath his white cowboy hat, but the hat wasn't brand-new anymore. The brim had been worked with his hands so that it made an almost sharp point over his face. It fit him now. When I'd first met him, the hat had struck me as a present from someone who hadn't really known him or wanted him to be more cowboy than he'd seemed.

He offered to take a bag so I could shake his hand, and I let him take it. I'd have done the same for him. "Thanks for flying out at the last minute, Blake."

"I appreciate you reaching out on this." I almost added "rookie," but he wasn't one anymore. He was newer than me, but then, most marshals in the preternatural branch were. There were only eight of us from the old days; everyone else was either dead, worse than dead, or retired.

"Thanks for helping me out, Jim," Newman said to the pilot, who was standing by his plane watching us.

"The Marchand family has been around here a long time, and Bobby is my friend, Marshal Newman. I appreciate you trying to give him a chance."

"You understand that if Bobby Marchand did this, then I will have to execute him," Newman said.

"If he killed old man Marchand, then he'll have earned it, but Bobby has been an Ailuranthrope since just after we graduated high school. He had it under control."

I was surprised that Jim knew the politically correct term for cat-based lycanthropy. Sorry, for Therianthropy, which was the new term for all of it since it didn't imply wolf like lycanthropy did. But a lifetime of using it as a general term was going to be hard to break for me.

"That's what everyone tells me. Thanks again, Jim. Marshal Blake and I have to get over to the sheriff's office." He started moving toward a big Jeep Wrangler that was parked in the grass beside the runway.

"Duke is a good man, Newman. He's just never seen anything like this."

Newman kept us moving toward the Jeep as he called back over his shoulder, "I'm not questioning Sheriff Leduc's competency, Jim."

"Good, but you watch out for his deputy, Wagner."

That made Newman stop and look back at the pilot. "What's wrong with Wagner?"

"He gets rough when he thinks he can get away with it."

"Does the sheriff know?" Newman asked.

"I don't know, but everybody else in town does."

"Thanks for the heads-up, Jim."

"Not a problem. I hope you and Marshal Blake work this out."

"Me, too, Jim. Me, too," Newman said as he opened the back door and tossed my bag of weapons in.

Since I already had the Springfield EMP 9mm in an inner pants holster, with my marshal's badge on the belt next to it—so if I had flashed it on one of the larger planes, they'd see my badge—plus two extra magazines in the cargo pockets of my pants, a folding Emerson wave knife from Gerber in another pocket, a small tactical flashlight, a very slender man's wallet, and my smartphone, I was okay being out of easy reach of the rest of my weapons and body armor. I went around to the passenger-side door and let myself in. I'd add two more knives and switch the EMP for my Springfield Rangemaster full frame .45 in a drop leg holster when I got the chance. I had a hip holster for it, but if I had to wear the body armor, I'd have to change to the drop holster anyway, just like the EMP would switch to a holster on the MOLLE strap system on the chest of the vest. Inner pants holsters were for concealed carry when you didn't want to spook the civilians. On an active warrant, by the time I was all geared up, concealed carry was an impossibility.

"Did you know that this Deputy Wagner had a rep for roughing people up?" I asked.

Newman settled himself behind the wheel of his Jeep and shook his head. "I hadn't heard the rumor, and as far as we know, that's all it is."

"How well do you know Jim the pilot?"

"Well enough to roust him out of bed on a Saturday and get him to fly you from the main airport to here."

"You knew he was Bobby Marchand's friend, so he'd be moti-vated."

"I did."

"Is this your home base now?"

"It is."

"It's not exactly a great post for a marshal. Did you choose it, or did you piss someone off?"

He smiled wide enough for me to see it as he pulled the Jeep out on the runway and drove like we were a plane getting ready to take off. I realized that there didn't seem to be any other paved area nearby. We passed a shed with a windsock, but that was it. It was the definition of middle of fucking nowhere.

"I chose it."

I looked at him and he laughed. "Don't look at me like that, Blake. I know it's not a hotbed of career opportunities, but I met a woman on a case, and it sort of rearranged my priorities."

I grinned at him. "And she's local to here, I take it."

"Yeah."

"So, you sank your career to follow the love of your life to the Michigan wilderness?"

"No, but I decided that a quick rise through the ranks wasn't as important as being near the woman I wanted to spend the rest of my life with."

I spread my hands and said, "Hey, I don't throw stones at anyone's love life, Newman. My house has too much shiny glass on it, which reminds me, I promised to text them when I finally landed."

That made him laugh. It was good to hear the sound; it meant things hadn't gone completely to hell. It was bad, but he could still laugh. Some crime scenes stole laughter along with everything else. "It's nice I'm not the only one that has to text home. Some of the other marshals give me grief for it."

"Fuck them if their relationships aren't as good as ours," I said.

He laughed again. I smiled reflexively, typing on the phone. I was metaphysically tied to all the people I loved, which meant I could have just dropped my psychic shields and contacted at least some of them mind to mind, or they could have reached out to me, or in an emergency they could crash my shields, but that was damn distracting in the middle of a fight, so the deal was I'd text and call more like a regular Joe or Jill. Also, the other police were giving me enough grief about dating supernaturals, which was one of the politically correct terms for vampires, wereanimals, and any-thing else that wasn't strictly human. Once I'd have said *straight human*, but I'd been chastised for using the word *straight*. Between actual vocabulary guidelines for the job and civilians getting butt-hurt because of my word choices, I was thinking of just substitut-ing the word *fuck* for the word they didn't like to see if they liked that better. If I was going to be offensive, I might as well go for broke.

I erased several texts and finally settled for "Landed safe. Love you. Miss you already." It seemed inadequate, but it was all true, and at least I'd remembered to text. Staying in touch when I was on the job out of town wasn't one of my best things, to say the least. Micah

Callahan, one of my fiancés, was as bad as I was about it and traveled as much. Our mutual lovers had recently done an intervention to let us know we needed to do better.

The first return text binged on my phone. I wasn't surprised that it was Nathaniel Graison, one of my other fiancés, because he had been one of the main instigators of the intervention. His text said simply, "Thank you for texting. I know you don't understand why I need it. Love you back. I like that you miss me. Looking forward to the call tomorrow, or you back home before that." And there it was, the loving text turned into a nagging push. We had all agreed that I'd text when I arrived and that I'd call once a day if possible, or text again. Nathaniel was reminding me of what I'd agreed to do, which turned a loving text or phone call into an obligation, which kind of bugged me. The return texts came fast and furious after that, because the group text contained eight people, not including me. I'd actually been surprised at some of the lovers who had insisted on getting more long-distance attention and at the ones who were content with the status quo. Some of them answered in the group text, but others answered privately. I typed an answer to each one of them; only two made me smile. Jean-Claude's *"Je t'aime, ma petite,"* and Nicky Murdock's "I know you love me. You don't have to keep texting me to prove it."

"I know it's none of my business, but how many people are you having to text while you're gone?"

"Enough," I said, and sighed. I scrolled through all the texts and realized I wasn't sure whom I had to call tomorrow morning if I was still here. I wouldn't know how long I'd be on the ground here until I knew more about the case. I put my phone away and said, "You didn't invite me here to talk about our personal lives, so what's up first on the crime busting?"

He smiled as he said, "Sheriff Leduc requested I introduce you before we head to the crime scene. We have to drive right by the sheriff's office, so it's not out of the way. Hell, you can see Bobby Marchand. Maybe you'll think of smarter questions to ask than I did."

"You were exactly what your name says when I met you, Newman, but that was a couple of years ago. You do okay on your cases."

"You checked up on me?" he asked, glancing away from the night black road; the headlights seemed to carve their way through the moonless night.

"I keep an eye on the newbies I meet."

"And I keep an eye on the careers of the marshals that I want to grow up to be," he said.

That made me laugh. "If you grow up any more, I'll need a ladder to shake your hand."

He joined me in the laughter, and we drove for a few minutes in companionable silence.

"It's a dark night up here," I said.

"The cloud cover is thick tonight, but if it clears off, you'll see stars here like I've never seen outside of the desert or the ocean."

"It's not just cloud cover, Newman. Last night was the dark of the moon, and tonight won't be much brighter. If Bobby Marchand has been a wereleopard—sorry, Ailuranthrope—for this long, he shouldn't even shift form this far from a full moon."

"It's one of the things that bothered me enough to try to delay executing him, and don't worry. I'm having trouble remembering all the new terms, too. Besides, we know that Bobby Marchand is a leopard, so we don't have to use the generic terms between us."

"Great. I appreciate that. I hate the new vocabulary. Do you have the warrant of execution in hand already?"

"Yeah, the judge e-mailed it to the sheriff's office and got it signed through DocuSign just hours after the body was discovered."

"I remember when getting the warrant faxed over was high-tech," I said.

"Yeah, it's all high-tech most of the time now. Fast and efficient, maybe a little too efficient."

"How much time is left on the warrant?" I asked.

"About sixty hours out of the original seventy-two. I should have called you sooner."

"Should isn't helpful, Newman. Concentrate on what we can do here and now. Second-guessing yourself just eats up your energy and time."

He glanced at me, then back at the road. "Maybe, but they've started to get really picky on extending the timeline on a warrant of execution."

"Yeah, since they stretched the window for a warrant from forty-eight to seventy-two, they don't like extending the time unless it's a live hunt where you can't lay hands on the murderer, and you've got this one locked up in jail. There won't be grounds for more time, and if you don't pull the trigger in a timely fashion, it will be seen as refusing to perform your duty as a marshal of the preternatural branch, and that will be a career killer."

"Better my career than an innocent man's life."

"You told me you don't believe he did it, but we didn't have time for you to tell me all your reasons over the phone."

"No, I needed you here ASAP so you could help me figure out what's wrong with this case."

"I'm surprised that the first police on scene didn't just kill him on sight. They would have been able to make a good case for it being a clean shoot."

"If they'd found him covered in blood right beside his uncle's body, they probably would have, but he was in his bedroom passed out. I'm not sure they'd have even suspected him if he hadn't had blood all over him."

"I looked at the crime scene photos you e-mailed me. First glance, the victim was clawed to pieces. Why wouldn't the local cops suspect the only wereleopard living in the house with him? I'm not complaining that they didn't jump to the conclusion, but it's simple cop math to think it."

"Like Jim said, Bobby is a local boy. He's well-liked. Doesn't drink too much, doesn't do much of anything to excess, and his family is rich enough that he could afford a lot of excess."

"A lot of shapeshifters are careful about doing anything that will lower their control of their inner beast, like drinking or drugs or even strong emotions," I said.

Newman nodded. "Which means that Bobby is careful and doesn't take chances with his beast."

"He sounds like a model citizen," I said.

"He is. I know you were traveling so you couldn't just open the files without risking civilians seeing the crime scene photos, but did you get a chance to look at them, really look at them?"

"Yeah."

"What bothered you about them?"

"No bites, for one thing. If a leopard of any kind had killed him, it should have taken a bite or two."

"The family says that Mr. Marchand was on heavy painkillers for an old back injury and arthritis. The theory is that the wereleopard could smell the meds in his body and wouldn't eat it."

"Maybe. I have some friends I can call and ask later if they'd smell meds on someone, but I'll need to know the exact prescriptions."

"I've got it written down. I'll give you the list."

"I do know that people poison carcasses to illegally kill lions and other big cats, and they take the bait. People use poison to get rid of rats, mice, moles, and then the local cats eat them and die. I'm not sure a wereleopard would be any different."

"They found Bobby passed out cold in his bed, nude, covered in blood, but his bed wasn't as messy as he was."

"You mean the sheets weren't stained with blood, just his body?"

"Yeah."

"Were there bloody handprints, knee prints where he crawled into the bed just before he passed out?"

"No, there weren't."

"Well, he didn't levitate into bed. Even most vampires can't do that," I said.

"I know, and also his human body should have been cleaner than that. It was his beast form, which killed the uncle, that should have been drenched in blood, but if he left the area before switching back to human, then the blood should have just been absorbed during the change."

"Were there bloody footprints leading from the crime scene to the bedroom?" I asked.

"Yes, but there's something about them that's off, too."

"What do you mean, off?"

"I don't know, but it looks like the foot is a bigger shoe size than Bobby's. If this was a normal human-on-human murder, there'd be time for forensics to gather evidence and tell me if I'm right, but because it's a supernatural-on-human crime, they won't even bother with forensics unless I can make a case for needing them."

"If this went according to plan, Bobby Marchand would be dead long before the forensics could be processed," I said.

"I know, and we're too small an area to have much in the way of forensics. The sheriff would have to ask the state cops for their help with the forensics, and he doesn't see the need for it." Newman sounded deeply unhappy about the whole thing.

"Once the warrant of execution arrives, you are duty bound to act on it."

"I know that, Blake. I know that the only thing that could add to the time limit is if Bobby escapes and we have to hunt him down."

"That doesn't add to the time we have to finish a warrant, Newman. The suspect just gains the time it takes for us to hunt him down and execute him."

"He's shackled and inside a cell. He's not going to escape, which is why I called you. I don't mind executing Bobby Marchand if he lost control and killed his uncle. If he's that dangerous, then it's for the best, but I do not want to put a bullet in his brain and then find out that the footprints don't match, that the blood evidence all over him is wrong for the crime, that . . . It just doesn't feel right, Blake."

"That's why I just flew in the smallest plane I've ever been on to come and help you figure out if he did it."

"The warrant gives me the right to ask for the backup I need," he said.

"It gives you the right to deputize people if their skill sets will help you carry out your duty in a safe and timely manner, with the least possible loss of life."

"I know that normally that wording is for getting better hunters and trackers to help you find the monster, but I thought the wording would give me enough room to call in someone to help me make sure that Bobby Marchand doesn't lose his life unless he deserves to lose it."

"It's commendable thinking, Newman."

"You saved my life the first time I met you, and you just flew across the country to help me save a life. Call me Win."

"I've never heard that as short for Winston."

"I was Winston until sixth grade when I started my growth spurt. By the end of seventh, I was on the basketball team."

"A winning basketball team, I take it," I said, smiling and shaking my head.

"Yeah, everybody started calling me Win, and I preferred that to Winston," he said, grinning at me.

"Fine, Win. If I remember right, you helped ride to my rescue, too, but I didn't fly here to save a life. I flew here to maybe save a life, but if we look at the evidence and Bobby Marchand is guilty of this crime, then the execution will have to move forward."

All hints of smiles vanished, and when oncoming headlights flashed across his face, he looked tired and years older. "I know, and if he's guilty, I'll do my duty. But I want to be certain that killing Bobby Marchand is my duty first."

I agreed with Newman, but I also knew that once the warrant arrived, there'd be a lot of pressure to finish it. This was probably the most horrible murder this tiny area had seen in years, if ever. They'd want the murderer caught and punished; they'd want to feel safe again. We had a few hours to figure out if there were enough grounds to vacate the warrant, or at least get a legal stay of execution under extraordinary circumstances while the evidence was processed.

Hanuman's sheriff's station was roomier than I'd expected after the airport. It had a front area big enough for two desks with room to add another if they were careful around the coffee machine. There was one door in the back wall. I sort of assumed that if they had a jail cell, it was back there, but you never knew in a place this small.

Sheriff Leduc had to be at least five-eight, because my head didn't come up to the top of his shoulder, but the weight he was carrying around his middle made him look shorter. He'd had to fasten his duty belt underneath his stomach, so it fit more at his hips than at his waist. You don't have to hit the gym like you're on SWAT, but being able to run at a medium pace without having a heart attack seems like a minimum for a police officer. I wasn't sure Leduc was at that minimum.

He smiled and offered his hand, and we shook like we were actually on the same team. I liked that and hoped it was true. "Call me Duke. Everyone does."

In my head I thought, So your name is Duke Leduc, but I didn't say it out loud. I didn't want to tease the man. I could be taught.

"Everyone pretty much calls me Blake when I'm working," I said. I smiled when I said it, but I didn't want him calling me Anita. That was for my friends, or at least acquaintances, when I was wearing a badge. Using last names also helped keep that professional distance that every woman in a mostly male-dominated field needs to keep.

"Now, Anita—I can call you Anita, can't I?" He smiled at me as he said it.

I wanted to ask if he called Newman by his first name, but I didn't. Sheriff Duke Leduc was being friendly, and that was good. We'd need him on our side if we decided the warrant needed to be delayed. It didn't cost me much to let him use my first name.

"Sure," I said, and tried to make sure I smiled instead of gritting my teeth.

Newman was smiling, too, and he looked like he meant it. We were all being so damn pleasant, as if they hadn't found one of their leading citizens butchered fourteen hours ago. We were all being so nice, it was almost unnerving, as if we were there for a reason totally different from murder.

"How's Bobby holding up?" Newman said, and the smiles vanished from everyone's faces.

Leduc—I couldn't think of him as Duke; unless you were John Wayne, you could not be Duke—shook his head. The light went out of him, and he just looked tired. "I think if we didn't have him shackled to the bunk in his cell that he might do himself a harm."

"He didn't seem suicidal when I interviewed him," Newman said.

The sheriff shrugged his big shoulders, and again there was the hint of his size and how maybe once there'd been an athlete in there somewhere. "I think he's beginning to believe he did it. Ray was the only father that Bobby really remembers. How would you feel if you woke up and found out what you'd done?"

"You say woke up, but I'm told that Bobby Marchand typically passes out after he changes from animal to human form," I said.

"It's typical of most lycanthropes . . . Therianthropes. The fact that they pass out cold for hours after they change back to human is the only edge we have when they start killing people."

"Not all shapeshifters pass out after they shift back," I said.

"Well, God help us if Bobby had been one of them. We'd probably still be hunting him through the woods."

"Is he a big outdoorsman in human form?" I asked.

Leduc nodded. "He grew up camping with Ray. They were both big into anything they could do outdoors even before Bobby caught lycanthropy. The boy knows these woods."

"How serious do you think Bobby is about hurting himself, Duke?" Newman asked.

"Well, now, it's hard to tell. All I can say for certain is he sounded serious enough for me to mention it to you, but Frankie has been sitting in there with him for the last bit, so you'd need to ask her how he's doing now. He's all over the board emotionally. One minute he sounds like normal, like Bobby, and then he'll start getting worked up about things, and there's no telling what he'll say. He said if he killed Uncle Ray, that he deserves to die. He said that a lot."

"That's not exactly suicidal talk," I said.

"It's been my experience that when folks start saying they deserve to die, it doesn't take long for them to get around to making the wish come true. They may not succeed. It may just be a cry for help, but sometimes those cries turn out to be permanent."

"A permanent solution to a temporary problem—suicide, I mean."

Leduc looked at me, eyes narrowing. "Sometimes, but Ray isn't temporarily dead, and nothing Bobby can do, or say, is going to undo what he did. There's nothing temporary about the emotions that are tearing that boy up."

"I stand corrected, Sheriff. You're absolutely right. I think you must deal with more suicides than I do."

"We've had more than you'd think in a town this size," he said, and he looked suddenly weary. Tired didn't cover it. He hitched his duty belt up again, as if trying to move it back where it used to ride. It looked like a habitual gesture that didn't quite work anymore, like brushing your hair back from your face after you cut it short.

"The only people that die on my watch don't die by suicide," I said.

"The first uniform I wore was army. I saw combat. I thought that was bad, but sometimes I miss it. It's cleaner than dying by inches in a backwater town." Duke sounded wistful, or way too honest to be talking in front of a stranger.

It was Newman who asked, "You okay, Duke?"

It's against the guy code to ask things like that, but sometimes when you start off talking about suicide and hear such bitter defeat come out of someone's mouth, you break the rules. Most of us who wear a uniform have learned that we can't keep the guy code of silence when one of our own is in pain. We lose too many people that way, both male and female. Twenty-two combat veterans die every day in the United States alone from suicide, and it isn't just soldiers who have just come home from their tours of duty. There is no statute of limitations on nightmares and depression. With numbers like that, we need to start talking to one another more.

I was still glad that Newman had done the asking. I didn't know Duke well enough to be that personal.

Duke shook his head. "I've known Ray for over thirty years. I was here when his sister and her husband died and left Bobby an orphan. Kid was two, three back then, and Ray had never had time for children of his own. He was all career after college, but he changed his life so he could be a dad to that little boy. That's when he sold his company, because he couldn't be a CEO and a dad. He told me that once, just like that. Selling when he did meant he got the most money he'd have ever gotten for the company, and he was out of it when the crash came, but he didn't know it when he did it. He loved that boy like he was his own, and now he's dead, bad dead. Last thing I saw that bad was a bear attack, and that was nearly ten years ago. It was no way for Ray to die, and now Bobby's going to die, too." He shook his head again. His eyes were a little shiny as he got his hat and said, "I'll take you out to the crime scene."

"I know the way, Duke," Newman said, voice gentle.

"I know you do, Win, but all the same, I'll go along."

"I'd like to talk to Bobby before we go," Newman said.

I did not want to talk to the prisoner, because right now he was abstract, not as real as Leduc, who had just let us see his pain. I didn't want Bobby Marchand to be real to me. I needed as much emotional distance as I could get, because I was beginning to realize I might be the only badge in town who wasn't emotionally compromised. I still believed that Newman would do his duty in the end, but I was beginning to understand how much it might cost him. It would stay his warrant, but if we both agreed that it would cost me less to execute it, then it might be me staring down the barrel of a gun at the prisoner. If I was going to have to kill someone who was chained up and couldn't get away, then I'd want all the emotional distance I could get. Give me a straight-up hunt after a monster that was trying to kill me, and I was fine, but shooting chained-up fish in a jail cell, that would be a new one even for me. I did not want to speak with the prisoner, not if I was going to have to shoot him later, but when Newman went through the door in the back wall, I followed him. It took a lot more courage than I'd have admitted out loud. There was no win here for me, or for Newman. Hell, there was no win for anyone.

2

THERE WERE TWO cells, with a narrow hallway leading to a closed door at the end. A deputy sat in a chair by the wall with a shotgun across her lap. She stood as we entered, the shotgun held loose in one hand, the barrel pointed safely at the concrete floor. All the skin that showed around the uniform was a deep brown. I thought she might be Mexican like my mother, or at least some flavor of Hispanic, but a second look showed that the nice dark skin tone didn't come from south of the border but somewhere more east.

Her hair was as black as mine, but straight and tied back in a neat ponytail. My curls never went back into a ponytail that neatly, which is why my fiancé had helped me French-braid it before I got on the plane. Sheriff Leduc introduced her as his deputy, Frances (call her Frankie) Anthony.

We all shook hands as if there wasn't another person in the room— well, in the cell. You don't have to have a badge long before you start to think differently about prisoners. It's partially self-preservation, especially for marshals in the preternatural branch like Newman and me. It's harder to kill someone if you think of them as people just like you and me. Everyone but me knew this prisoner, and yet they still introduced me to the deputy first as if Bobby Marchand weren't within hearing distance. I wondered if they even knew they'd done it.

Newman turned to the cell without introducing me to the man inside it. "How are you doing, Bobby?"

Bobby Marchand blinked at us with blue eyes so large that they dominated his face to the point they were all you saw at first, like he was an anime character. Of course, it might have been the mask of dried blood surrounding his baby blues that made them so startling. The contrast must have been even more extreme when the blood had been fresh and red. Now it was a tired sort of brick red heading toward brown; most people would have thought it was dried mud. They'd never have guessed it was blood until they saw what happened in a shower. Water would bring it back to *life*, and suddenly the mud would look like something far more liquid than dirt. Bobby's short blond hair had one spot of drying blood in it; the rest was disheveled but clean. He had a gray blanket wrapped around himself, so most of him was covered. The hint of chest that showed had blood drying on it, but the shoulders and arms that were holding the blanket in place were clean; his hands were not. There was even blood dried on the cuff around his right wrist. The chain from it went to the metal frame of the bed beside him. The bed was chained to the concrete floor, and there was a second chain that trailed underneath the blanket toward the leg of the bed, so he was shackled on at least one ankle, too. They looked like ordinary restraints, not the new stuff specifically designed for supernatural prisoners with their supernatural strength, which meant that if Bobby wanted to break his chains, he could, even in human form. Even the bars wouldn't hold if he really wanted out, but it would take longer—long enough for the officer on guard duty to shoot him and hope they could kill him before he could finish shifting into his even stronger other half. That they had the deputy on watch outside the cell with a shotgun meant they understood some of it, and they probably didn't have the budget for the new special restraints. Even some major cities couldn't afford more than a couple of full sets.

Bobby fidgeted, clutching his blanket tighter. He'd tried to clean his hands by wiping them on the blanket in a few places, but the blood had embedded around his nails and into the pores of his skin.

Even a shower wouldn't get it all now. I knew from experience that if you didn't wear gloves when there was that much blood, it was a serious bitch to get it cleaned out from around your nails. Under your nails you could do, but the cuticles and the edges of the nails were the challenge. It was just his hands that were covered in dried blood; it didn't go past either wrist. In that moment I believed that Bobby Marchand was being framed. Whoever had done the blood evidence on him hadn't known that if someone plunged bare hands into a still living body, or even a freshly dead one, the blood wouldn't stop neatly at the wrists. It would climb up the arms, and there would be blood spatter on the chest, not the thick coating that someone had painted on Bobby. It was all wrong, but unless you'd seen as many lycanthrope kills as I had, or waded through enough gory murder scenes, you wouldn't think about the right things. You wouldn't know where to put the blood.

"How am I supposed to be, Win? I killed Uncle Ray."

"We're not convinced of that, Bobby. I'm still gathering evidence," Newman said.

Bobby turned those blue eyes in their gory mask to the sheriff. "Duke, you told me I did it. You told me I killed Uncle Ray."

"I'm sorry, Bobby. I'm really sorry, but we found you covered in his blood, and you're the only wereanimal in these parts."

Bobby looked back at Newman. "Duke is right. If a wereanimal killed Uncle Ray, then it has to be me. There isn't another shape-shifter for a hundred miles."

"Let us worry about finding other suspects, Bobby. I just need to make sure you don't do anything stupid while I'm out there trying to prove you're innocent."

"Now, Win," Leduc said, "don't get the boy's hopes up like that."

I debated on whether to remark on the blood evidence now, but I wanted to tell Newman in private first. He'd known the blood wasn't right, but he didn't have my field experience to say exactly why it was wrong. This was his warrant, his case, and, almost more important, his hometown, his friends. I didn't want to undercut his authority here. I wanted to know only one thing: Had they photographed the blood patterns on the prisoner? I wasn't besmirching Leduc and his people's police work, but when you know a warrant of execution has been issued, sometimes even the best officers don't collect evidence like they would in a regular murder case. I mean, what's the point? There's never going to be a trial.

"I don't mean to get your hopes up, Bobby, but I believe there's a chance you didn't do this. That's why I called in a more experienced marshal to look over your case."

"It's commendable that you want to be sure, Win, but you wasted Marshal Blake's time getting her up here," Leduc said.

Deputy Anthony and Bobby both said, "Blake," at the same time. They looked at each other, then back at me as she said, "Anita Blake?" and he said, "Not Anita Blake?"

"Yeah, that's me." I was the scourge of the supernatural set, so it wasn't entirely surprising that Bobby Marchand recognized my name, but I wasn't always on the hit parade for nonmarshal local law enforcement, especially for local law enforcement, LEOs, in more rural areas.

"You're here to kill me, because Win doesn't want to have to do it," Bobby said, and he seemed completely defeated. There wasn't even any fear that I could detect, and there should have been. Even guilty people are afraid to die. The sheriff might be right about the suicide risk after all.

"How do the two of you know Marshal Blake?" Leduc asked.

"She's our bogeyman. If you break the law, she's who they send to kill you," Bobby said, voice thick with sorrow, but still no nervousness, just a hopelessness as if it were already over.

"I'm just one marshal from the preternatural branch, not the only one," I said.

Deputy Anthony said, "You still have the highest number of successful executions in the entire preternatural branch."

"I was part of the old vampire hunter system years before I got grandfathered into the Marshals Service, so I had a head start."

She shook her head. "Even Death doesn't have as high a kill count as you do, and he started earlier than you did."

If Marshal Ted (Edward) Forrester and I weren't best friends and partners, it would probably bother him that he, Death, was behind me on legal kills. Of course, if you added in illegal kills, he was ahead of me. Short of a true apocalypse, I'd never catch up with his numbers if you included all of them.

"Death gets everyone in the end, Frankie, so what the hell are you talking about? No one has bigger numbers than death," Leduc said, and he sounded frustrated, bordering on angry. He was more on edge than he was showing, but then I think they all were. I was the only one without a personal stake in the murder.

"The other police nicknamed four of the preternatural marshals the Four Horsemen: Death, War, Hunger, and Plague," she said.

Leduc made a *humph* sound. "I know what the Four Horsemen are called. I know my Bible, and Marshal Blake isn't in it."

"Of course not, sir. I didn't mean the real Four Horsemen."

Leduc looked at me, and it was a slightly different look now, more appraising—not the way that a man looks at an attractive woman, but the way a man looks at another man when he's wondering if he could take him in a fight. Leduc decided he could take me in a fair fight and didn't try to keep the knowledge off his face and out of his body language. I was okay with him thinking he would win. I knew better, and that was enough.

"So, if someone else is Death, who are you, Plague or Hunger?"

"I'm War," I said.

That made him frown harder and then he laughed. "You're too small to be War, Blake."

"Even a little war is a very bad thing," I said, and smiled.

3

NEWMAN LAUGHED. DEPUTY Anthony laughed. Sheriff Leduc did not. Apparently, I did not amuse him. That was okay. My sense of humor didn't work for a lot of people.

"Did anyone take pictures of the prisoner when he was brought in?" I asked.

"No need," Leduc said.

I knew what he meant, but I took him out of earshot of the prisoner, which meant out in the office area. Newman trailed us, leaving Anthony alone with the prisoner again. I really didn't think he was going to try to escape. He seemed to have given up completely. The thought of this jail holding a shapeshifter who hadn't given up and still wanted to live was just such a bad idea. They'd gotten lucky this time. Hopefully there wouldn't be another time if, like they all said, this was the only lycanthrope within a hundred miles.

Leduc leaned against the edge of his desk as I talked, so that he didn't tower over me. "Photographs will help us get size for the wounds and stuff later, just in case there's any questions about us going ahead with the warrant."

"Why should there be any questions about that?" he asked.

"From what Newman told me, the Marchands are *the* family around here for money and power. It's not fair, but that can mean more lawyers get involved. I'd rather cover all our asses."

That seemed reasonable to Leduc; if it didn't to Newman, he

didn't show it. Either he'd learned to hide his emotions in the years since I'd met him, or he trusted my more experienced call. Either way, he agreed to help me take pictures of the prisoner that we could use as reference photos at the crime scene. It was pretty much bullshit. Even in half-man form, the size of hands, feet, teeth, mouth, everything is different from the full human form. The only reason these photos would be useful was if there was a regular trial later, and they could be used as proof that someone had tried to inexpertly frame Bobby Marchand. I was almost certain that Newman understood why we wanted the extra photos. I'd ask him in private later, because if he didn't, I'd share the info, and if he did, then his level of trust in me was a little scary. Trust but verify, even if it's me.

It's standard procedure in any "prison system," no matter how small, that you never take weapons into a cell with you. You just don't want to run the risk of a prisoner grabbing your gun and using it against you. There are exceptions to all rules, but tonight wouldn't be one of them. I gave my .45, Gerber folder, and both wrist sheath blades to Anthony. The sheriff got impatient and said, "Oh, for Pete's sake, you're disarmed enough. Get in there and take your pictures or measurements or whatever so I can drive you out to the house."

I was actually done disarming myself, but I didn't bother to explain that to Leduc. Let him wonder what else I might be carrying.

"We can find the house on our own, Duke. I told you that," Newman said.

"And I told you that I'd take you out there," Leduc said, sounding defensive, or angry, or just cranky.

Anthony asked, "Can I put some of your stuff on the floor, Marshal Blake?"

I looked at her and realized the pile was a little unwieldy to carry in your arms. "Sure. Just don't scuff anything."

"Oh, I'll be careful," she said, and she sounded way too earnest about it. I shaved a few years off her age. You just don't stay that eager much over the age of twenty-five.

The sheriff unlocked the cell, and Newman and I walked in voluntarily. I'm never a fan of disarming myself and walking into a cage.

It just seems bad on principle. The big metal door *cha-chunk*ing behind us didn't make me like it any more, but over the years, I'd learned not to startle when it happened.

We'd already explained to Bobby that we wanted to take pictures of him for evidence later. He was fine with that. His reaction had been so flat, it made me want to ask him something outrageous to see if he'd react more.

Newman helped Bobby hold the blanket and put his arms out to his sides at the same time. Apparently, they hadn't given him anything to wear but the blanket, and either Newman was modest, or he knew that Bobby was, because they worked hard at making sure that he didn't flash me or the deputy. What glimpses I did get showed that Bobby Marchand worked out and kept himself in good shape. Some people believe that becoming a wereanimal or a vampire automatically gives them washboard abs and a lean, muscled body, but it doesn't. Yes, supernaturals are stronger than human normal, but they don't automatically come with bigger muscles. Those you still have to go to the gym and create yourself even if you're a shapeshifter. If you're a vampire, you can't even do that. If you want a good-looking corpse, you have to do the work before you cross over, because once you become one, you're stuck with what you look like on the day of your death for all eternity. Some vampires, my fiancé Jean-Claude being one of them, are powerful enough that exercise can cause the same changes to their bodies that humans experience, but it's an enormous use of energy. And even if you're willing to use the power, most master vampires still can't do it. Jean-Claude is the exception to a lot of vampy rules.

Something about the blanket moving let me see Bobby's feet and one leg, which made me say, "I need to see anywhere there's blood, Mr. Marchand."

"Call me Bobby. Everyone does," he said automatically without even making eye contact.

I didn't really want to call him Bobby, just in case I had to pull the trigger on him later, but I'd already looked into his eyes from inches away. He was becoming real to me and not just a job, so why not?

"Okay, Bobby, I need to see anywhere there's blood evidence. I got your feet, but I saw some higher on your legs on one side. I need a picture of it, okay?"

"Okay," he said in that same emotionless voice he'd had the whole time. He gathered the blanket close to his body and lifted it up almost like an overly long dress. There was blood smeared on his right lower leg. I got an image of it.

"Is this all the evidence?"

He nodded without looking at me. He had avoided eye contact the whole time. He didn't remind me of a criminal; he was reacting more like a victim. If he'd been a woman, or even a man under other circumstances, I'd have wondered if he'd killed in self-defense after an attack. That was the sort of vibe I was getting off of him and his reactions. I couldn't figure out how to ask if his uncle, the man who'd raised him from a toddler, had molested him. Had he fought back finally? No, that didn't feel right, and that wouldn't explain the blood evidence on him being so wrong. A shapeshifter would know that his human form wouldn't have blood on it from the kill. Only someone who didn't know much about wereanimals would do it this way.

"Are you sure these are all the pictures I need?"

He nodded again but stared at the floor.

"Bobby," I said, "what aren't you telling me?"

He shook his head this time, still staring at the floor.

"Bobby, is there blood evidence somewhere else on your body?"

He went very still in the way that trauma victims can go deep inside themselves as if they believe that if they're still enough, quiet enough, they won't have to answer any more questions. If they go away in plain sight, then the worst thing won't happen or won't have to be shared. Everything about him screamed victim, not perpetrator. What the hell was going on here? What had happened to Bobby Marchand to make him react like this? I'd ask Newman later in private if Bobby was usually this quiet and withdrawn; if he was, then that usually indicated long-term abuse. If it wasn't normal for him, then something bad had happened to him very recently, like yesterday recently. Maybe waking up covered in blood and being accused of murdering the only father you've ever known would be enough? Yeah, that sounded like enough. I was just used to looking for horrors, as if tragedy alone wasn't enough.

"Bobby, we're trying to help prove that you didn't kill your uncle. Don't you want us to prove that?" I asked softly, gently, the way you do with victims when you don't want to spook them.

He answered, still staring at the floor, "If I killed Uncle Ray, I don't want you to save me."

"But if you didn't kill your uncle Ray, then someone else did, Bobby. Don't you want to catch them?"

He looked at me then, eyes startled, but trying to see me, really see me. He looked into my eyes—trying to see if I meant it, I think.

Sheriff Leduc said, "Don't you go lying to him, Marshal. He did it, and he's going to have to die for it. Giving him false hope is just . . . cruel."

Bobby looked at Leduc. "You know I did it, don't you?"

"I'm sorry, Bobby. I'm truly sorry, but I know what I know. I know what I saw at your house."

Bobby started to look down at the ground again, but I waved a hand in front of his face so close that he startled back from it. He frowned at me, a moment of anger flashing through his eyes. And with that anger came the faintest warmth of his beast, like the hint of heat when you walk too close to an oven. There's no need to open the door to know it'll burn you.

My own inner beast rose toward his. Oh, I knew the oven was on, but there was something sweet baking inside it, and my own inner leopard wanted to find out if it was cookies or cake. I had better control than that normally, but something about Bobby had unsettled me.

His eyes went wide with surprise. "How can you be . . ." he started to whisper, and then stopped himself, glancing toward the officers outside the bars. He thought I was a wereleopard like him, but he didn't want to out me. It was still legal grounds for dismissal from most police forces or military. The preternatural branch was the exception, but Bobby didn't know that. Just like he couldn't have known that I carried multiple strands of lycanthropy inside me, but never changed form. The doctors thought that catching so many types of the disease so close together had made me a medical miracle, so I was a carrier but didn't have a full-blown case of any of the inner beasts I carried.

I stared into his blue eyes in their mask of blood and said, "There's more blood on you somewhere, isn't there, Bobby?"

"Yes," he whispered as he met my gaze.

"Show me, Bobby, please."

"I don't want everyone to see," he whispered, voice even lower.

Newman said, "Can you give us some privacy, Duke, Frankie?"

"Privacy, what the hell do you need privacy for? We brought Bobby in here jaybird naked. We seen the show."

Bobby flinched at that and went back to looking at the floor. What little animation had been in his face just drained away.

"Humor us, Sheriff," I said.

"I won't leave you in there alone with him unarmed, but we can turn our backs if that will help."

"If that's the most privacy we can get, then we'll take it," I said.

The sheriff turned his broad back first, thumbs in his duty belt. He had to tell the deputy to turn around. She seemed puzzled, but she turned around with my weapons still dangling off of her.

I leaned in close to Bobby and said, "They won't see now, Bobby."

"They already saw. You heard Duke." He sounded stricken; that was the only word for it.

Newman spoke slow and soft; he'd caught on to what I was doing. "We want to help you, Bobby, but you've got to help us do that."

Bobby shook his head, still staring at the floor.

I called just a hint of leopard back so that it glided along my skin and trailed like warmth between us. It made him look at me again. "Bobby, show me, please."

He stared into my eyes as if he couldn't look away, and he slowly began to drop the blanket. Newman didn't try to catch it this time. He just let it fall open to expose the front of Bobby Marchand's body. There was blood on his groin, caked into the short hairs around him.

He started to shake, and if Newman hadn't caught him from

behind, he'd have fallen as much as his chains would have let him. "What did I do? What did I do to Uncle Ray? God, please tell me I didn't do that to him. I don't know why I would do that. I never, ever thought about anything like that. He's my dad. I would never, but if I didn't, then why is there blood there? What the hell happened last night?" He wailed his grief and horror. More than a scream, it was what people meant when they used to say *keening for the dead.*

Bobby's grief tore through him, and like all strong emotions could, it brought out his beast. Newman was still trying to get him on the bunk with the chains, with Bobby's nearly deadweight hampering him, when I felt the rush of heat. It was as if I'd opened the oven instead of just walking past it. That blast of heat washed over me in a skin-prickling rush. Bobby raised his face upward and wailed again, but this time his eyes were pure yellow. His leopard looked out of his human face. It was the first part of his humanity to go, but it wouldn't be the last.

4

"HIS EYES. LOOK at his eyes," Anthony said.

Leduc yelled, "He's shifting. Get out of there!"

Newman dropped Bobby and let him fall to his knees and one hand. The other hand was still chained to the bed and couldn't touch the floor. Newman went for the door, but I could tell that the heat wasn't enough yet. Bobby was still fighting his beast, still trying to win control back. I let myself glance at the door. Anthony had her shotgun to her shoulder like she knew how to use it. Leduc had opened the cell door for Newman. He barked an order at the deputy, telling her to put the barrel through the bars, not to hold it outside them. As soon as Newman was in the open doorway, Leduc drew his side-arm and aimed it at the fallen man. They had no idea that Bobby was still fighting to stay human. They couldn't feel it. If I left the cell, they'd just shoot him, and I couldn't even blame them.

I went to my knees beside Bobby and spoke low. "I'm here, Bobby. I'm right here."

His yellow leopard eyes stared at me from inches away. His voice came out as a growl. "Get out. Can't . . . hold it."

"Get out of there, Blake!" Leduc yelled.

"He's still fighting not to shift," I said, but I never looked away from those bright yellow eyes. I touched Bobby's arm, and his power jumped from him to me. It called my own inner leopard like I knew it would, but I trusted my control. I'd played this game before on both sides of the problem. My energy made his stumble, for lack of a better word.

"Anita, get out of there!" Newman's voice was urgent. I didn't look at him. I knew he'd have a gun in his hand by now, too. If I stopped blocking their aim, Bobby Marchand would die.

The man kneeling beside me blinked, his human face showing that he was already losing his words, because leopards don't think in words.

"Your name is Bobby Marchand. You live in Hanuman, Michigan."

He stared at me, frowning, as if he knew I was talking to him but in a foreign language that he couldn't understand.

"Come on, Bobby, I know you're in there. Talk to me."

"If he shifts with the door open, we will have to shoot, and friendly fire is a bitch, Blake," Leduc said from behind me.

"Then close the door."

"Anita, no!" Newman said.

I just kept looking into Bobby's face and willed him to answer me. "Bobby is still in there. He's still fighting to stay human. He doesn't want to hurt anyone. Do you, Bobby?"

He gave the smallest shake of his head; it was a start. I was so happy that he'd responded that I added my jolt of joy to the energy. It jumped down my hand into him. He shivered and then gripped my arm back where I still held on to him. The energy of our beasts swirled across each other's skin, and when he blinked at me next, I saw his eyes widen in surprise. He didn't whisper it, more breathed it out with his lips barely moving. None of the humans at the door heard him say, "Your eyes."

I blinked and knew that if I'd had a mirror at that moment, my own eyes wouldn't have been human either. My eyes were the only thing that ever changed for me. To save himself, he couldn't find his words, but to warn me of danger, to save me, he'd found his human half.

I leaned in close to him, using his body to hide my eyes from the door, because if they saw us both with inhuman eyes, I didn't know what would happen. No, I did know: They'd shoot us both. Maybe Newman would try to save me, but Leduc would shoot first and sort it out later, and his deputy would follow his lead. I hugged Bobby, resting my face in the bend of his neck on the side opposite the door. It gave him a perfect opportunity to tear my throat out, but I could feel the heat of his beast withdrawing like we'd finally found the knob to turn the oven off. From the doorway, people were yelling just my name or demanding to know what I was doing. But in that second, I knew if I looked back at my fellow officers with leopard eyes, they'd kill us both.

5

I RAISED MY voice to make sure all my fellow officers would hear me, but I was careful not to yell and startle the man in my arms. "We're okay. We're both okay. No one is shapeshifting. Right, Bobby?"

"Right," he said, voice low and hoarse. He had to clear his throat to be loud enough for them to hear him say, "Yes. I mean, no. I mean, I'm okay. I'm not going to change."

Newman said, "His eyes are blue again, Duke, Frankie. Let's everyone calm down and lower the weapons."

I drew back enough for Bobby to see my eyes. I thought they were human again, but I wasn't a hundred percent certain.

He nodded and then said, "We're okay. We're both okay." It was his way of saying we were both safe to look at the armed police on the other side of the bars. I took his word and looked back at them.

Newman's gun was aimed at the floor. Deputy Frankie's shotgun was lowering. It was Sheriff Leduc who still had his handgun wedged between the bars so he'd be sure not to miss us by bullets ricocheting against the metal. His eyes were wide, lips parted, breath coming a little too fast. I could almost see the pulse in the side of his neck thudding against his skin. He was the veteran officer of the three, so why was he the one who was freaking out?

I looked at him, met his brown eyes with my own so that I was giving him eye contact about as serious as I'd given anyone in a while. "Hey, Duke, I'd feel better if you lowered your sidearm or at least stopped pointing it in my direction."

"Just move away from him, Blake."

"I don't think that would be a good idea, Duke," I said. I tried to make my voice as unemotional as I could. He was emotional enough for all of us. I did not need to add to it.

Newman said, "Duke, the danger is over. We can all stand down."

A nervous tic started under one of Leduc's eyes, and the tremor that ran down his hands was strong enough that the barrel of his gun scraped against the bars. "You saw Ray's body," he said in a voice that was choked with emotion.

"I did," Newman said, his voice gentle, the way you'd talk to a spooked horse or a jumper on a ledge or a man with a gun.

Frankie said, "Duke, what's wrong with you? Just lower your gun. It's over."

"It's not over, Frankie. It won't be over until someone pays for Ray's death."

His face showed so many raw emotions, I couldn't read them all, but he was still thinking about pulling the trigger. If I hadn't been kneeling in front of Bobby, he'd have done it even now with the danger past. Hell, he was thinking about shooting through me, and he hadn't even seen my eyes change. As far as Leduc knew, I was just a U.S. Marshal here to help with the case, and he was still thinking about shooting me just so he could shoot his prisoner. I'd thought that being a fellow officer would mean something. It usually did, but as I looked into his face, I knew it didn't mean enough.

"Duke, put down the gun now," Newman said, and his voice was as serious as the gun he'd raised to point at the sheriff.

I shifted my gaze enough to see Deputy Frankie. Would she threaten Newman to back her boss, or would she understand that Duke had lost it?

"Duke," she said, "please, there's no threat from the prisoner, and you're pointing a gun at a fellow police officer."

"Duke," Newman said, voice sliding down to a lower tone than I'd ever heard from him, "do not make me do this."

"I know you, Win. You won't shoot me."

"I like you, Duke, but if you think I'll stand here and let you shoot another marshal, an unarmed fellow officer, then you are full of shit."

"Duke," Frankie said, "you taught me not to let my emotions get in the way of the job. It's a rookie mistake."

I watched the emotions war across his face. Either he'd been closer to Ray than anyone knew, or he had some personal history with lycanthrope-related crime. You had either to have lost someone to a beast or to have witnessed something that haunted your dreams to have this kind of reaction. Or, like Frankie had said, be a rookie. Leduc wasn't a rookie.

"Stand down, Duke!" Newman said, and his sidearm was pointed very steadily at the sheriff's head. If Leduc pulled the trigger he might miss us, but Newman wouldn't miss. He was too close. If he pulled the trigger, the town would be looking for a new sheriff.

The gun lowered as the tension ran out of Leduc. It was as if all the strong emotions just leaked away and what was left on his face was decades older, the skin pale. He was shaking visibly as he went for the door that led out to the offices.

I waited for the door to close behind him and then said, "Get me out of this cell."

Deputy Frankie started to fumble in her pocket for the keys while trying to balance the shotgun. It's not as easy as it sounds. Newman used his free hand to take the shotgun so she could get the keys out. He was still holding his gun in his other hand. I appreciated that he hadn't holstered it yet. Leduc could still come back through the door, and I didn't think any of us was sure what would happen if he did.

I turned to Bobby. "I don't believe you killed your uncle, so hold on to your humanity. Don't shift. Don't give them an excuse to kill you before we can prove you're innocent. Okay?"

He nodded, and then he hugged me. "Thank you."

"You're welcome," I said, and hugged him back.

Deputy Frankie got the door open. I walked out through the door and let out a long, sharp breath. I'd come close to dying more than once, but not like that, not from friendly fire.

"I've never seen Duke lose it like that," Frankie said as she made sure the cell locked securely behind me.

"Me either," Newman said.

I started collecting my guns, which were in an unceremonious heap on the floor now. Frankie had needed her hands free. I started putting my weapons in place and even checked that the 9mm was still loaded, as if somehow magically the bullets would have all disappeared. You always assume a gun is loaded, as if the ammunition fairy was real and would load your empty gun when you weren't looking, but now I needed the reassurance of just handling my weapons before I put them back in place.

"Did Leduc ever lose anyone to a shapeshifter attack?" I asked.

"Not to my knowledge," Newman said, and then glanced at the deputy. "How about you, Frankie? You know if Duke has any bad history with supernatural citizens?"

She shook her head. "No, or nothing bad enough to cause him to . . . I am so sorry, Marshal Blake."

"Is there anything happening in the sheriff's personal life? Is he under pressure from somewhere else?" I asked.

"Well, everyone knows about Lila, his daughter. She's sick, really sick."

"She's dying," Newman said. "She's got some rare form of cancer."

"That's awful, and I'd say that would be pressure."

"Lila's been sick for over two years. Last I knew, she wasn't any worse than she had been," Frankie said.

"Would he tell you if she was?" I asked.

Frankie looked at the floor like she was thinking, and then up to meet my eyes. "I thought so, but now I'm not so sure."

"Uncle Ray was helping with some of the medical bills," Bobby said.

We all turned and looked at him as if he'd just appeared. I know it sounds weird after just being up close and risking a bullet for him, but once the cell closed, he went back to being the prisoner. I felt bad that I'd let him slip back into that category so easily. Maybe I'd been on the job too long?

"They've used up the insurance that Duke gets through the town."

"What happens if Duke can't pay for the treatments?"

"I don't know," Bobby said. "I guess . . . I guess Lila will die." He looked like that bothered him, and then I realized he'd probably known her all his life.

"She's already dying," Newman said.

"But without the treatments, she'll die sooner . . . a lot sooner," Bobby said.

"How old is she, his daughter?" I asked.

"Twenty or maybe twenty-one," Bobby said. He was sitting on the edge of the bunk with the blanket around him again.

"She's twenty-one," Frankie said.

"So, whoever killed Ray Marchand basically killed the sheriff's daughter, too," I said.

"I think that's how Duke sees it," Newman said.

"Well, fuck," I said.

"Yeah," Newman said.

"Go see if you can find Duke, and check on him," Newman said.

Frankie shook her head. "We're a small force, but we're professionals. Duke made sure of that. He left me on guard duty here, and until he tells me otherwise, I'm going to follow orders. I know that you think he's lost it, and maybe he has, but until I'm sure, I'll stay at my post."

"He must be a good man for you to be that loyal to him," I said.

"He is, and I hope you get to see how good a cop he is and don't judge him just on the last few minutes."

"I hope I get to see him at his best, too."

"All right," Newman said, and his voice was heavy, "we'll go check on Duke and then drive out to the crime scene."

"Don't tell him that I told you Uncle Ray was paying Lila's medical bills. Duke hated taking the money."

"Are you seriously telling me that you're worried about the sheriff's hurt pride after he nearly shot you?" I asked.

"He's been sheriff here as long as I remember."

"He's a good man," Frankie said.

"No one should have to bury their child. That's what Uncle Ray said when he talked about it at home to Joshie and me."

I took a deep breath, let it out slowly, and looked from one to the other of them. I glanced up at Newman, and he answered my unasked question.

"Yes, until this minute, I'd have said Duke was a good man, a good cop, a good husband, and a good father."

"Then let's go find him. He still needs to drive us to the crime scene."

"I can drive us, Anita."

I shook my head. "I want Duke where we can keep an eye on him."

"I won't let a prisoner be killed on my watch," Frankie said.

I studied her face. "So if Duke comes back in here and tries to shoot Bobby again, you'll shoot him to protect your prisoner?"

She nodded. "It's my job." She sounded sure of herself, but her eyes weren't so sure.

"Maybe you would, but let's not force you to make that choice, Deputy."

She let out a breath and some tension went out of her shoulders. "I appreciate that, Marshal Blake."

"So would I, if our roles were reversed."

Newman holstered his gun and went for the door. "Let's go find Duke."

I used my body to hide the movement of my right hand from Frankie, because I drew my gun. I thought the danger was over, but I hadn't much liked being a fish in a barrel for Leduc. Maybe he was a good man, but even good men can be pushed to a point where they go bad.

6

WE FOUND DUKE leaning against the side of his big SUV. I smelled the bitterness of the cigarette smoke before I saw the bright orange-red tip glow with the intake of his breath. He threw the cigarette to the paved road with a practiced flick of his fingers.

"I gave up smoking twenty years ago, but it's just like riding a bike." He fished breath mints out of his pocket and popped several in his mouth.

Newman walked up to him as if the last few minutes hadn't happened. I hung back, my gun held against my thigh. Leduc seemed calm enough that I could probably holster it, but it might be a little awkward if he noticed me doing it.

"You're holding that gun against your thigh nice and sneaky, Blake."

"Not sneaky enough," I said, and changed how I was holding the gun to a more natural position, business end pointed politely at the ground, as I moved up behind Newman. I kept my distance from Leduc. Guns are great from a distance, but too close and it can turn into a wrestling match. Struggling over who has control of your gun is a bad idea. I tried to avoid it.

"I'm just an old hand at this, Blake. I've seen all the tricks and lived to talk about it."

He wasn't calling me Anita anymore. It's easier to shoot Blake than it is to shoot Anita. You think first names don't matter, try looking down the barrel of a gun at a perfect stranger. It's easier to pull the trigger. Let them tell you Hey, I'm Jimmy, or Armand, or Gustav, and it's a little harder to go bang. Leduc knew how close he'd come to shooting me, and he was trying to distance himself from it, from me, from whatever emotional mess was inside him. I felt sorry for him and his daughter, but not sorry enough to forget or forgive what had happened.

Leduc offered the breath mints to Newman and me, but we both shook our heads. He seemed utterly calm. It was such an abrupt change of moods that to most people it would have seemed impossible, but I'd seen other police officers, soldiers, first responders of all kinds go from that level of emotionalism to outwardly cool and collected. Is it healthy to stuff our feelings that hard and fast? No, but sometimes it's the only way you can hold your shit together enough to do your job. When first responders fail at their jobs, people die.

Normally you're supposed to act like nothing happened. They ignore it, and you ignore it, but I couldn't do that today, or not entirely. I wouldn't break Bobby's confidence about his uncle helping the sheriff out, but beyond that, we needed to talk.

"What the hell were you trying to prove in there, Blake?" Leduc asked. His voice was still calm; it even held an edge of amusement. It was a very good act.

"Nothing to prove. Just trying to keep our prisoner from getting shot."

"You're going to be executing him. Does it really matter when and how?" The amusement was leaking out of his voice.

"Yeah, it matters," I said.

"If Bobby attacks someone else, then we can shoot him in self-defense, but if he's not a danger, then it's manslaughter at best and murder at the worst," Newman said.

"Frankie and I would both testify that we thought Blake was in danger. Hell, Win, you had your gun pointed along with us."

"Once Blake told me that she had the situation under control, I believed her."

"Well, I haven't worked with the marshal before, so forgive me if

I didn't feel so confident." Leduc looked at me then and asked, "How did you get Bobby to calm down? Once a shapeshifter's eyes go, the rest usually follows."

"Do you have much experience with shapeshifters, Sheriff?" I asked.

He frowned hard enough that the dim light couldn't hide it. "Not personally, but when this happened, I did some research online." Something must have shown on my face, because he added, "I know you can't believe everything you read on there, but with a crime like this, I didn't have time to run to the library."

"Eyes are the first thing to go, but most Therianthropes with experience can fight their way back if the eyes are the only thing that changes," I said.

"How long is a person supposed to wait before we defend ourselves or another officer? Eyes, teeth, a tail? How are we supposed to know when the point of no return is, Blake?"

It was a good question, but I didn't have a good answer or a satisfying one. "It depends."

"On what?"

I sighed and holstered my gun. I couldn't stand there forever with it bare in my hand. This wasn't a matter of guns now, nothing as concrete as that. "How much control the individual Therianthrope has on his inner beast. How close it is to the full moon."

"I was told Bobby had perfect control of his animal side, but after what he did to Ray and what just happened in the cell, I don't think his control is perfect."

"Perfection is a pretty high bar, Sheriff," I said.

"When you turn into a man-eating beast once a month, I think perfection is the minimum I'd want."

I couldn't win this argument, if it was an argument. Whatever it was, I stopped putting energy or words into it. I was done with trying to convince Leduc that lycanthropes weren't monsters. A lot of people believe that supernatural citizens are people just like the rest of us until they see what preternatural strength and power can do to a natural citizen. Then suddenly they want to change their votes. I couldn't even blame them. I'd spent years thinking that the vampires I executed were soulless monsters, so it was okay to kill them. I was saving the lives of their future victims. It had all seemed so morally black-and-white until I'd met enough humans who were as evil and murderous as any vampire. Then I began to question my morality. It's a slippery slope once you start that kind of soul-searching. The kind that can lead you to fall in love and be about to marry one of the soulless undead. My grandmother Blake had informed me over the phone that I was damned if I married Jean-Claude, damned for all eternity. So many reasons I didn't visit home much.

"If Bobby is guilty, then he'll die for his crime," I said, "but I'm not convinced he is guilty."

"I told you, Blake, he is the only wereanimal we have in this area. It has to be him because it can't be anybody else."

"Did you check the body for signs of abuse?" I asked.

"It was abused all to hell."

"She means sexual abuse," Newman said.

Leduc looked at us both as if we'd said something so outrageous, he just couldn't believe his ears. "What the hell are you talking about, Win?"

"The blood on Bobby's groin . . ."

Leduc took a few steps away from us, then circled back like he was pacing in one of his own cells. "What the fuck, Win? Isn't it bad enough that Ray is dead and Bobby did it? I will not add to the scandal and pain for his family by even hinting about that kind of shit."

"Sheriff," I said, "the blood evidence on Bobby Marchand is all wrong. It's not in the right places even if he's guilty."

"That's your opinion, Marshal."

"It's an opinion backed up by a decade of working cases involving the supernatural."

"Anita has been called as an expert witness multiple times, Duke. It's one of the reasons I wanted her help."

"Fine, she's an expert on the supernatural. That doesn't give her the right to tell me we need to check Ray's body for sexual assault. That's just crazy talk. I believe that Bobby killed his uncle in some sort of animal rage, but I do not believe that he would . . . do that to the only father he's ever known."

I wanted to ask if there had ever been a hint, even the faintest whiff of talk, about the possibility that Ray Marchand had been abusing his nephew. I wanted to ask, but I didn't, not yet. I stuck to known facts. "Then how did the blood get all over Bobby Marchand's groin?"

"I don't know!" Leduc yelled, his voice raw with pain.

"We could have Dale look at the body," Newman suggested.

"Who's Dale?" I asked.

"Local coroner," he answered.

"I will not call Dale and ask him to look for signs of sexual assault on Ray's body," Leduc said. "I won't do it. We already have Bobby for the murder. We don't need anything else."

"We don't need it to get a warrant of execution and kill Bobby—that's true. But if the coroner checks for sexual abuse and doesn't find it, then the blood all over Bobby's groin has no reason to be there, just like most of the blood evidence on his body. It might give us enough to get a stay of execution," I said.

"He did it," Leduc said, and he was fumbling in his pocket for cigarettes even while he growled at me.

"But what if he didn't?" Newman said. "What if Bobby is innocent and we don't figure that out until after I kill him for the crime? I couldn't live with myself if I let that happen."

"Then give the warrant to Blake."

I thought about the feel of Bobby's skin, how warm he was, how alive he was, and I shook my head. "I came up here to help Newman get as much truth, justice, and the American way as possible. I did not come up here to take over the execution because he's gone squeamish."

"I'm not squeamish," Newman said, and he looked really unhappy with me as he said it.

"I know that, Newman. I just meant that I'm not up here to take over the warrant. I stopped pinch-hitting on warrants of execution a few years back. The only reason I'll take over a warrant now is if the first marshal is too injured to continue."

"Or dead," Newman said.

I nodded. "Or that."

"I won't talk to Dale about abuse of the corpse," Leduc said. "If you want to talk to him about shit like that, call him yourself."

"I will," Newman said.

"Good luck, because he won't believe you either, not about this."

"You'll believe that Bobby clawed his uncle to death, but not that he might have abused him either before or after death?" I asked.

"Death is clean and over. What you're hinting at is neither."

"I'll call Dale from the car when we follow you over to the crime scene," Newman said.

"You were right earlier, Win. You know the way."

"No, I think you were right the first time, Duke. I think you should take us."

Leduc looked from one to the other of us and then studied Win's face longer. Whatever he saw there made him stamp out his second cigarette and say, "I'd like to promise you I'm not a danger to Bobby anymore."

"You can't promise that, Duke," Newman said.

"No, and neither can Frankie or my other deputies. If he shifts in his cell, we will have to shoot him, because nothing inside there is strong enough to hold him, not even the bars."

"If he does a complete change of form, then it will be a justified shooting," Newman said.

"I didn't see any cameras in the cell area," I said.

"There aren't any," Leduc said.

I opened my mouth to say something that Newman obviously thought we'd all regret, because he said, "Let's get out to the crime scene. The faster Blake and I make up our minds, the faster we get this settled."

"Have it your way, Win." Leduc got in his SUV, rolled down the window, and was already lighting another cigarette. Apparently, he'd decided that quitting twenty years ago had been a mistake, and he was going to make up for lost time.

Newman and I got into his car and followed the sheriff out of town. It felt a little bit like we were being escorted out of town like in an old Western movie. I wasn't sure why I thought of that. Maybe too many Western-movie marathons with my dad when I was a kid, or maybe I'd had too many guns pointed at me since I got into town. Maybe.

7

WE FOLLOWED THE sheriff's taillights in silence for a few minutes. We sat in the darkness of the car with only the faint glow of the instrument panel to chase back the darkness. Once we left the town behind, it got seriously black, with the trees like half-seen giants on either side of the road. This far from the full moon on a cloudy night, the headlights seemed to carve tunnels out of the darkness.

"Damn, it's dark up here this far from the full moon," I said.

"Stargazing is good, and sometimes you can see the aurora borealis."

"Wow, that is dark," I said.

"What did you do to calm down Bobby's animal half?" he asked.

I don't know why, but the question caught me off guard. "Magic," I said.

"Really?" he said, and glanced at me.

I shook my head. "No, not really." Then I thought about it and wasn't so certain. Newman knew my background, so I tried for some of the truth. "I knew he'd smell my . . . the lycanthropy in my blood."

"How did that help?"

"Sometimes, if you can smell another beastie, it can bring you back to yourself."

"So, I couldn't do it?"

"No," I said.

He sighed. "I was hoping it was something you could teach me."

"Do not try hugging lycanthropes once their eyes have changed, Newman. You don't have lycanthropy, so you'd just smell like food."

"Is there anything I could do to keep someone from shifting, like through the cell bars maybe?"

He was so earnest about learning the job, it made me think harder and try to teach better. "If you knew them, if they were friends, you could talk about human memories and maybe bring them back in time."

"How about if I just knew the names of their spouses and kids, things like that? Could I talk them back to human by just reminding them about their lives, even if I didn't know them personally?"

"Maybe, but only if you're on the other side of the cage from them. And it depends on how long they've been a shapeshifter. If they're newbies, then it won't work. Once their eyes go, the rest will follow. They just don't have the control to do anything else at the beginning."

"What about bringing in family members to try to talk them down?"

"Absolutely not. You'd be endangering them. One, they're civilians, and two, think of the guilt if someone came to after being in their animal form and realized they'd killed people they loved. Don't ever put anybody in that situation."

"Okay, you're right. That would be . . . awful." He shook his head hard enough that his hat slid out of place. He shifted it back with one hand, the other staying on the steering wheel, and he added, "Awful seems like such an inadequate word, but I can't think of another one."

"You don't have to find the right word to understand how terrible something will be or why you want to avoid it," I said.

"Terrible. That's a good word," he said.

"Horrifying, heartbreaking, anguish, torment, suffering: I've got dozens to describe some of the things I've seen over the years."

"Why do you still do it, then, if it's so terrible?"

And just his asking that so early in his career after moving up to bumfuck nowhere, which had sidelined his career, let me know that Winston Newman was contemplating a change.

"So that I can help people like Bobby Marchand."

"I couldn't have saved him back there. I barely saved you," he said. I couldn't see his face clearly in the dimness of the car, but I saw his hands tighten on the wheel and knew some of the emotions prompting it.

"I got into this job to kill monsters so I could save lives, and then a weird thing happened. I stopped being certain of who the monsters were."

"You fell in love with a vampire," he said as if that explained it.

"No, I knew a man named Willie McCoy. He was a two-bit hustler, not a friend, but I knew him before he died and after he came back as a vampire. He was still Willie, still himself. That's what started me rethinking things. If vampires were soulless monsters, then Willie should have been very different after he died, but he wasn't. So, if that part was wrong, then maybe it was all wrong."

"How long ago was that?"

"Before I started dating Jean-Claude. Honestly, I think if Willie McCoy hadn't died and come back as himself, then I might never have dated Jean-Claude or any supernatural."

"Wow, I never think that clearly about what I'm feeling. It's impressive," he said.

I laughed. "Neither do I. Neither do most people, but I'm in therapy now. It's helped me realize a few things."

"You're admitting to another marshal that you're in therapy?" he said, and made it sound almost joking.

"When I got cut up on the job, I went to the hospital for stitches," I said.

"I was there for one of those," he said.

I smiled a little, though he probably couldn't see it in the dark. "Yeah, you saw me get hurt. I remember. This job doesn't just mess us up physically, Newman. It messes up our heads and our hearts. Some of this shit feels like it stains the soul. If you got a broken leg, you'd go to an orthopedist, right?"

"I guess so," he said.

"So why don't we look at a counselor or a therapist as just another specialist like an orthopedist or a dentist?"

"I don't know. I mean, when you say it that way, it sounds so logical."

"Maybe it is logical, and all the rest is just illogical, emotional bullshit."

He laughed then, and it was almost shocking after the heavy topic.

"I didn't think I was that funny," I said.

"You aren't funny. You're honest, and you go straight at a topic like a shark or something."

It was my turn to chuckle. "I've been described as a lot of things, but never a shark. I think they circle more than I do before taking a bite."

He just laughed and then, with the sound of it still in his voice, asked, "How far can we trust Duke with him this emotionally invested?"

"He's your friend, not mine, so shouldn't I be asking you that?"

"Yeah, but I figured I'd save you the trouble. I called you in on this. If you had gotten shot in the cell like that"—he shook his head—"it would have been my fault."

"No, Newman, it would not have been your fault. It would have been the fault of the person who shot me, and that wouldn't have been you."

"Duke has always been professional, kind of down-home and country like he'd read what a small-town sheriff should be like and wanted to play the part right, but always a good cop."

"Even good cops get confused when their family is impacted by a crime," I said.

"That's a kind way of looking at someone that nearly shot you."

"His daughter is dying. That's going to mess with anyone."

"You have this reputation for being a hard-ass, unpleasant person, but you're not like that. You get the job done, and you don't let bullshit stand in your way. And if someone is shoveling the bullshit, you're pretty merciless. But if they do their job, if they aren't part of the problem, you're kind."

"I'm as kind as people let me be," I said.

"Exactly," Newman said.

"Sheriff Leduc has used up my milk of human kindness for him. You understand that, right? I won't be an asshole about his daughter and the deceased paying for her treatment, but I won't let pity endanger me again."

"I wouldn't expect you to give him another pass, Blake. I honestly thought he was going to kill you both for a minute."

"I know you would have shot him to save us, Newman."

"I would have. I really would have, but damn, I would not have wanted to explain to his wife and daughter how it happened."

"You didn't have to shoot him, so there's nothing to explain."

"No, but you know how I worried that I was compromised because I knew everyone involved?"

"Yeah," I said.

"I'm not, but Duke is compromised six ways to Sunday."

"Six ways to Sunday. I haven't heard that expression in years."

He gave the small laugh that I was hoping for and said, "How would you say it?"

"Sheriff Leduc is fucking emotionally compromised."

"My grandmother would kick a fit at how much you cuss."

"Mine would, too," I said.

"I can't break my early training. How do you do it?" he asked.

"I'm still rebelling against my family."

"By saying the f-word so much?"

"By doing a lot of fucking things," I said.

"What are we going to do about Duke?" he asked.

"I think I'll start by calling another marshal," I said.

"Do you think we need more backup?"

"No, but I'd like someone besides us to know what happened tonight."

"You going to call Ted Forrester?" he asked.

"How did you know?" I asked, but I was already getting my cell phone out of the pocket it lived in when I was wearing work clothes.

"He and you are partners, or as much partners as this lone-wolf crap lets us have." And again, there was that note of discontent about how the preternatural branch was run.

I didn't argue or debate it. I just went to my favorites list on my phone. Ted's name was near the top of my list. His cell phone number was the one attached to his contact in favorites, because when you're calling for backup, you don't want to talk to the kids or the wife. One, it was business, not social, but two, just like Newman didn't want to have "the talk" with Leduc's family, I didn't want to have it with Edward's family either. It was easier not to think about the finalities of the grave when we just talked to each other.

8

My CALL WENT to Ted's voice mail. I left a very vague message, because I didn't know if he'd play it where one of his kids could hear it. Okay, where his stepson, Peter, would hear it. The two of them didn't seem to have any secrets from each other, which should have been a good thing, but I didn't want Peter joining the family business or feeling that he needed to ride to my rescue if Edward was unavailable. Peter had nearly died saving me from a weretiger when he was only sixteen. He was about to turn twenty. I did not need more heroics from him. If I didn't want to tell Donna, Edward's wife, that he had died in the line of duty, I sure as hell didn't want to tell her that her son had gotten himself killed.

Newman parked behind the sheriff's car on a wide gravel area beside the main road. The only streetlight I'd seen for miles shone down on a gate and a wall that peeked out from the trees on either side, as if the wall had been there long enough for the forest to grow up around it.

Sheriff Leduc was punching a keypad, but nothing was happening. He pushed a larger button and yelled into an intercom.

"We have the code to the gate," Newman said.

"Who could have changed it?" I asked.

Newman shook his head. "No one but one of the other deputies is supposed to be at the house."

We both started to get out of the car, but my phone rang, and it was Edward's ringtone, "Bad to the Bone" by George Thorogood.

I answered with "Hey, Ted."

"You talk to Forrester," Newman said. "I'll find out what's going on at the gate."

I gave him a thumbs-up as Edward said, "Anita, I take it you're not alone." He sounded slightly out of breath, which was unusual.

The car door closed, and I was suddenly alone in the quiet, night-dark car. "I am now."

"Social or business?" He still sounded out of breath.

"Business. Did I catch you working out?" I said.

"Yes, but if it's business, I'll get some water while you talk." I could hear sounds in the background and debated if they were from weight machines or something else.

While I gave him a thumbnail sketch of the case, especially what had just happened in the jail, he found a quieter place to listen. So when I was done, it was truly silent on his end.

Edward's first question was "Do you believe the sheriff would have shot you?"

"Yes."

"You need more than just Newman for backup," he said.

"The kid did good," I said.

"Would he really have pulled the trigger on the sheriff?"

"Yeah, I think he would have."

"I trust your judgment like I trust my own. You know that," he said.

"I know that."

"But I don't want to trust your life to Newman."

"Me either, but he had his gun aimed at Leduc's head. I think he would have pulled the trigger, Edward. I really do."

"And yet you're calling me."

"Newman is doing a good job, but there's no other marshal I trust as much as I trust you."

"I think just having more preternatural marshals on-site would protect you from the sheriff."

"Are you ass deep in alligators and not able to come out and play?" I asked.

I could almost hear the smile in his voice as he said, "No, but it will take me nearly five hours to fly to you, or almost twenty-four hours driving. What I need to know from you is how fast you need backup."

"And if I said sooner than five hours?"

"Put out a general call through official channels, and they'll send the closest marshal from our section to your location."

"You're talking round your ass to get to your elbow. It's not like you, Edward. Newman said I was direct like a shark, but you're part of what taught me to be direct. What are you trying to say or not say?"

"The nearest marshal to you is Olaf."

"No. Just no. I'll go without backup before I invite that psycho here."

"I figured you'd say that, but I had to be sure."

"How do you even instantly know where he is? I don't know."

"I make it my business to keep track of him."

"Do you keep track of me like that?"

"No."

"Do you keep track of anyone else like that?"

"No."

"You want to know where he is in case you decide to kill him," I said.

"No, I want to know where he is in case I have to kill him."

There was a time in our friendship when I wouldn't have understood that distinction, but that had been a while ago. Olaf, aka Marshal Otto Jeffries, was a serial killer. Edward and I both knew that, but neither of us could prove it, and Olaf had never committed that particular crime on American soil to our knowledge. I'd never even caught him in the act. Edward had once. If Edward caught him at it again, he would kill Olaf. They both knew the rules of the game. So far Olaf hadn't done anything illegal that Edward could use as an excuse, but he kept tabs on him, waiting. Olaf had fallen off the radar when he first contracted lycanthropy, even from Edward's resources. When Olaf reappeared, he had a level of control of his inner beast that most shapeshifters would have envied. Olaf was a scary, sociopathic suspected serial killer, but no one had ever accused him of slacking when it came to training.

"So, if I put out a general call for aid, he's the nearest help," I said.

"I'm afraid so," Edward said.

"Fuck," I said.

"Agreed," he said.

"I don't need backup that badly, Edward. Newman is good enough."

"Good to know," he said.

"Yeah," I said, but I was mentally cursing. "I thought Olaf was out west somewhere at his home base. What the fuck is he doing in the upper Midwest?"

"He's hunting a rogue shapeshifter."

"How close to me is he?" I asked.

"Close."

"How close?"

"Very close."

"Just tell me, Edward."

"If he dropped his hunt, he could be there in an hour, maybe less."

"Flying or driving?" I asked.

"Driving."

"Well, fuck."

"You said that."

"I'll probably be saying it a lot more if I have to deal with tall, dark, and psycho."

"You won't have to deal with him, Anita. You and Newman can hold the fort, and I'll be there in six hours or sooner."

"I think having you come in as backup for this may be overkill," I said.

"If you really believed that, you wouldn't have called me."

"I don't think Leduc is dangerous enough to need you here."

"Then why did you call?"

I thought about that for a few heartbeats and finally said, "If Newman hadn't had a gun to his head, I think Leduc would have shot into the cell. I'd given up all my guns before I stepped inside."

"Giving up your weapons is standard procedure," Edward said.

"I know. That's why I did it. I've done it before. I'll do it again for a different case, but usually the danger is the prisoner, not the other officers."

"Leduc spooked you," he said softly.

"He would have done it, Edward."

"I'll be there in six hours or less," he said.

"Sounds like a plan," I said.

"It is, but if things go south while I'm in the air trying to get to you and your choice is dead before I land or calling for more backup, promise me you'll call for the backup."

"No, Edward."

"Anita, if you're in the hospital or dead before I can get to you, I will be pissed."

"I've never worked with Olaf without you there to help keep the distance or the peace between us."

"I know, and it's not my favorite idea either, but he's a good man in a fight."

"He's evil."

"Sometimes evil will keep you alive."

"Being alive isn't always enough, Edward. You've got to live with yourself afterward."

"Promise me, Anita."

"Damn it, Edward."

"If the situations were reversed and you knew Olaf was close enough to save me, what would you want me to do?"

"That's not fair. He doesn't want you to be his serial killer girl-friend."

"Just answer my question, Anita."

"You told me once if I saw him to just shoot him dead and not to wait for him to hurt me, that you'd rather I be on trial than dead at his hands."

"I remember what I said."

"Then how can you want me to promise this?"

"Because I think you can negotiate the emotional baggage that Olaf has with you for six hours, but you can't outrun a bullet. He acquitted himself well last time both professionally and with you."

"I won't give up my guns again, not to Leduc or his people. I'll just wait for you."

"Anita, just promise me you'll do it. I don't want to have to explain to Jean-Claude, or Micah, or Nathaniel, or any of your people that you died because you were too stubborn to take the closest help."

"It's not stubbornness, Edward, and you know it."

"If we let our fear master us, Anita, then we're already dead."

"You're afraid of the big guy, too."

"I didn't say I wasn't, and the thought of him being near you when I'm not there scares the shit out of me."

That stopped me. He almost never admitted out loud that he was personally afraid of anything. "Okay, okay, I promise that if things get so dangerous that Newman and I can't handle them, I'll put out a general call for help, even if that means Marshal Otto Jeffries is the help."

"Thank you," he said.

"You're welcome," I said.

He got off the phone to check flights, and I finally got out of the car to join my fellow officers. It turned out that some of the family had come home, and the deputy guarding the scene had let them change the gate code. Leduc was yelling at someone over the intercom as the gates swung open. He was breathing heavily as he turned back to get in his car. Something must have shown on my face, because he said, "Looks like your personal phone call didn't go well."

"My personal business is none of yours."

"No need to snap at me because one of your boyfriends is getting out of hand."

I stepped up to him, invading the hell out of his personal space. He was so much bigger than me it probably looked ridiculous, but I didn't care. "Fine, I was trying to be nice, but if you don't want nice, we can do it the other way. I was calling another marshal for backup, because after having a fucking gun pointed at me by you, I felt we might need more guns on our side."

I was sorry I'd said the words as soon as they left my mouth. I didn't even have to see the pain in Leduc's eyes to be sorry. The cold, dead stare that replaced the pain was chilling, like someone had walked over my grave. I'd given him a target for all his rage and fear—me. So stupid, so avoidable, so my own damn fault.

9

WHEN WE ALL got back in our respective cars, Newman tried not to be angry with me, but he was upset and couldn't hide it. I finally saved him the struggle and said, "I behaved badly back there, and I'm sorry."

Newman's hands were gripping the steering wheel a little too tight as he tried to keep his voice even. "Aren't you the one who told me, 'Don't be sorry. Do better'?"

"One of the reasons I'm more patient with other people's rookie mistakes is that I had my share of them. Having a temper that made my mouth run away with the rest of me was one of them."

"We had things calmed down with Duke," he said as he eased between the now-open gates and followed the sheriff up the driveway.

"I know, and I am sorry that I lost my temper and made things worse again." Some sense of movement made me look behind us in time to watch the gates ease shut.

"I called you in to help make things better, not worse," he said. The trees were huge on either side of the gravel driveway. Again I got the sense that the estate had been here long enough to become one with the forest around us.

"I'm aware of that," I said, and I could already feel myself getting irritated with the fact that he was harping on it.

My temper is better than it was a few years ago, but I will always have it bubbling close to the surface. One of the things I'd learned in therapy is that fixing your issues isn't the same thing as getting rid of them. You discard the things that no longer serve you, but some things are so much a part of you that you can't get rid of them without destroying who you are and how you function as a person. My temper was one of those, but more than that, it was part of my aggression, and aggression was how I did my job and protected the ones I loved, how I succeeded more than I failed. Society views aggressive women as bitches, but sometimes being a bitch is the only way to survive. I'll take survival over being Miss Congeniality any day.

"You were visibly upset when you got off the phone. You can't blame Duke for noticing that."

"No, but I can blame him for making the remark about my boyfriends."

"I've seen people say worse to you, and you let it go," he said.

"Yeah, I know."

"So why now? What did Forrester say on the phone that got you so rattled?"

I shook my head. "I don't want to talk about it."

"You know, I defend you when people say that you're sleeping with Forrester. I tell them, 'She wouldn't have been best man at his wedding if his wife didn't trust Blake,' but you're acting like the phone call was more personal than just partners."

"Are you asking me if I'm sleeping with Ted?"

"No," he said, "absolutely not." He sounded offended, almost panicked in distancing himself from the question, which meant either he really didn't want to know or he really did.

I debated how much to share with him and finally realized that if I was truly afraid of Olaf and he might become our backup, Newman had a right to know at least part of it. I was still debating when the driveway spilled out into a circle with a huge fountain in the middle of it. The house rose up like a dark cliff face. Even the few lit windows didn't take away from the sensation that the house was part of the landscape like the forest that bordered everything.

"Is that just a huge-ass fountain or a moderate-size swimming pool?" I asked.

He gave a small laugh, but it was a start. "It's a fountain. The water around it is too shallow for anything but wading."

Leduc was out of his car and yelling at another man in a similar uniform. We couldn't hear what he was saying, but the porch light above them let us see their faces. The second man was fighting not to recoil from the sheriff's pointing finger, which was stabbing at his chest. If it had been a knife, it would have gone through his heart.

"Who's Leduc yelling at?" I asked.

"Rico Vargas. Deputy Rico Vargas." Just the tone in Newman's voice made me raise an eyebrow.

"I take it he's not your favorite deputy," I said.

"No," Newman said, and got out of the car before I could ask why.

I guessed we were both allowed to keep our secrets. I got out on my side of his car and had to double-time it to catch up with his longer legs.

"What the fuck were you thinking, Rico? This is the kind of shit that Troy usually pulls. You're supposed to be the smart one," Leduc was thundering, or maybe it was just the acoustics of the stone arch they were standing under that made his voice into a bass rumble of noise like having a verbal rockslide thrown at you.

Deputy Rico mumbled something, but Leduc yelled, "No, I don't want to hear one more goddamn excuse from you, Rico!"

We were close enough to hear the deputy say, "But it's their house. How can I tell them they can't come into their own house?"

"This is not their house. This is our crime scene!" Leduc said, pushing the flat brim of his hat into Rico's forehead so that the only thing that kept them from touching faces was the hat.

It took me a second to realize that the hat brim was almost cutting into the skin of Rico's forehead above his eyebrows. He was taller than the sheriff, so he had to be careful not to stand as straight as he could or the hat's edge would have cut across his eyes. On some police forces, it would have crossed the line from getting your ass chewed to talking to your union rep, but I guessed on a force this small, there wasn't a union. Who do you complain to when there's no one higher than the boss?

Thanks to the sheriff yelling at the gate intercom earlier, I knew that Deputy Vargas had not only allowed family members into the house, but had allowed them to change the security code, which meant without it the police didn't have access to the crime scene unless the family let them in. Family is almost always the first suspected in a murder. You don't really want them running amok at the crime scene until you're certain they didn't do it.

Newman didn't exactly yell, but he raised his voice enough to be heard. "When did they release Jocelyn from the hospital?"

Leduc stopped yelling, just stood there with his hat brim shoved into his deputy's forehead like a knife-edge poised to strike. He nearly growled his next words into Deputy Vargas's face. "Answer the marshal's question, Rico."

Rico swallowed so hard, I could see it from yards away. "I don't know, Sheriff."

Leduc moved back minutely so that his hat wasn't actually touching the other man. He closed his eyes and took a deep breath. I think he was counting to ten. He spoke in a very careful voice, as if he was afraid of what he'd do if he lost his temper again. "How long has Jocelyn been here, Rico?"

"It's not Joshie, Sheriff."

"You said the family was inside," the sheriff said, frowning at him.

"Yeah, Muriel and Todd Babington are inside."

"God give me strength," Leduc said. "Muriel and Todd don't live here, Rico. It's not their house. The only one that should be changing the security is Jocelyn Marchand, not Ray's little sister and her husband."

"They said they were worried that whoever murdered Ray had the security codes and that there were a lot of valuable antiques in the house."

"Yeah, and they've had their eyes on the valuables in this house for years," Leduc said, pushing past his deputy. The door wasn't locked, thank goodness. I'm not sure what Sheriff Leduc would have done to Vargas if he'd allowed himself to be locked outside of the crime scene by possible suspects. Of course, maybe Leduc didn't see Muriel and Todd as suspects, but I did. If Bobby hadn't done it, then Aunt Muriel and Uncle Todd had just made the top of my list.

10

LEDUC MOVED SO fast through the house that I got only glimpses of it, but what I saw looked like antiques, with real crystal dangling from every light fixture and candleholder, and there seemed to be a lot of those everywhere. The paintings looked like originals, and the statues, from life-size people to tabletop designs, were marble and metal. It was like rushing through a mini museum. Leduc was like a tour guide who had forgotten his job, but he certainly knew his way around the place, because he opened doors only to certain rooms, checked they were empty, and then rushed to another one.

There seemed to be no order to the rooms he was looking at downstairs, and finally he headed for the upstairs, but he didn't go back to the front of the house and up the grand staircase that was near the front door. He went through a small hallway tucked under an archway. I got a glimpse of a kitchen sitting dim and empty, and then he led us round a sharp turn to a much smaller set of stairs that was so narrow, I wasn't sure Leduc's waistline would fit, like Santa trying to squeeze through a chimney. Maybe I've always been so small that I just don't understand how to navigate the world if you're big. Leduc had no issues; he just had to duck a little on the tight turns of the stairs. Newman, who was nearly a foot taller than me and a few inches taller than Duke, had to take off his hat and bend over a little so he didn't hit his head. I caught movement around the edges of him and realized that Deputy Vargas was behind us rather than staying at his post. He was as tall as Newman, with broader shoulders, but he seemed to be squeezing through just fine, which meant he was a lot more agile than he'd looked while the sheriff was chewing him out. Meanwhile I was keeping one hand touching each wall so that I could feel how rough the plaster was, because it was narrow enough that my claustrophobia wasn't happy. I knew from experience that my eyes might tell me the walls were collapsing in on me, but my hands would stay the same width apart. So as long as my hands didn't move, I could talk my brain out of believing the optical panic. Maybe the stairs weren't as narrow as they felt, but I could keep my fingertips on either side as I followed Leduc up them, and with my smaller shoulders—the stairs were narrow enough.

Leduc opened a door at last, and he was through it before I had time to take a deep breath and let my body know it was in a broad, richly carpeted hallway instead of on the torturously narrow stairs. A heavyset man was carrying a small suitcase out of an open door. He saw us, or maybe just the sheriff, and froze like a deer in head-lights. He blinked, and his round head with only a fringe of dark hair left made him look owlish, all big eyes and round face. He drew the suitcase into the curve of his arms protectively.

"Hey, Todd," Leduc said all friendly, as if they were in town just bumping into each other.

"Hello, Duke. What brings you here so late?" Todd's voice wasn't as matter-of-fact as Duke's, but he tried.

"Work."

"Oh." Todd glanced back at the open door. I kept expecting him to call out and warn the mysterious Muriel, Ray Marchand's sister.

I was fighting not to push past Leduc and see what was in the case and what Todd's other half was doing in the room behind him. New-man moved up beside me enough for me to look at him. He gave a small shake of his head. This was his town and his warrant. I could chill—for a while.

Duke took the few steps he needed to be within reach of Todd. He held his hand out wordlessly. Todd hugged the case to himself a little tighter. Duke turned his hand upside down and moved his fingers in a give-it-to-me motion.

Todd glanced back at the open door and called out, "Muriel, we have guests."

It was so not on my list of things I expected him to say. It was the politest thing I'd ever heard anyone say when confronted by the police in the middle of committing a crime.

"Guests," a woman's voice said from inside the room. "What do you mean, we have guests? Rico would have asked our permission before letting anyone else into our house."

I felt Deputy Rico shift uneasily behind us without having to see around Newman. The sheriff moved so he could keep an eye on Todd and still give Rico a dirty look. Leduc got some of his brownie points back because he kept Todd in his sights as he moved. The man in front of us looked harmless, but a lot of "harmless" people end up killing cops every year. Just because Todd was clutching the case to his chest like a baby didn't mean there wasn't a gun tucked into his belt.

A woman—Muriel, I assumed—walked through the doorway. An angry scowl crossed her face before she got it under control and smiled pleasantly at us, but she couldn't quite get her eyes under control, while the rest of her nearly perfect face was all gracious hostess. She was tall, with blond hair that was almost the same shade of yellow as Bobby Marchand's. The family resemblance was strong enough that I'd have thought they were mother and son, not just aunt and nephew, if I hadn't known better. She was a handsome woman, like a blond Jane Russell, but slenderer, fewer curves. But some things even good cosmetic surgery can't change, so the thin arm she held out to Leduc had more loose skin in places than the rest of her seemed to promise. She kept herself thin but didn't worry about muscle tone, and without that, you can nip and tuck anything you want, but age will catch up. Maybe it always catches up—I didn't know yet—but Muriel Babington had done her best to stay ahead of time.

Thanks to Jean-Claude's love of jewelry, I knew that the gold chain with its simple diamond and the pair of understated antique earrings in gold and more diamonds cost more than most people's yearly salaries. The watch on her left wrist was a vintage Rolex. It complemented the cream pants and vest buttoned over a blue silk blouse that made her gray-blue eyes look closer to Bobby's brighter blue. I didn't know the designer of the clothes, but I was betting that everything she was wearing was designed by a name I should have known. Jean-Claude would have known, even Nathaniel might have known, but I didn't. The best I could do was recognize expensive when I saw it.

As Muriel glided down the hallway toward us, her pants gave glimpses of pale leather boots with stiletto heels, though once heels go that high, I think they're just high heels with boot fronts. Boots imply practical, and these shoes were not, but they did give her slender frame more feminine swish, which was the goal of heels like that. I had a few pairs that did the same thing, but after a few date nights when I danced in them, I was beginning to rethink the sexy-heels-to-comfort ratio. The closer the wedding got, and the more Jean-Claude insisted on dressing me up, the more I wanted to rebel against the whole impractical idea of women's fashion.

"What brings you by so late, Duke?" Muriel asked.

"Like I told Todd, work."

"You have the murderer locked up. Case solved," she said.

If I hadn't known that it was her brother who had been brutally murdered and her nephew locked up for the crime, I'd have thought she was an uninterested bystander, maybe a distant family acquaintance.

"Muriel, you know you can't be in here right now."

"I know no such thing. My brother is dead, and that's awful, but I warned him about Bobby."

"What did you warn him about?" Leduc asked.

She gave him a pitying look, as if he were being too stupid for words. Disdain dripped off her well-manicured hand as she put it on her hip. "You know what Bobby is, Duke. Don't play games after you saw what he did to Ray."

I fought to keep my face and body very still and not give away the spurt of adrenaline I'd felt because of the wording. If they knew details about Ray Marchand's body, then they had been here before the cops were called.

"What did he do to Ray, Muriel?" Leduc asked.

Her look went from disdainful to scathing. "Come on, Duke. I didn't see Ray's body, but seeing the study where he was killed was enough. It looks like a damn butcher shop."

Duke looked at the husband still clutching the small case to his chest. "What did you think of Ray's body when you saw it, Todd?"

Muriel touched her husband's shoulder. "We didn't see the body, Duke. Todd wouldn't even come into the study with me." Her voice held scorn and disappointment, as if she was often scornful of and disappointed in her husband.

"I saw the bloody footprints in the front hallway up here," Todd said. "That was enough for me."

"It would be for you," she said, and her tone was humiliating. I couldn't imagine being married to someone who would talk to me like that in front of strangers or at all.

Todd didn't say anything in return, just huddled more tightly around the small case in his arms.

Duke said, "What's in the case, Todd?"

Todd glanced at his wife and then at the floor but didn't meet anyone else's eyes. He didn't answer the question either.

Duke held out his hand. "Give me the case, Todd."

Muriel pushed in front of her husband so that Leduc either had to back up or let her invade his personal space. He didn't move back. Underneath the panic and pain of earlier was a good cop. I hoped to see more of that side of him and let the bad cop be an unfortunate moment we could all forget.

In the heels, she was a few inches taller than Leduc. "We don't have to let you see inside the case, Duke. It's our case. We brought it into the house. Rico there will tell you he saw us bring it in. Didn't you, Rico?"

The sheriff was already standing so he could keep Muriel and

Todd in his peripheral vision and see the deputy, but Newman and I had to move to the other side of the hallway opposite Duke so we could help keep an eye on everyone.

Rico gave her a less-than-friendly look, and something about the darker emotion made him look better or more real. I realized he was handsome in that generic Hollywood way, if you were going for a mix of old-fashioned Latin lover and Midwestern college athlete. The hair I could see around his Smokey Bear hat was as black as mine and had curl left even though it had been cut short. He looked like he'd tan darker than I did, but I was betting that his heritage was mixed like mine. The last name Vargas should have been a clue. Sometimes I'm slow, but mostly if you do your job, I just don't care.

"Yes, they had it with them when they drove up," Rico said.

"Where did they park, now that you bring it up? It's only your cruiser out front," Duke said.

"Your deputy was kind enough to let us use the garage," Muriel said.

Duke's eyes narrowed at the deputy. "So, you have no idea what they may have taken from the house and put into their car?"

"I was made to understand that it was their house and their stuff," Rico said. His face showed that he didn't like giving the answer, because he knew he was wrong now. He took off his hat and started running his hands around the brim like a comfort gesture. He looked better without the hat, showing that he had more curls left than the short sides had promised.

"Well, you were made to understand wrong," Duke said.

"I know the will hasn't been read yet, but our father always meant the house and contents to stay in the family," Muriel said.

"Not waiting for the will to be read is one thing, but your brother's body isn't even cold yet. That's jumping the gun more than I can overlook, Muriel."

"I'm about to become the wealthiest person in this county, Duke, and sheriff is an elected position."

"Are you threatening me, Murry?"

"Don't call me that awful nickname."

"How about El? You didn't mind that nickname once."

Her face became even more superior, but there might have been a slight blush underneath the perfect foundation. It was hard to tell, but she didn't like him calling her either nickname. That was for sure.

"It's not a threat, Sheriff Leduc. It's just a reminder of the politics around here."

"Well, now, Mrs. Babington, your brother, Ray, was the richest person in the county. That's for certain. But you and Todd are usually broke."

She put one delicate hand to her necklace. "It's Mrs. Marchand-Babington, and do I look like someone who's broke?"

"You're wearing and driving your money, Muriel. I know that. You know that. Now everyone in the hallway knows it. If you don't want the whole town to know it, I suggest Todd hand me the case so I can see what's in it, and then we'll mosey down to your car and see if anything else got packed away."

"You will regret this, Duke."

"I regret a lot of things, Muriel, but this isn't going to be one of them. Now, hand over the case, or I'll have to take it from Todd. You know I can."

"You could have twenty years ago," she said, and tried for the same disdain that she'd aimed at her husband.

Leduc laughed at her, and if it had a bitter tone to it, it still surprised her. She'd meant to hurt him. "Even with a few extra pounds, he's no match for me, Muriel. You know that. Don't make me prove it."

"Because you know you'll lose," she said, and tried to sound triumphant but failed.

It wasn't all about weight and waist sizes. Just because Todd was smaller didn't change the fact that he was soft and doughy. There was no muscle tone underneath his weight, and there was underneath Leduc's. But more than that, one man was huddled in on himself, and the other man was standing up straight and tall, confident in the moment. You didn't have to know either of them to know which side would win a physical encounter or even an argument.

"Todd, just hand me the case." Duke's voice was almost gentle as he spoke.

Todd started to offer the case to Duke, but Muriel snapped at him, "Don't you dare! He has no rights here."

Todd held the case tighter again and sighed.

"Are the contents of the case breakable?" Duke asked.

"That's none of your business."

"Well, now, if Todd and I start playing tug-of-war with it and it falls, I just wanted to be sure there wasn't anything fragile before we start this."

Todd looked up at his wife. "Muriel, honey, we don't want to risk damaging it."

She made a disgusted sound. "Fine. Fine, give him the case. Fail me like you always fail me."

Wow, I thought, that was harsh and cruel and out loud. Why would anyone stay with a spouse who talked to them like that?

"It's okay, Todd," Duke said, and this time his voice was kind, a hell of a lot kinder than Muriel's had been.

I realized that Duke felt sorry for the man. I think we all did, but it felt more personal with Duke. Just the few remarks between him and Muriel had implied they'd dated semiseriously twenty years ago. Did he look at Todd Babington and think, There but for the grace of God go I? I couldn't imagine anyone wanting to be married to the bitter beauty of Muriel Marchand-Babington.

Duke took the case from Todd Babington's hands gently but firmly. There was no weakness to his kindness, just a different kind of strength. Whatever was happening between the three of them had a long history, and I felt like something between a voyeur and unneeded backup, the police equivalent of a third wheel.

Leduc started to kneel in the middle of the hallway, but then seemed to think better of it. "Come here, Rico. You might as well be useful for something." He laid the case on the younger man's arms and made sure he had a good grip on it before hitting the locks.

When the case opened without needing to be unlocked, Muriel said, "How could you forget to lock the case, Todd?"

"I'm sorry, Muriel," he muttered, staring at the floor like a dog that had been hit once too often. His reaction to her wasn't love—at least not to me.

Duke opened the case carefully and then sighed heavily. Newman was tall enough to see what was in the case, but I wasn't. All I could do was guess as Duke said, "These are worth more than I'll make in the next ten years, maybe more to the right buyer. I'm assuming you have a buyer lined up."

"I don't know what you're talking about," Muriel said. "I just thought that it would be wise to remove some of the most valuable pieces from the house, with all the police and other strangers having access to it."

"So, you're only removing the small valuables that could be pocketed by the riffraff?" Duke said, voice tired and a little angry as he looked up at her.

I whispered to Newman, "What is it?"

He whispered back, "Porcelain figurines."

"Sorry, Marshal Blake. I guess you can't see," Leduc said.

"Maybe on tiptoes, but I'd hate to overbalance and knock the case."

"That would be a shame," Leduc said, and lifted the case out of Rico's arms so I could see two figurines nestled in gray foam that had been cut to hold them.

They were a male figure and a female figure, and there was just enough of the clothing to make me say, "They're Harlequin."

He looked surprised. "You know your porcelain," he said.

"No," I said, "but I recognize the costumes and colors enough to guess that they're supposed to be some sort of harlequin based on the old Italian commedia dell'arte."

Newman asked, "How do you know any of that?"

"I have friends old enough to have seen the actors live onstage."

I didn't add that the Harlequin was also a code name for the vampire equivalent of secret police and for the bodyguards of the queen or king of the vampire council. They'd once been the vampire equivalent of the bogeyman, and now what remained of them belonged to Jean-Claude and I guess technically me as his soon-to-be queen. I had managed not to share any of this with fellow police officers, and I didn't intend to start now. I don't know what made me say it out loud to begin with. Had I been showing off? Did Muriel's treatment of all of us as thieving riffraff bother me? Maybe. I wondered if later she'd planned on trying to blame some of the emergency responders for the disappearance of the figurines.

"They are based on actual actors that played the parts," Todd said, and he looked at me, really met my eyes and looked at me as if I'd done something interesting enough to get through the fog of emotional abuse.

"You know people old enough to have known the actors these are based on? That's impossible. Oh, you mean vampires," Muriel said, and managed to imply by tone alone that she thought even less of me now.

"Yeah, I mean vampires," I said.

Todd's eyes glazed over, and he looked at the floor again. His eyes were brown, which I hadn't been sure of until that moment. Jesus, he really was an abuse victim, so hurt that he didn't want to meet anyone's eyes. Could just verbal abuse destroy a person like that, or did Muriel add physical abuse behind closed doors? Spousal abuse is illegal, no matter what gender everyone is. It made me wonder if Todd might need a little rescuing. I filed it away for later. Once I'd helped save Bobby Marchand and found the real killer, I'd see about rescuing abused husbands, if Todd wasn't guilty of anything worse than attempted grand larceny. If he'd helped Muriel kill Ray Marchand and frame Bobby, then I couldn't save him. No one could.

"I thought marshals killed the monsters," Muriel said.

"That's part of the job description," I said.

"Then they can't be your friends."

"It does tend to complicate things," I said.

Muriel looked at me as if trying to decide if I was kidding her. I wasn't, or not much. "I am surprised that anyone with your job would recognize Nymphenburg porcelain."

"Figurines like this, some drawings, paintings are all that's left of people my friends knew centuries ago. It's a way of them showing me snapshots of some of the people they talk about." I didn't add that Jean-Claude had a figurine of an actress he'd been in love with once. It was in a glass case in a room of treasures that I hadn't even known he had until recently. The closer we got to the wedding, the more he tried to make sure he had told me everything that I might want to know before we said *I do*. But since he was over six hundred years old, his backstory was a little longer than mine. It wasn't that he was keeping things from me; it was literally that there was so much to remember, he forgot things. Scientists were starting to study vampires to try to figure out how they could remember so many centuries as well as they did. They were hoping it might lead to a cure for Alzheimer's and other brain-deterioration issues.

Duke had Newman take a picture of the statuettes nestled in their case, before shutting it carefully and taking it from Rico. "Let's go see what's in your car that you felt needed to be saved from us poor policemen. Sorry, Blake. Police persons."

"That's really not necessary, Duke," Muriel said. Apparently they were back on a first-name basis again.

"Oh, it feels necessary to me, Muriel. I mean, what would the insurance company say if some of these valuable antiques went missing? They might blame the wrong people, like some of the hardworking emergency personnel, and we wouldn't want them to blame the wrong people, would we, Todd?"

"Um, no, of course not," Todd stuttered.

"Shut up, Todd!" Muriel snapped.

"Let's all go down to the garage and take a peek," Duke said.

Muriel actually touched his arm, her body language changing to something softer. "We don't need all these other officers, Duke."

"Oh, I think we do."

She sidled closer to him so that a lot more of her body touched his than seemed appropriate for the circumstances. "We're old friends, Duke. We don't need a crowd."

He stared at her as if even he couldn't believe she was trying to seduce her way out of the situation.

I laughed; I couldn't help it. It was just so damn ballsy.

Muriel managed to stay snaked up against Duke and still give me a hard look. "This is none of your business. You've got your monster locked up in the jail. This is regular police business, just Duke and me."

"I don't think so, Muriel. I think I like the marshals tagging along while we're securing the scene."

She traced a perfect fingernail around the edge of his ear underneath his Smokey Bear hat. He jerked back then and stepped away from her, putting a hand on her arm to keep her from cuddling up again. "We don't need them, Duke."

"Two United States Marshals make fine witnesses."

"Witnesses to what, Duke?" Even her voice had gone lower—sultry, like she really thought she had a chance in hell of convincing him. Either this kind of shit had worked on him once upon a time, or she had a very high opinion of herself. Maybe a little of column A and a lot of column B.

"Marshal Blake, I hate to ask, but can you keep an eye on Muriel? She's less likely to try her womanly wiles with you."

"Glad to help a fellow officer out." I stepped up beside the woman. In her heels, she towered over me, but I managed not to be too intimidated.

"Duke, I don't want to go with her. I want to go with you."

"Did that vampy baby-girl voice ever really work on me?" he asked.

"It's just the side of me you bring out," she nearly purred.

Leduc sighed and called Todd up with him. "Let's go to the garage."

Muriel reached out toward both men, though I was pretty sure she was aiming at Duke. I gently blocked her arm and said, "If you can't keep your hands to yourself, I'll cuff you—and while we're at it, we should search them."

"There's no need for that," Rico said, but it was like his heart wasn't in it, as if he was saying it because he felt he had to say something.

Duke turned on him. "You let them into a house they don't own. You let them change the security code and not share it with you. You'd have let them drive out with this." He raised the case in his hand.

"They can't steal something that already belongs to them," Rico said.

I wondered if Rico was really that stupid or just . . . Nope, I was going to have to go with stupid, because I couldn't come up with another explanation.

"It doesn't belong to them, Rico. Nothing in this house belongs to them. This house doesn't belong to them. Ray and Muriel were estranged. That means they didn't like each other. We have no way of knowing what is in the last will and testament of Ray Marchand until the will gets read. Until that time, we treat this as his house, his things. Jocelyn and Bobby were the only family that lived in this house with Ray, and even they can't take things out of it except for personal items. Am I being clear?"

Rico glared at him, his lower lip going under a little as if he was literally biting down to keep from saying things he'd regret later. It looked like there was a lot of ego inside the tall man, and he'd already been humiliated once tonight by his boss. His voice was low and careful and the words tight as he said, "Yes, Duke, you're being clear."

I didn't know Vargas, but even I could hear the subtext of *Go fuck yourself.* I guess it doesn't count as insubordination unless they say it out loud.

"Rico knows that it's just a matter of paperwork and everything in here is mine."

"Maybe, Muriel, but until that paperwork happens, assume the position."

"What?"

"He means put your hands flat against the wall and lean," I said.

"What?" she asked again, and sounded suitably outraged. So I helped her lean against the wall, though kicking her feet farther apart in the stilettos almost brought her to her knees. Once she realized we were actually going to search them both, she tried to lure Duke over to do her, but he stayed with the husband and left me to the femme fatale. Newman stayed close by in case I needed backup, or maybe he just wondered if Muriel would offer to let him pat her down, or he thought I'd be too rough with her. She kept telling me how important she was, or her family was, and how I'd regret this someday. She also kept pushing off the wall and trying to turn until I pinned her against the wall with an elbow in a pressure point on her back and threatened again to put on the cuffs. She cried for help about the pressure point, and Newman helped hold her while I got my cuffs off my belt. I could have held her without the help, but I'd have had to take her to the floor, and it would have been a lot rougher ride for Ms. Marchand-Babington. The cuffs made that nice little metallic sliding sound as I found the right size for her wrists. She had slender wrists for such a tall person. She was actually screaming as Newman and I brought her off the wall with a hand on either of her arms. She tried to stomp my foot with the stiletto. I avoided it. Newman didn't, but no lasting damage. She fought like, well, an untrained girl. Besides, the cuffs were rated for supernatural suspects; she wasn't getting away.

11

TODD BABINGTON HAD werewolf spray in his pants pocket. Despite what it was called, it was rated for any shapeshifter, which meant it was pepper spray's tougher, uglier cousin. It was new on the market, because a couple of people had died after trying to use human-defense spray on shapeshifters. It had just pissed them off and made them more violent, so a new product had emerged to fill the void. Edward had experimented with it and declared it too dangerous indoors unless you put on a gas mask first. This from the man who burned a house down around us once because he used a flamethrower inside on a group of vampires.

Duke said, "Why do you have this, Todd?"

He gave a quick eye flick toward his wife and then said, "I didn't want to come back here without some protection."

"You're a fool, Todd. You didn't need anything to protect you," Muriel said.

"Ray was killed by a wereanimal."

"They have the wereanimal that killed Ray locked up. He can't hurt anyone anymore," she said.

"Bobby loved Ray like a father, Muriel. I just don't think he could do this."

"You were always overly sentimental about the boy."

"We should have taken Bobby when your sister and her husband died. He would have had two parents, and he'd have never gone on that safari trip after graduation."

"So you're saying it's our fault that Bobby got attacked in Africa?"

"Not our fault," he said, but his voice held a note of angry strength, and his eyes were less unsure.

"Good. I thought you were blaming us for Ray endangering the boy on all those adventures."

"No, not us," he said, and just for a second, his hatred for her showed in his eyes. I saw it as I stood there with a hand on her arm. Did she see it?

"Me? You're blaming me?"

"Yes," he said, very clear and precise.

"Don't blame me that we couldn't have children of our own. It's your sperm that doesn't work."

Todd flinched as if she'd hit him, crumpling a little forward as if it had been a gutshot, and maybe it had been in a way. It was a low blow—something that should have been on the list of things never to say in a fight. Every couple has a list of things that should never be said in anger, because once said you can't take them back, and the damage is done. Some words, even true words, are relationship killers.

Muriel didn't even look sorry. She looked triumphant, as if she knew she'd gotten the last word, and she had. That little spark of angry defiance evaporated, and Todd was back to being her whipping boy.

But whipped or not, Todd got handcuffed after Duke found the spray. If he'd used it in the hallway, it would have gassed us all. We took Muriel and Todd down the main staircase, which would have been wide enough for four horses to have gone down abreast, if their hooves wouldn't have slipped on the marble. I was very happy that I was in my heavy-soled boots and not Muriel's heels on the slick stone, because she struggled periodically. If Newman and I hadn't had a hand on both her arms, she might have fallen headfirst on the hard stone with her hands cuffed behind her. She wasn't even technically under arrest yet, so it would have been a shame for her to die in our custody. Though since they weren't under arrest and hadn't been read their rights, it wasn't the legal definition of custody, but it would have been good enough for the Internet if she hurt herself cuffed like this. After she almost fell on the stairs, she stopped struggling for the most part, but she made up for it verbally. By the time Duke led us to the garage connected to the house, I was very tired of listening to Muriel.

"I know my rights! You can't search our car without a warrant," she said from between Newman and me.

"One, you parked your car in someone else's garage without their permission," Leduc said.

"Rico let us in. He knew we parked back here," she said.

"Deputy Vargas and I will be discussing that in more detail later. Two, you have more suspicious packages in the backseat of your car. They're plainly visible, so I have reasonable cause."

"We were shopping earlier. That's all that's in the backseat," Muriel said.

I had to give her points for sheer audacity. She wasn't a good liar, but she was damn persistent. By the time the car was emptied out, there were two more porcelains: one more like the two in the case, and a plate. There was also a series of jade figurines that turned out to be ancient Chinese. A series of four small oil paintings turned out to be originals painted for the first Marchands back in Europe, so they'd been in the family awhile. There were also two larger oil paintings in the trunk painted by a contemporary of Rembrandt. I would have said Todd and Muriel were stealing a small fortune, but I wasn't sure it was a small one.

We ended up separating the couple so we could question them. Sheriff Leduc still believed that Bobby was the murderer, but we'd caught Muriel and Todd stealing red-handed, so to speak. Even Duke thought it was suspicious behavior. He had the one deputy I hadn't met yet, Troy Wagner, trade duties with Deputy Frankie so they could have at least one woman with Muriel. He let us go see the clues from the first crime, while he and his small force started gathering up new evidence for the new crime. Murder and grand larceny in the same location less than twenty-four hours apart was spreading his small force to its limits. We'd help them again after Newman took me through the murder scene and the blood evidence.

We started with the bloody footprints, but to get to the upstairs, which held the "kids'" rooms, was like a freaking maze. "How many square feet is this place?" I asked when we finally came to a white-carpeted hallway that had crime scene tape wrapped around one doorknob and the post of a third staircase. This one had a dark wood banister that curved in a spiral near the top, the wood gleaming with years of polish and care. The wood was so lustrous that it made me want to stroke my hand down it, but since I was already wearing latex gloves and booties over my boots, there was no point. I was trying not to leave evidence behind; it made petting things difficult.

"There are two estimates online and one in the last architect's plans. None of them is the same."

"I've never been in a house with three separate staircases before," I said.

"Me either. This was the original main staircase before one of the great-grandfathers started building onto the house. When the master suite moved to the new section, the kids got this wing to themselves."

I thought about what it must have cost to heat and cool a place this big and almost wanted to know, but not enough to ask. I was here to try to solve a murder or at least find enough reasonable doubt to delay executing Bobby Marchand, not to get nosy about how the other half lived. Jean-Claude had money. As I'd watched him spend money for the wedding, I had begun to realize just how much he might have. We were keeping separate bank accounts so far, but he'd told me that I could know his finances if I wished to know. I was almost scared to find out. Was he this kind of rich and I just didn't know it, and why did that thought bother me so much?

"Are you all right?" Newman asked, and I realized I'd just been staring into space for a few minutes. I had to get my head in the game, not keep poking at my insecurities about the wedding.

"Yeah, I'm fine. Just thinking too hard and not too productively."

I could see the footprints on the white carpet down the hallway, but since there were supposed to be prints on the stairs, I decided to start with them. The stairs were all hardwood with only a narrow burgundy carpet runner. The color hid the prints a lot better than the white hallway did.

I bent over on the second step so I'd be able to see it and the one above and below it better. I didn't kneel, because for so many reasons, I didn't want to accidentally kneel in blood. I had coveralls in my main gear bag in case things got very messy, but those were mostly for vampire stakings or zombies. Most crimes scenes were less bloody than doing the killing yourself. I used my gloved fingertips to steady myself as I looked for footprints on the burgundy runner. The carpet was held in place by metal bars that snugged in against the bottom of each step. The bars could be unfastened so that the stair runner could be cleaned or replaced without having to tear up carpet and damage the wood underneath. I filed it away to remember if we ever replaced the carpet on the stairs in the house back in St. Louis.

I could smell the blood before I saw it clearly enough to be certain what it was: a bare footprint or at least no obvious shoe tread. I got the small flashlight I carried in one of the many pockets on the tac pants and shone the light down on the blood. The light was bright enough that at night it looked like a prison-break searchlight; on the dimly lit stairway, it highlighted the footprint against the dark carpet nicely. It was a clear footprint, and the stair steps were deep enough that the entire foot showed.

"That's weird," I said.

"What's weird?" Newman asked.

"Let me check another print before I answer you."

I moved down a step and then more, until I finally moved all the way down to find where the footprints began on the floor below. Newman waited patiently at the top of the stairs. I didn't need the footprints trailing off away from the stairs to know that I was close to the murder room, because I could smell the blood and meat. It had that thick, beefy smell that comes only when at least one adult human being has bled out in a room. I have to say that one plus for vampire kills is that they are usually neater; less blood means less smell. Then I realized all I smelled was meat and blood. I didn't smell the outhouse smell that usually comes with someone who has been ripped open by a wereanimal. It didn't mean that Ray Marchand's body hadn't emptied itself, which is what usually happens, but the intestines hadn't been pierced at all or the smell would have been a lot worse. If Bobby had lost so much control of his beast that he had killed the man who raised him, the man who had been his father figure, then it should have been brutal. If the stomach hadn't been opened up and none of the body had been eaten, which is what the crime scene photos had shown, then it had been a controlled attack. If Bobby had had that much control, he'd have remembered the kill.

I walked back up the steps toward Newman, using the bright flashlight to make sure I didn't step in the footprints. "The footprint evidence is all wrong. I might buy that the leopard form walked through the blood and up the stairs, but he'd remember what happened once he changed to human form."

Newman came carefully down the steps in his own plastic booties, trying to avoid the prints, as if anyone ever collected that much evidence at a crime scene when the perpetrator would be dead in less than two days. "Also, Bobby still passes out when he changes from animal to human form. He should have been passed out next to the body, not in his own bed."

"Yeah," I said. "Are you sure he always passes out right after changing back?"

"Are you wondering if he did it now?"

"No, but I like to cover my bases. I like Bobby, but just because I like someone doesn't mean they aren't capable of doing bad things."

"That's fair. I interviewed some of the people that work in the house. They've got three people who live on-site. They've seen him come over the garden wall in back and then collapse and change back. He's human, but it's like a coma. He's out cold for hours."

"Would the domestic help lie for Bobby?"

"The gardener and his wife, Mr. and Mrs. Chevet, have worked for Ray Marchand since Bobby was a toddler. They can't believe that Bobby would do something like this, because they're used to shooing him out of the house if he's in leopard form. They talk about him like he's a big house cat. Until this happened, they weren't afraid of him."

"Were they around him when he first got lycanthropy, or did Bobby go somewhere else until he got it under control?" I asked.

"He was sent to stay with a wereleopard pack that could train him up, is what I've been told by Bobby and everyone else."

"It's called a pard, not a pack, when it's wereleopards. Pack is werewolves," I corrected him without thinking about it.

"I'll make a note," he said.

"So, the domestic help never saw Bobby when he was uncontrollable," I said.

"Apparently not."

"Did other people say that Bobby ran around the house in leopard form or was it just the Chevets who said that?"

"Everyone says he had the run of the house in animal form. You know how cats will bring home mice or birds sometimes?"

"Yeah," I said.

"Except for the fact that Bobby brought home deer to stuff in the tree outside his window, he was like an indoor-outdoor cat."

"Did he have only the one cat form, no bipedal form?" I asked. *Bipedal* was the new politically correct term for wolfman, or leopardman in this case. Bipedal wasn't sexist and was about as gender-neutral as it was possible to be.

"No, just a leopard form. He's actually almost the same size as a regular leopard."

I stared at Newman. "Wereanimals are bigger than normal leopards."

"When we get into the study where the murder happened, I can show you pictures of Bobby in animal form with his uncle and his cousin. If he's bigger than ordinary leopards, it's not by much."

"Hmm, I've never known a wereanimal that wasn't larger than its wild counterpart."

"Well, Bobby did contract the disease in Africa from someone who had lived there all his life. Could it be a different kind of wereleopard from the ones we have here?"

I thought about that for a second or two, then shrugged. "I don't know. I've never actually been anywhere out of the country except Ireland, and I didn't see any lycanthropes in animal form on that trip. Come to think of it, the wereleopards back in St. Louis trace their original lineage to India, not to Africa. I didn't think it would make a difference in the size of their beast, but maybe I'm wrong. I'll ask when I get home if there's a size variant depending on where your strain of lycanthropy originates."

"If you find out, tell me please, because now I want to know."

"Yeah, me, too," I said. I directed the flashlight at the prints for him. "The prints on the downstairs floor and the first few steps are okay, but then about here"—I shone the light on the fifth step—"it's wrong."

"You mean the whole foot being on the step," he said.

"Yeah," I said.

"I noticed that, too."

"You don't place your full foot on every step so that it's perfectly aligned like that," I said.

"No, you don't," Newman agreed.

I shone the flashlight up near the top of the steps. "And then here it goes back to someone walking on the front of their foot, which would be more normal on stairs."

"It was one of the first things that bothered me," he said.

"There are a lot of old-school marshals that started out as vampire hunters that wouldn't have looked at any evidence. They'd have just killed the lycanthrope, and that would have been that."

"Well, good that I'm one of the new marshals," he said.

"Yeah, it is." I was one of the old-school. If it had been me, would I have walked the stairs and really looked at the prints, or would I have just executed the warrant and flown home? The prints might have slipped by me, but the blood on Bobby's human body, especially placed where it was, would have struck me as wrong. Would Edward have looked for another answer? I knew Olaf as Marshal Otto Jeffries would have executed Bobby by now and been done with it.

"What are you thinking so hard about?" Newman asked.

I shook my head. "Let's look at the hallway upstairs and the room where they found Bobby. Then we'll go downstairs to the main crime scene."

I didn't have to stoop much to go under the crime scene tape in the hallway. Newman had to bend almost double like he was doing reverse limbo. He stayed near the tape and let me walk alone, studying the footprints. The blood was drying to rust and would eventually look brown even against the white carpet.

"Who puts white carpet on the kids' side of the house?" I asked.

"I asked Duke that. He said that they'd remodeled once Jocelyn and Bobby were both in high school. They let the kids choose the colors up here."

"What teenage boy would choose white carpet?"

"Maybe it was Jocelyn's pick?" he said.

"Maybe," I said, and then gave my attention to the bloody footprints.

They were bare feet, and they looked a similar size to Bobby's feet, though honestly I'd been looking to see if there was blood on his feet, not sizing him for shoes. There weren't that many steps until they turned into the open door of a bedroom. One of the prints crossed the threshold, but then the floor was covered in short beige or maybe taupe carpet. It wasn't as pretty as the white in the hallway, but it was a lot more practical. It also acted like a nice neutral to the blue walls of the bedroom. I stood peering in the doorway but didn't walk inside the room. Something was bothering me, and it was outside the room. What else was bugging me about the prints?

"You've got that thinking look again," Newman said from down the hallway.

I turned around and went back to the footprints in the hallway, but this time, I tried to match the stride pattern. I had to damn near do splits to take them step for step. I got all the way to Newman, who to his credit hadn't remarked on me funny-walking my way down the hallway.

"Bobby Marchand is maybe five-ten at best, right?" I asked.

"I'd say five-eight, maybe five-nine," Newman said.

"Come walk beside the footprints in the hallway, and let me watch where your stride hits."

He didn't argue, just did what I asked. When he got to the end of the hallway prints, he turned back to look at me. His face was expectant, as if he just knew I'd explain it to him.

"How tall are you?" I asked.

"Six-two."

"Are you a solid six-two or like a fraction below it?"

He smiled and looked almost embarrassed. "Okay, technically, I'm six feet one inch and three-quarters."

"I thought so."

"You thought what?"

"Most men round up on size."

He grinned. "I promise I only round up on how tall I am. All other questions are answered accurately."

It took me a second to realize what he was implying, and then I had to shake my head hard to stop myself from speculating. Newman was not and never would be more than a coworker and work friend at best. It meant that I would not, could not let myself speculate about certain things. I'd found that where my thoughts went, the rest of me usually followed, so I'd started being a lot more careful about certain thoughts.

"No offense, but not pertinent to what we're doing," I said.

"It was a joke, Blake."

"I know, and it was funny, clever, whatever, but unless Bobby has a weirdly long stride for his height and inseam, then whoever made these prints is closer to your height or maybe just your leg length."

"Do you think it's enough to get a judge to grant me a stay of execution?"

"No, but if we take prints of Bobby's feet and they don't match these prints, that would probably get a judge to extend the window by at least forty-eight hours beyond the original."

"That's only two extra days, four days total, before I have to kill someone that neither of us thinks is guilty."

"Yep," I said.

He raised eyebrows at me in a classic exasperated look.

"It's still two days extra to figure out who did it and who framed Bobby for it, but before any of that happens, the prints have to not match his feet."

"You think someone walked through the victim's blood not because they forgot, but because they wanted to frame Bobby?" he asked.

"It's a working theory," I said.

"How tall do you think Muriel is?" he asked.

"So you didn't like her either," I said.

"How would anyone like her?" he said.

"No arguments from me."

"Todd is taller than he looks. He slumps. It rounds his shoulders and makes him look shorter."

"He's not slumping to hide his height, Newman."

"I didn't say he was. I'm just saying that if we get a viable print, we can ask them both for a sample to match with."

I shook my head. "Muriel is about the same height as Bobby. Her high heels have to be adding at least five inches."

"They didn't look that tall to me."

"You've never had to wear stilettos," I said.

He frowned at me. "What has that got to do with anything?"

"Once you've worn enough high heels, you're a better judge of them on other people, that's all. Just like I didn't realize the husband was slumping, and you did."

"I'm tall and a man. I notice height in other men."

"They'll never agree to letting us take prints of their feet," I said.

"They might if Duke told them it was to clear them of suspicion. Since we found them in the house stealing, they're now suspects," Newman said.

"Maybe, but only if they're not guilty."

"I was regular police for two years before I became a marshal. Trust me, Blake, guilty people do a lot of stupid things, just like innocent people."

"I've been a lot of things, but never a regular cop, so if you tell me that it's worth a try for them to possibly implicate themselves, I'll vote with you."

"Thanks. I appreciate the vote of confidence."

"You're welcome." I glanced at the bedroom and finally let myself go inside to see if I could find anything else that would buy us more time. I couldn't really see either Muriel or Todd walking barefoot through Ray's blood. It was one thing to walk through your brother's blood in shoes, but barefoot was more hard-core. Of course, if they'd killed him and framed their nephew, what was a little barefoot promenade compared to a double murder? Because make no mistake: If we couldn't get Bobby free of this, he was going die within days of the man who raised him.

12

I STARED DOWN at the bed. The bedspread was crumpled to one side of the bed along with most of the pillows. The sheets were so tangled that it was impossible to imagine anyone sleeping in them or on them without smoothing them out first. There was blood on them, but not as much blood as had been on Bobby's skin when we saw him in jail.

"There's a little bit of blood where someone touched the sheets, but the front of his body is way more coated than that," I said.

"Did you notice that it was down one leg past the knee?" Newman asked.

"Yeah."

"So how did he get into bed without getting more blood on the sheets?"

"He could have just sat down on the edge of the bed and lain back," I said.

Newman shook his head. "If he used his hands to scoot backward, then the blood that covered his hands would have left more marks."

"And if he crawled into bed, then the blood on his leg and feet would have marked the sheets more," I said.

"Exactly."

"Like you said earlier, the blood evidence is wrong."

"I saw that, but it didn't occur to me that those weren't Bobby's footprints. I should have realized that if part of the blood evidence was wrong, then it was all fucked."

"Don't beat yourself up, Newman. None of us sees everything all at once. That's why in a normal murder case you have so much time to look over the evidence before trial."

"But this isn't a trial, Blake. It's an execution."

"Not yet it's not," I said.

"I don't want to take Bobby's life if he didn't do this."

"I don't want anyone to take his life if he was framed for this murder."

"People don't frame other people outside of murder mysteries," Newman said. "They blame other people, but they don't actually frame specific people."

"They do to throw suspicion off of themselves sometimes," I said.

"Maybe in Agatha Christie mysteries," he said.

"Are you on board with this being a frame or not?" I asked, looking at him.

"It just seems so elaborate. I mean, if they'd just killed Ray and then found Bobby with blood on him, that would have been enough."

"Crime makes people stupid, and committing murder makes them insecure, so they have to overdo it, I guess."

"But they had to know that footprints are as individual as fingerprints," he said.

"I bet most people don't know that, but maybe they were counting on you just pulling the trigger on Bobby and not overthinking it. Once he's dead, then the case is over. The carpet gets cleaned or ripped out and replaced. The room where the murder happens gets deep-cleaned, and all the evidence, real or fake, just goes away."

"Murders when I was just a uniform cop meant everything got bagged and tagged and saved for trial. It was worth your badge to mess up potential evidence. Now it's like none of it matters except hunting down the killer and executing them."

"By the time we're called in, there are usually a lot of bodies in the morgue, Newman. Our job was designed because putting vampires and wereanimals in regular jail to await trial didn't work, because they used supernatural powers to escape, usually causing the death of even more people on the way out the door."

"I know that, Blake. It's one of the reasons I wanted to become a marshal in the first place." His words were okay, but the tone and his face weren't.

"Sounds like you're having second thoughts about your career change," I said.

He looked surprised and just stared at me for a second. "It's like now, this case. There's only one person dead, so it's an eye for an eye, but we both think that someone is using the system, using our job, to commit a second murder, because they know if we believe Bobby is guilty, he's a dead man."

"Yeah, there's a lot of room for corruption and miscarriage of justice in the system," I said.

He stared at me again. "You say that so matter-of-fact, as if it's just business as normal."

"It is, Newman."

"How can that be okay?"

"I didn't say it was okay. I said it was normal. A lot of what people take for normal is very not okay."

"Then I don't understand," he said.

"It doesn't matter if it's good or bad or sucks ass. It only matters that we do our jobs to the best of our abilities."

"I don't think I can kill Bobby Marchand. I don't think he did this," Newman said.

"Then let's get some of the forensic people that are coming to help bag and tag on the theft charges for the wicked aunt and uncle to make a print of the footprints that we can use to either get a stay of execution for Bobby or prove that he's a great liar and guilty."

"What do you mean by the great-liar part?"

"If these are his footprints, then he woke up next to his uncle's body and walked in human form from there to his own bedroom to pretend to be passed out hard enough that you and the sheriff carried him 'unconscious'"—I made air quotes around the last word—"to the jail. That's some Oscar-worthy acting."

"I'd swear he was out cold, Blake. I've seen a few other humans that passed out after the change. They were out of it. You could burn a house down around them, and they wouldn't wake up to save themselves."

"I know. I've seen it, too." In my head I thought, *Not in a few years.* I'd been hanging around with too many powerful shapeshifters. Once you reached a certain power level, you didn't pass out when you went back to human. You could be tired, but it wasn't the coma state that new shapeshifters fell into or, like Bobby, never outgrew. It meant he was a seriously low-level cat. No wonder he hadn't wanted to stay with whatever leopard group had trained him to control his beast. No one wants to be the lowest man or woman on the totem pole.

"I don't think he could fake that," Newman said.

"And I'd swear that his emotions in the jail were real, but if these turn out to be his footprints, then he lied, and he fooled both of us."

"Even if he lied, even if he did this—and I still don't think he did—I'm not sure I can look Bobby in the eyes and pull the trigger."

"Well, that's honest," I said.

"Have you had to kill someone you knew?"

I nodded. "It sucks."

"It sucks. That's the best you can do?"

"What do you want from me, Newman? Do you want to know that his face haunts my nightmares? Do you want me to cry on your shoulder and say, 'Woe is me'?"

"Knowing you have nightmares actually makes me feel better about my own."

"Well, then, yay for you, Newman, but fuck you, too."

"Why are you mad at me?"

"Because I didn't come here to do therapy with you. I came to help you save Bobby Marchand if we can."

"I agree that's our priority," he said.

"Good, and if you need therapy help, find a counselor or a doctor. Like I said, I'm seeing someone to help with a lot of issues, not just the job. No shame in getting help when something's broken," I said.

"But you're mad at me for wanting to confide in you?"

"No, I'm mad at you for wanting me to trot out my inner demons so that you'll feel better about your own. I don't owe you that."

"Is anger always your go-to emotion?" he asked, sounding angry himself.

"Yeah, it is, because anger will help me keep moving until the job is done. Sadness won't. Grief won't. Anxiety won't. All those touchy-feely emotions that are supposed to be what make us human or whole or whatever will cripple you in the middle of a battle."

"This isn't battle," he said.

"Fuck that, it's not. We are fighting for Bobby's life. It's a battle between good and evil, Newman, and we're the good guys, so we have to win."

The anger just leaked away from him, and he got a soft look on his face that I didn't understand. "You still believe we're the good guys even after all the lives you've taken?"

"Yes, I do."

"Even when they cry for help and beg you not to kill them?" he asked, and his eyes filled with the horror of it.

We did not have time for this, but in a way, we didn't have time to ignore it. I finally realized that Newman had asked me here to save more than just Bobby. Damn it. "Those are bad," I said finally.

"Monsters aren't supposed to beg for their lives and say they're sorry," he said, his face still holding the horror of that moment when he began to question if he was the monster. I remembered my moment. Hell, I was still having them.

"Everything wants to live, Newman, even monsters."

He looked at me, frowning, and the bad memories in his eyes began to fade, replaced by that dogged determination to learn, to get better, to listen, that was one of his best qualities as a marshal.

"I've had a vampire beg me not to kill her while she was covered in the blood of her victims. It wasn't her fault. Her master made her do it," I said.

"Was it true? Did her master make her do it?"

"Maybe, or maybe vampires are just like any criminal. It's never their fault. You were a regular cop for a couple of years. Did you ever

arrest someone who believed they were guilty and deserved the punishment?"

He thought about it, then shook his head. "No, either they didn't
do it, or it wasn't their fault. They'd blame the victim. If she had given
me her purse, I wouldn't have had to hit her. If my husband hadn't
cheated on me, I wouldn't have stabbed him. Or my favorite: the man
who kept saying, 'I hit her before, and she never died.' He just kept
saying that as if it was a defense of some kind. It was like he really
believed that she'd died out of spite, just to put him in jail. He slammed
her head into the edge of a metal table until her brains leaked out the
front of her skull, but it wasn't his fault that the bitch died." Newman
was angry as he said the last, righteously angry at the everyday evil
of it.

"Now, think what that abusive shit would have said if you could
have legally aimed a gun and killed him there and then."

I watched the anger deepen as he said, "He'd have said, 'Why you
killing me? What'd I do? It's not my fault the bitch died.'"

"Turning into vampires or werewolves or whatever doesn't stop
them from being the people they were before. If they were evil and
petty before, they're still evil and petty afterward."

"What about the nice model citizens that turn evil after they
become vampires?" he asked.

"You know that old saying 'power corrupts, and absolute power
corrupts absolutely'?"

"Yes," he said.

"I think a lot of people are only nice because they don't think they
have a choice. Give them supernatural powers, the ability to control
people with just their gaze, and they don't have to play nice anymore.
They can take what they want, so they do. Of course, all that is pred-
icated on them being undead long enough to regain their minds. The
newly risen aren't deep thinkers."

"New vampires are like rabid animals. They kill everything they
find," Newman said, and again there was that haunted look in his eyes.

"Yeah, the newly undead need a master to control them. There
are rules in place that if you turn someone into a vampire, you have

to stay with them until they gain enough control to function safely. If you abandon them, the other masters will hunt you down and make sure you don't do it again, or they did in the old days before law enforcement was supposed to do it for them."

"Sometimes I wish it was the old days," he said, voice low.

"Sometimes me, too," I said.

"Really?" he asked.

I nodded.

"You wouldn't be marrying Jean-Claude if it was the old days," he said.

"There is that," I said, and smiled, thinking about my tall, pale, and gorgeous fiancé.

Newman smiled back at me, which meant maybe I could stop hand-holding and get us back to business.

"Do you still do morgue stakings?" he asked.

"No, vampires chained down, dead to the world, it's like shooting fish in a barrel. I leave the easy kills to the new marshals."

"It's not easy when it's nightfall and they're begging for their lives."

I counted to ten, because I went right back to being angry. It was my go-to emotion and had been since my mother died or maybe even before. I just couldn't remember me that clearly before my mother's death. I was only eight when it happened.

"Refuse the morgue stakings and tell any new marshals that they don't have to agree to nighttime morgue kills."

"I didn't know we had a choice."

"We're the vampire experts. All you have to do is tell the local cops that it's too dangerous when they're awake. You don't want anyone to get caught by the vampire gaze. Or, as a more senior marshal, you can literally say you're leaving the less dangerous assignments for the newbies."

"I'll try that next time." His face was all serious, but his head was so not in the game.

"When all this is over, I'll be happy to sit down over coffee and talk. I'll share all the tips I've learned over the years for keeping the personal horror level low, or as low as possible on this job, but right

now we have work to do. Bobby needs you, Newman. I need you present and accounted for, not lost in the nightmares. Can you do that?"

He nodded, taking a big breath and letting it out in a big rush.
"You're right. We have to try to buy time for Bobby. I'll take you up
on that coffee later." He shoved the anger down so that his eyes were
almost friendly as he looked at me. "Let's go see if the state forensic
people are here yet."

His voice was even, unemotional, except for that lingering anger.
If I hadn't known he'd take it wrong, I'd have patted him on the back
and said *Atta boy.* Men stuff their emotions because life and death
are more important than any emotion. If you don't survive, then what
the fuck does it matter? I was one of the boys in more ways than one.
I'd teach Newman how to survive; any emotional damage from the
survival was someone else's job.

13

NEWMAN AND I, along with some of the state police and Sheriff Leduc, were almost having a fight in the living room of the Marchand mansion, aka the crime scene. The living room was the size of my first three apartments combined, with elegant furniture done in silky-looking brocade in shades of pink, cream, and pale mint green. The carpet was deep burgundy with hints of the same pale colors swirling in shapes that I think were supposed to be flowers. There were real oil paintings on the walls, and I'd have bet that all the knick-knacks were real antiques. It looked more like a movie set than any living room I'd ever seen, so maybe it was a drawing room. There were chairs, two couches, and a love seat, but none of us was sitting down. I think we were all afraid to muss the furniture.

"You cannot put one of our people in the cell with a wereanimal that is already suspected of killing someone," Captain Dave Livingston of the state cops declared loudly. He wasn't quite yelling yet, but he was getting more forceful every time he said no.

The urge to say *Captain Livingston, I presume* was very strong. His parents had actually named him David Livingston, like the famous missionary and explorer, even though the last names weren't spelled the same. The original was Livingstone, but they were pronounced the same, so he'd probably heard the joke a bajillion times. It made it easier for me to resist.

It had seemed like such a simple idea to get prints from Bobby

Marchand to compare to the ones at the house, and half of it was simple. The forensic team from the state police was happy to collect evidence at the house, but we needed evidence from Bobby's body. At minimum we needed his feet to be printed, and that meant either one of the techs went inside the cell with him, or he came out of the cell to us.

"I will not let that monster out of the cell and endanger anyone else," Sheriff Leduc said, also not quite yelling.

"Well, you're not endangering one of my people by sending them in with a shapeshifter," Livingston said.

He was looming over the sheriff, not from height since he was only a couple of inches taller, but where Duke had let himself go after getting out of the military, Livingston had not. The captain was big, lean, and if his short, nearly buzzed hair hadn't been mostly gray, I'd have thought he was at least ten years younger. Once he took his hat off and I could see the hair, I'd known to notice the extra smile lines near his steel gray eyes and the parentheses around his mouth, which suggested that every sentence he'd spoken had left its mark around his lips. His mouth was wider than it looked, because the angrier he got, the thinner his lips seemed. I was never sure how some people's mouths did that when they were angry or sad.

I was letting the sheriff and the captain argue with each other, because neither of their viewpoints was going to help us gain more time on Bobby Marchand's execution warrant. Until I figured out a way to get what we wanted, I was content to let the men yell at each other rather than me, because anyone who interrupted the "discussion" was going to have both of them angry with them. I really didn't want to fight with both the sheriff and the captain until it would gain us something. Of course, Newman was newer at this than I was in every way. He still thought he could save the world if only the world would let him.

"Marshal Blake and I will be in the cell with drawn weapons," Newman said. "If Bobby tries to hurt anyone, we will take care of it."

Livingston turned on him, happy to have another target for his aggression. "Why haven't you executed your warrant, Marshal Newman? If you had done your job, we wouldn't need to be having this discussion."

Leduc moved in beside Livingston. "I've already had to save Blake's ass from that damn wereleopard once."

"That's not what happened," Newman said.

"Duke already told me that he and his deputy got you out of the cell, but the shapeshifter grabbed Blake. She's lucky to be alive. Hell, she's lucky she got out of there without getting cut up. Now you want me to let one of my people go into the cell with that thing. No. Just no."

I wondered if Leduc really believed his heroic version of the incident, or if he'd knowingly lied to make himself look better. If he believed the story, then we were fucked, because that would be how he wrote it up later. If he knew he was lying, then I might be able to get him to back down and use that to get some wiggle room with Livingston.

"You didn't tell me that the suspect attacked you, Marshals." This came from Kaitlin, the crime scene tech who had volunteered to help us. She was a few inches taller than me, five-five, maybe five-six, which made her short compared to everyone else in the room but me. Her straight blond hair was tied back in a tight, perky ponytail that bobbed in the air when she spoke. Most of the people I knew who did ponytails had longer hair, so the weight of the hair held it down more. If she hadn't talked with her hands, maybe the hair would have lain there like normal, but she was so animated when she moved that her hair was, too.

"He didn't," Newman said.

"I saw him start to change form," the sheriff said.

"You saw his eyes change," I said, finally joining the conversation. I'd try for logic but didn't hold out much hope that logic was what would win the day.

"You didn't tell me he started to shift in the cell after the murder," Kaitlin said.

"Eyes can change from strong emotions," I said. "Finding out you're accused of killing your father is pretty emotional."

"He killed his uncle, not his father," Livingston said.

"Bobby was raised by his uncle," I said.

"Bobby's parents were killed in a car accident when he was a baby. Ray is the only dad he remembers," Newman added.

"I'm aware of the family history, and you can call him by his first name all you want. It will not humanize him to me, because only half of him is human. The other part is a murdering animal," Livingston said.

"Legally he's human, and I don't want to kill another human being unless he's guilty," Newman said.

"You can be a bleeding heart on your own time, Marshal, but that animal has already killed one person and attacked another marshal. How many people have to die before you do your duty?" Livingston asked.

"Bobby Marchand did not attack me," I said.

"I was there, Blake. I saw it," Leduc said.

"You pointed a gun at both of us, Sheriff."

"I was aiming at the monster."

"Then why did Newman have to point his gun at you to save my life from your bullet?"

"You are both full of shit," Leduc said.

"Your own deputy told you to calm down and lower your gun," I said.

"I'm sorry as hell that Bobby did this, but I will not let you and Newman drag my reputation through the mud in some misguided attempt to get a stay of execution for him. Bobby has to pay for what he did."

I wondered if we got Deputy Anthony in here whether she'd tell the truth or lie for her boss. I'd be leaving town, and she'd have to deal with the fallout. Apparently, Newman had no doubts that she'd do the right thing, because he said, "Call Anthony up here. She'll tell you that Bobby didn't attack anyone in the jail."

I was glad that he didn't say that the deputy would admit that Leduc had pointed a gun at me until I felt in danger for my life. If she just backed us up on Bobby not attacking me, I'd take it. We just needed Kaitlin of the perky ponytail to do her job on the evidence that was Bobby's body.

"His eyes had changed to kitty-cat eyes. I wasn't going to stand there and let him do to Blake what he'd done to Ray," Leduc said.

"I had the suspect under control when you continued to aim your weapon at me," I said.

"He was starting to shape-shift, Blake. You didn't see Ray's body. I did. If I had to choose between that and being shot, I'd take the bullet."

"I wasn't in danger from Bobby Marchand—only from you, Leduc."

"Well, that's gratitude for you," he said, and he was so calm—calmer than he should have been unless he already knew that Anthony would lie for him.

"Let's get your deputy up here. Once she backs you up, then this discussion is over," Livingston said.

"Deputy Anthony is with our female suspect," Duke said.

"I'll have one of our female officers stay with the woman."

"We are wasting time here," Duke said.

"Yeah, it would be a shame to waste time when we could just kill the suspect and find out he's innocent later," I said. I should have saved the sarcasm, but sometimes old habits die hard.

"I met Bobby when he was playing peewee football. I've known him all his life. I don't want to see him executed like this, but he's proved himself too dangerous to be living beside other people. He has forfeited his right to live by killing someone else. It's as simple as that, Marshals. If I thought he could spend his life locked up, maybe I'd vote for that, but the only thing the law allows for this crime is death. If that's all we can do to punish the crime and protect the rest of the people, then we need to do it. The two of you need to do your damn job."

"I didn't realize you knew Bobby that well," Newman said in the sudden almost uncomfortable silence.

"My son was the same age as Bobby, so I saw a lot of him and the other boys that were close to my son's age."

Leduc spoke of his son in the past tense. He also didn't mention a name, just *my son*, as if the name was too painful, too real. If his son had been a friend of Bobby's when they were boys, and then the son had died young, seeing Bobby all grown-up must have been hard. Having Bobby be the one who had killed the man who was paying for Lila Leduc's medical bills was just rubbing salt in old wounds. No wonder the sheriff was all over the board emotionally. If he hadn't been the only sheriff in town, I'd have tried to get him to take himself off the case, but their force wasn't big enough to take anyone off the roster.

I wasn't sure what we should have said in that suddenly silent room. I knew I wasn't about to say a damn word. I did not know Duke well enough to risk saying anything in the face of such possible grief. A purposeful knock at the double doors ended the awkward pause.

"Come in," Livingston said, voice a little gruff. I didn't think I was the only one who was happy to have an interruption.

"You texted, sir," a woman in a state trooper uniform said as she came through the door.

"Yes, I want you to relieve Deputy Frankie Anthony and send her up here."

"Will do, sir," she said, and closed the door behind her much more softly than she'd knocked.

"So you don't believe me," Leduc said.

"I never said that," Livingston said.

"You're about to double-check my story with my own deputy. Fuck that, Dave. You and I have known each other too many years for you to doubt my word."

"It's not your word I'm doubting," Livingston said.

"Then what is it?"

"Some cases are harder on us than others, Duke," he said. It took me a second to realize the gruff voice was Livingston's version of kind.

"You think I can't handle this one? You think I've gone soft?"

"No, Duke, I'd never think that."

"Then, what the hell, Dave? Frankie is going to back me up, and then what? Is your heart bleeding for the poor wereleopard, too?"

"You know me better than that, Duke."

"I thought I did."

I realized that Livingston had caught on that maybe, just maybe, Duke was too emotionally involved to oversee this murder investigation. If I hadn't thought someone would see it, I'd have crossed my fingers that we could get Livingston on our side and that Deputy Frankie wouldn't throw us under the bus to keep in good with her boss.

14

DEPUTY FRANKIE ACTUALLY sat in one of the pretty stiff-backed chairs. It was as if we'd been waiting for someone to be the first, because Duke sat down on the edge of the couch closest to her. Kaitlin sat down in the matching chair beside her.

"The suspect did start to shift in the cell with both Marshal Newman and Marshal Blake still locked inside with him," Frankie said.

"His eyes changed, but that was all," I said.

Livingston held up a hand and said, "Let the deputy finish answering the question before you add your two cents' worth, Marshal."

"No, the marshal is right about that. It was only his eyes that turned yellow like a cat's, but we're all trained that it's the first sign of them changing form, so Sheriff Leduc and I told the marshals to get out of the cell. Newman did, but Blake wouldn't leave the suspect."

"Which is exactly what I said," Leduc added.

Livingston said, "If Blake can't interrupt, then neither can you, Duke. Let your deputy finish before you all jump in."

Frankie looked at her boss with nervous eyes, her hands clutching each other a little tighter. You didn't have to know her to figure out those were nervous fidgets. "Marshal Blake was in front of the suspect, so there wasn't a clear shot without endangering her."

"And you had your weapon drawn by then?" Livingston asked.

"Yes. I'm sorry, Captain. Yes, we all had our guns drawn, even

Newman. We were all urging Blake to get out of the cell, but she wouldn't do it. She told us to lock the cell door, that she thought she could talk the suspect out of changing into his animal form."

Livingston looked at me. "Blake, why did you refuse to leave the cell when your fellow marshal did?"

"I thought they would shoot and kill Bobby Marchand, and I no longer thought he was guilty of the murder. I didn't want to let them kill an innocent man."

"You put yourself in harm's way to save a suspect that a warrant of execution has been issued for?" Livingston asked.

"Yes."

"Why?" he asked.

"One, because I think he didn't kill anyone. Two, because I didn't want the other officers to kill him and then find out later he was innocent. That's a level of guilt that no one deserves."

"Are you speaking from experience?" Livingston asked.

"Not for sure, but in the early days of the warrant system, I took it on faith that if the law declared them guilty, it was fact. Let's just say that without evidence collection or any proof but he said/she said or eyewitness testimony, I'm beginning to wonder if some of my early executions were justified."

"You had a warrant of execution. That makes them legal," Livingston said.

"You and I both know that legal isn't the same thing as justice."

"We aren't in the justice business, Marshal. That's for the lawyers."

"There won't be any lawyers to help us find justice for Ray Marchand, or for Bobby if we kill him as soon as the warrant arrives."

Newman said, "I'm not asking to let Bobby go free. I just want another couple of days to make certain he deserves the bullet I'm going to put in his brain."

"And if the prints are his?" Livingston asked.

Newman sighed. "Then he's a lying bastard, and he probably did it. If the prints come back as his, I'll execute the warrant, but if they aren't his, then I'd like your help to convince a judge to grant a forty-eight-hour extension on the warrant."

"Why just forty-eight hours?" Kaitlin asked.

"Because that's all the law allows," I said.

"You can't refuse a warrant even if you find out the person isn't guilty?" Deputy Frankie asked.

"We can refuse a warrant if there are other marshals in the area that it can go to," I said, "but even then, you have to have a good reason why you want to pass on it."

"I was the only marshal in this area not already on an active warrant, so I couldn't pass it along," Newman said.

"You could pass it to Blake now," Frankie said.

"Theoretically he could sign the warrant over to me," I said. "They will let personal involvement with the target of the warrant be grounds for refusal. Newman knows Bobby as at least an acquaintance, and that makes it hard to put a bullet in him."

"What would you do if Newman tried to sign it over to you?" Livingston asked.

"I already told him that I stopped taking over warrants just because the newer marshals found it morally or emotionally difficult. The only grounds that I would accept a warrant on now are if I thought my expertise would be a better fit for an active hunt, or if the first marshal is incapacitated so that they cannot finish their own warrant. Neither of these circumstances is true in this case."

"So why did Newman ask you to come in on his warrant?"

Newman answered, "I wanted a more experienced marshal to double-check me. The facts of the case just didn't add up from the beginning, but since this was my first time having a warrant of execution for someone I knew, I didn't trust myself. When Marshal Blake had the same reaction to the evidence at the scene of the crime as I did, then I knew I had to find a way to make sure that this warrant of execution had the right name on it. I don't mind killing murderers who are going to keep on murdering people, but I don't want to be manipulated into being someone else's murder weapon."

"What do you mean, murder weapon?" Frankie asked.

"If Bobby has been framed for Ray's murder, then whoever framed him is the real killer, and they are using the preternatural branch to kill Bobby. They are using me and my badge, my duty, to finish their murder plot. That, I do not and will not be a part of if I can legally avoid it."

"I hadn't thought about it that way," Frankie said.

"I don't know why you both have such a problem with the bloody footprints he left at the scene, but before Blake goes all soft on the beast that did this, I think she should see the room where Ray was slaughtered," Leduc said.

Livingston looked at me. "Have you not been in the actual room?"

"No," I said.

He gave me a look. I gave him one back and said, "Normally it would be the first stop, but we were already upstairs, so we started there. Once I saw the prints, they seemed like our best bet to get a delay in the execution timeline. If we don't get extra time, then this is all moot."

"The warrant hasn't been faxed to my office yet. You get forty-eight hours after it arrives—there's plenty of time to waste on this footprint nonsense," Leduc said.

"Most warrants start their countdown from the moment the document is written, not when it's received," I said.

"So, if there's a delay on the judicial end, you could end up with a warrant that's past due?" Frankie asked.

"I've heard of it happening, but most of the time, the warrant arrives with the clock already ticking on how long the marshal has to complete the job, but not expired," I said.

"Is it just two days to complete the execution, or does the warrant become null and void after that time period, so killing the suspect would be murder?" Livingston asked.

"The ability to kill the suspect or suspects with legal impunity remains until the warrant is completed by their deaths," I said.

"So why does the warrant have a timeline written into it?" Frankie asked.

"Some of the marshals were delaying fulfilling their warrants," I said.

"The newer ones," Newman said, "like me that were cops before, but had only classroom experience with the monsters. You spend years training to keep the peace and do your best to save lives, and then you join the preternatural branch and suddenly it's all about taking lives. Not all of us can make the transition."

"What happens if a marshal doesn't make the deadline?" Kaitlin asked.

"If it's a hunt and the marshal in question just can't safely locate and destroy the target, then no harm, no foul. They may send in more experienced marshals to help with the hunt, but it remains the original marshal's warrant, and they remain in charge of the hunt," I said.

Newman added, "But if it's someone like Bobby that's already in custody, then refusal of the warrant by the marshal gets written up. If you refuse to complete three warrants, then you're given a chance to transfer to normal Marshals Service or you're fired."

"Is the preternatural branch losing a lot of personnel that way?" Livingston asked.

Newman shrugged.

"Some," I said. "Not everyone has the stomach for it."

"But now do you understand why it's so important for us to find reasonable cause to lengthen the warrant timeline?" Newman asked.

"So you can avoid getting written up for dereliction of duty," Duke said.

"It's not dereliction of duty, Duke. How would you feel if you let me kill Bobby and then we do find out he was framed? Could you live with that?"

Duke shook his head, but I'm not sure it was an answer to the question. "Let Blake see the room where Ray died. Let her smell it. Then see if she still wants to save the poor wereleopard."

"Fine, let's go," I said.

We left Livingston and Kaitlin discussing if she was getting in the cage with a wereleopard. Frankie stayed behind to answer questions about what had happened back at the jail. I hoped she was willing to share that Duke had lost it, but in the end, I guess that didn't matter. What mattered was that the state cops helped us delay long enough to either kill Bobby Marchand with a clear conscience or save him.

15

IF THE LIVING room was big, this room was cavernous. I'd never been in a regular house that had a room this large. Jean-Claude and I had looked at some wedding venues that had ballrooms, and even most of them weren't as big as Ray Marchand's study. It was big and dark, with only a handful of lamps around the room giving off golden pools that seemed to make more shadows rather than illuminate the darkness. Maybe the smells of blood and death in the air made the room feel grim. Maybe, but I'd have given a lot for an overhead light. There were chairs and a couch that looked like leather, more masculine versions of the living room furniture. There were two lamps: one beside the couch and the other, a reading lamp, curved over the back of the room's comfiest and highest-backed chair, which was closest to the fireplace. That chair looked cozy. I shone my flashlight near it and found beside it a short stack of books on a table. Very cozy. I caught a shape at the edge of the light and had my gun out and pointed before I'd really shone the light full on it.

My heart was in my throat, beating so hard, it almost choked me as I stared into the eyes of a full-grown bobcat. Newman said, "Don't shoot. It's stuffed," about the time I'd already decided that the yellow eyes staring at me were glass.

"Shit," I said softly but with feeling.

"There's a lot of taxidermy in here," Newman said, and swept his flashlight up along the right side of the room to show a herd of animal heads on the wall.

I recognized water buffalo and more kinds of antelope, or maybe they were gazelles, than I could name, all silent and staring, their horns curving gracefully in the still air. The rhino head did not look graceful; it just looked big. There was a pair of lion heads—a big maned male and a lioness snarling beside him. She looked shorn next to her mate. My own inner lion flared to life just at a glimpse of amber eyes in the darkness of my mind or maybe my gut. I had a second of smelling the sun and heat on grass halfway around the world that I'd never smelled as a human being, and then it was gone. The leopard head didn't seem to offend my inner one, because it didn't react.

"Wait until you see what's in the corner," Newman said. I joined my flashlight beam to his, and we swept across animal heads from almost every continent, and then in the corner was the showstopper: a full-grown elephant. I mean a full-size bull elephant complete with tusks gleaming in the dark like huge white fangs.

"Well, fuck," I said.

"Elegant as always," Newman said. He was smiling when I glanced at him.

"I'm glad you're enjoying the stuffed toys," Leduc said, "but could you look at the blood and actual crime scene?"

He seemed offended that I'd ignored the signs of new death to goggle at the old. But I'd seen more wereanimal attacks than I could count now. I'd never seen this many taxidermied animals outside of a natural history museum. I mean, who has a stuffed adult African elephant in their house? It was u-fucking-nique.

But I dutifully moved toward him in the plastic booties that we were all wearing so we wouldn't contaminate the crime scene. If it had been a normal warrant of execution, we might not even have bothered, because what did it matter if we contaminated everything if we were just going to shoot someone and leave?

The blood was beside a huge wooden desk that dominated the center of the room. The desk was obviously an antique. It had that rich, much-loved patina to it that only time and care will give to wood, like the banister on this side of the house. The wooden printer stands were nice but modern. The wooden file cabinets were a mix of old and new. They formed a half wall behind the big leather office chair. It was a complete office in the middle of the room; its "floor" was differentiated by a large square Persian or Oriental, or whatever the politically correct term is for it now. The carpet looked as old as the desk and as well-made, but they'd never get all the blood out of it.

There's more blood in an adult human being than any forensic show will ever be able to put on TV or in a movie. You'll have some horror films that go overboard and cover everything in gore, but no fiction hits that middle ground of truth. No episode of *CSI* has ever shown the viewer how much blood there would actually be. No visual can give you its raw-meat smell—it smells close to raw hamburger to me—but if I ever had any doubts that our bodies are just so much meat, violent murder scenes take any illusion away.

The top of the desk was completely clear because everything that had been on it was on the floor, as if the struggle had knocked it all off. A stapler, a desk lamp, and a real, honest-to-God corded telephone landline were in among the smaller office supplies and the blood. The office chair was set so that the victim would have been facing the door when he was sitting at his desk. He might have turned his back to check the file cabinets, but other than that, he had to have seen any-one coming into the room.

I moved carefully around the debris on the floor. The only thing that seemed to be damaged was the desk lamp. It was shattered as if someone had picked it up and slammed it against the floor or some-thing else. Had our victim tried to defend himself with it? Except it was on top of the blood. All the things that looked like they'd come off the desk were on the blood, not under it. I knelt down, perching on the balls of my feet so I had less chance of stepping in or on evi-dence as I peered at the lamp.

"There's blood on the lamp," I said.

"There's blood on everything," Duke said.

"No," I said, standing back up, "there isn't. There should be blood all over the things that got knocked off the desk, but they're all on top of the blood, like they fell to the floor after he was dead or at least after he was on the floor."

"So what?" Duke said.

"So, if the things were knocked off the desk during a struggle, some of them should have blood on them," I said.

"You are so busy trying to make this into something it's not that you don't see what's in front of your face," Duke said.

I faced him. His brown eyes looked almost black in the dim light. "Or maybe it's you that's trying to make it something it's not. We're trying to save a life. What's your motivation?"

"What are you trying to say, Marshal?"

"I'm just asking why you are so set on this being a wereanimal kill."

"Because that's what it is, Blake. It's you and Newman who are complicating things, not me."

"Not every case is simple," I said.

"Do you complicate the rest of your life as much as you do your professional one?"

I almost answered an automatic no, then realized it wasn't true. "The older I get, the more I realize that most people's personal lives are complicated, but professionally my job is usually dead simple, Sheriff. I hunt down murderers, and I kill them."

He made a harsh sound that was almost a laugh. "The older you get, Blake? You haven't hit thirty yet. You don't even know what older means yet."

"I'm thirty-two. Does being over thirty automatically gain me more respect?"

"Yeah, it does," he said.

"Why? I understand that you gain experience as you get older, but growing wiser and better at being a human being isn't automatic with age."

"Is that a jab at me?" he asked, trying to hook his thumbs in his belt and failing because of his weight. It made me debate again how rapid the weight gain had been if he was still trying to use his body like it was far smaller. Had he eaten the stress of his daughter's illness, and this was the result?

"No, but you've been in uniform long enough to have met losers and idiots of every decade. Older doesn't mean wiser for some people. Hell, some people live hundreds of years, and they're still idiots."

"Vampires don't count, Blake. They aren't people."

"Is that a jab at me because I'm about to marry one of them?"

Duke looked surprised and then got his angry, arrogant look back in place. "How the hell would I know who you were going to marry? Contrary to what you might think, Blake, not everyone follows your personal life on social media."

"Fine, but now that you do know I'm about to marry a vampire, do you want to rethink your comment?"

"Why? It's the truth," he said, and he stared at me as if waiting to see if it hurt my feelings.

I laughed. It made him jump as if I'd poked him with a stick.

"That wasn't meant to be funny," he said, and his tone had gone from angry to hateful. I don't think he liked being laughed at, which was fine with me.

"You just called vampires not people. That's a step up from soulless monster, which is what my grandmother called my fiancé. She told me I'd be damned forever if I married him. My father isn't sure he can walk me down the aisle, not in good conscience. He's a devout Catholic, and the Church still considers vampires unconsecrated dead like suicides at best and at worst a type of minor demon."

The hatred in Duke's eyes softened a little. Maybe I'd surprised him, or maybe it was sympathy. "I would give anything to be able to walk my Lila down the aisle to someone she loved. I'd hate it if I hated him, but I'd by God walk her down on my arm and be proud to do it." His eyes seemed to glimmer in the dim light. He shook his head a little too fast and said, "I'm going to go make sure that everyone is doing their jobs. These are the two biggest cases that Hanuman has seen in . . . hell, maybe ever." He turned his head so that we couldn't see his face before he turned the rest of him for the door and walked out.

16

"If HE WASN'T being a pain in our asses, I'd feel sorry for the sheriff," I said.

"I feel sorry for him anyway," Newman said.

"Yeah, me, too. I always hate it when people that are making my life difficult turn out to have real emotions and real lives. Makes me feel all conflicted about wanting to kick them in the ass."

Newman snorted a laugh. "You do have a way with words, Blake."

"Yeah, sarcasm is one of my best things." I shone my flashlight around the room. It was a bright light, but the far end of the room just swallowed it up.

"How big is this damn room, and why aren't there more lights?"

"The floor-to-ceiling windows behind the drapes give plenty of light in the daytime, and there are more lights. You just have to walk through the room and turn them on one by one," he said.

"Let's do that."

"I didn't think you'd be afraid of the dark, Blake."

I started to say I wasn't but then changed my response to "I'm not afraid of normal darkness."

"What other kind of darkness is there?" he asked.

"Trust me, Newman, you don't want to know."

The memory of blackness that had a voice and a mind of its own tried to become a clearer memory, but I chased it away by finding a lamp to turn on near the wall of weapons. That warm golden glow chased back the literal darkness and helped me short-circuit the memory of the Mother of All Darkness. She was dead now, or as dead as we could make her. It's hard to kill things that have no corporeal body to destroy.

I gazed up at the wall of weapons. There were antique guns, and there were swords of every shape and size with blades that were round, jagged like a lightning bolt, or curved like a wave of the ocean cast in metal. I even saw things that looked like bladed metal whips that I couldn't even figure out how to wield. The guns started with what I thought were blunderbusses, but they might have just been muskets. I wasn't the weapons expert that Edward was; he'd have probably known what everything was, along with its historical accuracy or inaccuracy. I knew just enough to confirm that the weapons were certainly not arranged by time period or culture or any other criteria except that they fit on the wall. It was like a museum display designed by a person who had been doing way too many drugs—or maybe it was supposed to be an artistic design?

I tried standing farther back from the wall to see if there was a pattern to the weapons that made sense to my eyes. I'd have settled for just a pretty design, but nope, it was just a wall covered in weapons without any rhyme or reason that I could see.

"They have some weapons that belonged to actual Marchand ancestors going back centuries," Newman said from behind me.

"How did they hold on to things like this? My grandparents came from Germany, but most of the family heirlooms went to finance the trip," I said.

"Was your family nobility?"

"No," I said.

"The Marchands were, and not just land rich and money poor but wealthy and noble. They had enough money to keep the family jewels and stuff together."

"Did you know all this about the family before the murder, or did you learn it afterward?" I asked.

"Some before. I mean, how often do you see a room like this in real life in America? There may be tons of houses with this kind of stuff in Europe, but you don't see it here."

"True," I said, and walked farther down the wall to find new animals mounted in the far corner. There was a black leopard head on the wall this time, and a skin that matched stretched up on the wall beside it. The paws were missing, but someone had done a good job of stretching out the skin so there wasn't much shrinkage. It had been a big leopard, probably a male. It would have looked even more impressive if there hadn't been a full-size tiger skin right beside it. Tigers are the largest land predator, not just the largest big cat. The huge striped skin made the rich black of the leopard look smaller than I knew it was, like Mutt and Jeff in fur. The tiger's head was mounted on the other side of its skin.

Newman turned on a pole lamp in the far corner, and more animals sprang to "life." There were monkey heads with impressive canines visible. There was a glass case full of brilliant birds that were unknown to me. In fact there were several cases of birds. Then, in the corner, was an elephant head with smaller ears than the ones on the full-body version across the room. The tiger had clued me in that this group of animals was from the Indian subcontinent, but the Asian elephant was the other clue. If I'd known more about the birds in that area of the world, or the monkeys, I'd have probably figured it out from those specimens. The first corner had felt like trophies, but this one had more of a scientific feel to it. I mean, what Great White Hunter collects birds? Apparently this one, because more than anything else in the room, this corner felt like one hand, one mind, had put it together. I wondered if this Marchand ancestor had done his own taxidermy. That might explain why it was just heads and skins for the bigger animals and full bodies for the birds. My understanding is the bigger the animal, the more challenging it is to stuff and mount.

There were a few primitive-looking weapons scattered among the heads, but they were more carefully placed, with the same eye for detail that had arranged the birds in lifelike poses behind glass. The other animals just looked dead—impressively preserved, but dead. The birds looked like they should have moved or had just stopped moving a moment before. I could recognize the art here.

Newman turned on two other floor lamps, and there were full-size family portraits that wouldn't have fit in Muriel's car. I assumed the paintings were of family, because though the people in them were attractive for the most part, they looked grim, except for a pair of young women in one painting and a couple with five small children plus the family dog in another. That one was the most natural and gave you a sense of an oil portrait rather than just an oil painting. There were four small spaces on the wall, all in a row, that were bare, but the frames had been there so long, the wall was a different color underneath, so that their loss stood out even on a wall full of art.

"They were here when I first toured the room," Newman said.

"Do you really think that Muriel and her husband planned on blaming the police and emergency responders for the thefts?"

"I think they would have tried," he said, turning on a smaller lamp that was on top of a full-size grand piano.

If we'd started with the piano, I would have been impressed, but after all the rest, I shrugged it off as no big deal, though the wood gleamed with years, maybe decades, of polish and care. There were more pictures on top of the piano, but these were photos. Some looked like women in nineteenth-century clothes. Others had men posing with what might have been some of the specimens in the room, but the animals were freshly killed and limp with death. The tiger's head was propped up so it was looking at the camera. The black leopard that a mustached man had just caught was hung upside down like a fish. It looked so terribly dead. The man's arm was in a sling, and there were bandages along one side of his face. It looked like the leopard had given him a run for his money and for both their lives. It made me strangely happy that the leopard had cut the man up before it died. I'd grown up hunting with my father, but we'd hunted deer and rabbits, never predators. He'd raised me with the belief that if you couldn't eat it, you didn't need to hunt it. I tried not to feel like I was on the leopard's side as I looked at that long-ago man standing so upright beside the animal that he'd hung by its hind legs like a deer. I guess dead meat is dead meat, and certainly the animal had been beyond caring, but it seemed like an insult. The leopard had marked him, hunted the hunter. To me that made it a foe. You should respect your opponents even in death. Hanging them up like a big fish for a photo just felt wrong to me.

The pictures went through the centuries. A lot of the family was blond. There were a couple of redheads, then a brunette or two, but they were predominantly pale of hair, skin, and eye. I guessed if you kept marrying among your white-bread roots, that was what you ended up with, but it bothered me. Maybe I was letting my own personal issues interfere? Probably. I'd been dealing with my family more than normal because of the wedding planning. My stepmother, Judith, was as blond and blue-eyed as her daughter, as my father, and as their shared son, my half brother. I was the only dark, ethnic note in their German white bread, and Judith had never, ever let me forget it. She'd been so rude about it that by the time we were teenagers, Andrea, Judith's daughter from her first marriage, had started correcting the racism in front of her mother and whomever she was talking to. Andrea and I had never really gotten along that well, so I'd been surprised that she'd come to my defense. In hindsight I wasn't sure she'd been defending me as much as she was just embarrassed by her mother's obvious white-supremacy leanings. Either way, it had left me with an ethnic chip on my shoulder that I never let Judith forget.

"Here're Bobby and his parents," Newman said, pointing.

There was a smiling couple with a baby and then a picture of them with a slightly older version of the baby. The next picture of the baby was with a man alone, just him and the baby.

"Is this Ray Marchand with baby Bobby?" I asked.

"Yes, those are the last of the older photos."

Newman led me back to the office area. There was a smaller corner table between the file cabinets and the desk that I'd overlooked, too busy looking at the blood and mayhem. There were pictures of Ray with a progressively older boy. Bobby at somewhere between six and eight, holding up a bigmouth bass almost as big as he was, a huge grin showing that he was missing some of his baby teeth. Ray was helping him hold the fish, a look of pure happiness and pride on his face. There were pictures of them with skis someplace cold, and then there was a wedding photo: Ray Marchand with a statuesque woman so beautiful, she didn't look real. From cheekbones to carefully waved hair, she was model perfect, movie-star gorgeous. Her hair was black, her skin the color of coffee with cream in it. Bobby stood beside her in a tiny tailored tuxedo complete with tails that looked to be a match to the one that Ray was wearing. His smile was flashing the same missing teeth as the fishing photo. He had a white cushion in his hands held loosely so that if the rings really had been on it, they'd have rolled away. I guess that's why there's a ribbon on ring bearer pillows. The easiest choice for Jean-Claude and my wedding party had been the ring bearer. There was a little girl clinging to the side of Ray's pants leg. The girl was younger than Bobby, so maybe four or five? She looked like a tiny replica of her mother, except her black hair was a short mass of curls and her skin tone had less cream to it and more coffee. There were no other pictures from the wedding. Maybe Ray and his new bride had been as tired of the drama llamas in their lives as I was, and just said *Screw it. We'll have a flower girl and a ring bearer and be done.* Of course, the flower girl position in our wedding had turned into a hotbed of drama, so maybe we'd just have a ring bearer and be done.

There were pictures of all four of them in the summer with a lake behind them, all smiling and happy. Ray was holding the little girl, and the woman had her hands on Bobby's shoulders. Without any obvious makeup, the woman was still gorgeous, just less dramatic. Close-ups showed her eyes were a startling shade of green. The daughter's eyes were a deep, rich brown, but except for that, she looked remarkably like her mother. The pictures jumped around in the years as if they'd been arranged more for ease of viewing than for chronology, or maybe favorites were in front. A picture of Ray with his wife entwined in a hug, both of them laughing, wasn't a professional photo, but it had been blown up and placed in the center of it all. The family photo beside it was of the four of them in bathing suits still wet from the Caribbean blue sea that gleamed around them. The kids were teenagers in that photo, and both Ray and his wife were in great shape. They looked like a happy, healthy, outdoorsy, athletic family. There were pictures of the two children growing up—Christmases, Easters, school track meets with them both winning ribbons, Bobby in football gear with his teammates holding a trophy. It took me a few minutes to realize one of the cheerleaders in the shot was the daughter. Then there was a photo of Ray and the girl jogging with a leopard bounding alongside them like a dog. Another picture had the girl lying back with her head against the leopard's side, its head turned so that his furred cheek was against her black curls. The leopard had bright yellow eyes. The photos of just Ray and the children seemed not to care if Bobby was in human form or animal. I'd never seen any family treat someone's beast form so casually. I liked that a lot, but I also liked that there were almost no professionally posed shots in the entire collection of photos. Maybe professionals had taken some of them, but they were remarkably candid looking, moments of people's lives frozen and happy. They seemed more like real memories than the stiff family photos that marched up the wall by the stairs in my father's house. It made me think about the photos that Jean-Claude wanted for the wedding. Was there such a thing as unposed, natural-looking professional photos?

"They looked happy," I said, at last realizing I'd probably looked at the photos longer than I would have at most crime scenes. "Do you know what happened to the wife?"

"Her name was Angela Warren."

I frowned. "Why does that name sound familiar?"

"I'm surprised you didn't recognize her in the wedding photo," he said.

"Did you?" I asked.

He looked almost embarrassed. "One of my favorite movies as a kid was her one and only starring role in an action flick."

"Oh, yeah, *The Model and the Spy* or something like that."

"Model Spy," Newman said.

"Why was it her one and only starring role?" I asked.

"It became a cult favorite, but when it was first released, apparently it didn't make that much money."

I studied the wedding photo again; she wore more makeup in that one than in any of the other photos. "I should have at least thought I knew her from somewhere."

"You weren't a little boy, so the fact that she got the cover of the swimsuit issue twice probably escaped you," he said.

I smiled. "Didn't she put out an album while she was a model?"

"She did, and she wrote all the songs on it, plus an extra song that she wrote for her boyfriend at the time, Tucker B."

"Him, I know. He does R and B and rap."

"He tops the charts in both," Newman said.

"You can't turn on a radio without hearing some of his stuff," I said.

"Angela wrote a lot of his biggest hits, and she continued to write for him and other chart-topping singers even after she married Ray and moved here."

"What is one of the world's top models and a singer, songwriter, and actress doing living in Hanuman, Michigan?" I asked.

Newman chuckled. "I know, right? But Ray and she met in New York or LA at some party that friends had dragged him to while he was traveling for business. He was twice divorced and, according to the local gossip, had vowed never to marry again, but once he met Angela, all that changed."

"I remember this. It was in all the tabloids in the supermarket and on the celebrity gossip shows. My stepmother loved those kinds of shows. I was still trapped at home with her in charge of the remote. 'Backwoods Millionaire Marries Supermodel.' Wasn't that one of the headlines?"

"Yes. The headlines called Ray a recluse, which he wasn't from all accounts, but they painted him as backwoodsy and primitive as they could."

"Didn't they use photos of him on hunting trips?"

"Yeah, they made it sound like Angela was marrying Grizzly Adams," Newman said.

"Do you know how she died?" I asked.

"Don't you? It made world headlines."

I shook my head.

"'Famous Model Mauled to Death by Leopard on African Safari with Her Family' was one of the news stories," he said.

"And it turned out to be a wereleopard, because one of the kids popped for the disease," I said.

"I thought you'd remember it for that at least."

"I was still in college getting a degree in preternatural biology when it happened. It was the talk of our department, especially for those of us wanting to be field biologists with a specialty in the supernatural."

"I never knew that you ever wanted a career outside of law enforcement."

"If I hadn't had the psychic ability to raise the dead as zombies, I'd have probably gone for at least my master's and been living out in the wilderness somewhere, studying trolls or helping track invasive foreign species like gargoyles."

"Why did raising zombies stop you from being a biologist?"

"A man named Bert Vaughn had started up a company called Animators Inc., where 'The living raise the dead for a killing' was the motto at the time. He found out my abilities and offered me a lot more money than any summer job I could find that year. I needed to earn money to help put myself through grad school, and I was also meeting postgrads with their master's degrees working for five dollars an hour, feeding seals at SeaWorld. It made me realize I'd need at least a doctorate, and that takes money."

"So your summer job turned into your career," he said.

I nodded.

"You ever think of going back?"

"No, not really. I miss camping and the outdoors though. I haven't been bird-watching in so long, my binoculars are outdated."

"Jean-Claude much of a bird-watcher?"

"No. Even if he wasn't a vampire, his idea of roughing it is a hotel that doesn't offer turn-down service."

"Haley does like those little chocolates they put on your pillow, but I'm glad she loves the outdoors more."

"I tried to find someone to go hiking and camping with me. He has his master's in preternatural biology, and he's even a bird-watcher."

"What happened?"

"His self-loathing trumped our love," I said.

"Ouch, sorry."

I shrugged. "I'm happier now than I've ever been in a relationship, so no bitching from me. At least my ex just left in a therapy-rich huff and didn't die like Ray Marchand and Angela Warren."

"He vowed never to marry again, and this time he made it stick," Newman said.

"How old was he when he died?"

"Just turned sixty-five."

"Did he continue to hit the gym and take care of himself like in these photos?"

"Yeah, Ray took care of himself."

"Then why was he on medication for arthritis and a bad back? That makes him sound decrepit and old."

"I'm not sure which family member told the sheriff that Ray was on medication for pain."

"How much other family is there besides Muriel and Todd?"

"Just Jocelyn and Bobby."

"Jocelyn is the girl in the photos?"

"Yeah, though you'll hear a lot of people call her Joshie. Apparently, she was a serious tomboy and tried to keep up with Bobby even though he was a couple of years older."

I looked at the picture with her reclining against Bobby's leopard. She looked like a slightly darker version of her mother, which meant she was beautiful. There was an unfinished look to her face that only age and experience would cure, but from the bone structure to the curve of her mouth and the big, dark eyes, she had everything she needed to be devastatingly gorgeous.

I turned so I'd be where the office chair was. The chair was so out of place that I didn't have to move it to stand close to the main desk. I'd have rolled it over and sat in it so I could have the actual view that Ray Marchand had when he was working, but in case this turned into an actual murder case with evidence gathering like with a normal crime, I didn't want to contaminate anything. I was wearing booties and gloves, not a full-on coverall, so no sitting or leaning.

"He set this room up so that he could see anything that came through the door," I said.

"So whoever came through the door to kill him was someone he trusted," Newman said.

"Statistically it usually is," I said.

"If I believed all the stats on violent crime, I'd be a hermit in the woods and avoid all humans," Newman said.

"Look up the stats on death by household accidents. Even living alone is dangerous," I said, but I was looking out from the desk toward the door as I said it. I'd noticed that detectives did that at crime scenes, talking without looking at you, as if the conversation wasn't as important as what they were looking at and thinking in their heads. When I started helping the police, I thought it was weird, but now I understood that the conversation was like background music to help your brain work on the niggling idea that's almost a clue if you can just drag it out into the front of your head. But it's like the things you see out of the corners of your eyes. If you look directly at them, they vanish.

"Did you look through the drawers yet?" I asked.

"No, I mean . . . this was someone I knew." The tone in his voice made me look at him so I could see the embarrassment on his face.

"It's okay, Newman. Was this the first time you've seen someone you know dead from violence?"

He shook his head. "My first was one of the officers that helped train me. He was the first person I saw killed by a wereanimal." His eyes had closed down, face grim with remembering.

"Is that why you wanted to become a marshal with our branch?"

He nodded, face still bleak. That's the best word I have for his expression. Victims and first responders can look haunted sometimes, but there's a certain look that only people in uniform who have seen the big bad get in their eyes. *Bleak* is the closest word I've found to what it looks like, even in a mirror.

"You never forget the first time you see the amount of damage that supernatural strength can do," I said.

"Which is one of the things wrong with the way Ray was killed," he said. The bleakness in his eyes began to fade to something closer to depressed anger or angry depression. You stay on the job long enough, you have your own version of it.

"I've seen the crime scene photos," I said, "and the murder was bloody and awful, but it didn't take superstrength to do it."

"I admit that when I first saw Ray lying there, all I saw was the blood and the damage to the body. It wasn't until we started taking pictures to help us get the warrant that I realized the blood wasn't hiding more damage. Usually there're pieces torn off, eaten. The victim is savaged, so when they start picking it up to wrap it up for transport, I expect bits to fall off the body."

"Yeah, sometimes the damage isn't obvious until you start trying to move it," I said.

"The body was too intact, Blake. It was too . . . whole. I told that to Duke, and he told me I was crazy. Wasn't Ray's throat being torn open enough damage?"

"No," I said, "it's not. I've never seen a wereanimal kill that was that clean. Vampire yes, but not a shapeshifter."

"Exactly," Newman said.

"The sheriff says he's seen what a wereanimal can do. Has he?" I asked.

"I don't know, but why would he lie about it?"

I shrugged. "Some people do."

"Duke can brag with the best of them, but he always lets you know when he's pulling your leg. He's never claimed expertise he didn't have to my knowledge."

"Maybe whatever he saw wasn't someone he knew. That can make a difference," I said.

I opened the top left-hand drawer and found the usual office bits and bobs. The drawer below it was deeper and had hanging file folders in it. I've worked so few cases where this kind of evidence mattered that I wasn't entirely sure if I messed with the files whether it would hurt the case later. A warrant of execution covered almost any kind of violence and death, but I wasn't sure about regular evidence.

"If the evidence didn't look like a shapeshifter attack, you'd have gone after the money angle?" I said.

"You mean, who inherits?" Newman said.

"Yeah."

"Like Muriel and Todd?" he said.

"Oh, yeah. I'm wondering if messing with the files in the victim's desk will mess us up if it turns into a financial case."

"Warrants of execution let us kill almost anyone or anything that's associated with the crime, but the legalese doesn't mention papers and files," Newman said.

"We can look at anything in plain sight, or if we have reasonable suspicion of something specific, but we're just fishing here. If we find something, it could get thrown out on the grounds of the warrant not covering what we discover," I said.

"So, we leave the drawers alone," he said.

"We can peek inside them, but I'd rather not move shit around without a different kind of warrant."

"You're the senior marshal on this one."

"I've got seniority, but it's your warrant, so technically you're the lead on this one," I said.

"It seems like every time we work together, the warrant starts out as mine," he said.

"No shame in signing it over to someone with skills you don't have," I said.

"Have you ever signed a warrant over to another marshal?"

"No, but remember, I'm one of the old-timers in this business. You young whippersnappers have things to learn. I've learned them already."

"You're only two years older than me, Blake. You don't get to call yourself an old-timer or me a whippersnapper. Who uses that word anymore?"

"Apparently I do," I said, but I was smiling as I opened the right-hand drawers to look but not touch.

The second drawer down had a gun in it. I actually reached out to touch it but stopped myself. It hadn't been in plain sight, and since there had been no shots fired in self-defense, we had no reason to think that Ray Marchand had a gun in his desk. I called Newman over to see it.

"Why didn't he use the gun?" he asked.

"We already said it: He trusted them and didn't think they were a threat."

"A shapeshifter that has lost control looks like a threat," Newman said.

"Maybe Bobby moved too fast for him to go for the gun?" I asked, playing devil's advocate.

We both looked at the door, trying to visualize the scene. The leopard could potentially make the leap from the door to the desk. "Were all the drawers closed like this?"

"As far as I remember, yes."

"Ask around to anyone else that was a first responder. Just ask if they noticed anything moved, disturbed, or open in the desk area besides the stuff on top being on the floor," I said.

"And if no one remembers the drawer being open?" Newman asked.

"Ray was prepared to defend himself. Even if the leopard hit the door and made the leap to the desk, the drawer should have been open. I'm not saying he'd have had time to draw the gun and aim, let alone shoot. You know how fast shapeshifters move."

"So, he opens the drawer, and then the leopard is slashing at him. He does have defensive wounds on his arms."

"The leap could have knocked over the lamp, and the struggle cleared the desk," I said.

"Are we trying to figure out how Bobby did it, or how someone else did it?" he asked.

"We're trying to get to the truth," I said.

He nodded. "Okay. Now what?"

"I'd really like to make sure that gun is loaded and if it's silver-plated ammo."

We looked back down at the gun. Could we check the gun for ammo by saying we didn't want to leave a loaded gun unattended in a house where there'd already been one murder, or was it outside the purview of our legal authority?

The doors opened, and Sheriff Leduc came through like he owned the place. Whatever had been wrong, he'd stuffed it back into its box. He was Duke Leduc again as he said, "Troy found your warrant on the computer, Marshal Newman. Time to take you back to town so you can do your duty."

"Having the warrant just makes it legal to kill the prisoner. It doesn't mean I have to do it as soon as I get the paper in my hands," Newman said.

"Troy says the date on the warrant is the night of the murder. So your original seventy-two hours is down to less than sixty according to the information on the warrant. You have to finish the warrant before the deadline's up. You're running out of time to do your duty, Win."

"Don't you mean Bobby's running out of time?" Newman said.

"I'm beginning to think you're a coward, Win."

"And I'm beginning to think you're an asshole," I said, "but let's not go calling each other names." I used my phone to take a picture of the gun. If it was loaded with silver bullets, then it just pointed more guilt at Bobby, because it meant that his uncle had been afraid of him.

"What are you taking a picture of?"

"A gun," I said.

"Ray always had a loaded gun for protection in his desk."

"Nice of you to share that," I said.

"Well, us assholes aren't big on sharing."

"I'm sorry I called you a name, but compassion isn't the same thing as cowardice."

"No, he's right, Blake," Newman said. "I don't know if I'm brave enough to kill Bobby."

"That doesn't make you a coward, Newman."

"What does it make me?" he asked.

"Human."

17

THE ONLY GOOD thing about the time on the warrant starting the night of the murder was that it convinced Kaitlin and Livingston to help us. They would meet us at the jail after Kaitlin made an impression or copy of the bloody footprints at the house. If they matched, Bobby was a lying bastard and almost certainly guilty, but if they didn't, then at least our little group would have reasonable doubt. It would take longer to get the judge on the warrant to be on board, but you have to start somewhere.

Duke was still in his vehicle as Newman and I pulled up. Because of the overhead light, we could see him talking on his phone. The driver's-side door was open already, as if the phone call had caught him in the middle of exiting his car. We parked and walked toward him.

He hit MUTE on the phone and said, "It's my wife. You two go ahead. Tell Troy that you need your warrant. He said he'd printed it out for you."

We both nodded and started toward the building, but not before we heard him say, "I'll be home as soon as I can, honey. I know she's in pain, but she doesn't want hospice-level meds yet."

Newman and I both hurried just a little, as if we'd eavesdropped on something too personal, and I guess we had. I didn't have kids, but I couldn't imagine having to watch someone I loved die like that.

Newman paused at the door of the tiny police station. "Jesus, hospice-level meds."

"I'm not sure what that means," I said.

He put his hand on the doorknob but didn't turn it. "It's when they give them so many pain meds they just sleep pain free until the end. When doctors offer you hospice care, then it's over. You're just waiting for the body to give out."

It sounded like Newman had experienced it personally in some way. I debated whether I should pry or keep to the guy code of never asking about personal stuff. I was still debating when we heard the gunshot. It sounded like it had come from inside the building. Our guns appeared in our hands like magic, and we went through the door toward the gunfire.

18

I WOULD HAVE checked the room as we entered to make sure nothing was hiding behind a desk or something, but Newman ran straight toward the far door and the cells. I stayed at his six because I was his backup, but it was careless, and careless could get us both killed. We had seconds to see that the office area was empty, and then we both went for the door to the cells. Newman didn't even check if it was locked; he just reared back and kicked the door right next to the doorknob and lock. The door burst inward, because not only hadn't it been locked, it hadn't been securely shut, so the door smacked into the wall and came back at us with way too much force. Newman caught it with one arm, and with the other kept his gun pointed into the room. I was at his back with my gun out, pointed at the floor, but the safety was off, finger on the trigger. Shots fired meant "gun safety" was hitting what was shooting at you.

There was a man in the now familiar uniform of the local cops aiming between the bars of a cell. I had a second to notice he was tall, thin, but I was mostly trying to aim around Newman's body without crossing him with the barrel of my gun. I didn't even bother to look inside the cage. Whatever had been done was done in that second. There was nothing at the end of the short hallway but the man, shoulders rounded, gun still in hand. It wasn't pointed at us, but Newman and I were both yelling.

He yelled, "Put the gun down!"

I yelled, "Drop the gun!"

The deputy turned and looked at us. I had a moment to see he was pale, with huge eyes in a face that looked shocked, but his hands with the gun still in them turned with him, and I yelled, "Drop it!"

Newman yelled, "Don't make us shoot you, Troy. Don't make us do it!"

I finally went to one knee against the wall opposite the cell, so I had a clear shot at the deputy without endangering Newman or accidentally shooting into the cell. It'd be a bitch to accidentally shoot the person we were trying to save.

If the shooter hadn't been another cop, I'd have shot him moments before, but then he dropped his gun. The only thing that had saved him was the uniform. Newman kicked the gun toward me. I changed my grip on my gun from two-handed to one- and picked up the dropped gun. Loose guns were bad guns. I clicked the safety on, got to my feet, and moved around so I could keep an eye on the deputy as Newman put him on the ground and secured his hands behind his back.

I heard something behind us, and I had the second gun up and pointed before I could think anything. I just reacted. I even thumbed the safety off, and my finger was on the trigger. I didn't have time to wonder if Wagner had messed with his trigger pull and lightened it from out-of-the-box standard. If he'd made it a hair trigger, then potentially someone else was about to get shot. I was okay with it, because a cop should have known better than to walk up on people when the guns came out.

Sheriff Leduc put his hands up without me asking; he also stopped moving closer. Good, it would be a shame to have to shoot him in his own jail.

My peripheral vision is above average. I could keep half an eye on Newman kneeling on the deputy and still watch the sheriff. Newman pulled the cuffed man to his feet.

I spoke very carefully, each word as cautious as the touch of my finger on the unfamiliar trigger. "You got that one?"

"I got him," Newman said.

I turned toward the sheriff, bringing my gun up to bear on him as I lowered Wagner's gun toward the floor. I took my finger off that trigger but left the safety off. One of his deputies had just shot one of his prisoners in his own jail. It might mean that Duke would be okay with it. Besides, he'd already pointed a gun at me once. I wasn't going to let him get the drop on me twice.

"Ease down there, Anita," the sheriff said.

"Fuck you, and it's Marshal Blake to you."

"Yes, ma'am," he said.

He stood very still, hands up. He was doing his best to not piss us off further. That was great, because we needed to look in the cell and know if we were calling an ambulance or the coroner. How had I not looked in the cell before? The armed person always takes my attention first. Enough people shoot at you and it's like you acquire this tunnel vision that cuts out all the unnecessary shit. The exception to that rule is if someone you love is involved. Then you're fucked because you notice too much. You're never at your best if you love someone in the room, unless they're as well armed as you are. Then it's like gangster date night.

"Ease down, Blake," Newman said. "It's over."

I thought he meant our prisoner was dead, which made me gamble a quick glance into the cell. Bobby wasn't there. What the fuck? I looked back at the sheriff to make sure he was still holding his hands up like a good boy, and risked a second, longer look into the cell. My eyes had registered the broken chains because when I saw them now, I wasn't surprised. A corner of blanket underneath the bunk let me know that Bobby had taken the only cover the cell offered. He was hiding under the bed like a little kid who's afraid of the closet monster, but this monster had a badge and a gun, and there was nowhere to hide. I had to look back at Leduc, but there'd been no visible fresh blood in the cell. That didn't mean much, but it was the only hope I had for Bobby's survival, so I took it. He could be dead later, but until I saw him that way, I'd keep believing that he was alive and that we could save him.

"I am not a danger to you, Marshal Blake, I swear," Sheriff Leduc said.

"I know, because I'm pointing a gun at you."

He sighed hard enough for the bulk around his middle to go up and down. "May I put my hands down?"

"No. If you want a different position, lace them over your head."

Deputy Wagner was babbling as Newman got him on his feet. "I couldn't do it. We were teammates. Got all the way to states our junior year. I know he's a monster, but he's still Bobby, too."

And there in the babbling of a soon-to-be ex-deputy was the real problem with shapeshifters: They turned into big, dangerous beasts at least once a month, but the rest of the time, they were still themselves. It made it so much harder to put them down in human form, but only a fool with a death wish waited for them to turn furry before trying to kill them.

Leduc had put his hands on his head, but it looked like it was an effort for him to keep them there, or at least his uniform strained when he lifted his arms that much. He needed new uniforms or to start exercising so he actually fit into the ones he had. Either way, the tight sleeves would cost him a second or two if he had to draw his gun, which was still sitting on his duty belt.

Newman was calling out, "Bobby, Bobby, are you hurt?"

I risked another glance and saw an arm wave from under the bunk. I hoped that was an I'm-okay wave, but we'd need to see more of him before we'd be certain. He started crawling out from under the bunk, and what showed around the blanket still looked okay. I went from being happy that the deputy had missed to wondering how he could have missed from that close.

"Bobby, are you all right?" Newman asked again.

"What?" Bobby asked, frowning.

I said to Newman, "The shot in this small a space probably rocked his hearing."

Newman yelled his question louder, and I heard Bobby Marchand say, "I . . . think so. I'm okay."

"May I put my arms down now, Marshal Blake?" Leduc asked.

"No," I said.

"I think the danger is over, Blake," Newman said.

I glanced back and found Newman standing with the handcuffed Deputy Wagner in front of him. I double-checked the safety on Wagner's gun and tucked it into my belt. It wasn't perfect, but it would hold. I moved forward with my own gun still aimed at the sheriff.

"Did you know that your deputy was in here trying to kill Bobby Marchand?" I asked. It was a stupid question to ask him, because all he had to do was say no, and I had no way to prove otherwise.

"No. I was very clear with all my deputies that unless he started to change into animal form, they were to leave him for Newman."

"Blake, it's okay," Newman said.

"You can put your arms down now," I said, and holstered my weapon.

Leduc did it slowly, as if he didn't want to spook me even without a gun pointing at him. It meant he believed I might actually shoot him. It's always nice when other cops take you seriously.

"What the fuck, Troy?" Newman said. He sort of shook Wagner. "What the fuck were you thinking?"

Duke said, "You didn't find Raymond Marchand. Troy did. You didn't find the boy in bed sleeping nude and covered in his uncle's blood. We did."

"I came as soon as you called me, Duke," Newman said.

"I know that. You always come when we call. It's been good having another lawman to call when we needed backup."

"You knew I was on the job, Troy. You should have let me handle it."

"But you weren't handling it, Win. You called in Blake to help you save the monster, not kill it," Troy Wagner said.

"If I did that to Uncle Raymond, then I am a monster, and I deserve to die." Bobby sat up on the bunk, huddling the blanket around him as if he was cold. Sometimes getting shot at makes you cold with shock. If we weren't going to kill him, then we needed to find him more to wear.

Leduc pointed at him. "Even the monster agrees with me."

"I said *if* I did it, Duke. I haven't had a complete blackout in over ten years. I remember what I do when I'm in animal form. I remember what I did before I changed back that night, and none of it includes hurting Uncle Raymond."

"We found you covered in his blood, Bobby," Wagner said, and his voice sounded like he was crying now.

"I can't explain that, but I wouldn't hurt my uncle. I wouldn't hurt anyone. I was with Jocelyn most of the evening. Ask her. She'll tell you that she left me in the bedroom as I started to pass out from shapeshifting."

"Joshie hasn't stopped crying since she found her stepdaddy's body in a pool of blood. She was so hysterical, they had to sedate her," Leduc said.

"I would remember if I had done what you're accusing me of, Duke."

Wagner said, "I can't stop seeing Jocelyn kneeling on the floor, cradling her daddy, blood everywhere, her screaming, blood all over her, all over everything."

"Are you saying that Jocelyn was the one who found Uncle Raymond?" Bobby asked.

"Yeah," Wagner said, looking over his shoulder at the other man.

Bobby Marchand looked stricken. That was the only word I had for it. "God, that's awful."

"Shoulda thought of that before you left him in one of the main rooms in the house for someone to find. Didn't you think it would be her? Only people that live at the house are the three of you and servants," Leduc said.

"There were no servants last night," Bobby said.

"What did you say?" I asked.

The sheriff said, "Last night was the regular night off for most of the staff."

"Did everyone in town know that?" I asked.

"Probably. Why?" the sheriff asked.

"Don't you find it suspicious that the one night all the servants are gone is the night someone murders Raymond Marchand?"

"We're just lucky that no one else was home when it happened. Otherwise we'd have had a massacre on our hands."

"Even Carmichael was gone," Bobby said.

"Who's Carmichael?" I asked.

"The live-in handyman. You know, a dogsbody," Newman said.

"Dogsbody. I haven't heard that term outside of an old British mystery novel."

"I like old British mystery novels," Newman said.

"You're just full of surprises, Newman. How unusual was it for Carmichael to be gone?"

"Unusual," Bobby said, "or it used to be before he started dating his new girlfriend. It was still part of his job to be there most nights."

I turned to the sheriff. "Did other people know Carmichael was going to be out of pocket?"

Newman answered, "Carmichael is dating Hazel Phillips. She's a waitress at the Sugar Creek."

"What does Carmichael's personal life have to do with my question?" I asked.

"Carmichael spent the night with Hazel. Sugar Creek's the most popular restaurant in town for breakfast and lunch. If he talked to her about his plans to spend the night at her place while she was at work, then half the county could have overheard it."

The sheriff shook his head hard enough for his jowls to shake. He reminded me of a tall bulldog. "If Ray had been shot, I might agree with you, but he was cut to pieces with claws. We don't have any other shapeshifters in this area."

"Come on, Sheriff. If it wasn't death by wereleopard, what would you think about it being on the one night when everyone else was gone?"

He scowled at me. "I know what I saw, Blake. No human being could have done that to a man."

"You might be surprised what human beings do to one another," I said.

"You think I'm just some hick cop that hasn't seen anything."

"That's not what she means," Newman said.

"I just meant that I've seen some shit normal people do to one another that made me wish it had been monsters."

Leduc took in a lot of air and let it out slow. "All right, I aimed a gun at you once, and you've aimed one back at me. Let's call it even and start aiming at the real monster."

"I thought if I did it, then it would all be over," Troy said, face still wet with tears, though the actual crying had stopped.

"Bobby would be dead, but you'd be up on murder charges, Troy. It wouldn't be over for you," Newman said.

"I have the warrant in my pocket," Troy said.

Everyone in the hallway with a badge looked at the deputy. Leduc spoke slowly like you would for a very young child who had done a bad thing. "Troy, what difference does it make if you have the warrant in your pocket?"

"You called it a get-out-of-jail-free card," he said, and his eyes were guileless, like he didn't realize his mistake.

"For the marshal whose name is on the warrant, yes, but not for you or anyone else."

Troy blinked at Leduc. I was beginning to wonder how bright Troy was or wasn't. He certainly wasn't catching on fast.

Newman tried. "Troy, the warrant has my name on it. If I'm part of the hunt, then and only then is it a legal execution. Anything else is murder."

"Now, Newman, if Bobby goes changing into his beast in the cell, then we will shoot him to make sure he doesn't get out and hurt anyone else," Leduc said.

"Deputy Wagner, was the prisoner changing shape when you fired at him?" I asked.

Troy looked at me, shaking his head. "No, but he killed Ray, and I had the warrant in my pocket."

"Troy, damn it. I know you're not a deep thinker, but ya gotta think better than this," Leduc yelled.

"Troy Wagner, we're holding you on suspicion of attempting to murder Bobby Marchand," Newman said. Newman said all the words that normal cops say to suspects all the time. I'd actually never read anyone their rights. You only did that when you took suspects into custody. I didn't do that. The vampires had nicknamed me the Executioner. I didn't take prisoners.

19

CAPTAIN LIVINGSTON AND Kaitlin the crime scene tech were a little surprised when they found Deputy Wagner in the cell beside Bobby's, but when we explained what he'd done, they didn't question it.

Livingston did say, "I heard you were a shoot-first-ask-questions-later kind of person, Blake. I'm surprised you didn't just shoot Troy."

"You know, I'm a little surprised about that, too. Must have been something to do with the uniform he was wearing."

"Don't believe the bad stuff you hear about Marshal Blake. She's one of the best preternatural officers I've ever worked with," Newman said.

I smiled at him and said, "Thanks, Newman."

"If I believed it all, I wouldn't be here helping the two of you," Livingston said.

"You'd really let an innocent man be executed rather than help the Whore of Babylon out?" I asked.

"I never used that word or anything like it," Livingston said.

"And I really appreciate that," I said.

"Are you saying that other officers have called you that to your face?" Kaitlin asked.

"I am," I said, and I smiled when I said it, because sometimes you have to smile when you say the bad stuff out loud, or it gets too deep a hold on you. Smile and think Fuck you as you say it.

"Wow, that's . . . awful," she said.

"Agreed."

"I'm sorry you experienced such a lack of professionalism at the hands of other officers," Livingston said. He seemed to mean it, so I thanked him.

"Weirdly, the insults have gotten fewer since we announced the wedding. If they were upset I was sleeping with monsters, I thought marrying one would make it all worse," I said.

"You're marrying him," Livingston said. "We don't bad-mouth one another's spouses. That's sort of off-limits."

"I've never had a spouse before, but good to know. Now, what do you need from us to take the prints from Bobby?" I said.

"I want Kaitlin safe while she gathers evidence, and I'd like to avoid killing the prisoner to keep her safe since that would defeat the entire purpose of why we're doing this."

"I'm sorry I had to break the chains," Bobby said.

"You were trying to take cover while someone shot at you. No apology needed," I said.

"I don't have anything stronger to chain him up with," Duke said.

"I have cuffs rated for preternaturals," Newman said.

"It's a start," Livingston said.

"I can get more chain to go around the cuffs," Duke said.

I shook my head. "It won't hold him."

"Well, then, Ms. Expert, tell me what will hold him."

"That's Marshal Expert to you, and the cuffs that Newman and I have are it."

"I thought silver chains worked," Livingston said.

"One, you got any silver chains that big?" I asked.

Livingston looked uncomfortable, and it took me a second to realize that it was his embarrassed look. "No."

"Second, silver rubs their skin raw like a mild corrosive agent, or a metal allergen, but it doesn't actually make the chains any stronger against them."

"I thought silver burned them," Kaitlin said.

"No, nothing that spectacular. It takes time for the silver to damage the skin unless it's the edge of a silver blade or a bullet with high silver content. Then the weapons work against them as if they were plain human."

Bobby added, "We can wear silver next to our skin to hide what we are or wear it with clothing between us and the metal."

"Well, aren't you just being helpful," Duke said.

"You've known me most of my life, Duke. I'm still me."

"What slaughtered your uncle wasn't human, so the boy I helped coach is gone. He died in Africa when that leopard got him and what came home was a monster."

"That's enough," I said.

"You don't get to tell me what's enough in my own jail."

"I think I just did."

"The two of you don't have to like each other to work together," Livingston said.

"Oh, good," I said. "For a minute there, I was worried that Duke and I would have to make nice."

"Blake," Newman said, and the one word was sort of pleading.

"If I have to call you Marshal, then you call me Sheriff."

"Duke," Livingston said, not pleading, more warning.

I sighed, took a deep breath, and let it out slow. "You're right, Newman, Captain. We don't have to like each other to be professional on the job."

"Fine," Duke said. "Then let's get this done, so you can go back home and we can dislike each other from a distance."

I nodded. "Works for me."

20

WE KEPT KAITLIN safe by having Livingston stand over them with a shotgun aimed at Bobby's head. The barrel of the gun was so close to Bobby that if Livingston had pulled the trigger, it would have pretty much decapitated him. It was one of the few absolutely sure-fire ways to kill a shapeshifter or a vampire, so it seemed even more important that Bobby stay in human form and not give Livingston an excuse to do it, which was why I was in the cell with them to meta-phorically hold Bobby's hand. I couldn't really do it, because Kaitlin was taking evidence from more than just his feet, and holding his hand would have put me in the line of fire.

Newman was standing outside the locked cell with Leduc. The sheriff had tried to get us to give up our weapons because it was pro-cedure. He'd conceded that Livingston needed his to shoot the mon-ster, but he tried to insist on me giving up mine just like the first time I got into the cell. Not only no, but fuck no.

"Once someone's pointed a gun at me, Duke, I don't give up my weapons to them again."

"And I don't let weapons just waltz into my holding cells for the prisoner to take."

"Duke," Livingston said, "just let it go. If the prisoner so much as twitches wrong, I'll kill him before he can grab for anyone's weapons."

I could have added that if Bobby had started to change into a leopard, he wouldn't have been going for our weapons. He'd have been too busy growing his own. But I didn't say that out loud. They were spooked enough without me overexplaining.

Deputy Wagner came to the bars on the wall that the two cells shared. "Do you really think that Bobby didn't do it?"

Newman answered, "We think it's a possibility."

"You mean, I could have killed him, and he was innocent?" His voice rose with the edge of guilt and panic that it had had earlier when he was hysterical in front of the cells.

I flicked my gaze to him. His hands were wrapped so hard around the bars, they were white. His face looked anguished. God, he was emotional.

"You didn't kill Bobby," I said. "You didn't even shoot him."

"But I tried."

"It's okay, Troy," Bobby said, and his head moved as if to look back at the other cell.

"Don't move that much," Livingston said, and his words were almost a growl, which meant he had a lot more testosterone floating through his body than the outward calm, cool, professional demeanor showed.

"You don't have to see Wagner to talk to him," I said.

"Right," Bobby said, but his pulse had sped up against the side of his neck. He'd been playing it as cool and calm as Livingston had looked until that moment.

"Duke, go calm your deputy down," Livingston said, still in that low bass growl.

"Troy, stop being an ass."

"Is his bedside manner always this awesome?" I asked quietly enough that it was mostly for the people in the cell with me.

"He's usually pretty nice," Kaitlin said as she drew a small piece of thread or fiber from the palm of Bobby's left hand. She'd already filled other plastic bags and containers with tiny crystals, or maybe they were rocks. I was a little fuzzy on the difference, just like thread and fiber. I mean, were all threads fiber the way that all poodles were dogs, but not all dogs were poodles, or were thread and fiber totally interchangeable?

"You're not catching Duke at his best," Livingston growled, and his voice had an edge to it that made me glance up at him. His eyes stayed focused on where the shotgun was pointed, which I appreciated, but if I hadn't been afraid that I'd set Bobby's beast off, I might have reached some energy into the big state cop. Was his voice going lower because of the tenseness of the moment, or was it something more?

I couldn't sense any animal energy off him, or off Bobby, for that matter. If your control was good enough, you could pass for pure human even to someone who had their own beast. That level of control was rare, but I'd met a few people who could do it. The only thing I couldn't figure out was how Livingston could have passed the blood work that was mandatory after you survived an attack on the job. Blood work didn't care how good your control was, or maybe I was just looking for monsters where there weren't any . . .

Bobby had dropped the blanket so that Kaitlin could get whole-body pictures. It meant that he had to stand up, which made us all have to readjust our positions. Livingston had the shotgun barrel pressed against the bottom of Bobby's skull, but at an upward angle so that he'd miss me. If he had to pull the trigger now, he'd paint Bobby's brains on the ceiling instead of on the wall. I stepped back while Kaitlin took her own pictures of the visual evidence on Bobby, but Livingston stayed put so that he was probably in at least some of the images. It would have been interesting if they'd had to be presented in court. I hoped they did get used in court, because that would mean Newman hadn't had to execute Bobby and that we'd found someone else to put on trial for the murder.

Bobby had been a good sport about Kaitlin looking for trace evidence in the dried blood on most of his body. He even managed not to get overly embarrassed when she knelt in front of him so that her head was placed in front of the bloody mess of his groin. Then she found something in the blood there that she wanted to pluck and put into a plastic Baggie. I don't know if it was the tweezers coming toward his junk, or if he still didn't know why there was so much gore caked on him there, but whatever the reason, he tried to back up, which made Livingston dig the gun into his head. Bobby pressed back against Livingston and his gun barrel as if he didn't feel it.

"Stop moving," Livingston said in that low, gravelly voice.

Bobby kept trying to back away from Kaitlin and her tweezers. I felt his energy spike with the fear that I could see on his face. It wasn't his beast yet—his eyes were still human—but the energy prickled along my skin, raising goose bumps.

"I will shoot you!" Livingston growled, and he had to change angles again to keep me out of harm's way.

I appreciated his attempt, but Bobby was acting as if the threat was the woman in front of him, not the man behind him with the shotgun. This was going to get out of hand, and Newman was right there outside the bars, so it would even be a legal kill.

"Bobby," I said. "Bobby, look at me."

I watched yellow pour through his irises like golden water drowning the human blue. His leopard eyes stayed wide and focused on Kaitlin.

"His eyes are gold," Kaitlin said, voice low.

"Do something, Blake, or I will have to shoot him," Livingston said.

He was talking through gritted teeth as he tried to hold his ground with the gun changing its aimpoint as Bobby pushed backward. The hair on Livingston's arms was standing to attention. He was reacting to the energy rush; most people didn't. Bobby's hands were in the cuffs Newman had supplied, but I wasn't honestly sure what would happen if he started to shift. Would the cuffs stay on, or would the sliding bones and ligaments help him slip the only restraint he had? I'd never actually seen those cuffs used on anyone during the change. I promised myself that when I got home I'd remedy that. Nathaniel would probably enjoy helping me test the equipment.

I waved Kaitlin back, and she scooted back behind me slowly, like she didn't want any sudden movements to spook him. I gave her brownie points for not just scrambling away or running for the door and yelling for them to open it and let her out.

I yelled, "Bobby!" He finally looked at me, golden eyes so wide, you could see white all the way around them, like the eyes of a horse that was about to bolt. The irises had changed color, but the structure was still human, though you had to be this close to realize that. To everyone else, his eyes were leopard eyes. They'd sign statements to that effect, and they'd all believe it.

"How could I do that to Uncle Ray?" Bobby whispered so low that I think only Livingston and I could hear him.

"We aren't sure you did anything to your uncle," I said, "but to prove that, we need to collect evidence. We need you to let us do our jobs, okay?"

"It's a hair—a hair caught in all that blood. It's not my hair."

I didn't try to argue with him. I hadn't realized it was a hair. I just said, "It doesn't mean it was your uncle's hair. Hell, if you share a washer and dryer with someone, you can get trace evidence on your sheets and then it transfers to you. Not all fiber and hair mean anything." I was babbling at him, trying to get his energy to calm down without me having to add to it, because if Livingston could feel just Bobby, I wasn't sure what he'd think if he felt me, too. I wasn't afraid that I'd out myself to him. I was afraid that he'd think my extra energy was Bobby changing, and shoot him because of that. Could I explain the metaphysics to Livingston in time?

Newman said, "I had Dale, our coroner, look, and there were no signs of abuse on your uncle's body."

Bobby tried to turn and look at him, but the shotgun barrel dug in so hard that he'd have had to push the barrel partially into his skull to see Newman and the sheriff on the other side of the bars.

"I don't believe you," Bobby said, and he kept turning toward Newman as if a gun weren't pressed to his head.

Livingston tried to stand his ground. I saw the metal imprint on Bobby's temple. If he'd been plain human, he'd have been bleeding, but the metal of the gun barrel wouldn't cut into him that easily. He kept pushing until a trickle of blood trailed down his skin. It would heal almost immediately, but that he was cutting himself at all meant he was really trying to hurt himself.

I glanced at Livingston and realized he was bracing his body and the gun to prevent the force of Bobby's head from moving him. Livingston's eyes flicked to me. He seemed to be asking me what the hell was going on. Bobby was either totally oblivious to the pain, or he was trying suicide by cop. When Wagner had shot at him, Bobby had reacted automatically, trying to hide and save his own life. But now, with more time to think, he wasn't trying to save himself. Maybe it wasn't in the front of his head, but the back of his head wasn't thinking survival anymore. If he changed tactics from slow pushing to sudden moves, Livingston would kill him.

"We called the coroner from the car on the way to your house," I said.

Bobby moved his head toward me, which was just enough to help Livingston stop having to fight against moving another inch, or maybe he was fighting not to hurt Bobby more. Maybe both.

"I told you not to call Dale about any abuse nonsense," Duke said.

"You're going to bitch about that now," I said, still staring at Bobby and Livingston. I didn't have to see Duke to fight with him.

"This is my case, Duke," Newman said.

"And this is my town," Duke said. "You're just visiting your girl-friend."

"Are you telling the truth about Uncle Ray's body?" Bobby asked. "It wasn't . . . hurt that way?"

"You're a wereanimal. You should be able to feel that I'm telling the truth." I didn't say we were telling the truth, because to my knowl-edge the coroner hadn't gotten back to us yet, so Newman couldn't know if our victim's body had been raped.

"I should be, but I can't feel anything, except that I'm afraid of what I did to Uncle Ray."

"He just confessed. You all heard him," Leduc said.

"No," Bobby said, and tried to turn back to look at the hallway again. "I don't remember."

"Confess, Bobby, and it'll all be over," Leduc said.

Bobby opened his mouth, but Newman said, "I won't execute Bobby because you trick him into confessing."

"I keep telling you that we don't have any other shapeshifters in this area. It had to be him."

"And we keep telling you that it doesn't look like a shapeshifter kill to us," Newman said.

I kept my attention on Bobby and Livingston. Kaitlin had moved to the far corner of the cell, as far away from us as she could get without asking to be let out. A lot of people would have asked for someone to open the door by now. Points for her.

"Win, you can't make it something it's not just because you don't want to have to kill someone you know," Duke said.

Bobby's eyes shifted completely. Only years of watching that change in people's eyes made me positive of what I was seeing. The march of energy down my skin confirmed it. Livingston let out a breath loud enough for me to hear it. I did that sometimes just before I squeezed the trigger, too.

"Don't shoot him," I said.

"Give me a reason not to," Livingston said, voice careful and controlled so that even his breathing didn't accidentally make his finger twitch.

"Bobby, help me save you," I said.

"What if I don't want you to save me?" he asked. A shudder ran down his body from the top of his head to the soles of his feet. He was starting to give himself over to the change. Fuck!

I grabbed his wrist and the energy poured over my hand and up my arm like I'd plunged it into a tub of warm water. If I didn't do something now, it would just get warmer. I lowered my shields and poured my own energy back into Bobby's, like trying to stop a fire with a firebreak.

"Livingston, I'm putting energy into Bobby to keep him in human form. Don't shoot him because of my energy, okay?"

"How do I tell the difference between your energy and his,

Blake?" Livingston asked. His eyes were showing a lot of white now, too, but there was no answering energy from him.

"You probably can't."

"Fuck that," he said, and he was gritting his teeth again, as if even his jaw muscles were holding on for dear life.

"If he starts to shift, you have to shoot him," Duke said from the safe side of the cage bars.

"Shut the fuck up, Duke," I said.

He protested, but Newman made him back off and stopped him from commenting on us, which was good since I needed all my attention to keep Bobby from shifting. Usually when I was doing this, the shapeshifter wanted to stay in human form, so they took the help like a lifeline, but Bobby didn't.

He poured his own "fire" into mine as if he wanted to burn us both up. It took me a few minutes to realize that if I couldn't contain Bobby's beast, he might trigger my own. If I'd been a full-blown shapeshifter, he might have brought on both our beasts and gotten us both killed, but I didn't change form except for my eyes.

"Blake, your eyes. What the fuck is wrong with your eyes?" Livingston said.

"She's one of them!" Duke yelled.

"Don't shoot me, Livingston."

"Don't change, and I won't."

"Bobby, you're going to get us both shot," I said.

"I don't want to get you hurt," he said, but his voice had the edge of a growl to it.

"Then swallow your beast back down."

"If I hurt Uncle Ray, I need to die." His voice was barely human. He opened his mouth and flashed fangs.

Kaitlin screamed. I heard the door open but didn't dare look away from the two men in front of me.

Newman said, "Get out of there!"

"Get out of here, Livingston," I said.

"I won't leave you in here alone with him."

I stared at him with eyes that I knew were almost the same shade of yellow as Bobby's, and said, "I won't be alone with him, Livingston. He'll be alone with me."

That was enough for him. He backed away with the shotgun snugged against his shoulder still aimed at Bobby, though I was in the way of that aim.

"Don't shoot either of us," I said. I wanted to look at him as I said it, but I had to keep my eyes on the shapeshifter in front of me.

"If either of you starts bending bars, all bets are off," Livingston said.

"Deal," I said.

Really powerful lycanthropes change shape rapidly, almost gracefully, like ice melting to reveal a new form. But for the rest of them, it's slow and painful and kind of horrific. If you've ever dislocated a joint, broken a bone, torn a ligament, or ruptured a muscle, you know how much that hurts. Now imagine that every joint, bone, ligament, and muscle in your body is tearing itself apart all at the same time. That's what a slow shape change is like, and that's why even the most experienced of lycanthropes will lash out while the pain rips them apart. The bones begin to slide under their skin like they're trying to stab their way out.

Bobby threw his head back and shrieked his pain to the heavens.

I jerked my hand off of Bobby as blood started running down his hands, and claws forced their way out over his fingernails. I hadn't been near anyone who changed like this in years. He might be safe once he was fully leopard, but until then . . .

I dropped to one knee so two things could happen: Livingston had a clean shot that didn't include part of me, just in case, and I could come up under what was left of Bobby's chin with as hard an uppercut as I'd ever thrown. If the bones of his face had still been solid, it might have knocked him cold, but it just staggered him. I drove my other fist into his diaphragm, and leopard or man, if you can hit the right spot, it will knock the wind out of him. Since he was still standing on two legs, it bent him over a little, and I hit him in the face with my elbow on the right side of his face and then used my other elbow on the left side of his face. I grabbed the back of his neck to help his face meet my knee twice, and he was still moving. I drove my knees into his face until he slid out of my hands in a smear of blood, and I couldn't tell whether I'd broken all the bones in his face or he was still trying to change into a leopard when he passed out. Either way, the fight was over.

21

THERE WAS ONLY one bathroom in the sheriff's station, so that was where I went to clean the blood off my hands and dab cold water on the knees of my pants. I was hoping the blood wouldn't set. I liked these pants. Not all the blood had come off my hands either, because some of it was fresh and mine. I'd managed to cut my hand on one of the surprise bones underneath Bobby's skin. Normally hitting under the chin isn't where you cut your hand in a fight. It's usually the cheekbone or the teeth that are the problem. Hell, maybe it had been one of those moved down into his chin, or maybe it had been leopard bones out of place when I hit them. I stared at the cut on my knuckle and didn't know what part of Bobby and his beast that I'd cut myself on. And just like that, I started to shake. The emergency was over. I could have my moment now. I'd been arrogant thinking I could control Bobby. When you're hunting, you want the target to be as powerless and animalistic as possible, but when you're trying to talk to them, you don't want to talk to the animal. You need a human being in there who can hear you and think about what's happening.

I found tears in my pants where Bobby's claws had poked through. I hadn't even known it happened in the heat of the fight. Even if my hand hadn't been bleeding, I'd have been forced to get tested for lycanthropy, except that there was no need. I'd popped as having leopard-based lycanthropy years ago. Lucky it hadn't been Newman in there, but of course he wouldn't have been stupid enough to let them lock him inside once Bobby's bones started sliding around. No, just me being so abysmally stupid.

I rested my hands on the cool edges of the sink and watched the blood begin to well up in the chunk I'd taken out of my knuckle. I let out a breath and stared at myself in the mirror. My skin was paper white; the dark brown of my eyes looked black, like holes burned into paper. I'd always thought that my hair was what made me look so pale afterward, but my hair was still back in its braid. Maybe it wasn't the hair after all. Shock is what happens when your mind decides that it needs to protect you from experiencing everything around you, or when your body begins to shut itself down for the same reason. As far as I could tell, Bobby's claws hadn't cut anything but my clothes. Lucky for me he'd been in manacles. If he hadn't been . . . No, don't even think it. Well, don't think too hard about what might have happened if I'd been just a little slower or less well trained. Nope, just don't think about it too hard.

We still had a few hours until Edward would get here to back me up, but even he couldn't protect me from my own arrogant stupidity. I'd never have taken such a terrible chance once upon a time before . . . before what? The only psychic ability I'd started with had been the ability to raise the dead as zombies. Of the eight of us old-time vampire hunters who had transitioned to being U.S. Marshals, three of us were animators, as in could animate the dead, which probably meant that our ability to raise the dead had given us more help against vampires than we'd first thought. Before I had fallen under Jean-Claude's spell and eventually in love with him. Before he'd shared his vampire marks with me and I'd become more than human. Before I'd caught lycanthropy and held a rainbow of beasts inside me. We weren't even sure why I didn't shapeshift completely, but we thought it had something to do with the vampire marks getting to me first. Now I was going to marry Jean-Claude. Yes, we were in love, but he was also technically my master, which made me his human servant, though due to my own abilities with the dead, there was some debate on who was in charge of whom. Last year I'd raised a zombie army to combat one raised by an ancient evil vampire. So what was my short list? Necromancer, vampire slayer, Mistress of Beasts, Queen of the Dawn were all titles I'd earned among the supernatural community. It was a lot of power, a lot of magic. I'd let it give me delusions of grandeur, and those delusions had almost gotten me killed. All the wedding plans and any other plans I had almost went up in bloody ruins, because I thought I was the biggest, baddest thing in the pool. Fuck.

There was a soft knock on the door, and Newman said, "You all right in there?"

"Yeah, yeah, I'm fine." I got more paper towels and pressed them to the wound on my hand. I needed the bleeding to slow more before I could put a bandage on it.

"Can I come in, or would you prefer Kaitlin?"

"Why would I prefer Kaitlin?" I asked and saw myself frown in the mirror.

"She's a girl. Some women prefer other women when they're hurt."

"I don't know her," I said.

"So, can I come in?" he asked again.

I glanced back at the mirror, but knew I wasn't going to look better anytime soon. "Sure."

He opened the door and had about as neutral an expression as I'd seen on him. "Are you hurt?"

I shook my head.

"Then why are you holding pressure on your hand?"

I think I gave him an unfriendly look, because he held up his hands in a little push-away gesture.

"What'd I say wrong?"

"Why ask if I'm hurt if you already know the answer?"

"That's fair, but I already asked if you were all right, and you said yes."

"Then stop asking me questions I've already answered."

"Okay. Are any of the all-right, not-hurt parts of you needing a doctor?"

I almost smiled at his wording but fought it off. "No, thank you."

He smiled then and stepped a little farther into the room. "Can I help you with your all-right and not-hurt hand?"

"Yes, once the bleeding slows enough for a bandage."

"How badly are you bleeding?"

I tried to motion toward the wastebasket, but since I was using one hand to press paper towel to the other hand, it was an incomplete gesture at best. "I thought one paper towel was enough, but apparently not."

He walked to the wastebasket so he could see what I was talking about. "That's not bad," he said.

"Like I said, I'm all right."

"I think your definition of *all right* may not match mine."

I smiled and shook my head. "It'll match Ted's when he gets here."

"I'll keep that in mind if either of you decides to slug it out with another shapeshifter."

I sighed and looked at the floor before I made myself meet his eyes. I hadn't been this embarrassed on a case in years. "There won't be another time. I've learned my lesson."

"Aren't I the one who's supposed to learn lessons when I'm working with you?"

"Don't rub it in, rookie," I said.

He grinned at me. "If it's any comfort, it was impressive as hell to watch you beat a lycanthrope unconscious in the middle of shapeshifting."

"It was arrogant and stupid, and if my reflexes weren't more than human normal, I'd probably need that doctor."

"I've never seen anyone move that fast in a fight."

"Don't you ever watch the new shapeshifter MMA fights?"

He shook his head. "I see them when they're trying to kill people. That's enough."

"The fighters aren't like Bobby. They have more than one shape, and they're in control of their change."

"I've heard it's a hell of a show," he said.

I nodded. "Yeah."

"Are the fighters on TV scarier than what I saw Bobby do in that cell?"

"No, but they fight a hell of a lot better than he does."

"He didn't fight you at all that I saw."

"Yeah, there was enough of Bobby still in there somewhere that he didn't want to hurt me."

"I think you nearly broke his jaw with your first punch, and he never recovered enough to hurt you before you knocked him out."

"Or that," I said. The paper towel stuck to the wound a little as I pried it off gently. I didn't want to jerk it off and stop the blood from clotting this time. I threw the paper in the wastebasket with the first one.

"What did you cut your hand on?" Newman asked.

"A bone that was someplace it wasn't supposed to be."

"Is it always like that, fighting them while they're in the middle of changing?"

"I don't know. This was my first time doing it."

Newman stared at me, and I watched the blood begin to drain out of his face. "Sweet Jesus, Blake. I don't know if you're one of the bravest people I've ever met or the stupidest."

"Today I'll vote stupid," I said. "Now, help me bandage my hand." When my hand was bandaged, I went out to Newman's Jeep for more of my gear. This was an active warrant and I needed to start treating it like one.

22

I CALLED MICAH from inside Newman's Jeep, because it was the closest privacy I could find. It seemed weird that it was still black night outside, so much had happened, and the sun was still hours from rising. Shit, it felt like more time had passed than that. I wasn't calling Micah for reassurance as my sweetheart. I was calling him because he was the head of the Coalition for Better Understanding Between Lycanthrope and Human Communities, which was now the Coalition for Better Understanding Between Therianthrope and Human Communities. I needed backup with Bobby and not the kind of backup that Edward would give me in a few hours. I needed someone who was better with shapeshifter energy than I was, and there was almost no one better at it than Micah Callahan. He'd become a wereleopard by surviving an attack; his uncle and cousin hadn't been so lucky. One of the things the Coalition did was help survivors and their families cope with the aftermath of attacks. It wasn't until his voice answered thick with sleep that I thought about the time difference. "Anita, what's wrong?"

"I'm sorry I woke you," I said.

"That's fine. What's wrong?" His voice was climbing into normal range, the sleep slipping away from him as he started to focus on the perceived emergency.

"Why do you think anything's wrong?"

"Because you just left to fly out on marshal business. When you're hunting monsters, we're lucky if you remember to text. A call means something's wrong."

I'd have liked to argue with him that I was more considerate than that, but he was right. I try not to pick fights with the people in my life when they're right and I'm not. "I need help keeping our suspect in human form. I thought I was good at this, but he's not like you and Nathaniel. He's low level, only one form. I'd forgotten how different that could be."

"Tell me what happened." Micah's voice was serious, thoughtful, a voice you'd trust your secrets to, and I had almost from the moment I'd met him.

It had been so unlike me to fall for someone so fast and so hard, but I guess what they say is true sometimes about when it's the right one. Micah was my one, but he'd come into my life too late to be my only. He and I had been an item for five years, but we'd never been a traditional couple. We'd always been a threesome with Nathaniel, not a twosome. If we could have legally done it, we might have tried a four-way marriage, but legalities and public opinion being what they were, I was marrying Jean-Claude, and Micah was marrying Nathaniel. They would be my intended forever, and I would be theirs. We would intend to marry one another indefinitely while we waited for the law to catch up with our hearts.

Micah listened to me without interrupting, except to ask for clarification a couple of times. He was a good listener and didn't waste time on stupid questions or accusations. He didn't even tell me that I could have been killed or ask me what I had been thinking, slugging it out with a wereleopard without backup from another supernatural. If the tables had been turned, I probably would have said something along those lines to him, but then I never questioned which of us was the better man. Micah was the most reasonable person I'd ever met. He was more logical than I was, and I was very logical as long as I didn't let my temper get the better of me. We were both calm and cool under pressure and ruthless when it came to survival. He would never accuse me of being a monster for resorting to violence like one of my ex-fiancés had. I would never call him a monster for being a shapeshifter like his ex-fiancé had. We valued each other completely, even the parts that scared other people—maybe especially those parts, because those were the parts that would keep you alive when the real monsters came.

"I can't bring the Coalition into this unless local law enforcement invites us in," he said when I'd finished.

"This is Newman's warrant. He'll invite you in if I ask him to."

"Send it through official channels, and I can be there in two hours or less."

"Less would mean you were borrowing Jean-Claude's private jet," I said.

"One of the perks of the three of us dating him," he said like it was a given, when just a few months ago he wouldn't have said it that casually.

Micah had been working his therapy hard to come to terms with certain things, and one of those things was our vampire master, who was the kind of man who had been making heterosexual men doubt their sexual orientation for centuries. Micah was lucky that Jean-Claude wasn't into force, either metaphysically or in any other way, because he had the power to have rolled over my Nimir-Raj, my leopard king, and just about anyone else he wanted to seduce. Jean-Claude didn't want anyone in his bed who didn't want to be there. He believed in willing partners and true love, luckily for all of us.

"How long do official channels take?" I asked.

"Anywhere from two hours to two days. It depends on how much the other local cops don't want the Coalition there and how much your friend Newman is willing to rock the boat."

I thought about that for a second. "Newman is engaged to a local girl here. He's hoping to make this his forever home, so I'm not sure on the rocking-the-boat thing."

"Then what do you suggest until the boat gets rocked?" he asked.

"I need help keeping Bobby Marchand alive while the rest of us try to figure out if he did it or if he's being framed."

"A lawyer could try to get an injunction . . ."

"It won't help us if Bobby transforms in his cell. I haven't been around any shapeshifter that uncontrolled during his change in years. If I hadn't been there, they'd have shot him, and it would have been a clean shoot."

"You wouldn't have blamed them for killing him?"

"No. The only thing that kept him from changing was me knocking him cold."

"He doesn't sound that controlled after ten years," he said.

"It surprised me, too."

"Did he hurt you?" Micah's voice was neutral as he asked.

"I skinned my knuckle when I hit him, but other than that, I'm fine."

"If the other marshal invites us in on the case and the local sheriff will allow it, we could put one of our people outside the cell to monitor Bobby's energy, but what you really need is more time on the warrant until we can get there, right?"

"Yes."

"Amanda Brooks, the lawyer we worked with to get people out of the government safe houses, has been wanting to try to throw a kink into the execution-warrant system. Are you willing to have me aim her your way?"

"You mean, am I willing to risk her fucking up the warrants of execution and basically screwing my job up?"

"Yes," he said.

I thought about it and finally said, "I'd like more options than just killing people if I get on the ground and think they didn't do it."

"How much of the situation can I tell her without getting you in trouble?"

That was a different question. "I'm not sure. I'd say give her the broad overview. I'll give her name to Newman and see if he can get Bobby a phone call."

"Try it," he said.

"I will. I love you."

"I love you more."

"Our mostest is still at work, I take it," I said.

"Yes, Nathaniel was onstage tonight."

"Give him a kiss for me when he gets home."

"I will."

"Love you."

"Love you more."

"Love you mostest," we said together.

That made us both laugh, and we hung up with the echo of it in our voices.

23

I WAS STILL smiling when an SUV pulled in beside me. I didn't know the vehicle, and it was still dark enough that I couldn't see inside the SUV, but the driver was most likely male and tall. Then he opened his door, and the overhead light illuminated him. My stomach fell into my shoes, and my pulse rate soared. I suddenly couldn't swallow right. It was Olaf. He was perfectly bald, with a mustache and a Vandyke beard framing his lips. When I'd first met him, he'd been clean-shaven. He looked better with the facial hair; it gave his face definition and complemented the thick black of his eyebrows. Before, he'd looked like a henchman in some big-budget action flick. Now he looked like the main villain. I hadn't understood what other women seemed to see in him until he grew the Vandyke. Then I could finally see that he was handsome in a scary-bad-guy sort of way.

Olaf, aka Marshal Otto Jeffries, unfolded himself from the SUV and stood all damn near seven feet of him on the other side of the vehicle from me. I had a gun naked in my hand, held against my thigh like I had for Leduc after he'd threatened me. Olaf hadn't done a damn thing to me; he was even smiling at me as he started to move in my direction. I opened the passenger door and slid out so that I wasn't sitting there staring at him like a mouse caught in a cobra's gaze. I even holstered my gun, because he had his badge on a lanyard around his neck. We were both U.S. Marshals in good standing. He hadn't done anything wrong yet, so I put up the gun that my fear had made me draw, but I did start moving toward the building behind me. I tried to make it casual, like I was just going to stand on the porch with its light and people just inside to chat with him, not so that I wouldn't be alone with him. He was one of the only people on the planet who could make me feel like a victim waiting for a crime to happen. I hated that I was afraid of him. I fought to quiet my pulse rate, though it was probably too late to hide my physical reactions from him. He was a werelion now, which meant he'd probably tasted my pulse the moment my heart rate spiked.

"Anita," he said. He had a deep voice to go with the size of him, and it sounded like the rumble of a Great Dane.

I almost called him Olaf, but remembered in time that we were on the job, and when other cops were nearby, he used his legal identity. I could hear the murmur of voices just inside the building. I couldn't understand what they were saying, which meant I probably could have called him anything without being overheard, but it was his secret, not mine.

My voice was even and neutral when I said, "Otto, what are you doing here? I thought you were on an active warrant somewhere else."

He smiled again, and it almost pushed its way into the black depths of his eyes. They were set deep in his face like twin caves. Maybe it was the color of them? If he'd had bright blue eyes, would he have looked less intimidating? Maybe I could have talked him into colored contacts and see. Though any color would have ruined his style of all-black assassin chic. Whether he was out of work clothes or in them, I'd never seen him wear anything but black. There might have been a white T-shirt thrown in there once, but when I thought of him, I thought of black.

"The warrant is complete." Which meant he'd killed someone recently, but I really couldn't throw stones at him about that. We were both executioners with badges.

"Good for you," I said. "Ted told me you were chasing down bad guys close to here." I mentioned Edward on purpose, because he was one of the few people in the world Olaf respected man-to-man. Pretending to be my lover, Edward had helped me keep Olaf from pursuing his crush on me further.

Olaf smiled as if he knew exactly why I'd dropped Edward's legal identity into the conversation. "Ted told me you were nearby as well."

"No, he didn't," I said, and my voice was still neutral; even my pulse and heart rate were even. Good for me.

"How can you be so certain?" he asked.

"Because he would have told me that he'd talked to you."

He gave a small nod. "There was a second crime attached to Newman's warrant. As the closest U.S. Marshal, I was notified."

I nodded, and some tension I hadn't realized I was holding eased out. He wasn't stalking me; he was on the job. "I thought the new protocol only alerted the nearest marshal if there was a second attack connected to a warrant."

"As did I, but apparently it alerts for any major crime associated with the warrant."

"So the attempted theft at the same crime scene was pushed through channels to you," I said.

"Yes."

"So you knew the second crime was just theft with no violence," I said.

"Yes."

"Then you knew that Newman and I didn't need any more backup."

"We're supposed to contact the marshal in question and ask if they need help before we leave the area," he said.

"I think that means a phone call, not a face-to-face."

He smiled, a brief curling of lips in the black beard-mustache frame. There was emotion in the depths of his equally black eyes, but it shouldn't have gone with the smile. I fought the urge to shiver as he stared down at me.

"I am following the new protocol, and I get to see you in person, Irene."

"I appreciate that . . . Sherlock."

I took in a deep breath and let it out slow. I'd made a side comment to him once that I was the Woman for him—well, the only one he actually wanted to date instead of kidnap, torture, rape, and kill. He had never read the Sherlock Holmes stories by Sir Arthur Conan Doyle, so he hadn't understood the comment. I'd explained, and to my surprise, he'd gone off and read the stories, so the next time we met, he'd suggested we have pet names for each other. I'd be his Irene Adler, and he wanted to be my Sherlock Holmes. I'd suggested he should be Moriarty instead of Holmes, but he didn't think that made sense as terms of endearment since they'd never been a couple in the stories. My opinion had been not only no, but hell no. Edward had persuaded me to go along with it as a way to stave off the day when Olaf finally realized we'd never be a couple, or he just decided to move me from would-be girlfriend to victim.

"You know, I'm still thinking that Holmes might work better as a term of endearment," I said.

"Have you decided that you would prefer Adler to Irene?"

"Let's try it that way and see if it rolls off the tongue better."

"Very well, Adler." But he shook his head. "I prefer Irene."

"I prefer Moriarty, but you said no."

"You do not seem comfortable with our nicknames for each other." His voice had gone lower, softer, and his face was sliding to something more neutral. I did not want him to look at me coldly; that could go badly for both of us. Damn it.

"I don't have cute nicknames for any of the people in my life," I said, which was absolutely true.

"Jean-Claude calls you *ma petite*."

I rolled my eyes before I could stop myself. "He has cutesy nicknames for everyone. It's just the way he is, but I've never come up with anything to call him."

"You call him master."

"Hell no, not unless there are other vampires around we need to impress, and even then, I usually forget."

He smiled again, which even with the creepy expression in his eyes was better than him shutting down and going into full-sociopath mode. "I also have never given pet names to anyone."

"Maybe we're just not that kind of people," I suggested.

"I enjoy calling you Irene, or Adler."

"And I'm good with you using it for me, but I'm just saying that Sherlock Holmes doesn't quite work on my end for you. That's all."

"And you think Moriarty would be better?" he asked.

"I'd like to try it if you're game." I couldn't believe that I was standing here discussing pet names with him. He scared the fuck out of me. Under no circumstances did I want to call him anything but far away from me.

"Why Moriarty instead of Holmes? Give me your reasons." His voice was serious, the smile gone. He studied me with those pitiless eyes of his.

I took a deep breath and concentrated on keeping my pulse and breathing even. He'd enjoy my fear if he could detect it, and I didn't want him to enjoy it. "Moriarty is the bad boy, the mystery man. It seems to fit you better than Holmes's cold logic."

"He is addicted to cocaine. That is not cold logic," Olaf said.

"True, but I see that as weakness, and you're not weak."

He smiled, and this time it was a real one or the closest his little black heart had to offer. It was good enough that I smiled back at him.

"Your reasoning is sound," he said. "I will be Moriarty for you."

I wondered if he understood just how true that statement was, but I kept my smile. Maybe it was more relieved than romantic, but it was still a smile. "Moriarty. Yeah, that I can call you and be happy with."

"You are right. It does roll off your tongue better than Holmes ever did." He managed to do that thing that men do sometimes when perfectly harmless statements turn into creepy sexual double entendres. But since we were supposed to be romantic in some weird way, I couldn't call him on it or say something snarky in return. I lost my battle of will with myself and shivered.

His smile changed somehow, or maybe it was just the look in his eyes. He was staring at me like he wondered what I'd taste like, and not in a double-entendre kind of way but just straight-up taking a bite out of someone. Fuck, fuck, fuck.

"I am glad that our new closeness has not made you unafraid of me." He took a step toward me on the tiny porch, sniffing the air above me.

I backed away from him before I could stop myself. I was so close to him that with his new literally catlike reflexes, I'd never get to a weapon in time. I knew with good reason that he wouldn't hurt me here and now, that if he decided to do it, it wouldn't be like this, but damn it.

"I like the scent of you when you're afraid, Adler."

"I know you do." I couldn't keep the anger out of my voice as I said, "Moriarty."

He took another step forward, and this time I made myself step forward to meet him. We stood so close that it was almost more awkward not to touch. I glared up at him, putting all my rage and defiance into my eyes. I would not cower for him.

He bent over me, not like he was moving in for a kiss, but so he could smell my hair. His voice was a low rumbling whisper against my hair. "I am torn with you, Anita, my Irene. You would make a magnificent hunt to end as all my hunts have ended. To take all that rage and power away from you is exciting, but I can have you like that only once, and I do not think I want you only once. You are the first woman that has ever made me think I would want her more than once."

I think I held my breath. I had no idea what to say to him in that moment, and we were standing too close for me to just pull a gun and shoot him. He'd been fast for a human before, but now he was a werelion, one that was trained in hand-to-hand combat and who outweighed, outreached, out-everythinged me.

My hand found the doorknob behind me. I could still hear the voices inside, so close, but they might as well have been on the moon at that moment.

I found my voice, and it was breathy and shaking. I hated that, too. "And you wonder why I wanted to call you Moriarty."

"Not anymore," he whispered, and laid his lips against my hair again.

I turned the doorknob, and he had to move back or risk us both stumbling through the door. I did half-fall through, my hand on the door handle the only thing that saved me from tripping to the floor. Olaf came through the door gracefully like the big predatory cat he was. Oh, hell, he'd always moved like that. I could bitch about a lot of things, but the man knew how to move.

24

"So, THOUGH THE shapeshifter listed on the warrant by name is in a cell in the next room, he is still alive," Olaf said from the chair that he'd folded all that height into. He had a cup of coffee in his hands, but he seemed to be holding it more than drinking from it. He hadn't drunk coffee or tea when we first met, so maybe he was just doing it to be social, the same way he'd decided not to kill me so we could date.

I was drinking mine with my back leaned against the wall near the open door to the cell area. I'd been offered one of the chairs but chose to stand in case I needed to draw a weapon or move quickly. Olaf might try flirting again, and I wanted to be prepared. We didn't have enough people to guard the prisoners and explain everything to Olaf and argue about what our next move was, so Duke had told Deputy Wagner to yell if Bobby woke up. If Bobby had been plain-vanilla human, I'd have been worried that I'd done more than just knock him out, but since his brain and heart were still in his body, I knew that whatever I'd done to him would heal eventually.

"Yeah," I said, and took another sip of coffee. It was good coffee, strong but not too strong—right on that edge of wake-me-up bitter and too acrid to sip and enjoy. Bad coffee you drank because it was coffee; this was good enough to drink slowly and savor each mouthful. It was helping settle my nerves as well as yummy and warm. I didn't like Leduc, but he made a nice pot of coffee.

"Why?" Olaf said.

"Why what?" Newman asked.

"Why is he still alive?"

"That's what I've been asking. Maybe you can talk sense into Win and Blake here or take the warrant over yourself," Leduc said from his swivel chair behind his big desk.

"Win is Marshal Newman?" Olaf said.

"Short for Winston," I said.

Newman sighed heavily from where he was perched half sitting, half leaning on the far corner of Leduc's desk. "But everyone calls me Win." He gave me a pseudo-hard stare as if giving me grief for sharing the name he disliked, but his heart wasn't in it. We'd joke for real later when we'd saved a life and figured out who the real murderer was.

"I will call you Newman."

"That works for me, Jeffries."

Olaf took a sip of coffee and turned back to Leduc. "I cannot take Newman's warrant from him, Sheriff Leduc. He has to sign it over to me, or he has to be so badly injured that he cannot complete it."

"What happens if a marshal that's serving a warrant dies before it's complete?" Kaitlin asked from the chair behind the deputy desk.

"That would fall under too injured to complete," I said, sipping my coffee. I was debating whether I should drink slowly and make it last, or quickly and grab another cup before someone else emptied the pot.

"Oh, of course," she said, and she looked embarrassed. She'd refused coffee and taken water. The glass of clear liquid sat on the desk in front of her, looking sad and incomplete, as if it had been cheated of its destiny to be made into coffee. Or maybe I was just fixating on coffee so I wouldn't think too hard about Olaf being here without Edward to act as a buffer, or any of the men I was actually a couple with to help keep the big guy at arm's length.

Livingston spoke from the other comfortable client chair, which he'd moved so that he sat by Duke's big desk. His coffee was on a coaster at the edge of the desk. "It's not about which marshal has the warrant now, Duke. The footprints at the crime scene don't match the prisoner."

Duke said, "And how do you feel about testifying in court about the innocent shapeshifter, little lady?"

For a second, I thought he was talking to me, but then Kaitlin answered, "Duke, I've told you before not to call me little lady." I liked that she corrected him.

He rolled his eyes and sighed like she was being silly, but replied, "Fine. Have it your way, Kaitlin. Just answer the question."

"I could testify that the prints don't match Bobby Marchand's. They're close in size, but the shape of the foot itself isn't even close. I could absolutely testify to that, but that doesn't make him innocent or guilty of the crime. I don't know for certain it's the victim's blood that was tracked from the crime scene to the bedroom. We assume it is, but for court, we'd need to be certain."

"Since there were no other bodies or large pools of blood found at the scene, it's a safe assumption that the bloody footprints were made from Ray Marchand's blood," Livingston said.

"We can assume that here and now. I'll be happy to talk to the judge that issued Newman's warrant to try to buy us more time to figure out if Bobby Marchand deserves to die for this crime, but you know that if we do find other viable suspects and have a trial, we assume nothing. You taught me that." Kaitlin smiled at Livingston and took a sip from her sad glass of water.

"If we find another shapeshifter is guilty of the crime, there will still be no trial," Olaf said.

"Only one name is on the warrant," Kaitlin said. "If he didn't do it, then you need a new warrant with a new name on it."

I shook my head. "The warrant is worded to cover any supernaturals involved in the crime and any accessories to the crime, regardless of straight-up human or not."

"But if Bobby Marchand is innocent, then he doesn't have any accomplices, because he didn't commit the crime," Kaitlin said.

"True, as far as it goes," I said. I'd finished my coffee, and no one else was headed for the pot. Would it be rude to take the last cup, and did I care?

Newman explained, "What Blake means is the warrant will still cover anyone involved in the crime, even if the person named isn't involved."

"I don't understand," Kaitlin said.

"The new time-limited warrants are in place because some of our newer brethren have refused their kills," Olaf said, "but the warrants remain what they have always been: legal documents to cover any violence we do in the course of our jobs."

"We understand that," Livingston said.

"You would think that if we prove Bobby is innocent, the warrant is void," Newman said, "and I will act as if that's the case, but Blake and Jeffries are right. It's a choice I would make not to execute the warrant to the absolute limit of its legality."

"What does that even mean?" Leduc asked.

"It means that Newman will void the warrant if we find out that Bobby was framed. Even if we know who the killer is, he will not execute them," I said.

"Why would you refuse to execute the shapeshifter guilty of this crime?" Olaf asked.

"I wouldn't refuse to execute a shapeshifter that lost control and started killing people," Newman said.

"Now I do not understand," Olaf said.

"Newman and I don't think the murder was done by a shape-shifter. We think humans did it to frame the only shifter in town," I said.

"Why does that affect Newman's ability to complete the warrant? The crime remains the same, and the warrant allows him to bring justice to those that committed it."

"Are you really suggesting that Newman should kill any humans involved in the crime?" Kaitlin asked.

"Why should humans be treated more lightly by the law than shapeshifters?" Olaf asked.

"Because humans don't have claws and teeth to tear your throat out," Leduc said, and he sounded outraged.

"They may not grow their own, but if it wasn't Bobby, then it was humans using something to mimic claws, and they still slit the victim's throat," I said.

"When you say humans, who do you have in mind?" Leduc asked.

"The only people that have a motive for the killing and have broken the law in front of me are the aunt and uncle."

"Are you seriously suggesting that we execute Muriel and Todd Babington if they framed Bobby Marchand for murder?" Livingston asked.

"No, I'm just saying that legally we could."

"Well, I couldn't," Newman said.

"You mean you would not, not that you could not," Olaf said.

"Yes, that is what I mean. If I have issues killing a wereleopard that happens to be someone I know, then I sure as hell don't want to kill human beings that could be safely kept in jail for life. We only kill the supernaturals because they have proved too dangerous for prison. Muriel and Todd can rot in jail or be executed after a trial. We don't have to kill them to keep the prison staff safe."

"True," I said.

"I did not say that we had to kill them. I said we could kill them legally," Olaf said.

"No, just no. We don't know they're guilty of anything except being greedy and stupid," Newman said.

He pushed away from the desk and went to stand so he was looking out the window by the door. I realized the night wasn't quite as inky black in the window. It wasn't dawn, or even light, but more as if the darkness was lessening. I thought about it, and I could feel the press of dawn like a promise out there. The air would smell different if we opened the door, as if night and day had different scents the way that dogs and cats smell different. I couldn't tell any other time without a watch, but I could sense when the sun was close to rising. I think it was all those years of fighting vampires and praying for the light to come and help save us. It was still dark enough that there was nothing for Newman to look at out there, but I don't think the view was the point. He just didn't want to look at any of us right that minute.

"No one is killing Muriel and Todd on my watch," Leduc said.

"Because you know them? Because you have a history with them?" Newman asked without turning away from the window.

"Not just that, but they're harmless. I don't believe they hurt Ray."

"But you don't know they didn't," I said.

"I know them, Blake. They might have been able to kill Ray if they needed money bad enough, but they wouldn't have been able to cut him up like that. Todd wouldn't have had the stomach for it, and Muriel wouldn't have had the strength."

"Do you have any other suspects besides them and the wereleopard in the cell?" Olaf asked.

Newman turned around so he could look at me. I looked back at him but had nothing helpful to share.

"No," I said.

"Not yet," Newman said.

"What if you don't find anyone else to blame?" Kaitlin asked.

"Let Newman check with the judge about extending the warrant deadline. Then we'll worry about figuring out whodunit," Livingston said.

"You cannot be on board with this, Dave," Duke said.

"Duke, if there's even a chance the wrong person's name is on that warrant, we need to figure it out before anyone else gets killed."

"I didn't figure you for one of those liberal bleeding hearts that feels sorry for the poor wereanimal," Duke said.

"You know me better than that, Duke."

"I thought I did."

"We need to figure out whose prints those are," I said.

"Well, they aren't Jocelyn Marchand's. That's for sure. She's tall, but her feet are dainty compared to the prints," Newman said.

"Who else was in the house?" I asked.

"According to her and Bobby, no one but them and Ray." Duke looked at Olaf and added, "Ray Marchand is the victim—was the victim."

Olaf nodded, as if thanking Duke for clearing up his confusion. Once I'd have thought that he didn't really care about any part of a case except the killing at the end, but he was actually good at the job and a great person to have on your side in a firefight. Edward put his abilities close to his own, which was damn high praise. If you could keep him from wanting to go all serial killer on you, he was good backup. Of course, the *if* was pretty serious when it happened.

"Whoever left the footprints was trying to point the finger at Bobby," Newman said.

"Maybe," Duke said, which was more than he'd conceded before about Bobby's innocence. We were making progress.

"All I can say for sure is that the footprints don't belong to him," Kaitlin said.

"Is it enough to buy us time on the warrant?" I asked.

We all sort of looked at one another.

"I've never tried to get extra time on a warrant except when the suspect fled the area. I know I can get an indefinite timeline for a pursuit across the country. I'm not really sure what will be enough to get an extension for proof of guilt," Newman said.

"Tell me why you are trying to save the shapeshifter listed on the warrant," Olaf said.

We explained it in more detail to him until he held up a hand. "If Anita thinks it is not a shapeshifter kill, then I will trust her expertise."

"Thank you," I said.

Olaf nodded at me.

"When I looked Blake up, your name was in some of the online articles. I thought you'd be on my side and want to end this fiasco," Duke said.

"I am not on anyone's side. I was alerted that there'd been another crime associated with the warrant. I was nearby, and I came to offer aid if it was needed."

"Thank you," Newman said.

"Don't thank me. If Anita hadn't been listed with the warrant, I would have just gone home."

"You sweet on Blake or something?" Duke asked.

Olaf gave the sheriff an unfriendly look. "I have never been accused of being sweet on anyone."

"You know what I mean."

"Anita and I have hunted together before. We've killed together. I was nearby, so I came to see if she needed my help. That is all."

"What's your opinion as a marshal, Jeffries? Do you agree with Blake and Newman about the course of action?" Livingston asked.

"I think it is not our jobs to decide guilt or innocence. Our job is to kill who the warrant tells us to kill. Unless the hunt is difficult, our jobs are very simple. Newman is complicating it."

"That's what I said. Keep it simple. You go in, kill the murdering monster, and get out. Bing, bang, boom," Duke said.

"Bing, bang, boom?" Newman said, staring at him.

"Yeah."

"If you think it's so easy, Duke, then fine. If I can't get extra time, I'll let you do the honors," Newman said. He let his anger ease into his voice just a little.

"What are you talking about, Win?"

"If the judge won't grant a stay of execution long enough for me to be certain Bobby wasn't framed, I'll let you do it. You can look him in the eyes and pull the trigger. I'll stand right outside the cell so it'll be legal."

"It's your warrant, Win."

"And if I'm convinced that Bobby is guilty, I'll act on it. But until then I don't want to kill him and find out later that he was innocent. Do you?"

"It won't be legal if I do it. It'll just be murder," Duke said. I couldn't read the expression on his face, but it wasn't happiness.

"Technically, if the named marshal is present, then it's all legal," I said. I looked at Duke as I spoke, watching his reaction.

Duke shook his head. "That can't be right." He was a little pale around the gills.

"It's not what the lawmakers meant when they wrote up the execution-warrant system, but it's how it's been interpreted in court over the years," I said.

"See, in court, which means it's not legal for me to do it."

Newman, Olaf, and I all shook our heads. "It's got court precedents so long and so accepted that it won't be a problem," I said.

Duke looked at all of us. Whatever he saw on our faces didn't reassure him. "That doesn't seem right."

"See, Duke, you don't want to shoot someone you know either," Newman said.

"It's not my job to do it."

"It's my job to kill dangerous supernaturals, not to kill innocent ones that have been framed using the law as a weapon," Newman said.

"Let's call the judge and see if Newman can get an extension on the deadline," Livingston said.

"And if I can't?"

"We'll cross that bridge when we come to it," Livingston said.

"Is the shapeshifter a close friend of yours, Newman?" Olaf asked.

"Not really," Newman said.

Olaf looked at him, shaking his head. "Then why do you care about him?"

"Wouldn't it bother you if you had to kill someone you believed was innocent?" Newman asked.

"No," Olaf said.

"I don't believe you."

"I don't care if you believe me."

"Newman, you have to make the call to the judge to get the ball rolling," I said, trying to derail the conversation. It was going to go somewhere creepy with Olaf involved. I was kind of done with his creepiness for tonight.

"Have you lost your taste for killing?" Olaf asked Newman.

"I'll kill people if I have to, but I won't let someone use me to do their murder."

"So, you object to them using you," Olaf said.

"Yes. Wouldn't you?"

Olaf took a sip of coffee and then nodded. "I would."

"Then let's see if we can buy ourselves enough time to figure out who's framing Bobby," I said.

"We aren't a hundred percent sure that anyone is framing him," Livingston said.

"Fine. Time to figure out if someone is framing Bobby."

"And to avoid killing him if he's innocent of the crime," Newman added.

"That, too," I said.

Newman went for his phone to call the judge who'd put his name on the warrant. I went to get the last cup of coffee out of the pot. Maybe I could persuade Leduc to make a second pot. We were going to get to see the sunrise, and no one was talking about sleep. We were going to need more coffee.

25

LEDUC MADE COFFEE, and we helped him finish off a second pot before Newman got anyone to answer a phone at any of the numbers that he had for this area. They were all still asleep an hour past dawn on a Sunday, lazy bastards, and we still hadn't gotten the actual judge on the phone. Clerks were useful, but they couldn't change the parameters of the warrant; only the judge who signed it could do that. In all the time I'd been hunting monsters, I'd never tried to get a judge to change a warrant, so I had no idea how it worked or even if there was a step in the legal system to cover it. Surely there was, or if not, there needed to be, but I honestly didn't know. I wasn't used to this much downtime when I was hunting monsters. It had given me enough time to text Edward and let him know Olaf was here. Since he hadn't texted back or called, I had to assume he was on a plane on his way here.

Olaf came to stand next to me against the wall. I tensed up, waiting for something creepy, or at least sexist, but he asked, "Do you normally just wait like this?"

"Wait like what?"

He motioned with his coffee mug at Newman trying yet another phone call and Kaitlin trying to get the images of the two very different footprints up on the computer so they could be sent to the judge when he finally returned the call. Livingston and Duke were talking quietly together in the far corner.

"While they gather evidence and talk to lawyers, do you just wait and do nothing?"

"I don't know."

He frowned down at me.

"I've never been on a case like this. I come into town, round up the bad guys, hang 'em high, and get out of Dodge."

His frown became a scowl. "You meant that as a metaphor of some kind, didn't you?"

I had a minute to remember that his first language wasn't English, though he spoke it perfectly now. The one thing that travels least well between languages is slang. I'd grown up watching old Westerns, and he probably hadn't.

"Even I have never hung one of my victims," he said.

I sighed. He just couldn't help himself; he always had to push it to the next level of disturbing.

He noticed my expression and knew it wasn't happy. "Have you hung one of yours? Vampires can't even die from suffocation. It seems very inefficient even for shapeshifters."

I shook my head. "No, I have never executed anyone by hanging them. What I meant is that we're like Old West lawmen. We ride into town, shoot the bad guys, and then we leave. I'm not used to waiting around like this either."

"Ah," he said, and took a drink. I think he drank to give himself time to think about what he wanted to say next. He cared about how I reacted to him. He didn't always care in the way I wanted him to, or the way that a non–serial killer would, but within his limits he was trying.

"The monster is locked up and maybe innocent. I've never had that happen before."

"The way the law is written, his guilt or innocence doesn't matter," he said.

"If you mean the warrants of execution are worded in such a way that we could kill him and not go to jail, you're right. If you were any other fellow marshal, I wouldn't say this, but it's not about covering our asses legally. It's about doing what's right."

"You do not think I have a sense of right and wrong?" he asked, his voice low, and I realized that to the rest of the room, we looked like Livingston and Duke: just two cops talking shop.

"I think your sense of right and wrong isn't the same as most people's."

"That is true," he said.

"I want to kill the person who killed Ray Marchand, not the person who was framed for the crime."

"So, you agree with Newman that it's about not allowing the murderer to use you."

"That's part of it."

"What is the other part?"

"I took this job believing that if I killed the monster, it would save the lives of all their future victims. Killing the monsters keeps the rest of us safe. But killing someone that hasn't gone rogue doesn't save lives. It just takes a life."

"You see yourself as the protector of the innocent," he said.

"I guess so."

He took in a deep breath so that his chest rose and fell noticeably with it. "I do not see our job that way."

"I know you don't."

He looked down at me, those deep-set eyes so intense that I wanted to look away from them. It took more willpower than I'd admit out loud to stare back and not flinch. "How do I see our job?"

"Do you really want me to answer that?"

"I never ask questions unless I want the answer, Anita."

I fought the urge to lick my lips, but I was trying to keep my heart rate slow and even, and if I was going to waste energy doing that, I'd be damned if I'd show any secondary signs of nervousness. "It's a legal way for you to indulge in your violent fantasies and get paid for it."

He smiled, and it was one of the best and most normal ones I'd ever seen from him. It changed his face like a shadow of what he might have been if he'd been a completely different person. "Yes, exactly."

I licked my lips and added, "You're also like Ted. You like testing your skills against the most dangerous prey, and there's nothing more dangerous to hunt than vampires and shapeshifters."

Even his eyes sparkled with his happiness as he said, "I've never met a woman that understands men as well as you do."

"I'm just one of the guys, I guess."

He nodded, the smile beginning to fade into something more serious but not yet disturbing. "That is truer of you than of any other woman I have ever met."

I shrugged, not sure what to say to that.

A voice called from the open door to the cell area. "Hey, I think we need some help back here." It was Wagner, the deputy who would be seeing real jail sometime soon.

I called back without moving from the wall. "What do you need?"

"Can you beat a wereleopard to death?"

"What? Why do you want to know that?" I pushed away from the wall and moved around Olaf toward the doorway.

"Because Bobby hasn't moved at all, and I'm not sure he's breathing."

26

BOBBY LAY ON his side on the floor of his cell. I'd moved him onto his side so that he wouldn't choke on his own blood, as Olaf had said they could suffocate. I hadn't put him on his bunk because he'd have gotten blood all over it. He should have healed by now. He should have been up and moving by now. I tried to see if he was breathing under the blanket I'd pulled up over him. I wrapped my hands around the bars, willing him to move.

Olaf touched my hand, which made me jump and look at him. "He is alive, Anita."

"How do you know?"

"I can hear his heartbeat."

"I forgot you could do that now."

He placed his hand over mine. I think if he'd had room through the bars, he'd have held my hand, but the metal protected me from a more intimate gesture, just like it was supposed to protect us from the man on the floor I'd beaten senseless.

"Can someone please go in there and check on Bobby?" Wagner said.

Newman yelled back, "Duke, we could use the keys to the cells."

Duke's voice came a little muffled. "I'm working on it."

"Please hurry, Duke!" Wagner yelled.

"You're awfully worried about someone you tried to kill earlier,"

I said, and used talking to Wagner as an excuse to pull away from Olaf and walk toward the other cell.

Wagner was pressed up between the bars that separated his cell from Bobby's, as if pushing hard enough would let him touch the other man. His concern seemed as real as the hysteria had earlier. Maybe he was feeling guilty. I knew I was.

"I know. I was stupid and crazy, and I'm sorry, but Bobby hasn't moved at all since you guys left him there. Shouldn't he have moved or done something by now if he was going to be all right?"

"Yeah," I said, and I was suddenly afraid not of Bobby's beast but of what I might have done to him. I wasn't as strong as a real shapeshifter or vampire, but I was stronger than a normal person. I'd hit Bobby as hard as I could. I'd been fighting for my life, so I hadn't held back. Had that been more than Bobby's body could handle? God, it would suck if I'd accidentally killed him when we were trying so hard to save him.

"Could you have snapped his neck?" Newman asked.

"The uppercut was the most dangerous for spinal injury, and he moved just fine after that."

"If he was human, I'd worry about some kind of brain injury," Livingston said from the doorway.

"You mean a concussion?" I asked.

"Can shapeshifters get those, and if they can, do they heal from them better than humans do?"

"He is not dead," Olaf said.

"Good to know, but I've never seen a shapeshifter take this long to heal from something like this. If he's not seriously injured, he should be moving by now," I said.

"Can he change into a biform?" Olaf asked.

"I can't keep up with the new politically correct language. I thought biform meant any shapeshifter and bipedal was what we used for half-man forms?"

Olaf seemed to think about my question and then gave one nod. "Bipedal would be for leopard-man form, but that we are debating it proves that biform and bipedal are too close."

"I prefer that for correct speech to Therianthrope for shapeshifter and Ailuranthrope for all werecat forms just because some humorless humans decided lycanthrope is an insult to anyone who isn't an actual werewolf."

"Does the prisoner have a bipedal form?" Olaf asked.

I shook my head. "He's got the leopard form, and honestly it was one of the smallest beast forms I've seen in a wereleopard. It was about the same size as a regular leopard."

"That makes him very weak."

"Are you saying he's not powerful enough to heal from a beating like this?"

"I am saying that he will not heal like a more powerful shapeshifter would—that is all." He even spread his hands for me in an it's-okay gesture. I realized that he was trying to soften the blow for me emotionally. The Olaf I'd first met years back would not have bothered.

I yelled, "Leduc, get in here with the keys!"

"And if I do let you in the cage, what are you going to do, Blake?" He spoke from the door as Livingston moved back to make room for him.

"See how hurt he is."

"And then what?"

"We call—" And I stopped. "We can't call an ambulance."

"We have to," Wagner said.

"I agree with Troy," Newman said.

"Newman, you saw what Bobby almost did to me," I said. "We can't put EMTs or paramedics in there with him."

"He's unconscious, Blake, thanks to you, so no danger to anybody."

The comment pissed me off, and I let some of the anger into my voice. "I thought he was going to kill me, Newman, and so did you." I gave him the look that went with the tone in my voice.

Newman glared back for a second or two, and then all his defiance seemed to wash away. "Damn it, Blake, we're trying to save him."

"I know that, but if what we saw in that cage is all the control he has during the change, then I'm amazed he hasn't hurt anyone before now."

"You saw all the pictures of him in leopard form with the family," Newman said.

"I did, but all I can tell you is the wereanimals with good control that I know don't change form like that."

"What do you mean?" Kaitlin asked from outside the door. There just wasn't room for all of us in the hallway in front of the cells.

"He does the really painful, violent change where you see all the parts rearrange themselves. It's grotesque, like a medical textbook where a body is dissected and put back together. If that was the way they all changed form, no one would want to see it onstage."

"Don't go bringing up the unnatural businesses that your fiancé has in St. Louis," Leduc said.

I turned and stared at him. "Did you miss the point of all the new politically correct speech, Duke? Because calling supernatural citizens unnatural sounds awfully insensitive." My words were calm; my tone was a little warm.

"One of the perks of being the boss on a small force like this is that I don't have to read the latest memo about the new politically correct vocabulary. We wouldn't want to offend anyone by calling them what they actually are, now, would we?"

"The men in my life are fine with being called vampire or shapeshifter. Hell, none of the werewolves in my life has bitched about being called lycanthropes."

"How about calling them soulless demons and rampaging beasts? Let's call a spade a spade," Duke said.

I shook my head, not even angry anymore. "The only people who throw around the term demon are people that have never met one for real."

"You haven't met a real demon," Duke said, but his tone wasn't as sure as his words.

"The fuck I haven't." I stepped into him then, and I let myself get angry as I said, "You can live here like this and insult the men I love because people like me are hunting shit down and keeping it away from you and this nice little town of yours."

"Win doesn't hunt shit like that."

"I can't speak to what cases Newman gets called up on, but I can tell you that I deal with shit like that and worse. I'm War, and Otto is Plague. You don't call in the horsemen unless it's some apocalyptic shit." I was angrier than I'd meant to get, angry enough that my beasts swirled inside me like a rainbow of shapes. I had to step back from Leduc and take some nice even breaths. I hated that I'd let his racist, intolerant assholery get to me like that. I knew better.

Leduc watched me regain control of myself. I couldn't hide that he'd gotten to me, but he didn't look pleased by it. I expected him to gloat, but he didn't. "I don't know about all that, Blake, but I guess you and the big guy here have earned your reputations. I'll try not to use words like *demon* unless one pops up for real."

"Thank you," I managed to say.

"Open the door to the cell, Duke," Newman said.

"And what will you do once I open it?" He'd apologized for his words, but his actions continued to be just as obstructionist as before. One apology doesn't an open mind make.

"I'll check on Bobby," Newman said.

"I can call an ambulance and tell them what we've got for them, but they can't take him to the hospital. The local one doesn't have an area rated for supernaturals, and since he's already under a death penalty for murdering someone, they cannot transport him to the nearest supernatural trauma center. It's too far away for them to risk him waking up on the way, Win."

"Open the door, Duke," Newman said, and he sounded like he meant it.

Leduc came forward with the keys. "It's your funeral."

I touched Newman's arm. "I hate to agree with Duke—you know I do—but he's right about one thing."

"What is he right about?"

"Newman, come on. You've seen me in there with him twice."

"You risked your life to save him twice."

"Yeah, I did, but the second time, he spooked me, Newman. I was too close, and it all happened too quick to go for a weapon, but if he hadn't gone down when I stepped away from him, I would have."

"Are you saying you would have shot him?"

"With the damage I'd just done to him, if he had come after me, I'd have been grateful to get to a weapon in time to kill him before he killed me."

"Have you changed your mind? Do you think he murdered Ray now?" Newman asked.

"No, I still think he was framed, but that doesn't mean he's not dangerous."

"You did this to him bare-handed?" Olaf asked.

"She hit him with one of the prettiest uppercuts I've seen in years," Duke said.

"I used mostly my elbows and knees, but no weapons, no," I said.

Olaf smiled at me as if I'd spoken sweet nothings. He always reacted like that to the weirdest shit.

"I've never seen anyone move as fast as she did," Kaitlin said.

"You've never seen a real shapeshifter move," I said.

"No, I haven't, but if they're faster than you, I'm not sure I want to."

"If Blake had been any slower, we'd have been putting her into an ambulance," Livingston said.

"You can't just let him die like this," Wagner said.

"Shut up, Troy. You're in enough trouble," Duke said.

"Troy's right," Newman said. "We can't just let him die."

"Boy, you have a warrant in your pocket that says you can shoot him full of holes until he dies. You saw him in the cell. You were afraid for Blake's life, too. Don't tell me you weren't."

"Yes, I thought he was going to hurt Blake, but that doesn't give us the right to let him bleed out like this."

"We don't even know that's what's happening," I said.

"Then why hasn't he moved? If he hasn't got a concussion or a damaged spine, then why hasn't he come to?" Newman moved toward me, hands in fists at his sides. He wasn't going to start a fight. He was just upset, and it was coming out in his body.

"I don't know, Newman!" I had to swallow my own anger down before I lost it. My voice was calmer as I said, "I would never have hit him like I did if I hadn't thought he would heal."

"You are used to the shapeshifters in St. Louis," Olaf said.

I looked at him. "What does that mean?"

"All of them would have healed by now."

"Are you saying that Bobby won't heal?"

"He should heal, but it will not be one of the miracles of healing that you are used to at home."

"Why won't he heal like that?"

"First, he is not part of any group, so he does not share in their larger energy. Second, he has only one small beast form, which proves he is not a powerful shapeshifter in and of himself. Third, he is not tied to a master vampire, so he doesn't have that energy to draw upon. I do not think you understand how unique St. Louis is for all these reasons and more."

Olaf looked at me very pointedly when he said the last part. He seemed to be trying to tell me something with that look, but I had no idea what he was hinting at. I'd ask him later in private, or maybe I wouldn't. I focused on what was in front of me, one problem at a time or they gang up on you.

"Fine. So I play with too many big dogs to play nice with the small ones. How do we help Bobby here and now?"

Olaf shrugged. "I do not know."

"Open the damn cell, Duke," Newman said, and the anger was back. I couldn't really blame him. We were working so hard to save Bobby, and now it might all have been for nothing.

"Who goes inside with him?" Duke asked.

"I will," I said.

"You'll need backup," Livingston said.

"No," Newman said. "He's not a danger to anyone like this."

"If he wakes up suddenly and sees you bending over him—" Duke started to say, but Newman cut him off.

"Open the fucking cell, Duke!"

Livingston got his shotgun again, and once he had it ready to aim, Duke opened the cell.

"It's your funeral," Duke said again as Newman pushed past him.

I followed him into the cell. He'd called me for backup, so I'd have his back. Olaf stayed in the cell doorway so that Leduc couldn't close it behind us. Good, I was tired of being locked in this damn cell.

27

LIVINGSTON HAD HIS shotgun to his shoulder, though it was aimed at the ceiling while Newman knelt to check Bobby's pulse on the side of his neck. I stood on the other side of Bobby from him. Bobby looked so pale and so still. I held my breath as if that would help Newman find a pulse. Bobby's face was a bloody mess, and I'd done that to him. Had I done more? Had he died while we tried to call the judge, slowly bleeding to death inside his head? Or maybe I'd broken his spine badly enough that the trauma had acted like a decapitation. Yeah, Olaf said Bobby's heart was still beating, but I couldn't hear it. In all the years I'd been hunting, fighting, and dating people with lycanthropy, I'd never heard of one of them dying from a spinal injury or a concussion. I thought you had to see brains on the outside of the skull for the brain to be injured enough to kill. It was going to be a hell of a time to be wrong.

"Pulse seems slow, but it's there."

I let out the breath I'd been holding, but the tightness in my chest wasn't fooled. It knew that a pulse just meant Bobby wasn't dead yet.

"I told you he was not dead," Olaf said from the door, where the sheriff was still trying to get him to move so he could lock the door again.

"If that monster comes to and rushes the door, he could kill us all before we get him," Leduc said.

"No," Olaf said.

"You hunt these things. You know how fast they can be," Leduc said.

Newman was opening one of Bobby's eyes. I prayed that the pupils weren't uneven and fixed, because if either of those things was true, then I'd killed him. It was just going to take him longer than normal to die.

"Anita would slow him down until I could join the fight. He would never reach you and the others," Olaf said.

"You can't know that."

"Blake beat him without help last time, Duke. I think we're safe to leave the cell open," Livingston said.

"Pupils are even and reacting to light," Newman said.

The tightness in my chest loosened. "Good," I managed to say, and I sounded breathless, as if I still couldn't get enough air. Killing someone on purpose was one thing; doing it by accident was something else. It's funny how you don't know what will bother you until it does.

Newman looked up at me. "I still want to call an ambulance."

"If we can get some paramedics that are willing to look at him, I'm good with that," I said.

"They have to do their job if we call them," Newman said.

I shook my head. "Not if it will endanger them. Legally they can refuse."

"They'd just let him die because they're afraid?" he asked, sounding outraged. He suddenly seemed years younger than I knew he was, or maybe I just felt years more cynical.

"If they think he'll kill them, yeah," I said.

"He's unconscious," Newman said.

"Even if they look at him here, they won't transport him."

"They might," he said, and again I felt so much older than he was, not in years, but in experience. That will age you faster than any number of birthdays.

"She's right, Newman," Livingston said.

Newman glanced back at him, a hand protectively on Bobby's shoulder. "We could take him to the hospital ourselves."

"You'd have to take him all the way to the county hospital. It's the closest one with a trauma unit that could hold him," Duke said.

"Fine. We'll do that," Newman said. "Help me move him, Blake."

I thought about being in Newman's car when Bobby came to and how close the fight had been in the cell. I realized I didn't want to be in the car with him if he started to shift. "On one condition."

Newman gave me outraged eyes. "Conditions? You nearly beat him to death, and you want to give conditions for saving his life?"

"Maybe condition was the wrong word, but I want you to understand one thing before we start for the hospital. If he starts to shift in the car like he did in the cell, I'm going to shoot him in the head, probably multiple times."

"He'd never survive that."

"That would be the idea."

"You think he's a murdering monster now?"

"No, but I think he would have killed me if I hadn't stopped him. I'm glad I didn't kill him by accident, defending myself. I hope we prove that he's innocent and find out who really killed Ray Marchand, and if Bobby just wakes up in the car like normal, then we'll take him to the hospital. But I will have a weapon drawn and aimed at him in the car. If he goes apeshit again, I won't risk fighting hand to hand with him."

"You can't blame Blake for that, Newman," Livingston said. He was still holding the shotgun at the ready.

"Yeah, I can."

"Newman," I said.

He looked up at me with angry eyes.

"If it had been you in the cell with Bobby when he started to shapeshift, what would you have done?" I asked.

The anger started to fade in Newman's eyes as he said, "I'd have gone for my gun."

"You'd have shot him to save your life," I said.

He sighed and nodded. "I guess I would have."

"Then don't blame me for not wanting to push my luck and try to survive a second slugfest with a shapeshifter."

Newman looked down at Bobby, still touching him protectively. "Who am I fooling? I'd never have gotten my gun out in time. It's why you didn't draw yours. There wasn't time. I don't have your fight training, Blake, or your speed. If I'd been the one standing next to Bobby when he went animalistic, you'd have been taking me to the hospital or the morgue."

"And we'd have had to shoot Bobby to save you," I said.

He nodded. "I know."

"Do you think he'll go crazy when he wakes up like he did before?" Kaitlin asked from near the door to the offices. She hadn't come too far into the cell area this time. I think she'd decided that she didn't want a repeat performance with Bobby. Me either.

"There's no way to tell until he wakes up," I said.

"He had to have control of his change before this," Newman said, "or his family wouldn't have let him walk around the house in leopard form."

"He was trying to suicide by cop when he started to shift," I said. "He may have carried that thought over as he started to change."

"Would that have been enough to make him lose control like that?" Newman asked.

"I think it was," I said.

"Yes," said Olaf. When the others looked at him, he explained, "If he were a normal person that was intent on suicide by police, he would raise his gun instead of putting it down, so we would have to shoot him. His beast is his gun. That is the only difference."

"Win, don't put yourself and Blake in a car with him. I don't want to have to explain that to Haley," Duke said.

"Don't do that, Duke. Don't bring Haley into this."

"I know you want to help Bobby, and I know you believe he didn't kill Ray, but is any of that worth not having a lifetime with the woman you love?" Duke seemed so reasonable, even caring and gentle. It was another glimpse of a good person, a good cop who was in there somewhere. Maybe I really hadn't seen him at his best.

"Damn it, Duke," Newman said.

"I'll call an ambulance and see if they're willing to look him over. Okay, Win?"

Newman nodded and lowered his head until it was almost touching Bobby's. If the wereleopard woke up now, it could go badly. But Newman was as aware of that as I was, so I let him be. Duke went into the office to call for an ambulance just as Bobby took a long, shuddering breath.

28

NEWMAN STARTLED SO badly, he sat down hard beside Bobby. I was beside Newman before I'd thought about it, grabbing him under the arm and pulling him to his feet and moving both of us toward the door. Even though he had been damn near crying over Bobby a second before, he didn't fight me. He wanted to save Bobby, but that didn't mean he wasn't scared of him. Livingston moved smoothly away from the door so that the two of us could get out. Olaf closed the door behind us, and we all watched as Bobby coughed and sputtered awake.

"You broke my nose," Bobby said in a voice that was thick with blood and all the things that happened when someone smashed your nose into their knee repeatedly.

"You're alive," I said from the safety of the cage bars.

"What the hell does that mean?" Bobby asked as he lay on his side, raising his manacled hands up to touch his face. He winced and jerked his hands back from his nose.

"Do you remember anything about the fight?" I asked.

He rolled onto one elbow, but apparently having his head hanging down was bad, because he moved so his face was pointed more upward. He pushed stiffly to a sitting position, wrapping the blanket around his shoulders. If we didn't kill him soon, we really needed to give him some clothes.

"No," he said.

"Nothing?" I asked.

"No."

"You said, 'You broke my nose,'" Newman said. "Who broke it?"

"She did."

"Who's she?"

"Her," Bobby said, and pointed toward me.

"If you don't remember anything, how do you know I broke it?" I asked.

That seemed to stop him, his blue eyes blinking confused in their mask of fresh blood. "I don't know."

"You're lying, Bobby," I said.

"Wait," Olaf said.

I hadn't expected him to join in much, so that one word made me look up at him. He was studying Bobby. "Wait for what?"

"Let me try."

"Be my guest."

"Tell us exactly what you see in your mind."

"I don't know," Bobby said. "It's darkness and flashes."

"Tell us what you see. Do not edit yourself. Just talk."

Bobby frowned and then winced again as if even frowning hurt. "Anger. I was angry, and then I started seeing in leopard vision."

"What the hell does that even mean, leopard vision?" Leduc said from the doorway to the offices. I think he'd delayed the ambulance call now that our suspect was awake and talking.

"My leopard eyes don't see color the way my human eyes do. That's usually my first clue that I'm changing."

"What do you remember next?" Olaf asked.

Bobby drew the blanket around him as close as he could and shivered. I wasn't sure if it was from coldness or from what he saw in his own head. "I could smell the gun, feel it against my head. It scared the animal part, but the human part wanted it." He stared up at Olaf with confusion in his eyes. "I tried to get . . . I wanted to die for what I'd done to Uncle Ray."

Bobby tried to wipe his hands over his face like he was going to hide, but it hurt too much, and his blanket began to slide down. He seemed very serious about the blanket staying in place. Again, it made me wonder about some kind of abuse background. He could have just been that modest, but he was a good-looking, fit man in his early thirties. I hadn't met many of them who were this modest. If he'd just tried to keep his groin covered, maybe. But he seemed equally intent on keeping his upper body covered, which was usually more a woman's problem unless something had happened to make the man self-conscious of his body.

"Do you remember the fight now?" Olaf asked, his deep voice as serious and calm as I'd ever heard it.

"Yes, most of it. I'll remember all of it in a few minutes."

I looked up at Olaf. "How did you know to question him like that?"

He met my gaze with his own, but for once the eyes were thoughtful and serious, nothing more. "Even the best of us sometimes need a few minutes to reorient ourselves when we awake."

"Are you saying that I didn't knock him out? He just passed out from the change?"

"No, but even a partial change can be disorienting. Add several blows to the head and even a human might have trouble remembering the last few minutes."

Olaf was right. "Damn it, you're right. I was so busy thinking of him as a wereleopard that I forgot that his human half could be knocked silly, too."

"If you hadn't been here to help us question Bobby, I might have thought he was lying about not remembering," Newman said.

"Which would have made us doubt his whole story," I said.

Kaitlin piped up from the doorway. "Guess he's not just a pretty face after all."

It startled me that she was referring to Olaf. Pretty was so not an adjective that I would ever have used for him.

"I am not a pretty face," Olaf said. He made it a statement.

"Handsome, then," she said.

I nodded. "If you like."

"I like," she said, and I realized she was flirting with him.

He seemed to realize it, too, because he scowled; *frown* just didn't cover that look. He'd reacted badly to compliments from women when I'd first met him, but I knew he could flirt and pretend because I'd seen it. I wondered if the reason he didn't bother was that Kaitlin wasn't his victim preference. I mean type. He liked petite women with dark hair, and preferred darker eyes. Yeah, I fit his *type* to a T. The only thing Kaitlin fit was the petite part, so she was safe and apparently held no interest for him. He didn't even pretend to flirt back. He ignored her. Kaitlin would probably take that as a snub, but she didn't know how lucky she was that he wasn't interested in her. I wondered if dyeing my hair blond would make him lose interest. I'd never dyed my hair before, but to get Olaf off my back, I'd dye it Technicolor rainbow. If I did it before the wedding, Jean-Claude would never forgive me, but afterward he might agree. Anything to move me off Olaf's dating menu seemed like a great idea.

"Thank you, Marshal," Bobby said.

"Marshal Jeffries," Olaf said.

"Marshal Jeffries, thank you for helping me remember."

"You are welcome."

"Now that we don't need an ambulance," Duke said, "what next, Marshals?" Again, I got that glimpse of the good lawman I would have seen if things had been different.

"I've done everything I can until someone calls me back," Newman said.

"If we have all the pictures and samples we need from Bobby, I think he needs clothes and maybe a chance to clean up," I said.

Livingston said, "Kaitlin, have you collected everything we need?"

"Yeah. He can clean up," she said.

Duke shook his head, pushing back through the doorway so the rest of us had to adjust farther down the hallway to give him room. "Clothes we can do, but if you mean a shower, I can't sign off on that. It's too big a security risk."

"Not your call," I said.

"It's my jail," he said.

"If my vote counts, it would be awesome to wash all this blood off me, though I'm not sure about my face. That may hurt in the shower."

"Don't put your face directly in the water," I said, "because that will hurt."

Bobby touched his nose gingerly. "Did you really have to break it?"

"I could have just killed you."

"You don't have a mark on you, so it couldn't have been that bad," he said.

I pulled my pants leg out enough that I could put a finger through some of the holes his claws had made.

"Jesus, did I cut you?"

"A nick here and there, nothing major."

Bobby closed his eyes and took a deep breath. "Okay, I remember now."

Something unhappy passed across his face, and since his eyes were still closed, it was like watching someone have a bad dream. You always had to debate whether you should wake them and end the nightmare. Of course, when Bobby opened his eyes, the nightmare was real.

"I've trained for years to remember what I do in animal form, but it's always harder when it's a memory that makes you look bad or frightening," he said.

"I thought the amnesia was something that shapeshifters couldn't help," Newman said.

"At first, but later it's like any traumatic memory or a memory that makes you feel bad about yourself. People edit it to make themselves look better or block it if it's too painful. Shapeshifters aren't any different."

"You have a disease. It doesn't make you into a different person," Kaitlin said.

It was weird that I could hear her, but the others had moved, so I couldn't see her. I wondered if that was how I was in a crowd, just a voice. Since I was about three inches shorter than she was, probably. Of course, everyone else in the hallway was tall enough to see her, so maybe it was just she and I who couldn't see each other.

Bobby looked toward her voice, but I think from the cell he couldn't see her either. "Yes, it does, because you're not all human anymore."

Kaitlin pushed her way in between the men so she could see him.

"Of course you are. Don't let anyone tell you that just because you have lycanthropy—Therianthropy—that you're not human. That's just prejudice."

Bobby shook his head, then winced and stopped the movement. I think more than just his nose hurt. At least he was alive, and he'd heal if we didn't have to kill him first. The more we did to take care of him, the harder it was going to be if we did have to pull the trigger.

"It's not just prejudice," Bobby said. "I carry a leopard inside me, and that's not metaphorical. That's just true. I become that leopard once a month or more, and while I'm in that form, I am that cat, just like I'm me now. I'm not a human being in a costume. I become something else that isn't human." He was so reasonable, with the blood, both old and new, spread across his face and into his hair. He looked like an accident victim trying to calm down a doctor.

"But you're still yourself," Kaitlin said.

Bobby looked at me. "Can I have a shower and you explain it to her?"

I almost smiled but wasn't sure if Kaitlin would take it wrong. She was trying so hard to be liberal and progressive; she meant well. "Therianthropy isn't like other diseases. It's not a virus that makes you sick once a month. It's literally another being inside you."

"They change into their beast form once a month, but in between they're still human," Kaitlin said.

"Yes, and no," I said.

Olaf said, "The beast is not separate and gone in between full moons. It is always inside waiting, watching, seeking a way out."

"Do you have pets?" I asked.

"A cat," Kaitlin said.

"Okay. Does your cat ever try to dart through a door and get out?" She nodded. "Sometimes."

"And what do you do to stop it?"

"I grab her. I push her away from the door."

"Now, think about the cat being inside you. You're the house that it's trying to escape from. If it gets out the door, you turn into the cat, and the cat becomes the house now, and it wants to keep you inside so it can be free."

"That's a good analogy," Bobby said.

"I can't take credit for it. It's Micah's. He has to explain this a lot."

"Micah Callahan, right? The head of the Coalition," Kaitlin said. I nodded.

"The analogy stops too soon," Olaf said. "If you have the force of will to truly control your beast, then you keep your human mind in both forms."

"So you're the cat and the house and you all at once," Kaitlin said.

"Yeah, it's like a supernatural version of Schrödinger's cat," I said.

"Sort of," Bobby said, "but if you force your human mind on your beast all the time, then you can't be a good cat. You can't hunt and jump and be a leopard if you keep trying to think human."

"You must find a balance between beast and man," Olaf said.

"Yes. Now can I have a shower, please?"

Duke said no and the debate or negotiations or argument began. We ended with Bobby getting to shower. Livingston suggested that Duke could go home and have breakfast with his family, and that seemed to be a deciding factor. Duke called one of his deputies who was still at the crime scene to bring clothes for Bobby, and then refused to leave until after they arrived.

"This is my place. That means one of my people needs to be here." Duke was being so reasonable that none of us argued with him.

Newman escorted Bobby into the shower and took off the cuffs, but Olaf stayed in the room with him. I'd already beaten Bobby sense-less with my bare hands. If I could do it, Olaf wouldn't have a problem handling the prisoner. Duke insisted that the door to the bathroom stay open the whole time in case Olaf yelled for help. I think every-one but Duke was aware that Olaf wouldn't need help, but it was Duke's jail and Newman had to live here after I flew back home. It didn't hurt us to concede enough to keep everyone happyish.

In all the moving around, I found a quiet moment to give New-man the name of the lawyer Micah had recommended for helping

Bobby. "It's your warrant, so I can't invite Micah and the Coalition into this, but you can."

"Duke is going to be pissed enough if I give Bobby a phone call to a lawyer. If I invite the Coalition in, he'll never forgive me."

"Do you care?" I asked.

He nodded. "I want to live here with Haley for the rest of my life, so yeah, I care."

"Do you care about that more than Bobby's life?"

"That's not fair, Blake."

"It's not, but I'm stating that I need help if Bobby goes apeshit again."

"You've got backup with Jeffries."

"If we want to kill Bobby, sure. I want help keeping him in human form, keeping him calm. Otto doesn't know how to do that."

"And your fiancé does?"

"Micah does, yes."

"If it was almost anyone else, I'd think they were trying to find a reason to get their lover into town."

"I actually don't want any of my lovers near this case."

In my head, I thought, *I don't want them near Olaf without Edward here.* I sure as hell didn't want Micah near him. I loved him to pieces, but he was my height, within, like, a couple of inches or less. He was in good shape and trained to fight, but so was Olaf. If skills are equal, the bigger person will win a fight unless the smaller person gets lucky. Olaf wasn't the kind of fighter who would leave room for luck. I realized I really didn't want Micah here with Olaf.

"That case in Washington State where I met you for the first time makes this one look safe, Blake. You invited some of your people in for that one—maybe not Micah Callahan, but still people you cared about. So what makes this one scarier? What aren't you telling me?"

I couldn't tell him the whole truth about Olaf, so I was left not knowing what to say. I could have lied. I was even pretty good at it now, but I wasn't good at complicated lies, and even the truth about Olaf was complicated.

I finally settled for a half-truth. "I know how to kill the monsters, but keeping them alive is harder, Newman. More things can go wrong."

He shook his head. "No, Blake, killing them is harder. If I can help save Bobby, then maybe it will wash away some of the blood on my hands."

"Newman, you knew what this job was before you took it."

"I knew the facts, but nothing prepares you for killing people, Anita, for just killing them."

"We save future victims by killing the predators," I said.

"That's a great thought. I even believed it once."

"It's the truth, Newman."

"Maybe, but I don't get to see the future victims we save. All I get to see is the people I kill now."

"When a shapeshifter tries to kill you like they did in Washington State, do you think of them as people?" I asked.

"No, that's survival, just like hunting vampires after dark. If they turn into monsters, it's easier to pull the trigger, but when they're like Bobby, it feels like murder."

"You're too close to Bobby to be on this warrant, Newman."

"I know, but since so many of the newer marshals have refused warrants or quit, you need a good reason to pass on a warrant."

"Being friends with the name on the warrant is a valid reason to pass on it," I said.

"And if I had passed, then it turns out that Jeffries was next closest. Do you really think he would have waited to figure out that Bobby had been framed?"

I answered truthfully, "No, he'd have just executed him."

"I took the warrant because I thought it was the right thing to do. I figured if Bobby was guilty, I could make sure his death was as quick and painless as possible. If there'd been a mistake and he was innocent, I figured that if I was the marshal in charge, I could help him."

"It was good thinking as far as it went," I said.

"I forgot the third option, didn't I?" he said, face so sad.

"Yeah," I said, "you did."

"That he could be innocent, and I'd still have to execute him."

"Yeah, that would be what you forgot."

"What am I going to do, Blake?"

I started to say he should sign the warrant over to me, but I didn't want to kill Bobby either now. He was too real to me. I'd put my body in harm's way to protect him. I'd risked my life for him. Executing him now would seem wrong, like a violation of the natural order of things. There are three types of people in this world: those you protect, those who fight with you, and those who fight against you. You killed to save those under your protection and to defend your own life and the lives of the people who fought beside you. It was simple math until the monsters became your friends and the people who were fighting beside you still wanted to kill them. Then it all went to hell.

29

I FOUND ANOTHER quiet moment, but this time I needed more privacy than anything the local police station could offer, because the person I most wanted to avoid eavesdropping had super-duper hearing. I could have asked Newman for the use of his car again, but the woods were right there, and I was feeling strangely claustrophobic. I needed a breath of fresh air, literally. I took the time to put on the tac vest. It was technically a plate carrier, but since I was police and not military, I'd probably never put a plate in it, so I just called it a tac vest. I didn't like the feel of the vest, and I'd spent some time in the gym trying to fight in it, because it restricted my movement, but it would stop most bullets and the MOLLE straps all over it were awesome for carrying extra gear. I had the 9mm on the chest holster, which was great for drawing if I was sitting in a car, but it was my secondary handgun once the full battle rattle went on. The .45 in its drop thigh holster was the main handgun now, sitting snug to my leg and out of the way of the tightness of the vest. My AR-15 hung on a tactical sling strap so that I could push it behind me to get it out of the way, or let it swing forward to be snugged to my shoulder and used. I'd carried the AR in my hands as I walked through the woods so it wouldn't get caught on anything, but once I stopped moving, I slid it behind me. I had extra ammo in the pockets of my tac pants, like cargo pants but tougher and better designed for carrying dangerous, helpful things. I had the wrist sheath blades on under the windbreaker; they'd saved my life more than once. Guns ran out of ammo, while knives stayed sharp and ready. I could admit to myself that I wasn't just armed for an active warrant; I was armed for Olaf. I guess I was armed for bear, too, but I wasn't really worried about them. If I wasn't armed enough for a quick walk in the woods, then I needed to give up my tough-ass nicknames. I was the Executioner. I was War. I either deserved my rep, or I didn't. Damn Olaf for making me doubt myself.

I expected the air to smell like evergreens because there were so many more of them here than back home, and there was more of that Christmas tree scent, with the sweeter undertones of cedar, but over it all was an earthier smell. It was somewhere between fresh-turned earth and slow water, like a marsh that I remembered from childhood. I'd always known spring was really here when the frogs started to sing in that little marsh. It had smelled like a pond, but also like land. Even by smell I knew that the water was in transition between pond and soil. What I was smelling now let me know that there was something similar close by, except it was even earthier, like peat. I wondered if I just started walking through the trees and underbrush, I'd find a bog somewhere nearby that would be even less water and more land than that long-ago marsh. Was that marsh even still there, or had some housing developer buried it under fresh construction? I hoped not. I hoped the frogs still went there every spring, and the red-winged blackbirds were still singing and nesting in the cattails there. I wanted Micah here with me so much, but the comfort of him and even the help he could give Bobby weren't worth the risk.

Micah's voice was wide-awake this time when he answered the phone. "Hello, my love. Newman just asked us to come help on the case."

"That's great, Micah, really."

"Your tone says it's not so great. What's wrong?"

I sighed and let myself lean my back against the thick trunk of the tree beside me. It felt solid and real and good, though with all the weapons and body armor, it wasn't as cozy as it might have been, but you can't have it all. I had a moment's peace by myself out of sight of everyone but the birds and the wind. "I want and need the Coalition's help with keeping Bobby Marchand in human form and alive so we can find out if he was framed and who framed him, but I don't want you to come."

"I'm confused. Do you or don't you want the Coalition to help you?"

"I do."

"That usually means me, Anita."

"You've been delegating more out-of-town assignments since Nathaniel requested we both try to cut down."

"I have, but you're there and if I come, we'll be there together. You usually like that."

"Olaf is here, Micah."

"Did you call him for backup?"

"No."

"Is he there officially as a marshal?" His voice held a note of urgency now.

"Yes."

"You scared me for a minute, Anita." I could hear the relief and the puzzlement in his voice.

"I'm sorry, Micah, that . . . I didn't mean to."

"Okay, apology accepted. If he's there as Marshal Otto Jeffries, then why are you spooked? Because that's how you sound."

"Can't you just accept that I don't want you near him?"

"We were near him in Florida at Edward's wedding, and nothing bad happened."

"We were all there for the wedding. Then Olaf crashed the party. This time he's here first, and now that he's a werelion, I want you to be able to make an informed decision. You're a grown-up and one of the most competent people I know, so I'll let you make the final call."

"I can understand you calling and telling me he was there, because it would change the security I'd bring, but telling me not to come personally, that surprises me."

I tried to put what I was thinking into words and finally gave up. "I don't know what to say, other than he's different this time. He's more insistent about the relationship stuff. The last macho, super-violent werelion that had me as his first-ever true love was Haven, and you know how that turned out."

"I agree that werelion society is one of the most violent cultures we have, but Haven lived all his life as a criminal, Anita. He was a mob enforcer starting in his teens and moved up to being a body-guard for the mob boss and head vampire for Chicago."

"I know all that," I said, and sounded pissy even to me. There was no reason to be angry with Micah.

"Olaf has been in some kind of military service, a bounty hunter, and now a U.S. Marshal. He's done things besides be a criminal. It gives him more life skills than just beating people up or killing them."

"I'm not sure Olaf was ever in the real military. He may have only been a mercenary or a contractor of some kind, but I take your point."

"Good," he said.

"But Haven didn't have hobbies that scare the fuck out of me."

"Are you calling being a serial killer a hobby?" he asked.

"Yeah, I guess."

"It's not his hobby, Anita. It's more his sexual preference."

"Gee, Micah, that makes it way less creepy." He laughed at my tone, but I didn't laugh with him. "I really don't think this is funny."

"Anita, honey, what has he done this time that's different? You seem shaken in a way that's not like you."

"Haven almost killed Nathaniel before I had to kill him, and he wasn't nearly as dangerous as Olaf."

"Do you really think he'd try to hurt me?"

"I don't want to find out, and I don't want to have to worry about your safety while I'm trying to keep myself safe while working on a murder investigation."

"Has Olaf threatened me?"

"No, none of you. In fact he's behaving himself pretty well for him."

"And yet you don't want me there with him."

"No, I really don't. I can't explain it, and maybe I'm being para-noid, but I love you, and I want us to spend the rest of our lives to-gether. If it's a choice between Bobby Marchand or you, I've already made my choice."

"I have good people on the Coalition. Thanks to Nathaniel wanting us home more, I found out that I have some great people that had just been waiting for me to delegate more responsibility to them."

"Then delegate this one . . . please."

"I'll miss seeing you, but all right, since you said please."

There was an edge of a smile in his voice, and I managed to put some of the same tone in my voice as I said, "I'll miss you, too, and thanks for listening to me."

"Listening to each other is part of being a couple," he said.

I laughed then. "If only more people understood that."

"It only matters that we understand it."

"True," I said.

I was smiling, and then suddenly I wasn't. Something was wrong. I couldn't have said what, but the hairs on the back of my neck were up. The woods had gone quiet as if everything was hiding. I spoke so low that if Micah had been vanilla human, he wouldn't have heard. "Gotta go, love." I pressed the button to disconnect without waiting for a response.

I stood there in the silent woods, fighting not to tense up, but to force myself to relax against the tree, into the bushes beside it. Tension catches the attention of a predator, and I knew that was what I was sensing. It wasn't vampire or beast powers; it was the same sense I'd had years ago in the woods with my dad when there'd been a cougar. They weren't supposed to be in the Midwest, but every once in a while one of them would wander through. You can't hide from wild animals; they have better senses than you do. So make noise and let them know they can't sneak up on you. Most ambush predators give up when they realize their element of surprise is lost.

"I know you're there, Olaf," I called out.

"You did not hear me," he said from the cover of the woods so close to me that I jumped. I couldn't help it.

"You didn't see me." He sounded puzzled as he stood and stretched that tall frame upward.

I wanted to ask him if he'd combat-crawled that close to me but didn't want to admit I hadn't realized he was within twenty feet of me. My pulse was in my throat like it would choke me. I couldn't hide it from him, not this close. He'd smell my panic. So I let my fear turn to anger, because I'd always rather be pissed than scared.

"What do you want, Ol . . . Otto?"

"You," he said.

And suddenly I wasn't angry or scared. I was just tired of the games. "I walked right into that one, didn't I?"

He frowned at me. "You were frightened, then angry, and now you smell . . . neutral. How?"

"Even I don't understand what I'm feeling all the time, so I can't explain it to you."

"That makes no sense," he said.

"Emotions don't make sense most of the time."

"It must be terrible to be at the mercy of so much illogic."

"Sometimes," I said.

"I know I am supposed to want a full range of emotions like everyone else seems to have, but I don't."

"Do you ever wonder what you're missing?" I asked.

"Doesn't everyone?"

I nodded. "Most people do, yes."

"Do you?"

"Do I what?"

"Ever wonder what it would be like to be less emotional, to be a sociopath?"

"Sometimes. I used to think I already was one until I met enough of you, but it does seem more internally peaceful than what the rest of us are doing."

"Much more peaceful," he said, staring at me with the full weight of his attention. "How did you know I was here if you neither heard nor saw me?"

"Maybe I smelled you."

"I'm upwind, not down-."

"I sensed you."

"You didn't see, hear, or smell me, and I'm too far away for touch or taste. There is nothing left."

"You're biform now, Otto. You should know better than to just count five senses."

He stared at me, and I stared back.

"You have been afraid of me in rooms full of people, and now we are in the woods alone and you are not afraid. There is no logic to that either."

"Witnesses protect us both, Olaf."

He frowned at me, and then he smiled. It looked like a real smile, as if he was genuinely happy. "You're threatening me."

"Just explaining."

"Do you believe you could draw, aim, and shoot before I closed the distance between us?"

"I don't know, but if you run at me, we'll find out."

I stood there and let the breath out of my body until I felt quiet inside. It was like white static inside me, empty and peaceful. It was how my head always used to go when I killed. Lately I hadn't seemed to need it, but as I looked at Olaf in the quiet trees, I didn't try to hide what was happening inside my head. I figured if anyone would understand, it would be him.

"You continue to surprise me, Adler."

"Good," I said, voice low and controlled.

My hand was hanging loose and ready next to the full-frame .45, and then I realized no, my AR-15 was on a tactical sling. All I had to do was move my body for it to spill into my hand. I could aim and start firing with it at my side. It wouldn't have been as accurate that way, but I was sure I'd at least wound him before I got the rifle snugged to my shoulder. Once it was there, I was sure I could finish him. The plan helped quiet even the static, so I felt calm inside my head, no fear, no anything. I wondered if that was how it was for Olaf most of the time. It seemed like a peaceful way to go through life, empty maybe, but peaceful. Maybe you couldn't have peace and give a damn.

He stood very still, hands spread wide to show he had nothing in them. "It is not time to answer this question between us, Anita."

I liked that he used my real name. I hated that fucking nickname, and I hated that I didn't feel free to tell him so even more. And just like that, the anger was back, and I knew if he rushed me now, I would be a little less quick, a little less focused, which meant it was a luxury I couldn't afford.

My voice was almost neutral as I said, "Then let's head back to the sheriff's station."

"After you," he said.

I smiled. "Let's go together but not too close until we have witnesses again."

"Agreed," he said.

We started walking through the trees back toward the road, the police station, and the witnesses who would keep us both from doing something the other one would regret. I wasn't a sociopath like Olaf, or even one like Edward, but I had my moments, because part of me thought about shooting Olaf where no one could see us. If I lied and said he'd attacked me, I could probably sell it. The fact that I even thought that said just how much I wanted to be free of my Moriarty. Fucking nicknames.

30

DEPUTY RICO BROUGHT Bobby's clothes and took over guard duty, so Duke felt he could go home for food and a little rest. Everyone seemed convinced that Rico could hold the fort, even Newman, though he said quietly to me, "Whatever I think of him as a person, he can handle guarding Bobby for a couple of hours."

"I thought you didn't like him back at the house," I said.

"He's one of Haley's ex-boyfriends."

"Oh," I said, because I couldn't think of anything else to say.

"He cheated on her. He cheats on all of them, but he never seems to run out of women to date."

"Fresh meat," I said.

Olaf spoke from too far away to have heard our conversation. I'd forgotten about his new supersecret hearing. "I will bet that it is not just women who do not know his reputation."

Newman looked startled but didn't ask how Olaf had heard us. He knew that Otto Jeffries had popped positive for lycanthropy after the case in Washington State. "You're right, but I don't understand it. I mean, he's good-looking, but not that good."

"No one is that good-looking," I said.

Olaf stalked toward us on those long legs that just seemed to eat up distance. "Most women will believe a handsome man when he lies."

"Most men do the same thing for beautiful women, and the same thing goes for the gay community on both sides of the aisle," I said.

Olaf nodded as he towered over both of us. "I will concede that beauty distracts everyone."

"Thank you," I said, and meant it. When we'd first met, he'd have been pissed if I'd tried to bring men down to the same level that he thought women deserved.

"You're both right. I saw it enough when I was a regular cop. Women believe that they will be the one that a bad man will reform for, that he'll never beat me like he did his ex-wife or cheat on me like he did on the last girlfriend. The women believe that it's the other woman's fault and not the man's. He just needs the right woman in his life, and that will be them," Newman said. "No matter how many times he has cheated on others, he will not cheat on them, because their love is true."

"Just like some men want to be a white knight for every damsel in distress they meet, because they believe they'll be the one that can save them from their terrible lives. They will be strong enough to succeed where all the other boyfriends failed," I said.

Olaf nodded. "The women take advantage of the men's good intentions."

"And men like Rico use the women they date," I said.

Kaitlin came up behind us and said, "Amen to that."

We turned to her. "I didn't know you were one of his exes," Newman said.

"It's all right. He's charmed most of the dating-age females in the county by now." She grinned and shook her head, managing to look both embarrassed and genuinely amused.

"I've always believed that if someone was too good at charming me, he'd had a lot of practice, and when he got tired of me, he'd be just as charming to the next one," I said.

"Well, you're right about that." Kaitlin frowned. "I've seen your Jean-Claude being interviewed on TV. He looks pretty darn charming."

It was my turn to grin. "It was one of the reasons I refused to date him at first. He'd had six hundred years of practice at being a ladies' man. He was so smooth that I instantly distrusted his motives."

"You were right to distrust him," Olaf said.

I frowned up at him. "What's that supposed to mean?"

"You should distrust everyone."

"Including you?" I asked.

He nodded, face solemn. "Everyone, Anita. Distrust them all."

"Well, that's a grim way of going through life," Kaitlin said.

Olaf gazed down at her. "It is the truth."

She shivered as she looked up at him, as if at some level she'd seen something to make her afraid. Good. Even though she wasn't his type, I didn't really want any women too close to Olaf. His idea of fun was just too frightening.

"I think there are people you can trust," Kaitlin said, but she looked away from him as she spoke.

"And that is why you dated Deputy Rico when you knew better," he said.

"I guess so, but no regrets. It was totally worth it."

"Why?" Newman asked.

Kaitlin grinned. "The sex was great."

That made me laugh out loud. Newman frowned, looking angry, and Olaf just looked neutral. Ordinary sex really didn't move him much.

"Great but not great enough," I said, still laughing.

"The sex was like the dating," Kaitlin said. "He had a few great moves that swept you off your feet, but once you'd seen all the tricks, he didn't have anything to back it up."

"A lot of serial daters are like that," I said.

"Serial daters—what are those?" Newman asked.

"It's like serial monogamy, except you don't marry them."

"I've never heard of serial monogamy either," he said.

I think it surprised us all when Olaf answered, "The ones who marry and divorce repeatedly."

"Yeah," I said, surprised he knew the term or cared enough to define it out loud.

"And shit like that is why I've never been married," Kaitlin said. Her phone pinged, and she checked the text. "Livingston texted that he's got us a table."

"I'm surprised he's the one saving the table," Newman said.

"You mean instead of sending me," she said, smiling.

"I didn't mean just you, Kaitlin. There are plenty of other state cops in town. Captain Livingston has a lot of lesser rank to send on errands right now."

"Livingston and the owner are good friends. If he'd sent anyone else in to get a table for this many people during their breakfast rush, we'd be lucky to get seated by lunch."

"I take it this is Sugar Creek," I said.

"Best breakfast in three counties," Kaitlin said.

"I wonder if the waitress that's dating the handyman at the Marchand place is working today," I said.

"You thinking of doing a little police work over breakfast?" Newman asked.

"I was thinking about it," I said.

Kaitlin took a deep breath of the air for effect and said, "I smell clues."

"I didn't think about Hazel Phillips being there this morning. I was just thinking about bacon," Newman said.

"And that is why you called Anita to help you," Olaf said.

"Would you have thought to question the waitress?" Newman asked.

"That's not fair. He doesn't know about her dating the man of all jobs at the Marchand home," I said.

"That is true, but it doesn't matter," Olaf said. "I would not have questioned her anyway."

"Why not? You just implied that you think it's a good idea," Newman said.

"I would have already completed the warrant of execution."

"So no reason to question anyone," I said.

Olaf nodded.

Newman looked at me. "Told you."

"Told her what?" Kaitlin asked.

"If Newman had passed on the warrant, it turns out that Otto here was the next closest marshal."

"Oh," Kaitlin said, and looked up at the big man, then back at New-man, and then finally at me. She smiled and put her arm through mine as if we were friends. "Well, then, you would be missing the best pan-cakes I've ever had."

"Pancakes, huh?" I said, letting her keep my arm, because women get weird about it when they try to be all huggy-feely and you don't want to be.

"Please tell me you're not one of those people that doesn't eat carbs," Kaitlin said, damn near hugging me.

"I eat carbs."

"Great. Pancakes for everyone!"

"I do not like pancakes," Olaf said from behind us as Kaitlin moved us to the door.

She called back, "Then you can have waffles."

"I do not like them either," he said, but he was following us out the door.

"What do you like for breakfast?" she asked.

I resisted saying, "The blood of his enemies," because it wasn't true. That was Edward's style and mine. Olaf was much more a blood-of-the-innocents kind of guy.

31

SUGAR CREEK RESTAURANT and Bakery was so crowded that the sound of the customers made white noise like crowds at a sporting event or a concert. The waitress at the podium in front said, "We're at a two-hour wait and longer for large groups. Sorry."

Kaitlin said, "Our party is already here at a table."

"Name?" the waitress said as if she didn't believe Kaitlin.

"Livingston."

"Oh, sure. Just follow Mandy. She'll take you back."

Mandy—who was either a second hostess or our waitress; only time would tell—took the menus the first woman handed her, and we followed her back through the tables and booths. The place was a lot deeper than the narrow front had hinted at, so we got to go through several rooms until we finally found Livingston sitting with his back to a wall in the center of a horseshoe-shaped booth. There was a dark-skinned woman in a black suit jacket sitting with him. His arm was across her shoulders, and their faces were so close together that her thick black hair had swung forward to hide her face completely and some of his. Her hand, with its perfectly red nails, caressed the side of his face. What I could see of his face was smiling.

He pulled back, and his professionalism came over him like he had put on another set of clothes. One minute all cuddles and romance, and the next Captain Livingston was there again. "Pamela, you remember Kaitlin."

Pamela looked up at us and smiled with lipstick the same crimson as her nails. The black suit jacket framed a crisp white shirt, and there was an engraved gold nameplate on her lapel that read MANAGER. I was beginning to see how we'd managed a table during the restaurant's busiest time of day.

"Of course I remember her," Pamela said as she started scooting out of the booth. Since it was a deep booth, that took some doing, but she did it with ease, even grace. I'd have looked like a five-year-old getting down from the dinner table. Of course, when Pamela stood up, she was about six feet tall. Longer legs help the whole scooting thing, or so I'm told.

Pamela shook Kaitlin's hand graciously. I could see she was wearing red designer flats that matched the lipstick and nails, so the height was all her. Her hair was black like mine, but a different shade and texture. I couldn't imagine what kinds of hair products she used and what careful blow-drying she'd done to get her hair to lie in a smooth, shoulder-length hairdo. Maybe I was wrong, and Pamela's hair in its natural state wasn't as curly as mine, but I'd never met anyone with her skin tone and rich facial features who didn't have my curls or more.

Livingston scooted out on the other side of the booth and introduced us one at a time. It wasn't until Pamela was shaking my hand and giving me great eye contact out of big brown eyes that I realized she was wearing very nice and understated makeup, except for the red lips. But thanks to Jean-Claude's lessons in color and style, I knew the red gave just the pop of color that the severity of the black-and-white outfit needed. You also had to be staring right in her face to feel the full force of her personality and let the impact of it change her from pretty to beautiful, or maybe it wasn't beauty exactly, but whatever it was, the force of it made me smile as she shook my hand.

The only one who didn't smile back at her was Olaf, and he frowned, which meant he felt her beauty, her personality, whatever it was, but he didn't want to be moved by it. Or maybe he just didn't like tall women, and I was way overprojecting.

"I'll leave you to talk business, but unless it's a life-or-death emergency, you'd better come find me and give me a kiss good-bye."

Livingston smiled. He was wearing a line of her lipstick already. "Unless it's an emergency, you know I will."

Pamela used her thumb to rub the lipstick off his lips, which was a strangely intimate gesture. It made me sad that I wasn't wearing my own shade of red and that I was too far away from any of my sweeties to paint it across their mouths. It's funny what can unexpectedly make you homesick for the people in your life. I was suddenly almost aching to be home.

Livingston waited until Pamela had disappeared to the front of the restaurant before he sat back down. I was pretty sure he watched her ass as she walked away, but apparently, he was allowed to do a lot more than just watch, so it was okay. Then it was the fun of sitting down. When you have a bunch of police, or certain types of military, sitting down in public is harder than it sounds. The booth was against the wall, so that was good for everyone, but there were pros and cons to it all. Sitting in the middle of the booth meant your back was securely against a wall and you had a clear view in all directions; the farther from the center you were, the more easy viewing you lost on one side or another. Of course, if you were in the middle and there was an emergency, you were trapped behind the table. You couldn't run either toward the emergency or away from it, depending on what was happening. You were sort of committed to doing something from where you were sitting. On the ends of the booth, you could move easily if you needed to, but you had your back toward one side of the room or the other. Did you keep your field of view and sacrifice maneuverability, or lose the view and maintain your ability to move? I expected that sitting arrangements would be complicated. What I hadn't expected was for Olaf to complicate them even more. I shouldn't have been caught off guard; that I had been meant I was in a certain amount of denial about him and me.

Livingston went back to the center of the booth, which surprised me until I noticed that the table moved freely as he scooted into his seat. Obviously the table wasn't bolted down, which gave him an option if he had to move fast. He could just tip the table over and get out. Despite what you see in movie shoot-outs, most tables won't stop bullets from hitting you, because they are soft cover, not hard cover. Hard cover is what it sounds like, something so hard or dense that it will absorb or block bullets before they hit you.

Kaitlin slid in on Livingston's left side, and Newman slid in on his right. I started to slide in beside Newman, and it would have been normal for Olaf to sit beside Kaitlin on the other side so we'd be even, but he slid in beside me. I scooted as close to Newman as I could get, or thought I had until Olaf moved all the way in and suddenly Newman's sidearm was digging into my hip. I was also in danger of hitting my head against Olaf's shoulder.

"Can someone please move down? I'm getting squished," I said.

Everyone else moved down enough for me not to be in danger of getting stabbed by Newman's holstered weapon. I moved over enough so that my face wasn't pressed in against Olaf's shoulder or any other part of him. Of course, I could only go so far before I bumped into Newman again, and I was not going to make them all scoot down again. I had enough room—we all had enough room—I tried to convince that part of me that wanted to crawl under the table and go to the other side of Kaitlin, but I wasn't a child. I could do this with a modicum of cool. Sure, I could, and I told that tight feeling in the pit of my stomach that it could fuck off and let me be a grown-up.

I really expected Olaf to push the chance to sit close to me, but he didn't try to put his hip or leg up against mine. Even with him behaving himself, it felt tight. I think it was the height difference, and his shoulders, though not as broad as Livingston's, still crowded me. Olaf seemed to realize that he was a little close because he raised his arm and put it across the back of the booth. He wasn't trying to be smooth or even aggressive; his shoulder was just at a bad height for us to be this close. With his arm up, we fit better. The span of his arm was so long that his hand went all the way past Newman to the edge of Livingston's shoulder. God, Olaf was just so big. Even if he hadn't been creepy, he was over my height preference for dating. I didn't like to feel this physically overwhelmed just sitting next to someone.

"I don't have cooties, I promise," Kaitlin said. She tried to make a joke, but I saw her eyes flick to Olaf, then to me. She was doing some sort of girl math in her head, or maybe just girl-plus-boy math. I did not want her to come up with an answer on this one.

"Anita and I work together frequently," Olaf said, "and I prefer dark hair to light."

That last remark made me glance up at him. He was wasting a smile on her, the one that filled his eyes with warmth. To me, it was like one of those fireplace channels where you can watch TV images of a crackling fire. It was pretty to look at, but you couldn't warm yourself by it.

"I always wanted to know what I'd look like as a brunette," Kaitlin said, and she gave him a smile that said, *Yes, I am flirting with you.* Was she serious or just teasing him? He wouldn't like either much.

"Brunette would be dark enough," he said, still smiling at her.

She wiggled her eyebrows at him, which meant she was teasing, but enjoying it anyway. I looked into her gray-blue eyes and knew that as long as she stayed away from colored contacts, she was still safe from Olaf's darker intentions. It helped me fight the tension that was trying to build in my shoulders.

Apparently, I wasn't the only one who wanted to change the conversation. "You know how to fight, Blake," Livingston said.

"Thanks. Just part of the job," I said.

"No, it's not," Newman said. "We're not supposed to get that up close with any of the supernaturals."

I looked up at him and nodded. "True, but then I don't think I've ever been on a lycanthrope—Therianthrope—case where we managed to get the rogue in a cage. Usually we're hunting them and they're hunting us, so we shoot them before they get that close."

"So, you don't learn serious hand-to-hand fighting for the job?" Kaitlin asked.

"Not in official training," I said.

"Where'd you learn it?" she asked.

"Ted started teaching me, um, Marshal Ted Forrester. He was one of my mentors back when I first started."

"You were one of the first, weren't you?" Livingston said.

"Vampire executioners?" I asked.

"Is that what they called you at first?"

"No, we were just vampire hunters. The job title didn't change until after the law changed and made vampires legal citizens with rights. You can't hunt citizens like animals, so they started calling us executioners."

"Wikipedia says that the vampires nicknamed you the Executioner. Is that true?" Livingston asked.

I nodded.

A waitress with long dark hair pulled back in a ponytail came up to fill our water glasses and hand out menus.

"Hi, I'm Hazel, and I'll be serving you today."

I looked at her name tag, and it did read HAZEL, which was an unusual enough name that she had to be the waitress Carmichael, the Marchands' handyman, was dating. We hadn't been waiting so long because of slow service; we'd been waiting for our potential witness to be free to wait on us. Brownie points to Livingston. Dating the manager hadn't just gotten us a table; it had gotten us another person of interest.

Knowing who the waitress was made me notice her more. Hazel had hazel eyes that had more gray in the brown than green, as if the original color had faded. I wondered if her parents had known ahead of time that Hazel's eye color would fade, or if she'd been born with her eyes that way. Was that even possible? Something had etched harsh lines at the corners of her eyes and the edges of her mouth like unhappy parentheses, but even with that, I put her on the young side of thirty-five. She seemed hard-lived rather than old. I caught a faint whiff of cigarettes as she moved around the table. Ah, a smoker; that will age the face and skin. She probably couldn't even smell the bitter scent of it on herself anymore, but a nonsmoker like me, I couldn't not smell it.

I'd have started interrogating her, but Livingston ordered his food, which meant the rest of us had to look at our menus ASAP. For future reference, I hate to be rushed when choosing food, especially at new restaurants. I ended up ordering pancakes, because pancakes are like coffee. They're all good; it's just a matter of how good. A side order of extra-crispy bacon, orange juice, a regular Coke, and coffee and I was set.

"Think you ordered enough caffeine?" Kaitlin said, smiling.

"Probably not," I said.

That made her laugh. I was beginning to wonder whether she was just that cheerful or she was flirting with me. I wasn't always able to tell when women aimed at me. The fact that women were included in my poly group at home still caught me by surprise sometimes. I was beginning to think that if I hadn't been metaphysically connected to Jean-Claude and a half dozen other people who preferred women, I might not have ever found the same sex attractive. But then again, maybe I was just a late bloomer.

Olaf ordered an omelet with mostly meat in it, a side of fruit, and coffee. I wondered if he'd have ordered differently if we'd had more time to look the menu over. I know I probably would have.

When Hazel left with our orders in hand, Livingston took up the conversation as if we'd never stopped. "So, you're *the* Executioner to the vampires."

"Among other pet names, yeah," I said, and sipped my water. Nathaniel was starting to pester me about not drinking enough water.

"Doesn't that make marrying their king sort of awkward?"

"I thought it would, but it turns out that they're used to being afraid of their rulers, so me being their bogeyman and their queen will probably seem like business as usual to them."

"When do we question Hazel?" Newman asked.

"After we get our food and eat it," Livingston said.

"Why eat first?" Newman said.

"I thought you were a regular cop before you became a marshal."

"I was."

"Then you know that you always eat first, in case you get another call and have to leave."

Newman smiled and looked down at the table, nodding. "I can't even argue. The food is good here. I didn't know you were dating Pamela."

"We both decided we were ready for people to know."

"Well, congratulations."

"Thank you and congratulations on the engagement."

"You know all the local gossip now that you're dating Pamela," Newman said.

"More than I did before, but I had to swear not to use anything I overheard unless I run it by her first, or someone's life is at stake."

"Smart woman," I said.

"She is," Livingston said, smiling as if the fact that she was smart made him happy. Pretty is good, but pretty and smart are better.

"Frankie told me that the other marshals call Ted Forrester Death, and I heard you say you're War," Kaitlin said.

"Yeah," I said, sipping my water and hoping the coffee got here soon. If I was going to have to answer twenty questions about myself, then I needed more caffeine.

Kaitlin turned to Olaf. "She said that Blake and Forrester were half of the Four Horsemen and that one of the others was Marshal Jeffries."

"Yes," he said, and sipped his water. Maybe he wanted something stronger, too.

"It's you and Marshal Spotted-Horse. I would not forget such a great name, but I can't remember which of the horsemen you are."

"He's Plague," Newman said.

"Why are the four of you named the Four Horsemen of the Apocalypse?" Livingston asked.

"Doesn't my Wiki page say?" I asked, and didn't manage to keep the sarcasm out of my voice.

"It's mostly vampire stuff and your love life," he said.

I rolled my eyes. "Friends told me to stop looking myself up online, especially with all the publicity about the wedding, so I don't know what people are saying about me."

"Probably best you don't know," Livingston said.

"So friends keep telling me," I said.

"I promise not to look you up online anymore if you'll answer my questions," he said.

"Depends on the question, but sounds fair."

"Why the Four Horsemen of the Apocalypse?"

Olaf answered, "The four of us have the highest kill counts."

"And we're some of the most senior marshals still on the job," I added.

"You both seem awfully young to be the most senior," Livingston said.

I looked up at Olaf, and he noticed, so he looked down at me. I'd never really thought about how old he might be. He seemed sort of ageless, not literally like a vampire, but as if he would always be like he was when I'd first met him. It had never occurred to me to wonder if he was closer to Edward's age or mine. He had to be somewhere in that nearly ten-year age difference, didn't he?

"What?" he asked me.

I shook my head, and said to Livingston, "There were never many of us, but once they added a physical requirement along with the shooting requirement, that took out most of the real old-timers. They could shoot, but they couldn't pass the obstacle course and calisthenics part."

"Some of them are teaching classes to the newer marshals," Newman added.

"I was glad when they invited them to teach you new guys. That much field experience shouldn't go to waste."

"A lot of them are stake-and-hammer guys though," Newman said. "Old-fashioned doesn't begin to cover their methods."

"The hunter that taught me the ropes was like that."

"I thought Forrester was your mentor. He's known for his gun knowledge," Livingston said.

"You get that off his Wikipedia page?" I asked.

"No, he worked a case that a buddy of mine was on. My friend is a gun nut, and he loved Forrester's arsenal. He said that Forrester even used a flamethrower."

"Yep, that's Ted," I said, shaking my head.

"So, he wasn't your first mentor?"

"No, Manny Rodriguez was. He taught me how to raise zombies and how to kill vampires."

"What happened to him?" Newman asked.

"His wife thought he was getting too old and forced him to retire from the hunting side of things."

"It is not a job for old men," Olaf said.

"I guess it isn't, but I wasn't ready to fly solo when Manny retired. I was lucky I didn't get killed doing jobs on my own at first."

"When did Forrester start training you?" Livingston asked.

"Soon enough to help me stay alive."

"Ted spoke highly of you from the beginning," Olaf said. "He does not give unearned praise. Are you being humble?"

"No, I don't . . . I really did have some close calls when Manny first retired, or maybe I just missed having backup."

Hazel brought our coffee and my Coke. "I'll be back to fill those waters up, and with the juice," she said before she left again.

I so wanted to start questioning her, but this was Newman's warrant and everyone else besides Olaf was local. They knew Hazel. I didn't. I'd let them play it for now.

The coffee was fresh and hot and surprisingly good for a mass-produced cup. I did add sugar and cream, so it wasn't great coffee, but I didn't add much, so it wasn't bad either. Olaf put in way more sugar than I did, so his cup would have been too sweet for me. He didn't take cream. I guessed we could be snobby about each other's coffee habits later.

"But it was Forrester who taught you how to fight empty hand?" Livingston asked.

"I had some martial arts when we met, but he started me on more real-world training that worked outside of a judo mat or a martial arts tournament."

"I thought he was out of New Mexico," Livingston said.

"He is."

"And you're in St. Louis, Missouri."

"I am."

"Hard to train long-distance."

"I have people I train with at home."

"How often do you train?" Kaitlin asked.

"At least three times a week in hand-to-hand and blade."

"Really that often?" Newman asked.

"Yeah. How often do you train?"

"I go to the range two, three times a month."

"Any martial arts?" I asked.

"I go to the gym three times a week."

"Weights?" I asked.

"Interval training with weights and cardio."

"That's more than you were doing when I first met you, isn't it?" I asked.

"Yeah. How did you know?"

"You've put on muscle."

"Thanks for noticing."

"Is that all you do?" Olaf asked.

"Yeah. What do you do?" Newman asked.

"More," Olaf said.

"Blake only trains three days a week. Why are you giving me attitude and not her?"

"She trains in close-quarters combat three times a week, but that is not all she does."

Newman looked at me and raised an eyebrow.

"Three days a week for weights, sometimes with cardio between sets, sometimes straight weights," I said. "I run at least twice a week, three if I have time. I do gun training of some kind at least twice a month, and I try for every week."

"So you're in the gym or training every day of the week?" Newman asked.

"I try to take one day off a week."

"How can you keep that up?"

"How can you be happy with three days a week of cardio and weights? Seriously, Newman, what kind of workout are they using in training now?"

"What were they using when they grandfathered both of you in?" he asked.

Olaf and I looked at each other. "They needed to keep as many of us as possible until they could get you newbies trained and in the field, so the physical requirements were the regular ones for the Marshals Service."

"Same for me," Newman said.

"They were talking about doing a physical-training program that would help prepare new recruits for the job. Are you telling me that they didn't do that?" I asked.

"Once we become marshals, as long as we keep meeting physical requirements, there's no forced PT."

"That's typical of most law enforcement," Livingston said.

"They don't force us to train," Olaf said.

"Well, no, but"—I tried to think how to put it into words—"but if you don't train and train hard, you won't make it in this job."

"Do you mean you'll fail when you get retested?" Kaitlin asked.

"No, I mean if you can't run, fight, just have the stamina to make it through a hunt, you'll get hurt or worse."

"It's not just that, Anita," Olaf said. "The new executioners lack mentorship. They have only classroom experience with the monsters and no one to show them how to stay alive in the field."

"They are sending the newest marshals out with older marshals now," Newman said.

"They haven't asked me to babysit anyone, so who are they asking?" I said.

"They contacted me," Newman said.

"You've been doing this barely two years."

"I know. That's why I told them that I didn't feel I had the experience to help anyone newer than myself. I told them that I'd found you, Forrester, Jeffries, and Spotted-Horse to be the most help to me. They didn't like me crediting working with all of you as a reason I was better than most of the marshals that joined at the same time I did."

"Why don't they send out the Four Horsemen with the new recruits?" Livingston asked.

"They do not trust us," Olaf said.

I nodded and said, "Yeah, what he said."

"Don't trust you how?" Kaitlin asked.

"They think we will corrupt the recruits," Olaf said.

I glanced up at him. "Not the word I'd have chosen, but yeah, that's sort of it. They think we'll train the new marshals to be as independent and lone wolf as we are."

"Will you?" Livingston asked.

"Probably. Almost all of us that were grandfathered in were freelance operatives that were only marginally with the police. I was a consultant with the police, but a lot of the other marshals were bounty hunters before they got badges. Those of us that passed fitness training and the firearms test were grandfathered in, but that didn't make us police officers. We don't have the training, and most of us don't even have a police background."

"What background do you have?"

"Military," Olaf said.

"Magic," I said, "or technically psychic gifts that made us good with the undead or shapeshifters or both."

"So none of the people grandfathered in was a cop first?" Livingston asked.

"Not to my knowledge."

"No," Olaf said.

"Surely some police were hunting vampires before the laws changed and made them legal citizens," Livingston said.

"They were some of the first, actually," I said.

"So why weren't they grandfathered in?" Kaitlin asked.

"One, cops weren't allowed to be bounty hunters. Two, they were dead."

"So you're saying that you're better at this job than regular police," Livingston said.

"Yes," Olaf and I said together.

"That's just insulting all your brothers and sisters in blue," Livingston said.

"I'm not insulting them. I'm stating that police are trained to save lives. Most officers can do their twenty years without ever having to shoot anyone. I know every shooting makes the news now, but if you do the math between how many police are in this country and how many people die by gun violence, it's mostly civilian-on-civilian crime. Police are trained to keep the peace. You need to think very differently to do our job."

"You were a cop before you became a marshal, right, Newman?" Livingston asked.

"Yes."

"You're good at the job."

Newman shook his head. "My first hunt in the field was with the Four Horsemen. I got to see how the job is supposed to be done, not what our bosses want the job to be."

"What do they want it to be?" Livingston asked.

"They want cops that kill on command like the dog half of a canine team attacks, but the rest of the time, we're supposed to be good dogs, man's best friend, until they tell us to kill again." His face as he talked got more and more unhappy.

"Wow," Kaitlin said, "that's grim."

"It feels grim," Newman said.

"But you're not dogs. You're police officers," Livingston said.

"And that's the problem, sir. Part of the time, they want most of us to be regular marshals, but then they push the button, and we're supposed to become something else—something that I don't understand how to be. And the fighting you saw Blake do in the cell, that's her training with Forrester and Jeffries and others like them. No one is teaching that to the rest of us."

"You're saying that you need to be more like SWAT than regular police," Livingston said.

Newman shook his head. "No, sir. SWAT is still about saving lives, containing the violence, but that's not what the preternatural branch does."

"Preternatural branch goes out with SWAT to serve warrants on known preternatural citizens," Livingston said.

"Only after the marshal goes through extra training closer to our Special Operations Group, SOG. Once you pass that, you can be picked to accompany local SWAT on regular police warrants to known or suspected supernatural citizens."

"You sound like you're quoting," Livingston said.

"I am."

"Have you gone out with SWAT?" Kaitlin asked.

"No," Newman said.

"Yes," I said.

"Yes," Olaf said.

"Sounds like a good idea to send the supernatural experts out with SWAT on warrants like that," Livingston said.

"It is. It's a great idea," said Newman, "except we're supposed to be protecting SWAT in case the supernatural citizen goes completely rogue and tries to kill them, but most of the newer marshals are greener than me. They think like cops, and that's not what a SWAT unit needs if the monster tries to eat them."

"What do they need from the marshals?" Livingston asked.

"They need them to kill the monster, not contain it, not handcuff it, not put it in a cage or into the back of a cruiser. This job isn't police work at all. It's closer to special operations units like SEALs or Delta Force. Or maybe it isn't even that. Maybe we're just assassins with badges, like Blake says, but whatever we are, it's not police. When they nicknamed Blake War, they were being honest about what the preternatural branch does. It's war. It's deep, dark, behind-enemy-lines shit that our government is allowing us to do right here on American soil. But you have to want to be a SEAL, and you have to know what one is and what one does. Same for any of the other special operations units. You don't end up on one of them by accident. They don't recruit you for regular service and then throw you out into the dark with Delta Force and expect you to be okay." When Newman finished talking he was not looking at any of us but staring off into space, and whatever he was seeing inside his head wasn't anything good.

I looked at the side of Newman's face. I wanted to touch his arm, to let him know he was all right, but it would have been a lie. I caught Livingston looking at him, too. Our eyes met for a second, and I think we both thought the same thing: Newman needed a new job.

"Newman, Win, you can go back to being regular police or transfer to the other side of the Marshals Service," I said.

"You said 'back to' like it's a step backward, lesser."

I opened my mouth, closed it, and tried to think of something to say. "I'm an assassin with a badge, Newman. I couldn't be a regular cop. I don't have the temperament or training for it."

"And I don't have what it takes to be an assassin with a badge," he said, and looked at me. His eyes were shiny, and if it had been allowed, I'd have said he was nearly in tears. But I pretended I couldn't see them, and he pretended they weren't there. Even if the tears started, we'd all pretend we couldn't see them unless Newman let us know it was okay to acknowledge them.

He excused himself for the bathroom. Olaf and I would have moved, but Kaitlin started the scoot-out first, so we let Livingston and her clear the way for Newman. I watched him walk away until he turned a corner and was lost to sight.

I don't know what we would have said out loud, because the juice and the food all came at once. The bacon was perfectly crisp, like a hard look would make it fall apart, and Kaitlin was right. The pancakes were great. We all ate as if Newman hadn't bared his soul moments before. One, we were all hungry and the food was that good. Two, how would it have changed anything to talk about it?

When Newman came back to the table with his face damp but clear, he sat down to his food as if nothing had happened. That was our cue to do the same. We talked about the food and made harmless small talk until the food was gone and Hazel came back to the table to ask if there was anything else we needed. Why, yes, there was. Let's talk murder.

32

HAZEL DIDN'T WANT to sit down with us. "I have tables to wait on."

"You know what Kaitlin and I do for a living, Hazel?" Livingston asked.

"Yeah," she said, and the one word was sullen, like a shadow of the rebellious teenager she might once have been.

"Do you know Marshal Newman?" Livingston nodded toward Newman, and since they were sitting next to each other, it was a small gesture.

"I know him." Again her demeanor was sullen and instantly guarded. It didn't mean that she knew a damn thing that we needed to know. A lot of people are just naturally suspicious of the police. Go figure.

"This is Marshal Anita Blake and Marshal Otto Jeffries," Livingston said, motioning down the table toward us.

I said, "Hi, Hazel." I was going to try to be the good cop, because Olaf sure as hell couldn't do it.

She mumbled, "Hi," before she could stop herself. A lot of people will do automatic social cues if you give them a chance. She frowned harder, showing where some of the harsh lines around her mouth had come from. To get such deep lines, she must have frowned a lot more than she smiled.

"We just want to ask you a few questions, Hazel," Livingston said.

"I don't know anything," she said. She hadn't asked us what it was about, just gone straight to not knowing anything about it. Either she did know something, or she'd had a run-in with the police before.

"I bet you know lots of things," I said, smiling.

Hazel frowned harder, looking at me. "I don't know anything."

She put a lot of emphasis on *don't*, and again there was that echo of sullenness that teenage girls seem to specialize in, as if a part of Hazel was stuck at about fifteen or sixteen. If you have something bad happen to you, sometimes you can get stuck at the age when it happened, and without therapy, you can stay stuck for the rest of your life. I was beginning to want to know more about Hazel's childhood. If it wouldn't help us figure out who done it, I'd leave it alone, but if we needed leverage to get her to talk to us, then I was pretty sure her past would give us a lever to move her or at least to try.

"I bet you can figure out the math on a good tip faster than I can."

She frowned even harder so that the lines in her face looked almost painful, more like scars than lines, as if her unhappiness was a wound that showed on her face.

"And I bet you know this menu backward, forward, and sideways."

She gave a half smile that softened the pain in her face. "I've worked here for over three years, so yeah."

"Please have a seat, Hazel. We just want to talk to you," Livingston said.

The smile vanished, and she was back to sullen and wary. "I have other tables, Dave. Sorry." She actually started to walk away.

"Hazel, we can talk here, or we can talk at the station. It's up to you," he said.

She turned and looked at us all. The scorn on her face was epic. I wondered what she'd have been like if she was really mad at someone, and I realized we might find out. "Unless you're arresting me, I don't have to go with you or answer your questions."

"Do you know Bobby Marchand?" Newman asked.

Hazel narrowed her scorn onto him. I would not want to date someone who had that look and attitude in them. "Of course I do."

"We're trying to save his life."

"I thought you were one of the supernatural marshals."

"I am."

"Then isn't it your job to kill him?"

"I have a warrant for his execution."

"Then why do you want to talk to me about anything? It's a done deal. Bobby killed his uncle, and now you have to kill him so he doesn't attack anyone else."

"What if Bobby is innocent?"

"The whole town knows he did it." Hazel rolled her eyes at Newman, as if to ask how stupid he could get. Again, it was that echo of a teenage girl, because no one does scorn as well as they do.

"If I kill him and find out later that he didn't do it, then whoever had knowledge of the real murderer and didn't speak up to save Bobby's life could be charged with manslaughter or even third-degree murder."

I wasn't sure that was strictly true, but watching Hazel with hesitation in her eyes, I just sat there and kept my doubts off my face. Newman might have found a way through all that scorn and bad attitude.

"That's not true." But her eyes said plainly that she wasn't a hundred percent sure of that.

"Sit down and talk to us, Hazel, and we won't have to find out," Livingston said.

She finally sat down on the edge of the seat near Kaitlin. She looked at all of us and then said, "You wanted to talk, so talk." Most people chat and get themselves in trouble, but apparently, she was going to make us do the talking. I'd have bet money this wasn't her first police rodeo.

"Carmichael said that he slept over at your place the night of the murder," Newman said.

"Yeah, he did. Now, I have other customers waiting for their food." She moved to the edge of the seat like she was going to stand up.

"Don't he and the Chevets usually check with one another to make sure that someone is at the house just in case?"

"Yeah. The one time they don't, and the shit hits the fan." Hazel stood up.

"Why didn't Carmichael coordinate with the Chevets?" Newman asked.

"How am I supposed to know?"

"I thought you and he were serious about each other," he said.

"We were. We are." She said the last part fast, as if hoping we'd miss the grammar change.

Livingston asked, "Did you break up?"

"No," Hazel said. She glanced behind her, and there were people at another booth trying to flag her down.

"You said you were serious, past tense," I said.

"I said we are serious. Now, I have people waiting for their food and their tickets. My tips are getting smaller every minute."

"Okay, Hazel. Thanks for talking to us," Newman said.

Hazel hurried away to wait on other tables. When she was out of earshot, Kaitlin said, "I thought Hazel lied better than that."

"She usually does," Livingston said.

"Does she lie a lot?" I asked.

They both nodded. "She can put on a great act as a waitress. She can pretend to be sweet as honey while she's trying for a bigger tip," Kaitlin said.

"She's a good waitress," Livingston said, "but she's lied to Pamela about why she's late to work. Lied so well that Pamela believed her more than once, only to find out weeks or in one case months later that it wasn't true."

"She was hiding something," Newman said.

"And hiding it badly," I said.

"You say she is normally a very accomplished liar?" Olaf said.

"She can smile to a customer's face so that they request her to wait on them next time, but behind the scenes she's bitching about them the whole time. I've seen it. She's not just a good liar. She's good at hiding how she feels."

"So why was she nervous and making mistakes today?" I asked.

"She was pretending," Olaf said.

"Why pretend to be nervous?" Kaitlin asked.

"Lying to your boss about why you're late to work is one thing," Newman said. "Lying about a murder investigation is different."

"You think she's in over her head?" I asked.

"When I questioned Carmichael, he seemed genuinely torn up about Ray's death and Bobby being under a death sentence," Newman said.

"So what does his girlfriend have to hide?" I asked.

"I've seen true remorse in murderers before," Livingston said.

"I don't think Carmichael killed Ray," Newman said.

"Did you get the feeling he was hiding anything?" I asked.

Newman shook his head. "No."

I looked across the table at Livingston. "Is Carmichael a good liar?"

"I don't know him as well as I know Hazel, but he's always seemed pretty straightforward."

"Honest, you mean?"

"Yes."

"What is he doing with that woman?" Olaf asked.

"She's twenty years younger than him," Livingston said.

"So, he's sixty-something?" I asked.

"No, fifty-something."

"Okay, I give—how old is she?"

"Just turned thirty."

I blinked at him. "I'm older than she is. I wouldn't have called that."

"Me either," Kaitlin said. "I thought you were my age."

"How old are you?"

"Twenty-five."

I smiled and shook my head. "I've got you by seven years."

"Wow, you've got to tell me your secret sometime. Please tell me it's not an all-natural diet and virtuous living."

I laughed. "Hardly. It's part good genetics, part not smoking or drinking or partying. I burn in the sun and don't tan worth a damn, so no tanning. And all my friends that are my age or older that hit the gym seriously are aging better than my friends that don't exercise. I try to eat semihealthy, but I love fast-food burgers and French fries. I'm not giving them up until I have to."

Kaitlin laughed. "Yay! I love fast food. How about junk food like chips and desserts?"

"I'm not big on snacks and sweets. Sorry."

"I've seen your intended on TV, so I won't ask about the virtuous living. If you're abstaining from that gorgeous vampire, I don't want to know, and if you're having the wild and crazy sex that the Internet claims you are, then I don't want to know that either. It'll just make me jealous." Kaitlin smiled when she said the last part, because she didn't really mean it.

"This area is too rural and you're too cute to have any problem getting dates."

She grinned at me, tried to look modest, and failed. "I do all right on dating but finding someone to settle down with, that's a different story. Like you said, the county is pretty rural, so a small dating pool means I can have my pick within reason, but finding 'the one,'"—she made little air quotes around the phrase—"in the same small pool is harder."

"I didn't know you were looking for Mr. Right. I know a few fellows that are ready to settle down," Livingston said. He smiled when he said it, like he didn't think she'd take him up on it.

She laughed. "I'm not ready."

"You were joking about being jealous of Anita and Jean-Claude," Olaf said, and I couldn't decide if he was stating a fact or admitting that he'd just figured out that she'd been teasing me.

"Yes. I'm happy if she's ready to settle down, but I want to be able to date whoever I want, to be with whoever I want, to have fun with whoever I want." Kaitlin took a sip of her coffee and gave him the full weight of her big gray-blue eyes over the rim of the mug.

If I hadn't been sitting right beside Olaf, I might have missed the extent of the look, but I saw it and I knew he had to have seen it. I was happy all over again that Kaitlin wasn't his type. I liked her, and it would suck to have to protect her from the big guy. I had enough trouble protecting my own boundaries from him. As if the thought had caused it to happen, I felt a hand on my knee. I looked down, and there his hand was, having to maneuver around my holster and gun, but still that big hand cupped my knee like he had a right to touch me there.

I looked him in the eyes and didn't even try to look friendly. My voice was low and careful as I said, "Move."

He stared down at me with his cave-dark eyes, and for the first time, I wasn't afraid. Part of it was being in public, but the other part was simply that I had to draw the line now, because he was one of those men who would keep pushing until I did. Whispers, threats, but he'd never just touched me like that before. It was a small thing. He hadn't grabbed my breast or something. But to some men, if you don't say no at a knee, they'll take a breast or more the next time.

"Now," I whispered because I didn't want to humiliate him in front of our fellow officers. That would have been dangerous.

He moved his hand, and he wasn't angry. He studied my face as if searching for a clue.

"Everything all right over there?" Livingston asked.

"Yeah, I'm fine."

"We need to talk," Olaf said.

"Yeah, we do."

"Are you sure you're all right?" Livingston asked.

"Otto and I just need a minute," I said. I gave a pushing motion, and Olaf slid out of the booth while I scooted out after him.

"The porch out front is good for privacy," Newman said.

The porch was where a lot of the customers waiting for tables were sitting. We could find a private corner to talk, but we'd be surrounded by people. The fact that Newman had suggested it meant he knew something was up between Olaf and me. He gave me a very serious look, and his head was turned so that Livingston and Kaitlin couldn't see. I realized he'd seen Olaf put his hand on me. In that moment I wasn't unhappy he'd seen it. Now I could tell him the same cover story that Edward had told a fellow cop at his wedding when I'd been best man/person: Olaf had a crush on me and was starting not to take no for an answer. So Edward had pretended to be my boyfriend even in front of other cops to back Olaf off. It had been half true; the only lie was that Edward and I had ever been more than just best friends. I didn't want Newman playing white knight for me, but him helping me not be alone with Olaf would be helpful until Edward got here.

But right now I was going to lay down some ground rules for the big man. He wanted to try to date me. The fact that it would be a cold day in hell before I actually let him date me was beside the point. If he was serious, then he needed to understand basic consent. You didn't get to touch me anywhere unless you asked first, and I had to agree to the touch. Then and only then could you do it. I was about to try to teach a sexual sadist and serial killer about asking before he touched a woman. Since his idea of a great date up to this point had been kidnap, torture, and rape, I wasn't sure how he'd take the lesson, and worse, I was beginning not to care. He had done far scarier things before, but for some reason, his touching me under the table like he was my boyfriend with other cops sitting right there had just pissed me off.

33

WE WENT TO stand at the end of the porch far enough away from the screaming toddlers and the families dressed like they'd just come from church. Newman, Livingston, and Kaitlin stayed on the other end of the porch so we'd have privacy, but they were watching us, so we'd have to be careful of what we let them see, and there would be no shouting.

"There is no fear in you, just anger. Why?" Olaf asked.

"Why am I angry? Or why am I not afraid?"

"Both."

"Look, if you really mean it that I'm . . . the Woman for you, that I'm your Irenie, or whatever, you need to understand the basics of consent."

"I touched your knee. That is not a sexual area."

"The fuck it's not," I said, lowering my voice as I saw a toddler race past us with a harassed woman chasing him. "If I let you touch me someplace that isn't technically an erogenous zone, then you'll touch me again without my permission, and maybe next time, it will be somewhere that's more sexual. I learned a long time ago with men that I have to draw the line early on, or they just keep pushing."

"It was not a big deal."

"It's my body, so if you want to touch me anywhere, then you need to ask me first, and I have to say yes."

He stared at me. "You are joking."

"No, I'm not. Jean-Claude had to learn to keep his hands to himself, too."

"He had to ask permission to touch you?"

"When we first started out, yes. I'm a little confused on boundaries with some people because of the metaphysics involved, but if I have a choice, I go slow. Besides, Newman saw you, and the other two knew something happened."

"If you had not reacted to it, they would not have known."

"Maybe, but I'm not going to sit quietly like a good little girl while anyone touches me without my permission. Anyone in my life has to earn the right to touch me."

"But you do not have to earn the right to touch me. Women can do anything to a man, and we are just supposed to be flattered at the attention."

"No, that's not right either."

"Am I wrong about everything?" He was starting to be angry now.

"No. I mean, it's not fair. It's a double standard that women can grope men and not be in trouble, but men get in trouble in the reverse. I think everyone should keep their hands to themselves until they have the other person's consent. It's about mutual respect of one another's bodies and personal space."

"I would not mind if you touched my knee."

"Even if we were to the point of casual touch like that, I wouldn't do it at a business breakfast with other cops."

"So your objection is that it was unprofessional?"

"Part of it, yes."

"I am sorry if it was unprofessional."

I'd been ready to start yelling, but his apology caught me off guard. "If you don't do it again, then I accept your apology, and thank you for saying it."

"You are welcome, Anita. You know I do not understand consent."

"I think you understand it, Ol . . . Otto. You just ignored it until now."

He seemed to think that over and finally nodded. "I will accept that. I did not care about a woman's consent, because it wasn't necessary."

"You took what you wanted," I said.

He nodded. "I do not want to take from you, Anita."

"Then that means I need to offer it. Personal intimacy is like a gift that you give each other. Does that make any sense to you?"

"I think I understand what you mean."

"Good," I said.

Olaf leaned in close and smelled my hair like he had over at the sheriff's office, but I wasn't afraid this time. I don't know if it was the bright sunlight and the crowd of families with kids, or other cops being nearby, or maybe I was just done with being scared of him.

"You do not smell like fear now. Do you think you've tamed me?"

"No, never. You are what you've always been: a big, dangerous predator. Do your preferences toward women scare me? Yes, but you keep saying you want to date me or have a relationship with me. I finally realized when you touched me in there that I've been so busy treating you like the big bad wolf that I haven't taken the time to tell you any of my preferences. If this is supposed to be some kind of relationship, then you need to know my dating rules, just like I need to know yours."

"I do not think I have dating rules, since I have never truly dated anyone."

"Fair enough, but since I've dated more people than you have, maybe it's my job to help you figure out your dating rules."

He took in a deep breath and let it out slow. "Dating you is going to be difficult."

"You aren't the first person to say that."

"Dating me is far more than just difficult, Anita."

"Yeah, I know it's potentially life-threatening."

"Yes," he said, face solemn, as if the answer made him sad.

"Just promise me one thing."

"What?" he asked.

"If you realize you can't fight your serial killer urges when it comes to me, warn me."

"I will give you my word, if you will give me your word on something else."

"What?" I asked.

"That you will truly give me a chance to date you."

"Maybe we should figure out what dating means to us before I give my word. I'd hate to promise something and then find out that you meant something very different."

"That is both fair and logical," he said.

"Thanks."

"Then first we need to define what dating means to me," he said.

"Just you?" I asked.

"You know what dating means for you, because you've done it. I have not dated in any way that you would approve of for yourself."

"You've never taken a woman out to dinner or a movie or anything, not ever?"

"I've only done that if I was pretending to be someone else and the woman was necessary to maintain my cover."

"I keep forgetting that you and Ted used to be in the same business." In my head, I thought of them as supersecret assassins.

"We still are."

"Okay, so then we have to figure out what dating really means for you."

"How do I do that?"

"Figure out what you enjoy doing that someone else could do with you."

"Something that we would both enjoy?" he asked.

"Preferably, yes."

He nodded again. "I will think on it."

"Good. Now let's join the others and get back to work."

"I enjoy killing people with you. Could that count as a date?"

I shook my head. "No, nothing illegal counts."

He sighed. "Dating is harder than I thought it would be."

"Always," I said.

34

Newman told Olaf that he wanted to ask my advice about his fiancée and combining his career with a serious relationship. He even had a lead-in question ready to go, as if that was the only reason he wanted some private time with me.

"I mean, how do you get your fiancés to be okay with you spending so much time in the gym every week?"

"They work out with me or are doing their own workouts while I do mine."

"Simple," he said, "but I'd like to pick your brain about a few other things."

"Sure," I said.

"Jeffries, if you wouldn't mind riding back with Livingston and Kaitlin, I'll do the couple talk in the car, and that way, when we get back to the sheriff's station, we'll be ready to work."

Olaf was suspicious and not particularly happy about it, but Newman just vibrated with sincerity, so in the end, he rode with the state cops and I got into the car with Newman. He smiled and was perfectly normal until he saw them go out of sight; then he turned to me. He wasn't smiling anymore.

"What do you really want to talk about?" I asked him.

"I saw Jeffries touch your leg at breakfast."

"I thought you did."

"You told him to move it, and he did."

"Yep."

"Normally I'd leave it alone. I mean, I know you're not monogamous, and you handled it at breakfast."

"I hear a *but* coming," I said.

"But you didn't like him touching you, and there's some tension between the two of you that seems to get worse every time I see you together."

That was way too perceptive for comfort or for Newman's safety. The last thing I wanted him to do was try to talk to Olaf for me. "Like you said, Newman, I handled it."

"I'd say you could handle yourself with any man on the planet, but . . . Jeffries is a scary motherfucker."

It made me laugh. I wasn't sure why.

"Why was that funny?" Newman asked.

"I think I've just never heard you cuss," I said.

"I was a cop for four years before I became a marshal. Not much spooks me, but Jeffries does."

"I'm glad, Newman. I'm glad you understand he's scary. Whatever else we say here and now, I want one thing clear between us: Under no circumstances do you play white knight and talk to Otto for me. One, it will undermine me in his eyes, and I can't afford to look weak to him. Two, I'm not sure what he'd do to you if he thought you were somehow in his way."

"If it was anyone else but you and him, yeah, I'd be having a man-to-man talk with him about professional conduct," Newman said.

"But it's him and me," I said.

"Yeah," he said. He rolled his hands over the cool plastic smoothness of the steering wheel and watched them move as if it were important. I think he was just giving himself time to think. I sat in silence and let him gather his thoughts. "I really thought you would have been louder in the restaurant if anyone touched you like that."

"If it had been almost anyone else on the planet, I'd have probably dumped my water in their lap or made a scene at the table, but I don't want to humiliate Otto. I don't want to back him into that kind of corner ever."

Newman gave a little shiver, settling his shoulders deeper into his jacket. "Please don't, because I'd feel like I had to protect you, and I really don't want to fight him."

"I already covered this, Newman. Under no circumstances are you to try to protect me from Otto." There was a hard-tight feeling in the pit of my stomach at the thought of Newman being all gallant on my behalf with Olaf. I did not want Newman dying to protect my honor. If anyone was going to do that, I would do it myself.

"Are you telling me that if he gets out of hand with you, you want me to just leave the two of you alone? I know you're tough, Blake, one of the toughest people I know, but . . . I couldn't leave you alone with him if I thought he might . . . hurt you."

"I appreciate that, Newman. I truly do. But I don't want you getting hurt or worse because you stepped into Otto's crush on me."

"Is that what it is, a crush? That sounds like you're in junior high, and he wants to ask you out to the school dance. Whatever Jeffries wants with you, it's nothing that innocent."

Newman looked at me, and there was something in his brown eyes that was part pain, part knowledge of really bad things. He might not have seen everything I'd seen, but he'd seen his share. It was there in his eyes, raw. He was either honoring me by letting me see it, or he couldn't hide it in that moment. Either way, I'd treat it like the important thing it was. You don't parade your pain for just anyone in our line of work.

"You're right. It's not." Then I told him the lie that Edward had created to keep me safe from Olaf.

"So Forrester isn't your boyfriend?"

"No, but we let Otto think he is, because he respects Ted. Most of the cops that notice this whole dynamic, we let them think what they want to think about Ted and me, because we can't risk them telling the truth to Otto. If he ever finds out that Ted and I lied to him about being lovers, I don't know what he'll do, and I don't want to find out."

"Why can't you just say no and make it stick?" Newman asked.

It was a great question, and I didn't know how to answer it without telling Olaf's secret. It would be like giving away the secret identity of the Joker, if he had one. I'd have been okay with that, except Olaf, like any good villain, had made it clear that if his secret identity went up in flames, he'd make sure Edward's did, too. Burning Olaf was one thing. Destroying Edward's life with Donna and the kids was something else entirely.

"It's complicated," I finally said, and even to me, my words sounded lame.

"You've said no, haven't you?" he asked.

"I have."

"I really thought if any woman alive could make her 'no' stick, it would be you."

"So did I." Put that way, I hated it even more. I hated that Olaf was manipulating me into dating him, or at least manipulating me into manipulating him into thinking I'd date him.

"What aren't you telling me, Blake?" And again, Newman was too perceptive for comfort.

"Okay, I'll be as blunt with you as I can be. I don't want to have to kill Otto just to keep him from wanting to date me."

"Do you think it will come to that, seriously?"

I shrugged. "I think it might."

"Jesus, Blake, just report him to the higher-ups. They'll tell him to back off."

"You were a cop, right?"

"Yeah."

"How many women did you see that died with a court order of 'leave me the fuck alone' in their purses?"

Newman went back to looking at the steering wheel. "More than I want to remember." There was so much emotion in that one sentence that I could tell it had ghosts attached to it: all the people he couldn't save. That's the hardest lesson as a cop: You can't save everyone.

"I've decided that I'm a big grown-up marshal, and I'll handle Otto without going through channels."

"You let Forrester help you," Newman said, and looked at me again, the anger in his eyes still raw.

I almost asked, *Who couldn't you save? Whose death are you remem-*

bering and blaming yourself for? But I didn't. You learn early on not to ask certain questions.

"Ted is my mentor. I'm your mentor. I'm not letting my apprentice take this one for the team. It's tricky enough without me having to worry about you, Newman. I want to make sure that you and that fiancée of yours get to the altar."

"Are you saying that Jeffries would kill me?"

"Are you saying he wouldn't?"

"He's dangerous, yes, but I think he'd rape before he'd kill."

I had to fight to keep my face blank, because Newman was closer to the truth than I wanted him to be. "Well, you know the saying 'pillage first, burn second.'"

"Don't make a joke, Blake."

"I don't know what else to do, Newman. You offered help. I've refused it. If you keep helping me, then you're taking my agency away. You're in effect telling me that I am a helpless victim that needs you to rescue me, and that is not true."

"If Jeffries were into men, hell, Blake, I might take your help to rescue my ass."

The phrasing made me want to laugh, but I fought the urge off. "I appreciate you admitting that, Newman, but I'm a woman, and I had to get used to dealing with shit like this around puberty."

"That is a sad fucking statement, Blake."

"It's a sad fucking truth. Now, unless you want to explain to Jeffries where we've been all this time, you need to start the car and get us moving to meet up."

He started the car but didn't put it in gear. "I don't like this, Blake."

"I don't like it either, but we have a crime to solve and a life to save. We'll worry about the other shit later."

Newman put the car in gear. "Fine. What next on the crime solving?"

"I think it's time to talk to the only other person that was in the house when the murder occurred."

"You mean Jocelyn Marchand?" He started out of the parking lot and onto the only road through town.

"Yeah."

"There had to be more than just her and Bobby in the house with Ray, because the footprints don't belong to any of them," Newman said.

"Okay, let's go question the only other person who we know was in the house when the murder occurred."

"We could just go do that?" he said.

"You mean, leave Otto out of the crime solving?" I asked.

"Why not?"

"One, he's actually a good man in a fight, and he sees things at a crime scene that no one else will see. If he wasn't good at his job, I wouldn't put up with the other shit."

"So you think he'll be helpful."

"I do. I wish I didn't, but I do."

"Well, you are my mentor, so let's go get the big scary fuck and head to the hospital."

"Damn, Newman, you're even beginning to sound like me."

That made him laugh. My phone let me know there was a text. It was from Nicky. "Landed. Will head your way as soon as we get rental car." There was a heart emoji and a purple smiley face with horns after the brief message. The devil emoji made me smile, because it was so him. If it had been Nathaniel, the message would have been longer with way more emojis or a GIF. Micah would have just done lots of hearts. Jean-Claude wasn't big on texting.

I sat there staring at my phone, wondering who the *we* in the sentence were. I knew that they wouldn't include any of those three men, and they would include more bodyguards, because I'd texted Micah that we needed more muscle when I gave him the heads-up that Olaf was here. Nicky was a werelion, and he had the size and training to go up against Olaf if it came to that. I trusted Nicky and Micah to have sent the right people for the task.

"You smiled, and now you have a look on your face. Are you okay?" Newman asked.

"Yeah, Nicky and the rest of his people landed at the nearest major airport. They'll head this way once they get the rental car."

"Duke is going to be pissed."

"Tell him that I needed a booty call."

"More pissed," Newman said, smiling.

"Tell him I wanted more Therianthropes to help control Bobby."

"That, he'll believe." Newman looked at me, eyes narrowing. "You didn't just want me to invite the Coalition in to help with the case. You wanted more people to run interference between you and Jeffries."

"That last part is true, but I asked you to invite the Coalition in before Otto got here. Remember?"

"I remember, but it's still more backup for you with Jeffries."

"Ted will probably get here first, but yeah."

"Normally I'd either feel insulted or like you were manipulating me, but extra lycanthropes—Therianthropes—between us and Jeffries sounds like a great idea."

I agreed. He put the Jeep in gear, and we went to pick up Olaf.

35

We got good news when we pulled into the hospital parking lot. The judge had agreed to add another eight hours to the warrant of execution, thanks to Kaitlin's footprint evidence, but unless we had another name to put on the warrant by then, when the time limit was up, Bobby Marchand had to die. There would be no more extensions, so we had to find a clue and bust some crime. Newman had also given Bobby the name of the lawyer Micah had recommended. If all else failed, maybe the other branch of the law could come up with a delaying tactic.

Jocelyn Marchand lay against her snow-white hospital bed like the princess from a racially diverse cast of *Sleeping Beauty*. The pictures at the house had shown her as having grown up into a beautiful young woman, but they hadn't done her justice. She looked like her mother had cloned herself. I mean, I'd known she looked like her mother from the pictures, but when I saw her up close, the resemblance was almost eerie, or maybe it was her own beauty that was disturbing. Her skin was perfect without a drop of base makeup to hide flaws, though as far as I could see, there were no flaws to cover. Her hair lay in near perfect ringlets around her face. I'd never been able to get my curls to be that well-behaved. The only way to come close was for someone else to use a very narrow curling iron over and over until every curl was tamed and hung like bouncy spiral magic. Her hair wasn't black like the pictures had shown, but a nearly reddish brown. It looked natural, but you don't go from black to that without an expert dye job. I couldn't imagine what they'd done to take all that dark out of her hair to make it nearly auburn. Her eyelashes lay on her cheeks like thick black lace, as dark as the perfect curve of her eyebrows.

Olaf leaned in to whisper between Newman and me so that we could both hear. "She is awake."

Newman whispered back, "How do you know?"

I looked away from her face to her body and realized that she was feigning the deep, even breathing of sleep. The pulse in the side of her neck beat against her skin like it was racing. She was nervous, maybe even scared. Why?

"Pulse rate and breathing are wrong," I said.

Newman nodded and then said, "Jocelyn, I'm sorry but we have to talk to you."

She tried to keep pretending to be asleep, but the pulse in the side of her neck was beating so hard, it looked like a butterfly trapped under her skin and beating its wings to escape. Her chest stopped trying to rise and fall but went to something shallower.

"Jocelyn, you can't just pretend we're not here. I'm really sorry, but we have to talk to you," Newman said.

There was movement at the door behind us, and both Olaf and I turned toward it as a tall nurse stepped through the door. It hadn't been movement inside the room that had alerted me. I'd have sworn I sensed movement, but maybe it had been Olaf reacting to hearing her in the hallway that had made me turn. Whatever. He and I looked at the nurse as she came through the door.

She was well over six feet tall. I personally knew only one woman taller, and that was Claudia back home in St. Louis. Claudia was also a serious weight lifter, so she was the most physically intimidating woman I knew. The nurse looked to be in good shape, but she was as slender as most people her height. Words like *willowy* came to mind. Her pale brown hair was cut very short around a face devoid of makeup. She had high sculpted cheekbones and a wide mouth that made her brown eyes look smaller than they actually were. She wore a pink smock with little kittens on it as if it would disguise her size and make her more approachable, or maybe she just liked kittens.

"I'm sorry, but she's still sedated," the nurse said.

"She's feigning sleep," Olaf said.

"What he said," I said.

"We really do need to speak with Jocelyn. I'm sorry that it can't wait," Newman said.

"I'll get the doctor," the nurse said like someone who was going to tattle to your parents, as if the doctor would be able to convince us that Jocelyn was asleep when a mere nurse could not. She left in search of a doctor.

"Hi, Jocelyn. I'm Marshal Anita Blake. This is Marshal Otto Jeffries. We really need to speak with you."

Newman leaned over the bed and said, "Jocelyn, I'm sorry. I know you've been through a lot, but I need to talk to you."

She kept her eyes closed as she said, "Leave me alone."

"I would if I could, but it's a matter of life and death," Newman said.

That made Jocelyn open her eyes. She looked so much like her mother that her eyes being brown instead of extraordinary green was almost jarring. Until I saw her eyes, I hadn't realized just how well I knew her mother's face. I'd grown up seeing her mother in tabloids at the grocery store and on the celebrity gossip shows that my step-mother, Judith, had loved. It was almost like having a friend show up with the wrong eyes.

"What do you mean, Win? No one else could have died. It was just . . . Dad." The flicker of pain in her eyes when she said that last word was hard to watch, and I'd just met her. It had to be even harder on Newman.

"No, no one else is dead, and I'd like to keep it that way," Newman said.

"What do you mean?" Jocelyn asked.

Her voice was breathy and sounded far younger than I knew she was, or had I been expecting to hear the deep contralto of her mother out of that so-similar face? I hated to think that was it, but after my reaction to Jocelyn's eye color being different, I couldn't rule it out. I hated that I might be trying to put her mother over the top of her like a mask that she was supposed to wear, but if I kept the idea in mind that I might be doing it, maybe I could avoid actually doing it. I wasn't even sure that made sense really, but I'd lived as the ghost of my own dead mother for most of my life. Except for having my father's pale complexion, I looked like my mother's clone, too.

"We need to ask you about what happened, Jocelyn," Newman said.

"I told the police already."

"I know, but I wasn't there for the initial interview, so I need you to tell me . . . to tell us," he said, glancing behind himself at Olaf and me.

"I don't want to have to talk about it again, ever. It's done, over with. Dad . . . is dead and Bobby's dead. Everyone but me is dead," she said. Tears sparkled in her eyes; her fingers dug into the sheets like she was trying to find something to hold on to.

"That's just it, Jocelyn. Bobby isn't dead."

She stared up at him, eyes going wide, which made the tears slide down her cheeks. "He killed our father. You were supposed to kill him for what he did to Dad."

"And if he did kill Ray, then I'll do exactly that. But before I do something that I can't undo, I want to be absolutely certain that Bobby is guilty."

"What are you talking about? He did it. I found the body. I saw what his"—she made a gesture in the air like she was tearing at it—"claws did to my father . . . our father! How could he do that to Dad? How could anyone do that to their own father?" Her breathing was erratic, eyes too wide, pulse rising. She looked like she was on the verge of a panic attack.

I thought Newman would back off, but he didn't. He asked one of the questions we'd come here to ask. "Bobby said he was with you that night, that you left him in his bedroom about to pass out after shapeshifting. Is that true, Jocelyn?"

"I was not with him. What an awful thing to say! He's my brother."

Newman backed up both physically and verbally. "Of course not. All I meant was, did you see him start to pass out in his bedroom?"

"No, of course not! I saw his bloody footprints in the hall, and I saw what he did to Dad! That's what I saw!" She sat up and started flailing her arms, which put her in danger of pulling out her IV.

A shorter, dark-haired nurse came through the door, speaking soothingly to Jocelyn and telling us that we had to leave. She used one arm to keep Jocelyn's arm lower so she didn't pull out the IV, and then tried to get her to lie back down.

A dark-haired man wearing a white coat over business slacks and shoes came through the door with the first nurse behind him. Apparently, she'd found the doctor. "You cannot browbeat my patient like this," he said as he pushed us back from the bed so he could help the nurse soothe Jocelyn.

Newman said, "We did not browbeat her." His voice was firm and sounded convincing, but since Jocelyn was screaming, the doctor and the nurses probably didn't hear him.

The tall nurse who had met us first made shooing motions with her arms as if we were wayward children. We could have forced the issue, but it might literally have taken force, and they'd just put another needle of something into the IV tube. Jocelyn was going quiet and passive as we let the tall, brown-haired nurse usher us out. Her name tag read PATRICIA. She didn't look like a Patricia, far too athletic and forceful. Maybe a Pat or a Patty?

We walked far enough down the hallway to be out of earshot, and then we huddled together like a football team. We needed to figure out what had just happened and what we should do next.

"I didn't mean to imply that she and Bobby were an item," Newman said.

"Her reaction was a little over the top, don't you think? Or is she always this high-strung?" I asked.

"No, I wouldn't describe Jocelyn as high-strung or even the nervous type. She's usually very calm, cool, and collected."

"I guess finding your parent's murdered body would unhinge anyone," I said.

"By unhinged, do you mean, make hysterical?" Olaf asked.

"Yeah," I said, nodding as if he needed that to go with the word.

"She was not hysterical."

Newman and I looked at each other. "We just saw her act hysterical," he said.

"Saw her, yes, but her emotions did not match what you saw."

"Okay, explain," I said.

"When Newman asked his question, she was afraid."

"How do you know that?" Newman asked.

"I could smell it."

Newman sort of blinked at him and then went with it. Good for him. "She's been through a terrible event. Wouldn't she be afraid to remember it?"

Olaf shook his head. "The spike of fear happened when you asked her the first part of the question."

"You mean, 'Bobby said he was with you last night'?" I asked.

Olaf nodded.

"She sounded outraged," Newman said.

"She acted outraged, but her true emotion was fear."

"I could see disgust, outrage, anger, but why fear?" I asked.

"Maybe any memory tied to the murder is fear inducing?" Newman suggested.

"I might believe that, except that her emotions after that did not match the show of grief and emotional pain," Olaf said.

"How so or how not?" I asked.

"I smelled the fear, and there was panic to that, but then that went away. She smelled calm while she was screaming at us."

"Are you saying it was an act?" I asked.

"I am saying that she smelled different from her actions. I've learned that people can control most of their bodies, but not the change in scent."

"Do all emotions have a scent?" Newman asked.

"No, or if they do, I have not learned them yet. I am still relatively new at being a shapeshifter. Anita might ask one of her fiancés. They have lived like this far longer than I."

I appreciated Olaf conceding that Micah and Nathaniel might know more about something than he did. The Olaf I'd met years ago was too insecure, or too angry, to admit any weakness. Or maybe he just hadn't admitted them to a woman. Either way, this was an improvement.

"I'll ask them when we talk next."

Newman stepped into Olaf, which made me step into both of them. "Are you saying that Jocelyn was pretending to be more upset than she really felt?"

"She was."

Newman looked at me. "Do you think she was lying about something other than her emotions?"

"You got one question out, Newman, just one. Then she went hysterical, and the interview was over. The doctor won't want us near her again," I said.

"I might have to get a court order just to question her again."

"That takes time," I said.

"We have an extra eight hours, that's all. I don't want to waste that getting more judges involved. Besides, court order or not, if Jocelyn does another hysterical scene, we still won't be able to question her."

"Agreed," I said.

The doctor came around the corner, and you didn't have to be a shapeshifter to know he was pissed. It showed on his face and in his posture. "How dare you come into my hospital and threaten my patient?"

"We did not threaten her," Newman said.

The doctor held up a hand as if we should just stop talking now. "Nurse Brimley heard you. That's why she came to get me."

"Is Nurse Brimley the tall one, Patricia?" I asked.

"Yes."

"Did she actually say we threatened her?"

"She said you were browbeating my patient into hysterics. I don't know what gestapo tactics you people from the preternatural branch are used to doing in other places, but you will not intimidate anyone in this hospital. We had to sedate her again."

"I swear to you we asked one question," Newman said.

"I want all your names. I'm reporting you." The doctor got out his phone—to make notes, I think.

"For what?" I asked.

"For threatening my patient. She's been through enough."

"I swear to you that we did not threaten her," Newman said.

"The three of you looming over her bed would be threat enough," the doctor said. He had his phone out, and he was ready to type with his thumbs. "Give me your names."

"We didn't loom over her bed," I said.

The doctor motioned at Olaf with his phone still grasped in his hands. "How could he not loom? You should never have been in there alone with her!"

"Are you saying that someone over a certain height is scary just by being that tall?" I asked.

"No, but he is." The doctor had a point, but he'd pissed me off, so . . .

"Are you saying that someone's physical appearance, something they can't change or do anything about, like the color of their skin, is enough to cause you to be afraid of them?" I asked.

The doctor frowned at me, thinking through what I'd said. "I did not say anything about the color of his skin. He's white."

"Are you saying you have a problem because he's white?"

"No, of course not."

"Are you saying that you would have a problem if he wasn't white?"

"No, of course not!" The doctor was starting to be indignant.

"Blake," Newman said softly. I think he was warning me to stop poking at the doctor.

The doctor typed something on his phone. "Marshal Blake, what's your first name?"

"Anita," I said.

He shook his head. "No, he said his name was Blake."

"No, I was talking to Marshal Blake. I'm Marshal Win Newman."

"Can you spell your first name, please?"

Newman did. Then the doctor turned to me. "You're Marshal Anita what?"

"Blake, Marshal Anita Blake, and you are Doctor what?" I asked.

He typed my name before he said, "Dr. Jameson."

"Dr. Jameson, what?" I asked.

"Corbin Jameson. Why does it matter what my name is?"

"I just want to make sure your name goes on the wrongful-death suit along with ours. The more the merrier, you know."

That stopped him enough that he looked at me, really looked at me, maybe for the first time. "What are you talking about?"

"Tell him why we're here, Newman," I said.

Newman explained in the briefest terms that we were fighting a time limit, and when it was over, he would be forced to execute Bobby Marchand, but that we weren't convinced he was guilty of the crime. "That's why we're here, Dr. Jameson: to try to gather enough information to either clear the accused of the crime so we don't kill the wrong man or gather evidence that absolutely proves his guilt. Jocelyn Marchand is the only living witness to what happened that night, except for the accused. We can't trust that his information isn't self-serving, so that's why we're here."

"You are all just murderers with badges," Dr. Jameson said.

"Sometimes that's what it feels like, but this time I'm trying to save a life. Won't you help me save a life, Dr. Jameson?" Newman said.

The doctor looked at all of us, thinking for longer than I thought it should take, but we were ahead right now. I didn't need to do anything but keep my mouth shut. I think we all tried to look harmless and sincere. Some of us were better at it than others, but Olaf did his best.

"I want your name, too," Dr. Jameson said, looking at Olaf.

"I am Otto Jeffries, Marshal Otto Jeffries."

Dr. Jameson typed the name into his phone and then put it back in his coat pocket. He looked at us one at a time, studying us individually for a long time. It was like he was trying to weigh and measure our worth, or maybe he just thought if he looked at us long enough, we'd crack under his steely gaze. At least two of us looked at him calmly. Newman was having trouble with his blank cop face today.

"Very well. If you give me a number to reach you at, I'll let you know when the sedative wears off enough for Ms. Marchand to be able to speak with you, but only with myself and at least one nurse present. Is that clear?" He gave us his hard look again. It must have played hell on the nerves of his interns, but the three of us managed to remain calm.

Newman gave him his cell phone number and mine as a backup. We got the doctor's assurance that he would let us question Jocelyn when she woke up. It was the best offer we were going to get, so we took it and left.

36

"THAT WAS CLEVER," Olaf said as we walked across the parking lot.

"What?" I asked.

He looked at me. "Do not be falsely modest, Anita. You made the doctor falter in his anger and listen to us."

"I thought you were just teasing him because you didn't like him at first," Newman said.

"I wasn't sure which way it was going to go either, honestly, but I was hoping I'd find a way to slow him down. Sometimes if you can trip people up verbally, it's just like a foot sweep in a fight. You can make them stumble or lose their balance, and then you can move into the opening."

"Were you this good verbally when we met?" Olaf asked.

"No, not even close."

"Good. I did not like the thought that my hatred of women caused me to miss that much of your skill set."

"You hate women, and you just told that to a woman?" Newman said.

"I'm aware of how Otto feels about women," I said.

"We have no secrets from each other," Olaf said, looking down at me.

I met his eyes, shrugged, and said, "I guess we don't."

"I feel like I'm missing something," Newman said.

"Oh, you're missing tons of stuff, but it won't help save Bobby's life, so let's just focus on that," I said.

Newman hesitated outside his Jeep and then finally shook his head. "Keep your secrets. Today I don't care. Just help me find the real killer so I don't have to murder Bobby."

"It's not murder, Newman," I said.

"If I pull the trigger on Bobby knowing he didn't do it, badge, warrant, legal system, none of it matters, Blake. If I kill him knowing he's innocent, then I know it's morally wrong, and that makes it murder in my book."

"We are not the murderers here, Newman. Whoever framed Bobby is the murderer."

"You will be the method of murder, not the murderer," Olaf said.

That made Newman and me both look at Olaf. "What?" Newman asked.

"At the sheriff's office, you said the murderer was using you to complete their crime. That makes you the method of murder, or the weapon that the murderer is using to kill his second victim, but you are not the murderer," Olaf said.

"He's right," I said.

"I will not be the weapon they use to kill Bobby."

"Then let's find out whodunit," I said.

"How?" Newman asked.

"Ah, there's the rub," I said.

37

SHERIFF LEDUC MET us at the door to his office. "What the hell did you do? I got a call from a lawyer named Amanda Brooks telling me that we can't execute her client."

"It's a gray area, Duke. If Bobby is just going to sit in the cell for a while, then maybe he needs legal representation?" Newman said.

"No," Duke said. "No, he's supposed to be dead by now, and dead men don't get to call fancy lawyers to gum up the works." He was up in Newman's face, trying to put the brim of his Smokey Bear hat into his face the way he had with Deputy Rico.

Newman stepped to the side so that Duke almost stumbled, as if he'd been using the hat brim as support. He walked farther into the room past the sheriff, and I followed in his wake. Leduc was so angry with Newman that he didn't notice me. I got to see the rest of the room. Livingston was sitting in the client chair by Leduc's desk, and Olaf was in the chair at the deputies' shared desk. Kaitlin was leaning against the corner of the desk near Olaf. She had that friendly, relaxed look that some people get when they think their flirting is going well. Olaf was looking up at her. His expression must have been pleasant, or she wouldn't have looked so pleased.

Newman stayed near the door, talking to the sheriff. Since Olaf and Kaitlin seemed safe enough, I stayed near Newman in case he needed backup.

"I'm sorry you're upset, Duke, but it felt like the right thing to do."

"Doing your damn job is the right thing to do, Win!"

"I was a cop before I joined the preternatural branch. I'm trying to still be a cop."

"You never stopped being a cop, Win," Duke said.

"I still have a badge, but that's about the only thing that feels the same."

"Boy, you think too much."

Newman smiled, but not like he was happy with himself. "I know. My dad says I always have."

"If you know something's a weakness, then you need to work on fixing it," Duke said.

"I don't think it is a weakness. It's just part of who I am."

"A lawman that overthinks will hesitate when it's time for action."

"I've been in the field with Newman. He's just fine when the shit hits the fan," I said.

Olaf stood, leaving Kaitlin in midflirtation. "Newman does not hesitate in the middle of a hunt."

"High praise from the two of you," Livingston said.

"Praise where it's earned," I said.

"Many of the newer marshals think and weigh their morals more than is good for them on this job, but Newman will fight when it is time," Olaf said.

Kaitlin said, "Aren't we all supposed to use our moral judgment on the job?"

"On your job, perhaps, but on ours it is better not to have them."

"Not to have what? You mean morals?"

"Yes," Olaf said.

"But you can't help having a conscience," she said.

Olaf smiled at her and didn't try to push it up into the black emptiness of his eyes. She looked at him for a second and then shivered. His smile widened, but his eyes stayed the same: black and empty like the eyes of a shark.

"You're just playing with me, right?" Kaitlin asked.

"I do not know what you mean."

"You're pretending, right? Giving me the dead eyes like some kind of psycho."

Olaf smiled at her, and this time it was one of his real smiles, not the one he'd been using to pretend to flirt with her. It was one of the smiles he'd given me over the years—the one that said not only was he thinking about you without your clothes, but what you'd look like after your skin came off, or maybe after he took a real bite out of you. That wasn't his inner werelion talking. He'd thought shit like that long before he caught lycanthropy.

Kaitlin's eyes widened, her breath coming faster. I could feel her fear like something touchable that I could have dragged out of the air around her. I stepped between them, breaking their eye contact and taking her out of the game, because now Olaf was playing with her.

"We'll head back to the crime scene at the house. I need to check in with everyone," Livingston said.

Livingston hadn't seen the look that Olaf had given Kaitlin. Olaf was good at hiding in plain sight most of the time. I gave Kaitlin a little push toward her jacket, which Livingston was holding out to her. She moved and took it from him.

"Perhaps I could make an exception for you, Kaitlin," Olaf said.

She was putting on her jacket as she said, "What kind of exception?"

"Blondes. Perhaps I should try blondes just once."

When he said *once*, he looked at me. I knew what *once* with a woman meant for him. The thought of him taking all that intelligence, skill, and perky beauty away through torture made me sick to my stomach, and then the fear rose. I was afraid of him and what turned him on. His desires were so terrible, there was no way of taming what he wanted, no way of channeling it into dating. I saw the truth of him painted on his face aimed at another woman to get from her the kind of reaction he'd once gotten from me, and I hated him. Hated the complication of him, the fact that someone like him was one of only a handful of preternatural marshals who were as good as I was at this job. What did it say about me that someone like Olaf was one of my few equals at killing, or that I had more official kills than he did? Nothing good.

Behind us Newman was thanking Livingston for his help. If Kaitlin hadn't been spooked, only Olaf and I would have known how much of Olaf's mask had slipped. He enjoyed showing it like that in the middle of things to unsettle you, but only if he wasn't hunting you at that moment. If you were just prey, then he hid like a lion in the tall grass waiting until the antelope came a little closer. Kaitlin had gotten moved to my old category. It was more like a cheetah walking among the antelopes in plain sight, no cover, no pretense. The antelopes just didn't know when the cheetah was going to start running and which one it was going to run after. I was not a goddamn antelope.

I worked so hard to have control of my inner beasts, but in that moment, I wanted Olaf to remember that I wasn't food anymore. Yeah, he was bigger and stronger than I was, but that didn't make him king.

It was like the thought called my lioness, or maybe the thought came from her. Not in a human one-for-one way, but in her own way, she understood me and my world better than any of the other animals inside me. She'd made herself known to me in ways that were more about communicating than about trying to break out of the prison of my body and become more real. In the past she'd communicated her needs, and they hadn't been my needs, but this time I agreed with her: *Fuck you and your king of beasts, we both know who does most of the hunting.*

Olaf sniffed the air and shifted his gaze from Kaitlin to me. "I smell . . . I like your new perfume, Anita." He'd changed what he was about to say so that he didn't give our secret away. Yes, the others knew we both carried lycanthropy, but that wasn't the same thing as telling the humans that we smell like lion. Only lycanthropes— Therianthropes—seemed able to smell that phantom perfume when the beasts moved close to the surface.

"I'm wearing it just for you," I said, and my voice was an octave lower than normal.

"What's going on?" Kaitlin asked as she looked from one of us to the other.

Livingston rubbed his arms as if he was cold, but I was betting the skin on his arms was running in goose bumps. He'd sensed the power in the cell with Bobby and me, but that had been much closer to the surface. If he could feel it now, he was even more sensitive to it than I thought.

"You need any more help, Marshals?" he asked.

"No," I said, "but thanks for offering. We've got this." I was looking straight at Olaf when I said the last part.

"Do we?" Olaf asked, and his voice was a little lower, too.

"We do," I said.

My lioness stalked up that long path inside me, each footfall carefully placed like she was creeping up on a gazelle at a watering hole. We would not be able to sneak up on him, I thought. My lioness stared at me with those golden amber eyes, and I suddenly knew just what she meant: Olaf would not expect us to fight him. We were sneaking up on him in plain sight.

"If you both say so," Livingston said, and then, to the other men, he added, "Duke, Newman, why don't you step outside and see us off?"

"You go ahead," Newman said. "I just want to double-check something with my fellow marshals."

Duke started to protest, but Livingston took his shoulder and started talking about something to do with this year's chances for the local sport's team. It was enough to distract Duke and get him through the door.

"You should go with them, Newman," Olaf said.

"I'm good right here."

I had a moment of hesitation. On one hand, I didn't want to be alone with Olaf more than I had to be; on the other hand, I wasn't sure I wanted Newman at ground zero. The lioness gazed up at me with golden amber eyes, and thought/asked/translated my feelings that Newman was our cub, a big grown male cub, but still one we wanted to protect. She was right. I was treating Newman like a child, and he wasn't one. My confusion puzzled her, and she began to fade into that darkness inside me, but she left me with one thought: She wanted a mate but not one that would kill the cubs. No, it wasn't a word-for-word translation, but that was the gist of it.

I stood there, just me, the scent and the feel of her fading around me. But even with her gone, I still had the message. "Go out with the others, Newman."

"Blake, are you sure?"

"Yes," I said. I was strangely calm as I stared at Olaf.

He was still sitting down; even with my lioness thick on the air, he hadn't thought either she or I was danger enough to stand for. "You heard her," Olaf said.

"I wasn't asking you," Newman said.

"Go, Newman," I said. "We just need the room for a few minutes. It won't take long."

"It'd better not. I can't distract Duke for long."

I felt him move and heard the door shut behind him, but I kept my attention on Olaf.

"Where has your lioness gone, Anita?"

"She's still in there, here, and she has a message for you. We both do."

He smiled so arrogantly. He'd been the biggest kid on the playground for most of his life, and now he was a werelion. There's a certain arrogance that runs in them, too, because they're usually the biggest, baddest animals on the playground. I wondered if his attitude would have been better if he'd been turned into a wolf, or a leopard, but now we'd never know. The die was cast. Lion it was.

His smile was fading around the edges. I think I stared at him too long. He wasn't sure what I was doing, and he cared what I did now. It was a chink in his armor, just like my fear of him had been for me.

"What is the message, Anita?"

"She likes you. She thinks you would be strong enough to be my lion to call, and her mate."

The arrogant smile flared back. "Your inner lion is wise."

"She didn't understand why I didn't just jump at the chance to have you in Florida, but she understands why I hesitated now. We can't have a male that kills all the cubs. We'll be alone before we let that happen."

"Cubs? You have no children."

"Kaitlin is a cub, or a fellow lioness, and we are not okay with you playing cat and mouse with her."

"I was teasing. You know I do not like blondes."

"You did the same kind of teasing with me once."

"Are you jealous?"

I sighed and tried to think how to explain this to him. "Look, Moriarty. If I really am your Adler, then you know that I'm not okay with you threatening other women. You know that doing shit like that is not the way to my heart."

He frowned up at me now. "So now I cannot even tease and taunt other women? I have given up doing other things with them, because I know you will not approve. You have no idea what it has cost me to give up certain . . . things."

I took in a deeper breath and let it out even slower. "I have some idea, and I really appreciate that you're trying to behave yourself."

He stood up then, and he was angry. I had no idea why he was angry, but it made the heat in the room rise as if he'd turned up the thermostat. His beast's energy prickled along my skin. Jesus, he was powerful. My lioness stirred inside me, flashing golden eyes at me. If we could tame him, she liked him, but she finally understood that I thought he was a cub killer, and that wasn't okay with her either.

"I am not a child, Anita, to behave myself!"

"I didn't mean it that way."

"Yes, you did. All your men are pussy-whipped, but I will not be unmanned, not even by you."

Olaf took a stiff step toward me, his big hands in fists at his sides. I wanted to take a step back. The room wasn't that big, but he was so angry. It made me sniff the air as if rage had a scent, and in a way, it did for me now. His beast was warm, but his anger was hotter. A heat that would feel so good to drink down. My stomach almost cramped with the nearness of such a bounty. All I had to do was touch his skin with mine, and I could feed on all that rage.

I hugged myself, not trusting that I wouldn't do just that if he crossed the distance between us, because if anything would push me from would-be girlfriend to victim in his mind, it would be turning him into my gazelle.

I decided to try for truth between us. "You're not the only one that's trying not to make one of us into their victim, Olaf." We were alone, so I could use his other name.

He took another slow step. I should have been afraid, but I knew he wouldn't kill me just like that. He wanted too many things from me that a quick death wouldn't satisfy. "I have tried so hard with you, Anita. Harder than with anyone else."

"I know, and I'm trying to give you the same courtesy."

"What does that mean?" he asked, and there was a growl in his voice now.

My lioness was crouched inside me, ready to spring, but would that hurt me more than him? "It means I can feed on things besides sex, and I'm trying very hard not to feed on you."

"I know you are trying not to have sex with me."

Great. It was like he'd edited what I'd said and heard only the sex part. I should have known he would. "That's not what I said, Olaf."

"It is the truth."

"Yeah, because you can't guarantee that you would be satisfied with plain sex. Aren't we both worried that if we have sex, you'll want to push it to that next serial killer level?"

"I told you, Anita, there are things I want to do with you that require you alive and whole. I do not want just one night with you, but many, and for that, I have to find a different path with you."

The anger was beginning to fade a little. It helped that aching need inside me to let go of me. I'd eaten physical food recently. I'd fed the *ardeur* before I left home. I shouldn't have been having this much trouble with it yet. I was usually good for twenty-four hours at a time now with no ill effects. So why was his anger so tempting?

"And I'm trying to let you do that, but I feed off anger, too. Olaf, do you understand what that means for you and me?"

He frowned at me. "What do you mean, you feed on anger?"

"I mean I can feed on the emotion."

He frowned harder. "I don't understand."

"Have you ever fought a vampire that fed on fear?"

He nodded.

"Like that, but instead of fear, I feed on rage."

"So, when I became enraged just now, it tempted you?"

"Yes."

"But you do not want to feed on me."

"No, not like that."

"How long have you been able to do this feeding on anger?"

"A couple of years."

"Is this another of Jean-Claude's abilities you share?"

"No."

"Then where did you inherit it from?"

"We think another master vamp, but it may just be my own special thing. We're not advertising it, and I do my best not to use it."

"Why? Is it so terrible?"

"When it first started, I would wipe out a person's short-term memory, which was kind of hard to explain."

"And now?" he asked.

"It seems to weaken them physically, and either way they aren't angry anymore. It siphons that emotion out of them for a while."

"The vampires that feed on fear frighten their victims more, and each time it is more to feed upon."

I nodded. "Yeah. I had one guy that was pissed at what I was doing, and he just kept getting angrier. I drained him until he couldn't stand up anymore."

"Did you do it on purpose?"

"Not at first, but that last time, yeah."

"Why?"

"He sexual-harassed one of the other female guards, and then he disrespected me even after I told him who I was."

"One of your own bodyguards did this?"

I nodded.

"You had to establish dominance over him, Anita."

"Yeah, I did, but that's not what we're trying to do with each other. If I fed on your anger, it would be disrespectful and more than that. I think you're like me. I think that anger is the core emotion for you."

"I'm not certain I understand what you mean by core emotion."

"If I don't know what else to feel, I'm angry. There's this big end-less pit of rage inside me that's been there since at least my mother's death. I think you have your own version of that rage."

"Are you saying that I am some poor little boy angry at the world?"

"I share with you that my mother's death has fucked me up from childhood, and you try to take an insult from it." My own anger started to rise as it usually did.

"That is not what I meant to do," he said.

"Then stop taking insult where I don't mean it. I'm trying to ex-plain to you that I think we both run on a core of wrath."

"Perhaps," he said, face thoughtful, like he was trying to think with me, trying to understand.

"If we both run on rage, then feeding on yours would be like feeding on your soul. I don't want to do that."

He studied me, and I could almost hear the gears grinding in his brain as he tried to catch up with my reasoning. "I think you com-plicate things, Anita."

"I do, but that doesn't mean I'm wrong."

"You could have kept this ability secret from me and used it if I ever attacked you for real. It would have been a good defense."

"I thought about that, but we're trying not to get to that point, right?"

"Right," he said.

"I can't always control the feeding-on-anger thing. I've gotten better at it, but I've done it by accident more than any other ability that I have, and just now your rage smelled yummy."

"The sheriff has been angry enough. Why have you not fed on him?"

"I thought about it, but his anger didn't appeal to me. He doesn't appeal to me."

"But my anger did appeal to you?"

"Yes. I just said that, right?"

He smiled. "You did. You said it smelled yummy."

I rolled my eyes at him. "Maybe a different word would have been better, but it gets the meaning across."

"I like that you find my rage yummy, Anita." He took another step closer to me, but it wasn't a stiff, angry step. It was almost gentle as he reached out toward me.

I wanted to step back, but didn't want to give ground, and he hadn't done anything to hurt me yet. Part of me said *Back up! Hell, run!* But I couldn't keep running forever. I either had to make peace with him or kill him. If there was a third option, I couldn't think of it.

He started to touch my face and then hesitated. "May I touch your face?"

If he'd just touched me, I'd have accused him of not paying attention to the talk at breakfast, but he'd asked first. "Sure," I said. My voice wasn't sure at all, but it was the best I could do.

He put that big hand along the side of my face in a touch gentler than I thought he was capable of. He looked down into my upturned face. We studied each other; that was the only word I had for it. I admit that there was sexual tension between us, even on my end, but I thought, *What a shame he's so broken.* I don't know what he thought about me, but it couldn't have been too bad, because he asked, "May I kiss you?"

"I usually don't kiss until at least the first date," I said, trying for a joke, but my voice was breathless. You can't make a joke without the right delivery, and I had fumbled it.

"May I kiss you?" he asked again.

I didn't know what to say. Yes was logical, but no was safer, or maybe it was the other way around. I was beginning to lose the fight to keep my pulse and heart rate even. The hand on the side of my face was so big that he could have palmed me down to my neck, but the touch in that moment was gentle. He was playing by the rules I had so recently given him. I've always believed that effort should be rewarded.

I whispered, "Yes."

He leaned down toward me. I had a memory of the only two times we'd kissed before; both had involved us taking the heart and head of a vampire so that our arms were covered in blood. The violence and gore had excited him. How could I let him kiss me now? But I did. It was like his hand on my face, the gentlest of touches, and my pulse raced up into my throat so that I could feel his lips but taste my heartbeat on my tongue.

He drew back from me and whispered, "You're afraid of me now. Why?"

I had to swallow before I could answer, because my mouth had gone dry. "I remembered when we kissed before."

He smiled, and it filled the dark caverns of his eyes with happiness. "So did I."

I stepped back from him then and almost got hit by the door when it opened behind us.

"Are you coming outside, Blake?" Leduc asked as he looked at the two of us.

I nodded. "Yeah, just need some air." I pushed past him and stood in the cool air outside, taking in deep, even breaths of it.

"Are you okay?" Newman asked.

I don't know what I would have answered, because a rental SUV pulled up, and it was Edward.

38

I WAS RUNNING toward him before I'd thought it through. I had time to see that he was wearing blue jeans and well-worn cowboy boots but was missing the cowboy hat that usually covered his short blond hair. The whole outfit including the brown leather bomber jacket was so not Edward, but perfectly Ted Forrester. I wrapped my arms around his waist, because I knew Edward was in there somewhere. He hugged me back, but I felt that moment of hesitation in his body, because in all the years we'd known each other, I had never greeted him like that. The hesitation made me start to pull back, but he held me tighter, and whispered into my hair, "What happened? What did he do?"

We both knew who *he* was. I pulled back enough to see his face. His blue eyes were already starting to fade from bright to winter sky blue. That was the color his eyes were when he killed. I didn't want him to do anything unfortunate just because my nerves had gotten jangled. If we ever pulled the pin on the grenade that was Olaf, I wanted it to be for something real.

"Nothing. He's actually behaved himself well."

Edward moved us so that no one in the sheriff's office could see his face, and then he stopped pretending. The face was still the same face, but the expression on it was cold and matched the winter sky eyes. "Tell me the truth, Anita."

"I swear to you that Olaf has behaved himself. We've actually had two good conversations where he was reasonable and compromised."

His eyes narrowed. You didn't have to know him well to read the expression. He didn't believe me.

"My word of honor, Edward—Ted—that he has done pretty good, far better than I expected."

He settled his arms more comfortably around me and raised an eyebrow at me. I started to try to back out of the hug, but he held his arms in place. "You can get out of the hug when you explain to me why we're hugging in the first place. Are you lying about what he did so I won't go in there and shoot him?"

I frowned at Edward, my arms still around his waist. If he was holding on, then it was the most comfortable way to stand. "Well, if I actually thought you were stupid enough to kill him like that in front of witnesses, I might, but no, I'm not lying."

He gave me cynical eyes and raised the eyebrow again. "So why run into my arms for the first time ever?"

That was a good question. I tried to think of a good answer. You always seem to have more good questions than answers in life. I stared off into the distance rather than meet his eyes while I tried to put it into words. "I think maybe because he is being so reasonable."

"You realize that makes no sense, right?" he asked.

I nodded and looked back at Edward's face. "When we started letting him think I was or would be his serial killer girlfriend, I thought it was just a delay tactic until we had to kill him because he stepped over the line."

"It was," Edward said.

"But he's really being reasonable, Edward. I mean, like therapy reasonable, couple reasonable. I didn't think he was even capable of that, even to pretend."

"He's as good an actor as I am, Anita. Don't be fooled."

"You mean the way you fooled Donna?" I asked.

"Donna knows as much as she's comfortable knowing about who I am."

Since I'd been in their wedding and spent quite a bit of time around them and the kids, I could only agree. "Fair enough, and I'm sorry if I put you in the same category as Olaf, but he seems to really be trying."

"Trying how?"

I told Edward about the hand on the knee at breakfast and me reading Olaf the riot act. "And just now he asked permission before he touched my face."

I actually didn't want to admit that Olaf had asked for a kiss and I'd said yes. I was embarrassed or scared or something. The moment I realized just how conflicted I was about the last few minutes with Olaf, I knew why I'd run to Edward like some damsel in distress.

"You look calmer," he said.

"I think we can stop hugging now," I said.

"Why?" he asked.

"Because I figured it out."

He let me back out of the hug and then asked, "What did you figure out?"

"I'm not upset because Olaf behaved badly. I'm fucking freaked out because he's behaving so well."

"You said that already, and it still makes no sense."

"Yeah, it does, if you're inside my head."

Edward actually smiled at that. "Well, I'm not, so say it out loud."

"I'm trying to explain it." I stared up at him, frowning. "You once told me that Olaf agreed to try vanilla sex with me, which was the first time you knew of him being willing to try that with anyone."

"I remember."

"I can't remember if you encouraged me to just let him think I'd have sex with him or to have sex with him."

"Both at different times, I think," he said.

"Okay. Where are you on the question right now?"

"No real sex. Just play along."

"Good, but I can't keep pretending, Edward. Olaf is actually doing what I ask him to do so we can get to a point of going out on a date."

"No, Anita."

"I don't mean sex but dating, like doing something together to get to know each other better."

"He won't understand what that means, Anita."

"I agree, but if he's working this hard to try to meet me halfway, then it seems shitty that I won't go through with it."

"Run that by me again slowly," Edward said, studying my face.

"If I won't actually date him, then it's shitty to let him keep believing that I will."

"I told you, if he ever thinks you aren't his serial killer pinup, he will put you in the victim box. He'll probably kill me first, quick and efficiently, because he knows what I would do to him if he didn't. But then you would die, Anita, but it wouldn't be quick. It will be long and lingering and more terrible than you can imagine."

"I know you've seen what he does to women."

Edward grabbed my arm, and there was anger in his eyes, but there was also fear. Edward was afraid of almost nothing. "I have, and I never want to see it again. The thought of him doing that to you makes me want to go inside and kill him, witnesses or no witnesses."

I swallowed, because my mouth was suddenly dry. "Which is why the fact that he just asked, as polite as I've ever had anyone ask before, if he could kiss me scares the shit out of me."

"You ran out without giving him an answer? He won't like that, Anita."

"I gave him an answer," I said.

"He'll hate you saying no."

"I didn't say no."

"What did you just say?"

"I didn't say no."

Edward stared at me.

"Don't look at me like that, Edward. I feel bad enough."

He blinked, and I watched him fight to process it all. "So, you agreed to kiss him?"

I nodded.

"Anita, he's going to expect you to make good on that."

"I already did."

"What?" He looked shocked. I wasn't sure I'd ever seen him look quite that much at a loss.

"I said yes, and he kissed me."

Edward just stared at me for a few heartbeats, and then he finally asked, "What am I supposed to do with that, Anita? Do I ask how it was?"

"Gentle."

"What?"

"It was gentle. The kiss, the touch to my face—they were both gentle."

"He's not gentle. Don't let him fool you the way I've seen him fool other victims. You of all people know what he is."

I nodded a little too fast. "That's just it, Edward. I do know. So how the fuck do I tell if he's just pretending and setting me up for the kill, or if he's as sincere as he's capable of?"

"He is not capable of having a normal relationship, Anita."

I nodded again. "I think you're right."

That seemed to settle Edward down a little. It was rare to see his calm broken so badly. Once I'd lived for moments when I could make him drop his cool, but not now, not about Olaf.

"Good. Then we're still on the same page."

"Yes, but I'm not good at pretending things I don't feel. I will not be able to keep up this act for much longer, Edward. We're getting too close to me having to put up or shut up with Olaf, and I don't know what to do."

He took in a lot of air and let it out slow, as if he was thinking about our options because it wasn't just my life on the line. Yes, metaphysically the people tied to me might die if I died, but that wasn't all. Edward was right about Olaf probably starting with killing him. Olaf thought we were lovers, so if he was going to kidnap, rape, torture, and kill Edward's girlfriend and live through it, then he had to start by killing Edward. It was just logical, and underneath the pathology, Olaf was cold, dispassionate, and logical, just like Edward and me. Practical, we were utterly practical about survival most of the time. Of course, it wasn't logical for Edward to have tried to pretend to be my lover so Olaf would back off. It hadn't been logical of me to play along, or to keep talking to Olaf as if any change on his part would make him datable for me. It wasn't practical or logical that Olaf had been willing to compromise and grow as a person to get to a point where I'd been willing to agree to a kiss.

"I thought he'd cross the line with you before it got this far, Anita. It never occurred to me that he'd try this hard."

"Me either, but he is, so what the fuck do we do now?"

Edward shook his head. "I don't know."

Newman's voice rang out far louder than it should have for what he said. "Yes, Duke, Marshal Ted Forrester just arrived. Blake is filling him in on the case." Newman was telling us that the sheriff was about to get us in his sights. We weren't doing anything we didn't want him to see, but Newman didn't know that. Bless his heart, he was a good wingman.

I whispered fast, "What do I do when we go inside?"

"Did you kiss him in front of everyone?"

"No, of course not. Told him no romance in front of other cops."

"Then act like nothing happened and stay in sight of other people until we figure something out."

I might have said more about the mess of it, but I could hear the sheriff's feet crunching across the gravel of the parking area. He was almost here; we'd have to talk about the personal mess later. We had to put our cop faces on and catch the bad guys.

39

WE MOVED OUT from the SUV so that we were walking toward Leduc as he came rolling toward us.

"Newman and I have been on the ground since the start of this case, Marshal Forrester. We can fill you in on things that Blake wasn't here for." Leduc managed to sound belligerent and helpful, as if he was ready to cooperate or fight. The choice was ours or, rather, Edward's.

Edward went into full Ted mode, with a big grin, a hearty hand-shake, and an accent that was so down-home Texas, or what people thought cowboys from Texas would sound like, that it seemed over the top to me. "Well, that's mighty kind of you, Sheriff. Just let me get my hat."

He reached in and pulled out a cream-colored cowboy hat that matched the rest of the outfit. I refused to call it a white hat—it was off-white at best—but it was well-loved and well-worn, the brim shaped just so by his hands. Molded to his head by years of use, the hat fit him perfectly. The first time I'd see him wear it as Ted Forrester, I'd thought it had been going too far. He kept it even when everything else he wore was black. When he'd been just Edward, he hadn't even liked hats, and if he had, it would have been a black one. Edward was not a white hat, but strangely Ted was, as if the hat was to him what the glasses were for Clark Kent and Superman.

Ted patted the sheriff on the shoulder and got him talking and walking toward the office. Leduc opened up to him, answering questions about the area, though nothing about the crime. Ted was putting him at ease before we got down to crime busting.

Newman fell into step beside me. "I didn't know that Forrester had that kind of charm in him."

"Ted's full of surprises," I said.

Newman just nodded.

Ted and the sheriff went through the door, and Olaf came out of it. There was a small traffic jam as Edward and he shook hands, but then Olaf pushed past and came out on the small porch. He was suddenly between us and the office area. He was also between me and Edward, and I didn't like that one bit.

I stopped moving forward. Newman stopped when I did, glancing from me to the big guy. He ducked his head and spoke low to me. "Do you want me to stay out here with you or go inside?"

I patted his arm. "I appreciate the offer, but I don't want you to be part of my beard."

"Beard?" He seemed to think about it and then said, "Oh, that kind of beard."

He walked with me to the porch, but when I stopped on the steps, he tipped his hat to Olaf and kept going into the office. Edward hadn't come back out to check on us yet, and I was suddenly torn about if I was happy about that, but if we'd reached a point where I couldn't stand beside Olaf in public view, we were past the point of no return. We weren't there yet.

I did stay on the steps leading up to the porch for a moment, which made the height difference between Olaf and me even more ridiculous. I realized that part of what made me not want to step up was that I'd said yes to a kiss once. I didn't want him to ask again, because I didn't want to give the same answer, and I wasn't sure no was wise. It was like a weird game of sexual harassment, except that one of us would lose a hell of a lot more than just a job if we lost.

I finally made myself get on the porch, keeping the opening between the posts between us by leaning a shoulder against one of them, all casual-like. It also put my right hand closer to my main handgun at my side. It was probably overkill, but if it wasn't, seconds counted. I wasn't sure why the one gentle kiss had upped my anxiety this much, but I'd learned that I didn't have to understand my feelings. I just had to acknowledge them. My pulse was steady and slow, but I was more anxious around Olaf than I had been before the kiss.

He'd put his sunglasses on, so I couldn't see his expression. His face showed nothing. "Adler."

"Moriarty," I said, using the ridiculous nickname, and even that concession made me angry.

"I had begun to wonder if you and Ted had lied to me about being lovers. Attracted, yes, but in Florida at the wedding, I began to see how much he cared for Donna. It made me question whether he would betray her even with you."

I wished my sunglasses weren't inside the building, because I could feel my expression sliding away from blank. I decided I'd go for anger, always a good refuge for me. It was better than fear. "I don't understand what he sees in Donna either, but he loves her to pieces." I realized that, because I was talking to a serial killer, that might have been an unfortunate phrase, and just thinking that made me laugh. I think it was a stress reaction, but Olaf had never liked being laughed at.

His anger flared to life. "Do you think that is funny?"

"No, I mean . . ."

His anger burned hotter, and I felt the first stirring of his beast tickling along my skin. It made me tell the truth, because I couldn't think of a good lie. "It was my comment about him loving her to pieces. I just had a moment of thinking that was maybe an ironic phrase to use with you."

I fought not to rub at my arms where the goose bumps ran with his power, and the first stirring started deep inside me as my lioness woke to his energy. She was just a glimpse of golden fur in the dark sanctuary down inside me, where nothing should have been but me.

"Do you think that is how I like my women, in pieces?" Olaf said, and his voice was a few octaves lower. I wasn't sure if it was his beast getting stronger or if something had excited him. I was kind of hoping for his beast in that moment, though logically I should have wanted it the other way.

I sort of shrugged. "I know you like to cut the bodies up, so maybe it's not technically pieces."

"There is no fear when you say that."

My lioness flashed her amber eyes at me as she seemed to gaze up that long dark well that was my visual for where the beasts lived. She put one big paw on the ground that just suddenly appeared as part of my visualization. One of the ways you stayed sane with an inner menagerie was to have a visual that your human mind could understand, so my beasts always walked up a path toward *me*. It helped me keep them as their own separate beings and not deal with the fact that they were inside me like my tonsils or appendix, except that the beasts couldn't be removed, and the tonsils couldn't cut their way out of my body.

"I've watched your face while we cut up bodies together, Otto. I know that it excites you." That thought quieted my anger and my nerves so that the lioness hunkered down on the path, but didn't vanish back into the dark. She was waiting. We both were. We just weren't sure for what.

"Doing it together with you excites me, Adler."

"Come on, Moriarty, doing it on your own flips your switch, too."

He nodded. "I enjoy my kills very much." His voice was even deeper as he said the last two words.

"We'd better get inside before Ted runs out of charming things to say to Duke," I said, trying for casual even though my pulse had sped up. I pushed away from the post to move toward the door.

"I believe that you and Ted are more than friends now."

"Good," I said, and reached for the door without taking my eyes from him.

Eventually the nervous tension was going to get to me, and I would need action to work it out. I was ready to go through the door or fight—something, anything, to stop the rising tension and the nearly burning energy of his beast against my skin.

"And cool your beast, or you're going to change right here on the porch," I said, voice low.

"I am not even close to losing control of my lion, and you know that—just as you are not," he said, and sniffed the air like he was trying to get a stronger whiff of some delicious scent. "But I can smell your lioness." He caressed his fingertips down his own arm like he was touching something else. "I can feel your power on my skin, as you can feel mine."

If he'd been one of my fiancés, it might have been nice foreplay talk, but since it was him, it wasn't that kind of exciting. My pulse sped faster, my heartbeat starting to thud, but not because of sexual attraction, unless you thought fear was sexy. Oh, wait. He did.

The door opened beside me, and I was concentrating so hard on Olaf that it surprised me. I even made that little *eep* sound that only women seem to make. My pulse thudded in the side of my throat like a trapped thing. I couldn't swallow past it to say anything to Edward in the doorway.

His voice was Ted's drawl. "Y'all going to join us in here, pardners?" The expression on his face went from Ted's warm smile to Edward's cold one in seconds, so his affect didn't match his words at all.

Olaf spoke in a low, growling whisper. "You ran to him the way a woman runs to a man she thinks will protect her. Only prey runs to others for protection."

And just like that, I saw the danger. If I'd changed lists in his head from fellow predator to prey, then we were in deep trouble—the kind that meant that at least one of the three of us would not leave this town alive, and if things went really badly, it would be two out of three.

40

I LOOKED AT Olaf and all I could think was *This is it. We will have to kill him.* My lioness crouched inside me as if readying herself for a real leap, as if she could help me fight him. My hand touched my gun, but Edward came up with a better idea. He called back to the others in the office and said, "Give us a minute, pardners," and closed the door so we had some privacy.

"Anita trusted you to keep her safe in Florida when that car almost ran into us," Edward said, the Ted slipping out of his voice the way it had slipped from his face.

Olaf actually startled, his whole body reacting to it. My pulse slowed down, the fear of the moment replaced with the memory of older fear. We'd piled too many of us in a car on a hunt in Florida. Long story short, I'd ended up sitting in Olaf's lap because I didn't fit anywhere else. It sounded stupid and careless now, but it had made sense at the time. A car had nearly crashed into us and only the driver's car-handling skills had kept us from either being T-boned or flipping over. The fact that I had broken my solid rule about seat belts in that moment . . . I thought I was going to die, but Olaf had folded his arms around me. He'd kept me safe with the strength of his hands, his arms, his body wrapped around mine. His legs and body braced to keep us both in place. In that moment I had curled myself against him, burying my face against his neck, and held on to him, and weirdest of all, I had known that he would keep me safe even if it meant putting his body in harm's way. In that moment all the strength that I normally feared had been my shield.

"I did," I said, my voice a little breathy.

My lioness relaxed against the path inside me; she rolled herself on that dark ground, remembering the surety of Olaf's strength. She'd made no secret of the facts that she liked his lion and that she wanted a mate. I'd told her she couldn't have Olaf, but I hadn't found anyone else to put in his place. Of all my unmatched beasts, she was the "loudest" about missing her other half.

"You didn't see Anita as prey after you saved her in the car." Edward made his words a statement.

"No," Olaf said, like he wasn't sure he was happy with the answer, but it was still the truth.

"Being able to protect someone you care for doesn't make them weaker, Olaf. It makes you stronger," Edward said.

Olaf frowned, and even though he had sunglasses on, you could see him fight to understand the concept. "That Anita trusted me to keep her safe did feel . . . good."

"That's what it feels like to protect a woman that you care about."

Olaf stared at him, frowning so hard that his handsome face gained lines I'd never noticed before, like a preview of what he might look like in a few decades. "She did help me torture the waitress in the restaurant later, after that." His voice was hesitant, almost thinking out loud. He'd now lost me on his logic train, but apparently Edward was still on board, because he explained Olaf's thinking.

"Would you have played your part in threatening the suspect if you hadn't had that moment of trust with Olaf in the car?"

I thought about the question, like, really thought about it. I hadn't enjoyed scaring the waitress, but she'd helped kidnap other women, knowing that they were going to die horrible deaths. If we hadn't gotten her to tell us what she knew right then and there, more innocent women would have died. It had been necessary, and it had been frightening to me how easily Olaf and I worked together to gain her information. She was a lycanthrope, so nothing we cut off wouldn't grow back, and we'd saved the women who were still missing, so I counted it as a win, but it wasn't one of my proudest moments. Truthfully, I tried very hard not to think about it.

"No, I don't think I would have, but it wasn't just that. I saw him with your kids. I didn't realize he was Uncle Otto the way I was Aunt Anita to them until the wedding trip." I looked up at the big man. "I don't know how much was pretend on your part, but Becca and Peter trust and love you. They helped me be willing to stand on the other side of the woman in Florida and do what we did." There, that was the absolute truth.

Olaf nodded. "You stood beside me in the firefight and never faltered. I never thought to find a woman that would have such courage."

"Thank you." Now was not the time to lecture him on the fact that women could be just as brave as men. Edward and I were winning this discussion; never argue when you're winning. "I knew you wouldn't let me down in the fight either."

"You trusted me," Olaf said.

I nodded. "Yes."

The frown lines were smoothing out, but you could almost hear the gears working in his head again. Sometimes new thoughts can be almost painful, especially if they're fighting with older thoughts or, worse, older certainties that are no longer certain.

"I have had women trust me in the past, but they did not know the truth of me."

"You were hiding your truth from them," I said.

"I was."

"The lion has to hide in the long grass so the gazelle doesn't see it," I said.

Olaf nodded. "Yes."

Edward said, "But the lions don't hide from one another."

Olaf and I glanced at him. In my head I thought, *Well, sometimes they ambush other prides in the wild.* But again, we were winning, so there was no need to talk real-lion biology when we were ahead.

"No, they do not," Olaf said.

"The lions trust one another on the hunt," I said.

"Will you help me hunt the gazelles, Adler?"

"It depends on the gazelle, Moriarty."

"I don't understand."

I tried to think how to explain it to him without insulting him. "I can help you on legal hunts when hurting or killing people saves other lives."

"She won't help either of us hunt victims that she sees as innocent," Edward said.

Olaf made a derisive noise. "No one is innocent."

"How about children?" I asked before I could think if doing so was a good idea or not.

"I do not hunt children."

"Good to know because that would be a hard line for me, too."

"Child vampires are an exception," Edward said.

"They aren't children," Olaf and I said together. It made me smile, and after a moment of missing his social cue, so did he.

"Vampires will still kill their own kind for bringing over children. It's forbidden for so many reasons," I said.

The thoughts that went with that knowledge wiped the smile off my face. Kid vamps were always crazy as fuck and usually sadistic or broken in some other major way. Teenagers could sometimes manage to survive okay, but if the victims were younger than puberty, vampirism just fucked them up.

"I am disappointed that this case is about keeping the wereanimal alive," Olaf said. "I had hoped to help you kill him."

"Even though he's a he and not a she?" I asked.

"I told you before, I will help you kill your preferred victim so long as we kill together."

He had, which again was high praise from Olaf, just creepy-as-fuck high praise.

"From what I understand about the case, aren't we trying to find the real murderer so that we can save the suspect's life?" Edward asked.

"Yeah," I said.

"That is what Anita wants to do," Olaf said.

"The warrant of execution may have the suspect's name on it, but the way they're written, they leave us legally able to hunt anyone involved in the murder," Edward said.

I hadn't really thought that far ahead. Save Bobby Marchand, and then we'd see where we were legally.

Olaf smiled. "You mean we can still execute the real killer?"

"Legally," Edward said.

"Newman and I both think the killer is human. They could go to trial for murder."

"They could," Edward said, "but they already killed once and are trying to use the marshal system to kill a second victim. Do you really think they deserve more consideration from the law just because they're not preternatural?"

"Legally, that's the way the law is written," I said.

"It's just as legal to execute them for it here and now and save the taxpayers a trial," he said.

I looked at Edward, trying to figure out if he was humoring Olaf or really believed what he was saying. I finally said, "I'm not sure how I feel about your reasoning."

"You argued legalities, Anita. The law is on our side."

I sighed, and it was my turn to frown. "I'm fine with killing them if they're trying to kill us or others. I'm fine if it saves lives, but cold-bloodedly killing them just because we can if they aren't a danger to anyone else . . . Not sure I can sign off on that."

"I will hope that the murderer threatens more victims, then," Olaf said.

"Thanks for not saying you hope they kill more people."

"You are welcome," he said.

I still wasn't sure if Edward had said it all to give Olaf hope that we'd get to torture and kill as a couple again, or if he'd meant every word he said. I hoped he hadn't meant it. If we had time and privacy later, I'd ask Edward. I might not like the answer, but I'd like myself less if I was too afraid to ask the question.

41

WE INTRODUCED MARSHAL Ted Forrester to Bobby. In clothes, he looked less like a victim and more like a person. He wore jeans, a T-shirt, and jogging shoes, as if he were going to walk out of here soon. That wasn't true, but the clothes made him seem more real somehow. Bobby's attitude was more solid now, too, as if the clothes had given him more confidence, or maybe he just felt more himself in them. The deputy who had brought his clothes had forgotten a belt, so Bobby kept pulling his pants up as he paced in his cell. He'd started pacing when we asked him to give us more details about the night of the murder. I didn't need Olaf's supernatural senses to know Bobby was nervous and hiding things from us. Bobby ran one hand through his straight blond hair so often that if it had had any body to it, it would have been a mess, but lucky for him it was so straight and so baby fine that it just kept falling back into place.

The five of us watched him pace back and forth behind the bars like we were at a zoo. Newman said, "Bobby, we're trying to save your life here. Duke is pissed that I gave you the name of the lawyer that's willing to try to help you, but it doesn't matter what the rest of us do if you won't help yourself."

"I told you what happened that night." He gave a quick look up at us and then went back to staring at the floor as he paced. He couldn't even meet anyone's eyes for long. He must have sucked at bluffing in poker.

I tried. "You said that Jocelyn saw you pass out in your bedroom after you shifted back to human."

He nodded and stopped walking long enough to look at me, and then his eyes were back to the floor and the pacing recommenced as if he had lost something small and had to stare at the floor hard to find it.

"We talked to her, and she said she didn't see you in your bedroom that night."

That made him hesitate between one step and the next, then stumble. He studied my face to see if I was lying to him. I kept my face calm because I wasn't lying, so it was even easier than normal when interrogating a suspect.

"But she saw me pass out, or start to. I mean, I saw her in the doorway as I started to black out."

"Jocelyn says she wasn't in your bedroom that night."

"I didn't say she was in my room, just that she saw me pass out. She saw me change back to human, and she knows I came in the window like I always do. I never even went downstairs as a leopard that night. Joshie knows that."

I shrugged. "She says you did it, Bobby, that you killed her dad."

"Did she see me do it?" he said, and he finally seemed indignant.

"No, she just found the body," Newman said.

"Then I don't understand. I've been thinking about it, and I remember going hunting outside in the woods. The deer I killed should still be in the tree outside my window. It's where I stash kills that I can't eat all at once."

"Leopards in Africa put kills in trees so lions and hyenas don't get to them. What are you hiding your kill from here?" I asked.

He shook his head. "Coyotes mostly, though a lot of animals will scavenge. Even the animals that can climb or fly are less likely to try it with the carcass so close to the house. If there's a fresh deer in the tree, then what I'm remembering is true and I didn't kill Uncle Ray."

"You seemed pretty certain you did it when you first woke up in the cell," Duke said from the doorway to the offices.

"I woke up covered in blood, and you told me I'd killed Uncle Ray.

What else was I supposed to think? I've been trusting your opinions since peewee football league when you were just one of the other dads. You gave all of us on your . . . on the team better advice on how to play than our coach." Bobby had almost said *your son's*, I think. I wanted to know the backstory of Leduc's dead son, but not enough to pry into something that painful.

"You said you didn't remember before," I said.

"I didn't, except in glimpses—sometimes it's more like remembering dreams than real memories."

"You have been a shapeshifter for over ten years, and you still only remember as if it is a dream," Olaf said.

"Yes. Do you remember your full moons?"

"More clearly than you do."

"Bobby also shifts only into a leopard about the size of a normal one," I said.

"Really?" Edward said.

"That is not typical," Olaf said.

"I just thought it was because Bobby doesn't seem to be very powerful," Newman said.

"That just affects how many forms you shift into, not how big each of them is," I said.

Bobby looked at us, his hands wrapped around the bars of the cell, and I was suddenly aware that his hands fit through the bars and the hallway was narrow. If he'd been a regular shapeshifter, I wouldn't have wanted to be standing this close. I realized that Edward was standing farther away from the bars. Olaf had moved up with me, but then he didn't have to worry about Bobby's extra strength or speed, because he had his own. I had some of my own, true, but that wasn't it. I didn't see him as that dangerous, because he probably hadn't killed his uncle, and . . . he was so not in the same power level as the shapeshifters I lived and worked with regularly. But small dogs can still bite. When had I decided Bobby was more person than suspect? Oh, now I remembered: when I put my body between him and a bullet. Yeah, saving someone's life usually made me feel protective toward them, damn it.

Bobby leaned his face in closer to the bars and sniffed loudly, and then he rubbed his cheek against the bars. I wasn't even sure he realized he'd done the second part. "You must only hang out with really powerful shapeshifters if you think my leopard is small."

I moved back from the bars so I could give Edward better eye contact. Olaf moved back with me. Newman stayed near the bars. He wasn't being cautious enough either, especially after seeing Bobby go apeshit earlier.

"So you guys haven't seen many shapeshifters with animal forms as small as regular animals either?" I asked.

They both shook their heads.

"The wereleopard that was my mentor was my size in animal form," Bobby said.

"Did he contract lycanthropy in Africa, too?" I asked.

Bobby nodded. "He contacted Uncle Ray because he heard about my attack in the news. His story was almost identical to mine, except that they hadn't been able to kill the shapeshifter that attacked him and his friends."

"I was wondering if it's a different strain from the one that's here in the United States," I said.

"I've never hunted in Africa," Edward said.

"I have worked there," Olaf said, "but I had no business with any Therianthropes while I was there."

"We have a few low-level people at home that don't get that much bigger than a regular leopard, but even they're bigger than Bobby's beast."

"Then you may be correct: The African strain might be a different strain from the one we have in America," Olaf suggested.

"It would have to be different from most of Europe as well," Edward said.

"All the Therianthropes I know came from parts of Europe, so yeah, agreed," I said.

"I've seen them in Europe. They look mostly the same as they do here," Edward said.

Olaf nodded.

"Why does it matter how big he gets, or any of that?" Duke asked.

I answered, "Maybe it doesn't matter, but then again, sometimes the esoteric shit is what makes or breaks a case, or what helps keep us alive on the next hunt."

"Whatever happens here, Duke," Edward said with more accent than he'd used in the last few minutes, "we go on to other cases, other monsters. The things we learn here may help us save lives later."

"They are working on a cure for lycanthropy," Olaf said. "Perhaps investigating the African strain and comparing it to others would help in that search."

"They've been looking for that for decades," Duke said derisively.

"They are much closer than they were," Olaf said.

"Really?" Bobby asked.

Olaf nodded.

"How do you know?" I asked before I remembered that we weren't alone, and this should have waited.

"I was offered to take part in some of the research."

I so wanted to ask more questions, but I'd wait until it was just the three of us, because we had too many secrets from everyone else here to risk it.

"Did you try a cure?" Bobby asked.

"No," Olaf said.

"Why not?" Duke asked.

"Some of the side effects were worse than the disease in my opinion."

"What side effects?" Bobby asked.

Olaf shook his head. "I had to sign a nondisclosure agreement to be considered for the program."

This was all news to me. I fought not to show it or to glance at Edward and see if it was news to him. I knew that Olaf talked to Edward more than he talked to me. I'd ask later.

"Must have been some serious side effects for you to prefer being a monster," Duke said.

Olaf looked at the other man as he said, "I always prefer to be the monster."

Duke didn't seem to know what to say to that. "Well, suit yourself."

"In all things," Olaf said.

"Spoken like a man who's never been married," Duke said.

"Or in a serious relationship," Newman and Edward said together. Newman smiled at Edward, who smiled back automatically, but it didn't quite reach his eyes. If Newman noticed, he didn't show it.

"I am learning that if one wants more from a woman than what I have had in the past, some compromise may be necessary."

"You finally find someone that makes you willing to compromise, Jeffries?" Duke asked.

"I have," Olaf said, and he looked at me. To me it felt like he was making it painfully obvious.

Duke looked from Olaf to me, and then he opened his mouth to say something, but Edward stepped in and spoke first.

"Is there a room where we could question the suspect in private? I think we're all getting distracted," Edward said.

His accent was a little less thick and more him. It used to be that he lost the accent only when emotions ran strong, but lately I'd begun to wonder if he was tired of always being in character. It had been one thing when Ted was his part-time persona, but now that he was doing more marshal work than anything else, he was Ted more than he was Edward. Maybe he was ready to be himself even with a badge.

"The only way he's coming out of that cell is if a judge orders it or for Win to finally do his duty. We don't have anywhere else that's as secure as this," Duke said.

"Then maybe we need more privacy here," Edward said, and there was only the faintest hint of accent.

"You can't kick me out of my own jail," Duke said.

"We're not saying that, Duke," Newman said.

"It sure sounded like that was what Forrester was saying."

"I'm just saying that we all need to narrow our focus and concentrate on the job at hand. We can talk about African lycanthropy and other things later," Edward said.

"Agreed," I said.

Olaf nodded. "Agreed."

Edward looked at Newman and me. "Did anyone see a deer in a tree?"

Newman shook his head. "But we weren't exactly looking for it either."

"If you still have people on-site, call and have them check," Edward said. The words were his, but he kept his Ted accent. His own accent was middle-of-America nowhere, as if he could have come from anywhere.

"Rico was still there when I left. I can ask him to check," Deputy Frankie said from out in the offices.

Apparently, she'd been standing behind the sheriff the entire time. I was too short to see her there. Though since she'd just departed from the hallway in front of the cells because there wasn't room for all of us, I should have known she hadn't left completely. Once she'd realized that she had three of the Four Horsemen of the Apocalypse in front of her, she'd started to sort of quietly vibrate. I'd thought she'd been excited to meet a senior female officer, but apparently that hadn't been it. I was one of the horsemen!

"That'd be mighty fine, little lady—I'm sorry, Deputy Frankie." Edward even wasted a Ted smile on her, which meant he was tall enough to see her past Leduc.

"It's okay, Marshal Forrester. You can call me little lady if I can call you Ted."

"Ted it is, little lady."

Was she flirting with him? Or was she sort of hero-worshipping and flirting with all of us? It could be weirdly hard to tell the difference sometimes.

Deputy Frankie laughed; it was damn near a giggle. It made me frown at Edward, but he either missed it or didn't care, probably the latter.

She got Rico fast enough, but then the conversation began to go downhill. Rico couldn't seem to wrap his head around the idea of looking for a deer in a tree. "Rico, stop overthinking it and just look for a deer in the damn tree," she said. A few moments of silence followed as she listened to him, and then she said, "Because we're trying to check the suspect's version of things, that's why. Now, just go do what I asked." She lowered her voice a little, and said, "You're making us look bad in front of the feds, Rico."

Duke had moved out into the office—to make more coffee, I hoped. I was starting to need more. It meant we could see Frankie in the doorway. She hung up and sighed, shoulders slumping.

"It's okay, Frankie," Newman said. "We don't blame you because Rico is an idiot."

Edward and I both looked at him, but Edward remarked on Newman's comment in his best Ted voice. "Now, there, pardner, not sure that was very politic."

"I know Rico personally, Forrester. Trust me. I could have said worse, and it would still be true."

"Win, I know you don't like Rico, and I know why. He's always tomcatting around after some woman, but he's usually better on the job than this," Frankie said.

A laugh came from the other cell, which we were all sort of ignoring. Deputy Troy Wagner laughed like he meant it. "God, Frankie, that was the politest thing I've ever heard anyone say about Rico and women. He's a man whore, and everyone in town knows it."

"Well, at least Rico isn't in a cell with attempted-murder charges hanging over his head," she said.

The laughter died, and Troy leaned the top of his head against the bars of the cell. "Yeah, I guess you're right on that."

"I'm sorry, Troy. I shouldn't have snapped at you," Frankie said.

"Don't be sorry when you're right," he said.

"I still shouldn't have said it to you."

"I don't want Troy to go to jail," Bobby said.

"He tried to kill you," I said.

"I know, but if the only difference between it being legal and illegal to shoot me is having the right badge and the right name on a warrant, then it seems almost wrong to punish Troy."

"That's mighty decent of you there, Marchand," Edward said.

"I don't deserve any mercy from you, Bobby," Wagner said.

"I don't think mercy is something you deserve. I think it's just something you're supposed to give to people," Bobby said.

"If you'd done your job like you were supposed to, Troy wouldn't have gotten tempted to do something stupid," Duke said.

"Regardless of what I did or didn't do, what Troy did was against the law," Newman said.

"I can't make it up to you, Bobby. I can only say that I couldn't do it. Even when I thought you had killed Roy, I couldn't shoot you," Wagner said.

"I know, Troy," Bobby said, walking closer to the shared cell bars between them.

"He shot into your cell while you were chained to the bed, Bobby. I think he missed the first shot by accident," I said.

"Are you saying you wouldn't forgive him?"

"Yeah, I'm saying I wouldn't forgive him."

Bobby shook his head. "If my life is ruined, no sense taking Troy down with me."

"You aren't taking Troy down with you. He did that all on his own when he aimed at a prisoner that was already chained in a cell. If you hadn't been able to break your chains and hide under the bed where he couldn't get off a second shot, you might be dead now," I said.

"Some things you just don't do, pardner. Shootin' someone chained up in a cell is one of 'em."

"It is like a caged hunt," Olaf said. "There is no sport in it."

"No," Wagner said, "I swear I was done with that first shot. Doing it seemed to bring me to my senses. Thank God I missed."

"Yeah, otherwise it would be murder charges instead of attempted murder," I said.

"That's throwing a lot of stones for preternatural marshals,"

Duke said. He'd come back to peer over Frankie's shoulder at us. I could smell coffee brewing, which put me in a better mood, so I actually let it go, but Newman didn't.

"What's that supposed to mean, Duke?"

"You pound stakes through the chests of vampires chained up and covered in holy items in the morgue or in their coffins. That's more of a canned hunt than any cell."

We looked at him. Whatever Duke saw on our faces made him hold his hands up in a push-away gesture. "If I'm wrong, I apologize."

"You're not wrong," I said, but not like I was happy about it.

"We're busting Deputy Wagner's chops, pardner, because the morgue stakings are part of our sworn duty as preternatural marshals. Wagner was supposed to be guarding the prisoner, not trying to kill him," Edward said, smiling like Ted, but his eyes were starting to fade from the bright blue they had when he was happy.

"The morgue executions are the first kills they give to new marshals," Newman said, his voice sounding about as happy as mine had.

"Then isn't that worse than Troy trying to shoot someone in a cell, even chained up?" Duke said.

"Yeah, a vampire chained down and covered in holy items is more trapped than Bobby in the cell here," I said.

"But like I said, pardner, those are legally sanctioned executions," Edward said, accent still strong, but his eyes were leaving the blue range and entering gray. You didn't want him upset with you when his eyes got to their palest gray-blue, like winter skies before a blizzard falls on top of your head and destroys your world.

"So, if Troy had been one of you marshals and killed Bobby in his cell, then it would have been legal?" Duke asked.

"Yes, it would have been legal," I said.

"Does the legal part really make shooting someone in a cage better?" Duke asked.

"Boss," Deputy Frankie said as if she wanted to caution him but wasn't sure it was her place.

"I've never had a shapeshifter in a cage before. Everything about his case is different," Newman said.

"Are they tied down like a vampire for you, then?" Frankie asked.

"No, and it's always chains with supernatural prisoners. Rope is pretty much useless," I said.

"If they're not chained up or in a cell, how do you usually execute shapeshifters?" Frankie asked.

"Kill or be killed," Edward said, and his Ted accent was still there, but the cadence of the words was all Edward.

"What do you mean?" she asked.

"We're usually hunting them while they hunt us," I said.

"Don't you kill them while they're passed out after changing back to human form?" Duke asked.

The four of us looked at one another. "Doesn't usually happen that way," I said at last.

"I have," Olaf said, "but it is not preferred."

"Why isn't it preferred? Seems like it would be the safest way to do it," Duke said.

I shrugged. "I'm not saying I wouldn't do it. I'm saying it's never come up."

"I thought they all passed out after they shift back to human," Duke said.

We all shook our heads like planned choreography, and I said, "If it's a new shapeshifter that's too green to control their beast, then they're so apeshit that you, the local police, usually have to shoot them to save lives, long before a marshal can be called in. They're the ones most likely to pass out after changing back."

"If a shapeshifter is weak enough to still pass out after they change back, they don't usually kill anyone on purpose. We're usually only called in after there are multiple bodies," Edward said. His vocabulary sounded almost wrong with Ted's accent.

"How'd we get honored with this many of you, then?" Duke asked.

"I invited Blake in for backup," Newman said.

"But that doesn't explain why we need four of you."

Edward gave him a truly wonderful smile that warmed his face all the way to his blue eyes. I wondered if he knew that his eyes got bluer when he pretended to be Ted. "Now, Sheriff, you have three out of the Four Horsemen. There are cases all over the country that would be plum tickled to have us helping out."

"If the three of you were as hot shit as you're supposed to be, then he'd already be dead." Duke threw a thumb in the direction of Bobby without actually looking at him. At least he'd used a pronoun rather than calling him *the suspect*, and he'd trusted him not to try to break out of the cell. Duke could say that he still saw Bobby as a monster, but he was beginning to treat him as more than that.

"I already explained the warrant system to you, Sheriff. It's Newman's warrant," I said.

"I know, I know. It's Win's choice of how to do the execution until he's too injured to do the job, and then one of you takes it over."

"Yes," I said.

"I thought you agreed that the footprint evidence meant we should look for other suspects, Duke," Newman said.

"I didn't exactly say that, Win. I just didn't argue that it's peculiar, that's all."

"You didn't want to pull the trigger either, Duke," I said.

"It's not my job to pull the trigger, Blake."

"No, it's mine, and I don't want to kill Bobby and then find out he's innocent," Newman said.

"Eventually the time limit will be over, Win, and then you'll be out of options."

"Not if we find other viable suspects first."

"And if you can't?"

"Then they can have my badge. I will not execute Bobby unless I'm sure."

"Newman," I said.

"No, Blake, no, this is wrong. It's so fucking wrong. I've wondered before if the supernatural citizen I killed was the one that should have been executed, but at least I didn't know them. I know Bobby, and I will not have his face added to my nightmares."

I thought he'd say something else, but then I caught a shine in his eyes that might have been tears, or maybe it was just the lights in the cells. Either way he turned abruptly and pushed his way past Leduc and headed out. I heard the outer door open and close. There was a moment of silence while I debated whether to go after Newman or give him some room.

Edward surprised the hell out of me by saying, "I'll go check on him."

"I'm supposed to be his mentor," I said.

He gripped my shoulder and smiled at me. "Think of it as tag-team wrestling. My turn."

Was it cowardly to let Edward go after him? No, because I was running out of ways to comfort Newman.

"He is not meant for this work," Olaf said.

"He's too soft for it," Duke said.

"No," I said, "it's not soft, not like you mean. Newman isn't a coward when the bullets are flying and the monsters are hunting us, but killing under fire is different from this." I motioned at Bobby.

"How is it different?" Olaf asked.

I thought of several replies, but finally settled for "It would bother me more to kill someone who wasn't a danger to me."

Olaf nodded. "Why?"

Once I would have thought he was trying to be irritating, but now I realized he honestly didn't understand the difference.

"I'm not sure I can explain it to you."

"Try. I want to understand why it is important to you."

"I'll think on it and try to explain later. Right now I don't really know how."

Olaf thought about what I'd said and finally accepted it with a nod. "I look forward to the discussion."

I was glad one of us did. I was not looking forward to trying to explain what it felt like to have a conscience to someone who didn't. I'd tried with Nicky back home. He was tied to me metaphysically and could feel my emotions, so he behaved like he had them, but he didn't. He was a sociopath, and even feeling my emotions, he didn't

understand all of them. It was like explaining the color red to someone who had been color-blind all their life. Where do you begin?

Frankie's phone rang. It was Rico getting back to her on the deer
hunt. Great. Maybe real police work would interfere with explaining
feelings to sociopaths or hand-holding junior marshals.

42

I HEARD FRANKIE say, "Are you sure?" She made *hmm* sounds and then hit the button to end the phone call. Her face was serious, but I didn't know her well enough to read that as positive or negative.

"What did Rico say?" I asked.

She shook her head.

"The deer was in the tree where I left it, right?" Bobby asked from the cell.

"No, Bobby. I'm sorry, but Rico couldn't find a deer in the tree."

"Did he check the tree just outside my bedroom window? It's got a limb that was always great for sneaking out."

"Rico says he checked all the trees near the house and didn't find any dead animals in them."

"That's not possible. I remember the hunt. I remember the deer's heartbeat fading under my jaws. I can still feel it struggling under my claws, the sensation of the hair in my mouth. It was too real to be a dream."

Duke stepped back into sight. "Sometimes we remember things the way we want them to be, not the way they are, son. I'm sorry."

"What does that mean? What are you trying to tell me, Duke?" Bobby's hands were starting to mottle where he gripped the bars.

"Are you remembering a deer, Bobby, or something else under your claws and fangs?"

Bobby raised his face up, his blue eyes large and nearly perfectly round like whatever he was seeing or remembering was something awful. He started shaking his head. "No, no, I would remember the difference between a deer and . . . Uncle Ray."

"If a memory is too terrible, we change it, edit it even in our own heads until the lie replaces the truth. You said so yourself," Duke said to me.

"I remember what I said."

"Do you edit your memories that way?" Olaf asked.

"No, but a lot of people do."

"I do not," Olaf said.

Bobby kept shaking his head and backed away from the bars. "No, I finally started remembering again. I've never remembered the wrong thing before."

"Have you ever hurt anyone before?" Duke asked.

Bobby shook his head. "No, my mentor, my sponsor, was with me from my first full moon."

"Why did you change form on the dark of the moon? Even a new Therianthrope would have been safe that far away from full," I said.

Maybe if I could get Bobby talking about something else useful, I could head off the emotions that were all over his face and body language. I'd seen other shapeshifters when they realized that they'd killed someone they loved by accident. The realization was never pleasant, and the shock looked just like this.

Bobby blinked at me as if he was having trouble drawing himself back from whatever was in his head. "What?"

Olaf tried, "Why did you change so far away from the full moon?"

"She asked," Bobby said, and then he stopped talking as if he hadn't meant to answer.

"Who asked?"

Bobby just shook his head.

"Who is she?" Olaf asked.

Bobby shook his head again, lips held in a tight thin line as if he were literally holding his lips closed so he wouldn't say more. He was protecting someone, and I didn't think it was himself.

"You're remembering tearing Ray apart, Bobby," Duke said.

"No, it was a deer!"

"You're not sure of that, are you, Bobby?" Duke said.

Bobby frowned. "I was."

"Stop it, Duke," said Wagner in the other cell.

"You're on my shit list already, Troy. Don't pile it higher."

"No, Duke, you could always do that with Bobby and me and some of the other boys. You could talk us up for a game or talk us down for something you thought we'd done wrong, but this isn't who threw a ball through Miss Bunny's window, Duke. This is Bobby's life on the line. Don't fuck him over."

"I should let the staties take you with them when they leave, Troy."

"What happens to Wagner is up to you, but this isn't some regular crime, Sheriff. If you get Bobby to confess, he doesn't get held over for trial. One of us takes him out and fucking kills him," I said.

"Win should have done that when we were still cleaning up Ray's body."

I looked at Leduc, really looked into his brown eyes, gave him some serious eye contact. He met my look with a bored one of his own. I was betting that was his blank cop face; every officer had one if they stayed on the job any length of time. It was the face we used to hide anything we were thinking. Some looked bored, uninterested, distracted, even faintly amused, but we all had a version, like a mask we could hide behind. It was so suspects didn't know what we were thinking or other cops didn't read us when we were hiding things. Sometimes all we were hiding was that we were scared, or disgusted about the crime at hand, and to show it would be weak, but sometimes we were hiding things that made us bad cops, and we didn't want the other cops to find out.

I searched Leduc's eyes and tried to figure out which reason had made him drop the cop look over his face like a mask. I wasn't a suspect, but Bobby was, and Leduc had already shown all sorts of emotions in front of him and us marshals. It seemed a little late to be hiding his emotions behind the mask.

Bobby sat down on the bunk in his cell, head in his hands. He was muttering something that I couldn't understand.

"Sorry, Bobby. I didn't catch that," I said.

He looked up. "I remember the deer. It should be in the tree."

Frankie said, "Maybe Rico missed it?"

Duke said, "I've gone deer hunting with Rico. He knows what a deer looks like, and he's the best shot among all of you deputies."

"He's the only one of us that can outscore you at the range, Duke," Frankie said.

"You're nipping at our heels, Frankie. I'll take you out for practice when this is all over."

"Thanks, Duke," she said, smiling. She looked pleased in that dad-noticed-me-and-was-proud-of-me way. It wasn't the look you gave someone who was just your boss. Maybe that was why Duke and his officers all called one another by their first names? It was more family than business. I'd seen it before on small forces, but never to this degree.

"Who asked you to turn into your leopard?" Olaf asked. It surprised me that he was taking lead on the questioning when there were no threats involved. He didn't usually enjoy interrogation without them.

Bobby shook his head. "I shouldn't have said that. I didn't mean it."

"Bobby, just confess, and it'll be all over," Duke said.

"We're trying to get to the truth here, Sheriff, or don't you care about who really killed Ray Marchand?" I asked.

"We found him covered in blood at the scene of the crime, Blake. The only ones complicating this case are you and Win."

"If it was so open-and-shut, why didn't you pull the trigger while Bobby was unconscious, Duke? If you were so certain that he killed his uncle, then you'd have been justified in shooting him at the scene. No one would have questioned it. You could have written the report up almost any way you wanted it to read. This is your town. Your deputies think of you as a father figure. If it was so simple, why didn't you just take the simplest solution, Duke?"

He tried to meet my gaze with his bored-cop face, but he had to look away. Whatever he was thinking or feeling at that moment, he wasn't sure he could hide it from me. That meant it was a strong emotion. The question was, which one?

"Unconscious seems a lot more unsporting than shooting into a cell," he said at last.

"You couldn't do it," I said.

"Not like that, no." Duke raised his eyes and let me see the anger and confusion in them. It wasn't just the two younger men who had history with their "coach." It was Leduc's history with them. God, it was like family. No matter how this ended, damage had been done to the relationships, if nothing else.

Duke turned those angry eyes to the prisoner he'd known since he was in elementary school. "But if Bobby would man up and be the monster that tore Ray apart and spread his blood and guts all over that room, that I could shoot."

"I swear that all I remember was the deer," Bobby said.

"Your control should be better at the dark of the moon," Olaf said.

"It is."

"Then why change form?" Olaf had moved closer to the bars and was giving Bobby some of the most serious attention I'd seen him give anyone when they weren't a target or a victim.

"I . . . wanted to."

"Why?"

"I . . . can't say." Bobby's eyes flicked toward the sheriff.

"Duke, I think we need less of an audience for this," I said.

"I already told Forrester that you don't get to kick me out of my own jail, especially not when you're questioning my prisoner."

There was movement in the doorway. Then Newman poked his head in and said, "But he's not your prisoner, Duke. He's mine. You've made it clear that he's my problem to solve."

"He's yours to execute, but he's my prisoner as long as he's in my jail."

"You've got an interrogation room here."

"Not one that will hold a shapeshifter."

"You let us guard him in the bathroom," I said.

"That was different. If you're not going to kill him, then making him sit around covered in God knows what probably goes under cruel and unusual or something," Duke said.

"If he starts trying to change form and escape, I'll shoot him, just like you want me to do," Newman said.

"And how many more people will be hurt or dead or contaminated before you shoot him?"

It was interesting that Leduc listed death as preferable to catching lycanthropy. I'd almost died more than once and finally popped positive for lycanthropy. It wasn't worse than dying.

"I'm already contaminated, so don't sweat my purity of blood," I said.

"I, too, am contaminated," Olaf said.

"If I was a betting man, Duke, I'd put my money on Marshal Jeffries if Bobby gets frisky," Edward said, back in smiling-Ted mode. He pushed Newman ahead of him through the doorway so there really wasn't room for all of us to be comfortable in the small hallway. He'd done it on purpose to make a point, I think.

"Not betting on your girlfriend?" Leduc said.

The smiling-Ted mask slipped a little through the eyes as Edward said, "If you mean Marshal Blake, then she and I always let Otto do the hand-to-hand with the other supernaturals first. He takes a lot of the fight out of them, and then Anita and I just come in and mop up."

"You never let me kill them with my bare hands," Olaf said, and I swear he sounded pouty. He was playing along, because we'd never let him wrestle a suspect.

"I know. We ruin all your fun," Edward drawled, or maybe Ted drawled. Even I got a little confused after a while.

"I've got three of the best preternatural marshals in the service as my backup, Duke. I think we can handle Bobby in the interrogation room," Newman said.

He hadn't batted an eyelash at the talk of letting Olaf go hand-to-hand with Bobby. It made me think that Edward had done more than just give Newman a pep talk outside; they'd made a plan. Since I didn't have a plan, I was just relieved that someone else did, especially if that someone was Edward.

Leduc tried to protest a little more, but Newman stood firm. Edward got to hold a gun on Bobby while Newman and I put the new supernatural strength shackles on him, which meant metal around his wrists and ankles with a chain going between them all so movement was limited. Then we shuffled Bobby out of the cellblock, though that seemed to imply more than two cells, and led him to the door that I'd thought was a closet. The room wasn't much bigger than one, but it was the only interrogation room we had, so we all squeezed in and shut the door. I was immediately claustrophobic. Yeah, it was that small.

43

THE TABLE IN the middle of the room took up most of the floor space. There were two chairs. We put Bobby in one, and then there was barely room to walk behind the chair. I could squeeze my hips between the chair back and the wall, but barely. Newman took the chair opposite Bobby, and that left the rest of us to figure out where to stand. There weren't a lot of choices.

Edward took up a corner behind Newman so he could watch Bobby's face, and then Olaf and I had one of those comedic moments of both trying for the other corner that would let us watch Bobby. Under other circumstances I'd have accused him of trying to rub up against me, but we both genuinely wanted the same spot. Edward solved it like we were kids to his adult.

"Anita gets shotgun," he said, and that meant I was beside him. Olaf took it gracefully enough, but even he couldn't ease behind Bobby's chair gracefully. He managed it, but it was one of the most physically awkward things I'd ever seen Olaf do. He finally ended up in the corner closest to the door so that he and I mirrored each other.

Newman smiled at Bobby like he meant it and said, "Bobby, I need to know everything that happened the night your uncle died."

"I told you before the other marshals got here, Win. I told you what I remembered."

"Bobby, you know that you've left things out."

"Do you think I did it?" Bobby's voice had more emotion in it, not exactly anger but something.

"No, but I think if you don't tell us everything now, then it won't matter in just a few hours. I only got an eight-hour extension on the warrant of execution. When the time is up, there will be no choice, Bobby. Do you understand that?"

"I don't think you'll kill me, Win."

"Maybe I can't, not like this, but I'll be forced to give the warrant over to one of the other marshals. Even if I give up my badge, the warrant will just go to the next marshal. I can't save your life by refusing to take it, Bobby, because if I don't do it, one of the marshals in this room will."

Bobby looked up at Edward and me and then turned his head so he could see Olaf. He turned back to look at me. "I don't think you'll do it either, Anita."

"Maybe not, but Ted will, and Otto will, but honestly, Bobby, after I nearly got shot saving you once, I'll be really pissed if that was for nothing because you won't tell us the whole truth."

He looked startled. Maybe I'd sounded angrier than I'd meant to sound, but what I'd said was still true.

"Why did you shapeshift at the dark of the moon?" Olaf asked.

"I wanted to." Bobby looked down at the tabletop.

"Who was the woman that asked you to shapeshift?" Newman asked.

Bobby shook his head.

"Are you still trying to suicide by cop?" I asked.

Bobby looked up then and again he was startled, or maybe it was confusion on his face. I didn't know him well enough to be certain. "I didn't—"

"Bullshit. I nearly died protecting you when you decided to lose control and let us shoot you."

He looked down again, but this time he murmured, "I'm sorry. I wasn't thinking clearly then."

"Are you thinking clearly now, Bobby?" Newman asked.

"Yes, I am."

"Then who is the *she* that you mentioned before?"

"It doesn't matter."

"Let us decide that."

"I promised I wouldn't tell anyone until we're both ready."

"What did you promise not to tell?" Newman asked, voice soft.

"I gave my word."

Olaf spoke from the corner. "Will you die to keep her secret?"

"It's not like that."

"Why did you change into your leopard form on one of the few nights that almost nothing could make you do it?" I asked.

Bobby licked his lips and swallowed. I realized that I hadn't seen him drink or eat anything since we'd been here. I guess I'd assumed that someone else had taken care of that, but I didn't know that for certain. I just wasn't used to having prisoners, and dead bodies didn't need to be fed.

Edward must have noticed, too, because he said, "Do you need a drink, pardner?"

"That would be nice. Thank you," Bobby said.

It took some maneuvering past me, but Edward finally managed to get the door opened without hitting the table. He shut the door carefully behind him.

Bobby was way too at ease. He should have been scared, and he wasn't. I realized that he was a lot more relaxed outside the cell. Had it been a mistake to bring him out of it? We could always take him back and do it the other way, but we had to either get him relaxed enough to let his guard down, or we had to up the emotion and scare him into talking.

Newman talked to Bobby but didn't push too hard until Edward got back with a soda. We waited in silence while Bobby opened the can and took a few drinks. He actually laughed and said, "You're all staring at me. I'm not doing anything that interesting."

"In seven hours . . ." I made a big deal out of looking at my watch. "Oh, wait, in six hours and forty minutes, you're going to die, because you won't tell us the whole truth about that night."

"But I'm not holding back anything that can help save me."

"How do you know?" Edward asked.

"What do you mean?"

"How do you know that we won't find a clue in what you're not telling us?"

Bobby seemed to think that through as he sipped his soda.

"We're cops, Bobby," Newman said. "It's our job to make sense out of stuff like this. You never know what might help us to help you."

"You've never been a police officer, right?" I asked.

"You mean me?" Bobby asked.

"Everyone else in the room is a police officer, so yeah, you."

"Sorry, yes. It's just you all asking questions from all over the room is sort of disorienting."

I filed that thought away for future interrogations and asked, "So you don't know how to do our jobs, right?"

"No, I don't."

"Then why don't you stop deciding what will and won't help us figure out whodunit, and just tell us everything you know so we can try to do the crime-busting part of our jobs?"

"I thought crime busting was your jobs." He smiled as he spoke as if I'd said something to amuse him.

"Only part," I said.

"What's the other part?"

"Executing people," I said.

"Killing people," Edward said.

"Killing," Olaf said.

Bobby looked around the room at all of us one at a time. "You're trying to scare me."

"If that will get you to talk, sure, but that last part wasn't planned. It's just the truth," I said.

Bobby turned back to Newman, who was the only one of us who hadn't said that particular truth. "Don't you want to scare me, too?"

"No, I want to save your life and find out who killed Ray and framed you for it, because if they'll do all that, then they are a danger to everyone else in our town."

"I don't know who killed Uncle Ray. I just know I didn't do it."

"Then tell us what you know, Bobby, please. Once you die for this crime, the investigation is over, and there will still be a double murderer free in our town to kill again."

"Double murderer? Only Uncle Ray died, right, no one else?" He was scared now, worried for other people.

I'd have let him sweat and asked whom he was worried about, but Newman was lead marshal and he didn't ask my opinion. "You're the second murder victim, Bobby."

"But I'm alive, Win. I'm right here."

"Not for much longer, Bobby, not unless you help us."

Bobby's emotions went across his face like clouds across a windy sky, too fast for me to catch them, but the shadows of them chased across his face as he fought through them all. Whatever he was hiding was important to him and came with an emotional price tag.

"Troy is one of the biggest gossips in town. I couldn't talk with him right there. I still don't feel right about it. I gave my word."

"Bobby, it's just us now, and I swear to you that anything you tell us won't leave this room unless it directly relates to the murder," Newman said.

Bobby looked at him and then at all of us in turn. "Do you promise?"

We all promised. He was so earnest, I half expected him to ask us to pinkie swear.

"Jocelyn and I grew up together. Her mother married Uncle Ray when she was five and I was eight."

That didn't seem to have anything to do with anything, but I was betting who the "she" might be.

"She saw me in leopard form after the accident every month. I know you've seen the pictures of me with the family in both forms, Win. I'm not sure about the rest of you."

"I've seen them. That's how I knew your leopard was the same size as a regular leopard," I said.

"Then you know that I'm in the pictures like the family dog. Joshie saw me in my animal form a lot, but she never saw me shift. I always did that in private, sort of like changing clothes. She wanted to see the change all the way through once." He looked back at Olaf. "Like you said, I had the most control at the dark of the moon, so that's when we planned it."

"Planned what?" I asked. If he said the murder, I was going to be both pissed and pleased: angry I'd almost gotten killed protecting a murderer and pleased we could solve the case.

Bobby looked back at me. "Um . . . to have her see me change form."

Olaf came up beside Bobby's chair and leaned over him as he said, "You're lying."

Bobby glanced up at him and then away. "I'm not lying. It's the truth."

"Then why did your pulse rate speed up? Your body is reacting like you are hiding something." Olaf leaned closer, bowing his bigger body over the other man's head so that Bobby reacted like the roof was getting lower.

"It's the truth," Bobby said.

"If it is the truth, it is not all of it," Olaf said, his face nearly touching the other's man's cheek.

"Win, tell him to back off."

"I'm not his boss," Win said.

Bobby's eyes flashed up at Win, and he was afraid as he tried to sit up straighter with Olaf's body almost touching him. For the first time since we had come into the little room, Bobby seemed to realize that he wasn't safe, that maybe bad things could happen to him and Newman might not be able to help him. Good. Maybe he'd stop playing games and tell us the truth.

Olaf asked the next question damn near curled around Bobby. "Why did your sister want to see you change form?"

"She's not my sister," Bobby said, and he sat up so suddenly that if Olaf hadn't moved back, Bobby's head might have hit him in the face. Why had that question upset Bobby?

"You were raised together," I said.

Bobby looked at me, and he was angry. "That doesn't make us brother and sister. Uncle Ray never formally adopted Joshie, just me, so even legally, we're not related."

"Everyone in town calls her Jocelyn Marchand," Newman said.

"We're the Marchand family, and when Joshie and I were younger we didn't even know that her last name wasn't Marchand."

I had an idea. It was kind of twisted, but his anger and defensiveness were coming from somewhere. "When did you start having sex together?"

Newman said, "Blake!" at the same time that Bobby said, "It wasn't like that."

"So, you and Jocelyn didn't have sex together?" I asked.

This time Newman didn't say anything. He was trying to do his best blank cop face, because his mind was having trouble with the detour.

"We love each other," Bobby said.

"How long have you loved each other?" I asked.

"I've had a crush on her since she was in her teens, but she still thought I was her brother, so I didn't say anything. I figured I was just wrong. I mean, you're right, we were raised together, but I didn't feel like a brother. But if she felt like my sister, then I could live with it."

"What changed your mind?"

"She said she had feelings for me, and I finally told her how I felt."

"Then what happened?" I asked, because apparently this line of questioning was my lead, or Newman didn't want to touch it.

"We couldn't date exactly, because people do think of us as siblings here. We were planning to tell Uncle Ray how we felt, and then we were going to move away to a big city where no one knew us. We weren't doing anything wrong, but Jocelyn didn't want to have to explain it to the people we'd grown up with. It bothered her more than it bothered me."

"Would you have just told everyone if she'd agreed?" I asked.

He nodded. "I'm in love with her. I've been in love with her for years. I was engaged once, but I realized that Joshie had been my first love and still was, so it wasn't fair to marry anyone else, not if I couldn't really love them."

"Noble," Olaf said. "Many men would have married and tried to forget what they could not have."

"It didn't feel noble. I thought maybe if she found someone else and married, I'd finally be able to let it go, but she couldn't find anyone either. We finally both realized that it was because we were meant for each other."

"But you weren't able to tell anyone," I said.

Bobby shook his head. "She knew we weren't really brother and sister, but to the rest of the town we were, and so she made me swear that I wouldn't tell anyone that we were in love."

"Or that you were lovers," I said.

He nodded. "Or that."

I was beginning to see why Jocelyn might have been a little hysterical in the hospital. She'd been hiding the fact that she was having an affair with the man who was raised as her brother; it's legal, but if she hadn't felt conflicted about it, she wouldn't have made Bobby swear not to tell anyone.

"Why did she want to see the whole transformation from human to leopard?" I asked. Maybe if I concentrated on what we didn't know, I wouldn't get hung up on what we'd just learned. Was it incest if you weren't blood relations? I mean, technically, legally no, but if you were raised together it just felt . . . wrong.

"I proposed, and she said she couldn't decide if she didn't see me change. She was comfortable with me being a wereanimal as her brother, but not sure about as a husband."

"What happened that night, Bobby?" I asked.

He told the story pretty much as he'd told Newman from the beginning up to a point. They'd sat down to dinner with Uncle Ray at seven o'clock like normal, but then all the hired help had left, even Carmichael, who lived on-site in a small house on the grounds.

"Except for Carmichael leaving, it was a normal Friday night up to that point. Uncle Ray went to his study to look over the stocks and write in his journal like he did almost every night. We had some television shows that we watched together, and sometimes we'd watch a movie as a family, but other than that, he went to his study and left Jocelyn and me to entertain ourselves. That's how he always said it: 'You kids go entertain yourselves. I'm going to do boring old-man stuff.'"

Bobby's eyes got shiny at that point. He raised his hands as if he'd rub the tears away, or pretend he had something in his eye, but the shackles brought him up short, and he couldn't complete the gesture. "I can't believe he's never going to hug me and say that ever again. I didn't see his body, so I don't believe he's dead. Does that make sense?" He looked at me.

"Yeah, makes perfect sense," I said.

He nodded, and the tears started down his face.

"Go on, Bobby," Newman said. "What happened after Ray went to his study?"

"We went up to my room and made love. She let me hold her for a while, and then she asked to see me change." The tears were drying on his face by the time he'd finished the sentence.

He hesitated so long that I was debating on asking a question while he struggled to find the words, but Edward beat me to it. "You said she let you hold her afterward. Was that unusual?"

Bobby nodded. "She joked that I was the girl, because I liked to hold her after sex and she just liked to clean up and be done like a boy." He smiled as he spoke, his face going gentle at the memory.

In my head I thought two things. One, if she could get up every time that fast, then she wasn't having that good a time. Two, if she didn't want to be held after sex, she had serious issues about the whole thing, or she was using him for sex or in general.

"How did she react to seeing you change shape?" Olaf asked from the corner to which he'd retreated.

Bobby glanced back at him, and there was an uneasy look on his face, but I think that had more to do with Olaf intimidating him earlier than anything else. "She didn't scream or run away. She looked happy, smelled pleased. I rubbed up against her legs. She petted me like she always does in leopard form, and then I went out the open window and down the tree outside my window like I always do."

"The same tree that you put your deer in?" I asked.

He frowned and nodded. "Unless one of the other animals in the area moved the deer, it should have been there."

"Rico looked in the tree. He didn't search the woods for it," Newman said.

Bobby smiled and then looked utterly serious. He glanced at me and then at Newman. "Does she really think I killed him?"

"I'm sorry, Bobby, but yeah, she does."

"Win, I did not do this. Maybe the deer fell out of the tree. Have Rico look on the ground around it. If the deer is there, then that's all I killed." He sounded so certain.

"I'll have Rico check again," Newman said.

"Thank you, Win." Bobby looked up at me. "Thank you, too, Anita, for believing in me when I didn't believe in myself. Thank you, too, Marshal Forrester and Marshal Jeffries." He started to lift his hands as if he'd offer to shake, but the shackles stopped him.

"Don't thank us yet, pardner," Edward said, pushing away from the corner and smiling his Ted smile at Bobby.

We shuffled him back to his cell and then Newman's phone rang. It was Dr. Jameson at the hospital. Jocelyn was awake and alert enough to talk to us.

"We'll be there in just a few minutes, Doctor. Thanks for the call." Newman hung up.

"Perfect timing," Edward said.

"What's perfect timing?" Sheriff Leduc asked as we moved through the office area on our way to the cars.

"We're off to chase clues," I said.

"Chase clues? Who are you, Nancy Drew?"

"I was always more of a Hardy Boys fan myself," I said.

"Me, too," Edward said.

"I had a crush on Nancy when I was a kid," Newman said.

"I do not know who this Nancy Drew is or the Hardy men," Olaf said.

"I knew you missed Sherlock Holmes, but didn't you ever read any kind of mystery as a kid?" I asked.

"No," he said, and that one word put a stop to the conversation.

We got our jackets and headed to the hospital. As I settled into the passenger seat of Edward's rental, I could have sworn I could feel Olaf's gaze on the back of my head. Maybe if Olaf and I had that coffee date, I could ask him what he liked to read. Yeah, that sounded swell.

I turned in my seat and managed a smile. "If you move over and sit behind Edward, I'll be able to look at you while we talk on the drive."

"Would looking at me please you?"

"Yes," I said, smiling even more brightly.

So long as he didn't ask why it would please me to look at him, we were good. He could think it was so I could admire his scary good looks, and I could feel safer, not having him pressed at my back in the car. He didn't question why I wanted him to move over. He just did it. Perfect.

44

SOMEONE HAD PROPPED Jocelyn's pillows up behind her, so she was sitting up this time. Her reddish brown curls were still almost eerily perfect, as if someone had done her hair before we got here. Maybe the back of her head was all mushed the way that my curls were when I lay down, but the front was bouncy and framed her face perfectly. If we hadn't been there for a murder investigation, I might have asked what hair-care products she used for such manageable curls. Her large brown eyes still bothered me, like I was still waiting for her mother's green eyes to appear in her face. Her wide, curved mouth was shiny and had a tinge of color like she'd used lip gloss. The color was wet and even and stayed put as she sipped diet soda through a straw, so it was high-end lip gloss.

Jocelyn stirred her fork through the tray of hospital food in front of her, but it didn't look like she'd eaten any of it. I wasn't sure if it was grief or a critique of the food. She stared at the food instead of at any of us. It reminded me of Bobby avoiding our eyes earlier. Maybe it was a family trait? I wondered if her mother or Ray Marchand had done it and Jocelyn and Bobby had both learned it as children. Since both parents were dead now, I guessed I'd never know.

Olaf stayed by the door this time so he wouldn't "tower" over the patient. Edward stayed a little back from the bed, too. Newman and I stood directly beside the bed. We'd all discussed our strategy on the drive over. We didn't want to give Jocelyn any extra reason to get spooked before we'd asked our questions. Newman and I were the least physically intimidating, and he was lead marshal, so we got to take lead on the interrogation.

Dr. Jameson stood across the bed from us with the tall nurse who had gone to fetch him on our first visit. He'd introduced her as Nurse Trish, as if her first name were her last. Nurse Trish was over a head taller than the doctor, which meant either she was even taller than I'd first thought, or the doctor was shorter than he'd seemed. I had a moment of wanting to see her stand next to Olaf so I could get a firm height on her. Her pale brown hair was styled more today so that the tips of the short haircut framed her face on purpose in delicate pixie-like points that seemed more club kid than RN. Her smock was pink again, but instead of kittens it was covered in unicorns. No, really, unicorns.

"In the interest of potentially saving lives, I will allow you to question my patient, but I warn you to tread carefully, or I will have security escort you off the property."

Dr. Jameson seemed serious. I almost wanted to see what would happen if hospital security tried to kick us out. On second thought, I didn't. We were here as U.S. Marshals. We'd have to behave ourselves, and that wouldn't be any fun at all.

"Thank you, Dr. Jameson, Nurse Trish. We really appreciate you understanding how important this is," Newman said.

I realized that he had his own version of Ted's "Aw, shucks ma'am/sir," except this was genuinely a part of Newman and not an act to manipulate people. Newman was as nice as he seemed, which wasn't necessarily a good thing in this job, but one problem at a time.

"Trish, just Trish," the nurse said with a smile, but it didn't quite fill up her brown eyes. There was discomfort in them. Maybe she hadn't liked being introduced as Nurse Trish. She hadn't felt free to correct the doctor, but apparently, she thought it was fine to correct a marshal. In the world of the hospital, the doctor had more clout.

"Well, Trish, thank you for taking the time to help us today," Newman said, giving a reassuring smile that must have melted the hearts of women who were looking for a nice guy.

She flashed him a smile that showed a dimple in one cheek. It made her look younger, lighter, as if the smile lifted some burden of seriousness that she'd been carrying. I hadn't noticed until her face lit up that she was pretty. There was a glimpse of a woman who, with her pixie haircut and darker eyeshadow, might go dancing. I was betting in a dance club she wouldn't be wearing kittens and unicorns on her clothes, but you do what you can to cheer yourself up when your job is dealing with other people's misery.

Dr. Jameson frowned at the nurse as if he'd caught her flirting, and maybe he had. "You said you had some questions for Jocelyn."

"Yes, sir," Newman said.

"I don't understand why you want to talk to me again," Jocelyn said, still stirring her food around on her tray.

"We just have a few more questions for you, Jocelyn," Newman said.

"What questions? You know what happened to Dad, and you know that Bobby did it. What else do you need to do your job?"

She looked up at us then, and I realized she had used more eye makeup than I'd thought. It was subtle, but it brought out her eyes. She aimed all that beauty at us like a shield. Her eyes were a deep, rich brown, large in the smooth perfection of her face. She was even more beautiful than she had been before, and it wasn't until I sensed how angry she was that I realized that was it. Telling women that they're beautiful when they're angry has become a cliché, but for some women, it was true. Jocelyn Marchand was one of them. I began to see how it might have been hard for Bobby to see her as just his sister, and the moment I thought that, I knew it wasn't right. Plenty of beautiful women and handsome men have siblings who never think a single incestuous thought about them. It was more than beauty that made the difference.

"We just want to double-check our facts, Jocelyn, that's all," Newman said.

"What facts, Win?" she asked, voice impatient. She half dropped, half tossed the fork onto her food tray as if what she really wanted to do was throw the whole thing across the room. Anger was the second stage of grief, and she had plenty of things to grieve.

"Bobby says that you and he . . . spent time together after dinner," Newman said.

Jocelyn shook her head hard enough for her curls to swing. She crossed her arms over the front of her hospital gown.

"Okay, then, what did you and Bobby do after Ray went to his study?"

"We didn't do anything together!" she said, and it was almost a yell. She closed her eyes, lowered her head, and breathed deep and slow as if she was counting to ten. She was so angry, and she was right there.

All I had to do was touch my hand to her bare arm, and I could feed on all that rage. I took a few deep breaths myself then, because it wasn't like me to see a crime victim as food. She was hitting my radar as food, and I didn't know why. I thought I had all the metaphysical hungers under control, but maybe not. Crap, I did not need this right now. Jocelyn Marchand had been victimized enough. I would not add to that because I was some creepy anger vampire. Just thinking that all the way through hurt my sense of self a little. I spent half my time thinking I'd already become a monster and the other half fighting not to make it a reality. I was a little conflicted about some of my supernatural abilities. Maybe Jocelyn was more than a little conflicted about having sex with Bobby?

"Bobby says you spent the evening together," Newman said, voice gentle.

"Well, he's a liar!"

"I know you went out with friends, and Bobby stayed home."

"Then you know I did not spend all night with him. You know he's lying." Jocelyn looked up at Newman with those big brown eyes, giving him the full impact of that lovely face, willing him to believe her.

"So you didn't see him change into his leopard form before you left the house?"

"No, I shut the door to my room so I wouldn't have to see any-thing across the hall."

"It must be hard with the rooms right across from each other," I said.

Jocelyn looked at me then, giving me the full weight of her eyes, the face. She knew the effect she had on people. Nothing wrong with that. I was marrying someone who knew it, too.

"I was hoping to get a job and an apartment of my own, but now I don't know what's going to happen." The loss and confusion filled her eyes before she looked down at her lap.

"Did you know Bobby planned to turn into his leopard that night?" Newman asked.

She shook her head without looking up. "It was the dark of the moon. He never changed form then."

"Any idea why he decided to change that night?" Newman asked, as if asking why Bobby had decided to change clothes instead of skins.

Jocelyn stared at her hands as they plucked at the white sheet. "I think so. I'm afraid so." Her voice was almost a whisper. The anger was fading into something else, but since I didn't feed on any other emotion, I couldn't tell what she was feeling.

"He told you his fantasy, didn't he?" she asked, voice somehow small, as if she didn't want to say her words too loud, because doing so would make them bigger, more real.

"He told us about your relationship," Newman said.

Jocelyn looked up then, tears shining in her eyes, but the anger was back blazing so that her brown eyes looked almost black like dark water glistening in sunlight as the first tear trailed down her cheek. "The only relationship I have with Bobby is as brother and sister."

"I'm sorry, Jocelyn. Bobby says it was a little bit more than that," Newman said, and he sounded almost apologetic.

"He wanted it to be more, but I said no."

"Bobby says that the two of you aren't genetically related and that

Ray only adopted Bobby and not you, so you're not even legally brother and sister."

She threw her hands up in the air, more tears trailing down her face from those angry eyes. "Bobby's my brother. He told me all that stuff about not being related, but I was only five when my mom married his uncle. To me they are my dad and my big brother."

"So you and Bobby never had sex?"

She looked disgusted. "No, I would never . . . That's a horrible thing to say, and I told Bobby that. I told him I was going to tell Dad."

"You planned on telling Ray?" Newman asked.

"I told him. He was shocked, but he said he'd talk to Bobby and get him to leave me alone."

"You told Ray the night he died that Bobby was wanting to date you?" Newman asked.

"Yes. Dad said he'd talk to Bobby after I left for the night." She started to cry in earnest. "Don't you see? It's all my fault."

"How is it your fault?"

"Dad must have confronted Bobby and told him to leave me alone, that I didn't feel that way about him, and he went crazy and killed Dad." She hid her face in her hands. The nails were that pale-pink-and-white French that always looked weird to me, like something you'd do for a wedding but not for real life.

Newman glanced at me as if for help, so I took the hint and said, "Bobby says he proposed, and you told him that you had to see him change into his leopard before you'd know if you'd be comfortable with it."

She looked up with tears drying on her face, but no new ones. Her voice finally held the angry scorn that I'd felt roll off of her earlier. "That's ridiculous. I've lived with his leopard for ten years. I don't have any problem with him being a wereanimal. Well, I didn't, but after what I saw . . . after what he did to our dad. Oh, God! It's all my fault. I should have told Dad sooner or stayed home, but I never dreamed Bobby would hurt him. We both loved our father, or I thought we did." She stared off into space as if seeing things we couldn't: maybe the sight of her father's bloody body or maybe things we couldn't have guessed at.

"Did you tell anyone else that Bobby was trying to be . . . inappropriate with you?" I asked, struggling to find words that wouldn't make it worse for her.

She nodded. "I told Helen that he was leaving his door to his room open so I'd see him undressing as I walked by, and that he'd peek at me if I left mine open. I couldn't tell her the worst of it. It was so wrong and embarrassing." She shuddered, hugging her arms to herself.

"Helen Grimes, the cook?" Newman asked.

"Yes, and I told my friend Marcy at a lunch a few days before the girls' night out. Bobby had tried to . . . He forced his way into my room, and he . . . he tried to make his fantasy a reality. It's what made me finally try to tell Dad. I didn't even know if he'd believe me. You hear about women telling their families all the time that someone is molesting them, but nobody believes them, you know. Dad loves us both—loved us both—and it was like making him choose between us."

"We believe you, Jocelyn," Newman said.

She smiled up at him, but it left her eyes empty and sad. "Did you believe Bobby, too?"

"He believes what he says," Olaf said.

His comment made her look past us to where Olaf stood trying to be nonthreatening by the door. "I know he does, which is what scared me, but I wasn't scared because he was a wereleopard. I was just scared because my own brother was trying to force himself on me, wanted me to marry him. It's crazy, and when Dad confronted him over it, Bobby killed him. So you see, I did it. I killed my father, just as much as Bobby. We killed him together!" Her voice rose in hysteria with the last two sentences until she started to sob—big, deep, hyperventilating sobs.

"That's enough," Nurse Trish said.

"I agree," Dr. Jameson said.

Newman nodded. "We're done for now."

The nurse looked at him with eyes shining with tears and said, "How much more do you want from her?"

Newman shook his head. "Nothing. We're leaving."

Dr. Jameson was already putting a needle of something into Jocelyn's IV line as she sobbed and screamed on the bed. I think in between wordless screams she was gasping out, "I did it. I killed him. I killed him."

We walked out into the hallway with her screams echoing after us.

45

NEWMAN WALKED AWAY down the hospital corridor, striding fast as if he wanted to run but wouldn't let himself do it. The three of us followed him, though I had to do some serious quick time to keep up. Newman was already in the open elevator when we got there. Edward put an arm in the door to keep it open long enough for us to join him. Two people were already in the elevator, so we still couldn't talk.

Newman stood pressed in the corner, looking pale and tense. In the mirrored surface of the elevator, the rest of us just looked bored as we rode down. The people looked at us with our badges in plain sight but didn't say anything.

The doors opened, and Newman pushed past all of us to head for the parking lot. We followed, and a glance back showed the couple watching us. It would be hospital gossip that the marshals looked upset, or maybe the story would grow and we'd be accused of brandishing weapons. We needed to be calm.

"Newman," I called, "I'm almost twelve inches shorter than you are. If you want me to run to keep up, I can, but I'll feel silly."

He stumbled and turned around to look at me, and a car honked its horn before it almost hit him. The three of us jogged up to be with him then. Be a shame for him to get injured in the parking lot by being careless. Our job had so many other more interesting ways to get hurt; being hit by a car was just too mundane.

Newman crossed to stand by our vehicles, hands on hips, hat in his hand as if it had become too heavy. "Jesus," Newman said, "I fucking hate this case."

"It's got all the awfulness of both regular police work and the supernatural," I said.

"Incest. Fuck, I do not want to put that in my report. If Bobby has to die and Ray's already dead, I do not want that following them to the grave."

"Jocelyn doesn't need that following her around the rest of her life either," Edward said.

"They aren't actually related to each other," I said.

The two of them looked at me.

"Legally it's not incest," I said.

"I double-checked—Bobby was seven and Jocelyn was only five years old when her mother married Ray. They have been raised as brother and sister. Jocelyn probably doesn't even remember a time when Bobby wasn't her brother," Newman said.

"So, you will simply accept that the woman is telling the truth because she cried?" Olaf asked.

I looked at him. "Are you saying she smelled like she was lying?"

"Yes and no."

"What does that mean?" Edward asked.

"She was disgusted with Bobby. She does not feel for him what he feels for her, but she also smelled like truth when she said she killed her father."

"Can you blame her for thinking she killed him?" I asked.

Olaf stared down at me and finally said, "If her version is true, then I can see why she might feel guilty."

Edward said, "But you said that Bobby is telling the truth, too."

Olaf nodded. "He believes what he says. There is no doubt or lie in him when he speaks of the love between himself and his sister."

"Is he delusional?" Newman asked.

"That's for a court-appointed therapist to say," Edward said.

"If Bobby were human, then we'd get him in to be interviewed by professionals, but he's a wereleopard. There won't be any doctors doing talk therapy with him," I said.

Newman leaned against the side of his Jeep, head down. "Jesus, have I been wrong all along? Did Bobby kill Ray?"

I went to him, touched his arm. "I'm sorry, Newman, but if the friend and the cook corroborate Jocelyn's story, then no judge is going to give another extension on the execution."

He looked at me with anguish in his eyes. "But did Bobby do it? Does he deserve to die?"

"If he was delusional, then he may not remember killing his father."

"Which means when I shoot him, he'll beg for his life, and he will believe that he's innocent and I'm killing him for nothing."

"I'm sorry, Newman," I said. It seemed so inadequate, but sometimes it's the best you have to offer.

He started to cry then, and though it was against all the male rules of cop life I hugged him, and because it was Newman, he hugged me back. I held him in the parking lot while he curled all that six feet plus of police officer around me and wept. He cried his grief out now, so maybe, just maybe, he could do his job later.

46

WHEN NEWMAN CALMED down a little, Edward tried to take over from me. Newman didn't hug him like he had me. Maybe it was a guy thing or a girl thing? Edward tried to get him thinking about calling the cook and the friend who was Jocelyn's alibi, and seeing if we could set up an interview ASAP. I thought it was interesting that Jocelyn had told only the one girlfriend, Marcy, about Bobby molesting her. Why not tell both? We'd find out. But in the end Newman asked me if I could catch a ride back to the sheriff's office with Ted and Otto.

"I may drop by the house and check on Haley, but I won't be long."

"Sure, Newman, whatever you need."

He nodded, managed a weak smile, then went for his Jeep. Edward ushered Olaf and me toward his SUV.

"Who is Haley?" Olaf asked.

"His fiancée," I said.

Olaf scowled so hard his sunglasses couldn't hide it. "Women make a man weak."

"I'm not sure he's really going home," I said.

"He wanted some time to himself," Edward said.

"Why did he not simply say that?"

"Pride," I said.

"Everyone in the car," Edward said, "in case he just goes straight back to the sheriff's office."

"I would respect Newman more if he hadn't used the woman in his life as an excuse," Olaf said as he opened the driver's-side back door. He was going to sit behind Edward, just as I'd asked him to do on the drive over. It was nice that he just did it without my having to debate with him about it. He really was trying his best not to piss me off this time.

I got my seat belt fastened, and Edward had even started the engine, before Olaf said, "I think you are weakening Newman."

I turned in the seat so I could look at him. It really was easier to talk with him sitting catty-corner from me. "Weakening? What are you talking about?"

"Some men will show emotion and weakness around women that they would never show around men. Newman needs to be strong, not weak right now."

"I agree with that last part, but not the first part."

"You're a woman. You do not understand the effect you can have on men."

Edward started backing out of the parking spot.

"What's that supposed to mean?" I asked. My tone was a little angry.

Olaf scowled at me. "It means exactly what I said."

"That's not an answer," I said.

Edward was paying a lot of attention to getting us out of the hospital parking lot. He hadn't tried to make eye contact with either of us. I was sitting right beside him, so he had to actually work at not looking at me.

"Is there a reason you're trying to stay out of this discussion?" I asked.

"You won't like what I have to say."

"You're joking," I said.

"Olaf may have a point, Anita."

"I really didn't expect you to agree with Olaf," I said.

"I know you didn't. That's why I didn't offer an opinion."

"I really thought you'd be on my side on this one."

"I'm on Newman's side, and he isn't doing well."

"I know," I said. "I don't think he's cut out for this job."

"I do not think he will be strong enough to kill the victim," Olaf said.

I wanted to argue about his use of the word *victim*, but Edward went right on as if that was an okay thing to call our executionees.

"I'm more afraid that he might feel he has to kill Bobby and finish the job," Edward said.

"Why afraid?" I asked.

"There are things that a person can do and survive intact, and there are things that will break them. I think killing Bobby Marchand will break Newman in a way that he won't recover from."

Olaf nodded. "I agree."

"Hell, I'm not sure I'll be okay if I have to kill him at this point," I said.

"You've talked to him too much, Anita. You know better than to interact with the mark before the hit," Edward said.

"It does not bother me to interact with them," Olaf said.

"You're a sociopath. Anita isn't."

"I enjoy the kill more sometimes if I have spoken with them, interacted with them."

"You're a serial killer, and Anita isn't."

"She kills as much as we do, perhaps more."

"She's a killer like I am, not like you are."

I thought about reminding them that I was sitting right here, but I found it interesting to watch them interact as if I wasn't here. Was this how they talked all by themselves? Probably not. It was that old conundrum that observing the experiment changed it—just by being present I changed their interactions.

"Agreed," Olaf said.

"I think it might be better if I spend some time with Newman," Edward said.

"Are you saying that I can't teach Newman what he needs to know just because I'm a girl?"

"No, it's not you, Anita. It's him. Olaf is right. Some men are just more . . . tender around women. I think Newman needs a man's touch."

"That's so chauvinistic."

"Why is it chauvinist to say that I'd be better at teaching New-man how to be a man than you would be?"

"He's a man already, all grown-up. We're talking about teaching him how to do this job. Yes, you helped teach me, but I'm good at the job now. So why are you a better teacher than I am?"

"I'm not saying I'm better at helping people learn the ropes. I'm saying that I think I might be better for Newman right now."

"It still seems like some macho bullshit that I didn't expect to hear from you."

"We don't have time for egos and feelings here, Anita. I think you'll sympathize with Newman and the Marchand kid too much to help Newman figure out what he needs to do. I won't."

My anger washed over me like heat, and I felt the beasts stir in-side of me like my soul writhing to the beat of my anger. Fuck. I did not need this right now, and just like that, I thought, But what does Newman need? Was Edward right? Would some man-to-man talk benefit Newman more than my marshal-to-marshal relationship with him? I didn't want to kill Bobby now. I knew what the skin of his neck smelled like when I held him close. It was always harder for me to hurt someone after a certain level of physical closeness. It was like, at some level, I equated physical with emotional intimacy. My therapist and I had been talking about that, among other things.

Thinking about things too complicated for my beasts could either quiet them or make them lash out in frustration. This time it quieted them. I could almost feel them thinking, *You complicate your life, hu-man*. I couldn't even argue with them.

I nodded. "Okay. How do we get you some one-on-one time in the middle of an investigation?"

"You're giving in just like that?" Edward asked, frowning at me as if he suspected a trap.

"You're right. I've gotten too close to Bobby Marchand. I saved his life once by putting my body between him and a gun. It would feel weird for me to kill him now, so maybe I can't help Newman work through his own feelings about it. It's not about being male or female. It's about me being emotionally compromised in a way that you are not, which makes you a better partner for Newman right now on this case."

"Exactly that," Edward said.

"I am impressed that you worked through your anger so quickly," Olaf said to me.

"Thanks. Therapy is a many-splendored thing."

"Whatever tool works for you," he said.

"Thank you."

"You are welcome."

"Normally, I'd just ride with Newman once we meet up with him again, but that leaves the two of you alone," Edward said.

Olaf and I looked at each other. Did I want to be trapped inside a car with him? No, hell no. I had a moment to realize that it wasn't him going all serial killer on me that made me hesitate. I believed he'd behave himself until the case was complete The problem was the kiss that I'd somehow let him manipulate me into, or I'd somehow been willing to do. He'd asked for my consent. I'd said yes. But once you say yes, it's harder to say no later without the man in question getting upset. I did not want to be trapped in a car alone with Olaf when he got upset with me, and I didn't want to kiss him again. I'd decided I'd say no and make it stick from now on, but the no would have been a lot stronger if I'd never crossed the line. What the hell had I been thinking?

"I think we will be fine on our own, but Anita's expression says she will not agree."

I didn't like his being able to read me like that, but he wasn't wrong. "You confuse me, Olaf."

"In what way?"

Edward pulled into the gravel parking area in front of the sheriff's station, and it startled me. I'd been so wrapped up in worrying about Newman and Olaf, that I hadn't realized we were there. Shit, I had to do better than this. "In a lot of ways." I saw Newman's Jeep coming up behind us. I nodded in that direction. "Newman's here. He didn't go home to get a hug."

"He wanted to be alone," Olaf said.

I just nodded and shrugged—about this he was right. We'd barely gotten out of the SUV, but Newman was parked and coming our way. He was excited about something.

Newman called out, "The women are both at their homes. I left messages for Helen Grimes, the cook at the Marchand house. We can interview them now and hope Helen gets back to us soon. I want to double-check Jocelyn's story ASAP. If they confirm her story, then Bobby is crazy and doesn't know what's real and what's fantasy." He'd sounded more certain of himself until he said the last part. He rallied though and gave us his tough-cop look. Sometimes the look isn't for bad guys or for hiding stuff from others. Sometimes it's for you to try to convince yourself that you're really as tough as you need to be.

I went toward Newman's Jeep, but he said, "It makes more sense if you and I split up so that one of us that's more familiar with the case goes on each interview. I'll take Jeffries with me, and you can go with Forrester."

"I think I should go with Newman," Edward said.

And just like that the moment of decision was here. I had to put up or shut up or something like that.

Newman shook his head. "I don't think so."

"Anita has explained why my earlier behavior was unprofessional. I give you my word that it will not happen again on this case," Olaf said.

"I don't know you that well, Jeffries."

"If Otto gives his word, it's good," Edward said.

My pulse was speeding, but my voice was steady as I said, "His word of honor really is good, weirdly."

"Great, but that doesn't mean that you should ride with him," Newman said.

I don't know what I would have said, because two SUVs, one white and the other red, crowded into the small parking area. Nicky was driving the white one, and the moment I recognized that blond hair, the mirrored sunglasses hiding his eyes, as Nicky's, I realized that it was Ethan in the passenger seat, with his white blond hair that had gray lowlights and a streak of dark red that didn't occur naturally in humans. People usually thought it was all a great dye job. The hair color was natural, but it was always fun watching people get angry with him for not being willing to share his hairstylist with them.

I was down the steps and moving through the parking lot almost before the cars had stopped. If I could run into Edward's arms while he was Ted, I was by God going to run into the arms of my actual lover. If the other cops thought less of me, fuck them. I wanted a hug and a kiss I wasn't conflicted about.

47

NICKY GOT OUT of the SUV. I had a moment of looking up into his face and seeing the newly shortened hair, the strong, oh-so-masculine line of his jaw, the sunglasses that hid why he'd worn his hair long for years, and then we were kissing, all lips and tongues, and then he bit my lower lip just a little. It made me make a small eager noise, and that made him tighten his hands against my body so that his fingers dug in, and that earned him another noise from my mouth to his. He swept me up into his arms and because he was nine inches taller than me, he literally swept me off my feet. If we'd both been wearing fewer weapons, I'd have wrapped my legs around his waist, but the best I could do was bend my knees as if I was kneeling in midair. I thought about kneeling for real later if we could find the time, and that brought another eager sound from me. The pain got too much on my lip, and I tapped out, literally the same way I would have in the dojo to let someone know that they needed to ease up or they might hurt me for real. It was our signal when he rendered me speechless in one way or another.

He set me back on the ground, but kept his arms around me, because he knew he'd made my knees weak. It was exactly what I'd needed to wash away the feel of that other, unwanted kiss. It was ironic that Olaf's kiss had been so much gentler than the one I'd just gotten, and yet the gentle one had spooked me and this one had helped me come back to the center of myself.

I could hear the murmur of voices on the other side of the cars. Ethan and whoever else they'd brought with them were trying to help Edward run interference for me with the other police officers. This wasn't exactly the best way to introduce the Coalition to Sheriff Leduc. He was going to hate them all interfering in his case without me playing kissy face with one of them. It wasn't like me to be so uncontrolled in public while wearing my badge.

Edward came around the front of the SUV. "We need you out here, Anita. Hi, Nicky."

"Ted," Nicky said with a nod of his head. Edward had paid Nicky the ultimate compliment of being willing to take him as backup even if I couldn't come.

"Your new guys have ex–special teams written all over them."

"Former SEALs," I said.

"Then get out here and help me back Duke off them before they do something we'll all regret. Also, I don't like the way that Otto is looking at the women you brought."

"What women?" I asked, glancing up at Nicky.

"Angel is one of the best at helping inexperienced shapeshifters keep human form," he said.

"You don't have to justify Angel. She's really good at helping newbie Therianthropes stay in human form. Who's the second woman?"

"Petra," he said.

I stared at him for a second, because he had to be joking. Petra's real name was Pierette. Petra was her Clark Kent alias, like Edward's was Ted or Olaf's Otto. And just like theirs, Petra was a law-abiding and government-worthy identity, but Pierette had been a spy and assassin for centuries. She was somewhere between Edward and Olaf on stability when she flipped from upstanding citizen to merciless killer, so not my choice for a traveling companion. She was also only a little taller than me with short dark hair and brown eyes. She fit Olaf's vic profile as well as I did.

"Why the fuck would you bring her here? You know what he is."

Nicky nodded. "We all do."

"I don't even know what that means, Nicky, but fuck, just fuck."

"Argue later, Anita. I need you policing your men and your women now," Edward said.

"Shit," I said, and started moving toward the problems.

The sooner I got things straightened out and maybe even apologized for the public display of affection (PDA), the better. It had been indulgent of me, but I still felt better, clearer-headed even. I walked around the cars with Nicky and Edward at my back. With them as backup, I could do anything if violence was the answer, so not great for Leduc, but potentially perfect for Olaf.

Leduc was literally up in the faces of Milligan and Custer, his big belly shoving at them aggressively almost the way he'd gone after Rico at the first crime scene. Ethan and Newman were trying to calm things down, which left Angel and Petra standing off to themselves with Olaf. Angel's shoulder-length hair was almost back to natural white blond; only the last few inches were still the raven black that she'd dyed it. Her hair was very straight, but she'd styled it into a faux-1940s hairdo.

Her clothes matched the hairstyle. Chunky black-and-white heels, with a black pencil skirt that hugged the generous swell of her hips and painted its way down the fullness of her thighs, making her look even curvier than I knew she was. A little white blouse with black lace tracing the short puff sleeves made her look like a retro sexy secretary from a soft-core porn. She was five-eleven; in the heels she had to be at least six-one. She glanced back at me, at us, and the makeup was the dark Goth makeup I knew she'd be wearing once I saw the clothes. It wasn't what she usually wore when she was going out of town on Coalition business, but it was one of her favorite fashions for date nights. I'd discuss with her why she'd dress for a date on Coalition business later.

At least Pierette was dressed for work, in black stretch jeans fitting into tactical boots identical to mine. They looked cuter with jeans than with my tac pants, but the tac pants had more pockets. She'd put on a short jacket that left her lower body with just the curve-hugging jeans. I had a second of realizing that I liked her ass in the jeans better than Angel's in the pencil skirt. Dating women was still so new to me, it still startled me when I noticed women at all. The fact that I was comparing the two of them the way I thought only men did bothered me, but not half as much as the look on Olaf's face. Angel was inches too tall for his preferences, even if she hadn't been wearing heels. With the hair color and the blue eyes, she wasn't his ideal victim, but she'd said or done something, or maybe Pierette had. Whatever the case, the look on his face was aimed at both of them. I wasn't even sure how I knew that, but I knew.

He'd turned so that no one else could see him but the two women. He'd dropped the mask so that they were staring into a face that wasn't just stripping them naked in his mind, but flaying the skin off their bodies, or maybe he was thinking things about them that I couldn't even imagine thinking. The look on his face was alien, other, in-fucking-comprehensible to anyone who wasn't a sexually sadistic lust killer.

My instinct was to go straight to the two women and mark territory hard, but Olaf wouldn't attack them here in front of witnesses. We'd established that in the woods earlier. He liked having his secret identity intact, so they were safe for now.

The energy coming off the two SEALs was so angry, their beasts were beginning to boil under the surface of their skin like water that was almost hot enough for coffee, tea, or third-degree burns. My beasts stirred wolf and hyena because Milligan and Custer were one of each, respectively. My inner wolf and hyena weren't the exact species as theirs, so the call was never as strong, but their energy still echoed through the cousin beasts I carried. If they started a fight with Leduc, then he'd never let anyone from the Coalition into his jail, so I started with the men. I'd leave the beast and the beauties for second.

I tried to step between Leduc and the two men, but the sheriff was literally pressed against them, so I stepped into him. I didn't hit him, didn't use force, just literally walked so that the front of my body touched the side of his, and the two SEALs moved back as I moved forward. Their energy prickled along my skin, raising the hair on my arms as I stepped into Leduc. He stumbled back, though I had done nothing to make it happen. It was like I'd startled him.

"What the fuck is wrong with you, Blake?" Leduc yelled it, but his voice didn't have the force it had had a moment ago. The stumble and me just walking into him had caught him off balance. If I'd been another man, the maneuver might have caused him to take a swing at me, but I was small and female, and sometimes that helped defuse situations.

"You don't get to treat my people the way you do your deputies, Duke," I said. "They aren't your whipping boys."

"Whipping boys? What the fuck does that even mean? You're over there playing kissy face with the big one and you lecture me on unprofessional conduct?"

"You're right on that. I'm sorry for the over-the-top PDA. I won't even try to excuse it."

The apology seemed to catch him off guard, too. "Well, I appreciate the apology and you admitting you were wrong."

"But please, from now on, don't take my bad behavior out on my people."

"I thought they were the Coalition's people."

"I asked Micah Callahan to send his people here. They are all at least work friends for me, so since Micah isn't here, they're my people, like your deputies are yours. I wouldn't disrespect your people the way you just did mine."

Duke seemed to think about that for a minute and then he nodded. "Fair enough, Blake."

I held out a hand, and after a moment's hesitation, he shook it, a little tentatively because his hand was so much bigger than mine. A lot of men have trouble with smaller hands like mine, so I didn't take it personally.

"This case has us all shook," he said.

I nodded. "It does me, too."

We said a few more pleasantries, and then the pleasantries were

over. I turned toward Olaf and the other women off to the side of the
porch. I flashed one of my best professional smiles at Newman and
Edward. "How about you guys all go inside, and Duke can make some
of that wonderful coffee so we can discuss how we can all help one
another deal with this fucking case?"

Newman started trying to herd everyone inside. He'd believed
the smile. Edward knew better.

"I'll stay out here," he said.

"No, Ted. You go help introduce everybody. I've got Nicky and
Ethan with me."

"Us, too, boss," Custer said.

I shook my head and stepped close enough to them that everyone
else wouldn't overhear. "You almost let the local LEO goad you into
a fight. That's not the kind of backup I need right now."

"Anita . . ." Milligan said.

"Boss," I said.

He blinked at me, and I watched the ego fight inside of him. Milligan was usually more reasonable than Custer, but I didn't have time
to worry about what Leduc had said to bring out the full special
team's ego issues. I did not have time to babysit that kind of ego right
now, so I just looked at him. Not aggressive, just steady, which some
people think is aggressive, but they would be wrong, because there's
a difference between direct and aggressive. Milligan would know
the difference; all the Team's guys did.

"Yes, ma'am," Milligan said as if he were back in uniform.

"That'll do, too. Now, both of you go inside and remember that
you are here to make things better, not worse."

"If we said that the LEO started it, would you get mad?" Custer
asked with one of his usual grins.

I didn't smile back. "He started, you started—I don't care who
started it. If it starts again, I will finish it for everyone."

They both had a moment of looking at me, of doing that guy math.
Physically they could totally take me—we all knew it—but it wasn't
about physical prowess. It was about other kinds of power.

"You are endangering our mission," I said, "so your superior skills mean shit to me right now. You are making me babysit your egos while Otto is over there looking at Angel and Pierette like they're fucking steaks. Get your priorities in order, gentlemen, or get the fuck off my team."

"You heard her," Nicky said. "Go make coffee."

Custer and Milligan had been calming down, but suddenly I felt their hackles rise. I pointed a finger at Nicky. "Don't you start. We are not going to play 'Who has the biggest dick?' right now."

"Sorry," he said, but not like he meant it, and there was the problem with this many big, dominant men working together. Until dominance was established, and sometimes even after, they'd push at one another. Add that they were all wereanimals, and it was just worse.

I walked toward Olaf and the women. I did not look back to see if everyone was doing what I'd told them to do. I was either the boss of them, or I wasn't. Looking back to double-check made me appear weak, and it wouldn't change a damn thing. Micah had already established his leadership over the new guys. I thought I had, but apparently I hadn't in the field. When I'd told Micah to stay home, I hadn't thought what that might mean with the rest of his crew. Ethan wasn't dominant enough to be the boss of these guys, and sometimes Nicky and the Team's guys clashed, which left me to be boss. Damn it, you fix one problem and then cause another. Fuck unintended consequences all to hell.

48

"ANGEL, PETRA, WHAT are you both doing here?" I said with a big smile that didn't reach my eyes. The tone in my voice matched my eyes, not the smile.

Angel turned with a smile until she saw the look in my eyes, and then it wilted a little around the edges. "Hey, Anita." She moved to the side so she could keep an eye on Olaf and still see me and the men with me as we came up through the cars. Her base makeup was almost white to highlight the scarlet lipstick and the black-and-red eye makeup. There was a tiny cluster of fake cherries pinned at the center of the rounded collar of the white button-up blouse. More black lace traced the collar. She had a red heart-shaped enamel watch pin on the left side of the blouse. The small touches of red brought out the red in the makeup, or maybe it was the other way around. Either way, it was adorable and sexy.

Pierette's makeup was subtle in comparison, a natural look except for the eyeliner around her dark eyes. The slight uptilt to them was emphasized and made her look more exotic than her original French and English ancestry. Though she might have been older than either country—I wasn't sure when France and England officially became countries. Pierette, through her vampire master's marks, was a lot older than that delicate triangle of a face looked.

I wanted to ask out loud, What the fuck are you doing here? You know you're his perfect victim, but that seemed a little blunt, so I tried, "I asked a question, ladies. What are you both doing here?"

"You know I travel with the Coalition to help new Therianthropes control their shifting," Angel said with a smile.

"You and Ethan are two of the best we have at helping the newbies. I need the help with Bobby, so great."

Angel smiled at me. It was a version of a smile that I'd seen a lot—mischief with an edge of evil. That expression reminded me so much of her twin brother, Mephistopheles, that it was disturbing. I still had some issues with the fact that both of them were my lovers now. It just seemed a little incesty. Was that smile on purpose to pull on Olaf's tail and see what would happen, or was it just her smile, too? When we got some privacy, the good Angel and I were so going to talk.

I turned then and said, "But Petra doesn't have your skills with keeping weak little Therianthropes in human form, so I'll ask the question one more time. What are you both doing here?"

Pierette gave me the full weight of those big brown eyes and said, "I have come to be whatever you need, my . . . Anita. Whether by sword or flesh, I am yours."

She'd almost used the title, my queen. She had lived more centuries with kings and queens than presidents, but I really hoped she didn't forget and call me queen in front of Leduc or even Newman. Oh, hell, anyone but the people who came with her on the plane.

"What does she mean by that?" Olaf asked.

"Oh, let me explain," Angel said, and the mischievous smile that went with the words blossomed until it was mostly just evil. It was the smile that Mephistopheles, our Devil, Dev for short, wore when he was about to do something unfortunate.

I shook my head at her. "No. Whatever you're thinking, just no."

"Well, you are the boss of me," Angel said, but the tone implied strongly that she was humoring me.

"You are not the boss of me," Olaf said, voice almost growling low.

I looked up at him, and for a second, he let me see all that creepy-as-fuck murder lust. The puzzlement at Pierette's phrasing hadn't been enough to dampen it, as if he was tired of wearing his civilized mask the way that Edward seemed to be getting tired of being Ted so much of the time.

"No, I'm not, but you heard what I told Duke about the SEALs."

"I did."

"That applies to Angel and Petra, too."

"I don't know what you mean," he said.

"The hell you don't," I said.

Olaf smiled at me, and he put all that happy creepiness into it that usually spooked me, but in that moment, I was done. Maybe later he'd creep me out again, but not now. For now I was done with this shit. My lioness raised golden eyes and stared up through me.

Nicky moved a little closer to me, and Ethan moved up on the other side so they flanked me.

Olaf looked disdainful. "You would let them fight your battles."

"That's what bodyguards are for," I said.

"I had thought better of you than this, Anita."

"If I ever want to just kill you, I'll do that myself, but up to that point, I'm going to need some help arm wrestling you."

His lips moved upward. Other people would have called it a smile, but it was a snarl, a warning. "I know that you sent the others inside. No witnesses." His body settled into a deep stillness like the breath before you leap into space.

"The women are mine. You do not play fuck-fuck games with them."

"And if they play them with me first?"

I looked at Angel. She tried to give me that grin again, but I let her see how unhappy I was with her, and she decided not to risk it. "I'll be talking to Angel in private later. She won't give you a problem unless you start one."

"Anita," Angel started.

"I give you my word," I said.

"Your word is good," Olaf said, "but I do not know this angel of yours."

I looked at her. There was no laughter in her voice or face now.

She was trying to tell me something wordlessly, but I didn't have the ties to her that I did with her brother. She couldn't whisper her message in my head like he could. All she could do was stare at me and try to tell me something with her eyes.

She laid her fingertips on my arm. The warmth of her golden tiger was instantly there, either from anxiety or on purpose. Angel had near-perfect control of her inner beast, so it was probably on purpose. I could have stepped away from Olaf and let her tell me whatever was so important in person. If she hadn't been standing there just minutes ago, flirting or pushing his buttons . . . if Pierette hadn't been standing there, the perfect prey for the big guy . . . if, if, if— It all translated into me being pissed at Angel. I'd sent for help, and now I just had more problems.

"I've given my word, Angel. You have to honor it."

I moved away from her so that warm rush of energy wasn't breathing along my skin. It had felt good, but I didn't want her to use her energy to calm me down. I was going to hold on to my anger at this whole situation. I'd invited the Coalition to town to make things better; this wasn't better.

"Don't make her promise, Anita, please," Ethan said.

I looked at him, surprised. I'd thought it was just Angel being Angel, but if Ethan was asking, then it was a plan, a plot. What the fuck was going on?

"They are playing both of us, Adler," Olaf said.

"I'm beginning to think you're right, Moriarty."

"They aren't playing you, Anita," Nicky said.

"I don't care what's going on. I gave my word. I expect anyone that's mine to honor that and not make me into a fucking liar." I looked at Angel.

"You're ruining my fun," she said, but there was no teasing look to go with the words.

"You keep saying that she is yours," Olaf said. "How is she yours? Is she one of your lovers?" He rolled the last word off his tongue in a way that would have pissed me off a few minutes ago, but I had the taste of Nicky's mouth lingering on mine, and Olaf always fucked with me. I wasn't used to my own people doing it.

"I told Leduc that Milligan and Custer were my people, too. You didn't ask if they were my lovers."

The lust-killer look slid into angry killer; it wasn't really an improvement. "Are they your lovers?"

I shook my head. "No."

He stayed angry, the tension trailing down his hands so they curled into fists. He wasn't getting ready to fight; he was just so angry, it had to come out physically. I was the same way sometimes. "Tell me which of them are your lovers, Anita."

I'd have liked to tell him to go to hell because it wasn't any of his business, but there was something in the way he held himself that told me not to play games. If we were going to pull the pin on this particular grenade, I wanted it to be over something important.

"You know about Nicky, and you were on the same warrant with me in Washington State when I met Ethan, so you know we're intimate." So there wasn't confusion later, I added, "Though Ethan has a serious girlfriend now, so he's emergency food for the *ardeur*, not on the main list."

"That is why you kissed Nicky hello and not Ethan?"

"Yeah."

"So, the women are not your lovers either?"

I sighed and so wanted out of this conversation, but truth was truth. I wasn't ashamed of my female lovers, but these were not the women in my life I was the most comfortable with. They were two of the newest, and we hadn't worked out all the kinks in things yet. Angel slept with Jean-Claude and Richard, Ulfric of the local werewolves, more than me. She and I had sex with the men in my life together more than sex with just each other. She was cheerfully bisexual, just like her brother. The only other person I knew who was as truly bisexual as the twins, without a strong preference for either sex, was Nathaniel.

"It's okay, Anita. You don't have to stake a claim you don't feel,"

Angel said, and there was no teasing or smiling now. Some of the light had dimmed in her blue-gold tiger eyes, because they were the eyes of a tiger caught in her human face. All the pure-blooded clan tigers were born with animal eyes, though most people just thought her eyes were exotic human eyes. People see what they expect to see.

I looked at her unhappy face, and I didn't want her unhappy. I closed the distance between us and slid my arms around her waist, which was surprisingly slender for someone so much taller than I was. I was still more accustomed to touching men. She smiled down at me and put her arms around my shoulders.

"The kiss has to be gentle," I said, "or your lipstick will be all over me."

She wrapped herself more securely around me, pressing her breasts into my face so I had to turn my chin up more not to touch my mouth to any of her. That mischievous smile was back on her face, and it made me happy to see it. She gave a little wiggle through the hips, which was usually an invitation to move my hands from waist to her ass, but I moved them up her back instead. Her back was strong and firm under my hands. I fought not to dig my fingers in, because I knew we'd both enjoy it. The mischief was suddenly evil, and I knew she was debating just how gentle the kiss was going to be.

"I mean it, Angel. The locals are already weirded out about the whole wereanimal thing. We don't need to ring the heterosexual insecurity bell, too."

"Promise me a kiss like Nicky got once we're in private?"

"Better kisses in private, I promise," I said, and I couldn't help smiling up at her.

"Deal," she whispered, and leaned over me.

I went up on tiptoe like I did for the tall men in my life. The biggest difference was that there were breasts to brush mine, though with me in body armor, it wasn't nearly as fun as usual. Her lips were soft and full, and because I wasn't wearing my own lipstick, I could taste hers. She wrapped her arms around me and pressed us together, and I returned the favor. She opened her lips, and I slid my tongue delicately inside. There was a moment when I forgot about being careful and started to kiss her like I wanted to, with teeth mixed in with tongue and lips until she made a small sound against my mouth. I returned the favor, finally letting my fingers dig into her back. Her hands responded to me, sliding over my body armor like she was trying to find me underneath it. When her hands touched my ass, I drew back first, laughing and a little breathless.

"Enough for now," I said.

I fought not to glance in Olaf's direction. If he was looking all serial killer at us, it would spoil the mood. If he looked at us like so many men who had that lesbian fantasy, that would piss me off, so I just concentrated on the excitement in Angel's eyes, her face alight with what we'd just done.

Ethan had Kleenexes in his hands to offer to both of us. Men's pockets hold so much more than women's pockets.

"Thanks," I said.

Angel laughed as she got a compact out of a tiny purse that had cherries on it to match her outfit. She started carefully cleaning her makeup. I just started to wipe the lipstick off. Since I wasn't wearing any makeup, I didn't need to be that careful.

I turned to Nicky and Ethan. "Did I get it all?"

Ethan shook his head. Nicky just took the Kleenex and started dabbing at the corner of my mouth and a little on my chin, which meant I looked like I was wearing bad clown makeup. He put his fingertips on my chin and turned my face to the side. "Clean."

"Thanks," I said, and turned toward Pierette.

I held my hand out to her, and she took it with a smile. I didn't have to look very far up to meet her eyes. They were as solid a brown as mine, though not quite as dark. I laid my hand on the side of her face; my other arm went up and over her shoulder. Her arms slid around my waist and up my back. She was one of the women in my bed who made me think words like *delicate, dainty, petite*. I liked that she made me think words like that as I stared into her eyes from inches away. We leaned in together, and I closed my eyes, though I knew Pierette didn't. She'd trained herself out of it for safety reasons, or so she'd explained one afternoon.

Her lipstick was neutral, mostly just a shiny lip gloss. It meant we could kiss without worrying about smearing it, so I did. I kissed her like I wanted to be in her arms. I let her know that I valued my hand cupping the delicate bones of her cheek, the press of her mouth against mine. My tongue slid between her lips and she opened wider, so the kiss grew as we explored each other's mouths. I thought the same thing I'd thought almost every time I'd kissed her: Her mouth was so small. Pierette didn't like rough kissing, so I was careful not to use teeth or dig my nails into her back. Her arms tightened across my back. I had a moment of feeling just how strong that delicate-seeming body was, and then she broke the kiss like she was coming up for air and I was water that she had to throw herself free of. She stood there with us just holding hands, her breathing ragged like we'd done more than kiss. I wasn't nearly as breathless with her as with Angel. I missed the teeth and nails.

"You are not bothered by this, any of you?" Olaf said. I didn't know whom he was asking, but Nicky answered.

"Why should we be?"

"She is only one woman. How can you be happy sharing her with so many others?"

Nicky smiled and let himself look pleased. "Do you think that the only person I have sex with is Anita?"

Olaf looked at him. "I did."

Careful not to compromise Nicky's gun hand, Angel came and slid her arm through Nicky's. Her lipstick was perfectly red once more; she'd retouched it while I was kissing Pierette. Angel leaned her head toward Nicky like they were posing for a couple's photo. She gave that smile she seemed to be able to do at the drop of a hat. Nicky smiled that guy smile. The one that said, *I get to hit this, and it still hasn't screwed up my primary relationship.* It wasn't a cat-with-cream smile; it was a have-your-cake-and-eat-it-too smile.

I looked at the two of them and thought of all the times we'd been together, usually with Dev or Nathaniel, and a couple of times with both of them. That had been fun. I gave a little shiver that went from my head to my feet, and now my breathing was faster just thinking about it.

"What did you react to just now?" Olaf asked.

"The possibilities," I said and smiled, and realized that maybe my smile was a have-your-cake-and-eat-it-too smile.

"Doesn't it bother you that Nicky is having sex with all the other women?"

Nicky corrected him. "Angel and I have sex together. Petra and I don't. It's a person-by-person negotiation."

Olaf looked back at me. "And it doesn't bother you that Nicky is fucking another woman?"

I don't know what made me be honest. Maybe it was the feel of Pierette's hand in mine or the memory of being with Nicky and Angel together. "I'm there when he does it, so no."

Olaf stared at me. "Now you are teasing me."

"I'm telling you the absolute truth, Olaf . . . Otto," I said, trying to get back in the habit of using the right name before we went back in to the other cops.

He looked from Nicky to me, then to each of the women, then back to me. He looked at Ethan. "Do you also negotiate individually?"

"I just have sex with Anita and my girlfriend. That's enough for me."

"At the same time?" Olaf asked.

Ethan gave a nervous laugh. "Not Nilda and Anita. No, just . . . no."

We all agreed with him, since Nilda was an ancient werebear with a temper that had required therapy. I was glad that she and Ethan seemed to love each other to pieces, because she was one of the most unstable of the Harlequin. Nilda and Ethan as a couple helped keep the rest of us safer.

"Is Petra only having sex with you, Anita?" I realized that Olaf was asking questions of me and the men, but that he hadn't spoken directly to either of the other women. It was the way he'd talked to me when we first met: sort of around me, talking more to Edward than to me.

If it had been almost anyone else, I'd have forced them to talk directly to the women, but if Olaf saw me and the other men as a gateway to the women, that worked for me. Maybe he wouldn't talk to them without one of us present. I especially didn't want him talking alone with Pierette.

"Not just me."

"So, if I wished to negotiate with her for sex, you would have no objection?"

My pulse was suddenly trying to jump out the side of my neck. He hadn't said anything wrong really. He'd been amazingly polite, so why was I scared?

"I do not wish to sleep with him, my queen. Please don't make me," she said.

There was fear in her voice. It surprised me enough to look at her, and the expression on her face matched the voice. She was scared of Olaf. I mean, he was scary, but she'd hunted scarier things than him for hundreds of years. Even if he scared her, she didn't have to show it this much. What was she doing, and why? She moved behind me like I would be her shield, which seemed weird for someone who was supposed to be my bodyguard.

I knew too many of the older vampires who treated their *moitiés bêtes*, beast halves, like slaves, but Pierrot didn't treat her that way, or I hadn't thought he did. I thought they were lovers as well as master and servant. Now I was suddenly wondering if he did abuse her. In old vampire society, animals to call had no rights. Jean-Claude and I were changing that and stopping the abuse when we found out about it, but some of the animals to call had centuries of being more possessions than partners to their masters. I had thought better of Pierrot, but Pierette's reaction let me know that better wasn't the same thing as good.

"No one will make you have sex with anyone, Petra. We keep telling you that's not how things work with us." I stroked her face, my other hand still in hers. She wouldn't meet my eyes. Her shoul-

ders were rounded; her entire posture was huddled in upon herself. Shit.

I felt the heat of lion, smelled it like grass baked under a merciless
sun. I looked at Olaf. He was watching Pierette like he'd seen a
wounded gazelle at a watering hole. Crap, crap, crap. Her reaction
had just made her even more his perfect victim.

49

LEDUC CAME OUT of the building, moving our way like he had a purpose. That purpose was probably to yell at us. Either Edward and Newman hadn't been wingmen enough to keep him busy, or Edward had decided Leduc interrupting us with Olaf was the lesser evil. I hoped the sheriff hadn't seen me kiss either of the women, but of course . . .

"What the hell, Blake? Are you going to kiss all of them? If you want a booty call, then get out of my town and go home."

Great, just great, he'd seen at least some of it.

Edward was trailing behind Leduc, and just the way he was moving told me that he'd let the sheriff out to distract Olaf, or maybe he'd been afraid of what we'd do once we were all alone with the big guy. Did he really think we'd kill Olaf and play the "We have no idea where he went" game? Or was that what Edward was beginning to debate doing himself? I'd ask him later if we were ever alone on this damn case.

I stepped away from everyone, and when Nicky tried to follow, I said, "Stay, and that goes for all of you."

I was pissed, so pissed, and before I'd worked on my anger issues, I'd have lashed out at Leduc and made everything worse, but I was in the wrong here. If I'd seen another police officer smooching someone while we were in the middle of a murder investigation and Bobby's life was hanging in the balance, I'd have ripped them a new one, so what could I do? I tried for a version of the truth, because I couldn't think of a lie that would help dig me out of the unprofessional hole I'd just fallen into.

"I'm sorry, Sheriff. I have behaved unprofessionally, and I'm embarrassed by it," I said fast as he was drawing breath to yell at me again.

He hesitated like he was rethinking what he was going to say, which was what I was hoping he'd do. "Hell, Blake, you keep apologizing for all the over-the-top PDA, but you're still doing it."

"I know and I'm sorry, but . . . You have a wife, right?" I said.

Leduc frowned at me. "Yes."

"What would you do if she showed up on the job and wanted you to give her a hug?"

"My wife would never do that. She knows when I'm working, I'm working."

"Did she know it when you began dating?"

He frowned harder. "I have no idea what you're talking about, Blake."

I leaned into him like I was confiding in him, and he leaned in to hear me. Let's hear it for social conditioning. "I was unprofessional with Nicky. I own that. But then I didn't greet the women the same way, because one stupid moment was all I allowed myself."

"So why did you kiss both of them? I can't even wrap my head around the fact that you're dating this many people."

"It's a lot of people even to me, Sheriff, trust me."

"Then why do it?"

I glanced back at the two women and Nicky. "Which of them would you kick out of bed for eating crackers?"

Leduc glanced behind me and got a considering look on his face. Then he grinned and started shaking his head. He gave me that guy-to-guy look that I'd gotten from a few of the police officers at home when they met some of the women in my life. I'd had two of them tell me, "You dog." I knew it was a compliment, just not one I'd ever thought I'd get.

"Well, now, can't argue that, but that much eye candy is going to be damn distracting." Leduc's eyes narrowed to nicely skeptical cop eyes. "You going to be too distracted to do your job?"

"I deserve that, but I promise the public displays of affection are over until we get a break in the case."

"You said the big guy was your mistake, so why kiss the others if you knew better?"

Then I lied, and I took a chance that a long-married man would understand something that you only learned if you dated women. "Some version of 'if you loved me as much as you love him.' Basically, those two kisses just kept me out of the doghouse with two women."

My answer wasn't strictly true. Angel wasn't that serious about me or anyone. Pierette would never have pushed her advantage. She saw herself as serving her queen, me. She'd volunteered and pursued the relationship, but she still wouldn't push that much. But I couldn't explain all that to Leduc. I could explain trying to keep the women in your life happy.

"But you're a woman, too, Blake."

"Trust me, what sex I am doesn't matter at all, only theirs."

"So, what if they get their feelings hurt and need more romantic reassurance again? They're going to distract you from the case."

"I'm going to make it really clear that this is the one and only PDA for this trip, and if they can't understand that, then I'll be in the doghouse when we get home."

"I can't quite picture a woman being in the doghouse the same way that a man ends up there."

"Trust me, Duke"—yes, I even stooped to using his nickname—"if you're dating women and certain men, the doghouse doesn't care if you're male or female."

He frowned at me. "Seems like women should be smart enough to stay out of trouble."

I shook my head. "Maybe, but I'm not."

He smiled. "I heard the rumors that you were sleeping around, but that's not it. That's casual, and casual doesn't give people the power to make you do stupid shit like you just did."

"Whatever I'm doing, it's not casual."

"Well, wouldn't want to get a fellow officer in the doghouse with two women at once."

"Thank you, Duke. I really appreciate that."

He shook his head and actually patted my shoulder. "Being with one woman is hard enough, Blake. Good luck to you."

"Thanks, and could I have a few minutes alone to explain the no more PDA for the rest of the trip?"

"How many of them are staying for the talk?"

I looked at them and realized that it was everyone but Milligan and Custer. "All of them, I guess, except for Otto Jeffries."

He laughed. "Then I can give you privacy, Blake, but this is not the definition of being alone."

"No arguments," I said.

Leduc went inside, but Olaf didn't want to go without us—okay, mostly me—so I told him a version of the same thing I'd told Leduc. "I need some privacy to talk to the women in my life, Otto. We need to make it clear that this is the last PDA while I'm working. I smoothed it over with Leduc once, but I can't do it twice."

"You have explained it to them," he said.

I shook my head. "One of the hard things about dating women is that it takes more explaining to explain things, especially emotional ones."

He stared at me, frowning, thinking hard. "You are admitting that women are not logical?"

"No, but they are more complicated than men when it comes to dating and romance."

He seemed to think about that and then finally shook his head. "I will agree, and I will leave you to speak to the . . . women in your life."

Olaf started walking toward the offices. When he walked through the door, Edward tipped his hat to me from the little porch and followed inside.

Once they were inside and the rest of us were as alone as we were going to get, I turned on them and said, "You have minutes to tell me why the fuck Pierette is here. Isn't it enough that I fit his victim profile? Did you have to endanger someone else?"

"I am your bodyguard. It is my duty to put myself between you and danger," Pierette said, and she didn't sound the least bit frightened now. She stood tall and certain, as if the woman who had just finished hiding behind me was someone else. It reminded me of how Edward could switch to Ted.

"What exactly does that mean?" I asked.

Pierette just looked at me with her brown eyes, made larger with the eyeliner, which she never wore at home. "I serve my queen in any way she requires."

I turned to the one person I knew had to tell me the truth. "What the hell is going on, Nicky?"

"It wasn't my idea. I knew you'd hate it," he said.

"What wasn't your idea?"

"To bring Pierette and Angel here to help you deal with Olaf."

Then I had a thought, and he was right. I hated it. "Pierette, you were pretending to be afraid of him just now. It's not enough that you look like his favorite type of victim. You're playing to it."

"I am afraid of him, my queen. I would not want to be helpless in his hands. I merely let him see the fear rather than hiding it." She was so calm as she spoke.

"Why? Why would you do that?"

"To tempt him."

"What?" Angel tried to put an arm around my shoulders, and I moved away from her. "And you, why are you flirting with him?"

"If you mean the clothes, I was at the concert. I didn't wear them for anyone here."

She sounded angry then, but I'd had my last emotional-blackmail moment from either of them. I'd already apologized once for her missing the night out with everyone. I was done with that.

"I don't mean the clothes, and you know it. Why are you flirting with him, of all people?"

"We wanted to see if he'd respond to normal flirting," she said as if what she'd done was a matter of course.

"Why would you want him to respond to it?"

"They're here to try to take some of the pressure off of you," Ethan said.

I took a deep breath and counted to ten as I let it out slowly. It didn't really help. "If you came to protect me from Olaf, and not to help me save Bobby Marchand's life, you can drive right back to the airport and get the hell away from me."

"If he responds to me flirting with him, then maybe he's datable in some weird, psychotic way," Angel said.

"He's not psychotic, and are you volunteering to date Olaf?"

She laughed. "I'm too tall, too blond, and too blue eyed, but if he wasn't fixated on his victims, then he'd be totally hot."

Whatever look was on my face made her laugh again, but this one was a nervous one. "Come on, Anita, if you just look at the physical, he's smokin' hot."

"I guess his whole liking to kidnap, tie up, torture, and rape women ruins it for me."

"I actually think the danger is part of what makes him hot."

I looked at Angel as if I'd never seen her before. "Well, forgive me as a woman that fits his vic profile to a T if I don't find it intriguing."

"And that is why Pierette is here," Angel said.

"This is ridiculous. We are not doing this. It is a stupid and dangerous plan."

"It's not stupid," Nicky said, "but I knew you'd hate it."

"It is stupid. I won't let Pierette endanger herself. I don't want anyone to be at Olaf's mercy—certainly not someone I've had sex with and actually like."

"I am honored that you care for me that much, my queen, but if I could end this threat to you once and for all, it would be worth the danger."

"You do not understand what he is, or you wouldn't say that."

"It is he who does not know what I am," she said. She let her face show the confidence of centuries of being one of the most feared assassins in the world. She and all the other Harlequin had been so frightening that even mentioning their name could have gotten bad little vampires executed. Now they were part of our bodyguards, and if they spied, they did it for Jean-Claude or Micah. Oh, how the mighty had fallen and all that jazz, but the arrogance naked in Pierette's eyes showed that at least the ego hadn't fallen that far.

"I'm not saying that you aren't fearsome on your own, Petra, but you can't understand what he is, or you wouldn't be this calm about using yourself as bait."

"I understand precisely what he is, and the fact that we've allowed him to continue living when he is a terrible threat to you is inexcusable."

"I'll say what is and isn't excusable," I said.

"That is your prerogative as queen, but if anyone had dared to threaten our old queen in such a manner, it would not have been tolerated."

"Well, I'm queen now, and that is not how I want Olaf handled. He's a fellow marshal, for the love of God. You can't just kill him."

"We will do nothing to him unless he tries to kidnap or rape me."

"But if you bait him into doing it, it's like you're setting him up to be killed."

"I will not harm him unless he tries to harm me first, and then I will merely defend myself. I am allowed to defend myself."

"Of course you are."

"Then if he behaves himself and passes on the bait, he will not get caught and slain," Pierette said, and she was still too calm.

I wanted to grab her and shake her until she showed the fear she'd let him see. Had it been an act? Was she an even better actor than Edward? If she was, then I couldn't trust anything she'd ever said or done with me. Damn it, didn't she understand this would make me doubt her?

Nicky said, "She understands."

"You read my mind," I said.

He nodded. "And both Angel and Pierette understood both the danger from Olaf and that it might damage their relationship with you."

"We all decided the risks were worth it," Ethan said.

I looked into his soft gray eyes. "It's wrong."

"Why, my queen?" Pierette asked.

"What she asked," Angel said.

I tried to think how to say it and finally said, "It seems . . . dishonorable. If I have to kill Olaf, I want him to know it's coming and why."

"If he kidnaps one of your girlfriends, he'll know why we're killing him," Nicky said. Put that way, it made sense, but it still felt wrong.

"I don't have time to argue about this anymore. We go inside and you prove to me that you're all assets on this case, or I will by God send you home."

"As you like, my queen," Pierette said.

She even bowed at the neck, which was as much bowing as I allowed her in public. In private she'd press her face to the floor like she was abasing herself before something holy. It was incredibly uncomfortable to have people drop to the floor in front of you. I never knew what to do. Did I tell them to stop that and stand up, or just get off the floor, ignore it, help them up? I didn't know, and I didn't want to know. I just wanted to break them of the habit.

"Don't bow to me where the other police can see it."

"As you like, my queen."

"And don't use any of my titles except for Marshal while we're here."

"Of course . . . Marshal."

"We're sleeping together. I think you can call me Anita."

"Thank you, my queen."

I started to correct Pierette, but then just started walking toward the sheriff's office. I had a crime to solve and a life to save. I wasn't letting anyone—not Olaf, not my bodyguards, not my lovers, not even my friends with benefits—interfere with this case. If they kept distracting me this badly, I would send them home, even the two women who were willing to fall on Olaf's serial killer blade. I'd handled him before with just Edward to run interference. I could do it again if I had to. There was a tiny part of me that wasn't so sure of that, and a very large part of me that knew someday I'd have to kill Olaf or he'd kill me. So why did it bother me so much that we were setting him up to fall back into his old murderous habits? I didn't know, and I stopped trying to figure it out. Later. I'd think about it later. Crime first, moral dilemmas later. Oh, wait. The case was a moral dilemma, too. Damn it all to hell.

50

WE WERE ALL in the office having more of Duke's yummy coffee, but none of my new people had been allowed near the cells. The cells were just a door away from us, but they might as well have been on the dark side of the moon. With the hours ticking away before we had to execute Bobby, we were stuck trying to play diplomats. I'd thought Leduc and I had had a "guy" bonding moment outside, and he had forgiven the PDA, but he hadn't even begun to harp on the fact that we'd brought members of the Coalition for Better Understanding Between Therianthrope and Human Communities to his town. Legally, Newman had invited them in, so he could simply show them to the cells, but he had to live here after the case was over, and he seemed to be chasing Leduc's approval like a black sheep that finally wants Daddy to love him more, or maybe that was just my natural impatience and crankiness talking. Since everything out of my mouth made Leduc angrier, I'd found a piece of wall near the door so I could watch the entire room and all the people in it. Edward had stayed in the diplomatic effort, playing Ted to the hilt to help Newman, Ethan, and Angel persuade the sheriff that he should play nice with us. The rest of us who weren't as good at playing diplomat were just trying to stay out of the way.

Olaf was in the chair by the smaller desk since Leduc was pacing by his big desk and gesturing angrily between offering refreshments. The sheriff was like a mix of hostess and pissed cop. Ethan was utterly polite, and Angel was that plus an attractive woman who played to it; they both seemed to bring out a hardwired part of Leduc that wanted to play Susie Homemaker.

Milligan and Custer had found a piece of wall to lean against near Olaf. He was studiously ignoring them while they were trying to casually keep an eye on him. It was the alpha-guy equivalent of women who showed up to a big party looking fabulous and wanted desperately to be prettier than the other women, but tried to act like it wasn't that big a deal. Milligan had cut his white blond hair so short that he looked nearly as bald as Olaf. Custer's brown hair was finally long enough for a short ponytail. The other three former SEALs who had survived the lycanthrope terrorist cell somewhere classified were giving him a lot of grief for growing it out. Millie was taller at over six feet. Custer was a little under six feet and broader through the shoulders and hips. Why was Custer nicknamed Pud? It was short for Puddin', which was a play on Custer being Custard. I'm told that some military nicknames stick with you for life. Millie was on the willowy side. All the guys in their unit were of similar builds, regardless of ethnicity. They both gave off that I'm-the-biggest-dog-in-the-room vibe like most of the Team's guys, but for once they weren't. Olaf would have towered over everyone if he'd bothered to stand up; that he didn't bother was an insult. He had nothing to prove to them, because he already knew he was bigger and better. Of course, all the SEALs had had to work on swallowing their egos when they joined our security team, because we had a lot of bigger dogs.

Nicky was staying the closest to me, the way Bram shadowed Micah back home. Nicky didn't travel everywhere with me the way Bram did with Micah, but when he was with me, he usually assumed the position of main bodyguard for me. The fact that he was also one of my lovers and metaphysically tied to me was almost beside the point for his job. He was probably about the same height as Custer, under six feet, but he was so muscled that he always seemed bigger. He'd removed his sunglasses and tucked them in the front of his shirt. The newly shortened yellow blond hair meant he couldn't use it to hide the scars that were all that was left of his right eye. When I'd met him, he'd grown his bangs out in a long triangle like an anime character. Of course, he'd had about twenty pounds less muscle on him then, so he'd looked more like a club kid, but a devotion to the weight room had made him too fierce-looking to match the club-kid disguise, so he'd cut his hair. He was looking at the world bare-faced. I'd been with him when people gawked or did the fast look away as if they were embarrassed they'd been caught staring. Watching Nicky walk through the world with his scars showing had made me love him even more. Bravery was one of my favorite things.

Olaf wasn't just ignoring the two men near him; he was also pretending that he didn't see Nicky as worthy competition, and I knew that wasn't true. It wasn't like they had ever discussed it in front of me, but they respected each other as warriors.

Pierette had found a corner of the room away from all of us. I couldn't even see her from where I was standing, and neither could Olaf, which I think was her point. She was back to playing would-be victim for him. I still didn't like it, but I hadn't absolutely forbidden it either. One disaster at a time. First, I had to get my people in to see Bobby.

Newman extracted himself from the discussion with Leduc to come talk to me. "I'm the one that has to deal with Duke when this is all over, so I have to be here for this part. You go and question one of the women. When you're done with the interview, text or call me, and I'll let you know if I can take the second interview or if you get both."

"Are you sure I can't help here?"

Ethan had come up to us, leaving Angel to be charming to Leduc. It was amazing how most men preferred to talk to an attractive woman, especially one who was willing to flirt a little while she did it. Angel could be almost as hard-nosed as I was, but she went the soft, flirty way much better than I did when it suited her purpose. It suited her purposes now. I knew she could flirt, but I hadn't realized she could use it as a negotiation ploy. I could never use it that way. I either flirted with intent to date or I didn't flirt. I just didn't flirt well enough for anything in between. Duke was an older man; they always liked a young, pretty woman paying attention to them. Hell, I guess most people who are into women do, but I've found that men above a certain age are more susceptible to it without expecting anything to come of it.

"You guys make a good team," I said.

"She's the only one of us that has college degrees in social work and psychology," Ethan said. "She's smarter about this than I'll ever be."

He lowered his voice and said, "Go question your witness. Try to find us more legal ammunition to give to the lawyer once she gets here. Angel and I will get us in to see Bobby."

With him bent over me, I was suddenly aware of the smell of his shampoo, the warmth of him so close to me. I wasn't in love with Ethan, but he was one of my *moitiés bêtes*, my animal to call, which meant touching him felt comforting. Touching any of my animals to call, or even a shapeshifter of the same species, would lower my anxiety level. It just felt good to touch the shapeshifters who were tied to us. I didn't want to kiss Ethan the way I had the others, but leaning against him so that we could touch without holding hands or getting all romantic would have been nice.

"I thought you were done with the PDA, Blake," Leduc said.

"We're trying to talk quietly so as not to interrupt you, Duke. That's all, no hand-holding."

Leduc narrowed his eyes at us. "I don't usually touch the people I'm talking to in the office. Maybe Flynn and Miss Angel here are more professional than I first thought, but I'm still thinking maybe you lied about it not being a booty call, Blake."

"You don't have to have a good opinion of me, Sheriff. If you let Ethan and the rest of our people help us with Bobby, then you can hate me all you want."

"I didn't say I hated you, Blake."

"Thanks, Le . . . Duke."

He nodded at me. "You're welcome, but I need you to tell me exactly how they can help you with this case."

Ethan started to say something, but Leduc held his hand up. "Not from you, from Blake." Leduc looked at me expectantly.

"If I step back into the cage with Bobby, I want more wereanimal backup."

"Therianthrope backup," Angel corrected automatically.

"Yeah, that, but I'm not going to risk my life again without better backup."

"I was here, and I am an Ailuranthrope, like Marchand," Olaf said.

"Yeah, you're both cat-based."

"I expected Micah or even Nathaniel to come and help you with the leopard in the cage. It's always easier to control the same internal beast, yet you bring another lion, wolves, hyenas, and a tiger. What can they do that I could not?"

"I'm a leopard like your prisoner," Pierette said. She managed to make her voice sound uncertain, as if it took bravery for her to speak up. She was good at pretending—like Edward good. Again I realized that maybe I didn't know her at all. It was interesting that Olaf hadn't been able to tell what animal she was by smell . . . or had he met everyone else before? I couldn't remember if he'd met Milligan and Custer or not.

"Come out where I can see you, little cat," Olaf said, his voice already full of what passed for teasing for him. It always came out as threatening to me.

"Are you saying you're not glad to see me, Otto?" Nicky said from his bit of wall near but not too near Olaf. He even smiled when he spoke. They'd run in the same mercenary—sorry, private contractor—circles at one point in their careers. They'd both had a certain reputation among their fellow contractors and had come to admire each other's work, though they'd never actually worked together. And just like that, Nicky took Olaf's attention off Pierette and put it squarely on himself.

Olaf unfolded from the chair and suddenly seemed even taller than normal, as if he slumped just a little bit most of the time. I don't think that was it, but he'd done something to make it very clear that he literally towered over everyone in the room. Nicky pushed away from the wall, still smiling. Milligan and Custer stood straighter; they'd already spaced themselves to have room to fight before they'd chosen their bits of wall. Ethan stayed by me like a good bodyguard; he looked fragile beside Olaf, but then he looked fragile beside Nicky, too. I guess everyone did, even the SEALS.

"Everybody, ease down," Leduc said, which proved that he was better at his job and more observant than this case was showing. Again, I got the idea I wasn't catching him at his best, whether it was years too late or just emotional issues.

"We're easy," Nicky said, grinning happily, as if saying, *Let's have fun, or let's get violent, or let's do both.* He'd had that grin from the first moment I met him.

Newman said, "Anita is going to go question the friends that went with Jocelyn to the club the night of the murder."

"I will go with her," Olaf said.

"And I'll tag along," Nicky said.

"You have some kind of badge?" Leduc asked.

Nicky smiled at him, giving full-face attention. Leduc's eyes did the slide thing as if he was trying to decide where to look on Nicky's face, because like most polite people, he didn't want to stare at the scars. Thanks to Nicky, I'd discovered that I always stared at just one eye on anyone I was giving good eye contact to, and it was always the right eye. I'd tried to change that for Nicky, but he'd thought I was being weird like everyone else. In the end I'd explained my discovery, and we'd both decided that I'd stare at his face the way I did at everyone else's even if that made it look like I was staring at his scars.

"As members of the preternatural branch, we have the ability to deputize people if we think they'd be an asset on a case," Newman said.

"It's your case, not hers, and I know you didn't deputize someone you don't know."

"I met him in the field on the same case where I met Forrester, Jeffries, and Blake."

Leduc looked Nicky up and down like he was taking measurements. "So, what's your specialty that makes Blake want you on her cases so often?"

"Tough motherfucker," Nicky said, face sobering so that he said it straight-faced and serious.

Custer laughed from the wall.

"Are you making a joke?" Leduc asked.

"No," Nicky said.

I smiled; I couldn't help it.

"Nicky is a good man in a fight," Edward said, finally coming forward instead of just watching us.

"Are we amusing you, Blake?" Leduc asked.

"No, sir."

"Then why are you smiling?"

"Nicky has that effect on me sometimes."

"He's part of her poly group," Olaf said, and that surprised me more than almost anything he could have done. I hadn't expected him to spill my secrets to the cops, if I couldn't spill his. I mean, the kiss had given things away, but him using the poly vocabulary probably wouldn't help with Leduc.

I shot Olaf an unfriendly look.

"What's a poly group?" Leduc asked.

Ethan answered, "Poly group and polycule are terms for the permanent members of a nonmonogamous group, a coupleness formed of more than two people."

We all got poly questions now, but apparently Ethan had heard Micah answer the question a lot, because Micah was the one most likely to have to answer on camera while he was trying to save lives or help lycanthropes—sorry, Therianthropes—get a more positive public image.

"Are you a member of her poly group?" Leduc asked.

Ethan shook his head. "I'm happily monogamous with my girlfriend back home in St. Louis." A look of nearly shining happiness crossed his face. Ethan had loved Nilda enough to go to couples counseling when they'd barely been dating.

The offer to help pay for therapy for any of our employees who wanted it was one of the best new policies of the last few years. As people had success and showed improvement, they encouraged others to go work out their issues and get healthier. I saw the policy as the same as dental or vision riders to health insurance, just another part of our bodies that needed care and attention.

"Then how do you know all that?" Leduc asked.

"I work with a lot of people that are poly, including my boss . . . bosses." Ethan smiled at him.

Leduc looked suspiciously at his pleasant smiling face. Ethan was handsome but not in a traditional way. I think it was the mixed hair color. Leduc probably thought it was some rebellious statement. At least Ethan's eyes were solid gray and not some of the more exotic colors that the rest of the clan tigers had. Unless you knew what tiger eyes looked like, most people's minds just saw human eyes in Ethan's face, because it was what they expected to see.

Angel came over to us and tried to help by touching the sheriff's arm lightly, enough to make most men debate on if you were flirting or just a touchy-feely kind of person.

He shook his head and patted her hand where it lay on his arm. "I appreciate the attention from a lovely young woman, Ms. Devereaux, but it's not going to get you in to see the prisoner."

"What will? And a minute ago you were calling me Miss Angel. I liked it," she said, smiling one of her smiles that wasn't real, but I'd seen her use it to make men back in St. Louis trip over their own feet. It was like she and her twin brother had come into the world knowing how to flirt.

Leduc patted her hand again and stepped out of reach. "Well, then, Miss Angel, I need proof that you can help and that you're not just here to screw up the warrant of execution. I read up on your Coalition. You do as much politics for supernatural rights as you do for attack survivors and their families. I don't want Ray's death turned into political sound bites."

"Let us take them back so they can meet Bobby, and we'll go from there," I said.

"Come on, Duke, what can it hurt just to introduce them?" Newman asked.

"I promise not to flirt if you'll just let us talk to him," Angel said, face solemn with her eyes very wide, like she was trying to look innocent and sincere. She failed, but it was cute as hell.

Leduc laughed, looking at the ground and shaking his head. "Damn, all right. Talking doesn't hurt."

He knocked on the door, and I heard Deputy Frankie unlock it. They hadn't locked it the entire time I'd been here, or I didn't think they had. Apparently, this many lycanthropes in the police station required more security. Whatever made them feel better. I decided not to point out that the door wouldn't have held against any of the Coalition shapeshifters. Hell, I wasn't sure it would have held against me if I wanted in badly enough. If it had been locked when Newman had kicked it in to stop Troy from killing Bobby, they'd have needed a new lock or a new door.

I'd never tried to get through a security door outside a cellblock before. I looked at the door sort of speculatively as we followed Leduc through it. I still wasn't used to being more than human strong. I still didn't know everything I could do without injuring myself. It was like being a new superhero. You never knew what you could do until you did it.

51

DEPUTY FRANKIE UNLOCKED the door for us, but we couldn't all fit into the area in front of the cells, so I introduced everyone a couple at a time while Leduc watched from the door and Frankie tried to stay small in the corner farthest from the outer door.

Bobby's eyes got a little wide when he was introduced to Nicky and the SEALs. Nicky was just big, so a lot of people gave him a wide berth. Without him wearing sunglasses and having hair to hide his missing eye, some people thought he was a pirate or a villain in a movie. The fact that Bobby reacted almost the same way to Milligan and Custer said that he wasn't judging the men on just size and scary-looking injuries, but on physical potential. That he didn't react to Ethan that way wasn't a mark against Bobby; it was a testament to how well Ethan could hide in plain sight. Ethan was fast, dangerous, and well trained like the other men, but his basic energy was pleasant, almost gentle. It was one of the reasons that he'd started going out on jobs with the Coalition: He didn't throw his energy around or try to dominate anyone. It just wasn't important to him.

Angel didn't play dominance games either, but when Bobby saw her, it was obvious he was thinking not if Angel could kick his ass, but how her ass looked in the pencil skirt she was wearing. It's good to be pretty and dress up, but so many people make the mistake of seeing only that part, as if there's no person inside the dress or behind the makeup. Maybe men don't deal with that as much because they don't wear makeup and pretty clothes. Who knows? Whatever. Bobby was solidly in that see-the-pretty-and-not-the-person camp. He was a good-looking guy who had been raised with money. Maybe appearance was all he ever had to see?

He was introduced to Pierette, too, but he liked either tall women or Angel's flashier fashion sense, because he didn't give Pierette half the attention he gave Angel. It wasn't just Olaf who couldn't sense her inner leopard, though I took points away for Bobby not sensing a beastie to match his own. Most of them would sense their own flavor faster than other animals. Pierette, like most of the old queen's bodyguard, was excellent at hiding what she was. Would her being too good at hiding her beast when she played so scared and weak give the game away to Olaf?

Of course, Bobby wasn't the only one who saw the pretty. Frankie stared at Angel like a teenage boy seeing the crush of his dreams. In this case, they were her dreams. I didn't usually see cops—or women, especially lesbians in small Midwestern towns who happened to be cops—on the job act that obvious. It was like Angel had gotten through all Frankie's defenses and left her gobsmacked. I had to turn my face so I didn't look too amused. I wasn't sure that Frankie realized how much of herself she'd given away in that one look.

Angel noticed, because she always noticed that sort of thing. She flashed Frankie a smile that made the woman blush even through her darker skin tone. Anyone can make a redhead blush, but making a dark-skinned brunette blush takes talent.

Leduc was scowling from Angel to Frankie as if this was all news to him, and he wasn't very happy about it. I hoped that Frankie hadn't hurt her chances of having a police career here in Hanuman.

"Well, now we're all nice and friendly," Leduc said, "but what the hell good are you to me and this investigation?"

"Bobby," I said, "if you'll give Angel your hand through the bars, she can demonstrate."

He frowned at me. "What will she do to my hand?"

"It won't hurt. Promise," Angel said.

"You know how you lost control earlier and I had to hurt you to calm things down?" I asked.

He made a face. "How could I forget? I haven't been hit that hard since I stopped playing football."

I smiled at the compliment, because from an athletic guy, it was a compliment. "Angel and Ethan here can help you control your beast without resorting to violence."

"How?" Bobby asked, and sounded suspicious.

"She'll use energy instead of fists."

"Will it hurt?"

"Not as much as me breaking your nose again."

That made him smile, almost embarrassed. He walked up to the bars and held out his hand. Angel turned it palm up and rested it in her slightly smaller hand. Her energy breathed along the side of my body like a warm spring wind. It was as gentle as that sounds. Since, in full-blown golden-tiger mode, her energy could feel like you were putting your hand into live fire, it was always impressive to feel her be so delicate.

Bobby smiled. Apparently Angel's energy felt as good to him as it did to me. "It's like you're petting my leopard. I mean, that's not exactly it, but that's how it feels."

"That's a good analogy," Angel said, smiling at him like he'd said something smart, which he had.

Bobby smiled back. In the corner, Frankie frowned as if she thought Bobby was cutting into her time. It was too early for that kind of crankiness, at least in my opinion, but then I'm a poly. We share better than most.

"I can help you control your beast, but not as well as Angel and Ethan can, and Petra is another wereleopard," I said.

Bobby looked at her more seriously then. "I can't sense it."

"Thank you for the compliment, Bobby," Pierette said, and there was that touch of humbleness and just a hint of gentle flirting.

If I hadn't been standing right next to her, I might not have noticed the slight turn of her head, the smile coupled with the shy glance quickly turned to the floor. It was part her own body language, but not all of it. It matched the fear she kept letting Olaf glimpse. She was masterful at playing her part, a mix of truth and lie that was far more subtle than Edward and his Ted persona.

Bobby took the shy-flirting bait and wasted a nice smile on her. Sometimes it's not the big showy rose that wins the day. Sometimes it's the violet underfoot or the daffodil nodding in the breeze. The moment I thought of the analogy, I wondered what kind of flower I was and decided a thistle. A big prickly purple thistle, definitely not a flower to pick for a bouquet.

"Are you going to show me your energy?" Bobby asked.

Pierette did that shy eye flick and smiled a little bit more as she shook her head. "I'll only step in if I feel your leopard rising. Angel and Ethan will do the energy work until then."

Bobby looked at Ethan. "Is your energy as gentle as Angel's?"

Angel answered, "Gentler."

Bobby looked like he didn't believe her. She shook her head and said, "I've learned to be gentle, but Ethan seemed to come that way. Didn't you, dearie?"

She put her hand through his arm, which compromised his gun hand, but in the narrow confines of the hallway, if things went sideways it would be empty hands or blades, not guns. I knew Ethan had blades that he could reach with either hand, just like I did. We all practiced shooting with both hands, but most people carried for their dominant hand.

"Are you a gentle man, Flynn?" Olaf asked from near the door. He broke the one word into two—not *gentleman*, but a *gentle man*—and he made sure they sounded like an insult. I knew Ethan wouldn't rise to the verbal bait.

"I try to be," Ethan said with a smile.

Olaf made a sound that wasn't complimentary. I felt strangely like I needed to come to Ethan's defense. I actually opened my mouth to say something about how good Ethan was with weapons and hand-to-hand, but Angel put her hand through my arm and drew us to-gether, almost close enough to be PDA again. Was it just the casual touch of most of the wereanimals, or was she trying to tell me some-thing? Until I could ask her in private, I let it go. Besides, I didn't need to defend my people to Olaf. They were good in a fight, or they wouldn't have been working as bodyguards for us. Angel was an exception. She could fight if she had to, because she was gold tiger clan and they insisted that, male or female, you had to know the ba-sics, but she had other skills that made her good with the Coalition. A background in social work and psychology just to name two.

"That's it? That's all you can do?" Leduc asked.

Angel looked up at him, smiling, and Ethan and I both pulled away to stand on our own. "I'm sorry, Sheriff. I didn't realize you couldn't feel the energy."

"It wasn't much energy to feel," Olaf said, and sounded almost sul-len. Did he really resent me calling in other shapeshifters that much?

"You're too new to understand how impressive it is," Nicky said.

"My control is not that of a newcomer."

"Your control isn't what I'm questioning, Otto, old buddy. It's your lack of experience I'm questioning."

Olaf scowled at Nicky, and there was a flare of energy like the swat of a lion's paw. It didn't actually hurt, but it didn't feel good either.

"Now I'm questioning your control," Nicky said.

Olaf made a sound low in his throat that was almost a growl.

"Enough, Nicky," I said.

"So, what was your last name again?" Leduc asked.

Nicky answered, "Murdock, Nicky Murdock."

The sheriff turned to me. "So, Murdock, is your energy all gen-tle, too, like Mr. Flynn's over there?"

"No," he said.

Leduc looked at me. "Is Murdock another 'fiancé' like Jean-Claude or Callahan?" He gestured to make little quote marks when he said the word *fiancé*.

"No," I said.

I thought, *Nicky is my Bride, as in Brides of Dracula.* Brides of Anita just didn't have the same ring to it, and Nicky would be more a groom, but even Dracula couldn't make groom as cool sounding. If I'd been a real blood-sucking vampire, Nicky would have been a vampire, too, but a weak one who obeyed my every whim. I didn't want blind obedience, lucky for him, and somehow we'd ended up falling in love, which is something you're never supposed to do with vampire Brides. They're supposed to be cannon fodder you sacrifice to save yourself as needed. You can always make more.

Leduc said, "So if he's not what Callahan and Jean-Claude are to you, what is he to you?"

"He's my lover," I said, though I still fought not to squirm.

I really hated introducing people like that, because it implied just sex to most strangers. Nicky and others in our poly group thought lover meant love as well as sex, so that was what we'd settled on. Nicky would have been fine without a specific label, but most of the rest of our group had started to get weird as the weddings approached since we weren't putting rings on most of their fingers. If they couldn't be my husband, or my fiancé, then they wanted to be something.

"And what are you, Petra?" Olaf asked.

The woman seemed to shrink in on herself from just that much attention. I'd seen her pound the hell out of people in fight practice back home, but now she played the meek mouse to perfection. I sort of hated how good she was at it. It made me doubt her more and more, but it also felt like manipulating Olaf when he'd been behaving himself admirably.

"I am a friend with benefits," she said as if it was just true with no emotion attached. Pierette was content with being on the edges of our poly group. She and her master had been partners both in battle and in bed for so long, she didn't really want to be dating anyone else. I was good with that; I was dating enough people.

"And what are you, Angel?" Olaf asked, and managed to make her name seem like either a romantic nickname or a naughty one.

She gave him that mischievous smile that held a touch of evil in it, because she thought he had started it. I knew that Olaf didn't see what he'd done as starting anything.

"I'm fabulous. How are you?"

Custer laughed, and I sighed. I did not want Olaf to think we were making fun of him, but he surprised me, because he got the joke and upped the ante.

"I'm very good," he said, and his voice was even a little lower as if he could make his testosterone rise at will. I wouldn't have put it past him.

The corner of Angel's mouth dropped, and she suddenly had a look I'd seen before as she worked her way through the dating pool in St. Louis, both male and female, because she was as bisexual as her brother. It was a considering look, a can-you-back-up-the-brag? look. She knew who and what Olaf was, so she should have known better, but the look seemed genuine.

If we'd been alone, I'd have asked her what the fuck she was thinking, but we weren't alone, so I concentrated on business. "Otto, are you coming with me to question the witnesses?"

"Perhaps Angel would want to come with us?"

"She's needed here," I said.

"What about Petra?"

"What about her?"

"She could come with us."

"No, she can't," I said.

Olaf smiled at me, and something about the look made me want to say, I'm not jealous of you and other women. I'm scared for them. But Leduc was there, and Newman. I couldn't talk in front of the sheriff, so I didn't try. I just went for the door with Nicky at my heels.

We were almost to the SUV that Nicky had driven up in when Olaf called to us, "This is official marshal business. One of us should drive."

"I don't have a rental car, so you mean you should drive," I said, turning around.

He just stood there in the sunshine with his glasses hiding his eyes and looked at me. I don't know how long we would have waited for someone to blink first, because Nicky moved between us and literally broke the eye contact.

"The clock is ticking for the life you want to save, Anita." He was right, so very right.

"Fine, you can drive."

"Anita gets shotgun," Olaf said, the way Edward usually said it.

Maybe because of that, I didn't argue with him. I just got in the passenger door when he held it for me. Nicky opened his own door and sat behind Olaf.

"You will have more leg room if you sit behind Anita."

"I don't need as much leg room as you do. I'll be fine."

"No," Olaf said.

Nicky smiled, but this time it was a baring of teeth like a dog snarling.

"Stop it, both of you," I said.

"Not precise enough for me to have to stop," Nicky said.

"Do you want me to make it so you have to obey me?"

"Not really," he said.

"Then please just stop for now. Okay?"

"I'm your Bride. Your wish really is my command."

"Is it that complete, the control she has over you?" Olaf asked.

"It can be," Nicky said.

"Can be, but isn't?" Olaf asked.

"I'm not into slaves, Olaf," I said, "and my power with Nicky seems to recognize that. Now, are you driving, or do we need to get in the other car so Nicky can drive?"

"I am driving."

"Fine. Then drive."

"He sits behind you, not me."

Nicky drew breath to protest and I said, "Nicky, please just sit behind me."

He did it then because I'd told him to, or because of the "please."

I wasn't sure which, and I wasn't sure I wanted to know. I also wasn't sure why Nicky was needling Olaf more than normal, or why Pierette had made herself look as close as she could to his victim preference. What the hell was going on, and why didn't I know about it? So much for me being anyone's master.

52

WE'D PLUGGED THE address into my phone, so the tinny voice was giving us directions. Except for that, we drove in silence. Normally Nicky and I are fine riding in silence, and Olaf was, too.

I was enjoying being able to see the forest and the trees in daylight. It looked like a good place to go camping if I ever had enough time for a vacation, or if I found anyone willing to camp with me, or if I still enjoyed camping. I mean, if it was really important to me, wouldn't I have done it by now? I hadn't been camping in nearly ten years. Was it an old hobby that I'd outgrown and my interest was just nostalgia, or was it something I needed to make time for and enjoy again?

Something about planning the wedding had made me think things like that. I mean, Jean-Claude was never, ever going camping on purpose. Even if daylight wasn't a danger to him, he just wasn't a backpack-and-hiking-boots kind of guy. He owned more high-heeled boots than I did. He was all about appearance, and I was so not. I hadn't thought that was a problem until he wanted a wedding very different from what I wanted. If he'd been the girl, it would have been easier. Then he could have had the fabulous dress, and I could have worn a tux.

"Are the two of you not talking because I am present?" Olaf asked.

I blinked and realized that I hadn't been seeing anything: not the trees, not the car, not Nicky, not Olaf. Shit, I couldn't afford to lose my edge that completely around Olaf. The thought of just how oblivious I'd allowed myself to be with him sitting beside me made the pulse in my throat throb and my heart race.

"What did I do to frighten you?" he asked, and sounded genuinely puzzled. He didn't even make a creepy remark about liking the way I smelled when I was scared.

Nicky answered, "She let her attention wander with you sitting beside her. She thinks it was careless."

"You're right behind her. You literally have her back."

"I take care of myself, damn it, and if I need backup it's not supposed to be because I get careless."

I was angry at myself, and that anger wanted to spill onto the men in the car. It wasn't logical, but then anger seldom is. Luckily for all of us, I had been working on my anger issues in therapy. Otherwise God knew what I would have said or done: something to hurt my relationship with Nicky permanently or accidentally pull the pin on Olaf. If I ever did the last part, I wanted to do it on purpose.

Olaf glanced back at Nicky and asked, "How did you know what upset her?"

"I felt her thoughts." Nicky said it as if his doing so was totally normal.

Olaf kept looking at Nicky and not at the road. He wasn't drifting out of his lane or anything. There were no cars in sight, but . . .

"Driving," I said, "you're driving. Looking at the road would be good, Olaf."

He stared at Nicky for a heartbeat more and then looked back at the road. "Did the car divert from its course?"

"No."

Nicky said, "Anita's nervous in cars."

Olaf nodded. "I remember."

The mechanical voice on my phone, which tried to sound vaguely like a British lady, gave us the next turn, which was coming up soon. Olaf slowed down to look for the next road, but all I could see were trees and more trees. It was beautiful, but I suddenly felt claustrophobic, as if another road or house would have been comforting.

"Can you hear Anita's thoughts?" Olaf asked.

"Sometimes, but her feelings, those're constant," Nicky said.

"Do you experience the feelings with her?"

"No, but I'm still impacted by them."

"Impacted how?"

"Anita is uncomfortable with us discussing her like this, so I need to ask if she's okay with me elaborating."

"Elaborating? I don't remember you knowing words that large once," Olaf said.

"I read more now."

I sat there debating how I felt about the conversation, other than it making me uncomfortable. I finally said, "Answer Olaf's question, and I'll see how I feel about it."

"I'm her Bride. Apparently that means my main job is to keep her happy and safe. The happiness is the hard part."

"Because you do not understand what makes her happy?"

"No, I understand exactly what makes her happy, or I do now. If I make her unhappy, it literally hurts me emotionally and almost physically until I fix it. Like right now she's uncomfortable hearing me say that, but she told me to answer you, so it can get tricky."

"It sounds . . . terrible," Olaf said. He slowed to let a car turn out onto the road from the turn we were supposed to make.

"I've never been happier in my life," Nicky said.

"But it's Anita's happiness, not yours."

"Is it? I can't really tell sometimes, but I know I feel happy. I feel loved. I feel safe. I feel like you're supposed to feel in a family when you're a child, or how they make it look on TV movies and family events at school. I always felt like an outsider or like other families lied better in public than mine did. Until I hooked up with Anita, I didn't believe in family or love."

"We are both sociopaths. You can't feel those things," Olaf said.

"That's what I thought, too, but something about the connection with Anita opened me up to feel things."

"Nicky tells me I'm his Jiminy Cricket, like in *Pinocchio*," I said.

"I know *Pinocchio*," Olaf said.

"Sorry. You don't always get the cultural references I use."

"True. Thank you."

"You're welcome," I said.

The road widened, and we were suddenly in a small neighborhood that looked like a million others anywhere in the country, except for the ever-present trees that hedged round it like someone had dropped it into the middle of a national forest.

I was thinking about how pretty the area was when Olaf asked, "May I touch your leg?"

He'd asked permission like I'd told him to do, but I didn't want him to touch me. So if I let him touch me, was I really giving permission or being coerced?

"Your body is reacting as if it is stressed. I have done nothing."

"You asked permission, and that's great. It's appreciated, but I'm sort of in work headspace, and I wasn't expecting you to ask anything date-y, so it threw me."

"Why is it a problem? No one from work will see us, so it will not hurt our professional standing. Nicky will not care."

"I might care," Nicky said.

"Why would you care if I put my hand on her thigh?"

"Because she cares, and she doesn't want you to do it."

I added, "I don't usually let people touch my leg until we've had a couple of dates."

"With all the people in your life, you still have such stringent rules?" He gave me a sideways look, keeping half his attention on the street.

I sighed; he had a point. "It depends on the person and the relationship."

"Do you overthink all your relationships this much?" he asked.

"Yes, actually, but you're the only one that started out threatening to kidnap, rape, torture, and kill me, so I'm a little fuzzy on which category to put you in for dating." I'd ended by letting my confusion turn into sarcasm.

Olaf either didn't get it or ignored it. He knew me well enough to know that I made smart-ass remarks when I was nervous or just because I could. "I can see where it would be confusing. You are also in a different category for me, and it does make things more difficult. I have never had to beg a woman to touch her before. I do not like it, but I am trying to learn the rules of ordinary dating. You tell me I must learn consent, so I am trying."

"You are, Olaf. I mean, you really are. You've surprised the hell out of me with the amount of effort."

"Thank you for noticing."

"But if I say, 'Yes, touch my leg,' just because you want to touch me, but not because I want you to touch me, then is it really consent, or am I letting you bully me into it? And if I'm letting you do that, is it really consent, or is it coercion?"

"That is so convoluted that I don't know what to say to you."

"Yeah, welcome to the inside of Anita's head," Nicky said.

"Are all women so complex in their thought processes?"

"More. I'm actually pretty easy for girl logic," I said.

"I may owe your sex an apology. I thought they did not think deeply, but perhaps it is that you all think so differently from men that it seems to be shallow but is actually quite deep in a way that makes absolutely no sense."

I thought about that for a second or two and then said, "Thanks. I think."

"You are welcome."

The tinny voice on my phone said, "Your destination is ahead on the left."

Thank God, we were here. Maybe doing our actual jobs would distract Olaf from trying for his version of touchy-feely. It was better than him trying to kill me, but I understood the rules for that, and dating anyone always confused me. Dating Olaf was ridiculous, like trying to date Godzilla and not expecting to get crushed right along with Tokyo.

Nicky reached up and squeezed my shoulder to let me know he was there. He was part of one of the least complicated relationships in my life. Listening to him explain it to Olaf made me realize all over again that simple for me was super complicated for Nicky.

"I don't mind. I love you, and I know you love me, because I can feel it," Nicky said, leaning in as close as his seat belt would allow.

"What don't you mind? Why did you say that?" Olaf asked as he pulled into the driveway of our destination.

"I'm replying to what Anita was thinking."

Olaf glanced back at Nicky and then at me. "When you told me that you were trying not to feed on my anger because you were afraid of what it might do to me, is this what you meant?"

I made a little waffling movement with my head and shrugged. "Sort of. Just feeding on anger isn't what tied Nicky to me, but it's made me cautious about who I feed on for anything. I rolled Nicky on purpose. I'd hate to do this by accident."

"I had kidnapped you and was helping my werelion pride threaten to kill the men you loved," Nicky said.

"I didn't say that I regretted using the only weapon you guys had left me to turn you into my ally, but the thought that I could treat you like a true slave and you couldn't do anything about it creeps the fuck out of me."

"You're a better person than that," Nicky said.

"Luckily for you," I said.

"I knew Nicky before you. If the positions had been reversed, he is not the better person," Olaf said.

I looked into the back at Nicky. He smiled at me. I smiled back. "Nicky and I have talked about that."

"And what do you think of his old ways?" Olaf asked.

"I think he was made into a sociopath by the bitch that called herself his mother. I think his ties to me just helped him find his own emotions, which the abuse damaged."

"Then Nicky is not like me, Anita. I have no emotions hiding inside me for you to find."

"If you didn't have more than you think you do, then you wouldn't be trying to date Anita," Nicky said.

Olaf startled visibly, hands tightening on the steering wheel so hard that it made protesting noises as if he might break it. He took his hands off the wheel. "I am not capable of love."

"Are you sure?" Nicky asked.

Olaf looked at him, his face unreadable around his sunglasses. We waited to see if he'd answer Nicky's question. He didn't. He just got out of the car and left us to follow.

"That was interesting," Nicky said.

I wanted to argue but said the truth since he could feel it anyway. "It was weird, disturbing, but interesting."

"I think you just described Olaf."

Again, I couldn't argue, so I got out of the car and Nicky followed me, because he had to and because he wanted to. I was dating one sociopath; surely that was my limit. I'd never intended to date Olaf for real, so what were we going to do with each other? Even for my dating history, this was a weird one.

53

BRIANNA GIBSON OPENED the door to the one-story ranch house wearing a purple sports bra and leggings, with lavender-and-white cross-trainers on her feet. She was at least five-eight, maybe a smidge taller, and was lean enough to look good in the exercise clothes. Her nearly black hair was back in a short ponytail as neat and smooth as her body, so the fact that she was wearing full makeup that seemed more weekend clubbing than afternoon gym was a little startling, like she wasn't sure if she was going to work out or head to the city for an evening out.

We introduced ourselves and asked if we could ask her a few questions. She opened the door farther and ushered us inside. "Of course. I was wondering if any of you would need to talk to me about what happened to Jocelyn's dad."

I nearly tripped over toys as I walked into the living room. Brianna Gibson was clean, neat, and ready to greet the world. The same could not be said of her home. There were toys and baby things everywhere, so it was like tiptoeing through a biological-clock minefield. A baby started crying from farther inside the house, and then a second cry joined the first, so there was a chorus of unhappy infants.

"Damn, they're up from their naps. I'm sorry, but I have to go check on them. Clear off a space and have a seat," the woman said, and then walked down a hallway that led directly off the living room.

There was also a door on the wall, which probably led to the kitchen, but who knew? And honestly, until someone cleared the debris away, the door wasn't going to open anyway.

We stared around at the couch and the two overstuffed chairs, which sat like islands that were in danger of being engulfed in the toys and bits of baby clothes. There were two of those baby chairs with trays and wheels that helped babies practice walking while having snacks or playing with small toys. The mess on the floor was so thick, the chairs weren't going to move. The babies could practice standing, but walking wasn't happening until someone picked up a little.

Olaf started moving things off the couch, so Nicky and I joined him. We each had an armful of toys and other baby debris, but now where to put it? Did we dump it on the floor with all the rest, or did we try to straighten some of it? I'm not the neatest person in the world, but I was overwhelmed with the mess in the room. It made me want to start shoveling things against the wall so at least the floor would be clear.

I whispered, "Where do we put it?"

Olaf put his armload in the corner to one side of the couch so at least it wasn't making it harder to walk. I didn't have a better idea, so I added my armload to his. The pile began to slide down like ice cream melting, and I couldn't stand it. I went down on one knee to push at it and place things until there was some stability to the heap and it didn't try to fall apart.

Nicky dropped the stuff in his arms behind the couch. I hadn't realized there was enough room to do that. I thought about picking up another armload and putting it there, too.

Olaf whispered, "She's returning."

I stood up to join him by the couch. I had my hands clasped in front of me, because the urge to start trying to straighten more of the chaos was almost overwhelming. If I hadn't thought the woman would have been insulted by it, I might have done it anyway, but I wanted information more than I wanted anything else from Ms. Gibson. Nathaniel would have been amused that anything could be messy enough to make me want to start picking up. It was usually he or Jean-Claude who started picking up before the rest of us even thought of it. That was about as domestic as Jean-Claude got before he paid people to be domestic for him, but Nathaniel enjoyed bringing domestic order out of chaos. I wondered what he would have thought of this.

Ms. Gibson came back down the hallway with a baby in each arm. One was dressed in lavender and the other in yellow. They both had the beginnings of dark hair like five-o'clock shadow on top of their heads. Their big dark eyes looked like their mother's, but the faces looked like someone else's, probably the father's, though there were no pictures anywhere, so that was just a guess. For all I knew, the twins could have been the spitting image of their grandpa. Genetics is like that sometimes.

Ms. Gibson had taken the time to put a lavender-and-yellow headband on each baby. There were tiny flowers and ribbons on the headbands. The outfits were equally girlie and pretty. It was the kind of stuff that most people reserved for baby photos or maybe Easter service at church. That's to say, the babies looked great. They were pink cheeked and healthy and dressed as neatly as the mother. Apparently, on Brianna's priority list, clothes ranked higher than housework. If the babies had come out as neglected as the living room, I'd have been upset, but they were smiling and happy, so I smiled back and let my parenting expectations go.

She glanced at each of them in turn, smiling, and they smiled back. "Who're my beautiful girls? You're my beautiful girls, aren't you?"

The baby in yellow made noises back to her, and the baby in lavender joined in. It was gibberish, but I could have sworn it sounded like the same gibberish, as if both babies were speaking the same arcane baby language.

She talked to them as she put them in their bouncy seats. They gabbled back at her and to each other. Was it my imagination, or were they more solemn when they talked to each other? It was almost as if they smiled and talked to their mother the way she talked to them, like she was the baby and didn't understand them.

"I'm going to get them a snack and myself a diet. Can I get any of you something?"

It took me a second to understand she meant she was getting herself a diet soda and not an entire diet, so Olaf answered first. "No, thank you." His voice rumbled even deeper than normal.

It made me glance at him, but his face showed nothing. I wasn't sensing his inner lion either. I shrugged it off and answered her, "No, thanks. I'm good."

"I'm good. Thank you," Nicky said.

She flashed us a dazzling smile that I'd have liked better if the makeup had been a little lighter. The smile seemed happy-girl-next-door; the makeup was more burlesque-stage. "Have a seat and let me know if you change your minds." She went to the door and the toys piled against it weren't an issue, because the door pushed inward.

We sat down where we were standing by the couch so that I ended up between the two men. Normally I liked being in the middle. I thought about making Nicky change with me so I wouldn't be sitting next to Olaf, but it seemed too second grade. I was a big, grown-up vampire hunter, not a child, damn it. Nicky picked up on my unease and moved a fraction closer so that his thigh touched mine, and just that helped me find my center. I was debating if I could touch Nicky's hand without Olaf getting weird about it when a small sound made me remember the babies.

They looked after their mother and then back at us. The one in yellow smiled at us, and I smiled back, because that's what you do. Nicky smiled at them, too. The lavender twin smiled with us, and then the one in yellow looked at Olaf. It made me look at him, too. He wasn't smiling.

If I'd thought he would think it was funny, I would have asked him what kind of sociopath doesn't smile when a baby smiles at him? But I was pretty sure he wouldn't get the joke. Luckily for all of us, the mother came back into the room. She sprinkled Cheerios across the trays in front of the babies and then curled up on the only other clean seat in the room, the corner of the couch beside Olaf.

It meant he could just turn his head and look at her, but I had to turn my entire body to see around him to get glimpses of her. If I hadn't been wearing so many weapons, I'd have curled up on my end of the couch like she was in her exercise outfit. Olaf noticed the issue and sat straighter against the back of the couch so I could see past him.

"Now, Ms. Gibson—"

"Call me Brianna, please."

"Okay, Brianna, how long have you and Jocelyn been friends?"

"Oh, since high school. We even went to the same college."

"So, the two of you are close?" I said.

She sipped her can of Diet Coke and seemed to think about the question more than I thought it warranted. "We are. I mean, not as close as we used to be. I got married, and she didn't, and then we had the twins. Marcy—Marcy Myers—and I got closer because we have husbands and babies. I know Jocelyn felt left out, but she didn't want what we had. She's not ready to settle down, and I'm not sure she ever wants kids."

"It's hard when some of your friends get married and start families and some don't," I said.

She nodded, sipped her diet soda, and said, "None of you is wearing a ring, but one of our friends is a cop, and he said that a lot of you don't wear wedding rings to work. Are you the married friends or the single friends in your group?"

"Engaged and living with," I said.

"Living with," Nicky said.

"Single but dating," Olaf said.

Nicky pressed his leg tighter against mine, which meant I'd tensed. I did my best to relax and be grateful that Olaf had at least added the single part.

Brianna flashed that smile again, but this time there was a hint of mischief in her eyes. "Living in sin, my mother called it."

"My dad's not too fond of it either," I said.

Olaf looked at me. He actually opened his mouth to say something, then seemed to think better of it.

Brianna had seen the interaction. "You didn't know her daddy disapproved?"

"We're not each other's usual partners. About the night of the murder," I said, hoping to forestall any more personal questions aimed our way.

It was like all the light just drained out of her face. The makeup looked flat but not harsh, which let me know that she was wearing more base makeup than I'd thought at first. Why was she wearing this much in the middle of the day at home? It did hide whether she paled to match the grim look in her eyes. Maybe she'd worn the makeup like camouflage to hide her expressions while we questioned her?

"Jocelyn talked Marcy and me into a night on the town like we used to do when we were all single."

"Talked you into? So this wasn't common for the three of you?" I asked.

"Not anymore. I don't think the three of us have gone out without spouses or kids since the twins were born." She smiled at her babies, who were dropping more Cheerios than they were eating and gabbling to each other in their baby language.

"So, over a year," I said.

Brianna nodded and looked back at us with the glow of her smile still on her face. "Jocelyn said she missed the old days, and so did I. I'm not sure about Marcy. She always had to get a little drunk to get wild, but Joshie and I were wild in our day." She looked at the babies again with a serious look on her face. "God, I hope neither of them takes after me—not in that way at least." She looked almost scared. If we hadn't been investigating a murder, I might have asked what put that look on her face, but I had to let it go and concentrate on the night in question.

"Jocelyn says you went to a club."

Brianna flashed that smile again. This time the look in her eyes was more than mischief—something untamed, naughty, not evil but a look I'd seen before on people who really were wild. Not the get-drunk-or-high-and-do-things-you'll-regret wild, but the kind that doesn't need an excuse, just an opportunity. Nathaniel had that look, and so did Nicky. I had to fight not to glance at him. If that was really part of Brianna's personality, she was going to have a tough time being a traditional wife and mother.

"Dare I ask what kind of club the three of you went to?"

"Strip club," Brianna said. The two words had a relish and happiness to them that seemed to fill her up until a little wiggle ran down her body so she moved on the couch without using hands or feet, just her wiggly core.

I dated women as well as men, and I suddenly couldn't help thinking that Brianna might be interesting in a nonbusiness kind of way. I pushed the thought aside, but it was in there now, and I couldn't unthink it. Even though I wouldn't act on it, it was still there, and it would make the rest of the interview weird for me. Would I have been less weirded out if she'd been a man who made me think about sex? Yes. I'd only added women to my dating pool in the last few years. It was still new enough to throw me off balance sometimes.

"Watching men take off their clothes," Olaf said, and there was just the faintest hint of disapproval.

I doubt that Brianna heard it, because she aimed that smile at him.

"No, my husband didn't like the idea of us watching other men, so we compromised and went to see women take off their clothes."

Her brown eyes were luminous with the happiness of saying it or of doing it. Was she just one of those people who enjoyed doing things that most people thought were risqué? I'd met people who liked to shock others. If she only knew that I was engaged to three men, and two out of the three were exotic dancers . . . Brianna couldn't shock me or out-thrill-seek me, but she wanted to, so I'd keep my mouth closed and let her.

Olaf and I started asking the routine questions about when Brianna and her friends had arrived at the club, how long they'd stayed, et cetera . . .

"Can anyone verify how long you were at the club?" I asked.

"I'd think most people in the club would remember us."

"Strip clubs get pretty crowded," I said, "especially on a weekend."

"Oh, they'll remember us," Brianna said with such relish that I knew she wanted to tell us the details, or maybe she wanted to tell someone the details, not necessarily us.

I smiled at her, because this made her more alive than even looking lovingly at her twins. Some people are wired that way.

Olaf asked, "How can you be so certain?"

Brianna looked at him with her brown eyes shining with her excitement about the memory. "They don't get that many women as hot as or hotter than the strippers getting lap dances."

One of the twins made a small sound that made Brianna look at them, which made me follow her gaze. The twins were bouncing in their seats. The twin in yellow was waving her arms excitedly, and the other twin was listening very seriously. Were personalities set that quickly? Did we come into the world already so formed, so us?

Brianna unwound her legs and turned at the waist to take a coaster out of the small container of them on the side table. She set her soda down carefully on it and then got off the couch. How could someone careful enough to use coasters let the floor get this messy? She picked up some small toys off the floor and put them on the babies' trays. The Cheerios had long since vanished. The twins seemed happy with the toys, staring at them as if they were brand-new and awesome. I guess when you're that young, every day is Christmas, because there are so many new things to see, touch, do.

Coming back to the couch, Brianna stepped on a toy and cursed, then looked guiltily at the babies, who were ignoring us, focused instead on the new toys. "The living room doesn't usually look like this. Promise. But Daryl, my husband, and I thought maybe if our families see how much they've bought the girls, they'll stop. The twins are the first grandchildren on either side of the family, and both sets of grandparents have gone crazy buying things for them. We're just out of space."

She was suddenly worried and anxious and not at all the sparkling, excited woman of a few moments before. Did having kids always do that to people, make them less of who they were and turn them into parents? Did you have to give up what made your eyes light up to have kids? Surely it didn't have to be that way, or I hoped not.

"It is good to know that this is not typical for you," Olaf said, his deep voice as serious as his tone.

Brianna smiled in his direction, but her attention was still on the babies and the mess. She picked up her can of soda and curled back up on the end of the couch, but before, her posture had been effortless and sexy. Now it was more like she was huddling around herself. She sipped the soda and looked at us, but the look on her face said she wasn't really seeing us. Whatever was in her head at that moment wasn't happy.

I finally prompted her with "So you, Jocelyn, and Marcy Myers all paid for lap dances."

Brianna focused on me, but it was like her internal dialogue was having trouble catching up with the conversation. What had just happened to make her go so serious? I had missed something. I'd ask Olaf and Nicky later, but if I didn't understand a woman's reaction, I doubted they would be much help.

"Yes, yes"—she gave a tentative smile—"it was so fun to watch Jocelyn with the dancers."

The light started to return to her eyes. She sipped the soda like it tasted better than I knew it did, or maybe that was just my opinion. Maybe she actually liked it. I felt the same way about most alcoholic drinks, too, so maybe I wasn't a good judge. One friend who liked both diet soda and alcohol suggested that I'd drunk so much coffee that it had ruined my taste buds for anything else. Maybe, or maybe coffee was just yummy.

"Why was it so much fun to watch Jocelyn?" I asked, because the only other thing I could think to ask was if she liked to watch, but that sounded like flirting or like I'd learn things about Brianna that I didn't really need to know.

"She likes attention. It brings out something in her that is . . . I don't know how to explain it, but she puts on a show. She knew one of the dancers well enough that they had planned to have her up onstage. It was so hot."

The last sentence brought back her earlier happy energy. Her face and eyes were alight with the memory of watching her friend onstage. It made me wonder if she and Jocelyn were friends with benefits or at least something more than just friends.

"It must have been a real moneymaker for the dancer," I said.

Brianna nodded happily and gave that little wiggle again like a happy, sexy puppy. I didn't think I had a wiggle in me like that, but one of my sweeties did. He was both a serious voyeur and an exhibitionist. I'm not saying the wiggle meant all that, but some of her mannerisms made me think of Nathaniel, and I knew what he liked. If Brianna was anywhere close to him in her preferences, I wasn't sure how well being a straight, suburban, married mom was going to fit her. Of course, maybe she and her husband were practicing some form of consensual nonmonogamy. It was more common than I used to think before I joined the nontraditional crowd. But I didn't ask Brianna if she was nonmonogamous, because some people found it insulting, and others took it as flirting. I didn't mean either.

"The men just ate it up, seeing two hot women together onstage, and one of them being a customer . . ." She sighed and did that little wiggle movement again.

"It was probably the closest that most men will ever get to the fantasy of having two women at once," I said.

"Most men don't know what to do with one woman in bed, let alone two," Brianna said, and then she caught herself. She looked startled, even embarrassed, at the men. "I'm sorry. That wasn't aimed at either of you, just my dating history."

She rolled her eyes and looked at me. I feared she was going to try for a moment of girl bonding that might not work with me. I was trying to think what to say to stop her from attempting to get me to admit to something that wasn't true for me, but Nicky stepped in and took the heat off of me.

"You dated the wrong men," he said, and he gave her that flirting smile that could make strange women blush. He was still wearing the sunglasses to hide his eye, so it was a very movie star moment.

Olaf surprised me by adding, "Do not judge us all by the failures of a few."

Brianna laughed, and I couldn't tell if she was embarrassed or pleased. "Maybe. Where were you before I married and settled down?"

"Dating all the wrong people," Nicky said.

"Perhaps I, like you, was chasing the wrong people," Olaf said.

Brianna swallowed and seemed to catch her breath for a moment. "I didn't chase my husband. He chased me." Her words were good; she'd reminded them she was married and desirable enough to pursue.

"But you allowed him to catch you," Olaf said, his voice lower, almost husky. Was he doing the voice thing on purpose?

"Yes, but don't tell my husband that. It makes him feel good to think he seduced me." She gave a nervous little laugh at the end, though I wasn't exactly sure why.

"You lured him in with your beauty," Olaf said in that deep growling voice.

"You think I'm beautiful?" Brianna asked, but the tone implied that she knew she was beautiful and was saying it more for form. Once, I couldn't have told the difference, but dating other women had taught me more about the different ways there were to be female than actually being a woman ever had.

"You know you are beautiful, beautiful bait," Olaf said, and the voice was almost achingly low, but there was no heat of his beast making him growl—it was testosterone or an act. I'd ask later, maybe.

"Bait," she whispered, and leaned her upper body toward him as if she didn't realize she'd done it, like it was gravity and he was a heavenly body pulling her inward.

I looked at Nicky for a clue. The last thing I'd expected was for Olaf to flirt with this woman. Nicky raised eyebrows above his glasses, which was a version of a shrug for him.

One of the babies started to cry, and just like that the spell, or whatever, was broken. Brianna got up and went to check on her baby. She picked up the crying infant, the one dressed in yellow, but then the one in lavender started to cry for attention. Brianna tried to just pick up the second baby, but the child had gotten her leg hooked on something and was stuck.

Brianna turned to me. "Can you hold her for just a second? I need two hands." She didn't wait for me to answer, but just shoved the baby at me. It was like having something thrown at you. You just automatically put your hands up. Suddenly I was holding a baby while Brianna knelt and tried to free the other one's leg.

I grasped the baby awkwardly, like I was afraid she'd break. That seemed silly, so I tried to hold her closer, a little less like I thought she'd explode and more like she was a small person who probably needed to feel like the adult holding her wasn't about to drop her. The baby still had tears drying on her face, but she stopped crying and stared at me with wide dark eyes like she knew I wasn't her mom. I stared back. I wasn't sure when I'd held a baby this young. Maybe when my younger brother was a baby, which had been when I was a child myself.

The baby was round and strong and very firm, but still strangely delicate. I couldn't explain it even to myself, but I could feel the potential of all she would ever be in my arms, as if her grown-up self was inside just waiting for time to let her out, but at the same time she seemed fragile and in need of protection so that she could grow into all that promise. Would she always be as solemn as she was right now, studying my face like she'd memorize it? It was like she was judging me. Would this adult take care of her? Would she drop her? Would she feed her? Would she leave her for the wild animals on some hillside, or would she love and protect her? And just like that I knew I would protect her, because she was small and couldn't protect herself and that was what you're supposed to do with babies. It was like some switch inside of me got turned on, and I suddenly wondered if I felt this about a stranger's baby, what would it be like to hold my own? For the first time, having that thought didn't scare me. Did babies give off pheromones or something that made having your own baby seem like a better idea? Fuckers, and yet I held the solemn baby in my arms, and it felt . . . right somehow. Stupid biological clock.

I tried to be angry about it, but I couldn't, not while I was holding her. I heard myself asking, "What's her name?"

"Heidi," Brianna said.

The baby didn't look like a Heidi to me, but then what did a Heidi look like? I guess newborns didn't look like any name; they were all so unfinished and tiny whenever I visited friends and their newborns. By the time they had enough personality to earn a name, it was too late, and they were Heidi, or Frankie, or Anita. Weird to think that the name I thought of as mine had probably not matched me once either.

"She likes you," Brianna said, standing beside me with the other twin.

"She seems like she's thinking serious thoughts," I said.

Brianna frowned and then said, "Thank you for saying that. I told my mother-in-law that, and she told me babies don't think that deeply at this age, but Heidi is always watching, studying the world like she's memorizing it all. Clara is the one who does everything first, and Heidi hangs back and waits to see how it goes. My mother says that Heidi is shy, and Clara is outgoing, and she's right, but it's more like Heidi is cautious like Daryl, and Clara is like me, trying anything once."

"Heidi and Clara, like the characters in the book *Heidi*," I said.

Brianna looked a little embarrassed but nodded. She hugged Clara and said, "It was my favorite book when I was a little girl. Most people don't even recognize the names or remember the book."

"I read it when I was a little girl, and I remember the Shirley Temple movie."

"I loved that movie," Brianna said.

"They played all the Shirley Temple movies in the afternoon on one of the old cable channels when I was little."

"I loved watching all those on summer afternoons with my sister and mother." When Brianna smiled, her face appeared younger and happier with the memory.

Her reaction made me smile back. "I watched them with my mother." In my head, I added, Before she died, but the memory of watching them with her on summer afternoons was still a happy memory. "I totally forgot about the Shirley Temple film festival. Isn't that what they called it?"

"Yeah, I think you're right. What was your favorite movie?"

"*The Little Princess*, I think."

"Oh, that was a good one. Mine was *Heidi*," she said, laughing, and I found myself laughing with her.

Clara joined in with the laughter, and after a second, so did Heidi. Nicky joined in on the laughter, because that was what you're supposed to do as a social animal. I watched the baby's face light up with laughter, and it made me happy. Damn it, hormones. My life would not work with babies, would it?

"And then puberty hit, and I forgot all about *Heidi* and Shirley Temple," Brianna said.

"My mother died before I hit puberty, and it was just my dad and me for a while."

"Oh, I'm so sorry," Brianna said, and she reached out and laid her hand on my arm.

Usually that would have bugged me from a stranger, but this time it was all right. It felt like she meant it and really was sorry about all the time I'd lost with my mother when she'd had all those years with her own.

"My dad was more into hunting than Shirley Temple, so I learned how to shoot."

Brianna took her hand back and studied me, and suddenly I could see that maybe Heidi didn't just take after her dad. "Funny how things work out. You grow up to be a cop, and I grow up to be a Realtor that meets her husband on the job."

"Things work out, I guess," I said, "and if you could give us the name of the club and the dancer that took Jocelyn up onstage, we'll get out of your hair."

"And the time you arrived and left the club," Olaf said from the couch.

I glanced behind me at him, and it was almost jarring that he was still there while I was holding a baby and remembering my mother. He seemed to belong to a different life from the one that had my mother and Shirley Temple marathons in it.

Brianna gave us the information. Olaf wrote it down in his phone while we girls continued to hold the babies. Normally I'd have given Heidi back to her mom, but she seemed content, and Clara was happy in her mother's arms. It just seemed logical to keep the babies happy and quiet while we got the rest of the information. Yeah, it was just logic, not that some part of me enjoyed holding the baby.

I handed Heidi back to her mother at the door, so Brianna had a baby in each arm. She encouraged them to wave bye-bye. Clara waved first and then Heidi. I waved back to them as we went to get in Olaf's rental. He threw a hand up in their direction, which made Brianna smile brighter, though Heidi stopped waving. She was going to be the smart one.

54

I CALLED EDWARD from the car and got put straight to voice mail, so I texted him. If they didn't need us to question the second friend, we'd head to the strip club to try to get an address for the dancer who was part of Jocelyn's alibi. I punched the address of the strip club into my phone so we could find it. We'd have to start there to find the dancer since they all used stage names.

I wasn't sure how I felt about taking Olaf to a strip club. It was like taking the fox to the chicken coop and trusting he wouldn't eat any of them, but he'd given his word he would behave himself. Either I trusted him to keep his word, or I didn't. After the interview with Brianna, it just seemed like a day designed to test his limits.

"You enjoyed holding the baby," Olaf said, and there was something in his voice that I wasn't sure of: accusation, surprise?

I fought not to squirm as I tried to figure out what to say. "It wasn't awful," I said finally, and even to me it sounded lame.

Olaf made a disdainful sound, somewhere between a snort and a growl. "Are you lying to me or yourself?"

"I'm not lying. I just don't know what to say, okay?"

"This makes you uncomfortable," he said.

"Yeah, it does, so can we change topics?"

"Why does it bother you that you enjoyed holding the baby?"

"Why does it bother you?" I asked.

"I did not say that it bothered me."

"Now who's lying?"

Olaf spoke to Nicky in the backseat. "You must have felt that she enjoyed interacting with the baby."

"Like Anita said, she didn't hate it, but she was too conflicted to actually enjoy it."

I didn't really want to share my biological-clock issues with Olaf, of all people. Or that one of my fiancés was pushing for babies. Nicky was almost neutral on the topic, which was a nice change from everyone else having an opinion about what I did with my womb.

My phone rang with Edward's ringtone, "Bad to the Bone," so I knew to answer it.

He didn't bother to say hello, just went straight to the point. "We're headed back to the sheriff's station. Meet us there."

"What happened?" I asked.

"The Marchands' cook, Helen Grimes, came into the station and backed up Jocelyn Marchand's story. She brought Bobby Marchand's phone in with more damning evidence against him."

"What kind of evidence?" I asked.

"Sheriff says we need to head that way and see it. He seems to feel it wraps the case up nice and tidy."

"Well, shit," I said.

"We're supposed to want the case finished, Anita."

"Usually I do."

"The sheriff has a hard-on for killing the Marchand kid, so don't count the evidence as conclusive until we judge it for ourselves." I think he was saying that for Newman's benefit as much as or more than mine.

"Fair point. Okay, we'll turn around and head that way."

Olaf found the nearest cross street without me saying anything else. He used a driveway to turn around in so we could head toward the sheriff's station. Then I realized what he'd done.

"Do you know where we're going?" I asked.

"Back to the sheriff's station," he said, eyes on the road, big hands at nine and three on the steering wheel, which thanks to airbags are the new safe positions.

"I didn't say the location out loud."

"I heard Edward say it on the phone."

"Did you hear both sides of the conversation?"

"Yes."

I looked back at Nicky. "Did you hear it all?"

"Yep."

"I have some of the special abilities of a real lycanthrope, but I wouldn't have heard the entire conversation."

"Perhaps the fact that you are only a carrier for the disease but do not change forms limits your secondary abilities," Olaf said.

"Probably. Even your hearing isn't as good in human form as it would be in lion."

"I have not tested it. Most people do not talk on phones around me when I am in lion form."

"I'll bet they don't."

"I would think people would treat all the lycanthropes in their lives the same way."

I didn't really like his putting himself in the same status as the other shapeshifters in my life, but I let it go. Sometimes you pick your battles with an eye to winning the war. "Actually, we talk on the phone around everyone in whatever form."

"Then their control of their secondary form must be perfect indeed for the rest of your people to treat them so normally."

"We've all been lycanthropes years longer than you have. It takes time to master your inner beast," Nicky said.

"I have been told that my control is admirable for one so new."

"It is. I was impressed with your control in Florida the last time we worked together," I said.

"Thank you."

"Praise where praise is due," I said.

"Do you want to have children?"

"We aren't going to talk about the case or speculate on what evidence may have shown up?" I asked.

"We will know soon enough, and we will do nothing but speak about the case when we arrive back at the station, so I would speak of other things."

"I really didn't think you and I would ever talk about babies, Olaf."

"Nor I, but I saw you with the baby, and something harsh in you softened. I hadn't expected to see that."

"It surprised me, too," I said, and that was honest.

"You talked to the woman in a way that surprised me as well."

"You mean Brianna?"

"Yes."

I said, "She surprised me because she named her kids after characters in her favorite book. I really didn't see her as a reader."

"She was different as a child. You heard her. She found boys, and books were forgotten," Olaf said.

"If they were forgotten, she would have named her twins something else," I said.

"That was unexpected," he admitted.

"I know. I thought she was just some sexy airhead, but there's depth in there if you get her talking about something besides strip clubs and her friends."

"She would cheat on her husband," Olaf said as if it was just true.

"You don't know that."

"I believe I could seduce her."

"I noticed you putting some effort into flirting with her."

"Did it bother you?"

"I wasn't jealous if that's what you mean."

"I am jealous of you."

I didn't know what to say to that, so I ignored it and said, "She fits your victim profile, except for being a little too tall, so when you started flirting with her, instead of being jealous, I was more worried that you were going to see her as a potential target."

"So your concern for her safety overrode any jealousy issues?"

"Yes," I said. I thought, I don't think I would have been jealous over you, but that was probably a fact best kept to myself.

"Why do you care about her? She is not your friend. She is nothing to you."

"Brianna's a person, Olaf. I held her baby and enjoyed it. I know what her favorite book from childhood is and that she named her kids after it. I know that her mom and mother-in-law are buying so much stuff for the babies that she's trashing her living room to try to get them to stop. I know she's probably a voyeur at the clubs. She's real to me now, and the thought that she's not real to you in the same way is disturbing."

"I am a sociopath, Anita. I do not feel empathy. You know that."

"Intellectually I know it, but that doesn't help me understand it."

"As I do not understand your sympathy for the woman we just left."

"I guess we just agree to disagree," I said.

"You are being very quiet, Nicky," Olaf said.

"I'm just listening," Nicky said from the backseat, where he had been unusually quiet.

"You are a sociopath. Do you feel anything for the woman we just left?" Olaf asked.

"I can feel what Anita feels."

"Do you have no feelings of your own anymore? Have you become only an echo chamber for Anita?"

I heard Nicky sigh. It made me reach back over the seat so he could take my hand. It was an awkward position for hand-holding, but any touch felt better than no touch. I didn't like that heavy sigh, and I really didn't like that I might have been the cause of it.

"I have my own thoughts and feelings."

"Can you act on them?" Olaf asked.

"Of course."

"If you wanted to hunt Brianna Gibson, could you do it, knowing that Anita would disapprove?" Olaf used the rearview mirror to glance at the other man.

"I have no interest in Brianna Gibson, so it doesn't matter." Nicky rubbed his thumb over my fingers as he spoke.

"Your reputation for forcing information from informants was almost as good as mine. You don't get that good at torture without enjoying it, Nicky."

I tried not to feel anything about that statement, because if Nicky felt how unhappy it made me, it would mess with his answer. His hand had stopped moving in mine.

"I enjoyed some of it," Nicky said, "but after a certain point, it stopped being fun and was just part of my job."

"I don't believe you," Olaf said, glancing back in the mirror again.

"I don't care if you believe me or not."

I said, "I know you took pride in that part of your job. You liked having the reputation for being a bad guy."

Nicky nodded and started rubbing my fingers again with his thumb. "I liked having a reputation that scared other bad guys. Yeah, I enjoyed that part."

"You enjoyed causing pain," Olaf said.

"Up to a point, absolutely, but beyond that point, not so much."

"What point?" Olaf asked.

"I don't think Anita would enjoy us talking shop until we figured out exactly what point it stopped being fun for me."

"I would enjoy it," Olaf said.

"Maybe over late-night drinks sometime but not now," Nicky said.

"I would like to understand how we are different from each other."

"We talked about that earlier. You're a born sociopath, and I was made this way. It probably means I have more of an emotional range than you do."

"Did you feel sympathy for your victims? Is that why it stopped being fun for you?"

"No, it just didn't please me anymore. I like rough sex, rougher than most people, but after a certain point, torture isn't sexual for me. It's just information gathering. It's taking pride in how long I can keep someone alive, how much pain I can cause them and get the truth out of them. I saw people in the industry that did shit that would make anyone talk, but making them talk isn't the same as getting the truth out of them. People will lie to save themselves, to get the torture to stop. They'll tell you anything you want to hear, but lies won't keep you and the people you work with alive. Lies won't help you accomplish your mission. Put people through enough, and they can start hallucinating from the pain. Once that happens, their information is useless."

"You can heal them and question them later," Olaf said.

"Most of my pride's jobs were time sensitive. We didn't have time to nurse our prisoners back to health. My job was to get useful information, details that helped our unit stay alive and accomplish our objectives."

"What did you do with the people once you had all the information you needed?" Olaf asked.

I fought to not feel, to try to be empty of emotion so Nicky could answer truthfully. I tried to go into the big static emptiness where I used to go when I knew I was going to have to pull the trigger on someone. It was an empty, quiet place.

"Killed them or let someone else kill them."

"Fast or slow?" Olaf asked.

"Fast. Once they talked, it was over."

"Didn't you enjoy the kill?"

"Not really. Killing them was just part of the job at that point. Sometimes I was glad to kill them."

"You enjoyed it."

"Not in the way you mean," Nicky said. He let go of my hand and sat back in his seat.

"You said you were glad to kill them," Olaf said. "That implies joy in the kill."

"I enjoy a good hunt. I enjoy killing people that are trying to kill me. I like proving I'm better than they are, but killing someone who's chained up or so hurt they can't do anything back to you, that's like a canned hunt. There's no enjoyment in that for me."

"Then why were you glad?"

"Glad it was over and done," Nicky said. "Glad we could get on with the next part of our job. Glad I could put the people out of their misery."

"Are you saying you felt pity for them?"

"Maybe."

"I saw some of your videos, Nicky. The man who did that had no pity for his victims."

"I've seen your videos, too, Olaf. You enjoy the work a lot more than I did."

"Do you think your victims hurt less because you did not enjoy it, Nick?"

"No."

"Do you think they were less afraid because you didn't enjoy their screams?"

"No," Nicky said, and there was no emotion in the word.

"Do you think you're better than me because you felt more for your victims?"

"No. If it's morals you want to split, then I'm worse, because I had some pity, some feelings, and I still did it. I think that makes me worse."

I looked at him between the seats. "Is it being tied to me metaphysically that makes you feel bad about it now?"

Nicky made a little waffling motion. "I don't remember feeling bad about it before, so probably, but I know that I didn't enjoy the harm I caused past a certain point. It stopped being exciting or sexual or anything remotely resembling an emotion I could explain to you, Anita."

"You're a werelion. You like blood and meat," Olaf said.

"In my food, not in my sex."

"I don't believe you."

"I've said it before, Olaf: I don't care what you believe."

I had a thought but wasn't sure if I should share it out loud. I forgot that, with Nicky this close, a clear thought was enough, and I didn't have to say it.

"Yeah, I think you're right," he said.

"Thank for you for admitting it," Olaf said.

"I wasn't talking to you, Olaf. I was talking to Anita."

"She didn't say anything— Ah, you read her mind again."

"I did."

"What did she think that was so right?"

"That I'm into edge play and risk-aware bondage, but you're a serial killer, so once my victims were hurt past a certain point, I didn't see it as sex, and you still do."

"Those don't sound like Anita's words."

"Nicky's paraphrasing," I said.

"What did you actually think?" Olaf asked.

"Nicky explained it better. Thoughts aren't always as fully formed before you say them."

"Do you do edge play and risk-aware bondage with Nicky?"

"If I say yes, will you drop this line of conversation?"

"No," he said.

I said, "Then I'm not going to answer the question."

"Nicky, do you need the bondage to have sex?"

"You mean, to get aroused enough for sex?" Nicky asked.

"Yes."

"No, I can get it up without it. How about you? Do you need the violence to do it?"

"For the physical act, no."

"How about to enjoy it?" Nicky asked.

"I will answer the question if you will," Olaf said.

"Without the rough, it's no fun, but I can do vanilla. I did it for some undercover work," Nicky said.

"As did I, but without the rough, as you put it, it is not satisfying."

I honestly hadn't been entirely sure that Olaf could get it up without the extreme violence. It was strangely positive that he could, better than the alternative.

I could see the sheriff's station up ahead. We were about to learn what the new evidence was, and I was going to get out of this conversation. Double win!

"Do you want to have children with Anita?" Olaf asked.

And just like that, we were back to being trapped in the conversation from hell.

"No," Nicky said.

"Why not?"

"The woman who calls herself my mother is the one who took my eye when I was fourteen, and that's just the scar I can't hide. It's not even close to the only one. She abused my younger brother and sister, too, but I was her special boy. My father knew and didn't do a damn thing to protect us. With that as my pedigree, I don't think I should breed."

"So, you do not care if Anita has a child with one of the other men in your lives?"

"That is none of your business," I said.

"No, it's all right," Nicky said. "I want to answer."

I tried not to sigh and just motioned him on.

"The men she's closest to are like family to me. Nathaniel calls me one of his brother-husbands, like the polygamist term sister-wife. If Anita wants to have kids with some of my brothers, then it's just more family to love."

Olaf parked in front of the police station and turned off the engine. I was already reaching for the door handle when he asked, "And do you truly love them as you love Anita?"

"No, I'm in love with her. I love some of the men like brothers and some as friends."

"What of the women in your poly group who are still back in St. Louis?"

Nicky grinned, but it was more a baring of teeth, like the reminder that he had sharper ones in his other forms. "Most of them are afraid of me, so no, I don't love any of them."

"What about sex with them?"

"See the first answer: They're afraid of me. And none of them likes rough sex or bondage, so what's the point?"

"Even Angel and Petra?"

Fuck, I thought.

"I don't love either of them," Nicky said.

"Have you had sex with them?" Olaf asked.

I wanted to get out of the car, but was afraid the conversation wouldn't stop, and then I wouldn't be here to know what answers Nicky had given. I might need to know both the answers and Olaf's reactions to those answers, so I stayed. Damn it.

"I've had sex with Angel."

"And?" Olaf said.

"And Anita is very uncomfortable with this line of questioning," Nicky said.

"Does that mean you won't answer or cannot answer me?"

"It means that Anita would have to tell me she's okay with me answering."

I looked longingly at the sheriff's station; it was right there. There were clues to see, but I knew Olaf wouldn't leave this question alone. Since both women were being set up as bait, it seemed like it was a question that would have to be answered. Oh, hell.

"Does Angel know who and what I am?" Olaf asked.

That made me turn and look at him. "She knows."

"And yet she is still flirting with me."

I nodded.

"How rough does she like her bondage?"

I fought not to squirm or blush and failed on the second part. It made Olaf smile, and I glared at him. I started to get angry and welcomed it. It was so much better than embarrassment. "Not as rough as you do." My voice was thick with anger, my skin warm with it.

He undid his seat belt so he could turn and look more fully at Nicky in the backseat. "But she is rough enough to satisfy you?"

"In a group scene with Anita involved, yes."

The blush that had been fading flared back to life. "And we are done talking about this topic," I said.

Olaf stared at me with his eyes lost behind the dark sunglasses, but the intensity of his attention was still like weight on my skin. "If we are to date each other, Adler, I need to know certain things."

"He can ask them when you're not around, Anita," Nicky said.

"No, if you're going to answer, then I need to know what's said, I think."

"Even if it makes you incredibly uncomfortable?"

"Even if," I said, and just like that, I got myself under control. It was just another kind of bravery, and I would be brave, damn it.

"Ask," Nicky said.

"Do you only have sex with the other women with Anita present?" Olaf said.

"With Angel, yes."

"What of Petra?"

"She's one of the ones who's afraid of me and doesn't like it rough."

"So, you haven't had sex with her?"

"No."

"Okay, we're done, right? We have a clue waiting for us, remember?" I said, and reached for the door handle.

"One more question," Olaf said.

I actually rested my forehead against the window glass. "What?" I asked, and sounded tired even to myself.

"Anita must enjoy sex and bondage rough enough to satisfy you, but does she enjoy it rough enough for me?"

"For me, she's great," Nicky said. "Our kinks match up really well."

"After seeing your videos, I'm surprised that Anita would agree to it."

"My videos were mostly about work, about being scary enough to make people believe my old lion pride's threat was good, or as an advertisement to what we could do for prospective customers. The stuff that Anita wouldn't survive without scars or worse was torture to gain information or to make a business point. That's what I meant earlier when I said that I enjoyed the interrogation only up to a point. After that point, it was just work."

I sat there trying to go to that static, white-noise, empty part of me so that I wouldn't care that a man I was in love with was saying such terrible things. I knew what Nicky was, or what he'd been when I met him. I knew that if I hadn't possessed him, he'd probably still be happily torturing and killing his way across the world with his old lion pride of mercenaries, but it was still hard to hear him talk so casually about it. I realized that I wasn't Nicky's Jiminy Cricket. I was more his road-to-Damascus salvation.

"My videos are what I enjoy," Olaf said.

"No one would survive that, so no, Anita doesn't like it rough enough to keep you happy," Nicky said.

"I would like to try," Olaf said.

"I'm not sure how we can test your sexual preferences and keep Anita safe," Nicky said.

"I would be willing to do a vanilla version of what I prefer, if there is such a thing," Olaf said.

I couldn't hold on to my peaceful white-noise place.

"Anita is too unhappy with this conversation for me to continue with it," Nicky said.

"We need to go inside now," I said. I opened the door and actually got my seat belt unbuckled and a foot outside before Olaf's deep voice dragged me back.

"I would like your permission to speak with Nicky later in more detail to see if our kinks match."

"I don't know what to say to that. The thought of Nicky giving you that many personal details makes me incredibly uncomfortable."

"But if we are negotiating for actual dating and sex between us, then more shared information is better, isn't it?"

I glanced back at him and fought to keep the panic from showing on my face.

He smiled then, a wide, happy, predatory one. "Don't hide your fear from me, Anita. You know I enjoy it."

And that was it for me. I got out of the car and kept moving. I needed more people around me. I needed not to be the only nonsociopath in the conversation.

55

LEDUC WOULDN'T ALLOW any of the Coalition people, including Nicky, to see the new evidence. It was police evidence, and they weren't police. None of us could argue with that, so Newman recommended a bed-and-breakfast just up the road. "It's also the closest and has the most pleasant rooms. There's a motel just up the way and some Airbnbs, but they aren't as nice, and I can't guarantee anything will have rooms."

Leduc reluctantly agreed and even called the owners of the bed-and-breakfast since he knew them like he seemed to know everybody. They had two rooms available for tonight, and a third would open up tomorrow. Nicky took all three rooms for the time they were available, and Angel called the motel. For security reasons, the SEALs didn't like splitting the group up.

Olaf asked Nicky, "Why aren't you worried?"

"I'll be wherever Anita is tonight, so she's covered."

I had a moment of worrying about who would keep the other two women safe. Pierette was one of our guards; she'd put herself up as bait because everyone thought she could take Olaf. The hard feeling in my gut wasn't so sure. Angel didn't fit his profile, so I was less worried about her, but once Nicky assured everyone that he'd be by my side when and if I got to sleep, they all stopped arguing about security and just went to check into the rooms at the bed-and-breakfast down the road. There were enough available rooms at the local motel that they didn't have to call anywhere else. No one kissed me good-bye, because Leduc was there watching for more PDA. Ethan and Angel did make me promise to text or call when the evidence reveal was done.

"We can't help you with Bobby if we aren't here," Angel had said.

"I know and I promise," I said, and I meant it.

Leduc made us wait until they'd driven away before he'd share the new evidence with us. He punched in a code to unlock a phone and showed us more damning evidence against Bobby: pictures of Joc-elyn asleep taken from the angle of someone who was looking down at her or who was next to her. Leduc wouldn't let the rest of us touch the phone so that the number of extra fingerprints would be lower. I couldn't argue with his logic, but he was acting as if the proof would actually see a courtroom. Every picture was another nail in Bobby's coffin, showing he was obsessed with his stepsister. There was even a selfie that Bobby had taken of him smiling up at the camera with Jocelyn obviously asleep beside him. It looked like he'd been sneak-ing into her room after she fell asleep and taking pictures for at least a month, maybe longer. There was even a video at the end in which he was lying in her disheveled bed with the sheets and covers crum-pled around him while he was talking into the camera.

"What's he saying?" I asked.

"Does it matter?" Sheriff Leduc asked.

He was probably right, but . . . "We're talking about killing him, so yeah, it matters."

Leduc didn't argue again; he just turned the sound up.

"We just made love, and it was amazing. I am so in love with her!" Bobby's face was full of emotion to match the words. His voice rose. "Nothing. No, just talking to myself, Joshie. Yeah, I know I'm weird. I'm just happy you love me." He laughed and then sat up, the phone half forgotten in his hand so that the angle was suddenly odd. He was shirtless at the very least, and she was within hearing range. "Any-thing you say, Joshie," he said, and then the video ended.

"What more proof do you want that he was obsessed with his own sister?" Leduc asked.

Newman looked pale.

"How did you get the phone?" I asked.

"Helen Grimes, the Marchands' cook, brought it in, along with her own eyewitness account of the stalking," Leduc said.

"She's in the interrogation room waiting to repeat it to the four of us," Edward said.

"Play the video again first," Olaf said.

"You've seen and heard all of it," Leduc said.

"I heard all of it, but none of you did."

"What are you talking about?"

"My hearing is superior to yours. There is another voice on the video."

"I'm older than any of you, but I'm not losing my hearing, not yet," the sheriff said.

"Otto's hearing is better than any straight human's, Sheriff," I said.

"You mean because he's a wereanimal?"

"Yes."

Edward said, "Let's hear the video again with the sound all the way up."

Leduc sighed as if we were all being incredibly demanding, but he did what Edward asked. The video played again, almost too loud. Bobby's declaration of love sounded worse, crazier, more delusional, and then just at the end, I heard a female voice.

"Play it again," I said.

Edward put his ear so it was almost touching the phone. "Anita" was all he said, but I took my turn almost touching the phone, straining to hear, and it was a woman's voice. I couldn't have sworn it was Jocelyn Marchand's voice, but I could hear what she was saying: "What are you doing in there?"

Bobby: "Nothing. No, just talking to myself, Joshie."

Woman, maybe Jocelyn: "Bobby, you are so weird. I don't know why I love you sometimes." She laughed, and I knew it was a sexy or, rather, an after-sex laugh. I heard water start to run. "Come join me in the shower, weirdo." She gave that sexy, intimate laugh again.

"Anything you say, Joshie."

Edward said, "Newman or Duke."

Newman let the sheriff go next. Duke was frowning before he finished listening. He stood up without a word. "What the hell?" he said softly.

Newman listened, and he looked relieved at first. "I'd swear that was Jocelyn's voice."

"I'd swear it was, too," Duke said.

"Then she's lying," I said.

"No, she's not just lying. She's setting him up," Edward said.

"Why would she do that?" Newman asked.

"If this was a normal case with no supernaturals involved, what would you say?" Edward asked.

"Money," Leduc said.

We all looked at him. "If Ray had been shot or stabbed or almost anything else, we'd be following the money," he said.

"Would the attorneys tell us who stands to gain from Ray's and Bobby's deaths?" Newman asked.

"Officially, I think we'd need a warrant, but I know the attorneys Ray used. I coached their sons."

"We need to know what changes if Bobby dies with Ray," Newman said.

Leduc nodded. "I'll try to find out. I just can't believe Joshie would do something this . . . cold-blooded."

"We'll talk to the cook, and then we have to talk to Bobby again," I said.

"This may not be enough to get another stay of execution, Anita," Newman said.

"I know."

"We can't kill Bobby if we have evidence of a conspiracy to murder by someone else," Leduc said.

"Conspiracy?" I asked.

"If Joshie was out with girlfriends, then she wasn't home killing Ray. If Bobby didn't do it, then someone else did. She had to have an accomplice, so it's a conspiracy."

"Unless she was able to leave the club long enough to do it herself," I said.

"We need to talk to the dancer she was with," Newman said.

"Wait a minute," Leduc said. "I'll believe what I heard on the video, so she's involved, but she couldn't have done that to Ray. Human hands and fingernails could not have done that."

"Duke is right," Newman said.

"We need to see the body and the crime scene," Edward said.

"We need to find a murder weapon that would explain the wounds," I said.

"If I'd used something to commit murder, I'd have dumped it by now," Newman said.

"What do you need to help Bobby?" Duke asked.

"We need a smoking gun, and we need it soon," Newman said.

"I'll chase the money," Duke said.

"We'll talk to Helen Grimes," I said.

Olaf said, "Could she be the accomplice?"

"We'll find out," I said.

"Yes," he said, "we will."

And then he smiled, an anticipatory, predatory smile. He was hoping that we'd get to hurt the cook to make her tell the truth. A few minutes ago, I'd have been certain that I'd never help him torture another person, but if it was a choice between terrorizing a woman I'd never met or having to kill Bobby, then I knew what my choice would be. I hate that sometimes the path to hell really is paved with good intentions.

56

THE MARCHANDS' COOK, Helen Grimes, was sitting behind the table in the small interrogation room. She was a little heavy—not like she was built that way, but like she was eating more of her own food than maybe was good for her. The lines in her face seemed harsh, with sagging skin, but I didn't hold that against her. Grief will do that to people of all ages. On a normal day she might have looked ten years younger, but today was not a normal day. In fact, she looked so shaky that Olaf put himself in a corner as far from her as possible without being asked. Edward took another corner, leaving Newman and me closest to her.

Helen huddled over the glass of water that someone had gotten her; she had a crumpled tissue in her hand. "I caught Bobby at Jocelyn's door one night. He made some excuse, but it didn't feel right. That was the first hint I had that there was something wrong between the two of them."

"What were you doing there so late, Helen?" Newman asked.

"Mr. Ray was out of town on business, and he asked me to stay over in case the kids needed anything."

"I thought Carmichael was the live-in handyman," Newman said.

She made a derisive sound. "Carmichael is spending most of his nights with his new girlfriend. I'd started staying over in one of the guest rooms off and on, but Mr. Ray made a special request of it when he was out of town last time. I think he'd started to suspect that something was wrong." Her voice broke at the end, shoulders hunching forward even more as if she was collapsing over the water glass.

"Would you like some coffee?" I asked. Maybe a little caffeine would help revive her. It always helped me.

She shook her head but gave me a weak smile. Her eyes were red rimmed with all the crying she'd done. "Thank you, but caffeine makes me jittery nowadays, and my nerves are bad enough right now."

"How about something a little stronger?" Edward asked from his corner.

Helen looked at him, and the smile got a little firmer. "I wouldn't turn down a little sip of something."

Edward gave her his best Ted smile, all bright and reassuring. She looked a little calmer from that alone. He asked, "Any preferences, little lady?"

She laughed, and I almost jumped, because her reaction startled me. "No one's called me little lady in quite a while."

Edward just grinned at her, putting all his good-ol'-boy charm into it. Color crept back into her face; her eyes were bright enough that I noticed they were hazel with so much dark green mixed in with the brown that she probably could have put either on her driver's license. She damn near giggled at Edward, and her expression didn't look silly. It was like a glimpse of a younger woman, back in the day when she might have matched the history behind her first name more. Helen, the beauty whose kidnapping started the Trojan War, always seemed like a lot to live up to, but suddenly there was a sparkle in Helen Grimes. Maybe it wasn't a matter of being younger, but of being happier.

"Well, then, the men in this town should be ashamed of themselves, Helen. May I call you Helen?"

The look on her face said he could call her most anything and she'd like it, but aloud she said, "Helen will be just fine, Marshal."

"Ted. The name's Ted." And he tipped his cowboy hat at her. It would have been over-the-top for me, but Helen ate it up.

"Do you have a preference on what flavor of stronger you would like me to fetch for you, Helen?"

He moved forward, and I moved back so that he was across the table from Helen. She smiled up at him, looking better by the minute. It would never have occurred to me that a little flirting would revive the witness, but then, that's why I'm still learning from Edward.

She damn near simpered at him as she gave her preferences on Scotch versus rye whiskey. I didn't drink enough to follow most of it. She was sitting upright, a healthier color in her face, as Edward went off in search of her order.

Newman smiled at Helen and said, "I'd like to be able to wait for your drink, Helen, but we need to know the truth before Bobby runs out of time."

Her face clouded and her shoulders started to slump, but then she straightened up and forced herself to look Newman in the face. "I hate the idea of you having to kill Bobby, but I think the animal in him just got too strong."

"What do you mean . . . Helen?" I asked. I'd use her first name if it made her feel better. Belatedly, I wondered if I should offer for her to call me by my first name, but she was answering, so I let it go.

Her face was grim as she looked at me. She gripped her hands together tight enough for the skin to mottle as she said, "First, he started sniffing around Jocelyn, his own sister, and then he lost control and killed his uncle. Bobby was a good person, but he wasn't strong enough to fight off all the animal urges."

"When did Bobby stop being a good person, Helen?" Newman asked.

She looked startled. "I didn't say he wasn't. It's the beast in him that's bad."

"You used the past tense: 'Bobby was a good person,'" I said.

"When did you decide he wasn't a good person, Helen?" Newman asked, his voice gentle.

"I got up in the middle of the night to use the bathroom and saw a flash of light coming from Jocelyn's room. The door was partially open. I walked closer, and Bobby came out, wearing just a pair of underwear. He had his phone in his hand. I remember thinking it was odd."

"What did he say when he saw you, Helen?" Newman asked.

"He said that he thought he'd left his headphones over in her room. He had insomnia and wanted to listen to music and not wake her."

"Did you believe him?" I asked.

"No . . . maybe . . . I don't know." She wiped at the tears on her face with the crumpled tissue, but it was used up. Newman got a plastic travel packet of them out of his pocket and handed it to her. I'd never thought to add tissues to one of the pockets in the tactical pants. I filed it away for later as a good idea.

"Thank you," Helen said, and wiped at her eyes and nose.

We waited for her to get control of herself. Sometimes you don't want witnesses to regain control, because the breakdown helps them spill what they know, but Helen wanted to talk to us. She'd come down to the station to tell her story and to bring new evidence. She wasn't going to clam up on us.

"What happened next?" Newman asked, voice so kind. He had a nice light touch, better than mine.

"I asked Jocelyn if she'd found Bobby's headphones in her room. If she'd said yes, then I would have left it alone. They're siblings. Things end up in the wrong room for a lot of innocent reasons, but she didn't know what I was talking about, so I told her." Helen gulped hard and tried to breathe deep as if the next part was harder. "Jocelyn broke down and cried in my arms. She'd woken up with Bobby lying in bed with her once, and he'd walked in on her when she was dressing or showering so many times, she tried to keep her door locked, but she'd forgotten the night I saw him. I told her she had to tell her stepfather, Mr. Ray, that he had to know. I tried to ask if Bobby had done more than look, and she broke down completely." Helen started to cry again.

"What did she say Bobby had done?" I asked, trying to keep my own voice as gentle as Newman's.

Helen shook her head hard enough that her short hair bounced around her face. "She was so upset that she couldn't talk, but her reaction let me know it was worse. I told her to go to the police if he'd touched her, and she completely fell apart. I told her that I'd go with her, that she didn't have to do this alone, but she refused to go to the police. She said if I went to the cops without her, she'd lie and say I'd made it up. She didn't want everyone to know, and if the police got involved, then it would be courts and lawyers. She was ashamed, said it was her fault, too. I couldn't convince her that it wasn't her fault or to go to the police, so I told her to tell her stepfather. I offered to go with her for moral support, but she wanted to do it on her own. She was so brave."

Helen raised her face and looked at me with an almost radiant expression, as if the memory of that brave moment from Jocelyn had been some magnificent gesture. I let the moment of shining sister-hood fill Helen's face and make her eyes look even greener.

"Do you know if she told Ray?" Newman asked.

"She came into the kitchen and hugged me that morning, said that Mr. Ray had believed her and was going to talk to Bobby that night. She was so happy. I offered to stay that night, but she said she was going out with friends and that Mr. Ray wanted to be alone with Bobby for the talk."

I glanced at Newman and our eyes met. I wondered if he was think-ing what I was thinking: It all sounded so reasonable. If Olaf hadn't heard Jocelyn's voice on the video, if we hadn't put our ears nearly touching the phone to hear her being seductive with Bobby, we'd have believed Helen's story. It would have been enough for one of us to go into the cell and end Bobby's life.

"I should have gone to the sheriff and told him that Bobby was molesting his sister. I should have done it, even if Jocelyn hated me or they fired me. I should have told someone. If I had, maybe Mr. Ray would still be alive." Helen started to cry harder again, shoul-ders rounding and starting to shake.

We were trying to reassure Helen that it wasn't her fault when Edward finally came back with her drink. I moved back to stand beside Olaf so that Edward could have the room to work his sweet Ted magic on her. I was out of sweet talk about this case.

So Jocelyn had lied about the affair with her brother because she was embarrassed about it. It didn't mean she'd killed her uncle. Ray

Marchand could have seen it as incest and told Bobby to break it off with Jocelyn that night. Nothing we'd learned—even Jocelyn's lying—helped clear Bobby of the murder. We needed another murderer to put in Bobby's place, with enough evidence to convince the judge, or we were still going to have to kill him.

I had a sudden urge to lean my head against Olaf's arm, because I couldn't reach his shoulder, just to touch someone. It's one of the ways that lycanthropes soothe themselves, and I carried enough beasts inside me to just want to lean against someone for a moment so I could think. As if Olaf had read my mind, he moved that small distance to me so that his arm touched my shoulder. Yeah, I knew it was Olaf, and he was a scary fuck, but I found myself leaning my head against his arm, resting my weight against him for a moment. It felt good, comforting in that puppy-pile kind of way that I'd grown to depend on when I was home with my polycule. I'd thought it was because they were metaphysically tied to me, but maybe it was just the physical closeness, the way stray dogs huddled together for comfort.

Whatever it was, it helped me think. Leduc had said that Helen Grimes had brought in Bobby's phone because it had evidence that proved Jocelyn was telling the truth, or something like that. How had Helen known what was on the phone? How had she been that certain that it was worth bringing in to the police?

Those were good questions—questions we should have thought of earlier. I stopped arguing with myself about what felt good and what was a bad idea and just leaned against Olaf, finally feeling in the front of my head what the back part had already noticed, a faint hum of energy: his lion to my lion. It didn't raise our beasts, it didn't do anything bad, it just was, and in that moment, it was enough. If he would only give up the serial killer stuff, maybe we could cuddle.

57

BY THE TIME Edward got Helen calmed down, I had stopped leaning against Olaf. Even if he'd been my sweetheart for real, I wouldn't have allowed myself to show affection in the middle of an interrogation. The other marshals would have made fun of me.

Helen was smiling at Edward, but when she turned to Newman, the smile vanished. "Why haven't you done your duty, Win?"

"I'm not sure what you mean, Helen."

"It's not Bobby's fault that the animal inside him is turning him into a monster, but it's still a fact. It started with him lusting after his own sister, and when Mr. Ray told him that it was sinful, the animal side of him went crazy and killed him. Ray Marchand raised that boy like his own, adopted him and everything, but Bobby still turned into an animal and killed him. He's not safe anymore, Win."

"Did you see him kill Ray?" Newman asked.

"No, I wasn't there that night. I told you that."

"Were you safe and snuggled up at home, Helen?" Edward asked in his best country drawl.

"I was with my quilting group. We're making a cathedral-window pattern. None of us has ever tried anything that intricate before."

"The one that meets in the basement of the Lutheran church?" Newman asked.

"Yes," she said, smiling and relaxed from talking about her hobby.

"Was it your night to bring refreshments?" he asked.

"No, I was on cleanup duty this week."

"So, you locked up and went home pretty late," Newman said.

I realized that between the two of them, they had Helen's alibi. I hadn't even thought of Helen Grimes as a possible accomplice in the murder, and I should have. I just wasn't used to looking at ordinary people for my murderer. Once you had a victim who had been clawed to death, normal human fingernails just couldn't do the job.

Helen leaned across the table and touched Newman's sleeve. "I know it's an awful thing that you have to do, Win, but it's your job to keep the rest of us safe from the monsters, and that's what Bobby is now, a monster."

He patted her hand but moved back so she couldn't touch him again. "If Bobby did everything you say he did, then you're right, Helen."

"If? What do you mean, if, Win?"

"If you had to walk into that cell and kill someone, wouldn't you want to be certain first?"

"Jocelyn said you didn't believe her, that you thought she was lying about what Bobby did to her, but you've seen the pictures and the video on his phone now. You know he was stalking her, or I don't even have a word for what he was doing."

I made myself smile at her. "How did you know that the pictures were on his phone, Helen?"

"Jocelyn told me."

"When did she tell you about the phone, Helen?" Newman asked.

"When I visited her at the hospital today. She's got no family left now."

Newman said, "There're still Muriel and Todd Babington."

Helen looked angry and shook her head. "They never treated Jocelyn like a niece, not the way they treated Bobby, though heaven knows they didn't treat him all that well. Did you know that they were supposed to take Bobby when Muriel's sister, his mother, died, but they didn't want him? Mr. Ray took him because Muriel was the only remaining sister and she didn't want children. She'd have let the state have Bobby and him just a baby."

"I didn't think you'd worked for the Marchand family long enough to know the history, Helen," Newman said.

"I remember when Bobby's mother died. We all assumed that her sister would take the baby. I mean, Ray Marchand had divorced twice because he was married to his career. Everyone knew that. We couldn't believe that he took the boy. Muriel Babington got asked a lot why she didn't take Bobby, and she told anyone that asked that she never wanted children, her own or anyone else's. We thought Bobby would end up raised by nannies or something, but Ray cut his hours and stopped most of the traveling and was the best father he knew how to be." Helen started tearing up again. "And to think that all that kindness and love ended up with the boy he raised killing him."

Edward patted her hand, and she grasped his hand. How did he do it? "How did Jocelyn know the pictures were on the phone?"

"She borrowed the phone to look something up and one of the photos was his background, if you can believe it. I mean, bold as brass, that."

"Did she confront him about it?" Edward asked.

"She told him he had no right to those pictures, that she never gave him permission to take them."

"How did you know the code to unlock the phone?" he asked, still holding her hand, or letting her hold his.

"Jocelyn gave it to me so that I could unlock the phone for the sheriff."

"If Bobby was hiding pictures from her, seems like he wouldn't want her to have the lock code to his phone."

"Bobby told her that he loved her so much that he changed his code to her birth date."

"Very romantic," Edward said.

Helen pulled her hand out of his, her face offended. "Not if it's your own brother, it isn't."

"I'm sorry, Helen. Of course you're right on that."

"Now you know that Jocelyn is telling the truth."

"It looks bad for Bobby," Newman said.

Helen's face clouded up, some emotion I couldn't read crossing over her face. Her moods were like clouds on a windy day, fast changing. "I hate the thought of him dying, but I'll feel safer when the animal inside of him is dead."

"The animal and the man are one and the same," Olaf said, still leaning against the wall.

Helen glanced at him, then away quickly, as if she didn't want to stare at him longer than necessary. Either she had good instincts, or she was just naturally intimidated by a man of his size. "I cannot believe that Bobby is the same thing that killed his uncle."

"You cannot kill the beast without killing the man."

"I know that," she said, sounding defensive.

"Do you?" Olaf asked, and he gave her a long look out of his hooded dark eyes.

She didn't try to hold the look but found the tabletop much more interesting.

Edward turned around with a smile. In a thick Ted accent, he said, "Why don't the two of you go talk to Bobby about those awful pictures? We'll join you in a few minutes."

His eyes were not nearly as friendly as his tone. I think he thought Olaf was making Helen nervous, and he didn't want the big guy talking to Bobby on his own, so . . . I got to stand in the hallway with him. Great, I was Olaf's battle buddy. What could possibly go wrong?

58

OF COURSE, EDWARD wasn't sending me out to stand alone with Olaf. There was still plenty of company in the outer office. Nicky was sitting at one of the empty desks with a chair angled so he could see us coming down the hallway from the interrogation room. He also had a view of the rest of the office, the front door, and the cells down their little hallway. It made me smile just to see him sitting there. He smiled back.

I wanted to go to him and kiss him so badly. It was just wrong to walk into a room and not touch someone you loved, but we were going to cool the PDA while we were working. Nicky and I would be sharing a room tonight, so we'd catch up on the displays of affection in private.

"That was fast on the rooms," I managed to say without going close enough to touch him.

"Ethan and the others are handling it. We all decided it would suck if you needed help keeping your prisoner in human form and none of us was here to help."

Deputy Frankie was on the landline phone. She put the receiver to her shoulder to say, "Everyone else is out on calls. I'm manning the phones and guarding the prisoners."

I realized the door to the cell area was open so she could be at the desk and see into the other space, though maybe there was more than one reason she wanted a good view.

I could hear Angel's voice. She was sitting in the little hallway on the chair that Frankie had been using when she was on guard duty earlier. She was leaning forward and talking to either Bobby or Troy; it was hard to tell which from a glance. Angel laughed at something that one of them said; she used a very feminine laugh that usually meant the joke wasn't nearly as funny as it was meant to be. Either a lot of women are socially conditioned to laugh at men's jokes, or they're flirting. I'd never been socially conditioned as a girl for much of anything, and I'd never been able to fake a laugh, and I made it a rule not to fake anything else, but I could recognize when others did.

Deputy Frankie hung up the phone and glanced back into the hallway. Maybe Angel's flirting wasn't really aimed at the men in the cells. Angel dated both men and women, so you never knew which way she'd swing. Maybe she had a thing for women in uniform?

"We need to ask Bobby a few more questions," I said.

The phone rang, and Frankie waved us through the open door while she took the call. Angel stood up as we walked into the cellblock. Did two cells count as a block? She smiled at Olaf and me. Some lingering energy from the flirting seemed to cling to her, or maybe it was the extra wiggle she put into her hips as she swayed toward us in her pencil skirt.

"I know the rules: The sheriff lets us sit with Bobby, but we're not allowed to be in on any official police business like questioning the prisoners." Angel wiggled her eyebrows as she said the last word like it was something naughty.

Olaf and I frowned at her as she left. I don't know what he was thinking, but I still didn't like her and Pierette making themselves bait for him. I closed the door between us and the office for what privacy it offered. Everyone outside except for the deputy was a wereanimal. The door was thick, but I wasn't sure it was that thick. Since I'd have let Angel stay in the room, I really wasn't worried about it. I'd closed the door because I'd made the deal with Leduc that only the people with official badges would be involved in official businesslike interrogations.

Bobby and Troy were sitting as close as the cells would allow, visiting through the shared cell bars. They looked at Olaf and me as we walked in, and there was something in their expressions that told me they were on the same side. The whole cop-and-criminal thing didn't seem to apply anymore. Maybe it was their shared history, or maybe they'd bonded because one of them had nearly killed the other one. Men can bond over some strange stuff. Of course, maybe they were just bored, and they didn't have anything else to do but talk to each other, and I was just overthinking it. Yeah, probably that.

"What's wrong?" Bobby asked. He started moving to the front of his cell.

"Why do you think anything is wrong?" I asked.

"You look grim." He stopped moving toward us and just stood looking at us. He went pale, and his voice was a little breathy as he asked, "Are you going to kill me now?"

I shook my head.

He let out a long breath, or maybe he just breathed again. I thought for a second he was going to go to his knees, but he managed to back up and sit on his bunk. "I keep thinking every time one of you comes in here that it will be the last time."

I had no honest comfort to offer him, because he was right. I could kill when people were trying to kill me, when I had to protect others, or even when I was sure that someone had murdered others and would do it again, but this . . . this wasn't right.

"You're right, Bobby. We're running out of time, so I'm just going to ask you what I need to ask. I'm sorry that we don't have privacy, but the interrogation room is full."

"I understand that you want to help me, Anita, so just ask. If Troy tells anyone my secrets, I'll tell everyone what happened at our senior prom."

"Oh, dude, that is low," Troy said.

Bobby smiled at him. "Just reminding you that I know where your bodies are buried, too." Bobby frowned and looked at us. "Wow, that sounded way better in my head. Now it just sounds creepy."

"About that kind of thing," I said, "you say that you and Jocelyn had a consensual relationship."

"We're in love," he said.

"Okay, then, why do all the pictures on your phone look like stalker pics?"

"What are you talking about?"

"She looks asleep in all of them, like you snuck into her room and took them without her knowing. That's not what couple pictures look like, Bobby."

He looked angry, embarrassed. "This sounds so weak, but she didn't want any pictures until after we went public with the relationship. She was adamant about no intimate pictures."

"So, you did sneak into her room at night and take the pictures?"

"No, we'd make love and she'd fall asleep and then I'd take a few pictures. I loved her so much—I love her so much—that I wanted something to prove to myself that it was real. I know that's not a good excuse for promising not to take pictures and then taking them anyway, but they're not all like that. I have some of her smiling at me during the day, and those are good."

"We didn't find any pictures of her except the ones you took when she was asleep and the one video."

He frowned at me. "I have dozens of pictures of her smiling and talking to me. I took them before she told me to stop."

I glanced up at Olaf, and he nodded, which I took to mean that Bobby smelled like he was telling the truth. So either Bobby was truly delusional, or Jocelyn had found time to open his phone and delete the other photos. We needed to know if Helen Grimes had seen Jocelyn do it, or if Helen had left the phone alone for any length of time with the other woman. Jocelyn hadn't been able to hear her own voice on the video, so she hadn't known to erase it. If we hadn't heard that one bit of evidence, we'd have had to believe that Bobby was truly delusional about her and probably had killed the only dad that either of them had ever known. But we'd all heard her voice inviting him into the shower for sex, so he wasn't crazy. Jocelyn might have been one of the most cold-blooded and manipulative people I'd ever met. Considering some of the people that I'd dealt with over the years, that was saying something.

"Okay, Bobby, we'll double-check the phone. Maybe we just missed them."

I didn't believe we'd missed them. I believed Jocelyn had made them disappear. A good computer forensic person could probably find them again with some techie magic, but since we were supposed to kill Bobby soon, they'd never have time to find the other photos, and once he was dead, so was the case.

I went for the door, and Olaf followed me like a big pale shadow.

"Anita, wait," Bobby called.

I turned back to look at him. He was at the bars at the front of the cell, holding on to them. "How long do I have until . . . you know?"

I gave him the countdown. "We're really trying to find another way, Bobby."

"I believe you and Win are, Anita. I do." He licked his lips as if his mouth was dry.

"You want some water or something?"

"No, Frankie made sure we had something earlier."

"Hang in there, Bobby. We won't just walk in here without telling you that we're out of options. Okay? You don't have to freak out every time we come through the door."

"Do I get a last meal or request or anything?"

In all the years I'd been doing this, it had never come up, because I'd never had anyone be alive and in custody this long before execution. I glanced up at Olaf and he looked at Bobby. "We could arrange something."

"I'll think on it. I mean, what the hell do you have for your very last meal?"

"It won't come to that, Bobby," Deputy Troy said from the neighboring cell.

"You tried to kill him recently, Deputy. I don't think you are in a position to help the situation."

"You're right. I'm an idiot, and I've probably ruined my career or my whole life. But if you let me out of this cell, I won't run. I just want to help Bobby. I want a chance to make up for what I tried to do to him, please."

"You're Leduc's problem, not ours," I said, and went for the door again.

This time no one called us back, and we went back to the inter-rogation room. I did the soft knock, which is the only time police don't knock on a door like they're trying to scare the hell out of someone inside the room.

Edward came to the door and stepped outside. I told him what we'd learned from Bobby. "Do you want to ask her or let me do it?" I asked.

"I'll do it, but you can be in the room. Otto needs to wait out here."

"I make her nervous," Olaf said.

"You do."

"She's not as naive as she sounds," I said.

Olaf shook his head. "She doesn't know what I am. She is simply afraid because I am tall and male and do not flirt with her."

"I don't think your style of flirting would work for Helen," Edward said.

"No, it would not," Olaf said.

"You can get coffee or something," I said.

"I will get 'or something,'" he said, and walked back toward the office area.

We went back into the room, and Edward went to work, trying to charm Helen into telling things.

Helen didn't know she was supposed to hide things from us, so she told the truth. "I gave the phone to Jocelyn so she could make sure he hadn't changed the code or deleted the evidence. She was afraid no one would believe her if the pictures were gone."

"And had he changed the pass code?"

"No, it was still her birth date."

"Did you leave the room for any reason, Helen?" Edward asked.

"Jocelyn needed more water. She'd pushed the call button for the nurse half an hour before I arrived, and no one had checked on her. Can you imagine, a half hour and no nurse?" Helen was indignant about the nurses ignoring Jocelyn. It never seemed to occur to her that Jocelyn might not have pressed the button at all and had just wanted Helen out of the room so she could maybe delete some pictures.

"Thank you so much for all your help, Helen," Newman said to her.

"I know it's awful, but can I go back and tell Jocelyn that she doesn't have to be afraid anymore, that you believe her and you're going to do what needs to be done?"

Newman blinked at her and then put a smile back on his face. It almost reached his eyes. "Are you going back to the hospital from here, Helen?"

"Yes, Jocelyn is going to be discharged. I told her I'd help her get home."

"That's very kind of you."

"Well, she doesn't have any family left now."

"I guess she doesn't," Newman said.

Helen got up and asked her question again. "Can I reassure Jocelyn that you believe her, and it will be all right now?"

"Let me take this one, Newman," I said.

"Be my guest, Blake."

"You can tell Jocelyn that we will follow the letter of the law, and she can be certain that we will do our job."

Helen smiled at us. She'd heard what she wanted to hear. She left still smiling and reassured. Edward gave me a look that said he'd understood exactly what I'd meant.

Newman shut the door behind her and turned to me, frowning. "What the hell did that even mean?"

"You heard exactly what I said."

"You cannot be thinking that you would harm Jocelyn."

"If you have to kill Bobby, don't you want to make sure that whoever is responsible for that pays the price?"

"If we have to kill him, then it's over. We're done."

I shook my head. "The warrant gives us the latitude to kill anyone involved in the crime."

"Are you seriously implying what I think you're implying?"

"I'm saying that if Bobby Marchand dies because we couldn't prove it wasn't him, then I want whoever killed Ray Marchand and used us to kill Bobby to pay."

"Once Bobby is dead, the case is finished, Anita."

"Are you going to be able to pull the trigger on him?"

Newman looked away and then back at me. His hands were in fists at his sides. "If he was trying to kill me or someone else, yes, but shooting him through the bars of a cage . . . I don't think I can do that."

"Then sign the warrant over."

"I was going to until this conversation. Now if I sign it over to you, I'm afraid you'll use it to kill Jocelyn and Bobby." He looked at me. I met his gaze and held it. He was the one who finally looked away. "Fuck, Anita, just fuck. I need some air." He opened the door and pushed past Olaf.

"What is wrong, Newman?" he asked.

"I had to tell him that there's no Santa Claus," I said.

"I do not understand."

"She overshared. Now he's spooked, and he won't sign the warrant over to any of us, Anita," Edward said.

"That isn't what I meant to happen."

Edward sighed. "You're used to working with me, or Olaf, or Bernardo. You can't talk that plainly in front of the other marshals, especially not the new ones that come through traditional police channels."

"What did Anita say to him?" Olaf asked.

We told Olaf, and he smiled a smile so big, it filled his black eyes with good humor. I wasn't sure I'd ever seen him look so genuinely happy. "Do you truly mean to kill the girl?"

"If she is only hiding the affair with her brother out of shame, then no, but if she is behind the frame job on Bobby, then if he dies, she dies."

"Only if Newman gives the warrant up," Edward said.

"Damn it, Ted, this is so wrong, all of it. Jocelyn or someone is using us like a murder weapon."

"We'll figure it out, Anita. We always do."

"Usually we figure out how to find and kill the monster, but the monster is locked in a cell awaiting execution like a model citizen."

"We are hunting the beauty this time, not the beast," Olaf said.

"Poetic," I said.

"Thank you."

"Fine. Let's go find a bevy of beauties at the strip club and see if Jocelyn's alibi holds up," Edward said.

"Save the beast. Kill the beauty," Olaf said, and smiled again. "I like it."

"It was poetic the first time. Now it's just creepy," I said.

His smile didn't dim, but his eyes slid back to a more predatory happiness, less kid on Christmas morning and more serial killer. "You are not the first woman who has said that to me."

"I'll just bet I'm not, big boy. I'll just bet I'm not."

"Do not call me big boy."

"Sorry. Totally understand. I don't let people call me little girl either."

"Now that you two have worked out the name-calling, let's go find Newman before he drives off without us, because the little woman here spooked his ass."

There wasn't a trace of Ted's happy accent as he said that last part. I realized he was angry with me, and he was right. If I'd kept my mouth shut, Newman would probably have signed the warrant over to me. Then I could have run the investigation the way I wanted to run it. Now our hands were still tied by Newman's scruples. He was a good cop, but maybe that wasn't what this case needed. Maybe it needed a bad cop, or maybe even a little bit worse.

59

I MANAGED TO convince Newman that I was just angry about all of it, and that I wouldn't really use the warrant to kill straight humans unless they were trying to kill me first. It was the truth, but if I had to be the one who put a bullet between Bobby Marchand's eyes when I was about ninety-eight percent certain he was innocent—that might change. I wasn't sure I could kill Jocelyn in cold blood, and I sure as hell couldn't give her over to Olaf, so what the hell was I going to do with her if she was guilty of murder? Damn it, I hated this case. What I hated almost as much was the fact that Leduc had put his foot down and wouldn't allow any Coalition members to go out and question anyone else.

"Our deal is that I let your people babysit Bobby in my station, on the condition that you don't involve them in any other police business."

"Nicky went with Otto and me to question a witness. Nothing bad happened."

Leduc had shaken his head. "You gave your word, Blake, so the deal's done."

I took in a deep breath and let it out slowly, but he was right.

"Besides, Blake, ya got three Horsemen of the Apocalypse plus Win here. Don't you think that's enough firepower?" Again, Leduc was right.

The four of us divided and conquered but ended up meeting at

the edge of a parking lot to discuss Jocelyn's girlfriends and the supposedly perfect alibi. Why a parking lot? Because though we weren't
allowed to let any of my St. Louis people be actively involved in the
case anymore, Leduc felt perfectly okay interfering with any discussion of the case we had at the office. The four of us wanted some
privacy from Duke and his deputies.

We found a tree to the side of the parking lot away from the whir
of passing cars; just the open space gave us privacy to talk. Newman
and Edward shared their intel, what little they'd gained, from Marcy
Myers, Jocelyn's other friend who had gone out with her the night
of the murder. Marcy had agreed with everything Brianna had said,
though Marcy had had to get very drunk to let a stripper do a lap
dance for her, so her details were fuzzy at best.

"Jocelyn could have left the club and come back multiple times,
and Marcy probably wouldn't have noticed," Newman said.

"So she doesn't help either way," Edward said.

"Brianna Gibson was bright-eyed and bushy-tailed for her night
out. She remembers more details than I wanted her to share," I said.

"So she vouches for Jocelyn?" Newman said.

"For a night out at the strip club, yes."

"Did she mention Jocelyn confiding in her about Bobby wanting
to be her boyfriend instead of her brother?" Newman asked.

In my head I thought, Technically he would have been both, but
I didn't say it out loud. The situation was creepy enough without
belaboring it. "No, Jocelyn never told her anything like that because
if she had, Brianna would have mentioned it. She's not shy about
sharing details. I think she would have mentioned it."

"Jocelyn told Marcy about a week before the club," Newman said.

"Why not tell both of them?" I asked.

"Marcy said that the twins were keeping Brianna too busy for
much socializing. Her two kids are older, boy in kindergarten and
the girl in preschool," Newman said.

"Twins under one would keep anyone busy, I guess."

Three of us nodded. Olaf just watched the surroundings the way
a cat looks for movement at a window, as if he were seeing every-

thing all at once. If he wasn't making an occasional comment, I'd have thought he wasn't listening at all.

"If Jocelyn had confided in her other friend that night, it might have put a damper on going to the strip club," Newman said.

We all agreed, even Olaf.

"We have to talk to the dancer that was with Brianna and Jocelyn that night. Friends will lie for you, but strippers that see you as just money in their G-strings, not so much, especially not about murder."

"But even if we can break Jocelyn's alibi for the night of the murder, we still haven't figured out how she made it look like a wereleopard killed Ray. Without that, the judge won't take Bobby's name off the warrant or vacate it," Newman said.

Edward said, "Then we need to break or prove Jocelyn's alibi, because until we do that, we're wasting precious time chasing her story."

"She lied about the affair," I said.

"Anita, she's sleeping with her own brother. Anyone is going to be conflicted about that."

"I think it's more than that," Newman said.

We all looked at him.

"I think she's afraid that Bobby did kill Ray. Remember that it was Jocelyn who insisted he change on the one night when almost every Therianthrope is safe."

"The dark of the moon," I said.

"Yes, so if she thinks Bobby killed Ray, she could blame herself."

"If she saw him change form and go out the window as a leopard, she has to know that when he shifted back to human, he'd be passed out solid for hours. He still passes out like a newbie shapeshifter. It's how the sheriff and the deputies got him to the cell without a fuss," I said.

"Maybe he just comes back into his bedroom and passes out without Jocelyn knowing," Newman said.

"She's lived with Bobby shapeshifting for ten years. Trust me, when you live with a shapeshifter, you learn their patterns."

"Lying about the affair could be embarrassing, but lying about

Bobby being in human form when she left the house has only one explanation," Edward said.

"To set him up for the murder," I said.

"Many people would believe he came back into the house and simply killed the victim because he was a wild animal," Olaf said.

"Everyone says that Bobby had really good control over his beast," I said.

"Humans always believe that shapeshifters are but an impulse away from murder."

"Besides, Anita, you saw Bobby react to the details about Ray's death," Newman said. "He almost shifted form in his cell with us there."

"I can debate the whole humans-think-all-shapeshifters-are-dangerous thing, but I can't argue that. So, do we believe that Jocelyn is hiding the affair because if Bobby killed their father, she's not in love with him anymore?" I asked.

"It could be simpler than that, Anita," Edward said.

I looked at him. "I'm listening. Simple would be nice on this case."

"She believes he's a murderer. She knows that means he's a dead man walking. She thinks he'll be executed within hours of the crime. She can either be the only survivor of a family tragedy or the girl who fucked her brother and drove him to kill their father. Which would you rather be when the dust settles?"

I thought about that for a few seconds and then finally nodded. "Point made, and if she had changed her story only after the murder, I'd agree completely, but she was telling the cook and her friend at least a week before the murder that Bobby was harassing her."

"Point to you, and there's the money. With Bobby dead, her share goes up."

"We don't know that yet," Newman said. As if on cue his phone rang. It was Leduc. Newman made some *hmm* noises, then said, "Thanks, Duke."

We looked at him and waited for him to share. When he didn't, I broke first and said, "Well?"

"Bobby got most of the money, the art and family antiques. Jocelyn got the house, the grounds, and contents that didn't fall under art or family pieces. The art and family heirlooms are another fortune if Bobby sold them for the appraised value. With him dead, she inherits most of the family fortune and still gets the grounds and a lot more of the contents. The family portraits and some of the other art goes to a museum along with an endowment for a new wing or building. Apparently, Ray didn't trust anyone but Bobby with the family history and the more important pieces of art."

"Muriel and Todd were trying to steal and sell the art before the body was cold, so he was right on that," I said.

"Ray never adopted Jocelyn formally because she inherits money from her father, but only if she retained his name. She also inherits a trust fund that holds her mother's money from modeling, acting, song copyrights, et cetera . . . She gets access to it when she turns thirty-five. But she's not legally a Marchand, and there are some trusts and older wills going back a couple of generations that make it impossible for her to get some of the family heirlooms, so the endowment was to protect it all from Muriel and her husband."

"Wait. Everyone calls her Jocelyn Marchand here," I said.

"But on her driver's license and all legal documents she's still Jocelyn Warren, or that's what the lawyers told Duke."

"How much more does everyone inherit with Bobby and Ray Marchand dead?" Edward asked.

"Ray's sister and brother-in-law go from nothing to about two million."

"And Jocelyn?" I asked.

"If she sold all the real estate and liquidated the investments, it's at least two billion."

"Did you say billion?" I asked.

Newman nodded.

"And what did she get if Bobby lived?" Edward asked.

"Just what she could sell the real estate for."

"Wow," I said.

"How much money does she inherit from her own father?" Edward asked.

"Under three million," Newman said, "and that's tied up in investments mostly."

"Which means it's not real money," Edward said, "and if the investments tank, she could lose most or all of it."

"Her mother's estate-trust-fund thingie?" I asked.

"Two million."

"Real money?" I asked.

"Yes."

"Two million versus two billion," Edward said.

"That's a motive," I said.

"The two million that Ray's sister and her husband get sounds small in comparison, but it's still two million more than they'll get if Bobby lives," Newman said.

"So we have our motives."

"Muriel and Todd don't even have good alibis," Newman said.

"We need to know if the girl has a solid alibi or if she could have done it," Edward said.

"We need a murder weapon, besides Bobby's leopard," I said.

"We need to see the body and examine the wounds," Olaf said.

I knew instantly that I wasn't going to be the only other marshal in the room when Olaf looked at the body. I'd played that game with him before, and he always managed to make it creepy as fuck.

"You and Ted go to the morgue," I said. "Newman and I will go to the strip club and see if we can get a handle on the alibi."

"What if I prefer to go with you to the strip club?" Olaf asked.

I was glad I was still wearing my sunglasses so he couldn't see my eyes, because I could feel the twitch beside one eye that would have given me away. I could control the rest of my face just fine. "Your expertise on cutting up bodies may be our only hope to be able to figure out what was used to kill the victim." That was actually true.

"What if the dancer lies to protect the alibi?"

"If Newman and I don't think the dancer is telling us everything she knows, then you and Edward can have a crack at her."

"If there is a need to speak with the dancer later, I would prefer that you and I do it," Olaf said.

In my head I thought, *Hell no*, but Edward saved me from saying it.

"Come on, Otto. You know what weapons can do to a human body, but Anita knows strippers."

"I am engaged to two of them," I said. I might have protested the teasing, but Edward was giving me an out with the big guy, and I was going to take it.

Olaf nodded. "Then each of us to our expertise."

"Yeah, that," I said, and then I started walking toward Newman's Jeep like I had a purpose. We were trying to save a life after all. The fact that it also got me farther away from Olaf and all his strangeness was just a bonus.

60

NEWMAN OPENED THE door to the strip club like we were just customers. No one stopped us, or yelled, *Cheese it, the cops*, or really seemed
to notice us at all. The interior of the club was so dark that even
after we took off our sunglasses, it still took time for our eyes to
adjust. At least there was no entry platform like in some bars where
you were silhouetted against the light while you were blind to the
room. That moment in some bars seemed like an invitation to get
shot, but that was just my cop paranoia working overtime, sure. I'd
never actually been attacked while standing and waiting for my eyes
to adjust in a club, and today was no different. I still felt better when
we could see well enough to move farther into the dim interior.

There was a dancer on the stage wearing a shiny G-string and
those clear plastic heels that so many strippers seem fond of. Jean-
Claude had banned them from Guilty Pleasures. He thought they
looked cheap. I just thought they looked uncomfortable, but then so
did most of the heels that dancers wore. The dancer was barely moving to the music, as if just showing up onstage topless was enough to
get customers to throw money at her. It wouldn't have been enough
at Guilty Pleasures, but then, Jean-Claude helped his dancers put
together acts for their routines. Some of them even had special choreography. If you were going to just gyrate to the music, your moves
had to be athletic, well-done, and at least on time to the beat. The
woman holding on to the pole in the middle of the stage was manag-

ing none of the three. Guilty Pleasures had really spoiled me for strip clubs.

The dark, faded interior of the club also made me miss the brighter, more upbeat atmosphere of Guilty Pleasures. Maybe if more owner-managers had started out as dancers, they'd pay more attention to the details, too. The bar was to the right as you entered the club, and the man behind it was inches taller than Newman, so at least six feet five or six. He was also twice as broad as Newman, and most of that was shoulder spread. He smiled at us like he meant it and said, "Bar's open, and we have some daily specials. What'll it be?"

I saw scar tissue on his knuckles as he handed us the menus. He'd either started as a bouncer and worked his way over to bartender and waitstaff, or he was a man of many talents. Since his fist was the size of my face, I'd try to make sure his talents didn't get aimed in our direction.

Newman flashed his badge discreetly. "We just need to speak with one of your dancers briefly." He smiled as he said it.

I just stood there, doing my best to look harmless. I'm usually pretty good at that, though admittedly the guns, blades, and body armor made it harder. Most people wouldn't see all the gear on me, but the bartender flicked a gaze in my direction that let me know he'd noticed.

He kept smiling, but his eyes went cooler and considering. "You got a badge, too?" he asked.

I got mine out and showed it to him. He tried to touch it or maybe my hand, but I moved just out of reach.

"I'm just trying to get a better look at your badges, that's all."

I kept my badge out where he could stare at it.

He made a face like he'd tasted something bitter. "Preternatural marshals. You must be at the wrong place. We don't let monsters dance here." He said monsters like it was a dirty word.

I felt myself stiffen and knew that my face wasn't friendly anymore.

The bartender noticed, because he said, "We have a right to hire who we want."

"Of course you do," Newman said, his voice lilting and cheerful. He'd turned and seen the look on my face, so he was playing good cop to my grumpy cop.

I'd try not to go from grumpy to bad, but I couldn't promise. It would depend on how much the bartender pissed me off and how cooperative he was. I'd worn a badge long enough. I'd handle the prejudice in exchange for enough information.

"She doesn't think so. Do you, girlie?" the bartender said.

"First, don't call me girlie. Second, we just need to talk to one of your dancers, that's all."

"I could call you a ball-busting bitch if you'd prefer."

I looked at Newman. "I'm being nice here, right?"

"For you, very nice," he said, and smiled.

I frowned at him but turned to aim it at the bartender. "Let's try this again. First, I have not even begun to bust your balls yet. When I do, you'll know it. Second, we're just here to ask a few questions of one of your dancers about an ongoing hunt. You haven't even asked which dancer we want. Makes me think you already know. Are you just pretending to be prejudiced against the monsters because you're really on their side? Are you a closet groupie of the supernaturals there . . . What's your name again? I mean, I could call you racist douchebag, but that seems rude."

"Fuck you. I'm not coffin bait." It was a very rude term for people who dated vampires. I'd been called that and worse over the years.

"Oh, you're a fur banger. Do you have a preferred type of were-animal, or do you like them all?"

He flushed, big hands gripping the bar so tight that his skin mottled. I couldn't be sure over the music, but I thought the polished wood gave a little whine of protest as if he was going to break off a piece of it. God, he was strong for a human.

"You fucking bitch." The bartender's voice was low with the dump of testosterone from his anger.

It was almost too easy to piss him off. He was livid, and I could feel his anger around him like an aura. Maybe the rage filled his aura like it was a balloon, and all I had to do was prick it and let out all that anger, and then I could feed on it. The moment I thought that, I knew I needed real food. How long had it been since breakfast? Shit.

"Now she's busting your balls," Newman said.

"What?" The bartender looked at Newman as if he couldn't follow the conversation.

"Marshal Blake told you you'd know when she was really busting your balls. Well, she is. See the difference?"

"Get the fuck out of here, both of you."

"Or what, you'll call the cops?" I asked. I actually leaned in toward the bar, but I was too short to lean over it. He was out of my physical reach, which was good, because his anger felt warm and good.

"If you really hate supernaturals, help us hunt this one down," Newman said.

"Are you saying there's a monster on the loose in our town?" His anger started seeping away to be replaced with fear. He was such a big, tough guy, I hadn't expected him to scare so easily.

As the anger faded and the fear grew, I fought not to pout. I couldn't eat fear. Fuck, this was a potential witness, not prey. I looked at him, so big and tough and scared, and wondered if that was why he hated preternatural citizens, because they were all stronger than he could ever be. No amount of weight lifting or gym work would give him what lycanthropy or vampirism could.

"No, nothing like that," Newman said. "We just need some information to confirm a few things so we can go back and execute this one."

"Help us out, and there'll be one less monster in the world," I said.

"Promise?" the bartender almost whispered, and for a moment, I wondered if he had a real reason to hate the monsters. I'd liked it better when I could just hate the bartender. I didn't want to think about what bad thing had happened to put such fear into him. Disliking him for being a prejudiced asshole had been so much more fun.

"Promise," Newman said.

"Who you looking for?" the bartender asked, and there was no fight left in him.

"She dances under the name Giselle."

"She's one of our headliners. She doesn't work days."

"Give us her name and address, and we'll go to her," Newman said.

The bartender shook his head. "I can't give out the girls' real names and addresses. I'm the head of security. I'd fire anyone else that did it. I can't break my own rule."

"Not even for the police?" I asked.

We tried to persuade him, but he stood firm. He felt responsible for the safety of the dancers at his club. I couldn't help admiring his determination to protect them, but that didn't change the fact that he was incredibly bigoted and sexist. His very desire to protect the women who worked at the club could even have been an outgrowth of sexism: Women are physically weaker than men, so men must protect them. I couldn't argue the fact that most men could beat most women on upper-body strength. The problem was that some men drew the conclusion that lesser body strength meant lesser in all things. That was what pissed me off, and I'd met a lot of men who couldn't seem to want to protect women without feeling they were lesser beings. It was one of the reasons I didn't let most men step between me and a problem. I was not lesser, just smaller. I was not less just because you could outlift me in the weight room. We all had our strengths and weaknesses. Some people could do the math for astrophysics; other people could drive a stick shift—no one person could do it all.

We settled for Barry the bartender calling the dancer and persuading her to come down to the club to talk to us. "How do we know she'll show up?" I asked.

"I take good care of the girls. They trust me. She'll come. I can't promise she'll give you the answers you're looking for, but she'll show up. Find a table and order something to eat. She'll be here." He seemed so certain of himself that I let it go.

Newman and I took the menus and walked deeper into the dark interior of the club. The narrow entrance with the bar widened out until you could see the room was a lot bigger than it had looked from the doorway. We found a table far away from the stage. I had no inclination to watch the woman on the stage. I had my own breasts; I didn't need to look at hers. Yes, I dated a few women, but that did not mean I wanted to see them all naked. The same went for men: Just because you like the gender doesn't mean you want to see them all. It's not Pokémon.

I sat so that Newman could watch if he wanted to, but he didn't seem interested either. He concentrated on his menu like it was important. I wondered if he was uncomfortable. I wasn't exactly uncomfortable, but I wasn't comfortable either. It just felt awkward, like I wanted to go up onstage and tell the dancer to clap to the beat of the music until she found it. The few men drinking near the stage seemed not to notice her lack of rhythm, which bothered me, too.

"I know what I'm ordering. How about you?" I asked.

"I thought I'd get coffee. Seemed like the safest thing to get here."

"It's not that bad."

"It's a strip club. They aren't known for their cuisine."

If Edward or even Olaf had been there, I'd have explained that I'd thought about eating the bartender, so I really needed to eat food. Since I couldn't say that to Newman, I just said I was hungry, which was true. It was bar food, which ran high to fried food, but I didn't have to sweat my cholesterol, so that was fine. I liked fried food.

I got a burger, fries, and a Coke. Newman chose chicken fingers with fries, water, and a Coke. I added water to my order, and Newman took both the menus and our orders to tell Barry the bartender. Newman and I had both decided that I didn't need to interact with Barry any more than necessary.

A blond woman wearing a very short black dress started walking through the room. Her hair was long, waving artfully over one shoulder so that it looked casual. I'd have had to touch the hair to know if it just lay that way or if hair-care product held it in place. She touched a shoulder here, a cheek there at some of the other tables. She stayed away from the stage area, where the other dancer was still doing her awkward wiggle. It would have been considered rude if she tried to poach one of the customers near the stage while someone else was dancing, but the tables where people were eating or ignoring the stage were fair game.

As the blonde got closer, I could see that she was wearing black satin stilettos. The black dress was satin and shiny, moving around her body as she walked until I was sure that there was no bra under the dress, just small, tight breasts. That hint of breast underneath the satin was so much more attractive than the nearly naked woman onstage. Maybe it was the confidence that the blonde had as she moved through the room or the grace of her walk in the heels, but whatever it was, she blew the woman onstage out of the water—at least for me. I dated mostly men, but every once in a while a woman would hit my radar, and this one did.

I looked for Newman, but he was still hidden around the corner, giving our order to the bartender. How long could that take? The blonde was laughing with her head back as if whatever the three men at the table had said was the funniest thing. They probably hadn't been that amusing at all, and no one laughed like that for real. It was as if she practiced it in a mirror the way comedians practice facial expressions for their standup, but whatever the blonde had been practicing in the mirror was elegant, sexy, and— Where was Newman?

I pushed away from the table so I could get up to check on him, and the blonde was suddenly standing in front of me. I was staring at the black satin of her dress and had to look up to see her face. It made her seem tall, but I'd seen the heels; they added at least five inches of extra height, which made her only a little taller than me. She smiled down at me. Her gray eyes looked huge, with thick lashes framing them. She'd done her eyes up in black, gray, and silver. It looked almost Goth or emo or whatever they're calling it these days. It should have looked bad with the yellow of her hair, but it didn't. Neither did the silver lipstick, or maybe it was just shiny lip gloss with little sparkles in it. Whatever it was, it matched everything else she was wearing just fine.

I realized I'd been staring at her, so I stopped and looked at the floor and then almost desperately in the direction that Newman had gone. You'd have thought after all this time I'd be less awkward around strippers, but being attracted to women was still new to me, and it threw me back to the old days when I was awkward around men. It was like starting over with a new gender was starting over completely. Or maybe it was just not having any of the men in my life with me that made me unsure of myself. I hadn't had to meet new people on my own in a few years, and apparently on my own, I was just as awkward as I used to be. Great.

"Hi, beautiful," the blonde said in a voice as silky as her dress.

Something about the tone reminded me of Jean-Claude back at the beginning when I'd been more a mark than a romantic possibility. The voice and the word choice were as fake as a three-dollar bill. I might be awkward with women on my own, but I was not a mark. My head came up, and whatever she saw in my eyes wilted the smile on her face.

"I didn't mean to make you angry," she said in a voice that was almost normal. She leaned her ass against the table, which made the bottom of the dress rise until it became doubtful if there was anything under it except for her. "Most women like to be told they're beautiful. I know I do."

"You're beautiful, sexy, and more attractive dressed than the dancer onstage is nude. Now go find someone else to flirt with."

"Why should I flirt with someone else when you say the nicest things?" The blonde was almost purring as she leaned her upper body toward me. She was giving me a chance to look down the front of the dress. I kept looking at her face.

I brought my badge up until it was in front of her big gray eyes. They widened a little bit, but then the smile was back to the sexy practiced one. "We get a lot of cops in here, but you're my first female detective."

"I'm not a detective," I said, pushing my chair farther back so I could stand up. I was going to hunt Newman down.

The blonde sat down on my lap, taking the chair push as invitation. Rookie mistake on my part. I knew better. She wrapped her arms around my neck and gave a little wiggle in my lap, which made the dress slide up again.

"You'd better be wearing at least a thong under that dress, because I do not know you well enough to have your body fluids smeared all over my pants." My eyes were back to looking angry, and I didn't apologize for it.

"You haven't got me that wet . . . yet," the blonde said, giving me the full sexy look out of her big eyes. It might have worked, except I wasn't kidding about not wanting her body fluids on me. The thought just creeped me, no matter how attractive she might be.

I saw Newman coming back with our drinks. "Get off my lap now."

"I saw how you looked at me across the room."

"What do you want?"

"You, darling," she said, leaning in to try to kiss the side of my neck.

I put my hands on her upper arms to hold her back. "Liar. I'm working, and you're working, so you need to find another mark."

"Just because we're on the job doesn't mean we can't have fun."

It was the phrasing that got me, *on the job*. It was a cop phrase. Made me wonder how many of the local police frequented the club. "Some of the local cops regulars for you?"

"If you want information, you've got to play nicer than this with me."

"This is me playing nice."

"Are you a tough girl?" she asked.

That made me smile. "You have no idea."

Something uncertain flickered through the blonde's eyes, and then she was back to being sexy and flirtatious. If she was as good at her job as I thought she was, she'd be able to flirt even if she was bored out of her mind. People think that the strippers' job is to dance onstage and take off their clothes, but that's not really it. Their job is to get money from customers whether they're onstage or off-. Some dancers enjoy the performance or are true exhibitionists, but not as many as you'd think. They dance for a lot of reasons, but the main one is to earn money to put themselves through college, to support their families, to support themselves. It's a job, and if a dancer is sitting in your lap, she wants something, usually money but not always.

Newman hesitated with the drinks as if he wasn't sure I wanted him at the table. I let go of the blonde's arms and waved him over. I did not want to be alone with her any more than I had to be. If I was going to be awkward with someone this smooth, I needed backup.

The blonde had taken her chance to sit more firmly in my lap and put her arms around my neck. She gave a little wiggle. "If you were a man, I'd ask if that was a knife in your pants or you were happy to see me."

"I'm not happy to see you," I said, smiling.

Again, her eyes were uncertain, but she snuggled closer to me, working around all the weapons just fine. I was so not her first police officer, but then, she'd admitted that already.

Newman set the drinks on the table and smiled as the two of us looked up at him. "Marshal Blake, introduce me to your lovely companion."

"I would if I knew her name," I said.

"Phoenix," she said.

"After the town or the legendary bird?" I asked.

"Both." She smiled at me like I'd said a smart thing. I wondered how many of the customers didn't know the origins of her stage name.

"Would you like a drink, Phoenix?" Newman asked.

"That would be lovely."

He asked what she wanted. She ordered something with ice in it. I wondered if she'd drink it for real or sip it and let the ice melt. Nursing her drink so she'd stay in control would win her points with me, not that she cared what I thought of her, not for real. As she wiggled her short skirt across my lap again, I really hoped we learned something worth this level of up close and personal with a strange woman.

Newman went to put her drink order in, and she snuggled her face against the side of my neck. Her breath was very warm against my skin. She smelled of good perfume. Her hair was clean, thick, and smelled of shampoo. If there were hair-care products in her hair that were keeping it to one side, they had left her hair soft to the touch.

Movement caught my eye at the table nearest us. It was four men who looked like they'd run in from work for a late lunch, or an early dinner. They were in ties and suits with the food in front of them, but they weren't looking at their food. They were staring at us. Shit, I was dressed for hunting bad guys, with more weapons than most people owned, so I hadn't felt like a woman in that strip club anyway, but the woman in my lap was dressed feminine enough to make up for me—or maybe the fact that I was dressed more like a man fed some lesbian fantasy? I tried not to think too hard about it.

I glanced farther out into the club. Some of the other customers were looking at us, too. The ones around the stage were still watching the girl onstage, which was good, because it was considered bad form to distract from the stage act. The woman on the stage was moving even less than before, and she still seemed to have no idea there was a beat to the song.

The blonde brushed her lips against the skin of my neck, not a kiss but still more reality than usual this early in the game. Maybe she was just flirting to try to get the customers more interested in her for the stage show later, or maybe she just liked girls better than boys.

I laid my cheek against her hair, her face still buried against my neck. "What are you doing here this early, Phoenix? You're too good for the early crowd."

That made her raise her face enough to look into my face. "Oh, Beautiful, you say the sweetest things, and you're right. Another dancer couldn't come in at the very last moment, naughty girl."

Her face was so close to mine. Her lips were parted just so, and her eyes held large like an anime character. It was so artificial, so practiced, that it didn't move me nearly as much as the brush of her lips had. That had felt real, as if she'd forgotten the act for a second. Or maybe that was part of the act, too. With strippers, you never knew. One of the reasons I'd been able to resist Nathaniel and Jean-Claude for so long was that they both flirted professionally, so I

470   LAURELL K. HAMILTON

hadn't been able to tell that they were serious with me. Only years
of living with them had finally helped me figure out the difference.
The girl in my arms was a mystery still.

"Were you working two nights ago?"

Phoenix nodded, managing to get more hair-bobbing action into
it than necessary. She had good hair, and she knew it, but then she
knew exactly what her assets were and how to use them for work. I'd
never have been that smooth, but that was okay. I had other skills.

I was debating if I could get to my phone without kicking her off
my lap when Newman came back with Phoenix's drink. He set it
down next to my water, which reminded me that I hadn't drunk
anything yet. I was just letting my ice melt, which was okay for the
water but not for the Coke.

Phoenix turned to flash Newman a very nice smile despite the less
than happy look on his face. Her reaching for her drink let me do the
same for mine. The Coke was already too watered down, so I reached
for the water. It tasted cold and far better than it should have. It was
another sign that I hadn't been meeting my physical needs, which
made all the metaphysical ones harder to control. Which explained
why I'd leaned against Olaf in the interrogation room, which was the
lycanthrope energy, and probably why I had a strange woman in my
lap, which was closer to the issues/abilities I'd inherited from Jean-
Claude. I'd gone from uncomfortable and almost angry about Phoenix in my lap to, if not enjoying it, at least not disliking it. It so wasn't
me, but to get information from her, maybe a little less me and a
little more Jean-Claude wasn't a bad thing?

I sipped my water and realized that my other hand was curled a
little possessively around the woman's hip. It did keep her steady on
my thighs, but I hadn't realized I'd done it. I needed to eat really
soon. I asked Newman to show Phoenix the picture of our person of
interest. It's considered prejudicial to call someone a suspect in front
of a possible witness, so everyone is a person of interest or someone
we're hoping can help us with our inquiries or some such politically
correct phrasing.

Phoenix's face clouded over. For a minute she forgot about being the sexy flirt and let us see the steel underneath the silk. "Oh, yes, she was here that night. She and her friends hung out with Giselle all night."

"Are you sure the woman in the picture was here all night?" Newman asked.

"I'm sure." Her eyes had darkened to the color of storm clouds. The anger rolled off of her, and suddenly she smelled even more like food.

I caressed my hand down Phoenix's hip, and she was so angry that she didn't react. For her job she should have either flirted back or told me I wasn't allowed to touch her. Instead she sat up straight on my lap as if I was a hard chair instead of a person. Her skin felt hot under my hand, as if she were cooking in her anger. I could feed on that heat, skin to skin.

"How are you so certain?" Newman asked.

"Because that bitch Giselle did a lap dance with her while I was onstage."

I rubbed my cheek against her bare arm, rolling my face through the warmth of her anger. "That's not allowed," I said.

"What do you mean, it's not allowed?" Newman asked.

I forced myself to raise my face away from her skin and concentrate on Newman as I answered. God, I needed our food to come soon. "Doing a girl-on-girl lap dance would distract the customers from the stage show. It's like stealing money out of the other dancer's pocket."

Phoenix looked at me then, really looked at me, not just as a mark, or as a way to make money, but like I'd said something interesting. "Exactly."

She managed to roll her hip as if asking for me to pet her hip rather than just rest my hand on it. I rose to the invitation, because I wanted her to keep talking. We might not need much from Giselle by the time she arrived, or we might even learn enough that we could catch her in a lie. We needed to know if Jocelyn's alibi was good or bust, and we needed to know it now, because Bobby was running out of later.

"Did Giselle give all three of them lap dances while other dancers were onstage?" I asked.

"No, because I complained to management."

"Barry must like you," I said.

Phoenix gave me a grin that was part sex and part fun. "Everybody likes me, Beautiful."

"I'll bet they do," I said, and stopped petting her hip, because if I wasn't going to move my hand and do more, it was just a little too much repetition for me.

I wrapped my arms around her as if I was making sure she didn't fall off my lap, just to have something to do with my hands. Again, Phoenix could have told me to keep my hands to myself, but she didn't. She was using me to get the other customers warmed up, which meant she'd let me take liberties that she probably wouldn't have a male customer or even a female customer whom she wasn't using to build the illusion of girl-on-girl sex. It's a fine line to walk, promising sex without giving it. I could never have done it, but Phoenix understood the game, and thanks to the men in my life, I could play for a while.

"So the other lap dances got spaced out through the night?" I said.

Phoenix nodded, settling herself more comfortably in my lap. "Your girl in the photo did her last lap dance onstage with Giselle."

"What time was that?" Newman asked, sipping his coffee.

"Between two and three a.m." She turned in my lap so she could take a sip of the drink Newman had bought her. She was going to nurse it and let the ice melt to weaken the alcohol, which didn't mean she didn't have a vice—just that alcohol wasn't it.

"Are you sure?" I asked, because if she was sure of the time, then Jocelyn's alibi was solid.

Phoenix put her drink down and turned to me. The look on her face was real again, not sexy but an unhappy frown that showed small lines on her face that the smiles didn't. "I'm sure. Until your girl and her friends left, I wasn't making nearly what I normally do. Even when Giselle wasn't with them, the three of them were making out. They were just giving the show away for free, so no one wanted to pay to just watch."

"All three of them were making out together?" Newman asked.

"Early it was just your girl and the tall, dark-haired one, but later the third girl got drunk enough that she joined in, too." Phoenix made a derisive snort that wasn't sexy but was very real. "If you have to get that drunk to do it, you're going to regret it later."

"Totally agree," I said, and I did, which was a little weird.

Phoenix was far more practical than I'd expected. It made me like her better as a person, but be less attracted to her. I debated asking her to change from my lap to a chair, but she'd have taken the request as an insult, so I didn't bother. But the longer she sat in my lap just talking, the less seductive she became. It was like we could talk about any ordinary thing, but instead of sitting in a chair, she was in my lap. The illusion of the sexy siren was vanishing under her real emotions. Her being real helped both the investigation and my ability to control my metaphysics.

Phoenix seemed to remember where she was and what she was supposed to be doing, because she touched the side of my face and looked deep into my eyes as she said, "I bet you don't need to drink to have fun."

"No, I don't need to drink," I said, smiling because she had gone instantly back into sexy siren mode like she had slipped a mask back into place. Edward and "Ted" would have been proud.

Phoenix leaned her forehead against mine, her thick hair falling forward on one side so that to most of the club it might look like she was kissing me. Stripping is all about the illusion. It's a bait and switch of the highest order, all sweet promises and no follow-through. It's like dating used to be before the terms *hook up* and *friends with benefits* were needed. Dating was supposed to be about testing the waters for a lifetime together, not just for fucking—ah, the good ol' days, or maybe just the old days.

"I'll go check on our food," Newman said.

"Yes, please," I said. I couldn't see him through the fall of Phoenix's yellow hair, but I heard his chair scrape and felt the air movement as he walked away.

Phoenix and I sat there alone with her face pressed to mine. We were still in full view of everyone else in the club. Nothing had changed, but suddenly the sound of the music, the noise and movement of the rest of the club, fell away. The two of us sat in a space of intimacy, as if it were just us. If I'd pulled back enough to see, there would have been no one else in the club but us. I knew it wasn't true, but the woman in my arms wasn't the only one who could create illusions. The only difference was she did hers on purpose, and I didn't have full control of mine.

My hands slid along the sides of Phoenix's hips, my fingertips tracing farther back to the soft curve of her ass. She put her hands on mine to stop me, rising enough to see my face. Her face was unhappy now, her mouth forming *no*, but she never said the word out loud, because she looked me in the eyes. Her face went slack for a moment, her gaze unfocused, and then an intensity that hadn't been there before filled her eyes. She wrapped her hands over mine and helped me cup her ass in my hands. Her breath came out in a low, eager rush. Her body seemed to soften; the careful control of distance she'd maintained with me melted away. Her in my lap had only looked intimate before; now it was real. It was like she let go of some invisible tension that had been holding her away from me, like the tension on a pond that an insect skates across. She'd decided not to skate above the water anymore. She wanted to drown.

Phoenix kissed me like she meant to climb inside me through my mouth. I had a moment of kissing her back. We were all hands and arms, and finally her body was on the table with me above her. My feet were still on the ground, but her legs were around my waist. If I'd been a man, we might have passed the point of no return, but two women make fast sex harder. Girl-on-girl sex is about foreplay, not fucking. Just the confusion of how to give her the pleasure she wanted helped me climb back into control of myself, at least enough to stand up straight and stop dry-humping her against the table.

That let me see Newman with our tray of food. He was staring at me like I'd grown a second, ugly head or maybe sprouted some other monstrous body part.

He said, "Your eyes, Blake. What's wrong with your eyes?"

I looked down at the woman lying across the table with her legs still wrapped around me. Her lipstick was smeared like Goth clown makeup across her face, and her eyes seemed to shine. But it wasn't her eyes that were shining; it was mine. I could see the glow of my eyes in hers like cognac diamonds reflecting sunlight into this room that never saw the light of day.

61

I STRUGGLED FREE of Phoenix's hands so I could slide my sunglasses over my eyes. I told Newman, "Help me get her off of me."

He laid the tray of food on a nearby table and came to help. I gave him points for that. I knew some fully human marshals who would have refused to touch her or me after they saw my eyes glow. He helped me peel her off without hurting her, which is a lot harder than it sounds.

She was saying, "No, no, please, please, don't stop. Please!" She struggled in Newman's arms, not trying to fight him, just trying to reach me. I wasn't exactly sure what I'd done to her, so I didn't know how to undo it. It was like the *ardeur*, which was feeding off of lust or love, but it should have stopped when she wasn't touching me or looking into my eyes. Why wasn't it stopping?

My stomach cramped so hard from hunger that it nearly doubled me over. Oh, that was why. I went to the table where Newman had set the food down and picked up my hamburger. It wasn't a great burger, but it was protein and the first food I'd had since breakfast, which was about seven hours ago.

"Blake, behind you!" Newman called.

I turned with the burger still in my hand. Barry the bartender was behind me with a baseball bat, as if being over a foot taller and a hundred pounds heavier than me wasn't enough of an edge. "Get out of my club! Badge or no badge, we don't serve monsters in here!"

Had he seen my eyes? No, if he'd seen my eyes glow from across the club, there'd be more people panicking, and everyone I could see was still watching the show. I mean, a girl-on-girl make-out session and now a fight—it was like a double feature. So why was Barry saying monster?

Phoenix called out behind me, "Let me go! Let me go to her! Please, please!"

"Let's all calm down," Newman said from behind me, projecting his voice above her pleading.

I looked at Barry through my sunglasses, and he avoided direct eye contact even through the darkness of the lenses. He recognized the symptoms of someone who had been mind-fucked by a vampire. Technically I wasn't one, but I was getting to the point of if it walks like a duck, quacks like a duck . . . well, you know the rest. I swallowed my bite of burger and tried to think of what to say to de-escalate things. If he swung on us with a baseball bat, then we could shoot him, because one good hit to the side of the head with a baseball bat can kill you just as dead as a bullet. I didn't want Barry to die today because I'd lost control of my metaphysical extras.

"Put the bat down, Barry," Newman said. If he hadn't had to hold the struggling woman, he'd have probably had his gun out by now, but he literally had his hands full.

"You swallowed that," Barry said, "but you can't eat solid food."

Barry had been around vampires enough to know that some of them pretended to eat. They were like people with anorexia who could cut their food up and move it around their plates so that it looked like they'd eaten, but it was another illusion.

I swallowed again and then opened my mouth wide enough for him to see there were no fangs. I even used a finger to draw my lips down so he could see better. "See, no fangs," I said.

"What are you?"

"Would you believe I'm not sure anymore?"

"What the fuck are you talking about?" Barry sounded angry now instead of just scared, but he was starting to point the baseball bat toward the floor rather than hold it in a batter-up position.

"Put the bat on the ground, Barry. No one needs to get hurt," Newman called out behind me. He still had to project over Phoenix's voice.

Whatever I'd done to her was still done, because she wanted him to let her go so she could go to me, so I could finish. I'd had my moments of being mind-fucked over the years. I had let a vampire nearly drain me to death once, and I'd enjoyed it. I'd probably have enjoyed it right up to the time I died.

"You don't call that hurt?" Barry asked, pointing with one finger past me at Phoenix. The bat came back up in a one-arm-swing position. Not an improvement.

I took another bite of burger, because until I had enough food in me, I was dangerous to others. I didn't mind hurting people on purpose. I didn't even mind using metaphysical abilities on them if it was the best tool I had, but doing it by accident, that wasn't okay. I wasn't even sure how to undo what I'd done to Phoenix. I'd had enough control to stop the *ardeur* from feeding on her, but I wasn't sure I'd ever bespelled someone this completely without feeding. Luckily for me, I could eat my burger instead of her. If I'd been a real vampire, I wouldn't have had that option. The real problem was I didn't know how to fix her. I ate the last bite of burger, hoping that if my physical stomach was full, maybe that would help undo what I'd accidentally done to the woman.

"Barry, please believe me," I said. "I didn't mean to hurt Phoenix."

"I'll believe you when she isn't crying for you to feed on her blood."

He almost snarled that last part, wrapping two hands around the bat. It was in a position to take my head off if I didn't duck. He was too close for me to even try for a gun. I'd never have gotten it out in time. When you're this close, a baseball bat beats a gun. I had knives on me, and I had enough training that my knife would beat a bat, but I didn't want to have to kill someone because of my mistake.

I felt movement behind me in time to move slightly to the side, so I saw Phoenix a second before I might have tried to deck her. She wrapped herself around me so tight that I had to struggle to keep one arm free to defend with and wrap the other one around her waist just so I could maybe keep her out of the fight if it started.

Newman had his gun out and pointed at Barry and his bat. Phoenix tried to kiss me again, but I turned my face so she had to kiss my neck instead. She didn't see the gun or the bat or the danger. She saw only me. No, not even me. She was chasing the power, the *ardeur*.

If Jean-Claude had been here, he'd have known exactly what to do, because the power was originally his—the rarest power that could appear in the bloodline he was descended from. Of course, he would never have lost control of it like I had done. I could have dropped my metaphysical shields and contacted him mind to mind, but would that have made things worse or better? Since I wasn't sure what was happening, I didn't know. Shit.

"Put the bat down now," Newman said. His voice was getting calmer.

I knew what that would have meant for me: I'd be getting ready to shoot. You have to control your breathing to aim well. It's as hard as fuck to shoot well while you're shouting. You have to control your breath, your heart rate, your pulse. Good aim comes from a place of deep silence. For me it was a place that had been filled with white static once. Now it was just quiet.

A second security guy came up, carrying a cross in his hand and holding it toward me. If I'd been a vampire with glowing eyes, it would have glowed like a star in his hand, but it was just so much metal now.

"Thought you were a true believer, Sam," Barry said, which meant he knew that holy objects work only if you believe in them, really believe, or if they've been blessed by someone holy.

"It should be glowing," Sam said.

"I'm not a vampire. God as my witness, I'm not a vampire," I said. I had to turn my face more toward Barry and Sam to keep Phoenix away from my mouth.

"Then let Phoenix go!" Barry said.

I moved my arm from around her waist, putting both arms out to my side. I managed to say, "I'm trying," before she kissed me so hard and so thoroughly that I couldn't breathe, let alone talk.

"Put the bat down. I won't tell you again," Newman said.

I prayed, *Please, God, don't let Barry die because I screwed up*, and suddenly I had an idea. I broke the kiss and said, "Phoenix, take the bat away from Barry."

She stopped trying to kiss me and launched herself at Barry. She went for the bat as completely and wildly as she'd tried to kiss me. Barry tried to fight her off without hurting her or letting her take the bat from him. He had his hands full, and now Newman wouldn't shoot him because Phoenix was in the way.

Sam, the other guy, was shaking his cross in his hands as if he thought the battery wasn't working.

"Your faith is fine," I said. "It just doesn't work on me."

"Phoenix, stop. Stop! I don't want to hurt you," Barry was saying.

Newman came up beside me with his gun pointed at the floor. "What did you do to her?"

"I'm not sure," I whispered because it was true.

"Can you undo it?"

"I don't know."

"We have to do something, Blake."

Newman was right. I drew my own cross out from under my T-shirt, and I prayed again. "God, please help me free her from whatever I've done to her." My cross started to glow—not the hot white glow that happened when a vampire was trying to eat my face, but a soft blue-white glow. Sam's cross started to glow with mine. We were both true believers.

I prayed out loud. "Please, God, help me undo whatever I did to her."

Phoenix stopped trying to drag the bat out of Barry's hands. She went very still, arms going to her sides. I knew without seeing her face that her eyes would be empty, face slack. I'd seen it on other vampire victims. God, I hated that I had done that to her.

The crosses started to glow brighter, but it was blue light, and it didn't hurt to look at it the way white heat could. I'd been in fights with vampires where my own cross had blinded them and me with its light. This was different, gentler. It felt peaceful, the way praying can when you get that soft touch, as if you can feel God listening.

Phoenix started to fall. Barry dropped the bat, and it clattered on the floor as he caught her. She blinked in his arms, looking around the room as if she'd just woken up. Her dark makeup was smeared over her face almost like bruises, but she wouldn't remember how that had happened. I wondered what the last thing she did remember was.

The glow of the two crosses started to fade, and I got that sense of peace that I sometimes get when a prayer gets answered. Sam had tears on his face trailing past an almost beatific smile. I knew then that he felt it, too.

"What's happening?" Phoenix asked. "Did they spike my drink?" So she remembered we'd bought her a drink. Good. She hadn't lost too much time.

"No, Phoenix," Barry said, "they didn't spike your drink." He was staring at me as if he didn't know what to make of me. That made two of us.

"Come on, Blake, let's get out of here," Newman said. He had holstered his gun.

I grabbed my fries off the table as I went toward the door. I wanted to make sure that I had enough food in me until I went home and had real vampires around me to help me control this shit, or at least had Nicky with me or someone who was already on my approved menu for metaphysical munchies.

62

MY PHONE RANG just as Newman hustled us through the door and out into the sunlight. Somehow, I knew it was Nicky before I answered it. I don't think it was metaphysics or at least not the vampire kind—more the couple kind.

"Anita, what just happened?"

"I'm okay."

"If by okay you mean whatever was happening stopped, then yeah, but what caused the *ardeur* to rise like that?"

"I don't know." I ate another French fry while I waited for him to respond.

Newman said, "Who is it?"

"It's Nicky," I said.

"Is Newman with you?" Nicky asked.

"Yes."

"I can feel that you're still hungry, Anita."

I swallowed and said, "I'm eating solid food as we speak."

"Did you almost feed on Newman? Is that why you were able to stop?"

I looked at Newman and almost choked on the French fry. "No, that's not what happened."

Newman leaned down and whispered, as if there was anyone in the nearly empty parking lot to hear us, "Can Nicky help you with whatever just happened in the club?"

"If you tell me exactly what happened, maybe," Nicky said over the phone, because of course he'd heard.

"Maybe," I said.

"Then talk to him while we wait for Giselle to get here," Newman said. "We still have to question her."

I nodded at Newman and walked across the parking lot to get a little privacy for the talk. Newman didn't need to know any more of my metaphysical secrets than he'd just learned inside the club. Of course, since I wasn't sure exactly what had just happened, *secrets* might not have been the right word. I told Nicky everything as I walked. I was hoping for some insight before we had to question the next witness.

"I'm putting you on speaker so Ethan can hear," Nicky said, and then I heard the change in the sound on his end. I could also hear other things a lot more clearly.

"Are you in a car?" I asked.

"We're headed your way."

"You heard the sheriff, Nicky. None of you can be involved in the investigation."

"I know. We're just supposed to help keep Bobby from shifting. Angel is babysitting him."

"Who's with her?"

My gut tightened at the thought of her being there without Nicky when Olaf came back. I didn't actually believe he'd kidnap her for nefarious purposes in front of the local cops, but there was part of me that was scared for the other women. Part of it was knowing Olaf, and part of it was that Angel and Pierette were making themselves bait to take the heat off me. I didn't want them to get hurt protecting me.

"Everyone but Ethan and me. She's covered, and so is Pierette."

I let out a breath I hadn't realized I was holding.

Ethan's voice: "You really are that frightened for both of them?"

"I guess I am."

"They're covered," Nicky said.

"We need to worry about you right now," Ethan said.

"I'm okay now," I said.

"We'll meet you at the strip club," Nicky said.

"How do you know which one we're at?"

"You know we have an app that connects our phones' GPS, right?" he said.

"Oh, yeah, I keep forgetting that."

"And Bobby knew what club Jocelyn liked to go to," Ethan said.

"She'd come back and tell him about all the hot girl-on-girl action she got, and then when they were both turned on, they'd fuck," Nicky said.

"That isn't how Bobby told the story," Ethan said.

"It's what he meant," Nicky said.

"Guys, why are you headed my way?" I asked.

"We've got some protein bars and sports drinks for you to keep with you so you won't miss any more meals," Ethan said.

"I just ate lunch."

"That would have been dinner, Anita," Nicky said.

"Did you guys have lunch?" I asked.

"Yes," he said.

"Look, I'm sorry I was too busy crime busting to eat."

"Anita, it's not just the *ardeur* rising early. You risk the lives of everyone that is tied to you metaphysically. You start by draining Nathaniel and Damian. I'm not close enough to Damian to really care, but Nathaniel is like my brother. I know how much you love him, because I can feel it. I didn't know anyone could love as much as you love him, so how can you keep risking his life like this?"

I couldn't even argue with Nicky, and God, I wanted to, but . . . "Jean-Claude and Micah both promised to contact me if I started to drain anybody. Besides, Nathaniel is getting better at managing the energy among the three of us."

"You're just making excuses, Anita." Nicky sounded genuinely angry. He never got mad at me.

"You're my Bride, Nicky. I thought it caused you pain if I was unhappy."

"Sometimes it does, but if Nathaniel dies because you were careless, you'd never forgive yourself, and neither would I. Neither would Micah or Sin or Dev or—"

"I get it, Nicky."

"Do you?"

"Yeah, I do." I was angry now, which was better than feeling guilty.

"Good. Then you'll let us shadow you while you keep crime busting."

"No, you heard Leduc. None of you can be part of the investigation."

"We'll stay out of the way, but you need us with you, Anita."

"What do you mean, shadowing me?"

"We'll follow you in our car. We'll be nearby in case you lose control again."

"Leduc can't see you following us. He'll lose his shit, and he has enough clout around here to kick the Coalition out of the area. Hell, he's got so many friends in the good-ol'-boy network, he might be able to keep the Coalition out of most of Michigan."

"Anita, you almost fed the *ardeur* on a woman you'd just met. What if you'd lost control in the strip club?" Ethan said.

I paced around the empty parking spaces at the edge of the lot. My pulse was too fast; the anger had gone onto the edge of fear. "I handled it," I said finally.

"Anita, do you really want to risk the *ardeur* rising when you're surrounded by cops without any of us nearby?" Nicky asked.

"No, of course I don't. That would be a nightmare, and you know it."

"So we'll shadow you, just in case."

A compact car turned into the parking lot; there was a dark-haired woman driving it.

"I think the dancer we need to talk to just drove up."

"We'll park and wait for you to let us know you're done talking police business," Nicky said.

"You'd be even less happy if you lost control of the *ardeur* and fed on Newman or Deputy Rico or one of the state cops," Ethan said.

"You've made your point," I said.

"Will you let us follow you?" Ethan asked.

"I'll take the snacks for later," I said.

"If you won't let us shadow you, then feed the *ardeur* off of one of us before you meet back up with Leduc," Nicky said.

"Absolutely not," I said.

"It would make the *ardeur* safe for at least four hours guaranteed."

"I cannot do quickies in the parking lot while I'm out with other cops."

"Newman is the only one with you, right?" Nicky asked.

"Yes, but—"

"He saw what happened in the strip club, Anita. I think he'll be okay with it."

"He won't be okay with me grabbing a quickie in the parking lot while we're fighting the clock for Bobby Marchand's life."

"Then we follow you," Nicky said as if the matter was settled.

"I haven't agreed to that, but the dancer that was with Jocelyn is here. Got to go question her."

"Try not to touch this one as much," Ethan said.

"You're afraid I'll lose control again?" I said.

"Aren't you?"

I didn't know what to say because I was worried. I didn't understand why the *ardeur* had risen in the club. I didn't know how I'd captured the dancer with my gaze like I was a real vampire and not one who fed off of energy, sexual or otherwise.

"Yeah, I'm worried, but I still have to go question the dancer. She's wearing street clothes and no makeup. She won't be sitting in my lap like the last one."

"You let a strange stripper sit in your lap? Wow, you are off your game," Ethan said with an incredulous tone in his voice.

Nicky would have sounded angrier, and he would have pissed me off. Ethan's amazement scared me a little.

I waved to get Newman's attention and pointed at the woman, who was still sitting in her car. He nodded and started walking toward the car.

"I won't let this one sit on my lap. Promise. But I've got to go help

Newman question her." I started walking toward the car so I'd meet him partway.

"Feed on one of us when we get there," Nicky said.

"I have to question a witness, not take a booty call."

"Feed on one of us when you're done questioning the witness."

"I am not going to make Newman twiddle his thumbs while I have sex in the parking lot."

"I'll ask Newman if he's okay with it."

"Nicky, no, and if I tell you not to do it, you won't be able to."

"That's true."

"I'll ask Newman," Ethan said.

"Ethan!"

"I'll be embarrassed to ask him, but if you forbid Nicky to do it, then I'll do it."

"I can't—"

"If Newman is weirded out, we'll try to shadow you," Nicky said.

"You'll really ask Newman if he's okay with me screwing one of you in the parking lot?"

"If there's a motel nearby, would that make it better?" Nicky asked.

"Yes, I guess, but that takes more time, and Bobby is running out of that."

"Then we're back to a quickie," Nicky said.

"No."

"Then eat more regularly in the next four hours, and we'll follow you," he said.

"I said I'd take the snacks."

"Quickie or we play escort for the rest of this trip, Anita."

"I have to go do my job now." I was angry and let it show in my voice.

"We'll be there as soon as we can," Ethan said.

"I haven't agreed to any of this."

"We know," Nicky said.

I hung up on him. No *I love you*, nothing, because I was pissed. I was angry at Nicky for forcing me to think so far outside my comfort zone. I was angry with Ethan for helping him. I was pissed that my metaphysics had gotten out of control, especially in the middle of a police investigation. I hated all my choices, but the thought I hated most was losing control of the *ardeur*, because feeding on Newman, or one of the other cops, was the worst choice of all.

63

THE WOMAN GOT out of the car, and I asked, "Giselle, right?"

The woman nodded. Newman stared at her, frowned, then looked at me. I knew the expression by now. It meant he believed me, but only because I said so. Strippers in street clothes with no makeup on don't look much like their stage personas. You have to pay attention to the bone structure. That's about the only thing that doesn't change and can't be faked by normal makeup.

I suggested we talk out in the parking lot in the sunshine, and Newman played along to open her car door and get her outside. I was pretty sure that if Barry saw us with her, he'd raise the alarm or even call the cops. After what had just happened, I couldn't really blame him, but we still had a murder to solve and another murder to prevent. It's all about priorities even if you've just had a major metaphysical oops.

Newman helped me walk her toward the Jeep. I started eating the now cold French fries not because they were good, but because they were food, and I didn't want Giselle or any other strangers to be on the menu. We asked her to get inside the Jeep to talk.

"I'm not under arrest, am I?" she said.

When we said no, she wouldn't get in with us. Her choice. So we leaned against Newman's vehicle.

Giselle's face was pale in sunlight. She blinked wide brown eyes almost owlishly. Her eyebrows arched dark and perfect, which made the rest of her naked face look even paler and more unfinished without some extra color. She put her hand above her eyes to shield them from the light. "Couldn't find my sunglasses this morning," she explained as if we'd asked.

I thought about offering mine, but I didn't know if my eyes had stopped glowing. We didn't want to spook her. Newman wasn't wearing his, but he didn't offer them to her. Maybe it was that awkward moment of asking for them back that he wanted to avoid.

Giselle, in her jeans, Nikes made for fashion not exercise, and a T-shirt tied in a side knot at her waist, squinted up at Newman. She also wore a checked flannel shirt that looked big enough to belong to one of the men in her life. It could have been a boyfriend or even her father. Not all strippers live wild lives offstage. She looked like a college student named Becky or Jennifer who had rolled out of bed and thrown clothes on to make an early-morning class. There was almost no trace of the exotic Giselle from the promotional photos on the strip club's website, but then, how many performers actually look like their head shots?

Even after we'd both introduced ourselves as marshals, Giselle still kept her attention on Newman, as if I didn't count as much. She wasn't the first person to discount the woman in the group of badges, but it answered one question for me: She preferred men to women offstage. If she'd been more bisexual except as part of her act, she would have looked at me more. She played it like the college-age woman she appeared to be: Newman was the cute guy, and I was something to be ignored like an obstacle to his attention or maybe less. Welcome to girl world, where there are no friends and all that matters are who's more attractive and who gets the man. I was glad for the umpteen-millionth time that I hadn't been indoctrinated into typical girl culture.

"I felt so bad for Jocelyn when I realized she was here, maybe even onstage with me, when her father was killed." Giselle gave a little shiver and hugged herself through the flannel. I debated whether her reaction was real or acting, and decided it was real. I didn't think she had the acting chops to fake her skin going even paler in the light.

"It's a terrible thing," Newman agreed.

Giselle shivered again. "It was such a good night, and then to go home to . . ." She looked up at Newman. "Is it true that she found the body?" Her voice lowered on the last part as if she was afraid to say the words too loudly.

"It was a shock for her, as you can imagine," Newman said.

Giselle nodded and hugged herself again.

"Did you have to clear it with Barry that you were going to take a customer or customers up onstage with you?" I asked.

She rolled her eyes, her pretty face looking sour and unhappy. "I cleared it with him."

"Why did you have to clear it with Barry?" Newman asked.

I answered, "Customers can get more unruly when you drag other women onstage."

Giselle looked at me as if I'd said something interesting and nodded. "How do you know that?"

"I'm engaged to a dancer." I said it just like that, no explanation that it was male, or more than one.

She gave me her first real smile. "You must have spent a lot of time in the club back home."

"Enough," I said, and smiled, letting her make of it what she would.

She was friendlier after that, more relaxed. We learned that the night had been planned a couple of months out, because of Jocelyn having to coordinate with her two married friends. Lap dances were planned for all, but only Jocelyn had planned to get onstage.

"It must have rained money," I said, smiling again.

Giselle nodded, face happy and satisfied like the cat that ate a big fat canary. "Best night I ever had."

"Jocelyn must be a regular for you to trust her up onstage like that," I said.

She nodded again. "She's here at least a couple of times a month."

"Always a lap dance with you?" I asked.

Giselle frowned then. "No, not always. Sometimes I'm busy when she comes in, and then she'll find another dancer, but she always comes to me before she leaves for the night."

"I'll bet she does," I said, and again let her turn my smile into anything she wanted it to be.

Newman started asking timing questions, but like Phoenix, Giselle confirmed that Jocelyn's alibi was solid. Most normal people rarely have good alibis when they need them, because they aren't planning on needing one. It's actually more suspicious sometimes when the alibi is too good, like this one, but two strippers and an entire club full of people had watched Jocelyn all night. There was no way to put her at the scene of the murder. Strike one murder suspect, which put us back to Bobby as our prime. Fuck.

Giselle had gotten so comfortable that she bumped her shoulder against mine as if I'd been another dancer, and then she said, "All the other dancers were so jealous of me that night. You get women in the clubs, and they usually take the attention away from us, but these were all mine."

"The other dancers must have been pissed."

She nodded happily as if it were the best thing.

Newman said, "Let me walk you to your car."

The change was so abrupt that I would have said something, but he looked at me and I trusted he had his reasons. He beeped the Jeep so it was unlocked and asked me to open the doors and let the heat out. It wasn't that hot, but I didn't argue. I just went to the car and opened both front doors. I'd finished the French fries a while ago, so I found a trash can in the parking lot and put the garbage in it while the car aired out or whatever.

Newman found me sitting in the passenger seat with the doors open. "Why the abrupt end?" I asked him.

"I didn't want you to bewitch another dancer."

"I'm in control now, Newman. Promise."

"Let me see your eyes."

I didn't argue. I just lowered my sunglasses enough for him to see.

He sighed as if a weight had been lifted off his shoulders. "Normal again."

I put the glasses back on because, well, sunlight, but said, "Good."

"Giselle started touching you and being all chummy. I just didn't want to see you roll another dancer. Besides, we'd learned what we came to learn."

"That Jocelyn's alibi is airtight," I said.

He closed his door, so I did the same. He started the engine and got the air going. "What happened in the club, Blake? I know you have some supernatural abilities, but I thought that was from the lycanthropy. What you did in there was vampire, not shapeshifter."

Newman and I were work friends, not friend friends. I trusted him with my life, but I wasn't sure I could trust him with all my secrets. "I usually carry protein bars and water with me, but I forgot this trip. I need to eat real food, not just coffee, about every four hours to keep the other metaphysical hungers under control."

"Other metaphysical hungers? What does that even mean?"

"It means that I've been dealing with the supernatural a lot longer than you have, and the more time I spend with it, the more of it seems to rub off on me."

He gripped the steering wheel. "Jeffries and Karlton both caught lycanthropy on the job on the same damn case. It was Karlton's and my first time in the field on an active hunt. It could have been me."

"They both got to keep their badges and their jobs," I said.

"I don't want to keep this badge enough to give up my humanity, Blake."

I didn't know what to say to that, so I let the silence grow until he filled it. "What I saw in the club, you with that dancer, that wasn't human, Blake."

"One should be careful fighting monsters, lest you become one," I said.

"You're going to quote Nietzsche to me, really?"

"It seemed appropriate."

"Tell me what happened in the club, Blake," he almost yelled.

"There are other things you can catch on the job besides lycanthropy, Newman. What you saw in there was one of them."

"What was it? Give it a name, Blake."

I told the truth up to a point. "There isn't a test for it like there is for lycanthropy, Newman. What you saw inside is a side effect of being around too many vampires for too many years."

"So it's a type of vampirism?"

"Not according to my medical file, and trust me, they take blood and check me out regularly just like everyone else in the preternatural branch."

"The regular marshals don't get all the medical checkups that we do. They're looking for . . . what?"

"Scary things," I said.

"What does that mean, Blake?"

"It means that the quote from Nietzsche wasn't just me trying to avoid answering your questions."

"So you're saying that to be good at this job, you have to become one of the monsters?"

"Yeah, most of the time. Yeah."

Newman leaned over the wheel, hands gripping it so tight they mottled. I let him sit there like that without saying anything. This was his moment of crisis, and I'd known it was coming. He needed out of this branch of the Marshals Service, but he needed to decide for himself.

He looked up and his face was so raw with emotion that I had to fight not to look away, but if he could feel it, I could look at it. "I don't want to become one of the monsters, Blake. I don't want to have to kill people any more as my job. I liked being a cop. I liked helping people, protecting people. I never had to draw my gun on the job until I joined the preternatural branch."

"I didn't start out wanting to be one of the monsters, Newman. I just did what was necessary to finish the job."

"I don't want to kill Bobby," he said.

"I don't either."

"If I sign the warrant over to you, will you do it?"

I thought for a minute and then finally shook my head. "If I was the only one here besides you, I'd do it, because it's my job. But I've got Ted and Otto, so I don't have to take this one for the team."

"But if you had to do it, you could look Bobby in the eyes and do it?"

I let all the air out in a long sigh and then nodded. "I could if there was no other choice."

"But it would cost you, hurt you to do it?"

"A little piece of my soul would be cut off, yeah."

"I would never ask you to do that for me."

"Like I said, Ted and Otto are here. It won't cost either of them what it would cost me."

"I wouldn't sign it over to Jeffries. He enjoys the kill too much for me to give Bobby to him."

"Agreed," I said.

"Do you want me to sign it over to Forrester or you?"

"Me. I can give it to him later if it comes to that."

"It's going to come to that unless someone else finds a clue or someone confesses," Newman said.

"Then we pray for a clue."

"You prayed in there, and it worked. How can you be able to use your eyes like a vampire and still have your cross glow and work?"

"I'm a special snowflake."

"That's not an answer," he said.

"It's the only answer I have. God doesn't see my abilities as evil, and my faith is strong enough that my cross works just fine."

"Then you can't be a monster."

"Pretty to think so," I said.

"'If God be for me, then who can be against me?'" he said.

I smiled then. "Yeah, that."

"How about we pray that we get some help on this case and save Bobby's life?"

"I can help you pray for the truth to come out and for us to find the real murderer."

"Do you still believe that Bobby could have done this?"

"I've been in this business too long not to believe that good people do bad things."

"Would you pray with me that we don't have to kill Bobby if he's innocent?"

"Sure," I said.

We'd started to bow our heads but hadn't quite gotten there when Newman's phone rang. "Captain Livingston. Afternoon, sir." Newman managed not to sound as surprised as his face showed for a second. It's not every day a captain in any police branch calls you on a case without it being for a bad reason. Usually it meant you'd screwed up big-time, but a captain in one law enforcement agency didn't mean or do the same job as in another.

Newman said, "May I put you on speaker, sir, so Marshal Blake can hear the information?"

Apparently, Livingston said yes, because I was suddenly listening to his voice over the phone. "Marshal Blake," he said.

"Captain Livingston." I had to fight not to say *I presume*. I was sure he'd heard it a million times since I'd been tempted twice already.

"My people are helping the insurance investigator run an inventory of items in the Marchand house that might have gone missing in the robbery."

I almost asked what robbery, but realized that legally what Muriel and Todd Babington had done might have been burglary or breaking and entering or robbery or a mix of the above. The definition would differ from state to state. The more I learned about regular police work, the more confusing it seemed. Usually my job was much simpler.

"You said you may have found something that could have been used in the murder," Newman prompted Livingston.

"Is either of you familiar with a bagh nakha?"

We both said no.

"It's like reverse brass knuckles with concealable claws that fit against your palm. It has rings that go over the little and index fingers to hold it in place. This particular one supposedly has papers proving it originally belonged to a maharaja. Story goes he used it to assassinate his rivals."

"I'm still having trouble visualizing it," I said.

"It's not like anything I've ever seen either. I've sent some pictures," Livingston said.

Newman's phone pinged, and he made the pictures fill the screen. The first things that caught my attention were the jewels. Seriously large, richly colored stones glittered in the photo. Once upon a time, I wouldn't have known they were real and how much money I was looking at, but thanks to helping pick out stones for the wedding rings that were being made for Jean-Claude and me, I knew how much rubies of that size and color would go for. I also knew the stones in the photo had to be antique because of their color and size. People just didn't find new rubies of that color anymore. The diamonds that encircled the smaller of the two rubies looked like carved ice caught in brilliant sunlight. The larger ruby was encircled with gold, emeralds, and other things I wasn't sure enough about to name, but it was all beautiful and as flashy as hell. The rings seemed to be attached by a metal bar between them.

"That's a small to medium fortune in just the jewels," I said.

Livingston's voice on the phone said, "With the provenance paperwork and history attached to it, it's worth even more."

Newman swiped to the next picture. This one showed the metal claws underneath the bar. "So the rings fit over your fingers and the claws are against the upper part of your palm?"

"Swipe to the next picture. It shows the bagh nakha being worn."

We swiped, and there was a man's hand with two brilliant rings on his fingers: the illusion was perfect. It just looked like he was wearing two rings. One was all ruby and diamond, and the other had a larger ruby encircled by a colorful mosaic of smaller jewels and gold.

"Someone went to a lot of trouble to make sure the rings didn't look like a matched set," I said.

"The bagh nakha was designed to be undetectable until it was used either as last-ditch self-defense or to assassinate someone," Livingston said.

Newman swiped to the next photo. This one showed the claws curled tight against the palm of a hand. They weren't gold. I was betting they were good-quality steel or the equivalent mix. The top of the weapon was a work of art, but the bottom was all utilitarian and meant for only one thing.

"Bagh nakha translates to tiger claw," Livingston said.

"It's beautiful and deadly, just like a big cat," I said.

"And so far it's the only high-ticket item that we can't find. There may be others, but when my people told me about it, I figured I should let you and Duke know ASAP."

"Really appreciate that, Captain Livingston."

"It's the least I can do, Marshal Newman. I wouldn't want to do your job, but if I had to, I'd want to make damn certain that I was executing the right person."

"This could be our murder weapon," I said.

"It could. We need to find it before they dispose of it," Newman said.

"If you're thinking the same *they* as I am, then they won't throw it away. They'll take the jewels out of it and sell them," Livingston said.

"Can I just say who we're all thinking is *they*?" I asked.

"We're all thinking it," Livingston said.

"The wicked aunt and uncle who were trying to take every high-end item that wasn't nailed down with the body barely out of the house," I said.

"Muriel and Todd Babington," Newman said.

"If it was just a murder weapon, then they'd throw it in the nearest lake or river, and we'd never find it," Livingston said.

"But they're desperate for money," Newman said. "They'll try to keep the precious stones."

"If you find the stones, it'll be enough to prove they had the bagh nakha in their possession," Livingston said.

"Rubies can take a beating and keep on ticking, but emeralds can't," I said. "If Aunt Muriel and Uncle Todd know their stones, then they will want an expert to help them take the thing apart, and they may not have had time to find one yet."

"How do you know so much about precious stones, Blake?"

"I just finished helping design wedding rings. I thought emeralds were pretty until I learned that they're only a seven to eight on the Mohs scale of hardness, and that it's a soft eight that doesn't always

stand up to everyday wear. Rubies and sapphires are a nine, and diamonds are a ten—one of the hardest substances on the planet. I'm
hard on everything I wear, so there went the emeralds."

"You're just full of surprises, Blake," Livingston said.

"So I've been told."

"We'll need a search warrant for the Babingtons' house ASAP,"
Newman said.

"Well, luckily we already started the ball rolling on that when
they got caught in the middle of robbing the Marchand house."

"Do we have the search warrant?" Newman asked.

"We do. Duke's people and mine are driving to the Babingtons'
house as we speak."

"We'll join them at the house," Newman said, and smiled. He
looked more like the man I'd met a couple of years ago. Younger and
fresher to the job.

"I figured you would. Happy hunting," Livingston said, and hung
up. Most cops don't say good-bye, at least not to one another.

I buckled my seat belt and Newman started the car. He looked at
me sideways. "Did you pray silently already?"

"Not me," I said.

He grinned. "Don't tell the other marshals I asked you to pray
for a clue."

"Mum's the word," I said, smiling back. But I offered a silent prayer
of thanks, just in case. God really does work in mysterious ways, and
it never hurts to say thank you when good things happen.

64

NEWMAN PUT THE car in gear, and I had to tell him to stop. "We have to wait for Nicky and Ethan to at least get here."

He looked at me like I'd lost my mind. "Why are they coming here?"

"Shit, I didn't tell you. I'm sorry, Newman. They're meeting us here."

"Leduc was clear, Anita. None of your people can be involved with this investigation."

"They're bringing me some protein bars and stuff."

"We're not going to go look for the murder weapon because your boyfriends are bringing us snacks?"

"We'll join the search for the possible murder weapon, Newman, but I just need to make sure I don't forget to eat again."

"You just ate," he said.

"It was only my second meal of the day, and it should have been my third. It's not good when I skip meals."

"Are you saying that what happened in the club just now was because you skipped a meal?"

"Not exactly, but it may have contributed to it."

"Okay, we can wait a few minutes."

"They want to follow us around the rest of the time."

"Duke will have a fit."

"I know, but they aren't coming to help with the police work.

They'll shadow us, but they'll stay out of the way for witnesses or clues or anything that touches the investigation."

"Then I don't understand why they want to be here, Blake."

"In case what happened in the club happens again."

"You said it has never happened before."

"It hasn't, and if it never happens again, then Nicky and Ethan will waste their time following me around at a distance, but if it does happen again, they'll be close enough to help."

"Help how?" Newman asked.

"If I vamp out, one of them will take one for the team."

"What does that even mean? I mean, I know what the phrase means, but what does it mean for your . . . whatever it is?"

"They'll let me feed on them."

"Blood?" Newman looked like the thought made him ill.

I couldn't help it. I smiled at him.

"Do you think this is funny?" he asked.

"No, I don't, but the look on your face when you thought I drank blood . . . I have to find it funny or I'll start feeling more like a monster than I already do."

"I'm sorry. Don't let me make you feel bad about yourself. I don't mean to do that, but the thought that you could need to drink blood from something you caught on this job scares the shit out of me."

I wasn't smiling when I said, "I don't drink blood, Newman. I drink . . . energy."

"What kind of energy?"

"The kind of energy that I'd rather not take from you or any of the other local cops."

"So you'll feed on Nicky or Ethan?"

"Yes."

"What do you mean, you feed on energy?" he asked.

I was debating how to explain and if I even owed him an explanation when Ethan drove into the parking lot with Nicky at his side. If I hadn't been afraid it would give them the wrong idea about the quickie, I'd have given them both a kiss.

65

I WALKED TOWARD the SUV like I was a grown-up police officer who wasn't going to embarrass herself in the middle of an investigation, but by the time Nicky was out of the car, I felt more like a teenager whose hormones were running high and common sense was running low. It was ridiculous to want to touch him this badly. We'd just seen each other a few hours ago. I balled my hands into fists at my sides to remind myself not to reach out until my bare hand touched his naked skin. What was wrong with me today?

Ethan walked around the front of the SUV to grin at us. "I used to be jealous when I saw you looking at other people like that, but now I've got Nilda at home, and she looks at me that way."

That made me smile at Ethan. He looked so happy. It made me want to hug him, because I loved it when my people were happy. Nicky took my hand in his and was smiling at me and at Ethan. "It makes you so happy that Ethan is doing the whole happily ever after with Nilda."

"Of course it does," I said, smiling at him.

Ethan laughed and threw an arm around both Nicky and me and hugged us. "I love both you guys so much."

"Anita loves you, too, so I have to," Nicky said, and hugged the other man back.

I was caught up in the group hug, and it was like all the shared happiness washed away the anxiety and the sexual overtones of my skin hunger of just moments ago.

"You guys are so cute," Newman said, smiling at us.

We all turned in the hug to smile at him, willing to share the happiness of the moment. We were like a happily married couple who just liked seeing everyone else as happy as we were, except that instead of us wanting everyone to be a happy couple like us, there were more options.

"Thanks. Now I'll take my snacks, and we'll go look for more clues."

"Let's sign the warrant over before we go clue hunting," Newman said.

I looked at him, the happy glow beginning to fade for me. I was glad he was signing the warrant over to me. It had been what I wanted, right? So why did it feel like I'd lost instead of won? But I let Newman take out the warrant and spread it across Nicky's back. Newman and I signed it, and Ethan signed off as the witness. I folded it back up and tucked it into one of the pockets on my tactical pants. It was mine now, which meant I was in charge, for better or worse.

"Anita says you're going to follow us?" Newman asked.

Nicky nodded. Ethan said, "Yes."

"If Duke spots you, he will lose his shit," Newman said.

"He won't spot us," Nicky said.

"How can you be sure?"

Nicky just looked at Newman with his sunglasses making him look tough and cool. Ethan smiled, ruining the tough part, despite his multicolored hair combined with his sunglasses and a body so fiercely in shape that body armor couldn't hide it. Just because I was happy for him to be in love with Nilda didn't mean I couldn't admire the view.

"They are as good as they look," I said.

Newman smiled and shook his head at us or maybe just at me. "You're not catching Duke at his best. He's better than he looks."

"Maybe he is," I said, "but I'd rather risk them being spotted than not have them nearby."

"I feel like I'm missing something here, Blake."

If only you knew half of what you're missing, I thought, but out loud I said, "You know that energy I feed off of?"

"Yeah, you were going to explain what kind of energy it was when they drove up."

"You know how you didn't want me cuddling with Giselle?"

"Yes."

"Do you want me cuddling with you?"

Newman gave me a very long look. "What are you hinting at?"

"I'm saying that I'd rather feed on people I'm already intimate with instead of embarrassing any of us by accident."

He frowned and looked at me and then at the other two men. "I thought Ethan here was monogamous with his girlfriend back home."

"Mostly," Ethan said.

"What does mostly mean?" Newman asked.

I really didn't want to explain that Ethan was emergency food, and I really didn't want to say that Ethan had been my lover first and then moved out of my bed not because of Nilda, but because I had too many people in my life I was already in love with. Ethan was a great guy, but . . . he wasn't my great guy. Luckily for all of us, now he was Nilda's perfect guy. But he was still on the list of people I could feed the *ardeur* on without blowing up either of our lives. Nilda understood the metaphysics and treated it like Ethan was a blood donor for one of the real master vampires back in St. Louis.

"It means rather than let Anita accidentally feed on a stranger in a strip club, she can feed on me without my girlfriend getting upset," Ethan said.

"If what I saw inside the club is the kind of energy Blake needs," Newman said, "then my fiancée would most definitely be upset."

"Which is why we're here," Nicky said.

"It's some kind of sexual energy. That's why there are all the rumors about you having affairs while you're working," Newman said.

I fought to keep my face blank. "I do not sleep with the local cops when I travel as a marshal. Anyone who says otherwise is lying."

"I believe you." Newman sounded like he meant it.

"Thank you," I said.

"You're welcome."

"We need to meet Livingston and the rest of the locals ASAP," I said.

Newman nodded. "Let's go."

We went, though I risked a quick kiss with Nicky before I hurried to catch up with Newman's long legs. Ethan and I didn't kiss because we weren't lovers. We were closer to friends with benefits, which sounded better than food.

66

I CALLED EDWARD from the car to tell him about the missing bagh nakha. I started to explain what it was, but he interrupted, "I know what it is, Anita."

"Of course you know what a bagh nakha is," I said, smiling and shaking my head.

Newman asked, "Did they learn anything from looking at the body?"

I asked Edward the question, and he said, "Only that it wasn't done by a wereanimal, and that whatever was used was only in one hand, and the killer is probably right-handed. We made a list of possible weapons, but I'll admit I didn't even put a bagh nakha on the list. It's too rare."

"If I told you that the Marchand family had moved from India to here in the eighteen hundreds, would you have put it on the list?"

"Maybe," he said.

"And if I'd told you that the murder was done in a room full of taxidermied animals from India and Africa and antique weapons of all kinds from all over the world?"

"Yes, Anita, that would have been helpful."

"My bad, and I mean it."

"No, mine for not insisting on seeing the crime scene for myself."

I heard the rumble of Olaf's voice, but couldn't understand what he'd said.

"Our bad for not looking at the original crime scene," Edward said.

"Well, we'll know for next time," I said.

"Where are you and Newman headed now?"

"To help with the search of Muriel and Todd Babington's house and anywhere else they could have hidden the bagh nakha."

"Text us the address, and we'll join you there."

I had to ask Newman for the address. "Address sent to you; we'll see you there."

"If the murderer is human, what is Newman going to do with his warrant?" Edward asked on the phone.

"It's my warrant now. He signed it over to me."

Edward was quiet for a second or two. "Much more interesting," he said.

"Yeah, I thought so, too. See you at the house."

"Otto says not to do anything fun before we get there."

"He didn't say fun."

"He said, 'Don't kill anyone before we get there.'"

"I'll do my best to restrain myself," I said. I meant it as a joke, but I heard Olaf's voice much closer to the phone, as if Edward had given it to him.

"Killing is what we do best together, Anita. Wait for me."

My pulse was a little faster suddenly, but I managed to say, "I'll wait for you, unless they shoot at us, and then self-defense trumps waiting."

"Do not die waiting for me, Anita."

"I won't," I said.

Edward was back on the phone. "Newman won't like you using the warrant to kill humans."

I fought not to glance at the man sitting next to me, driving. "We'll play it by ear," I said.

Honestly, I hadn't thought that far ahead. I hadn't been impressed with the Babingtons the one time I'd met them, and I actively disliked Muriel, but that was a long way from being morally okay with killing them in cold blood just because I had a piece of paper that said I could. If they were handcuffed and safely detained, I wasn't going to shoot them. Maybe they'd try to shoot at the police. Then it would be self-defense. Short of that, I had no idea what to do.

Newman broke into my moral quandary by asking a question. "Jocelyn's alibi is airtight for the murder, but she still seems to have helped set Bobby up to be framed, so is she working with her aunt and uncle? I mean, if they did the murder while she was at the club getting her alibi? Are the three of them in it together?"

"The aunt and uncle don't seem to have treated either Bobby or Jocelyn like a nephew and niece. Everyone that knows the family has confirmed that there was no love lost between them and any other part of the family," I said.

"That's true, but if Muriel found out she was cut out of the will, I think she'd do almost anything to get her hands on the money."

I looked at him; he was so serious. "I agree, but would she be willing to kill her own brother? I think she wouldn't have a problem framing Bobby, with her attitude toward his beast. She doesn't consider him fully human anymore. I can even see her paying someone to off her brother, but doing the deed herself, that is more of a stretch."

"What if she had her husband do it?"

"Maybe, but I honestly don't think he has the stomach for it."

"I think if one of them did it personally, it was most likely Muriel," Newman said.

"Honestly, I have trouble seeing either of them as the actual hands-on murderer."

"You like Jocelyn better for it, her own dad?"

"The level of cold-blooded manipulation and lying that she's had to do to convince Bobby that she loves him, is in love with him," I said, and shook my head, "if she could do that, I wouldn't put anything past her."

"He's a wereanimal. Why didn't he smell that she was lying?" Newman asked.

"I've seen powerful wereanimals and vampires that were fooled if the lie was in one of their personal blind spots or they were too emotionally involved. Just because you're supernatural doesn't mean you can't lie to yourself."

"And Bobby isn't that powerful a shapeshifter, so it would have been easier to lie to him, right?"

"There's some of that. Being able to smell a lie is usually shapeshifter territory. You can lie to low-level vampires more easily than to low-level shapeshifters."

"I'll keep that in mind," he said.

"Muriel seemed to believe that she'd inherit the family estate and artwork," I said.

"She and Todd are going to be charged with theft or something," Newman said.

"So why steal anything if they knew that Jocelyn was going to cut them into the lion's share of the estate? I mean, why not just wait until the will goes through probate and the dust settles?"

"Good point," Newman said, "but if they didn't do the actual murder, and Jocelyn was in full view of a club full of people, then who did it? Who killed Ray Marchand?"

"You mean, besides Bobby?"

He shook his head. "No, Forrester and Jeffries say the murder wasn't shapeshifter claws and teeth, so that means it's not Bobby."

"Not if Bobby knew he'd be the first suspect. What if he used the bagh nakha instead of his own claws?"

"Then it would be premeditated and utterly cold-blooded. I don't see Bobby pulling that off," Newman said.

"I agree, but I'll admit that I like him better than any of the rest of the family, so I may be prejudiced in his favor."

"Me, too," Newman said.

"So Jocelyn seems to have set Bobby up as being a crazy sexual stalker after his own sister, and when the father said to cut that shit out, Bobby went all wereleopard crazy and killed Ray."

"If Jocelyn is the one lying, then yes," Newman said.

"We heard her voice on the video. That was not a victim. That was a willing participant in a relationship," I said.

"She's lying about the relationship, but what if she believes that Bobby killed their father because of the relationship? Then maybe she's so traumatized that she's trying to distance herself from all of it."

I frowned at Newman. "Are you saying she's convincing herself that Bobby stalked her, or even raped her, so she won't blame herself for him killing their father over the affair?"

"Sounds far-fetched when you say it like that."

"I've seen weirder things, but it makes more sense for Muriel to believe she was inheriting the house and contents."

"But if she's inheriting all that, then why steal?" he asked.

"Maybe their debts are so high, or maybe they've borrowed from dangerous people like a loan shark, and they can't wait for the will to go through probate," I said.

"I'm not sure that Muriel and Todd would know anyone that dangerous."

"They have to know someone that could fence, or wants to buy, some very expensive and rare antiques and art," I said.

He nodded. "Good point. Okay, so either way, we think Muriel and Todd are in it somewhere?"

"Yeah, I like them for it, either as the murderers on their own or in a conspiracy with Jocelyn, because unless Bobby is dead or guilty of the murder, then he still inherits the majority of the fortune."

"Killing Ray only ever really benefited Bobby," he said.

"Yeah, which gives him another motive," I said.

Newman shook his head. "Don't say that, Blake. We're too close to saving his life."

I couldn't argue, but I also knew that even finding the murder weapon in Muriel's purse wouldn't take Bobby's name off the warrant of execution, and it sure as hell wouldn't put a new name on it. This case was so not what the warrant system had been designed to handle. I wasn't sure there was a legal way to void a warrant once issued. You could only change the target, not the intent, but if it was all humans involved in the murder, then what? I actually didn't know. Maybe we could solve a murder, save a life, and make new case law all in one fell swoop.

67

THE MARCHAND-BABINGTONS or the Babingtons, whichever, lived in a McMansion in a neighborhood of them. Each minimansion might have been beautiful on its own with a sweep of landscaped garden leading up to it. But stuck-on postage-stamp yards with the usual unimaginative suburban landscaping made the houses look out of place, like the house equivalent of trying to fit into a dress that was too small for you. Just because you could didn't mean you should.

There were so many of the bright blue state trooper cars that they spilled out the driveway and took up one side of the road; it looked like someone had sewn a blue border in front of every green yard on that side of the street. Newman had to pull into a driveway past the address and turn around; he finally parked close to the entrance to the subdivision. As we got out of Newman's Jeep, I caught a glimpse of Nicky and Ethan driving by the subdivision entrance.

Newman noticed them, too. "I didn't see them behind us until now."

"Like we said, they're good."

He just nodded, and we turned to start the hike toward the house. Olaf and Edward went past us, then stopped in the middle of the street and waited for us to catch up to them.

Olaf rolled down his window since we were on the driver's side. "Should we just park here?"

"There's no parking left farther up," I said.

He closed his window and backed up without another word, tucking his SUV behind Newman's. We waited beside one of the few unmarked tan cars in the line of blue. Unmarked wasn't exactly accurate since the passenger-side door was marked with the Michigan State Police insignia. At least it wasn't their trademark blue and was missing the big red light on top and the shark fin with its bold STOP on it. I wondered if all their "unmarked" cars were tan. I hoped not. Working in unmarked vehicles would have been hard enough with a big badge on one door; all the cars being the same color would have made the job harder.

Edward fell in beside me on the other side of Newman as we started walking back up the street toward the house we were supposed to be searching. Olaf was on the other side of Edward, but there was a flare of power from him like an invisible swat from his lion. It made me stumble a little.

"You okay?" Edward asked.

I nodded. "I just need a word with Otto, that's all. You and Newman go ahead of us."

I hoped that let him know that whatever I needed to say wasn't Newman-safe and he should please distract our newbie. Edward gave a slight nod and continued up the street, talking in his best Ted voice to Newman. I couldn't understand the words, but I knew the rhythm of his Ted patter.

"I did not mean for that to happen," Olaf said as soon as we had privacy.

"Why did it happen? Your control is admirable."

"It is, and I have no excuse for losing that much control."

"Then what happened, Olaf?" I asked, and stopped walking so that I could give him better eye contact. Yes, we were both wearing sunglasses, so that eye contact was more figurative than real, but at least I could look at him rather than at the ground or the surroundings.

"I wanted to be next to you, but it seemed . . . unprofessional to force Newman to move."

I blinked at Olaf, happy that he couldn't see my eyes. "You must have felt very strongly about it for you to lose control like that."

"You make me weak, Anita."

"I don't make you anything, Olaf . . . Otto. Your feelings for me may make you feel weak, but I don't control your feelings. That's on you."

"You are right, of course, but it is so much easier to blame the object of your desire for the desire rather than owning that it is all in your own head and heart. If I desired only your body, I would have taken it by now." He held up a hand, because my reaction to the comment must have shown on my face. "I would have tried, and you and Edward would have tried to stop me. I know. What I meant to say is that if all I wanted was sex and power over you, it would be easier from my perspective, but I want you to like me, to want me. For the first time I am at the mercy of a woman in the way that I have disdained in other men. What made me lose control of my beast for that second was that you did not look at me at all. You looked at Ed . . . Ted, but you did not see me as I saw you. In that moment I wanted to hurt you rather than feel like that."

I didn't know what to say. It was one of the most honest things that any man had ever said to me, and that it was coming from Olaf just threw me. I finally went for the truth. "You keep surprising me with your honesty, Otto. I mean, seriously, I appreciate it. "

"But," he said.

The fact that he knew there was a but coming meant he really was learning. I'd dated men in the past who, if they'd put this much effort into the relationship, might still be with me. Of course, they weren't serial killers. That did weigh heavily in the con column for Olaf.

"But telling me you want to hurt me, because I looked longer at Ted than you . . . What am I supposed to say to that? I've known Ted years longer than you. You and I aren't even dating yet, and you're already jealous?"

Olaf started to get angry. It rolled off him like sweet, musky perfume, and just like that, he smelled like food. "I am not jealous over any woman." His voice was growling, deep with rage.

Apparently accusing him of being jealous over me had been the wrong thing to do. I should have been afraid; instead my stomach roiled. I'd just had a meal, but I was hungry again, just not for burgers and fries.

I leaned in to him and spoke low. "Your anger smells like food to me."

His anger ramped up to rage. It made me want to lean even closer. It made me want to touch him, to lean my lips in and press them against his skin and drink him down. I almost put my face against his arm. I think if he hadn't been wearing the marshal's windbreaker, I'd have been rubbing against him like a cat scent-marking. I froze midmotion.

He stared down at me, the anger starting to fold away. I didn't know many people who could go from that level of rage to cold and calm that quickly. It spoke of years of practice. He reached toward me as if he was going to put his arm around me. I moved away, but his arm kept coming like the hug was still going to happen. I stepped back farther, out of reach unless he was willing to grab me.

I watched, or maybe felt, him think about doing exactly that. "How are we ever going to do this without one of us getting hurt?"

He seemed to take the question seriously, as he seemed to take almost everything I said seriously. Under other circumstances, a man who paid that much attention to what I thought and said would have been great, but it was Olaf, so instead it was intimidating and a little scary—okay, a lot scary.

"I do not know," he said.

Edward's voice in full Ted mode called out, "What's up, pardners?"

We turned and looked at him. He was standing far enough away that if Olaf had grabbed me, he could have gone for a gun if I wrestled Olaf for a few seconds.

Edward came a little closer and said, "The other cops are starting to watch. Decide what you want them to see."

"We don't have time to discuss this here and now, Otto," I said.

"No," he said, but he was still angry and uncomfortable. That was different. He was usually very certain of things, maybe too certain, but there was an unease about him I'd never seen before.

"Newman is waiting for us up ahead. We walk down the street now, and you're on the other side of me just like you wanted. Problem solved for now."

He frowned at me and then said, "I do not like caring about such petty things."

"No one does," I said.

"What petty things are we caring about?" Edward asked.

I looked at the bigger man. "Are you okay with me explaining to him?"

I think I surprised Olaf. "You would keep secrets from him for me?"

"Not big ones, but I'll give you this one."

"I wanted to walk on the other side of Anita but was unsure how to move Newman without social repercussions." Olaf's voice was empty of emotion as he said it, almost matter-of-fact. Again, he surprised me by being willing to be so honest. I knew a lot of people with a full set of working emotions who would never have been that straightforward.

Edward raised his eyebrows behind his sunglasses, then gave his best Ted smile. "Well, now, I appreciate you sharing that, pardner, and I'll help out in the future when I can."

I looked at Edward then, and wondered exactly what kind of help he had in mind, but I let it go, because Olaf liked the answer.

"Thank you," the big guy said.

"Oh, don't thank me yet, pardner, but let's go up to the house and help look for clues."

Edward came to stand on one side of me and started walking. I moved with him, and Olaf fell into step beside me so we walked down the street three abreast like some old-time Western movie. Newman fell in on the other side of Edward as we continued up the street. The four of us walked down the middle of the street like we owned it. I had a flashback to all those old Westerns I used to watch with my dad in which the good guys walked up the street to meet the bad guys for that final showdown. I knew from reading real history that that wasn't how gunfighting worked and the most successful lawmen of the Old West hid and shot at the bad guys from cover, but that wouldn't have looked nearly as good on the screen.

"Why are you smiling?" Olaf asked.

I shared the thought with everyone.

"I like it. Those old movies are part of why I wanted to be a cop when I was a little boy," Newman said.

"Except in the movies we'd be walking up for the final showdown now," Edward said.

"And in real police work, we don't even know who the bad guys are yet," Newman said, and he wasn't smiling now.

"If we find the murder weapon here today, we'll have our murderers," Edward said.

"But there's no triumphant march to justice if it's Todd and Muriel," Newman said.

"It's not about triumph, Newman. It's about saving the innocent and punishing the wicked," Edward said.

"That sounds biblical," Newman said.

"Well, you do have three out of the Four Horsemen," I said.

"Are you saying that your vengeance comes in biblical proportions?" Newman asked, and he almost laughed.

"It can be," Olaf said.

Edward and I just nodded. Newman stopped laughing and glanced at the three of us as if trying to decide if we were teasing him.

68

AN HOUR LATER I was standing in the middle of what had started the day as a master bedroom, but now looked like a fabric-and-homes-good store after a big sale. The pillows, comforter, sheets, et cetera were piled knee-deep, as if I had to wade through white-and-tan-flowered snow. I could glimpse the walk-in closet past the bedclothes. It looked like everything had been dumped on the floor. I wondered if the officers who had searched the closet understood that the clothes were probably the most expensive things in the house. Muriel was one of those people who wore or drove her money so people could see it. The house and the furnishings were nice in that modern way, but not as nice as the clothes she wore, the Porsche SUV, and the Jaguar parked in the three-car garage. I hadn't even known that Porsche made an SUV. The Jaguar was a beautiful, sleek machine, but the SUV looked like all the other SUVs on the road, so paying Porsche prices seemed silly to me, but then I wasn't a label whore. I wouldn't automatically pay more because a designer or a high-end name was attached to a car or a piece of clothing. Some designers made great wearable art, but my day-to-day living didn't really lend itself to wearing art. Jean-Claude despaired of my never truly appreciating the finer things in life. I'd told him that I appreciated him, and he was one of the finer things in life. He'd smiled and conceded the point to me.

"Where is the damn thing?" Newman said from behind me.

Edward had said the four of us should split up into pairs and he'd taken Olaf with him. Fine with me. I'd had enough of the big guy for a while.

"I don't know," I said.

"I'm sorry. I know you don't, but if we can't find it, then . . ." He let his voice trail off.

I finished for him. "Then we can't get more time on the warrant."

"Yeah, I thought signing the warrant over to you would make me feel better, but it didn't. I don't want anyone to kill Bobby if he's innocent, and I know that you don't want to kill him either. I just feel guilty that I've put it on your shoulders instead of mine."

"You're a good man, Newman."

He shook his head. "No, I'm really not, or not as good as I want to be."

"I think that's true of all of us," I said.

He shook his head again. "You know as well as I do that not everyone wants to be good."

"Most people want to feel like the good guy or at least feel justified. I'm sure you've seen it: the thugs that blame the victim for fighting back, for wearing a short skirt, for having such nice stuff to steal. You know the drill."

He made a small sound that might have been a laugh but was way too bitter for the description. "I had a carjacker that shot a banker and his wife so he could steal their Rolls-Royce. They were on their way to a charity event when they got lost. The perp's defense was 'What was he doing driving such a nice car in a neighborhood like this? He shoulda known someone would jack his ass.'"

I said, "Like it never occurred to him that maybe he shouldn't be stealing people's cars at gunpoint."

"He said he wouldn't have shot them, but the man wouldn't open the door when he pointed the gun at the window. He seemed so offended that the rich dude had tried to drive off instead of just giving him the car. Said he wouldn't have shot either of them if they'd just given up the car."

"Like I said, even the bad guys want to be able to feel like they aren't the bad guys."

"You're right about criminals, but I like to think that the rest of us try to be better than that," he said, staring down at the mess on the floor.

Edward's text tone sounded, so I checked my phone. The message was simple. "They found it."

I showed the message to Newman. He started for the door, and I followed him. I think we both wanted to see Muriel and Todd put in handcuffs. Would they break down and confess? I thought Todd might, and if we had that *Perry Mason, Matlock, Law & Order* moment, I wanted to see it. I'd yet to see one of those television-show moments, but if it happened, I didn't want to miss it. Legally I had a warrant in my pocket that could be expanded to save the cost of a trial for the murderer or murderers of Ray Marchand, but I was finally on a case on which I wasn't going to have to be the one who did it. I wasn't even sure Michigan had a death penalty for nonsupernatural crimes. Usually I didn't have to know, because I was a walking-talking death penalty all on my own.

We heard Muriel Babington before we saw her. "We did not kill my brother!"

Todd Babington said, "I don't know how that barbaric thing got in this house."

Barbaric thing? I had to see the bagh nakha in person before it disappeared into evidence. I had a feeling of relief that was totally atypical to the way I usually felt at the end of a case. Maybe it was the fact that it was ending without me having to kill someone. Yeah, that might have had something to do with it.

"Don't touch me!" Muriel yelled.

We were still on the stairs when the knot of people near the door parted, and we had a great view of Muriel struggling against the state cops trying to handcuff her. She was fighting harder than I'd have thought she had in her, but the staties weren't just physically bigger than she was. They had more practice putting cuffs on people than she had at stopping them from doing it. She wasn't going to win, but she didn't give up until they took her to the floor and knelt on her. It looked rough, but it was the safest way to handcuff someone who was struggling that hard—not just for the officers, but for Muriel. The more control they had of her, the less likely that someone would get hurt accidentally.

She was screaming, "You can't do this to me! I'll have your badges!"

Her husband, Todd, stood handcuffed and passive with Leduc holding one of his arms loosely. They were both watching as if it was interesting, but neither man looked upset. Todd did not look like a man watching the love of his life being professionally manhandled by the police.

Two officers raised Muriel off the floor, each of them holding one of her arms. I couldn't see if her feet were even touching the floor. They carried her through the door. Duke came behind them with Todd. If I hadn't seen the handcuffs, I would have thought they were just two friends strolling outside.

Muriel, on the other hand, was trying to kick the police on either side of her. They pulled her forcefully off her feet so that she was too busy not falling on her face to try to hurt them.

"Bastards! Let go of me!"

I was betting she hadn't thought that last part through, because if they let her go now, she'd fall on her face with her hands still cuffed behind her and no way to catch herself. She might want a lot of things, but she didn't really want them to let her go.

I saw Livingston standing in the midst of it all like a calm rock in the middle of the furious energy. It was like the excitement didn't even touch him. He was so steady that it helped keep the rest of the people around him steady.

I wondered where Edward and Olaf were. I might have missed Edward in the mass of tall, bulky cops, but Olaf would still have been the tallest person in the room, and I didn't see him either. Newman and I started down the stairs. He followed after Duke and the handcuffed suspects. I went to Livingston, because for once I didn't have to follow the prisoners and do a damn thing. I was relieved, and it wasn't just because I thought we had enough to set Bobby Marchand free.

"Captain Livingston," I said, projecting my voice so he'd hear it above the tumult.

He turned toward me and then had to look down to meet my eyes. He smiled and gave a nod. "Marshal Blake."

"So where was the barbaric thing hidden?"

He gave a small smile. "You heard that, did you?"

"Hard to miss."

"Garden shed on a shelf, wrapped in dirty rags."

He held out the evidence bag, and through the plastic, I could see it like a phantom made of gold and jewels. It swung heavily in the bag, and even in the interior light, it gleamed. I had an urge to ask to see it in brighter light, but it wasn't just jewelry and history. It was a murder weapon, or potentially one. The police would have to match it to the wounds on the body now. There'd be a chance for a really good attorney to try to get the murder weapon excluded on some technicality. Once the judicial side of things got involved, a conviction and punishment weren't a given, not even for murder.

"Chancy to hide it outside the house," I said. "What if some neighborhood kid found it by accident?"

"We almost didn't find it tucked up on a shelf hidden in what looked like trash. The real danger would have been the landscape crew throwing away the trash in the shed."

"Can you turn it over so I can see the claw part?"

Livingston turned the weapon carefully in his hands so I could see the metal claws that were supposed to sit tucked in against the upper part of the palm. "Forrester and Jeffries both thought this would match the wounds on the victim."

"Where are they, by the way?"

"Outside. If I didn't know better, I'd say that Jeffries is upset that no one is getting executed today."

He made his comment a joke, and I laughed with him, because wasn't it funny that Olaf might want to kill someone? Yeah, it was freaking hilarious.

69

I SPOTTED OLAF standing on the far edge of the yard near the street with its line of bright blue state trooper cars. The crowd of police shifted, and I could see Edward with him. I could tell that Olaf was upset, but if I hadn't known him so well, I might have thought he looked calm, just like Livingston had. It was Edward who seemed calm to me, but he was clearly trying to talk to Olaf in a serious way. They were framed by the crowd of civilians that had started gathering outside the perimeter of police. Once I would have thought it was the neighbors, but there were far too many people for this one small street. There were always more people at crime scenes than you could explain. I never understood where they all came from, and people had been gathering at crime scenes long before the Internet made it easy to spread the word about every damn thing.

Muriel was screaming inside one of the police cars, pushing herself against the window. Her husband sat quietly in the car behind her. Newman was talking to Duke to one side of the cars. They seemed intense but calm. The bad guys were all tucked away, so I walked toward Edward and Olaf to see if I could help Edward talk the big guy down or out of whatever he was upset about.

I was partway to them when there was a commotion in the civilian crowd. A tall woman was trying to push past the police line. She was dressed in white, which made her stand out in the crowd even more than her height. I mean, she wasn't Olaf tall, but she was over six feet. She had large round white-framed sunglasses that hid her face, so at first, I didn't recognize her. It wasn't until the crowd parted for her and she bent low over the policeman who seemed to be listening to her that I realized it was Jocelyn Marchand. Honestly, if I hadn't had her mother's face in my head from years ago, I might not have recognized her, but with the glasses covering the brown of her eyes, she looked like her mother's ghost since she was dressed all in white.

Sheriff Leduc must have recognized her, too, because he was walking that way. He made a small gesture at the officer who was holding her back, so he stepped aside. She strode forward on strappy stiletto heels that put a sway into her narrow hips that made her short skirt flare out and swirl around her with every long-legged step. Seeing her in a hospital bed hadn't prepared me for how long and shapely her legs were. I wasn't normally a leg person, but they seemed to lead straight up to that swirl of oh-so-short skirt like it was an exclamation point aimed at the swell of her hips and everything else that lay just under the narrow, dancing hem of her skirt. As she sashayed across the street, I realized it was more than just clothes, makeup, and hair. She knew how to move for maximum effect. I wasn't the only one who watched her with my head on a swivel as she met the sheriff in the middle of the pavement.

In her heels she was actually tall enough that she had to lean over for him to speak low to her. I couldn't see her eyes, but at a certain point, her shoulders stiffened, and I would have bet money that her eyes had widened behind the big sunglasses. She looked toward the police cars with her aunt and uncle in them, and then she opened that perfectly lipsticked mouth and yelled, "Aunt Muriel, how could you do that?" She took a suddenly shaking step toward the cars. "Uncle Todd, how could you kill Dad? How could you frame Bobby? You made me think he killed our dad!"

She slapped the window of the car that held Todd, and he winced visibly as if the blow had touched him. If we could get him away from his wife, he'd talk. He felt guilty, and that made you do stupid things like talking without your lawyer.

Jocelyn moved to the car with Muriel in it. Muriel didn't flinch when her window got slapped. Her head was turned away from me, so she was looking at her niece. I wished I could have seen Muriel's face, because whatever her expression was, it made Jocelyn press her hands flat against the window and bring her face close as if she wanted to push through the glass and get to the other woman.

"I knew you were coldhearted, Muriel, but how could you kill your own brother? How could you take our dad away from us? Framing Bobby for it, you evil bitch!"

We were all watching the show, but as if the insult was a signal, Leduc moved close to Jocelyn and started trying to soothe her or at least get her away from the cars. He took her elbow and got her onto the sidewalk so the cars could drive off. The Babingtons were going to someplace bigger and far less hometown friendly than the local jail.

The sheriff kept a hand on Jocelyn's elbow as if he didn't trust her not to run after the cars or throw something. I couldn't really blame her. I walked over to them. I wasn't sure if I wanted to talk to her or what, but I didn't understand why she'd lied to people about her sexual relationship with Bobby. It had made me like her for the murder, but maybe that was my issue with her trying to gaslight Bobby. I really wanted to understand why she'd done it, but it really wasn't any of my business anymore. We had our bad guys on their way to jail. The beautiful liar standing in front of me hadn't done anything to bring me down on her legally.

She was talking to Leduc. "I can't believe I let them convince me that Bobby had done that to . . . Dad."

"They fooled all of us, Joshie."

"Jocelyn," she corrected him automatically with no change in expression.

"Jocelyn. I keep forgetting that you're not the little girl I met all those years ago."

I'd heard people say that all my life, but I'd seen the family photos, and I didn't understand how someone could genuinely not see the difference between the little girl and this tall, statuesque beauty in front of us. Forgetting how old someone was, fine, but literally not seeing the difference when it was this stark, I didn't understand.

"I'm so glad that the marshal didn't execute Bobby. That would have made all of this even worse." Jocelyn buried her face in her hands, shoulders shaking as if she was crying. With the glasses on, it was hard to tell how many tears were actually flowing. I realized I still didn't like her. She was gorgeous, but pretty is as pretty does, and she'd told people that Bobby was stalking her, abusing her, rather than admit that she was having a sexual relationship with him. I understood the incest taboo, but her lies had made the case against Bobby stronger. I wasn't going to be able to forgive that. If someone is good enough to fuck, then they're good enough to admit you're fucking them. If not, then you probably shouldn't be fucking them in the first place.

Newman came up to them. "I'm glad, too, Jocelyn. I wouldn't have been able to live with myself if I'd executed Bobby and then we found out that he was innocent."

Jocelyn flung her arms around his neck and pressed herself against him like she was trying to melt through to his spine. He looked startled, but it's always hard when someone hugs you not to hug them back, so he put his arms around her, patting her awkwardly. Then her legs collapsed. She had passed out cold, and if I hadn't come in to help Newman, they'd have both gone down. He was strong enough to hold her up, but it's surprisingly hard to catch someone unless you're ready for it.

We laid her down in the back of one of the police cars while we waited for the ambulance to come and take her back to the hospital. Livingston had his female officers sit with Jocelyn until the paramedics arrived.

Leduc called over to us, "Marshals, can you join us over here for a minute?"

He was standing with Livingston near the front steps of the house. Newman and Deputy Rico were already with them. No one looked very happy. Since we'd just solved the worst homicide this county had had in decades, something else had happened. As we walked toward the knot of men, I fought the urge to ask, *Now what?* Olaf fell into step with us before we reached them. He didn't mention anything personal, and neither did we. We were going to be professional until all the police work was done. Good to know.

70

"CARMICHAEL TRIED TO kill himself," Leduc said.

"The live-in caretaker for the Marchands, that Carmichael?" I asked.

He nodded.

Livingston said, "He was found at a local motel just a few minutes ago. Looks like that's where he's been hiding since the murder."

"Is he going to make it?" Rico asked.

"The doctors don't know yet."

Duke asked, "Did he leave a note about why?"

"He did, typed on the computer in the room. It's a confession."

"Confession to what?" I asked.

"You didn't mention the note before," Newman said.

"I was getting to it, but Duke wanted the marshals here for it."

"Newman signed the warrant over to Blake, so it's her case now, and she doesn't go much of anywhere without the other two," Leduc said.

"I thought the execution warrant would be moot by now, but okay," Livingston said. "The note was on his computer. I'll hit the highlights. He stole the bagh nakha for the Babingtons. They promised him part of the money from selling the jewels off it. He didn't know they meant to hurt anyone with it, and he's sorry about what happened to Ray Marchand."

"If he'd come forward with the information, it could have saved Bobby's life," Newman said.

"Maybe he thought it would implicate him in the murder," Rico said.

"I can see him stealing something small and not knowing how much it's worth, but I thought better of Carmichael than to let Bobby be executed if he had knowledge that could save him." Duke shook his head and looked suddenly older and exhausted again, as if he'd learned one thing too many about human behavior.

"Maybe Muriel threatened to lie and say that it was all Carmichael's idea," Rico said.

"You think he'd really let Bobby die rather than risk coming forward?" Duke said.

"I don't want to believe it, Duke, but it looks like that's what he did," Newman said.

Duke took his hat off and wiped a hand over his face like he was trying to use the air to wash it. "It was easier to believe that Bobby lost control of the beast inside him and accidentally killed Ray than to believe this kind of cold-blooded shit."

"Sometimes it's easier if they're real monsters instead of your family and friends," I said.

Duke looked at me and almost smiled, but then his expression turned sad to match the look in his eyes. "Amen to that. I think we've got enough reasonable doubt to get that warrant of yours vacated or changed."

"I've never actually had a warrant where it turned out to be humans only, so I'm not sure how this works. I think I need a judge to vacate it officially before I can walk away."

"I'll call him now," Duke said. He moved away, pushing numbers on his phone. It was nice to have someone on our side who was so intimate with the local judges.

"Is this the end of the case?" Olaf asked.

"If the warrant is vacated by the judge, then yes," I said.

He took a big breath in and let it out slowly. "If we are not going to hunt together, then I am not sure why I am here."

"If the warrant is vacated, then we can all go home," Edward said. He smiled as he spoke.

When we'd first met, he lived for the hunt and the kill. Now he still enjoyed it, but he lived for his family, too. He, like me, had people he missed when he was away from home now. We had lives that we actually enjoyed. Watching Olaf's reaction reminded me that he had no one. If you kill everyone you've been intimate with, there isn't a lot to build on relationship-wise, I guess.

Duke came back to us with the phone still at his ear. He spoke his side of the conversation out loud for us. "Dill, are you seriously telling me that even though I'm assuring you that we have a murder weapon and suspects with a motive for the murder and for framing Bobby Marchand, that the warrant of execution is still live?"

He listened to the other side of the conversation for a few minutes and then said, "You have to be joking, Dill. You can't add more to the time limit for the warrant? Dill, I don't care what the legalese says. You can't be all right with having one of the marshals execute an innocent man just because there's not enough time to get a confession!"

He hung up the phone and then made a gesture like he was thinking about throwing it across the yard. "This is the most god-awful, messed-up fucking thing I've ever heard."

"Are you seriously telling us that Bobby is still going to be executed when the time runs out?" Newman asked.

"Dill, Judge Metcalf, has got every law clerk and lawyer he can find researching a way out of the warrant, but it turns out there's no legal precedent for it, and Dill has never liked to rock the boat."

Livingston said, "This isn't rocking the boat. This is legal murder."

"How do you think I feel?" I asked. "The warrant is in my name now, so if any executing has to happen, I'm the one who's supposed to do it."

Newman stared at me, looking shocked. "You can't mean that."

"Legally, I'll have no choice."

"You can't mean that you would really kill Bobby when you know he's innocent of any wrongdoing," he said.

"She'll sign the warrant over to Otto or me if it comes to that," Edward said.

Newman looked at him. "Could you do it?"

"I could," Olaf said.

Newman just stared up at him. "I hope you don't mean that."

Leduc said, "Dill said if our suspects confess to the crime, then he'll work with us on a stay of execution until they can figure out a legal way to make the warrant of execution null."

"The warrants are worded loosely," Edward said, "so we can use them to wipe out all the vampires in a lair and their human servants, or an entire pack of werewolves, not just the individual that did the killing."

"Which helps us how?" I asked.

"If we treat the Babingtons like human servants, then the warrant covers them," Edward said.

Everyone in the huddle of police officers except for Olaf and me stared at him as if he'd sprouted a second head with fangs and one eye in the middle of its forehead.

"You can't execute humans as if they were supernatural," Livingston said.

"But Muriel and Todd don't know that," I said.

Livingston frowned at me, but Duke smiled. "You going to try to scare Muriel into talking without a lawyer?"

"No, I'm going to try to guilt Todd Babington into talking without a lawyer, and if guilt doesn't do it, then I'll try to scare him."

"We have the murder weapon hidden in their house. We have Carmichael's suicide note implicating them. It's enough to charge them," Duke said.

"Can they be charged like it's a regular murder and still be covered under the warrant of execution?" Newman asked.

"I'm not sure," I said, and looked at everyone in our little group.

"Don't look at me," Rico said.

But it wasn't just Deputy Rico. None of us knew.

"Let's not charge them with murder, then, not until we've used the warrant to get a confession," Edward said.

"How can you be sure that we'll get a confession out of either of them?" Livingston asked.

"If you stay out of our way and let us do our jobs, we'll get a confession," Edward said.

"What do you mean, stay out of your way?" Duke asked.

"He means that under the warrant system we have total discretion on the level of . . . vigor with which we act," I said.

"What does that mean, vigor and act?" Duke asked.

"Violence," Olaf said.

"Yes, that is what I mean," Edward said.

"We can't let you hurt Muriel and Todd," Duke protested.

"Do you want us to have to kill Bobby?" I asked.

"You know I don't."

"Then let us do one of the things we do best," I said.

"Which is what?" Rico asked.

"Be scary."

"I won't let you abuse prisoners on my watch," Duke said.

"Not even to save Bobby's life?" I asked.

Duke shook his head. "If I let you abuse Muriel and Todd, then I'm no better than they are."

"You still don't understand what we are," Edward said.

"You're United States Marshals," Livingston said.

"We are, but we're with the preternatural branch."

"It means you hunt monsters," Rico said.

"It means we kill monsters," Edward corrected.

"We're executioners," I said.

"You can't kill Muriel and Todd in custody," Duke said.

"Technically the warrant would allow it," Edward said.

"No," Duke said.

"No," Livingston said.

"This isn't why I became a marshal," Newman said.

"We have complete discretion on how we complete the letter of the law on a warrant," I said.

"Like I said, you are not killing them," Duke said.

"Them dead may not save Bobby. Them alive to confess will," I said.

"I don't think Muriel is going to break," Duke said.

"Everyone breaks eventually, Sheriff," Edward said.

"Do I really have to say out loud that you can't torture anyone under my care?"

"You can say whatever you want, but legally we can use the level of force we deem necessary to complete our task," Edward said.

"Do you normally torture your prisoners before you kill them?" Livingston said.

"No," I said.

"Yes," Olaf said.

"It depends," Edward said.

"You guys are fucking creepy. You know that?" Duke said.

The three of us nodded. We knew.

71

OLAF, EDWARD, AND I headed over to the larger jail where Muriel and Todd Babington were being held. I didn't know if we could get a confession out of either of them, but that was the one way the judge had told Duke we could stop the clock on the warrant. It wouldn't vacate it, because there was no system in place to do that, but it was a start. I really hoped we could get a confession out of Todd without having to torture him for real. Threats. I was good with threats, but I didn't ever want to help Olaf torture another suspect for real. Yeah, the one in Florida had been a shapeshifter and all the parts had grown back, but the fact that I could do it at all had scared me. I wasn't afraid of Olaf at that moment, but of me and what I'd done and what I might be willing to do again.

The moment I saw Todd Babington sitting in the interrogation room, I was almost certain we wouldn't have to torture him; guilt might be enough. He looked ten years older than when I'd met him at the Marchand mansion less than twenty-four hours ago. His shoulders were rounded and hunched around himself as if he were trying to hug himself as much as the handcuffs attached to the table would allow. Normally one of the leading citizens of the town would probably not have been handcuffed like that, but he'd been taken in on suspicion of not just murder but a brutal murder. Everything about him said defeat. Perfect.

Edward and I sat across the table from him. Olaf took up his post in the corner so he could loom when needed. Newman had gone to the hospital to see what he could learn about Carmichael. It was the gaming equivalent of sending the paladin around the hill while you looted the bodies, except that Newman knew we might have to do bad things to get a confession. He might not have been able to be there while we did it, but he wanted Bobby alive more than he wanted to keep his sense of moral outrage intact. We'd agreed on our division of labor. Now we just had to live up to it.

The three of us had bought only one thing into the room with us that we normally wouldn't have had: a manila folder with pictures in it. The insurance pictures were on the top of the pile. After that it was crime scene photos. We'd start with shocking visuals before threats—conservation of energy and all that. I laid the folder on the table in front of me, closed and neutral. Anything could have been in it. Todd's glance slid to it. Then he gave quick nervous looks at all of us and then went back to staring at the tabletop.

"Was the murder your wife's idea or yours, Todd?" I asked.

He raised his head enough to look at me for a second, eyes wide and startled as if he hadn't expected the question. He should have expected it. It was why he was in handcuffs, but I had caught him off guard. If we were smart and didn't push him too hard at first, he'd talk to us. Muriel Babington had already called for her lawyer, but we weren't giving in to her yet, because technically she was on my warrant. The warrant of execution stripped you of the right to legal representation. It really was a civil rights nightmare. They'd used that nightmare to try to kill their nephew. Using it against them now was poetic justice . . . or poetic injustice.

Todd shook his head and stared at me with those large startled eyes. He was like a deer in the headlights. I waited for him to say something. I'd have settled for a noise, but he just sat there staring at me with his mouth slightly open, eyes full of nothing but shock and fear. It was like he'd been emptied of anything else, and there was nothing left to answer my question. In that second, I realized that pushing him too hard could shut him down if he hadn't already.

I hadn't anticipated that and wasn't sure how to go forward. Subtle and soft weren't my speed.

I glanced at Edward. He flashed that big friendly Ted smile and then aimed it at the man across the table from us. "Hello, Todd. How are you doing?"

Todd turned and stared at him with those big scared eyes.

"Weird day for you, huh, Todd?" Edward just radiated that good-ol'-boy charm.

"Yes," he said in a small, uncertain voice. He blinked, but when he opened his eyes, there was more in them than just panic.

"Todd, you don't strike me as someone who goes around planning murders."

"I'm not." He sat up a little straighter until the handcuffs brought him up short, and then his shoulders rounded again, but not as badly. "I mean, I didn't. We didn't hurt anyone."

"Your brother-in-law Ray was more than hurt."

He shook his head fast and too many times. "We had nothing to do with what happened to Ray. We are not murderers." He managed to sound insulted.

"We found the murder weapon in your house, Todd. How did it get there if you didn't use it to kill Ray?"

"I don't know, but I assure you that we did not have it in our possession."

"Then how did it get in your house?"

"If Muriel were here, she'd say you planted it."

"Your wife isn't here. What do you say, Todd?"

"I'm not accusing the police of planting it in our house, but I swear to you that I have never seen that thing out of its display case. Are you seriously saying that it was used to kill Ray?" He looked so earnest, and he kept using Ray's name. Usually murderers try to distance themselves from their victims, and one way to do that is to avoid naming them.

"That is exactly what we're saying, Todd."

He went pale and had to swallow hard before he said in a breathy voice, "I didn't want to believe that Bobby could hurt Ray, but to think of someone using that . . . thing on him." He swallowed hard again, breathing through his nose. I hoped he wouldn't throw up, because that would have made the rest of the interrogation unpleasant for all of us.

"It's called a bagh nakha," Edward said in his Ted accent, but pronouncing the foreign-sounding phrase perfectly so that it was like the down-home accent disappeared on the last two words.

I opened the manila folder and got out the insurance pictures that showed all that shiny gold and the gems flashing in the light. When I got to the one that showed the curved claws, Todd looked away. Was it a sign of guilt or just squeamishness?

"Look at it, Todd," I said.

He shook his head without looking.

"You used it to slice Ray Marchand to pieces, and now you can't even look at it?"

He looked at me then. His eyes were startled, but not as afraid as before. "I told you, I have never touched that thing, never seen it out of its case."

"Then why was it in your house?" I asked.

"You did not find it in our house." He sounded very certain.

"But we did," I said.

"Where?" he asked, indignant again.

"Where what?" Edward asked.

"Where in our house did you find it?"

"In the shed out back," Edward said.

Todd looked arrogant. "The shed where we store the lawn mower and the gardening equipment? The shed that we don't even bother locking so that anyone in the neighborhood could walk in and steal it?"

Olaf spoke, surprising all three of us, I think. "Your nephew is going to die in less than a day."

Todd turned those startled eyes toward Olaf. "But you found the murder weapon. You know that Bobby is innocent now."

"The judge won't vacate the warrant unless we can find the real murderer," I said.

He frowned at me, then at all of us in turn. "But you think that Muriel and I are the murderers. You've found the murder weapon. Isn't that enough to save Bobby?"

"We thought it would be, too, Todd," Edward said, "but the execution warrants for supernatural crimes . . . well, they aren't set up to let people live."

"Are you saying that you'll still kill Bobby, knowing that he's innocent?"

"I don't want to do it," I said.

"You'd do it?"

"Marshal Newman signed the warrant over to me, so yes."

"But he's innocent. You said so."

"I believe he is, but the judge won't give us any more time on the warrant. The local police will continue to gather evidence to prove you and Muriel killed Ray Marchand, but by then it'll be too late to save Bobby."

"That's . . . that's . . . that's monstrous," Todd said.

"Ironic choice of words, Todd, since we kill the monsters."

"But you know he's innocent."

"But we can't prove it in time." Edward shook his head sadly, looking younger and strangely innocently disappointed.

God, he could act. I'd never be that good, but I did my best to play up the whole female-and-small thing. To save Bobby's life, I'd bat my big brown eyes at his uncle.

"You can save Bobby, Todd," I said, and debated whether touching his hand would be too much and finally decided against it. I could kill suspects, but holding hands was frowned on.

"How?" he asked.

"Confess."

"I'll confess that we stole things and were going to steal more."

"Like you stole the murder weapon?" Olaf said.

Todd glared up at him, indignant again. It seemed like one of his go-to emotions. "I told you, we did not take it, and if we had, we would not have put it in the garden shed. Something that valuable would need to go someplace much more secure."

"Like where?" I asked, and widened my eyes at him, leaning in a little closer. I could play to my outward appearance in a good cause.

"If I tell you where we would hide things, will that help Bobby?"

"Maybe," I said.

"We have a safe in the house."

"It got opened today before they found the bagh nakha," Edward said.

"Not the safe in the master bedroom. The one in the basement."

I looked at Edward, but he shook his head. "There was no safe in the basement, Todd," I said.

"But there is. I promise you it's there."

"What's inside it?" Olaf asked.

"Small things, but not that boc whatever. I have never seen it outside of Ray's study before."

"Did Carmichael help you steal the small things?" I asked.

Todd nodded. "Ray barred Muriel from the house after she said some unfortunate things to Bobby about his condition."

"Why would Carmichael risk his job for the two of you?"

"For the money. For his cut of the money when we sold the items."

"Do you have a list of everything you sold and how much you got for it?"

"We do, and I'll give it all to you. Is that enough to save Bobby?"

"I'm afraid not, Todd," Edward said softly, gently, like a friend who's come to tell you your pet died.

"What will save him?"

"Absolute proof that someone else committed the crime," I said.

"There is no time for that," Olaf said from the wall. "We need a confession."

"But I didn't do it. We did not hurt Ray."

"Then Bobby dies while we look for other suspects," I said.

"God, that's monstrous. It's not justice. It's legal murder."

"I feel the same way you do. I don't want to pull the trigger on Bobby, but legally I have to do it before the time limit runs out."

"If I confess, then what happens?"

"If you confess to the murder, then that will get Bobby off the hook," I said.

"I'll confess, then."

"To murder?" I asked.

"Yes, if it will save Bobby. I should have fought Muriel years ago and taken him in. He should have been our son, not Ray's, and then he'd have never gone on that damn safari and gotten attacked by that witch doctor leopard. He'd be ours, and I'd have a son, but instead I let Muriel have her way like I always do, and now here we are."

He confessed to killing Ray Marchand. He would not implicate his wife. When Edward pressed him, he said, "I love Muriel. I've always loved her."

By the time we'd heard his confession, I couldn't decide if Muriel had committed the murder without him, or if neither of them had done it. Either way, I knew Todd hadn't, but we took his confession anyway. It would save Bobby's life, and because Todd was human, they'd have to collect evidence before his murder trial. He had time, and he'd get a lawyer, which was something that most supernaturals never got. The lawyer Micah had recommended for Bobby was still on a plane trying to get here, though she had been filing paperwork on Bobby's behalf. None of it would have been in time to save his life, though she was trying to use it as a jumping-off point for some sort of legal precedent to help the next supernatural citizen caught in the warrant system. Legal precedents are great, but they often don't save the person involved at the beginning of the fight.

We'd meet Leduc back at his office, because legally I had to let Bobby out of the cage since it was currently my warrant. The warrant wouldn't even be canceled. It would just be postponed while the legal sides of the equation argued among themselves.

My phone rang, and the caller ID said it was Newman, so I answered. "How's Carmichael?"

"Dead. He never woke up from the drug overdose. Did you get enough from Babington to save Bobby?"

"Full confession," I said.

"Thank God. Thank God." He sounded beyond exhausted, and it was as if hearing his voice let me suddenly feel how tired I was, too.

"We're going to give Bobby the good news," I said.

"He's free, but his uncle killed his father, so is that good news?"

"I don't have to kill him, so yeah, that's good news, or at least the best we're going to get out of this mess."

Newman sighed on his end of the phone. "The doctor wants to talk to me. I'll be there as soon as I can."

"Do you want me to wait for you to let Bobby out?"

"No, it's your warrant now, Blake. You do the honors. I'd like to drive him home though."

"Understood."

"Gotta go," Newman said, and hung up.

I turned to Olaf and Edward. "Carmichael's suicide attempt was a success apparently."

"Two dead," Edward said.

"At least it's not three. Let's go tell Bobby he's a free wereleopard."

"We're not going to get to kill anyone, are we?" Olaf asked. He sounded sullen.

Edward and I both told him no. You wouldn't think that someone who's nearly seven feet tall could pout, but you'd be wrong. Olaf pouted all the way back to Hanuman.

72

WE COULD HEAR Leduc yelling at someone when the three of us stepped up onto the little porch outside the office.

"The lawyer is here," Olaf said.

"You can hear what he's saying?" I asked.

"And what she is saying."

"I believe you can hear it's a woman, but how do you know the woman is the lawyer?" I asked.

"She is saying things that only lawyers would say."

I'd have asked for more details, but I'd listened to enough lawyers to know exactly what he meant. Edward opened the door to the office to a woman's voice threatening to sue Leduc, his department, the city of Hanuman, and I think she mentioned the state cops when Edward and Olaf stepped far enough into the room for me to see the person who went with the voice. She was about Edward's height, though about two inches of that was the heels peeking out from her pants suit. Her makeup was understated. Her dark hair was cut short and styled so that all the waves in it had been tamed. I could never get my hair to do that.

Milligan and Custer were watching the argument like it was a tennis match. Angel was standing in the doorway to the cells, one hip leaning against the doorjamb so that the swell of her hips was more pronounced, or maybe it was the pencil skirt. I'd have wanted to take off the high heels that went with it by now, but I knew that

Angel would wear them all day. It was an outfit, and she wouldn't ruin it by changing shoes.

"I'm following the letter of the law," Leduc said.

"Sheriff Leduc, are you really telling me that you're fine with following this particular law to its conclusion?"

"My job is to uphold the law, and that is exactly what I intend to do," he said.

"Oh, come on, Dukie. Don't be such a hard case," Angel said from the doorway.

Dukie? I thought.

Angel put a smile on her crimson lips that made Duke almost smile back at her. Then he seemed to catch himself and aimed a frown back at the lawyer. I was betting if I called him Dukie, he'd have included me in the argument.

"What are we arguing about?" I asked.

"I'm here to save a life and right an injustice," the lawyer said.

Angel said, "Marshals, meet Amanda Brooks, tilter at windmills, the Coalition's very own Ms. Don Quixote."

"That would be Doña Quixote," I said, but I held my hand out toward Ms. Brooks.

She half smiled, but her face was set for the fight with Leduc, so she never quite looked at me, as if the fight was more important. I wasn't offended, because I had my own version of that look.

I let her shake hands with Edward and Olaf as I explained to Leduc that we had a confession from someone else.

"Muriel didn't crack," he said, and it was a statement.

"But Todd did," I said.

He nodded. "I still can't believe that they would do that to Ray."

I just looked at him pleasantly; no reason to muddy the waters by agreeing that I didn't think they had done it either. I wanted Bobby out of jail and home until the judicial system could catch up with the warrant in my pocket.

The lawyer said, "Wait. You have a confession to the crime that my client is accused of. Is that correct?"

"That is correct," I said.

"I'm happy that Mr. Marchand is going to go free, but this would have been a good test of the warrant system versus due process," she said.

"It still can be, because he's not going free just yet," I said.

"What do you mean?"

Edward and I explained to her that the warrant of execution was still live and had Bobby's name on it, because the confessed killer was human, and we were all a little fuzzy on how to proceed now. I ended with "According to the judge who signed the original warrant, there doesn't seem to be any precedent for vacating a warrant on the grounds that you have the wrong person."

Edward added in his best Ted voice, softly puzzled and pleasant, "Fact is, the crime looks to be just normal human beings pretending to be a Therianthrope, so the crime itself doesn't fall under the execution-warrant system."

"It's not a supernatural crime, so the preternatural branch shouldn't be here," Brooks said.

"That's true," I said, "but we are here, and the warrant is live, and suddenly we're in legal limbo."

"You are not in limbo," Olaf said.

We looked at him.

"Legally you are still bound to kill the person named on the warrant within seventy-two hours from the moment the warrant is live."

"And the fact that legally my only option is to kill someone I now know is innocent just because he happens to be a wereanimal—sorry, Therianthrope—is why the supernatural-execution system needs more legal options."

"You complicate things, Anita. The law is clear."

"Marshal Jeffries, are you seriously telling us that you could go in there and kill Bobby Marchand knowing that he is innocent of this crime?" the lawyer asked.

"You know that rule in court that you don't ask questions unless you know the answer will help your case?" I asked.

She nodded. "It's not always possible, but yes."

"Otto's answer won't help you."

She looked at the big man. "Are you seriously telling me you would kill an innocent man?"

"I do my job to the letter of the law as written," he said, and he gave me a look that even hidden behind sunglasses was chilling, or maybe that was just me, because Ms. Amanda Brooks didn't seem to be afraid of him.

"The entire warrant system is just a due process and civil rights nightmare," she said.

Edward and I agreed with her. Olaf just listened to us talk after that. I think he was still upset because he and I weren't going to get to torture and kill anyone together this time.

"Go tell Bobby the good news," Edward said in Ted's thickest down-home-on-the-range accent. He even put a big smile with it.

"Oh, he heard you," Angel said from the doorway, where she was still leaning seductively.

I'd have looked like I'd broken my hip if I'd stayed leaning that long; she made it seem just right. She wasted a smile on me and then turned it behind her toward the cells and Bobby.

I was smiling by the time I got to the doorway. Angel didn't move, just turned that red-lipsticked smile back toward me. I expected her to move out of the way so I could get past, but she smiled at me with a glint in her eyes that almost dared me to comment. I ignored the challenge in her face and squeezed past her hip, rubbing my arm along the promising swell of it. If we hadn't had a lawyer and other cops watching, I might have put more body English into it, or then again, I might not have. I could see Bobby in the cell beyond her, and he was my goal. He was standing at the bars smiling, and I was smiling back like an idiot.

"Am I really getting out of here today?" he asked.

I shook my head.

His smile faded. "I thought . . ."

"You are getting out, but we can't let you out of your cell today. We're thinking tomorrow."

He wrapped his fingers around the bars. "You said you knew who killed Uncle Ray. Why aren't they in here and I'm out there?"

"They're in jail," I said.

Edward poked his head in the doorway without having to push his way past Angel. "They're human, so they'll be processed like any other criminal."

Deputy Troy Wagner, or maybe ex-deputy Troy by now, spoke from the other cell. "I haven't been processed like normal, and I'm human."

"Yeah, but you're a jackass," Leduc yelled from the other room.

"I've told Duke that I don't want you punished for what you did, Troy," Bobby said.

"I'd take it as a good sign that you haven't been processed yet," I said.

Troy looked at me, face uncertain. "Do you think I deserve to go to jail for what I tried to do to Bobby, Marshal Blake?"

I shrugged as much as the body armor would let me. "It's not up to me. I'm strictly about the supernatural stuff, so you'll have to ask the sheriff."

Leduc yelled from the office again. "I'm still thinking about it."

"If I get out tomorrow, then so should Troy," Bobby said.

"Like I said, that part isn't up to me," I said. "I'm strictly here for you, Bobby. Troy is going to have to take his chances with Duke."

"Are you really not going to kill me?"

"I'm really not going to kill you." I was smiling by the time I finished speaking.

Bobby uncurled his fingers and reached toward me. It seemed totally reasonable to touch my fingers to his until we were holding hands through the bars. "I just want to hug you. I want to hug everyone."

Leduc's voice came from the office again. "I think we can manage that."

Angel moved out of the doorway for the sheriff. Apparently her flirting with him hadn't gotten to that point. Good to know. I moved back out of the way so he could unlock the cell door. Bobby stepped back from the cell door like he'd gotten in the habit of backing up.

Leduc stood there just inside the cell, looking at the younger man, and said, "I'm happier than I know how to say that you didn't hurt Ray, and you're getting out of here." Then he held his arms wide, and Bobby got a huge grin on his face that made him seem years younger, as if some weight had lifted. They hugged, Leduc patting Bobby on the back as they ended it.

I was standing almost behind the open cell door, so when Leduc let Bobby out into the little hallway, Bobby went the other direction for the hug fest. He hugged everyone, including Olaf, which was fun. The bigger man just stood there with his hands sort of out to the side as if he was so unaccustomed to being hugged that he didn't know how to do it.

Bobby hugged Angel and kissed her on the cheek, and she returned the favor. When he came to me, he leaned down so that I could bury my face in the bend of his neck the way I had in the cell when we'd almost gotten shot. His skin was warm, smelling of soap and shampoo, of him, and underneath all that was the faint hint of leopard. My inner leopard looked up from deep inside me, flashing dark gold eyes as she sniffed the scent of him. We liked Bobby, and then I realized, we realized, it wasn't just his leopard we were sensing. I turned still in his arms to find Pierette at the doorway, almost hidden behind Olaf's big frame. Her eyes showed leopard green before she slipped her sunglasses on to hide the leopard eyes in her human face.

Bobby sniffed the air and then snuffled next to my face, searching for the scent, or confirming it wasn't me. Something about the movement against my neck tickled, so I laughed and squirmed against him before backing off with a laugh. Heat marched down my skin, and it wasn't coming from Bobby.

It wasn't Angel, who was standing farther into the hallway past us. It smelled like sunburned grass and hardened earth waiting for the rains to fall under a merciless sun. Some inner beasts smelled like the lands they had originated in, not like fur and skin—lions were one of those. I looked at Olaf, and he had his sunglasses on, too, but I didn't need to see his eyes to know they'd changed to lion.

Bobby shivered beside me, rubbing his arms. "What is that?"

The fact that he had to ask instead of being able to figure it out said either he was that weak or he had no practice with other shapeshifters. Maybe both. Olaf turned and went for the door, taking his skin-dancing energy with him.

Pierette stumbled in the doorway, as if she'd barely gotten out of his way or he'd bumped her, but I knew he hadn't touched her. Shit. Now that Bobby was safe, did Pierette think the honey trap for Olaf was back on?

Olaf stopped short of the outer door. Milligan and Custer were standing on one side of the room, arms a little out from their sides, feet already positioned for pushing off to give that first blow. Olaf's energy burned through the room so that my lioness began to sniff the air, taking in the hot scent of him. The scent of wolf and hyena spilled into the power-laden air, but it wasn't the same as the wolf scents of home. Those were evergreens and thick woods with deep leaves under cool trees. This was desert, dry and parched. This hyena had the same scent, like they were from the same land, and they were. Milligan and Custer had been attacked by the same werewolf pack somewhere in the Middle East, a pack that had at least one werehyena of the striped variety as opposed to the spotted that was the usual type in the wereanimal community.

"Now that you have saved his life, we can finally talk of other things," Olaf said.

I'd have liked to say I didn't know what he meant, but as he stared at me and lowered his glasses enough for me to see his eyes gone hot and orange, my lioness spilled upward. She drew the scent of him deep inside her and thought very seriously at me that it was time to decide if he was a cub killer or if he was in line to try out to be our king. I thought very hard at the lion inside me to explain that I had more than enough kings waiting at home. There was a second figure standing beside her in the dark. It was huge, even standing next to her, with a thick dark mane. The lioness knew exactly what she wanted, and what she needed me to do was decide if the big man standing by the door could be that.

Olaf sniffed the air in the room. "Where is the male lion? I can smell him."

I started to say it was me, but a voice spoke through the door behind him.

"Right behind you." It was Nicky.

73

"YOU ARE NOT the lion I am sensing," Olaf said, turning so that he could keep an eye on both Nicky and the two SEALS.

It was Nicky's turn to raise his face and take a deep hit of the air in the room. It hadn't been a very human gesture when Olaf did it, and it wasn't any more human when Nicky did it. It had bothered me when Olaf did it, but not when Nicky did it. But then I loved him, and I was sort of afraid of Olaf, which colored my interpretation of things. Weirdly, knowing that made me more patient with both of them. Or maybe it was my lioness that didn't want to be angry at them. We had two big males in the room who could match the shadow male that she created inside me. She'd done it once before; it was like she was showing her wish.

Nicky gave a smile that was more snarl than happiness. "I've smelled that lion before."

"Who is it?" Olaf said, voice gone even deeper with the nearness of his beast.

"Follow the scent. You'll figure it out."

Olaf raised his face to the air again, but this time he parted his lips so that he could draw the scent in over the roof of his mouth like a flehmen response in a real lion: Males will try in this way to scent females in heat. In human form Olaf didn't have the parts either between his lips with their frame of black beard and mustache or inside his head. Human beings just didn't dedicate enough of our brains to translating scent. Even if we could smell it, we couldn't understand what we were smelling. We'd sacrificed too much of our brainpower to sight and abstract thought.

He moved farther into the room, still scenting the air in that not very human way. I started moving back toward the cells. I needed Leduc to put Bobby back in his cell so the rest of us could go somewhere more private to talk about my inner lion. But the moment I tried to move back from them, the big male inside me gave a coughing roar that vibrated through me, staggering me. I reached out to grab hold of something and found a hand to hold. Energy flowed down that hand to calm my inner lions. I knew whose hand was soothing me before I turned and saw Angel.

She drew me in to her body, putting her other hand against my face so that we stared into each other's eyes. It must have looked like a prelude to a kiss to the rest of the room, but it was Angel soothing my inner beasts. The male lion vanished first, because he wasn't really there. My lioness on the other hand snarled up at Angel's calming energy. She didn't want to be soothed; she wanted the reality of the inner beast she'd created, and just feet away from us were two of them. Except that Nicky was out of the running, because he was my Bride. It meant he was metaphysically compromised and could never be my lion to call the way that Nathaniel was my leopard to call, which left only one lion in the room as far as my lioness was concerned.

Angel put her forehead against mine, because more skin contact was better for most metaphysical powers. The lioness snarled and lashed out, claws extended. It made me stagger against Angel; she wrapped her arms around me while I fought the sensation of phantom claws trying to cut me up from the inside. There was never any real physical damage from the inner beasts, but it hurt as if there was for seconds, minutes, while my body had to realize we weren't really hurt.

"Are you all right there, Marshal?" Leduc asked from the cell area.

I had to breathe through the pain to answer him. "Yeah, just . . . I'm fine."

The lawyer actually moved around to distract Leduc. Ms. Brooks had been around enough shapeshifters to know an issue when she saw it. She started to try to argue that Bobby should be released into her custody now, today, which was ridiculous and had no legal standing, but she restarted her fight with the sheriff. It gave me time to stand up straight and pretend nothing had happened.

Angel spoke with her mouth touching my face so that her whisper wouldn't carry to any of the humans and might not carry to Bobby. "We need to get you out of here."

Pierette came to stand with us as if it were a group hug and whispered, "We all need somewhere private to discuss things with the big werelion."

It took me a second to realize she meant Olaf and not Nicky. Out loud I said, "We need to leave at least one of you guys here with Bobby."

"The case is solved," Leduc said, "and as soon as we can get the legalities worked out, Bobby is going home. We don't need the Coalition to babysit anymore, do we, Bobby?"

"It was my doubts that made me lose control of my beast," Bobby said. "I don't doubt myself anymore. I know that I didn't kill my uncle."

"If you weren't a Therianthrope, you'd be able to walk out now," Ms. Brooks said.

I nodded and walked into the cell area like my lioness hadn't just sideswiped me. The dull ache of it was just that, dull. I wasn't hurt. "Sorry, Ms. Brooks, but Bobby has to stay in the cell tonight. Hopefully sometime tomorrow he'll be home and clear."

"You know he's innocent now. Why should he spend another night in jail?" she asked.

"Because he's still a shapeshifter accused of a murder. I can refuse to execute him even with the warrant in his name, but until we've cleared him more publicly, he's probably safer behind bars."

"Are you saying that people who have known me all my life would hurt me?" Bobby asked from the open door of his cell.

"I'm saying that legally let's not tempt fate. You stay in overnight and part of tomorrow, and by then we'll figure something else out."

"But no one is going to execute me?" he asked.

"You don't have to worry when any of us come back here now. We aren't here to kill you."

"We will be working to get you free as soon as possible," Ms. Brooks said.

"You know he has no legal right to counsel under the supernatural system," Leduc said.

"And yet here I am," she said.

"You're here, but you have no legal rights, because Bobby has none," Leduc said.

"Which is monstrous," Ms. Brooks said.

Leduc shrugged, spreading his hands wide. "You heard the marshal. He has to be locked up for his own safety as much as anyone else's." He shooed Bobby back into the cell and closed the door with a resounding clang.

Bobby put his hands around the bars. "You promise that I'll get out tomorrow?"

I wasn't sure whom he was asking, but I answered. "Yeah, you'll get out tomorrow."

"Anita, you can't promise him that. It might take a couple of days," Edward alias Ted said from the doorway.

"I will keep fighting to get you out," Ms. Brooks said.

"I'll stay until you're out of jail, too," I said.

Bobby flashed a very warm smile my way. "Thank you. I really appreciate that."

"She must stay nearby until she either executes you or the warrant is voided," Olaf said. He'd walked back in so he could peer through the doorway to the cells.

Bobby's face crumpled, going from happy smiles to confusion and fear. I touched his hands where they were still wrapped around the bars. He smiled at me again, but his eyes stayed scared. I squeezed his hands, and he moved his fingers so he could squeeze back.

"It's going to be all right, Bobby," I said. "We're all working to get you free."

"Thank you. Thank you all," he said, still holding my hands through the bars, but looking at everyone he could see.

I fought the urge to rub my cheek against his fingers like a cat scent-marking. My inner leopard was trying to rise and comfort him, too, but I'd had enough of my beasts getting out of control. I took a deep breath and stepped back, letting Bobby's fingers slide down my skin as I pulled away. He didn't want to let me go. I knew it was part just human comfort, but part of it was his beast recognizing mine. Every shapeshifter I knew said it was lonely without more of your own kind around, and he had been alone a very long time.

"We have to go, Bobby, but we'll see you tomorrow." I smiled when I spoke, and he smiled back.

We left him in smiles. I tried to get Angel or Ethan to stay behind, but the sheriff didn't want them there, and we were in a gray area legally. The case wasn't a supernatural case at all, so technically it didn't fall under the supernatural marshals' jurisdiction. If I hadn't still had a warrant of execution with Bobby's name on it, we'd have had no rights in the case at all. But none of my bodyguards wanted to stay and babysit Bobby. They didn't say it out loud, but I got the distinct impression that they were more worried about guarding me and one another than Bobby Marchand. I wanted to argue, but Bobby seemed relaxed and happy. Leduc had found a chessboard, and he was setting up the pieces for him and Bobby to play through the bars. The winner would play Deputy Troy. Apparently, Troy had been something of a chess prodigy back in high school, but football got him more dates than chess club. I just couldn't picture the deputy being a deep enough thinker for chess, but then, maybe I wasn't catching any of the locals at their best.

Ms. Brooks went to see if she could talk to the judge in person and get Bobby out of jail earlier. I took Leduc aside and asked him where Jocelyn was. I wasn't sure how that reunion was going to go. She was back at the hospital under observation after her little fit with Muriel and Todd. They were talking about keeping her overnight under sedation. Bobby was as safe as I could make him. He'd be a free man in a day or two, and then I could go home with the first ever warrant of execution canceled without a death.

We all trooped out with Olaf and Edward joining us. It was time to talk metaphysics and dating serial killers. I'd have rather stayed and played chess or checkers or Parcheesi, and I didn't even know how to play that.

74

"YOU ARE ATTRACTED to Bobby Marchand," Olaf said once we got outside. Of all the things he could have started with, that hadn't been on my list.

"I'm not attracted to Bobby," I said.

"Lies! I saw you with him just now."

His energy blazed around him so hot that I wanted to step back as if it were real fire and I was afraid of getting burned. God, he was so powerful. It really was a shame he was crazy. The moment I had that thought, I saw my lioness step out of the shadows. She stared at me with dark amber eyes.

"I'm not lying. I don't want to date Bobby."

"Why must you always make it about dating? I said you are attracted to him, not that you wanted a relationship with him."

"I don't know what you're talking about." My lioness took the first step forward, sniffing the air. So much power, such strength, he could protect us from the other lions. If we could only get him to hunt with our other lion, and I knew she meant Nicky.

"She doesn't want to fuck Bobby," Nicky said.

Olaf whirled toward him, all that power blazing bright and feeding on his anger. He suddenly smelled like food again. "I saw her with him! I saw her beast react every time they touched!"

"I don't know what you're talking about," I said.

"Your leopard did react to him, my . . . Anita," Pierette said.

"Well, yeah," I said.

"You admit it," Olaf said.

"That my inner beast reacted to his, yes, but that's not the same thing as being attracted to him."

Angel made a sound that might have been a laugh. I turned and glared at her. "Why is that funny?"

"Your beast doesn't react like that to just everyone," she said with a smile.

"Stop grinning at me, and just tell me what that means," I said.

"It means that you have more control over your beasts now, and they flare only if you are sort of attracted to someone."

"Or if she hasn't fed the *ardeur* in more than four hours," Pierette said.

Edward said, "Do you really want to have this talk in front of the sheriff's office?"

"Until he can control his energy, we can't get into a car with him," Custer said, nodding at Olaf.

"His energy is calming down," Angel said.

Olaf had been calming down, but now the energy flared again, and the anger flared with it. Damn it, why did his anger smell so good to me?

"If you can tone it down, we can go somewhere and talk in private," I said.

I fought not to rub my arms or move closer to Olaf. It was like I either needed to wash his power off my skin or touch it. It wasn't his lion I wanted; it was his rage. Yummy, yummy rage. My thinking of him as food confused my lioness, so she faded into the darkness with only a gleam of golden eyes to remind me she wasn't gone, just hiding in the dark like a good ambush predator.

"Privacy means no witnesses," Olaf said.

It took me a second to realize what he was saying and why. I nodded, trying to clear my head of hungers that had nothing to do with solid food. What was wrong with me today? "I'm not wanting privacy so there won't be witnesses to a crime. I want it because I won't talk about this shit in public."

"What shit is that?" he asked.

"Private shit."

Olaf actually smiled as if I'd meant to be funny.

"Anita doesn't like talking about intimate stuff in public," Angel said with a come-hither smile.

"I want to talk of such things with Anita, but I will not let my desire make me foolish," Olaf said.

Angel cocked a hip to one side so that the swell of her hips was even more promising inside the pencil skirt. She even put a hand on one hip as if to emphasize the swell of them. "It's not just Anita you get to be alone with." She literally stroked a hand down one hip. I knew she'd overplayed it before Olaf said anything.

"Two women at once is not one of my fantasies," he said.

"Then what is?" She made her come-hither go up a notch so that it was a little bit evil or promised to do evil things with you.

"Does this pretense work on other men?"

"I'm not pretending anything," she said.

"I let you see on my face what my fantasies are when we first met. You showed fear then, which was wise, and then you went back to flirting with me."

"I flirt with everyone," Angel said, but she'd moved her hands away from her hips.

"I have noticed. What I cannot decide is if you would carry through with all of it. Would you fuck them?"

She took a breath to answer, but I cut her off. "Angel likes to flirt, but no, she doesn't sleep with as many people as she teases."

What I'd said was true, but the last thing I wanted was for Olaf to think Angel was a whore. He tended to kill them faster.

Angel tried to say something else, but I held my finger up, and she took the hint. "We really need somewhere private for this conversation."

"How many of them will be joining us for the talk?" Olaf asked.

"Most of them," I said.

"All of them," said Nicky.

"I don't think we need everyone," I said.

"I think we do." Nicky gave me very direct eye contact as if I was missing something important.

"Then I need guarantees for my safety," Olaf said.

"What kind of guarantees?" I asked.

"Are you admitting that you couldn't take us all?" Nicky asked, and that was when I figured out what he'd been trying to tell me with his look.

"Normally I would not worry about four against one," Olaf said, "but you are all shapeshifters and two of you are former special teams, and one of them is you."

Nicky acknowledged the compliment with a nod.

"Why only four?" Edward asked.

"You want to know which of us is better. You cannot learn that attacking me in a group."

I glanced back at the offices behind us. "We need to go somewhere else for this talk."

"Agreed," Edward said.

"Sure," Nicky said.

"You're not going to protest that he didn't include you in either attack?" Angel asked.

"Not while we're standing in front of the sheriff's station. So let's try this again. What guarantees do you want, Otto?" I said.

"Your word of honor and . . . Ted's that I will come to no harm if I go with you."

"I'll give my word of honor on the condition that you don't try to hurt us first."

"I will not strike the first blow," Olaf said.

"Promise?" I asked.

"I give you my word."

I nodded. "Okay."

"You're just going to take his word, just like that?" Custer asked.

"Otto's word is good, so yes."

"Don't you want everybody's word of honor?" Custer asked.

"I know that Anita and Ted keep their word," Olaf said. "I am almost certain that Nicky's word of honor is worth nothing. He lies too well. The rest of you I do not know, so I cannot trust your word." He turned to Edward then and asked, "Will you give me your word, Ted?"

Edward actually looked at him for a few seconds and then nodded. "I give you my word."

Olaf smiled, and it almost looked normal, like he was happy about something. "Where shall we go for this conversation?"

"I expected you to want us to go to your room," Edward said.

"I did not get a room yet."

"There aren't a lot of room choices in Hanuman," Ethan said. "We have two rooms that have connecting doors at the motel."

We all looked at one another and just like that we had our location. It was just as well, because Leduc came out on the porch.

"What the hell?" Leduc asked. "I told you this isn't a supernatural case anymore, so the marshals can stay, but the rest of you can't."

"Preternatural branch can deputize, so they count as marshals," I said.

He shook his head, fingers in his duty belt again in a gesture that looked practiced yet awkward with the weight that had to be new, because he wasn't used to it yet. "Not if it's no longer a supernatural case. The only reason you're still here is that warrant in your pocket. Once that is no longer in effect, then you're all out of here."

"Sheriff, we're in a legal gray area so big that I'm not even sure when I'm supposed to leave."

That made him laugh in spite of himself. "Well, I guess I can't argue that, but I know you being able to deputize is meant for emergencies when a marshal is alone on a monster hunt and needs backup. I'm not sure anything about this case qualifies. You never had to hunt Bobby, and now no monsters are involved."

"Do you really believe that the people who killed Ray Marchand aren't monsters?" I asked.

The last of the smile vanished from Leduc's face, and he suddenly looked exhausted and years older. It was that kind of case. "You've made your point, Blake. Now get the extra personnel out of here."

Angel sashayed up to him. "Oh, Dukie, you'll miss me when I'm gone."

That put a smile back on his face. "Of course I'll miss you, Angel. If I said anything less, I would not be a gentleman."

She kissed him on the cheek the way you'd kiss your uncle, except that she left a perfect crimson imprint of her lips behind. "You're always a gentleman, Dukie," she said, voice huskier than it needed to be.

He blushed until his cheek was darker than her lipstick. Angel was good.

75

THE MOTEL HAD all the charm of a chain motel, which is to say none, but it was clean. One window in each room looked out on thick green forest with more evergreens reaching up toward the cloud-bedecked blue sky than we ever had in Missouri. The view made the generic room not matter. I could see getting up and going hiking, bird-watching, tracing down the scent of water on the air and finding the closest lake. So many possibilities and I wasn't going to get to do any of them. Traveling as a marshal meant that it was all about the case. Sometimes the scenery was pretty, even glorious like this, but it didn't matter. Unless I had to chase a shapeshifter through the forest outside, it might as well have been a big-screen TV set to New Age wilderness music.

"Anita." Edward's voice came from behind me, and just by the tone, I knew it wasn't the first time he'd called my name.

"I'm sorry, Edward. What were you saying?"

I turned from the window to look into the room. It was ridiculous that we were having this discussion at all, as if I would ever really have sex with Olaf. But since he was a shapeshifter and might be able to smell if we were lying, we all had to pretend that we weren't lying and that there was a snowball's chance in hell that Olaf and I could date.

Nicky was standing with his back to the wall nearest me so he could see the room and the window. We were five stories up, but I'd seen shapeshifters climb up and down the outsides of buildings higher than that. Edward was sitting on the corner of the queen bed closest to Nicky and me. Angel was sitting on the bed with him, but she had taken off her heels and scooted all the way up on the bed so she could sit with her back to the headboard and the pillows she'd propped up behind her. Olaf was sitting in the corner of the couch that was almost at the foot of the bed. Custer was in the doorway to the connecting room. He was leaning his shoulder against the doorframe almost the way that Angel had cocked her hip at the sheriff's office. I wondered if he realized that he was echoing her; with Custer, I was never quite sure.

Milligan was leaning near the outer door that led into the hallway. The fact that both of the ex-SEALs had taken up posts by the only two doors hadn't been accidental. Custer might not have realized that he was doing the guy equivalent of what Angel had done earlier, but he knew why he was in charge of one of the doors. I knew that Olaf was very aware that both of the men were between him and the exits; if he was bothered by their positioning, he didn't show anything.

Pierette and Ethan were on the other bed. Ethan sat on a corner of the bed, almost mirroring Edward. They both wanted their feet flat on the floor so they were ready to bounce up in case they needed to move quickly and decisively. Pierette sat against the headboard like Angel, but her back was against the bare headboard. The only pillow she was using was the one she was hugging to herself. Where Angel was stretched out and happy on her bed, Pierette was huddled in on herself. I'd seen her in the gym, at martial arts practice, on guard duty, and she never looked like this. It wasn't her. It was an act for Olaf's benefit, but she'd played it wrong. Olaf liked women to be afraid of him eventually, but I'd never seen him be attracted to anyone who already seemed so beaten down.

If everyone had run their big plan by me beforehand, I'd have been able to give the women pointers, but it was too late now. It was almost a shame, since Olaf had been willing to like them in that serial killer way when he first laid eyes on them. Now he watched the room, but his gaze didn't slow down when he ran it over the women.

We had sodas and water that we'd picked up from the shop downstairs, and a coffeemaker that was doing its best to make coffee. It made sad little sounds, and the aroma was anemic, as if the generic coffee the motel offered wasn't going to cut it. Almost everyone had taken water. I had a Powerade that Nicky had insisted I take. He'd also offered me a protein bar, which I would have turned down, but he gave me that look that people have been getting from their significant others since probably before written language. The look said I was being unreasonable, and after what had happened at the strip club, he was right. The healthy bars never taste right to me, and the unhealthy ones . . . honestly you might as well eat a candy bar and be done with it, but I took the bar. He opened the end of it before he gave it to me. Now he knew I wouldn't just shove it into a pocket and forget about it. He knew me too well. The wrapper said it was triple-chocolate good and it managed not to be, but it wasn't terrible. It certainly wasn't as terrible as me losing control again. I took another bite and a drink of the Powerade, which helped. It was almost like chocolate cake and Kool-Aid at a kid's birthday party—okay, it wasn't, but I looked at Olaf sitting on the couch and thought about losing control when he was the nearest snack. I finished the bar in record time.

Olaf sipped his water and looked at me. It was like he was waiting for me to say something. What had I missed while I was staring out the window?

"I'm sorry, really. It's not like me to be this distracted."

"Drink your Powerade," Nicky said.

"I ate a big lunch."

"You haven't eaten enough today, Anita."

"Stop fussing over me."

Ethan said, "Do you really want Nicky to stop fussing about your health and well-being?"

I realized what I'd done. "I'm sorry, Nicky. I don't mean that I want you to stop taking care of me. If that includes fussing, so be it."

"Thanks, Ethan," Nicky said.

"Would you truly have had to stop fussing over Anita if Ethan had not interceded?" Olaf asked.

"It was a direct order, so yeah."

Olaf made a movement that in anyone else I'd have said was a shiver. I'd never seen the big guy that unsettled. "I cannot believe you are happy with being Anita's Bride."

"If you had asked me ahead of time, I'd have said hell no, but now it's just peaceful. Like I told you earlier, I'm happier than I've ever been."

Olaf shook his head. "I do not think I would be happier as someone's slave."

"He's not my slave," I said.

Olaf gave me the full weight of his cave-black eyes. "He must obey your every word. He has no free will of his own. Your happiness means more to him than his own. If he is not your slave, then I have no word for it."

"If you're in love with someone, then sometimes their happiness is more important than yours," Edward said.

"Then love is just another kind of slavery."

"It's not," I said.

"It's really not," Edward said.

"It's wonderful," Ethan said.

"It can be better than almost anything," Milligan said from his piece of wall.

"Better than being out in the field with your brothers-in-arms?" Olaf asked.

Milligan smiled. "I said almost anything."

"If your wife was here, you'd say it different," Custer said.

Milligan shook his head. "No, I wouldn't. She understands. That's why we've been married for ten years."

"Congratulations," Edward said.

"Yeah, Millie here is the old married guy in our unit," Custer said.

"Ten years is a long time for one of the Team's guys to be married," Edward said.

Milligan smiled and nodded at the compliment.

"Olaf, if you see being in love as slavery, then why do we need to have this big talk?" I asked. I took a sip of my Powerade, too. I really did want to do better, but I'd still rather have had one of the soft drinks.

"I am offering sex, not love. We're having the big talk, as you put it, because you're afraid to have sex with me."

"Do you blame me?"

"No, but I am offering to have ordinary sex with you, not my normal way."

"What do you mean by ordinary sex?" I asked.

"Plain vanilla sex."

"We're going to have to define terms," I said, "because one person's plain vanilla can be someone else's rocky road with sprinkles on top."

Olaf frowned and sipped his bottled water. "I do not know how to answer that."

Angel said, "Some men that say straight vanilla mean missionary position with no foreplay and doing it for God and making babies."

Olaf made a face as if the water tasted bad, but apparently it was more Angel's words. "No, no, that is not what I mean by the phrase."

"That's what I mean about needing to define terms," I said, and leaned my butt against the edge of the window frame while I sipped my almost yummy sports drink.

"If we can have such different definitions, then yes, we need to discuss what vanilla sex means."

"Why are you fixated on vanilla sex?" Angel asked.

"Perhaps I am using the wrong words."

I glanced back at Edward. I raised eyebrows at him, hoping he'd understand that I needed a little help here.

"Anita doesn't really do vanilla sex," he said.

"What does she do?" Olaf asked.

Normally I'd have told Olaf not to talk about me as if I weren't sitting right there, but honestly, I didn't want to answer the question. I did not want to talk about my sexual preferences with him, ever.

"Multiple partners for starters," Edward said.

"I know that most of her men prefer a second man in the bed when they are with her. I would not need that." Olaf's voice held disapproval now, almost disdain.

"You make it sound like it's every man's idea to have another man in the bed with us," I said.

"Are you saying that it is your idea?"

"It depends on the man. Sometimes it's Jean-Claude's idea, and sometimes it's mine. Sometimes it's Nathaniel's."

"Sometimes it's mine," Nicky said with a smile so fierce and happy that it was almost a snarl.

"You are able to ask for things you want?" Olaf asked.

"Yes."

Olaf looked at me. "How is that possible if he has no will of his own?"

"I give Nicky as much free will as I can," I said.

"She feels guilty about trapping me forever," Nicky said, "so she works really hard at letting me be myself."

"You are a sociopath and a mercenary that took money to torture and kill people," Olaf said. "How can Anita let you be yourself?"

"I don't torture and kill people for money anymore."

"Don't you miss it?" Olaf asked.

"Not as much as I thought I would."

"What do you miss most?"

"Being able to fight full-out, no-holds-barred, and beat the shit out of another guy."

"You train with the other guards at home," I said.

Nicky shook his head. "It's not the same thing, Anita."

"When you say you want to beat the shit out of someone, you don't mean like an MMA fight with rules and a referee, do you?" I said.

He just shook his head.

"He means fighting for his life, Anita," Edward said.

"He means beating people to death," Olaf said.

I glanced at Olaf, but Nicky spoke up and got me to look at him. "I mean fighting when it's all on the line. When if I don't win the fight, he kills me."

I stared at him, studying his face and trying to see if he was serious, and of course he was. "I've fought people to stay alive, knowing if I lost, they'd kill me. I didn't enjoy it."

"I know you don't, and if your life is at risk, or the lives of any of the people we care about, then it's not fun."

"But you still miss it for yourself?" I asked.

Nicky nodded.

"I understand what he means," Edward said.

"Okay. Explain it to me," I said.

"It's the same thing that makes me want to test myself against the biggest and baddest monster I can find."

"It's a way of knowing who's the best," I said.

Edward nodded.

I looked from my best friend to one of the loves of my life and back again. Then I looked at Olaf. "And you understand what they're talking about, don't you?"

"I do."

I looked at Ethan. He raised his hands. "Don't look at me. That's not how I think."

I looked at the two SEALs still guarding their respective doors. "How about you guys?"

Custer shook his head. "I like to test myself, but not like that, and I don't want to ever fight Nicky for real."

Milligan laughed. "I'll second that part, and I'm not one of your lovers. I'm not even trying out for the job, so I don't have to answer the other question, or are there questions? Either way, I don't have to answer."

"You're right. It's pretty personal. Sorry. I have bad boundaries sometimes."

"You're just used to dating almost everyone in a room," Angel said.

"You didn't ask us the question," Pierette said, voice quiet but firm enough to fill the room.

"What question?" I asked.

"What we miss by being bound to you."

"I don't think Angel misses the kind of things that the guys do, but if I'm wrong, then say something."

"It was sexist of you to ask only the men," Angel said, "but I don't want to fight for my life with fists or weapons. I'll fight if I have to, and you know I train, because we all train, but I don't train like the rest of you do. It doesn't interest me the way it does you."

"You're a social worker and a counselor. You don't usually have to resort to fisticuffs in your line of work," I said.

"You'd be surprised, but it's not nearly as dangerous as your job."

"So, you don't miss anything?"

"I miss New York, even with the terrible rents and the terrible pay for jobs. I hated giving up my life there at first, but I really enjoy working with Micah and the Coalition. I think we do a lot of good work for a lot more people across the country than I could have reached as a standard social worker."

"I'm sorry that you had to give up your life in New York," I said. "Do you want to go back there? I mean, I know you said you enjoy working with the Coalition, but I want you to be happy, so . . ."

Angel slid off the bed and came to me, putting her fingers gently against my lips, so I had to stop talking. "And that is why we love you, because you really, truly want all of us to be as happy as humanly and superhumanly possible." She took her fingers away and kissed me gently; it was barely a brush of lips.

"She does not want us all to be happy if what makes us happy makes her uncomfortable," Pierette said.

Angel moved so I could see the other woman. Pierette wasn't huddling over the pillow now. She was more just sitting with it in her lap.

"I told you that you can start traveling out of the country soon."

"And I thank you and Jean-Claude for that, but I miss what we did when we traveled. You won't let us do the things we need to do to make all the vampires and shapeshifters fear us again. Jean-Claude tries to be a good king, a fair ruler, and he won't let us do what is necessary to keep our threat strong."

"Pierette," Ethan said, and reached a hand toward her.

"I know I am spoiling our plan, but it wasn't working anyway. I look the part, but I played it too scared. He likes to break his victims down, not start with them broken."

"You were the wrong bait," Olaf said, "and so was she."

"I'm serious when I say if we could find a way to guarantee my safety, I would totally fuck you—at least once," Angel said.

I looked at her. I think I looked shocked, or like I didn't believe her.

"Oh, come on, Anita, he's hot. If you weren't scared you'd end up on the menu, you'd have done him by now."

"I don't think so."

"I have offered sex to Anita without her being on the menu, though menu is incorrect," Olaf said. "I do not find cannibalism titillating."

"Good to know," I said.

"Should I be offended that you're not making the offer to me?" Angel asked.

"Anita is the Woman for me, the only one I want to be with more than once. The only one that makes me want to find ways to satisfy my desires without destroying her."

"She and the others tell us that you want her to hunt monsters with you so you can cut them up and kill them together as foreplay," Pierette said.

"Yes," he said.

"I miss hunting down vampires that have broken our laws. I miss tormenting them, making examples of them. I miss doing terrible things in the name of those I serve."

Pierette sat up straighter with every word. By the last one, her pillow had fallen to the floor, and she sat cool, confident, centered in herself in a way I hadn't seen before. Was it real, or was it an act? Would the real Pierette please step the fuck forward?

"This is much better bait for me, but I do not believe this lie any more than I did the other," Olaf said.

Pierette looked at him. "I'm not lying about this."

"You are good at hiding it. Your breath, your pulse, nothing changes, but your scent does. No matter how controlled you are, you can't control that. Even one of the great fallen Harlequin cannot control the smell. Lies smell bitter on your skin."

"You are only guessing that I was one of the Harlequin."

"You keep almost calling Anita your queen. Only the bodyguards of the old queen of vampires would do that."

"And if I was one of them, then I would be a spy and assassin extraordinaire. I would hunt monsters with you, Olaf, and I would have far fewer morals about it than Anita does."

"I think if you got me alone, you would try to kill me. You would say later that I had attacked you, and you were forced to defend yourself. How brave of you, how tragic for me."

"I admit that was the original plan, but as Angel says, you are attractive and far more compelling than I expected."

"You seek to distract me, but I am not that easily put aside from my goals." He turned back to Edward as if the women had ceased to exist. "Have you slept with Anita and any of her girlfriends?"

"No."

"I will not ask the other. It is insulting."

"It's not insulting. It's just a question," Edward said.

"Are you saying you have shared her with another man at the same time?"

"We usually have sex when we're in the field away from home, which means it's usually not an issue."

It was everything I could do to keep my face blank and not give away how big a lie he'd just told. I wished I still had my sunglasses on so my eyes wouldn't give it away, but luckily for us, Olaf's attention was all on Edward.

"So she is your work wife?" Olaf asked.

"She's my partner. Donna is my wife."

"I meant no insult to either woman. I am just trying to understand."

"It's not my relationship with Anita you need to understand. It's her relationship to the others that's important for you."

"Why is that more important?" Olaf asked.

"Because you and I will never be comfortable sharing Anita in a bed together, but I think for her safety, you will need to find men that you would be willing to do that with."

"I do not understand."

"The only way I would trust you with Anita romantically is if there were men in the room that I thought could win against you or at least fight you long enough for Anita to escape."

"I still do not understand."

I was beginning to, and it was both brilliant and frightening, but then it was Edward, and that was how his mind worked. "He means that I would never feel safe one-on-one with you, but with some of my other lovers with us, I'd have a fighting chance if things went wrong."

Olaf was disgusted and didn't try to hide his reaction. "The only thing I have ever enjoyed doing with other men is torturing them or winning against them. I enjoy causing anyone pain. It is simply better if it is a woman."

"The only other option I've come up with is if you allowed yourself to be chained down while Anita topped you," Edward said.

"No, I will not submit to anyone."

"Then how do we keep Anita safe?"

"My word is not enough for you?"

"Not on this, Olaf. I knew this day was coming, and I have been trying to think of ways that your needs can be met at least partway without risking Anita's life."

He was lying again, and Olaf didn't call him on it. Either Edward's body gave nothing away for the werelion to sense, or Olaf was so upset that he couldn't sense it. It might have been a bit of both.

"What of the *ardeur*? What of Anita's ability to feed through lust?" Olaf asked.

"What about it?" I asked.

"If she fed on me, would I be able to harm her while she did it?"

"I thought you told me that you weren't food, not for anyone," I said.

"It is merely a question, Anita. I am trying to understand what options are open to us."

"I can answer this one," Nicky said. "Once the *ardeur* is released, then all inhibitions go. For Anita it means she can take even rougher sex than without it."

"I asked in the car when the three of us were alone if you and Anita did bondage together. You avoided answering the question."

"I was embarrassed, okay?" I said. "I'm still embarrassed, but if we're really going to answer the question, then yes, we do bondage together."

"Do you dominate him?"

"No, he's my top."

"He is your dominant?"

I shook my head. "I'm a switch, which means I like to go both ways in the dungeon. I can bottom, but I don't do complete submission."

"She bottoms harder than most submissives I've ever been with," Nicky said.

I so wanted out of this conversation, but if we were going to have it, I'd be a grown-up about it. "I cannot imagine a set of circumstances where I would be willing to be tied up with Olaf in the room, let alone with him topping me. I have to trust someone completely to give myself to them like that, and I don't know how I would ever be able to trust you like that, Olaf."

"Even if I let you release the *ardeur* on me?"

I looked at Nicky. "You tell me. Does the *ardeur* make you safer as a lover for me?"

"The *ardeur* is what turned me into your Bride, so yeah."

"She feeds the *ardeur* on the rest of us, and it hasn't turned us into Brides," Angel said.

"And she has Brides that she has never had sex with," Pierette said.

"I think I make Brides when I'm desperate. It's like a Hail Mary pass."

"So you've never tried to make a Bride when you weren't in dire straits?" she asked.

"No."

"So Anita could feed the *ardeur* on me and not turn me into her Bride?" Olaf asked.

"I believe so," Pierette said.

"Only if I felt safe, and like I said, I can't imagine a set of circumstances where I would feel safe with you like that."

Olaf looked at Nicky. "If she had not unleashed the *ardeur* on you, would you have hurt her that first time you fucked her?"

"No, I can enjoy sex without pain."

"So can I, but that is not my question."

"Was it gentler lovemaking than I would have done on my own without her magic?" Nicky asked.

"That is what I am asking," Olaf said.

"It was gentler."

"But still satisfying?"

"The *ardeur* is a rush. It makes every touch more intense."

Everyone in the room nodded except Edward and the two SEALs. Edward caught it in time to say, "I don't let her feed on me."

"Why not?" Olaf asked.

"I am not food, not even for her."

Olaf nodded as if that made sense to him.

I was never, ever going to have sex with Olaf, but I didn't say so

out loud, because we were still trying not to pull the pin on the grenade. But it was like a game of chicken between a car and a train. If
you didn't get off the tracks, eventually you were going to lose.

"How can gentle be satisfying to you, Nicky?" Olaf asked.

"The first time was gentle, and sometimes it still is, but the bondage we do together is RACK."

"I do not know the term," Olaf said.

"Risk-aware consensual kink, RACK," Nicky said.

"I prefer the term edge play," I said, "but RACK is more descrip-
tive, I guess."

I fought not to squirm, because it had taken me a long time to be
comfortable with just how much I enjoyed rough sex and bondage. I
still wasn't entirely happy that was part of my sexual orientation, but
I was working in therapy at accepting all of myself, and that was part
of me. You didn't get to pick and choose your sexual orientation. You
could choose not to act on it, but it was still what flipped your switch.
It didn't go away because you stopped doing it or tried not to start
doing it.

"Does Anita do this with anyone else?" Olaf asked.

Angel raised her hand, smiling.

"I've co-topped Angel and Anita with Nathaniel," Nicky said.

"I'm really not wanting to do details in front of everyone in this
room," I said. I was fighting not to blush, but since it's an involuntary
thing, I was losing.

Nicky smiled at me. "You are so uncomfortable with the things
you enjoy in the dungeon."

I nodded. "Yep. Yep, I am."

"I thought Nathaniel was an extreme submissive," Olaf said,
"even a pain slut."

"He can be," Nicky and I said together. We shared a smile over it.

"Are you telling me that you have sex with Nathaniel?" Olaf
asked.

"I think that's for you, Nicky," I said. "He knows I'm with Nathaniel."

"It could be aimed at me," Angel said.

"I assumed you were having sex with the men in St. Louis," Olaf said.

She looked at him and raised an eyebrow. "I'm not doing all of them. Even I have my limits."

"Hell, so do I," I said.

Angel grinned at me, all pleased mischief. "We can't sleep with everyone."

I shook my head. "I know I can't."

"Are you having sex with Nathaniel, Nicky?" Olaf asked.

"I don't fuck him. He helps me top and fuck Anita and sometimes Angel with her."

"It's a recent addition," I said, and realized I was still embarrassed about it. I sighed. Would I ever really be comfortable with what I enjoyed in the bedroom or the dungeon?

"I did not think Anita would submit to or bottom for anyone," Olaf said.

"Neither did I, honestly," I said, and I was doing my best not to make eye contact with anyone.

"Is it only with Nicky?"

I glanced up at Olaf and then back down at some vague point in the middle of the room. "No, it's not just with him."

"Who else?"

"How is this conversation helping us figure things out with Olaf?" I asked.

"You know I wouldn't ask this if I didn't think it was helpful," Edward said.

I gave him eye contact. "You're the only one in this room that I would keep answering these questions for."

"I know, and thank you," he said.

"For Edward, but not for Nicky," Olaf said.

I glanced at Nicky, and he said, "I top her in the dungeon, but she takes Edward's orders outside of the bedroom better than mine."

I didn't like the wording, but I couldn't exactly argue with it, so I let it go. "What was the question again?" I asked.

"Who else dominates you or tops you?"

"Besides Nicky, you mean?"

"Yes."

"Does it really matter who?"

"Perhaps not, but how many besides Nicky?"

"Edward," I said, looking at him.

"Please answer him, Anita," Edward said.

"Fine." I counted mentally. "Two."

"I count more than that," Nicky said.

I frowned at him. "Asher and Richard, that's it."

"Jean-Claude joins you and Richard sometimes, or you and Asher, so he counts."

"Okay, three."

Nicky looked at me as if I was missing something.

"What?" I asked.

Angel said, "I've been with you when you had sex with a lot of the others, and you really don't ever do just straight vanilla sex."

"I do, too," I said, and meant it.

"Not often," she said.

I shrugged. "I don't know what to say to that."

"I'm probably the closest to straight vanilla that Anita has," Edward said.

Again, Olaf didn't know he'd just lied his ass off. But just his saying it made me want to squirm with embarrassment, which was probably what kept me from smelling like lies. I was so embarrassed, I was masking Olaf's werelion senses.

"Anita likes rough enough to keep me happy," Nicky said.

"So when I said I would be willing to do straight vanilla sex for Anita, that is not what interests her either?" Olaf asked.

"Not usually," Nicky said.

"I don't want to have edge-play rough sex every night," I said.

"No, you don't," Nicky said. "That's why I'm not your only lover. You have other people in your life to meet the needs I don't."

"It's one of the best things about polyamory," I said.

"Totally agree," Angel said. "I mean, I like rough from time to time, but I don't like it as much as Anita does."

"Edward, I need you to help us make some kind of point here, because I'm getting tired of talking about this in depth in front of everyone."

"Don't mind us," Custer said. "I'm finding it educational."

I glared at him. He laughed.

"Leave it alone, Pud," Milligan said.

Custer raised his hands up as if to say he was sorry.

Edward said, "The point is that I've seen what Olaf does to women when there's no one to stop him. I wanted to know if there was anything short of that that would satisfy him with you."

"I would need to know what Anita does in her RACK play before I could answer that question," Olaf said.

"I can answer some of it, but for other stuff, you'd need to talk to Nathaniel or even Asher," Nicky said.

"No," I said.

"Anita, if there's a way to do this without either of you dying, isn't it worth the embarrassing conversation?" Edward said.

Put that way, it seemed yes, but . . . "Damn it, Edward."

"Am I wrong?" he asked.

I sighed and just let myself lean against the wall. Okay, maybe I sagged more than leaned. I was so tired of all of this. Surely I didn't play over the edge enough to satisfy a sexually sadistic serial killer. I mean, I played rough, but not that rough.

"Fine. I can't argue with the logic of gathering as much information as possible on this."

"So, can I answer Olaf's questions or not?" Nicky asked.

"You can, but not with all of us here. Milligan and Custer don't need to know that much detail about my sex life."

"Aww," Custer said, trying to pretend to pout, but the smile ruined it.

"Leave it alone, Pud," Milligan said again.

Custer stopped talking, but the smile stayed. I could ignore him as long as he didn't talk.

"Ethan doesn't like this kind of stuff, and neither does Pierette," I said. "I think they'd rather not be here for details."

"I'm your bodyguard. I'll do my job," Ethan said.

"As will I," Pierette said.

"Fine, but I'm not sure I can be in the room with this many people and have this discussion," I said.

Nicky said, "How about if I give a list, and I stop when you tell me to?"

"I'd rather not have anyone here I'm not sleeping with."

"I've given my word of honor that I will not harm anyone unless you harm me first," Olaf said.

"That's his way of saying that Milligan and Custer can wait outside the door or in the other room," Edward said.

"I know what he means," I said, and my words sounded cranky even to me.

"She likes breath play," Nicky said.

"That does not interest me," Olaf said.

"And we have to clear the room before we do any more on the list," I said.

I don't know what we would have done next, because my phone rang. It was a number I didn't recognize, but I was hoping it was someone who would get me out of this conversation.

"Blake, this is Livingston."

"Hi. What's up?" I asked.

"I need you to meet me at Sugar Creek ASAP."

"Why is it an emergency to meet you at the restaurant?"

"Hazel just came from the hospital."

"Newman told us that Carmichael didn't make it. I'm sorry his girlfriend is having to deal with it."

"Yes, she came back here to talk to Pamela. I think you need to hear what she has to say."

"Did she talk to Newman at the hospital?"

"Hazel doesn't trust anyone local."

"You're local."

"She trusts me because of Pamela. You need to hear what she has to say, Blake."

"Care to give me a preview?" I asked.

"Just get over here, and don't mention this call to the sheriff or any of his people. And don't bring any of your deputies. It's a regular murder case now, and I'm not sure what involving deputized Therianthropes will do to any evidence we find."

"I've used them before on other cases."

"Those were supernatural cases through and through. This one isn't. Regular Marshals Service doesn't have the ability to deputize anyone, so let's not give a lawyer the chance to use preternatural deputies against us later."

"I've never had a case go from preternatural to ordinary murder, so I can't tell you that it won't negatively impact the case later."

"Then you agree to leave them out of the rest of the investigation?" he asked.

"I guess so."

"Then you, Forrester, and Jeffries are the only people I want to see from your branch of service."

"All right."

"Good. Now get down here ASAP." He hung up.

Olaf stood up. "I heard. We need to meet him at the restaurant."

I filled Edward in since he didn't have super hearing.

"I can't tell Livingston he's wrong about the extra manpower being a problem later in court," he said.

"Neither can I."

"We're your bodyguards," Nicky said. "We're not much use if we aren't with you."

"I gave my word," Olaf said.

"His word really is good," I said.

"It really is," Edward said.

Nicky and the others didn't like it much, but in the end, they agreed, so the three of us left them at the motel. They couldn't even finish the discussion about edge play, because we took Olaf with us, and without him there was no reason to have the talk. Edward and I rode together so I didn't even have to finish the talk with Olaf. Yay! I did have to ask Edward one question on the quick drive to the restaurant though.

"You know I'm never going to have sex for real with Olaf, right?"

"That was the original plan."

"I do not like the way you just said that."

"I've never seen him try this hard with anyone. I honestly thought he'd bail on the whole bondage conversation."

"So did I."

He glanced at me. "Olaf is being so damn reasonable that we may run out of reasons to say no."

"It's not *we* that he wants to fuck. It's me."

"True."

"True? That's all you're going to say?"

"What do you want me to say, Anita?"

"One minute you tell me to kill Olaf or you will, and the next, you make it sound like you'd sign off on me having sex with him. What the hell, Edward?"

"I'm sorry, Anita, but the big guy just keeps surprising me. I thought I knew who Olaf was, what he was, and that there wasn't enough human being left inside the monster to have a relationship with anyone, let alone my best friend."

"You'll miss him when we have to kill him," I said, and it sounded like an accusation.

"Won't you?"

I shook my head, and then I thought about it. "I'll miss him in a fight, but I won't miss the constant state of threat I feel because he's out there. If there was a way to have the useful parts without the scary-as-fuck parts, it would be different, but it doesn't work that way."

"Maybe it's the scary parts that make him useful," Edward said quietly.

"I know it is, and that's what makes it all so fucking awful. He's helped us on multiple serial killer cases, but you and I both know where his expertise comes from. It's like using the medical notes from the Nazi concentration camps to save lives today. Is the help worth what it cost? Can you take help from the devil without losing your soul in the process?"

"I'm an atheist. You know that."

"Don't even get me started on the fact that you don't have enough faith to make a holy object glow in the face of a vampire. The fact that you've survived this long without it just proves that God loves you, no matter how you feel about Him."

He pulled into the packed parking lot of the Sugar Creek Restaurant and Bakery.

"Is this place always packed?" I said.

He started searching for a parking place without answering me. I guess I didn't really need an answer.

"I thought I could come up with enough rules or things Olaf would hate that he would just drop the idea of sex with you," Edward said, "but he keeps surprising me."

"Yeah, I thought you'd come up with a great idea to make him back off, but then he hung in there through all the bondage-negotiation talk."

A dark blue truck started to pull out ahead of us. Edward put on his turn signal and vultured while cars started getting trapped behind him. The person driving the truck didn't seem to know how to back up without hitting the cars behind them. Big trucks were tricky. It was one of the reasons I didn't own one; that and I was too short to get into them without climbing. I didn't need to drive a daily reminder that I was shorter-than-average height for a woman.

"What if Olaf agrees to something that you'd do if it wasn't him?" Edward asked.

I stared at the side of his face, because it was all I could see. He tried to just look at the truck in front of us, but it was taking so long, he finally had to look at me. His face was empty and unreadable behind the sunglasses.

"You cannot be serious," I said.

"Petra, or Pierette, is right about one thing, Anita: Your beast doesn't react to someone unless you're attracted to them."

"And?" I said. The one word was as cold and empty as his expression.

"Your beast likes Olaf a lot."

"The last person my lioness liked this much ended up trying to kill Nathaniel. If Noel hadn't pushed him out of the way and taken the bullet, I'd have lost Nathaniel."

"I'm sorry you had to kill Haven to protect everyone, Anita. I know it cost you."

"Then how can you ask me to even consider another werelion that's even more dangerous? I will not risk the people I love or the people that I've given my protection to because we're too gutless to tell Olaf the truth."

The truck finally managed to exit without crashing into the cars in back of it. It took the truck even more time to finally get turned so it could start forward enough that Edward could begin to slide into the parking spot. The truck backed up again. Edward had to slam on his brakes and prove the seat belts worked, or the truck would have hit us. The truck began to try to go forward. Some people shouldn't be allowed to drive big trucks.

"And what is the truth, Anita?"

"I can't be his serial killer girlfriend."

"He doesn't want a girlfriend. He wants to try sex without killing the woman."

"Say we manage it. Say we find a set of bondage rules that keeps me safe enough to fuck him. Then what? If it satisfies him, then I'm stuck as his lover forever? If it doesn't satisfy him, then he still wants to fuck me, but now he wants to do it his way, which means he'll torture and kill me during the process? There is no win here, Edward."

"You're probably right."

"Probably?"

The truck finally left, and we were able to park at last. Edward reached for his door handle. "I'll just be sorry when we have to kill him, and I'll be sorrier if he kills us first."

With that, he got out of the SUV, and I was left hurrying to catch up. We were in the crowd on the porch of waiting customers by the time I caught up, so I couldn't say any of the things I wanted to say. But then, neither could he.

76

WE ENDED UP in the manager's office, Pamela's office. She'd brought in extra chairs so she could sit beside Hazel instead of at her desk. Hazel's shoulders hunched forward, her arms holding her stomach as if someone had hit her there and doubled her over, but it wasn't a physical blow that had hit her. Pamela sat beside her, one hand making small circles on the other woman's back, the way you'd soothe a baby to sleep. Hazel didn't react to the touch, but she didn't tell Pamela to stop either. Either it made her feel better or she wasn't even aware the other woman was touching her. Carmichael hadn't been dead two hours yet, so it wasn't so much grief yet as pure shock. The hard-core grieving—where you missed them forever and had to accept that it was forever and nothing you could do would change it, or bring them back, or let you feel their warm hand in yours ever again on this side of the grave—that was still to come.

I sat facing the women in one of the other chairs clustered in front of the desk. Edward and Olaf were standing farther down the wall as far away as the room allowed. They'd be able to hear, but we were trying not to spook her. Livingston had drawn a chair to one side of all of us girls, so he was leaning back against the wall. Hazel knew him, trusted him through Pamela, so he was more a big comforting presence to them both, I think.

Hazel's voice was low, thick with crying already, though the tears stopped as she talked as if talking steadied her, gave her something else to do besides cry. "They killed him. I know they did."

"Who's they?" I asked.

She looked up at me. Her eyes held some of that harsh distrust I remembered from the restaurant. "Rico and Jocelyn."

I gave her the long blink, the one I'd learned over the years when I couldn't afford to show shock or act like I didn't know what the hell was going on. "Tell me what you know," I said, keeping my voice even and neutral.

"Mike showed up to work high a couple of times, and Mr. Marchand put him on notice that if it happened again, he'd have to let him go. I begged Mike to not screw it up, but it was like he couldn't help himself. If there was something good in his life, he had to fuck with it, you know?" She looked up at me as if willing me to understand that the man she loved hadn't been bad, just flawed.

I gave her my best sympathetic face, nodding. "I know people like that, too," I said.

That seemed to be enough for Hazel to smile and sit up a little straighter. "Mr. Marchand was a good man, but his sister is a bitch. She heard what had happened and she asked Mike to take small things from the house. She told him she'd give him some of the money when they sold, and he could start saving for when he had to find another job. Mike didn't tell me what he was doing. I thought he was cheating on me when he was handing stuff over to them to sell." She made a sound halfway between a laugh and a sob. "I wish he'd been cheating on me. He'd still be alive."

Pamela made sympathetic noises, and I resisted the urge to ask Hazel what any of this had to do with Rico and Jocelyn. She had more color in her face than when we'd first come into the room. The more she talked, the stronger she seemed, and that meant eventually we could ask more questions, but she had to get there first. I'd learned a little patience over the years. Besides, there was no reason to rush. Bobby was safe. No one else's head was on the chopping block. We had time to let Hazel tell her story.

"Jocelyn found out he was stealing and threatened to tell Mr. Marchand unless Mike did what she wanted."

"What did she want Mike to do?" I asked, because Hazel seemed to want me to ask.

"To keep quiet about what she and Bobby were doing. Mike saw them doing things that brothers and sisters shouldn't be doing, but she told him if he told on them, she'd tell about the stealing."

Hazel shook her head. "Mike said that Bobby should have known what was happening, but Jocelyn had him so pussy-whipped, he couldn't see anything but what she wanted him to see. She thought she could have anything, or most anything, that she wanted, but there were a few that said no to her. She doesn't like anyone that tells her no."

"Did Mike tell her no?" I asked.

"No, he just kept quiet and started stealing bigger stuff for that bitch Muriel and her stupid husband. I've never seen such a useless man, and I've seen some useless men in my day. I've dated enough of them." Hazel sniffed and started to cry again. "Mike was saving up for us to go away together. We were going to go to Europe and see all those places you plan on seeing and never see, you know?"

"I know," I said, and tried to keep my voice soft, because I was beginning to run out of patience. My supply was never endless.

"Then Mike heard Jocelyn talking to one of the other people that worked at the Marchand place. She was talking like Bobby was stalking her, trying to rape her or something, but he knew that wasn't true." Hazel looked up at me, eyes suddenly direct. "We couldn't figure out why she was lying to people about her and Bobby. I mean, they weren't really brother and sister, not by blood. Mike said that she was chasing Bobby hard when no one else could see. Then Mike saw Jocelyn kissing Rico Vargas. I mean, most women in town have kissed him at one time or another, but Bobby was talking marriage. You don't mess with Rico when you've got someone serious about you, because Rico isn't serious about anyone."

There was a tone in her voice that made me want to ask if she knew from personal experience, but I let it go. If it mattered, I'd find out later.

"Rico does seem to think he's God's gift to everyone," Pamela said.

Hazel smiled at her, and there was a moment of normalcy, and then she remembered, and she hunched in the chair again as if the blow was fresh. When grief is new, you forget for seconds, and then it crushes you all the more because for a second you felt normal, thought that no one had died, that it hadn't happened.

"I told Mike he should tell Jocelyn that he saw her with Rico. Blackmail for blackmail, you know? But he said not yet. He wanted to wait until he needed something on her, and besides, if she was telling people that Bobby was trying to stalk her, then maybe she wouldn't care if he knew about Rico, you know?"

"Makes sense," I said.

"Then Jocelyn told Mike to find a reason to give them the house the night that Mr. Marchand died. He asked her why, but she told him to do what he was told, or she'd tell Mr. Marchand and he'd lose his job. He would have, too, but you can't blame someone for firing you if you steal from them, right?"

"Right," I said.

"He told Jocelyn that he'd seen her and Rico together, and she called him a liar. It was his word against hers, and he was stealing, but when Mike heard about what happened to Mr. Marchand, he blamed himself for leaving them alone. I told him that he'd have just died, too. We believed the police story about it being the wereleopard."

"We all did at first," Pamela said.

"Why did Mike hide after the murder?" Livingston asked.

"He thought when they did an inventory of the things in the house that they'd find out he stole things. He didn't want to go to jail. He'd planned on us being out of the country when Mr. Marchand figured out the things were missing, you know?"

I almost said that last *you know?* with her, but stopped myself in time. "That makes sense up to a point, I guess."

"Then Win Newman didn't think that Bobby did it, and then Mike heard that Jocelyn was telling more people that Bobby had been trying to rape her or something when he knew that was a lie. He felt like she was setting Bobby up. He just couldn't figure out how."

"Then he remembered the bagh nakha," Livingston said.

Hazel nodded. "He thought if he went to Marshal Newman and told him about it, then maybe he could work a deal about the stealing part."

"Why didn't he talk to Newman?" I asked.

"Rico found him. Mike had to climb out a window to get away from him."

"Why didn't he contact Newman after that?" I asked.

"Mike got scared. He wasn't sure who he could trust. I mean, it was his word against one of the local deputies. Mike was an addict and a thief. Why would they believe him against one of their own? Plus Jocelyn."

"After you get hassled enough by the cops, you don't trust any of them," Edward said.

Hazel looked at him. "Yeah," she said.

"What makes you think that Jocelyn and Rico had anything to do with Mike's suicide?" I asked.

"Mike was back on drugs. They made him think wrong things, but he always got high when he was stressed and"—she started to cry softly again—"he tried to blackmail Jocelyn. He wouldn't tell me where he was, but in his last call, he said he was going to get enough money from her for us to go out of the country where no one could find us. I begged him not to do it, to come in and talk to Pamela's boyfriend. If there was a cop we knew that was trustworthy, it would be him, but Mike was high. He wasn't thinking right."

Hazel started crying harder now, rolling forward in her chair. I think if Pamela hadn't put a hand on Hazel's shoulder, she'd have fallen to the floor. Pamela held her while she had hysterics. The interview was over for now.

Livingston motioned us out of the room to the hallway. "Do you believe her?" Edward asked.

"Pamela does, but it's all hearsay. Carmichael is dead, so we can't even get him as a witness to any of it."

"Can we prove any of it?" I asked.

"Not right now," Livingston said.

"Do you believe that Rico is capable of this kind of violence?" Edward asked.

"I don't know him that well, but I'd have said no."

"We thought Rico was stupid, letting the Babingtons into the crime scene when he was supposed to be guarding it, but he was already planning to frame them," I said.

"Framing them doesn't make Jocelyn a billionaire," Edward said.

"They need Bobby dead for that," I said.

"And Jocelyn not implicated in Ray's murder," Livingston added.

"We have a confession that clears her and whatever accomplice she had. Shit, we played right into their hands," I said.

"Rico found the murder weapon in the shed. It was the only stolen object in the house that wasn't in the safe," Livingston said.

"Did Rico plant it?" I asked, and we all looked at one another. "Did one of them help Carmichael with his suicide and his note?"

"Rico was with us," Livingston said.

"The woman made sure we would see her at the aunt and uncle's house," Olaf said.

"She did make a scene," I said.

"If she had just finished giving Carmichael an overdose and faking his suicide note, then she's one of the coldest customers I've ever met," Livingston said.

"If she planned the murder and the frame-up, then she was absolutely cold-blooded," I said.

"Her alibi is perfect for the night of the first murder," Edward said.

"Did anyone check Rico's alibi for that night?" I said.

"Why would we?" Livingston asked.

"We have her voice on the video," I said.

"You have a woman's voice on the video that most people won't even be able to hear without special equipment. Once they find out that a wereanimal—sorry, Therianthrope—heard it first and then told the human cops, it'll probably get thrown out as evidence."

"Why?" I asked.

"Because judges don't like supernatural witnesses or evidence that only exists because of something supernatural. It doesn't play well in court."

"I've been the zombie expert on more than one case. Evidence from supernatural witnesses can be presented in such a way that a judge will let it in."

"That's after the case is strong enough to go to court. We don't have a case against either Jocelyn or Rico," Livingston said.

"Damn it," I said.

"I know a judge that might be willing to hear the video, but I'll have to call in some serious favors," he said.

"If you can get us a warrant to search the Marchand house and Rico's house, I'm betting we'll find something," Edward said.

"I don't know if I can swing a warrant for both just on Hazel's story—it's hearsay—but I think you're right. If they are in it together, then there'll be something to find. I'm betting at his house, because why would we ever search there?" Livingston started punching buttons on his phone. We got his promise to call if he found a way to get us a search warrant.

Edward, Olaf, and I went out to the porch and stood among all the families and couples waiting for the best breakfast in three counties, which is, I guess, why they served it all day long. Some of the locals glanced at us, but then turned away if we looked back. We were all still wearing our badges out where people would see, because we were still wearing too many guns to hide. At least Edward and I were wearing our windbreakers with MARSHAL in big letters on them.

"I want to check on Bobby," I said.

Edward led us down the steps and out toward our car. I wasn't sure where Olaf had parked.

"Do you think Duke is in on it?" Olaf asked when we had some privacy.

"No, but it's a small force," I said. "I don't like the idea of Rico being on jail duty."

"They still need Bobby dead," Edward said.

"Or they killed Ray Marchand for nothing," I said.

Edward hit the button to unlock his rental SUV. Olaf started to go for his car, but I said, "Ride with us. We'll come back for your car."

"You're afraid for him," Olaf said.

"Yeah, my pulse is fast, and my heart rate's up. Now, get in the car so we can put eyes on Bobby."

I expected Olaf to argue, but he didn't. He just got in the backseat. I road shotgun, and Edward peeled out of the parking spot so fast, he almost hit the car vulturing behind us. Maybe it was the big truck. Maybe it was the parking spot.

77

EDWARD PARKED THE SUV in front of the sheriff's station without any conversation from us.

Olaf asked, "What's she doing here?"

I couldn't see whom he meant until I was halfway out the door of the SUV with my foot on the running board. Then I could see Jocelyn on the porch. She was still all in white, leaning against the railing of the little porch as if a photographer would be strolling by at any second. It wasn't just beauty or the outfit with its strappy sandals, but a theatrical quality to her. No, that wasn't quite it. She was dramatic, in that unnecessary-drama-in-your-life kind of way, not that I'm-going-to-be-an-actress kind of way. She gave off drama llama the way Olaf gave off violence. Neither of them had to do a thing except exist, and in their own ways, they would both fuck up your life.

She came toward us crying and talking a little too loud. "Marshals, I tried to talk to Bobby, tried to explain how I felt, but he's so angry at me."

"And you're surprised by that?" I asked as we got closer.

"His eyes changed. He told me to get out because I was upsetting him." She started to cry harder, covering her face with her hands.

A gunshot or maybe two rapid ones sounded. Hadn't I been through this before? We ran for the building with our guns out, pointed at the ground, but ready to shoot. Only training kept me from rushing through the office door without looking. But we were all trained. Olaf got to the door first, but he waited for us to catch up. He took high, I took low, and Edward followed us. As we moved through the door, we cut the pie, dividing the room up and staying out of one another's way. The office looked empty, but the desks were big enough for cover.

We made sure that nothing was hiding behind the desks, and then we separated. Edward pointed for Olaf to check the small hallway that held the interrogation room and bathroom. Edward went for the closed door to the cells, and I stayed at his six. It doesn't do any good to rush to the rescue if you get jumped before you get there. We got to the door leading into the short hallway and the cells beyond, and we were done with stealth or training.

The wereleopard was trying to pull Rico through the bars by his arm. I saw bone glistening white in among all the blood. Rico was firing the gun between the bars, but his angle was bad. I couldn't figure out why he didn't turn more toward the shot, but it didn't matter, because the three of us had the shot. We had to move up to aim through the bars so we didn't miss. The leopard gave a growling scream and tore the lower half of Rico's arm free in a spurt of blood. I heard the sound of tearing meat and bone, like the sound a raw chicken wing makes when you tear it away from the body except louder, bigger, and meatier. Rico screamed and fired a shot that hit the bars and ricocheted back at us. Olaf disarmed him while Edward and I moved up and shot between the bars. The leopard threw itself at us in a snarling, claws-out leap. Our bullets hit it, but its body hit the bars hard enough to shake them. I shoved Edward out of the way as a clawed leg reached through the bars. I shot into the wereleopard's body as the claws raked at me. Olaf shot it in the head, and blood and bone sprayed out the bottom of its jaw. That took some of the fight out of it, and it backed away from the bars. Edward fired from the knee he'd taken. The leopard coughed blood and then launched itself at the bars again. We fired in unison, and the big cat fell over on its side and stopped moving. All three of us popped our cartridges out and reloaded without trying to count shots. If it got up again, we'd need more ammo. If it didn't, we could retrieve our dropped magazines and save any unused bullets.

We couldn't hear one another over the ringing in our ears from firing in such a small space. Sometimes I think I should just live in my damn ear protection. I could see Rico's mouth open and knew he was screaming. His arm was a blood fountain spraying into the cell. Movement caught my attention, and I almost pointed my gun at Jocelyn, who was screaming in the doorway. I yelled for her to call an ambulance. Hell, I probably screamed it at her, but she vanished from the doorway, hopefully to do what I'd asked.

Edward motioned for me to watch the wereleopard. He and Olaf had to put their guns away to try to get Rico free of the bars, but his shoulder was wedged so tight that he was stuck. We were going to have to open the cell to stop the bleeding, or he would be dead before the ambulance got here. The wereleopard was still in animal form, which meant it was not dead, not yet. I was deliberately thinking of the furry body in the cell as the wereleopard. I couldn't afford to think of it as Bobby, because the leopard in the cell didn't have hands, and I was pretty damn sure that it had taken hands to pull Rico through the bars and wedge him there. Bobby had been in human form and known exactly what he was doing when he did it. No lack of control, no accident, just murder. Jocelyn had said that his eyes had changed. Had that been enough for Rico to try to kill him? Had Bobby believed he was acting in self-defense? Did it matter in the eyes of the law? It sure as hell didn't matter to Rico.

Leduc was there from wherever he'd gone. He opened the cell, and I moved in with my gun aimed at the wereleopard on the floor. It was lying in a pool of Rico's blood, and if it so much as twitched, I was going to shoot it again.

The blood slowed its spraying into the cell and then stopped. I gave the smallest eye twitch to see a tourniquet on the arm, but Rico was unconscious and sagging in the bars. Leduc was on the outside of the bars holding him up for some reason. Maybe there was a good first aid reason for it. I didn't know. I fought to keep my attention on the leopard.

Voices came back in pieces with some parts louder and then far-ther away like some kind of special effect. I'd had my hearing come back from shit like this before, so I wasn't worried. I didn't look around, trying to figure out if people were moving closer and farther away or if it was just my ears. It would pass.

I yelled, "Where were you, Duke?"

"I took Troy down to see a lawyer."

I realized that Troy wasn't in the other cell. Fuck, that was all Rico had needed.

"It was your job to keep Bobby safe, damn it!"

I knew I was yelling louder than I thought, because my hearing wasn't quite right yet, but honestly, screaming sounded like a great idea. All the effort to save Bobby Marchand and it was all for noth-ing, for nothing.

The ambulance arrived, but the crew members wouldn't go in the cell with the leopard. I couldn't blame them. The body on the floor moved, drew a breath that made the pale gold and black-spotted fur rise and fall. That one clean spot in the bloody mess of the rest of the body moved. It was alive, but if the paramedics and the firemen with the Jaws of Life didn't get in here soon, Rico wouldn't be. The leop-ard stirred enough that the first responders saw it. I felt rather than saw their panic in the hallway. I couldn't see it, because I couldn't afford to look away from the leopard at my feet. I shot into that body, making the change in angle for the heart in leopard form. I did my job. I did the job that Newman was supposed to have done before I ever got on a plane. Had Bobby been framed for the first murder? Yes, but that wasn't going to be much comfort to Rico if he lived.

The body turned human, which probably meant that Bobby was dead, but not always. If you'd have asked me if Bobby was powerful enough to heal from this much high-content silver ammo, I'd have said no, but I'd also have sworn that he wasn't a danger to anyone. I'd been wrong once. I didn't want to be wrong again.

Olaf was in the cell with me, his gun pointed at the body. I got my ear protection out of the pouch I kept it in and put it on. I cov-ered the body while Olaf did the same. He didn't question me. He didn't try to ask to decapitate the body or take the heart with a blade. He didn't do anything but back my play. I stared down at Bobby's body. Mercifully he was lying on his side so I couldn't see the front of him, and his head was turned so that I could see only the edges of his face. I didn't have to stare into his eyes as I shot into his skull until it cracked and burst, spreading gore and brains all over the floor. I put my boot against the shoulder and rolled the body more completely onto its stomach and then shot where the heart would have been. I clicked empty and stepped back to reload while Olaf moved over the body and started firing into the chest. I covered the body while Olaf shot through the chest until the body was almost bisected.

Olaf clicked empty, and I kept my gun on the body while he reloaded. It was a formality, me watching the body like that, because it was as dead as we could make it unless we wanted to burn the body to ashes. But it wasn't a vampire, so burning was overkill, both metaphysically and legally. The warrant was complete.

78

I STOOD OUTSIDE in the sunlight trying not to think, not to feel, and failing. Olaf was there almost blocking out the sun.

"We killed together after all," he said.

I turned my head slowly to look at him. Anyone who knew me well would have moved away or stopped talking. Apparently Olaf didn't know me that well.

"But it was not satisfying."

"Not satisfying? Not satisfying! What the fuck, Olaf? What the fuck!" I yelled, and realized I'd used his real name in front of the other cops.

I took a deep breath, trying to swallow the anger down enough to think and not just react, but I kept seeing Bobby's blond hair and his brains on the floor. I wanted to scream, not words—just scream wordless, hopeless, enraged. The only thing that kept me from it was knowing if I started to scream, I wasn't sure I'd stop. I didn't mean I'd say things to Olaf I would regret. I meant that I'd just scream until my voice was raw, and when the screaming stopped, maybe I'd cry, or maybe I'd think of something more useful to do.

Olaf said, "I am sorry."

I stared at him, because of all the things he could have said to try to calm me down, that was a good one, especially coming from him. I stared at him, speechless. His face was still the empty serial killer calm. It wasn't the face that went with *I'm sorry*.

I felt Nicky's energy before the SUV pulled up behind all the emergency vehicles and the gawkers. There's always an audience for tragedy. I hated them all today. But it had been the crowd and the lights that let Nicky and the others know to come find me. So maybe I shouldn't have hated the crowd, but I did. They weren't here to help; they just wanted to see the circus. Bread and circuses. Jesus.

Nicky was suddenly beside me. I'd missed some time somewhere in there. Shit. I had to do better than this. He was careful not to touch me, because he could feel what I was feeling, which meant he knew that hugging me now would either make me start screaming, crying, or hitting something. Touching was bad for the next few minutes.

"Anita, I'm so sorry."

I looked up at Nicky, and Olaf was still close enough that I could see him past Nicky's shoulder. They'd both said almost the same thing, and they were both still blank-faced and sociopathic.

"What are you sorry about, Nicky? You didn't kill him. I did."

"You didn't make . . . him kill Rico," Nicky said.

He'd been about to say *didn't make Bobby*, but he didn't want to remind me of names. It's never good to think of names after you've shot someone to pieces. They're bodies, meat, not real, not the people you knew or thought they were. It's just an it. It's just dead meat. You can't personalize it. I swallowed the scream that seemed to be stuck at the back of my throat. Nothing I had said had cleared it, as if I hadn't made the right noise yet.

I licked my lips; my mouth was dry.

Pierette dropped to her knees in front of me. "I have failed you, my queen."

"Get up!" I said.

Nicky grabbed her arm and pulled her to her feet. He said, "We have an audience."

"We're being filmed, Petra," Ethan said.

I looked for TV crews, but it was cell phones, smartphones, filming the scene, or as much as the police would let them. The state cops who had still been in the area had appeared like magic to help manage the crowd.

Leduc came toward us yelling, "You were supposed to keep this from happening!"

"You kicked them out, remember," I said.

"We could have kept this from happening if we'd been here," Ethan said.

Our mild-mannered Ethan saying anything meant he was as upset as the rest of us. He'd spent hours talking to Bobby, and now it was all for nothing. Leduc pushed into Ethan the way he had with Milligan and Custer earlier, shoving his bulk in against the slenderer man.

"Well, now he's not going anywhere except the morgue, thanks to you not being here."

I'd had enough, or maybe I just wanted a target I didn't care about to aim all my rage and frustration at. Whatever the case, I pushed between them, forcing Leduc back from Ethan, and yelled, "It's your damn jail, and you've had two of your deputies shoot at your prisoner. What kind of fucked-up shit show are you running here, Duke?"

He drove all that weight and extra height into me, actually forced me backward with his bulk. I pushed back with my hands so I touched him first. You don't do that when tempers are this hot, not unless you want a real fight. He shoved me hard, and I was off balance, so I stumbled. Then I went for him. Nicky caught me, one arm across my shoulders keeping me back.

I screamed, "Let me go!" and he had to do it.

Milligan and Custer grabbed me. Newman and Edward grabbed Leduc.

Custer yelled, "Boss!"

I struggled, but I didn't fight them. I had that much control left. I yelled, "You were supposed to be watching over Bobby. You want to blame someone, seems like there's a fuck ton of blame to go around!"

"I told you I took Troy to see a lawyer—that's why I wasn't here," he said, and he wasn't yelling now.

He was getting himself under control enough that Edward stepped away from him. Newman stayed on his other arm, but more like patting him on the back than holding him, though I don't think the audience that had pointed their phones at us were fooled.

"Why? He hasn't been charged officially yet."

"He's not going to be charged, or he wasn't. Bobby didn't want him to be charged. Now that Bobby is dead, I don't know what will happen with Troy."

I didn't want to get calm. I wanted to stay angry, because it had felt better than so many other emotions that were there just below the surface. I didn't want to feel any of them. I fed my anger and called it sweet names so it wouldn't leave me alone with the rest of the things I was feeling.

Edward said, "Anita, you're bleeding."

I frowned at him as if he were speaking a different language. He nodded down at my thigh. I looked where he motioned and saw the blood and the fresh claw marks in the cloth. My first thought was *So what? One more scar.* It didn't even hurt yet, which probably meant it was worse than I thought or I was still in shock. Then I remembered that I'd gotten wounded because I'd pushed Edward out of the way. I had lycanthropy already, couldn't hurt me any more. I looked at Edward's thigh, but the blood on him was lower, closer to the knee, because he was taller, I guess.

"I thought I saved you," I said.

"You saved me from maybe being crippled for life."

"Or maybe not," I said.

"Don't second-guess yourself, Anita. You put yourself in harm's way for me. That's what I'll remember."

"You'll have to get tested."

"I know."

We looked at each other.

"Did any of my blood get in your wound?" I asked.

"No way to tell yet," he said.

I nodded. He was right, of course, but all I could think was in trying to save him from Bobby's type of Therianthropy I might have given him mine. It was like the harder I tried, the worse things got.

"Rico gained consciousness and said something before he got in the ambulance," Edward said.

"What?" I asked.

"He said, 'I should never have listened to that bitch.'"

"What does that mean?" Leduc asked.

"Jocelyn was here when we pulled up," I said.

"Did he say anything else?" Leduc asked.

"I asked him what he meant, and he said, 'She's killed us both.'"

"What the hell does that mean?" Leduc asked.

When Edward told Leduc what Hazel had told Livingston and us, he said, "Son of a bitch, son of a bitch, are you telling me that Rico . . . Ray and Carmichael, and that Bobby was just defending himself?"

I shook my head. "Bobby pulled him through the bars when he still had hands. He wedged Rico in so that he couldn't get away. He made sure that your deputy got to watch him shift in his cell and was unable to escape, knowing what was going to happen to him. Bobby could have walked away from this. He was free, damn it. Why? Why kill someone now?"

"I'll go to the hospital and see if I can get Rico to tell me more about Jocelyn's part in it," Leduc said.

"Tell the hospital to use minimum heat on the wound, because if he's caught lycanthropy, then he'll grow the arm back if they don't burn the flesh and kill it," I said.

"Motherfucking son of a bitch," Leduc said, already on his phone to the hospital.

I looked around for Jocelyn so I could ask her what she'd said to Bobby that had made him lose control so completely. I could aim my anger at her next.

Nicky said, "She got in a car with the older woman who came in to be questioned. She works for the family."

"Helen Grimes," I said.

He nodded.

"What did Jocelyn say to Bobby to make him lose his shit like this?" I asked.

"I don't think it was what she said," Olaf said.

"What do you mean?" I asked, and I tried to stay angry, but I wasn't angry at Olaf for this. I could feel the adrenaline from the near-death emergency leaking away. When it left, I'd want to be sitting or lying down.

"I held the deputy in my arms. I was very close to his body, and I smelled the woman's scent on him." I looked at Olaf and realized that he was covered in Rico's blood.

"Woman—you mean Jocelyn?"

Olaf nodded.

"What do you mean you smelled her scent on him?" Milligan asked.

"The scent of her body was underneath his clothes on his skin."

"You mean they had sex," Custer asked.

"It is likely. I can tell you that their naked bodies rubbed against each other's, sharing scent back and forth, but I did not sniff his groin or hers, so I can't be a hundred percent certain of what they did while they were naked." Olaf said it all with almost no change of expression, as if it was all completely normal.

"That would mean that she smelled like Rico," I said.

"Probably," Olaf said.

"She didn't have to say anything if he smelled them on each other's skin," Nicky said.

"She didn't come here to have him smell their bodies next to each other," I said.

"She said something to Bobby that made him freak out," Ethan said.

"If she is as cold-blooded a schemer as this, then Ethan is right: She wouldn't have just chanced Bobby smelling their scents on each other's skin. She told Bobby of the affair before she left to let the deputy finish the kill," Pierette said, and the men all nodded in agreement.

"Where's Angel?" I asked.

"She's throwing up in the weeds over there," Nicky said.

I went over and held her hair while she finished, and then something about the smell of her being sick hit me wrong. I had time to stumble farther away from her and catch myself against a tree before I started throwing up, too. I ended up on my knees, throwing up until I was dry-heaving. Nicky held my hair and then brought me some water.

The paramedics in extra ambulances that someone had called insisted on Edward, Olaf, Angel, and me going to the hospital. Edward and I were hurt, though I didn't need stitches and he did. Olaf was just covered in so much blood, they didn't believe it was all someone else's, and when he found out we were all going, he agreed to go. Angel got to go because she was faint after she finished being sick. I'd really expected better of a weretiger. They put the men in the back of one ambulance and us girls in another.

Angel started to cry on the way. "I am so sorry, Anita."

The thick Goth eye makeup started to run down her face like black tears. She needed to switch brands. Mine didn't run like that. Thank you, Dior. I felt nothing, watching her cry. It was like the inside of me went to that quiet white-noise place where I could pull a trigger and take a life and not feel anything. Maybe it was shock, or maybe killing Bobby had been the last piece of my soul I could lose and not lose myself.

The paramedic kept trying to take our vitals, while Angel cried like her heart would break and I just stared at her. I finally moved beside her and got the paramedic to leave us alone long enough for me to hold her and let her cry on my shoulder. Somewhere on the drive to a hospital that had facilities for dealing with supernatural wounds, I started to cry with her. We held each other and cried like a couple of girls. I could never have done it with Edward. Part of me regretted that I wasn't with him, and part of me was ashamed of letting go like this, but a small part of me felt that every tear I shed got me a little piece of my soul back.

79

RICO DIED OF his wounds, so whatever secrets he had to tell died with him. He had a no-resurrection clause in his living will, so we couldn't even raise him from the dead and ask. Todd Babington's confession fell apart. Bobby Marchand was the official murderer of both Rico Vargas and Raymond Marchand. Jocelyn technically inherited two billion dollars. The lawyers in charge of the estate released a chunk of money, a small fortune, to her in anticipation of her assuming control of the estate.

Then Hazel Phillips came forward with a video that Carmichael had e-mailed to her in which he confessed not to murder, but to blackmail. He'd been blackmailing Rico and Jocelyn, because he had seen them together in a bad part of town at a motel and he used his phone to get pictures. They were included in the e-mail. He'd been blackmailing them about the affair, threatening to tell not Ray Marchand, but Bobby. Jocelyn had paid him to keep that quiet. It was only after the murder that Carmichael realized the reason: She'd been willing to pay him to keep quiet so she could set Bobby up for murder. Then Carmichael got greedy and tried to blackmail them because he saw Rico's car near the Marchand house the night of the murder. None of it was enough to prove that Rico was a murderer or that Jocelyn helped kill her dad, but it was enough to make the lawyers begin to argue that she couldn't profit from a crime. It would take years for the lawyers to fight it out, and Jocelyn decided to wait it out someplace tropical that didn't have an extradition treaty with the United States.

Two months later Edward and I both received postcards from that country. His read, "My first trip outside the country in years." It was unsigned.

Mine read,

Adler,

I went hunting and bagged my limit. I hope we can agree on a hunting trip to take together someday.

Moriarty

The headlines read, "Heiress to Marchand Fortune Vanishes!" "Model and Songwriter Angela Warren's Daughter Missing." "Billionaire Heiress Lost, Presumed Dead." There were a lot of other headlines; some of them even hinted that Jocelyn was a person of interest in her father's death. The majority of the Marchand fortune is going to various museums and charities now, though they'll have to prove Jocelyn's dead or wait seven years to divide up the money. They'll be waiting, because Olaf doesn't leave incriminating evidence behind, and that includes anything that could prove Jocelyn Marchand is dead.

I don't feel bad that she's dead. She deserved to die, but did she deserve to die the way that Olaf killed her? No, no one deserves that. I did my best not to think of what he might have done to her before she finally died. I'm still doing my best not to think about it.

Edward and I talked about it, but Olaf didn't break the truce between them. He didn't do the crime on American soil, or when we were working with him, or when he was working for any government. He took a vacation, and he indulged in his favorite hobby. Isn't that what vacation is for?

Edward got tested for Therianthropy. We expected either a negative or an inconclusive because it can take weeks for Ailuranthropy, cat-based lycanthropy, to show up in a blood test, but he popped hot but inconclusive. The only other marshal who's had results similar to that is me, so they're waiting for another two weeks before they test him again. By then, exactly what strains of Therianthropy he carries should be readable. There is a remote chance that it's a false positive from stray antibodies or something from Bobby's body or mine, but odds are that in a month, Edward will be coming to visit us so that we can help him through his first full moon. I'd tried to keep Edward safe and instead I'd made it worse.

We'd tried so hard to save Bobby Marchand, and we'd failed. What did Jocelyn tell Bobby to enrage him to that point? Did she leave before Bobby pulled Rico through the cell bars or after? Did she leave Rico to die at Bobby's hands? Rico hadn't meant to die. He just got too close and underestimated Bobby's beast like I had. I'd lived through my mistake. Rico hadn't. Most people don't.

Newman and I are both under review by the Marshals Service. We're not under review because we killed Bobby; that was legal. We're under review because we didn't kill him soon enough, and that negligence led to the death of another officer. Newman resigned from the preternatural branch, no big surprise. He's transferred into the regular Marshals Service currently, but there's some talk of him joining the state cops.

I'm still waiting for the preternatural branch to figure out if Deputy Rico Vargas's death is my fault for not executing the warrant sooner, and the fact that we think he was our original murderer might not make a difference. His guilt or innocence will never be proven in a court of law now, but Livingston did find that Jocelyn had left personal items at Rico's house, so the affair was true. Rico had no alibi for the night of Ray Marchand's murder, but that didn't prove he had done it. Livingston wrote up a report that made me look good, or so I was told by people in the Marshals Service who are supposed to be the boss of me.

Even Leduc didn't bad-mouth me as much as I thought he would. I think he believes that Rico killed Ray Marchand. That took a lot of the self-righteous wind out of his sails. I'm weirdly calm about being on suspension. I don't know if I could be a regular marshal like

Newman, but I'm not sure I can keep being a preternatural marshal either. I don't know if I want to keep being the Executioner. For the first time, the pride I take in being War to Edward's Death and Olaf's Plague doesn't offset the nightmares I'm having. I keep killing Bobby over and over in my dreams, except sometimes he's Haven, and sometimes he's my friend Jason, and sometimes he's Nicky or Nathaniel or . . . You get the idea.

I got an invitation to Newman's wedding. I may even go. Maybe I could take a few days and go camping and see what's left of the girl I was in college—the one who wanted to get her doctorate in biology and be a field biologist specializing in the supernatural. Jean-Claude couldn't come with me; vampires don't travel well like that. Nathaniel could come if I insisted, but he's a comfort-loving cat. Micah camped and hunted until the attack that changed him into a wereleopard; he'd go with me. Nicky grew up out west on a ranch, so he might be game. Who knew? Maybe some of the other people in our poly group would surprise me by being more outdoorsy than I thought. Or maybe we could go someplace more tropical, with a luxury hotel as our base camp and day trips for the more outdoorsy stuff? Yeah, that might work for the men and women in my life and me.

FANTASTIC HOPE

A collection of sci-fi and fantasy stories

EDITED BY THE INTERNATIONALLY
BESTSELLING AUTHOR

LAURELL K. HAMILTON

AND

WILLIAM McCASKEY

Includes new short stories from *New York Times*
bestselling authors Patricia Briggs, Kevin J. Anderson,
Larry Correia, Jonathan Maberry,
L. E. Modesitt, Jr. and more . . .

And an all-new ANITA BLAKE, VAMPIRE HUNTER
story and an all-new ALPHA AND OMEGA story

Available from

HEADLINE